**A MAGNIFICENT DREAM . . .
A RUGGED NEW LAND . . .
A FAMILY WHO WOULD MOLD A
ROWDY MINING TOWN INTO A GREAT
AMERICAN CITY**

DAVID KIRKLAND—A bold wanderer and a dreamer, he followed his restless heart to the Colorado Rockies. But he could never forget his blood tie to the Cheyenne. . . .

BEATRICE KIRKLAND—She escaped a life of domestic servitude to marry rugged David Kirkland, but life with the solitary mountain man was lonely and plagued with hardship. All that sustained her were her children and the legacy of wealth she was determined to create for them. . . .

IRENE KIRKLAND—Exquisite child of the sprawling frontier, her reverence for the mountains matched only by her desire for a man she could never love, Irene would never truly know herself until she discovered the truth about her past. . . .

RAMON VALLEJO—From the moment he met Irene, he knew no one could ever drive her from his heart, just as surely as he knew Bea Kirkland would never tolerate their union. His pride and family honor at stake, could he allow her prejudice to destroy the love he and Irene shared?

ELLY KIRKLAND—Deceitful and treacherous, ruled by her insatiable desires, she waited for the chance to destroy her parents' favorite, beautiful, golden-haired Irene. She would see Irene torn away from the man she loved and betrayed by the man she'd married—or die trying. . . .

CHAD JACOBS—Tortured by a shameful past, Chad harbored a tragic secret he dared not reveal to anyone—especially his wife. Unable to love, he was determined to take from the Kirklands . . . whatev

D1115755

Bantam Books by Rosanne Bittner

MONTANA WOMAN
EMBERS OF THE HEART
IN THE SHADOW OF THE MOUNTAINS

IN THE SHADOW

OF THE MOUNTAINS

by

Rosanne Bittner

BANTAM BOOKS
NEW YORK · TORONTO · LONDON · SYDNEY · AUCKLAND

IN THE SHADOW OF THE MOUNTAINS

A Bantam Fanfare Book / July 1991

ISBN 0-553-29033-9

Published simultaneously in the United States and Canada

PRINTED IN THE UNITED STATES OF AMERICA

RAD   0 9 8 7 6 5 4 3 2 1

For my "lunch bunch," faithful friends and fans:

Pat Hauch
Marilyn Reschke
Evelyn Gaines
Linda Honyoust
Helen Emery
Betty Lull
Rosemary Hill
Bea and Bud Kimball

> Time and places new we know,
> Faces fresh and seasons strange,
> But the friends of long ago
>> Do not change.

> ANDREW LANG
> *"The New Joy of Words"*

In this circle
Oh ye warriors
Lo, I tell you
Each his future.
All shall be
As I now reveal it
In this circle:
Hear ye!

TATANKA-PTECILA (SHORT BULL)
DAKOTA SIOUX MEDICINE MAN
"Touch the Earth"

PREFACE

Anyone who has been West more than once will begin to feel the magical spell the land, and especially the mountains, casts on all who dare to cross the Great Divide. They will feel the silent beckoning to return, again and again, as I do every year. I have no doubt that one day my home will be somewhere in the Rockies.

I have covered much of the West in my travels, since the American West of the 1800's is the theme of all my novels, but the area that has always attracted me most is Colorado. It has been the setting of several of my novels, and for years I have wanted to write a story set in Colorado's Queen City—Denver. *In the Shadow of the Mountains* is that story; it traces Denver's growth from its birth in 1858 through the end of the nineteenth century.

To write a story about a city is to write about people, dreamers who build and sustain a city through the many setbacks that could easily turn it into a ghost town; for Denver is a city that was built on gold and silver, and we all know what happened to most of those once-booming towns.

And so, *In the Shadow of the Mountains* becomes a novel not just about the growth of Denver, but something much more personal—the story of a wealthy founding family and how the building of a city sometimes took precedence over their personal desires, which was true for so many of those who built America's cities. But there were also those who realized that dreams of empires meant nothing without love. The heroine of this novel,

Irene Kirkland, is such a person, and *In the Shadow of the Mountains* becomes, then, a poignant love story.

In this novel I occasionally I refer to people who were actually part of Denver's history. In such references, I base my characterization and dialogue on factual history about that person.

I referred to a wealth of material for this story. Major references included: *The Queen City: A History of Denver*, by Lyle W. Dorsett and Michael McCarthy (Second Ed.); Pruett Publishing Co., Boulder, Co.; *The Birth of Colorado: A Civil War Perspective*, by Duane A. Smith; University of Oklahoma Press; *The Oxford History of the American People*, by Samuel Eliot Morison; Oxford University Press, New York; Time-Life's *Old West* series, such as *The Townsmen, The Railroaders, The Women,* and *The Miners; The Denver and Rio Grande Western Railroad*, by Robert Athearn; University of Nebraska Press; and *Hear That Lonesome Whistle Blow*, by Dee Brown; Holt, Rinehart & Winston, New York. I would like to thank the gracious people of the Coloma Public Library here in my hometown for allowing me to keep certain books for weeks and even months.

Although *In the Shadow of the Mountains* is based on historical fact surrounding the growth of Denver and the people who built the Queen City, all major characters and their personal stories in this novel are entirely fictitious and a product of this author's imagination. To the best of my knowledge, there was no major founding family in Denver with the last name of Kirkland. But there were many mountain dreamers with the same desires and quests as the characters in this story, many of whom felt the same love and hate and experienced the same victories and defeats. They loved the land and their city, as much as they loved life itself. I like to think the Kirklands did exist. For me they are as real as those whose names have gone down in history books.

PART

ONE

It is often said that a woman is most strongly drawn to the man who needs her the most.

MARGARET BOURKE-WHITE
Portrait of Myself

CHAPTER
ONE

1846

David Kirkland headed his buckskin gelding into Bent's Fort. The horse was big. It had to be. David Kirkland was a big man, standing well over six feet, shoulders broad, chest solid. His fair skin was a ruddy reddish brown, tanned and creased by years of living under the open sky. He was twenty-five years old, and he had lived in and around the Rockies for thirteen years, ever since running away from an orphanage at the tender age of twelve.

He had ended up in St. Louis, then hardly more than a small settlement of log buildings. An old mountain man had taken him under his wing, and David Kirkland had followed the man into the Rockies, where he learned how to trap beaver for a living.

Since then, Kirk, as he was called by all who knew him, had wandered the open plains and purple mountains, his life more like that of an Indian than a white man. He loved the great alone, loved his freedom; and the life he led made him a man of courage and wisdom that belied his young age. The creases about his eyes and his big build made him appear older than he really was. His thick, wavy blond hair, bleached even whiter from the Colorado sun, peeked out from under his floppy leather hat in wayward wisps, and he sported a full beard, which was a light sandy color, and which was always a topic of curiosity to the Indians, especially the young women.

He led a second horse behind him, a spotted Appaloosa, which was loaded down with deerskins and wolf pelts he had gathered over the last several months while living alone in the Rockies. It made his heart heavy to realize he could not live the life he loved much longer. Things were changing; the number of white settlers at the fort only verified that.

The days of trapping beaver for a living were over. Both supply and demand had dwindled. It had been six years since the last rendezvous. Kirk missed those gatherings, the wild, good times with white and Indian friends after spending a long winter alone. He missed sharing stories, missed the wrestling matches the Indians loved, missed the horse races and shooting contests and the general camaraderie.

He hung on to those days by continuing to trap and hunt alone in the mountains, collecting deerskins and other pelts that could be sold at forts and trading posts; but the money he got for them decreased every year. He had to give serious thought to finding some other way to make a living.

Kirk blamed the changes on too many people coming West from more settled places in the East. This was no longer a land of just Indians and mountain men. Civilization was creeping into his West, and Kirk didn't like it, but he knew he could do nothing to stop it. Many of his old friends had turned to scouting and hunting for the emigrants, selling their services to wagon trains headed for California and Oregon.

At least his mountains remained untouched and unsettled. That was how he thought of the Rockies, as his own personal home. He was one of only a few men who still lived up there most of the time, usually alone, except for the times he was able to barter for an Indian woman to share his bed, cook for him, and clean his skins.

The last Indian woman he had lived with was Gray Bird Woman, a Cheyenne. She had been a quiet, obedient partner, and he would have gladly kept her with him, but she had missed her people, and he had taken her back to them.

That had been more than a year ago. He had spent the last winter alone, thinking about a young woman named Beatrice, whom he had met in Kansas City last summer. He had gone there in search of a more modern repeating rifle not sold anywhere west of the Kansas–Missouri border. He had spotted Beatrice working at the supply store where he bought the gun. She was taller than most women, and there were some who were prettier; but her trim figure and the way she had looked at him had caught his eye. He had considered getting to know the woman better, but the look in her eyes had spelled *marriage* and *settle,* two words that had sent him running back to the mountains. Now he couldn't even remember her last name, but he could still see her face.

Kirk struck an imposing posture, drawing stares as he rode through the courtyard of the fort, which was alive with activity. His intensely blue eyes scanned the scene; soldiers milling about in one corner; Indians everywhere, mostly Cheyenne; several men dressed in buckskins and moccasins as he was; some white families heading for California, or maybe Mormons taking a different route to Utah, or people headed into the Southwest. It seemed strange to see whites in these parts. Most stayed to the north, following the Oregon Trail.

Wagons clattered, and he heard the clang of a blacksmith's hammer. Bent's Fort was always a bustle of activity, but it seemed especially full and busy now. He had noticed more soldiers outside, and what looked like an entire army camp. People laughed and conversed, and one man sat in the shade of the fort's second-story overhang and played a banjo, entertaining the fort's visitors.

The voice of the man who sang sounded familiar. "Red McKinley, I'll bet," he mused. He headed his horse toward the music, removing his hat to wipe sweat from his brow with the back of his hand. July had brought its usual unbearable heat to the plains. He much preferred the cool mountains in summer.

He passed a group of Cheyenne playing a hand game and sharing a bottle of whiskey. He nodded to one he recognized, shouting a greeting to him in the Cheyenne tongue. Fast Runner was Gray Bird Woman's brother. The man gave Kirk a strange, dark look that surprised him. The Indian quickly got up and left his circle of friends, then headed out of the fort.

Kirk turned to watch him leave, figuring to follow and find out what was wrong; but just then someone called out his name. He reined his horse back to the right, and the big gelding snorted and shook its mane.

"Kirk! You worthless bastard, where in hell have you been keeping yourself!"

Kirk grinned, realizing he had been right. The man playing the banjo was James McKinley, better known to all as Red because of his orange-red hair and beard. McKinley sported buckskins like Kirk's, and was a long-time friend with whom Kirk had hunted and camped many times.

Kirk dismounted, quickly tying his horse to a hitching post.

Then he turned to greet Red, who was younger than he by two years. The men exchanged a firm handshake. "It's been a long time, friend," Red said with a smile, a slight Irish accent in the words.

Red had come to America as a baby with his Irish parents, who had settled in New York. At an early age he had gotten the "wanders," as most mountain men called their peculiar "disease," and had struck out for the West, never to return.

"How have you been, Red?" Kirk asked with a wide grin.

"Doing all right. Mostly I've been scouting for wagon trains." He glanced at the skins on Kirk's extra horse. "I see you're still trying to make it hunting."

Kirk laughed. "Trying is right. I think I'm going to have to turn to something else, Red. The damn game is getting more scarce every year, and the price I get for these skins can hardly buy supplies for the next year."

"Hell, I told you four or five years ago we'd have to turn to something else, Kirk. You're just a slow learner. Come on over to the tavern. I'll buy you a whiskey. You're going to need it, friend." He turned to a young Indian boy and told him in the Cheyenne tongue to watch Kirk's horses and supplies. "Anybody bothers them, you come running." He handed out a piece of candy and the boy grinned and nodded, sitting down beside the animals.

Both men headed into one of the rooms of the huge stucco fort. Built in one great square, it held supply stores, a tavern, and even a restaurant where travelers could get excellent meals, including apple pie. On the second story of the buildings were rooms men could rent for the night, and watchtowers where guards kept a lookout for hostile Indians. Bent's Fort was a popular gathering place for anyone who traveled the West and Southwest along the Old Spanish Trail.

"What do you mean, I'm going to need the whiskey?" Kirk asked Red.

Red waved him off. "All in good time, friend." The man walked up to a bar made of cottonwood, practically the only kind of wood available in the area. The room was cool, the three-foot-thick stucco walls of the fort giving excellent shelter from heat and sun. The smell of whiskey, smoke and leather was pungent.

Red ordered a bottle of whiskey and two glasses. "Let's find us a table."

"How come soldiers are crawling all over outside?" Kirk asked as they found seats.

Red's eyebrows arched. "For God's sake, man, you been alone in the mountains again all winter?"

"Sure have. You know that's what I love best."

"Well, you're sure behind on the news. Hell, we're at war with Mexico."

"Again?"

"This is big, Kirk, the real thing. This time we're invading Mexico—going to them, instead of letting them come to us. Hell, they figure to add more territory to Texas and claim New Mexico and California before they're through. Oregon's already fixing to barter with England and declare itself a territory. Before those men in Washington are through, everything from the Atlantic to the Pacific will belong to the United States."

Kirk frowned, slugging down a shot of whiskey. "You know what will happen then. More of those greenhorns from the East will head out here."

"Manifest Destiny, our leaders call it. The United States is practically 'ordained' to claim and own everything between the two oceans and between Canada and Mexico proper, only they aim to reduce Mexico's northern border a mite." Red laughed lightly, pouring both of them a second shot. "Yes, my friend, things are changing fast. We've got to change with them. Me, I've turned to scouting, but I don't even know how long *that* will last. You mark my word, someday there will be railroads out here, and people won't use wagons anymore."

Kirk shook his head. "Railroads way out here? Never! I can't imagine those noisy things chugging through the plains, their damn whistles and black smoke scaring away everything in sight, spoiling the peace and quiet. Hell, they'd chase away the buffalo, and they'd scare the poor Indians half to death."

"Well, nothing would surprise me anymore." Red took another drink. "Before I take on another scouting job, I'm thinking of going down to Mexico and getting in on some of the action. Want to come along?"

Kirk shook his head. "I've got no interest in any damn war with Mexico."

Red leaned back and took a cigar from his pocket. "Well, I was thinking maybe I'd need you. You saved my life once. You might come in handy in combat and do it again. Fighting Mexicans will be a little more dangerous than fighting Indians. They'll have better weapons."

In a land where a man's life was almost constantly on the line, friendships ran deep—and they shared a special bond. Kirk had fought off six Crow warriors once to save Red, who had already been badly wounded; then he had taken an arrow from the man's side and burned out the infection, staying with him and nursing him until he was fully recovered. That had been four years ago.

"You could have gone off and left me, Kirk," Red said soberly. He lit the cigar. "You had a chance to escape before those Crow moved in on us. I would have just been another casualty, probably never missed and never found. Our kind die like that every day, and you knew it."

Kirk shrugged it off. "I did what any man would have done."

"Not any man, Kirk—only the really good, honest ones. I'll always owe you."

Kirk poured another drink, feeling embarrassed. "You'd have done the same for me."

An awkward moment of silence followed.

"What will you do from here?" Red asked then. "You won't get much for those skins out there, I hate to tell you. The time has come when a man's got to earn himself an honest living, and we're both getting to the age when we ought to think about settling."

Kirk stared at his whiskey glass, oblivious to the din of voices in the crowded room. His mind was in the mountains, where all was quiet, and a man was master of his own fate. He could smell the crisp, mountain air, pungent with pine and wildflowers; he could see the vivid blue sky; feel the rushing, cold waters of sparkling clear streams and lakes; see the vivid colors. He recalled the awesome power of the mighty Rockies, a magnificence to the immobile granite that made a man feel insignificant.

"I don't know," he finally answered. "Like you say, things are changing. I don't want to change with them. I want to stay in the mountains. I might do just that."

"Ah, Kirk, you have a lot of living to do yet. You can't spend the rest of your life in those mountains."

"Sure I can. I'll build myself a little cabin and go get myself an Indian woman when I'm in need of one, live off bear meat and deer, cut wood for fires. What's wrong with that?"

Red shrugged. "Nothing, I suppose. I just happen to believe a man's got to do more than that with his life, that's all. And I think civilization is going to move in and take over your prairies and mountains, my friend. Men like us, we have to be ready for that. You've got to flow with the tide, Kirk. My father used to always tell me that. I thought he was just preaching then, but I've come to realize he was right."

Kirk met his gaze. "I don't call marching off to war flowing with the tide."

Red laughed. "Maybe not. But it will be an adventure, and we love adventure."

"Fighting Indians and bears is plenty of adventure for me."

"I don't see anything good ahead for the Indians, either. More and more whites are coming out here. You know what that will mean for our red friends. It won't be like the days of the rendezvous, when all we wanted to do was trade with them and share in games with them, buy their women for a night. It's a new breed of whites coming out here, Kirk, and they've got no feelings for the Indians, no understanding of them, no desire to be friends and share the land with them. They'll want the land for themselves, and to hell with the Indians."

Kirk shook his head. "I'd fight on the Indian's side."

"Maybe. Depends on what is at stake at the time."

"What do you mean?"

Red drew on his cigar. "Well, what if you settled, had a family—married a white woman; and then Indians attacked you. A white man settles, he starts thinking the land belongs to him. He changes."

"Not me. I'll never change, and I'll never settle."

Red grinned slyly, and Kirk scowled. "You trying to tell me something, Red McKinley? What did you mean about that remark earlier—that I'd *need* a drink? Seems to me like you've been skirting around something ever since we came in here."

Red took the cigar from his mouth. "Well, I offered to have you come with me to Mexico. You'd better give it some thought, my friend, or you might find yourself more settled than you'd like. You see Fast Runner when you came in?"

"I saw him. He jumped up and ran off before I could say a word to him."

Red nodded. "He and the rest of his clan have been camped here for a week, hoping you'd show up like you usually do this time of year. You dumped Gray Bird Woman off here last year before you went to Kansas City, remember?"

Kirk sighed. "I didn't 'dump' her. She *wanted* to come back. She missed her people. I would have gladly kept her. What difference does it make?"

"I think I'd better let Fast Runner and Gray Bird Woman tell you. She's married to a Cheyenne warrior now—Standing Bear."

Kirk nodded. "He's an honored man among the Cheyenne. She

picked herself a good husband, and Standing Bear chose a good woman."

"I expect so. But I don't think he figured on inheriting a couple of half-breed pups along with her."

Kirk paled. "What?"

Red poured him another shot of whiskey. "You'd better take another slug of this stuff," he told the man. "You'll need it."

Kirk shoved the glass away. "Gray Bird Woman had my baby?"

Red sighed. "Not just one . . . two. Twins. I've been here about a week, but I haven't seen either one. All I know is what Fast Runner told me when he was asking if I knew where you were. Standing Bear wants to keep the boy. You know how the Cheyenne are about children, especially sons. But he thinks a half-breed daughter is worthless. Nobody else in the tribe wants her. They want to give her to you. Fast Runner says she's about four months old already. They've been waiting here, hoping you'd show up."

Kirk stared at the man in astonishment. He reached for the glass he had shoved away. "You're right," he told Red. "I do need this." He slugged down the hot whiskey, his mind whirling with indecision. A child of his own flesh and blood! It was a strange feeling. He had never given much thought to having children of his own, never thought he would care one way or another. Yet suddenly, the knowledge that such children existed gave him a strange, warm, almost proud feeling. He caught Red's look. "What the hell would I do with even one baby, let alone two?"

"One is all you'd have to be concerned about. Standing Bear wants the son. I wouldn't go demanding to have the boy. You'll get yourself in deeper than you can handle."

"Hell, I don't even know if I want the girl, let alone *both* of them!"

"You don't have a whole lot of choice, my friend. None of these white settlers will take on an Indian baby, and if he doesn't get rid of it soon, Standing Bear is going to abandon it. The only reason he hasn't so far is because of Gray Bird Woman. Fast Runner says she puts up such a fuss that Standing Bear gives in to her. But one of these days he's going to put his foot down. You want a child of your blood to die alone and helpless on the plains, tore apart by wolves?"

Kirk rose suddenly. "Let's get out of here." He headed outside without another word. Red quickly followed, hurrying to catch up as Kirk moved to his horses.

"You going to run out on your kid?" Red asked.

Kirk whirled, his eyes angry. "Hell no! I'm just—" He threw his hands up in the air. "I don't know. Maybe I *should* go off to Mexico with you."

"Kirk, my friend, I see something in those eyes. A bit of pride, maybe, that you're a father? I know you, David Kirkland, better than most, I think. You're a man with a conscience, a firm believer in what's wrong and what's right, and a man possessive of what belongs to him."

Kirk nervously checked his pelts. "Why don't you just shut up and let me think," he told Red. "This is quite a shock." He faced the man. "And how in hell do I know those kids are really mine?"

Red shrugged. "You're the one who lived with her last winter. Fast Runner says the little girl has light hair and blue eyes. You figure it out."

Kirk frowned. "Blue eyes?" Red nodded, and Kirk cursed himself for coming here at all, cursed his feelings of responsibility for those close to him. It almost got him killed the day he fought off Indians to save Red's life. Now he knew he had children of his own blood living among the Cheyenne—a little girl that no one wanted. He knew that feeling well. Bad memories of his life at the orphanage back East would stay with him forever. He looked at Red with a helpless, almost pleading look. "What the hell should I do, Red?"

The man just grinned and shook his head. "I know what I'd do. I'd run as fast as my horse could go. But I'm not you, and—" He hesitated, looking past Kirk toward the fort's gate. "I think the time has come to decide, my friend."

Kirk turned to look. Just outside the gate he saw Gray Bird Woman watching him. Fast Runner and Standing Bear stood on either side of her, and Gray Bird Woman held a cradleboard in her arms. Kirk's heartbeat quickened. "Damn," he muttered. He glanced at Red, who shook his head.

"I can't help you, friend. Do what you think is best."

Kirk scowled at him, then turned and walked across the courtyard to the gate. As soon as he came closer, he realized this was as difficult for Gray Bird Woman as it was for him. It was obvious she had been crying but was trying to be brave.

The noise of activity around the fort seemed to die away into a distant echo for Kirk. What a strange day this had turned out to be. He wished he had not come here at all. To have found out after the little girl was dead, or never to have known at all, would have left him free of guilt. He knew instinctively that although he had never thought of having children of his own, now that they existed, he could not turn away from them.

He stood before the Indians awkwardly, unsure what to do or say until Standing Bear barked a command to Gray Bird Woman in his own tongue, telling her to hand the child in her arms over to Kirk. She obeyed, keeping her head down to hide her tears. Kirk just stared at the infant for a moment before finally taking the cradleboard.

"It is a girl child," Standing Bear told him in the Cheyenne tongue. "We have waited here for you. You are the father. You have first right to her. I do not want this girl child with white blood."

Kirk didn't look down at the baby. He kept his eyes on Standing Bear. "What about the boy?" he asked, speaking in Cheyenne. "I have first rights to him, too."

"No!" Standing Bear said. "We keep the boy!"

"He's my son!"

Gray Bird Woman raised her eyes then, and Kirk was stunned by the sorrow in them. "Please," she begged. "Do not take both my babies from me, Kirk. To say good-bye to just one is more than my heart can bear. Do not try to take Yellow Eagle."

His eyes met hers, remembering nights of passion. Kirk had respected her, taken pleasure in her, but he had not loved her. He was a man who knew little of what love was supposed to be, but now that he held his baby daughter in his arms, he was beginning to understand it better.

"That's his name?" he asked. "Yellow Eagle?"

Gray Bird Woman nodded. "He is a fine, healthy boy."

"I want to see him."

"No!" It was Standing Bear who answered. "If you see him, you will try to steal him away. It is easier this way. It is done!" He folded his arms in a proud, determined stance, and Kirk knew the Indians well enough to realize that to argue further would only bring trouble.

Gray Bird Woman watched Kirk a moment longer. "I served you well," she told him. "We were good friends."

Kirk nodded. "That we were."

"Promise me you will keep our daughter. Promise me you will not abandon her or give her to someone who would not love her as much."

Kirk finally looked down at the bundle in his arms. The moment he set eyes on the little girl, he was smitten. She hardly looked Indian at all, except for her tawny skin. She gazed up at him out of a lovely, delicate-featured face, her eyes the same bright blue as his own, her hair light.

"My God, she's beautiful," Kirk muttered. He did not need time to think about whether or not he would keep his little daughter. He looked back at Gray Bird Woman. "I promise," he told her.

She dropped her eyes. "It is good. My heart will not hurt quite so much," she told him. "Her name . . . is Morning Star." She looked up at him again. "Good-bye, Kirk." She turned and quickly walked away. Standing Bear and Fast Runner remained for a moment.

"Do not try to steal your son," Standing Bear warned. "You will die, and I will kill the girl baby! Gray Bird Woman belongs to me now. I let her keep the son so that her heart does not die, and because the boy is stronger and someday will be a warrior. Soon Gray Bird Woman will have more children, and it will ease the pain of giving up the daughter. She belongs to you now, David Kirkland. See that you keep your promise to Gray Bird Woman."

The man whirled and left. "We leave soon," Fast Runner told Kirk. "Do not try to see the boy. It is best this way." He followed after Standing Bear, and Kirk stared after them until Morning Star made a gurgling sound. He looked down at her, overwhelmed with a myriad of emotions.

"What the hell do I do now?" he asked Red, who stepped up for a closer look. The sight of big, rugged David Kirkland standing there with a cradleboard in his arms made it difficult for Red not to laugh and he finally chuckled as he studied the beautiful little face.

"Well, friend, I suggest you ask some of the womenfolk here how to take care of her. Find yourself a bottle and nipple, if they're to be had around here, and buy yourself a milk cow or goat." He almost laughed at the helpless look on Kirk's face. "What you *really* need is a woman. You'd better think twice about saying you'll never settle. That pretty little thing you're holding there kind of changes things." He shook his head. "You could always leave her off someplace and come to Mexico with me."

Kirk smiled into the trusting blue eyes. He found it incredible that in an instant all the feelings of pride and possessiveness that came with fatherhood had flooded into him. He looked out at the Indian camp, longing to see his son but knowing it would not be allowed. This little girl he held needed him now, and he could not risk losing his life. Fast Runner was right. It was best if he never set eyes on the boy.

He studied the distant mountains. He had planned on heading back into them soon. Now, all that had changed. But he hardly knew any women. Then he thought for a moment about the young girl called Beatrice back in Kansas City, before little Morning Star started to fuss. He turned to Red. "I can't leave her with just anybody. I promised Gray Bird Woman. But it's not just that. Hell, Red, she's mine!" He looked back down at the baby. "You're right. I do need a woman."

Red grinned. "You got one in mind?"

Kirk nodded slowly. "I might, if she'll agree to take care of this baby like it was her own."

"You're talking about settling, Kirk. You going to be able to do that?"

Kirk looked back out at the mountains. "I guess I have to try, don't I?" He turned to walk back inside the fort, and an eagle circled overhead, casting its shadow over them. Kirk looked up, feeling an odd ache in his heart.

Morning Star fussed more, and he touched her mouth with a knuckle. She began sucking on it. "Sweet Jesus," he muttered.

CHAPTER
TWO

Sixteen-year-old Beatrice Ritter looked up from her sweeping when she heard her cousin Cynthia's voice. Cynthia and her mother had come dashing into her father's store so that Cynthia could show off her new pink morning dress.

Bea returned to her sweeping, fighting the hurt and jealousy. Cynthia was only one year older than she, and the girl was so spoiled and pampered that Bea could hardly bear to be around her; but she had no choice. Bea's parents were dead, and she was too young to be out on her own. Three years ago her uncle Jake had agreed to give Bea a home, but there had been no love included in the offer.

Jake Ritter was wealthy, by most standards. He owned two supply stores in Kansas City, and one of the nicest houses in town, although Bea shared little in her uncle's riches. For her the Ritter home was nothing more than a shelter where she got fed—slave's quarters, she considered it. Her room was on the third floor, the hottest part of the house in summer, the coldest in winter. She spent most of her time here at the store, working for Uncle Jake for no pay. She was expected to help him to "earn her keep," while Cynthia was never expected to lift a finger, not even at home; Jake's nineteen-year-old son, Charley, was off at college in the East.

Bea glanced up again as Cynthia whirled around for her father. Her mother, Bea's Aunt Marlene, carried on about how beautiful the dress was, and how pretty Cynthia looked in it.

"Oh, Jake, we must have a party for her," the woman told her husband. "It's time Cynthia was socializing more, and meeting eligible young men." The woman watched Cynthia proudly, explaining to Jake that the dress was the latest fashion. "Don't the bell sleeves look lovely," she was saying, "especially with the lace-edged engageantes?"

"I don't understand your fancy description, but it sure looks pretty," Jake answered, admiring his daughter. Cynthia's pretty blond hair peeked out from under her flower- and ribbon-trimmed bonnet in perfect curls. She turned her pale blues eyes to glance at her cousin Bea, who stood at the back of the store, still holding the broom. She smiled haughtily and looked down her nose at Bea's plain brown cotton dress.

Bea turned away to finish her sweeping, hiding tears and longing to be with her parents again. But that could never be. Her father, Jake's brother, had been killed in a riding accident five years ago. Uncle Jake had grudgingly taken in Bea and her mother; but two years ago her mother had become gravely ill and had died.

Suddenly Bea was an orphan, and her uncle made no bones about the "strain" on his resources, telling her she would have to "help out," to earn her keep by working at the store, while Cynthia spent her days doing embroidery and taking piano lessons.

Bea swept vigorously in her anger. Helping out was hardly the term for how hard Uncle Jake made her work. He kept her at the store for up to twelve hours a day, seven days a week, sometimes doing work more suited to a man or a slave than a sixteen-year-old girl. Even so, she knew she could bear it if she felt even a hint of love from her aunt and uncle. But she knew she was considered a burden. Uncle Jake never failed to remind her how worthless her father had been, how irresponsible he'd been to leave behind a wife and child and absolutely nothing of any value to help care for them.

Bea's most treasured dream was to get out from under her uncle's care and be on her own. Most of all, she wanted her own home, her own clothes, something of value that belonged only to her. She didn't mind working hard, but she wanted it to be for her own benefit, not someone else's.

She cringed when she heard Cynthia's footsteps approaching. She knew what was coming, and she dreaded it.

"Bea, do you like my new dress?" Cynthia asked in the sweetly artificial voice she liked to use to sound more feminine.

Bea glanced at her, then continued her sweeping. "It's pretty," she said casually. *Too pretty for you,* she wanted to add. Cynthia tried her best to be beautiful, but she could not hide her narrow eyes and sharp nose, nor could she do anything about her small mouth.

Bea realized she was no beauty herself, but she was certainly prettier than Cynthia and could be even prettier if allowed the same nice clothes and fancy hairdo. Her own hair and eyes were dark. She had high cheekbones and full lips, and a nicely shaped nose. But she thought she was too tall, her skin a little too dark ever to have the "delicate" look most men seemed to prefer.

"It's more than just pretty," Cynthia retorted, pouting slightly as she twirled around. "Mother is having some more dresses made for me. You can have some of my old ones if you want." She looked Bea over. "Of course, someone will probably have to lengthen them, since you're so much taller than I am. When will you be finished working? You can come to my room and try them on."

"You'll be off doing something else before I get home," Bea answered, checking her anger. *Someday,* Bea thought, *someday I'll live much more grandly than you, Cynthia Ritter, and my own daughters will be far more pampered.*

"Well, we'll find a time to get together and try on dresses," Cynthia told her mockingly. "Just don't go in my room if I'm not home. There are special things in there I don't want anyone to touch."

"I wouldn't think of going into your room, Cindy." Bea pretended to be busily sweeping as she suddenly pushed the broom hard, throwing dust onto Cynthia's shoes and the hem of her dress.

Cynthia gasped and stepped back. "Oh, I'm sorry," Bea told her, forcing back the urge to smile. "You'd better go, Cindy; it's too dirty back here for you."

Cynthia's eyes glittered with anger as she shook at her dress. "You did that on purpose!"

"I did no such thing. Besides, you're the one who chose to come back here where you don't belong. I didn't ask you."

Cynthia stepped closer, eyes blazing. "You're an ingrate, cousin Bea," she sneered, "and you're just *jealous*. You should be *happy* my father took you in like he did. It's only proper that you should earn your keep!"

Bea forced back the hurt, the longing to be loved. "Of course it is," she answered, "and that's what I'm trying to do, so get out of my way."

Cynthia sniffed and whirled, petticoats bustling as she stomped away. "Let's go, Mother," she said, her nose in the air. Marlene Ritter stopped talking to her husband and hurried after her daughter.

"Cynthia, wait! What's wrong?"

Cynthia was already out the door. Bea felt sick as she watched her cousin through the glass of the door. Cynthia was carrying on and crying. Bea could just imagine what she was saying to her mother. Her cousin could turn on the tears whenever she wanted.

Bea turned away and swept dirt toward the back room, taking down a dustpan. She felt dirty and frumpy and hot. She leaned down to sweep dirt into the dustpan, then stepped outside to dump it into a waste can behind the store. When she came back inside, her Aunt Marlene was standing in the back room. Bea was not surprised. She breathed deeply for courage, seeing the angry, accusing look in her aunt's narrow eyes.

"I'll not have you talk to Cynthia and treat her the way you just did, Beatrice," the woman said sternly. "This has happened before, and I've warned you time and again. You continue to show your ungratefulness for all we've done for you, and I have had just about all I can take."

Bea thought how much Cynthia looked like her mother, the same sharp nose and small mouth. "I'm sorry, Aunt Marlene. I'm just tired. How do you think I feel, all dirty and sweaty, and then Cynthia comes over to flaunt a new dress in front of me?"

"She was only excited about it. She even offered to let you come to her room and try on some of her old dresses, which are all quite lovely, I might add. Now you will stop upsetting Cynthia and you will show more gratitude. It's two years before you're of age, and unless you want to be turned out into the street before then to fend for yourself, you'll behave yourself. Am I understood?"

Bea often wondered if being sent out on her own might be better than life with her aunt and uncle, but the thought frightened her. Perhaps if she hadn't lost her parents so close together, it would be easier. The sudden, terrible loneliness and homelessness had made her cling to her aunt and uncle's household, in spite of their cold attitude and the hard work. At least they were family. "I understand," she told her aunt, facing her squarely.

Marlene turned and walked out of the back room, and Bea stood there fighting tears. "Someday I'll be a rich lady like you," she said quietly, teeth gritted. "No one will ever talk to me like that again." A tear slipped down her cheek, and she promptly brushed it away. She had two more years to put up with her aunt and uncle and Cynthia, unless she found a way out of this drudgery sooner. By the time she was eighteen, she would have figured out a way to do just fine on her own. Until then, she would not let them make her cry.

She set the broom aside and went into the main room of the supply store, where Uncle Jake glared at her. She stayed toward the back of the room, but his voice carried back to her loudly. "I want every piece of china on display along the back wall taken down and washed, Bea, and the shelves cleaned before you go home tonight."

Her heart sank. "But it's almost quitting time, and it's so hot, Uncle Jake."

"Well, maybe you'll think about such things before you get Cynthia all upset again." He untied his apron and hung it on a hook, "I'm going home to supper. You lock up and come along when you're finished."

Bea's own stomach growled with hunger.

"It will be dark by then. You've always said Cynthia and I shouldn't walk the streets after dark."

He gave her a disdainful glance. "I don't think you have to worry about any men bothering you. Besides, it isn't that far, and most people in town know you're my niece." He laid the keys on the counter. "Make sure you lock up properly."

The man left, and Beatrice stood staring after him. Had he forgotten she hadn't had anything to eat for six hours? She couldn't understand why her aunt and uncle resented her so. It was as though they blamed her for her situation, when there was nothing she could have done about it. Were Uncle Jake and Aunt Marlene ashamed of her?

She began taking down the china, carrying several plates to the back room. She would have to fetch some water from a pump outside. She hurried out, determined to finish as quickly as possible and prove to her uncle that the chore was not nearly as terrible or time-consuming as he meant for it to be. Hunger added to her haste. She wanted to cry so badly that she almost felt sick, but she decided she would be ill rather than shed a tear. No one was going to make Bea Ritter cry, and no one was going to destroy her dreams.

Bea set the last plate in place, the darkened store lit only by an oil lamp. Voices and piano music from a nearby saloon filtered into the store, and she dreaded going outside to walk home; but she had already decided she would show no fear once she got there. She had upset "poor Cynthia," and her Uncle Jake wanted her to suffer for it. She knew that making her walk home alone was his way of causing her anguish, his idea of a proper punishment on top of a sixteen-hour workday.

She carried the lantern into the back room, where she brushed dust from her dress and washed her face and hands. She opened a jar of cream that she had taken from a shelf in the store, not caring whether her uncle would be angry. After sixteen hours, he could afford to let her use some cream, and she decided she certainly deserved it. It was a small enough luxury.

She worked the cream into her skin, closing her eyes and pretending she was a beautiful, rich woman who could afford all the creams and perfumes she desired. Her dress was not a dull brown, but a beautiful pink like Cynthia's. Her hair was piled into curls on the top of her head, and her cheeks were rosy with rouge. Soon a fancy carriage would come for her and whisk her away to her mansion.

She sighed, opening her eyes to study the plain face in the mirror. She set the jar of cream aside and picked up the lantern, going into the main store and checking the china display once more before picking up the keys and going to the door. She blew out the lamp and set it down, made sure the closed sign was turned the right way, and carefully locked the doors, unaware at first that a man sat on a bench nearby. She slipped the keys into her pocket and turned, then gasped when the man rose. His presence was so commanding that Bea stepped back at first, afraid.

"Miss Beatrice," he said quietly. "Do you remember me? My name's David Kirkland. I was here about a year ago—bought a rifle from the owner. I think he said at the time you were his niece."

Bea looked around to see if anyone was close by in case she needed to scream for help.

"I don't mean you any harm, ma'am. I—um—I don't remember your last name, but I came here to talk to you. You'll probably give me a kick and send me off, but I wish you'd at least hear me out."

There was a sincerity in his voice that got her attention. She looked him over, her heart beating a little faster. David Kirkland! Yes, she did remember him, the tall, handsome mountain man in buckskins she had met so many months before. She remembered how he had looked at her, spoken to her. She thought he might come back to see her again, but he never had . . . until now.

"I . . . what on earth do you want, Mr. Kirkland? And why are you here at this hour?"

"I came earlier, but you looked awful busy." He looked around. "You alone?"

"Yes. I had some extra work to do before I could go home."

He frowned. "Your uncle let you stay here alone? He's letting you walk home alone?"

She felt her cheeks coloring, embarrassed for him to know the kind of man her uncle was. "I'm afraid my uncle considers me something of a burden. It's all right. I plan on getting out on my own soon."

"There's no reason for him to make you work this late and walk home alone. I'll walk you."

She felt suddenly shaky, nervous. "You . . . don't have to do that."

"Of course I do. Somebody ought to give that uncle of yours what for."

She smiled at the idea. "Mr. Kirkland, you haven't said why you're here. You said you had to talk to me."

He removed his hat. "Yes, ma'am. Let's walk farther down the street, away from the noise of the saloon."

She hesitated, then decided there was nothing to fear. He seemed genuinely concerned for her welfare, and his handsome blue eyes brought a flutter to her heart. She nearly trembled when he took her arm, and she walked on trembling legs past other closed shops, up the street toward the Ritter home. Kirk stopped at a bench in a quieter section of town and sat down, urging her to sit beside him. Bea obeyed, wondering if she was being careless—or foolish.

He studied her in the dim light of the street lantern. "Most people just call me Kirk," he said. "What is your last name?"

"Ritter," she answered. "Beatrice Ritter. You may call me Bea."

He nodded. "Well, Bea. . . ." He cleared his throat, seeming suddenly nervous. "Well, uh, the fact is, I never quite forgot about you after I left here last year."

Bea's pulse raced and her cheeks reddened slightly. She put a hand to her chest, feeling suddenly beautiful. She worked too many hours every day to give men much thought, but this man had been in her thoughts often since she first met him. Would it seem bold to tell him? After all, he had admitted the same to her. She swallowed before answering. "I have thought about you often, too, Mr. Kirkland."

"Kirk," he reminded her. His gaze met hers. "That true?"

She felt herself blushing again, and she dropped her eyes. "Yes."

He looked out at the dark street. "Bea, where I come from, things aren't done the conventional way. I mean, a man does what he has to do to survive. Folks do what's necessary to look out for each other. Why, I've seen men and women marry who are practically strangers. A woman with several kids loses a husband along the trail west, and some single man or some widower hooks up with her so he'll have a woman to tend to him, and she'll have a man to protect her and provide for her and the kids."

Bea frowned, unsure what he was trying to tell her.

Kirk fingered his hat nervously. "I—I came here with a need, Bea. I need a wife, and you were the first woman who came to mind."

Her eyes widened in shock. "What?" She could hardly believe her ears. It was true she had been attracted to this man, but that had been a whole year ago, and they had hardly spoken two words to each other! She started to rise. "Mr. Kirkland, I can't—"

"Please hear me out," he interrupted, grasping her arm and turning to face her. "Please sit down and listen to me."

Bea slowly sank back onto the bench, staring at him in wonder. His eyes took on a pleading look. "I've got a child," he told her, "a little baby girl. Her mother was Cheyenne, and her people wouldn't let her keep the baby. She came to me at Bent's Fort about a month ago and said I had to take the baby, made me promise to take care of it."

He let go of her arm and looked away again. "I thought about trying to give her to somebody else, but once I held her and all. . . ." He shrugged. "She's mine, my little girl." He met her eyes again. "She's beautiful, Bea, the most perfect child you'd ever want to see; and she doesn't even look Indian. She's got my hair and my eyes."

Bea scrambled to think straight. "You . . . you want *me* to be a mother to your little girl?"

His eyes moved over her. "I . . . um . . . I thought you might consider it, unless, of course, you're already spoken for. I mean, if I'm going to take care of her proper, she's got to have a mother. I had a hell of a time traveling with her. Why, I had to bring along a stupid goat for milk, and special rags for diapers. A lady at Bent's Fort showed me how to change her and how to feed her with one of those contraptions with a nipple on the end—" He stopped short, realizing he had embarrassed her with the word nipple.

Bea looked away, her cheeks feeling hot. She knew what was expected of a wife, and although she was attracted to David Kirkland and flattered that he had remembered her, she was not ready to be a wife to any man. "I—I don't know what to say, Mr.—I mean, Kirk. This is very strange." She studied his face. "You traveled all the way here from Bent's Fort with a little baby?"

"Yes, ma'am. And I'll tell you right now, I'm full attached to that child. Nothing could make me give her up now. If you won't marry me, I'll have to find somebody else. I just thought maybe you'd consider it. Last time I was here, I got the impression you weren't very happy. It looked like your uncle worked you hard, and he"—his eyes moved over her plain dress, and she felt embarrassed—"he doesn't seem to take very good care of you, leaving you alone to lock up and walk home like this. I asked about you when I was here last, and he told me your folks were dead."

He rose, turning to face her and leaning against a post. "I'll say it out, Bea. I need a mother for my baby girl, and since I'd thought a lot about you over the past year, I figured I'd come to you first. I know it's not a very romantic way to approach a woman, but where I come from, there isn't always time for romance. I know you don't love me—yet—and I don't . . . well . . . I have to get to know you better, too. But you're a handsome woman and a hard worker, and you need somebody to take care of you. You have my word that I wouldn't . . . well, I wouldn't expect you to be a wife to me in all ways—not right off. I'm not an animal, ma'am, and I've never hurt a woman. I've never lived a settled life, but I'd do it for you . . . whatever you wanted."

Bea shivered with a mixture of excitement and fear. "I just don't know, Kirk." She put a hand to her hair, wishing she weren't so tired and dirty. "I'll have to think about what you've told me." She looked up at him. "Where is the baby?"

"She's at Sadie's place, the other end of town." He saw the shock in her eyes. "Now don't get all lathered. I know what somebody like you might think of a woman like Sadie Blake, but she's a good woman, and she and the other women there are taking real good care of Morning Star."

Bea rose slowly. "Morning Star? That's her name?"

He nodded, searching her dark eyes hopefully. Bea Ritter was not beautiful, but she had fine, clear skin and solid features, with a good shape to her, except for being a little tall and big-boned. Compared to the kind of women he was accustomed to, Bea was beautiful, and he sensed a certain strength beneath her vulnerability. He figured that it was her youth and the loneliness she must feel losing her parents and living with an uncle who worked her practically to death.

"She shouldn't be over there," Bea told him.

"I know, but I've got no choice for now." He looked serious. "I'd be a good husband, Bea. I wouldn't even touch you at first. All I want is for you to love my little girl, not just take care of her, but really love her, like your own. A kid knows when it isn't loved. I know the feeling myself, and I reckon you do, too." He stepped closer. "You and I—we're a lot alike in some ways, Bea. I lost my own parents when I was real young, and I was raised in an orphanage. I ran off when I was only about twelve. I took up with a mountain man, and that's the only life I've lived since then. I'm twenty-five now. Could I ask how old you are?"

She swallowed, wondering if she wanted to belong to such a big man, a man who could break her in half if he chose to do so. Still, he seemed like a good man. Surely a man who willingly took his baby daughter to care for had to have a lot of good in him. "I'm sixteen," she told him.

He nodded. "Well, we both understand how it feels to be homeless and unloved, don't we? I don't want that for my little girl."

She searched his blue eyes, feeling a spark that she suspected could turn into love. "I would never make a child feel the way my aunt and uncle make me feel," she answered. "That much I could promise you. But . . . I need time to think about this, Kirk. It's all so . . . so unreal . . . such a surprise."

"I understand." He took her arm. "I'll walk you home. I ought to talk to your uncle."

"No, I . . . I don't want my uncle to see you, to know anything about you."

He frowned. "Why not?"

"I just . . . he wouldn't care one way or another. But I'm afraid he'd try to stop me from doing what I want. It's not that he cares what happens to me, but he wouldn't want to lose my help at the store; and it seems like he and my aunt always find a way to ruin any happiness I find." She held her chin higher. "I have a right to make my own decisions, don't you think?"

"I expect so."

She stopped walking and looked up at him. "If I accept your offer, can we do it my way?"

"Your way? What do you mean?"

"I—I'm not sure yet. I just want to know that if I promise to love the baby and raise her as my own, I can make certain conditions, certain requests that will be honored?"

He watched her closely a moment. "All right—long as you say them out up front, before we see a preacher."

"Fine."

"You'll do it then?"

"I don't know yet. Meet me outside the store again tomorrow night and I'll tell you. Wait until my uncle leaves."

"Whatever you say. But I still think he should know."

Bea stiffened. "He doesn't deserve to know, not until after it's too late." She turned to him. "I'd better get home. You can watch out for me but don't walk beside me. I don't want anyone to see us and tell my uncle, or he might not let me leave the house tomorrow. He and Aunt Marlene are afraid I'll be courted and get married before their precious daughter, Cynthia does. Uncle Jake doesn't let me see men."

Kirk smiled slightly. "Well, I'm kind of glad. I always figured if I ever took a wife, I'd want her to be just mine, if you know what I mean."

Her cheeks flushed hot again and she turned away. "Good night, Kirk." She hurried off, feeling a surprising jealousy at the thought of the man going back to Sadie's place tonight. Would he sleep with the woman?

She walked faster, deciding that what David Kirkland did tonight was the least of her worries for the moment. Out of a clear blue sky the man had come back to Kansas City to ask her to be his wife! She realized there was no way he could really love her—not yet, anyway. All he wanted was a woman to take care of his baby. But marrying him opened up whole new avenues for her. It could be her way to realizing some of her own dreams, and it was certainly a way to get away from Uncle Jake and Aunt Marlene.

She knew that marriage was not a pathway to independence for most women, but to her it spelled a certain freedom. Was she a fool to consider David Kirkland's outrageous offer? She turned to see him walking some distance behind her. He was a big, handsome, honest man. She believed him when he said he would make no demands on her; but what kind of future was there with a mountain man who had never held a regular job or lived in one place? Still, he seemed willing to settle for her sake.

She felt suddenly beautiful, desired, needed. Perhaps he didn't love her, but people could learn to love each other, couldn't they? Like Kirk had said, out in the great West where he came from, sometimes total strangers got married. She realized his offer seemed perfectly sane and acceptable to him, for he came from a world far different from her own, and that fascinated her.

She looked back at him once more, feeling protected and safe. One thing was sure—David Kirkland was a man who knew how to take care of himself and protect his own. That was a good feeling. She reached the house, then turned and nodded to him before going inside.

Kirk gave her a little wave. He had already decided not to tell her about his son. It was enough of a shock to bring her a baby girl and propose marriage and motherhood both at the same time. He would never know his Indian son, and the thought brought a heaviness to his heart, more painful because he would never be able to share the ache of it with anyone else. Only Red McKinley knew about Morning Star's twin brother, and it was not likely he would ever see Red again. If Beatrice Ritter accepted his offer, his whole life would change forever. He had no choice. He had a beautiful little daughter who needed him, and he would do what was necessary to raise her properly.

Night seemed a long time coming. Bea was hardly aware of her daily chores, dusting, taking inventory, waiting on customers mechanically, thinking with secret excitement and a feeling of victory that no one knew what she would do tonight. It was difficult to add up costs, count pieces of candy, or accurately measure bolts of cloth, for her mind was not on her work.

There was nothing logical about her decision. It was dangerous, foolish, risky—yet no argument she posed could change her mind. The thought of getting out of her uncle's house overshadowed all warnings.

No one had asked why she wore one of her better dresses today, not that it was especially fancy. Cynthia hadn't spoken to her at the breakfast table, just looked at her coldly. Bea wondered if Cynthia thought she had worn her pink flowered muslin just to try to look prettier after seeing Cynthia's new dress the day before.

Bea didn't care what she or anyone else thought. At least no questions had been asked. She had bathed before coming to the store, and she had sprinkled on lilac water. She had plaited her dark hair into one thick braid down her back, which she thought looked nicer than a bun, and she had smuggled extra clothes into the store under the skirt of her dress. She didn't have enough possessions to bother packing a bag; what she needed after tonight, David Kirkland would have to buy for her.

The time finally came when Jake Ritter turned over the closed sign on the door. Her uncle had hardly talked to her all day, still annoyed with her for upsetting his daughter. Bea offered to stay and finish inventory, apologizing again for seeming "ungrateful," and telling him she wanted to make up for it.

Jake accepted her offer with grudging satisfaction, and left. Bea pulled the shades down over the door windows. She waited until it was fully dark, then went to the back room and, just as she had the night before, gently applied more of the luxurious cream to her face. She pinched her cheeks to bring some color into them, wishing again her skin was pale and pretty.

She smoothed her dress and breathed deeply for courage, then walked to the front door. Opening it, she stepped outside onto the boardwalk. The streets seemed quieter than usual. She looked up and down the street, until she saw David Kirkland walking toward the store. He had kept his promise.

She quickly stepped back inside the building, and when he came to the door she quietly told him to go around back. After locking the front door, she carried a lantern to the back room and opened the door, letting Kirk inside.

He removed his hat, and Bea looked up at him, sudden doubts again filling her at the realization of what a big man he was. The small back room only emphasized his stature. She noticed he had shaved his beard but had left a mustache, and he had gotten a haircut. He wore trousers and a shirt instead of buckskins, and she smelled the pleasant scent of a man's toilet water. His blond hair hung in neat waves to his shirt collar, and his eyes seemed even bluer in the lamplight.

Whether the man would be a good provider was yet to be seen, but one thing could not be denied—he was indeed handsome. She reminded herself he must be good, or he wouldn't have kept his baby girl and willed himself to settle down for her sake.

"Have you made up your mind, Bea?" he asked.

Her blood rushed with a mixture of anticipation and fear. "Yes," she answered. "I'll marry you, David Kirkland, and I'll be a mother to your little girl, but I have certain conditions."

He nodded. "What are they?"

She wondered where she got her courage. Perhaps it was the deep hurt she had suffered at the hands of her aunt and uncle and Cynthia that drove her to do something so daring and outrageous. She took a deep breath, her bold gaze on his face.

"We'll leave tonight," she answered, seeing surprise in his eyes. "I don't intend to tell my uncle until we're far from here and we're married. Otherwise he might try to stop us."

He frowned. "If you think that's best."

"I do." She folded her arms. "I want to go to St. Louis. I've never seen St. Louis, and I hear tell it's a pretty big city. You could find work there."

Kirk refused to express his aversion to such a move. Farther east. The thought brought an ache to his insides. What about his beautiful mountains? Still, he knew he would have to find work. St. Louis was probably as good a place as any, and he was not a man to take to farming; but living in a city would not be easy for him.

"I want a home," Bea went on, "a real home—a house of my own that I can fix my own way and live like a proper wife. I want nice things. I don't mean that I expect to live fancy like my aunt and uncle, but I don't want to live like poor folks either. You've got to work like a proper husband, and in return I'll make a nice home for you. I'm a good cook and I'm clean. I'll love your little girl like my own, that you can count on. But I want folks to think she's ours. I don't ever want to tell anyone she isn't. I don't want folks thinking you only married me to be a mother to her, even if it's true."

His eyes moved over her, and he swallowed. "It wouldn't be the complete truth, Bea," he answered, making her cheeks redden. "I mean, if I didn't already have fond thoughts of you, I wouldn't have asked."

Her blood tingled and she suddenly felt too warm. She dropped her eyes. "Another reason I don't want anyone to know the truth about your little girl is because some folks aren't very nice to someone with Indian blood. It will be better for her not to know herself." She met his eyes again. "I think she should think we're her real parents. As long as she doesn't look Indian, like you say, why should she be burdened with knowing she's got Indian blood? She'll feel more loved if she thinks I'm her real mother, and she won't ever feel she has reason to be ashamed."

Kirk frowned, looking around the little room while he seemed to be thinking things over. "I never connected being Indian with being ashamed," he finally said, not looking at her. "Where I come from, white men and Indians mix like blood brothers. I lived with Morning Star's mother for over a year." He turned to face Bea, seeing a hint of jealousy in her dark eyes. "She was a good woman." He sighed deeply. "What I'm saying is many of my closest friends have been Indians, Bea, and I'll never talk against them. I don't like what I can see is going to happen to them as more whites settle out west. But at the same time, I think I understand what you're trying to tell me. Places like this, and cities like St. Louis, people think different. My little girl might get teased and abused. I wouldn't want that." He rubbed at his eyes. "Maybe you're right. She ought to think we're her parents. The only thing about her that's dark is her skin, but it's not near as dark as a full-blood Indian's, and you're dark. With my light hair and blue eyes, I don't see why we can't pass her off as our own."

Bea nodded. "No one needs to know when we got married. We'll go to St. Louis and tell people we've already been married a while. When we get there I'll write to my uncle and tell him where I am and that I'm fine. He doesn't much care about me anyway. He won't bother coming to find me once I'm married and he knows I'm all right."

"You sure?"

A look of deep hurt came into her eyes. "I'm positive. And I don't care if I never see my aunt and uncle and cousin Cynthia again." She raised her chin proudly. "I brought some clothes with me. I want to leave tonight. I'll let my uncle wonder for a while what happened to me. It serves him right to worry for a few days. We'll be married as soon as possible, and I'll be a wife to you." She felt her face reddening again. "I just want your promise that you won't be—that you aren't a man who would abuse a woman, hit a woman."

He shook his head. "No, ma'am. I'm not that kind. And I'll wait as long as you need—"

"No. If I'm going to marry you, I'll be a proper wife right off." She felt herself trembling, and she took another deep breath, trying to keep her courage up. "If my uncle *should* decide to come after me, I want the marriage to already be properly consummated so that it cannot be annulled. I want you to be a real husband to me, and I your wife. Maybe in time we'll even be able to say we . . . we love each other."

He stepped closer, and she prayed her legs would not give way.

"I don't think that would be too hard," he told her gently. "Feelings like that don't come easy to a man like me, Bea, but since I've had Morning Star with me, I've begun to learn what the feeling is all about." He touched her arm hesitantly. "And I already love you some just for what you're doing for me and my baby girl."

She read only sincerity in his eyes, and she stood rigid as he leaned down and gently kissed her cheek. He was so handsome, so strong and sure. She wanted to love him, to experience the strange passion he stirred deep inside her. But he was still a stranger, and she knew so little of men. She wished she would be able to give herself to him with total abandon, as Morning Star's mother probably had; but she knew that would be impossible for her, at least at first. She would just have to be brave and trust Kirk to teach her, to do whatever must be done.

"I would like to rename Morning Star," she said quietly. "I want to name her Irene, after my mother. Irene Louise."

He let go of her arm. "That's a fine name."

She smiled. "It's settled then. I've wrapped my things into a blanket. I'll lock up and leave the keys inside for my uncle. He has another set. We'll take the back way to wherever Morning Star—I mean, Irene—is being kept and we'll leave tonight. Don't tell the woman taking care of her where you're going, and tell her not to say a word to my uncle."

"She won't."

She turned and picked up her little bundle of belongings. "Let's go then. I've already locked the front door and laid the keys on the counter. The back door will lock when we close it. Take that cape from the hook there and put it around my shoulders, will you?"

Kirk obeyed, patting her shoulder reassuringly when he did so. Bea felt numb. For the moment nothing seemed real. She blew out the lamp, and they walked outside. She looked up at him in the moonlight. "Remember, you promised me a real home," she said.

"You'll have it."

"I don't want you running off on me. You're not much of a settling man, I suspect, David Kirkland."

"I won't run off, Bea. I'll never leave my little girl, and I'd never abandon you after what you've done. I'll provide for you the best I can."

She took another deep breath and shivered. Whether it was the chilly night air or the realization that she was running off with a mysterious mountain man, she couldn't be sure.

Kirk put a hand to her waist and led her away. Bea smiled thinking how worried and confused her aunt and uncle would be by morning, and suddenly the idea of never seeing them or the store again made her happy. She did not look back. There was nothing in Kansas City she would miss.

CHAPTER THREE

August 1849

Bea lay on the rough-hewn bed in the crude cabin, shivering with fear and pain. The baby was coming, and she was alone. Three-year-old Irene sat beside her mother, her cheeks covered with tearstains. She was confused and frightened by her mother's groaning and crying. Irene's little brother, John David, crawled around on the straw-covered floor, unaware of his mother's suffering.

Bea was in agony, not only because she was having her second birth-child alone, but that while she lay suffering and helpless, there was no one to look after Irene and little Johnny. She turned to her daughter and took the soft little hand in hers. "Don't be afraid, Irene. Mommy will be all right. You have to be a big girl and watch Johnny for me. Can you do that?"

Irene sniffled and nodded, giving her mother a pat before climbing off the bed. Bea watched her lovingly. It would be so easy to blame Irene for her predicament, but Bea knew there was no one to blame but herself—and Kirk. She had vowed she would never blame an innocent child for something she could not help, never treat a child the way her own uncle had treated her.

Irene had made it easy to keep that promise. It was impossible not to love the child. She was naturally sweet, a beautiful, loving little girl whose pretty blue eyes were full of innocence and trust when she looked at her mother. Bea had come to love her as though she was of her own flesh and blood.

No, it was not little Irene's fault that Bea lay having a baby alone in the Sierras. She had married David Kirkland willingly, realizing she hardly knew the man, knowing he was a wanderer. She had kept her promises to him, but in her mind Kirk had failed miserably. It seemed he was never there when she needed him most.

She'd grown to love her husband, but sometimes he made her so angry and frustrated that she hated him, and this was one of those times. As she had feared from the beginning, his restless nature had gotten the better of him back in St. Louis. The job he had found there—driving wagons for a freighting company—had not lasted long. For a while they had lived in a simple but pretty little frame house, and Bea had realized part of her dream of having her own home. Now that dream was shattered.

Life had been good in St. Louis. After her first startling initiation into womanhood, Bea had learned to accept a man in her bed and had gradually grown to love her husband, in spite of the fact that he had chosen a job that kept him away for days at a time. She had her house and Irene, who was a good, quiet little girl. Everyone in St. Louis thought Irene belonged to her and Kirk, and Bea had begun living the life of a happy wife and mother, attending quilting bees, joining a church, making friends.

In November of 1847, sixteen months after she had married Kirk, she had borne him a son, John David. Bea had thought that having a second child, especially a son, would help Kirk settle even more; but all along she had sensed his restless spirit, and when rumors that gold had been discovered in California hit St. Louis, there was no holding David Kirkland home.

"It's our chance to have all the nice things you really want," he had argued with her. "I could go back to the mountains, and you'd be a rich lady. We'd both have what we want, Bea."

Kirk had told her he would go out first and send for her once he found gold, but Bea had insisted he take her and the children along, fearing that once her husband was back in the mountains, she would never hear from him again. They had sold everything and set out for California, leaving in late 1848 and spending the winter at Fort Bridger, in Utah Territory. Some called it Nebraska Territory, unsure of the dividing line. Others called it Wyoming.

Whatever it was called, it was a big, wild, dangerous land. Bea had never seen anything like it, and she had often regretted insisting on coming along. To Kirk the trip was nothing short of sheer joy. His love of this land she hated was obvious. He had actually spoken to Indians along the way, and knew several of the rugged, dangerous-looking men who had visited the fort during the winter. He had hunted for meat and lived much as he had before he married Bea.

For Kirk the trip had been exciting, but Bea found the long journey to California difficult and miserable. She had feared losing one of the children to sickness during the horribly cold winter in the mountains. To make things worse, she had become pregnant again, and now she lay having her baby alone while Kirk was off digging and panning for gold.

She had learned to use a rifle, something she thought very unladylike, in order to protect her children. She often felt terror at night, listening to wolves howl and bears claw around the cabin looking for food. And there was always the threat of being harrassed by lonely, woman-hungry men in these mountains, which were flooded with prospectors.

This was not the life she had planned, not what she had expected. Kirk had made certain promises to her, and he had not kept them, although he had sincerely tried. She knew he meant to do what he said, and that trying to find gold was his way of trying to give her a good life. But she had little faith in that dream, and now that Kirk was living in the mountains again, she feared she would never get him back to civilization.

She groaned with another pain, furious that she lay here alone while her husband was off on his own adventure, not caring that his wife could deliver at any time. Her anger increased even as her pain grew.

Kirk should be here. This crude cabin was a far cry from the pleasant little house in St. Louis, and here there were no supply stores, no doctors, not even another woman to talk to.

She could not help crying out then, and Irene ran into the bedroom. "Mommy," she sobbed, touching Bea's arm.

Bea tried to reassure her everything would be all right. She wished she had the strength to get up and build the fire, but the pains were too close together now. She feared she would die or faint, and the fire would go out, leaving the children cold and hungry. It was August, but at high elevations in the Sierras summer nights were freezing. It would be dark soon. Dark . . . wolves . . . bears.

She took Irene's tiny hand in hers. "Find some . . . bread for Johnny," she told the child. "Can you do that, Irene?"

The child nodded and scrambled back into the main room. Bea

remembered little after that. Her pains grew closer together, and she fell into deep labor, hardly aware of anything around her. She vaguely remembered the baby being delivered, remembering pulling it to her breast and cleaning membrane from its eyes, nose and mouth, doing everything from natural motherly instinct. She covered the baby and held it next to her to keep it warm, letting it feed at her breast. She wasn't even sure whether it was a girl or boy.

"Bea?"

She recognized Kirk's voice. Bea opened her eyes to see him bent over her, his eyes teary with remorse.

"My God, Bea, I thought you weren't due for another week or two. That's what you told me." With an aching heart Kirk saw the hatred and resentment in her eyes. He told himself it would go away in time, that she was just hurting and afraid.

"What are we doing here?" she said, her voice weak but the words bitter. "This isn't . . . what you promised, Kirk."

He closed his eyes and sighed, reaching toward her, but she moved her head as though she didn't want him to touch her. He pulled his hand back. "Bea, I'm close, I'm sure of it. I'm doing this for you . . . for us."

"Are you? It's just . . . an excuse, Kirk . . . so you can live in these mountains again."

"That's not true. If I *did* plan to just live in the mountains, I'd be living in the Rockies. That's where I like it best. I came here for the gold, Bea, and I'm going to find it. I swear I'll find it."

She closed her eyes, too weak and tired to argue for the moment. "I don't want . . . any more children, Kirk . . . not for a long time. It's . . . too hard out here. I'm afraid . . . they'll die." Her heart filled with alarm, and she pulled the blanket away. "The baby—"

"Let me see it." Kirk gently took the child from her and examined it. "She's fine, Bea. I'll clean her up for you."

So, Bea thought, *it's a girl.* She wondered how long she had lain here, oblivious to anything around her.

"I've built up the fire," Kirk was telling her. "Don't worry about a thing. Irene and Johnny are just fine. They're asleep now. When I'm through with the baby I'll help you bathe and get you something to eat." He started to leave the tiny bedroom.

"Kirk," Bea spoke up. He turned to look at her, holding his tiny new daughter in one arm. "There must be . . . a town somewhere below. I want to go there. I'll . . . find a way to get by . . . while you're up here. The children and I . . . we can't stay in these mountains any longer. It's too dangerous." She closed her eyes again. "Besides . . . it's best if we're apart for a while. I want no more pregnancies. Our money is already nearly used up. You can't even provide for the children you already have."

The remark cut deep. He wanted to shout at her, but this was not the time. "I'm trying, Bea, the only way I know how," he answered. "If you want to go below, I'll take you; but I'm telling you now that I'm going to find gold, and I'll do more than just provide for you and the kids. You'll live like a queen, better than that aunt and uncle of yours back in Kansas City. Maybe then you won't regret marrying me."

He watched for her reaction, but she made no reply. He knew she didn't believe him, but he was determined to show her he could do it. "I'm sorry," he added, "about you having the baby alone. I'm sorry I made you leave St. Louis, but someday you'll be glad you did, Bea." He swallowed back the hurt of her silence and turned away.

He carried his new daughter into the main room of the cabin, where he stopped to look down at little Irene, who slept quietly in a corner on a pile of deerskins. He watched her a moment, a picture of innocence and beauty. It was because of Irene that he was burdened with a wife and two more children, but he didn't really mind, if only Bea wouldn't look at him with such fury. He was trying his best to be a good husband. He would continue living this life that was so foreign to him, not just for Irene now, but for his son and his new daughter.

Secretly, in his heart, Irene would always remain special, because she was part Indian, a part of the life he had left behind. It was not that he loved her more than his other children. He just loved her in a different, special way. Half of her belonged to the land, to his past. He had never been quite sure it was right not to tell her of her Indian blood, but Bea had insisted, and for now Irene was too young to understand anyway. He had often wondered about her brother, Yellow Eagle, the son he would never know. It was far too late to tell Bea about the boy now. She had put up with enough. The knowledge that he had another child somewhere out on the open plains near the Rocky Mountains was something he would never share.

He turned to pour some heated water into a pan so that he could clean up his new daughter. Then he would bathe Bea, if she would let him touch her. Perhaps she would allow that much, but it was obvious it would be a long time before she let him back into her bed.

Bea looked up from her scrub board to greet another man bringing her his laundry. She was not sure her hands and arms and back could continue the aching, difficult task she had chosen, but at eight dollars for a dozen pieces of wash, she could not resist, no matter how hard it was on her.

It was already September 1850, and she had not heard from Kirk in four months. She and the children had spent another winter in the mountains before Kirk finally brought them in May to the small settlement called San Francisco. Right after the baby was born, he had discovered gold along a creek and had staked a claim there. Suddenly, again, there was no time to get his family down to civilization until another terrible, lonely winter had passed.

It had been a winter Bea hoped she could someday forget; more than that, she hoped she could find a way to forgive Kirk for keeping her in the mountains another nine months, nine months of hell, during which she and Kirk had made love only twice, if it could be called making love. Her heart had been so full of resentment that she had shown no emotion. She had literally prayed she would not get pregnant, and was grateful that the prayer had been answered.

Now Kirk was back in the mountains. He was intent not just on panning the placer gold, as it was called, but finding the mother lode, the source of the gold he had panned from the creek.

Bea wondered if he really intended to come back for her. Sometimes she regretted the way she had treated him before he left. She had been bitter and angry and had hardly told him good-bye. Some of her ill feelings had not fully left her. When she considered the possibility that her wandering husband had abandoned her, she grew even more angry. She worked much harder now just to survive than she had ever worked for her Uncle Jake.

She had three children to keep fed and clothed. Husband or no husband, she was determined to realize her dreams. Someday she would write to Cynthia and tell her what a rich woman she was, how much she had accomplished. If any woman could become wealthy on her own, these mining towns were the place to do it, if a woman was willing to work hard enough. Bea was so busy that she had hired a woman to watch the children while she scrubbed clothes all day long, every day.

It was back-breaking work, but in the three months she had been taking in wash, she already had three thousand dollars saved, which she kept hidden under a floorboard of their cabin. It was hardly better than the cabin in the mountains, except that this one at least had wood floors. The man who had owned it had already given up on mining. He missed his wife and children, whom he had left in Michigan. Kirk had paid the man ten dollars for the cabin and helped Bea move in their few belongings. He had left her fifty dollars—all the money he had—and had gone back into the Sierras.

Living was expensive in mining towns, and the fifty dollars had quickly vanished, mostly for food. Bea had been forced to find a way to feed her children and herself. Little Eleanor, the daughter to whom she had given birth in the mountains, was still breast feeding. Bea had begun taking in laundry for others, discovering that the men in these parts were willing to pay outrageous prices to get their clothes washed.

She had considered cooking for the miners, another lucrative business in these parts. But that would mean spending part of her profits on new supplies of food, on plates and silverware. The money she made taking in laundry was almost pure profit, since she could make her own soap. It was harder work, but the money was better.

The business had grown quickly, but her days were long and grueling. Doing wash meant carrying heavy buckets of water, keeping a fire going to heat the water, scrubbing clothes on a washboard until her knuckles were raw, hanging out clothes, and sometimes even pressing shirts. She washed by day and ironed at night, and she soon put little Elly on a bottle. She felt a little guilty having so little time for her babies, but she was determined that if Kirk did not come back for her, she would have a good life, even if she had to do it all on her own.

She took the bundle of laundry from the man who approached her and counted out the pieces, noticing again how callused and ugly her knuckles had become. The hard work was putting muscles on her where a woman shouldn't have them. Having two babies in three years had changed her shape somewhat, and since she was already tall and big-boned, she knew when she looked in the mirror, even at nineteen, that she would never be dainty and feminine. The long, hard days were taxing what little beauty she once possessed, but that didn't mean she couldn't be rich. That was one dream anyone could realize if she wanted to work at it hard enough. Every time her back screamed with pain from carrying water and scrubbing for hours, she reminded herself how much money she was accumulating.

"Seventeen dollars," she told the man. "You have twenty-six pieces here. I take gold coins, gold nuggets, or gold dust, and I get paid up front. You can pick up your clothes tomorrow."

The man grumbled. "For those prices, I might as well buy all *new* clothes."

"That's your choice, sir. But I think you'll find the price of new clothes is much higher. And don't try to fool me with pyrite. I know the difference between fool's gold and the real thing."

"I'll bet you do, lady," the man answered, scowling as he took a leather pouch from his gear. He handed her ten dollars in gold coins, then gave her another pouch. "This is gold dust, a good ten dollars worth."

Bea took the pouch and inspected its contents. "I'll go weigh it," she told the man. She took the pouch into the cabin, setting it on a little assayer scale she had purchased.

"More gold, Mommy?" Irene asked, her blue eyes wide with curiosity. She was four and a half years old now, a sweet, caring little girl who was always offering to help her mother with chores. Irene didn't quite understand why her mother had to work so much that another lady had to watch her and her brother and sister. She missed her mother and wished Bea would spend more time with her.

"Yes, Irene," Bea answered. "More gold. Someday soon we'll have lots of money and live in a pretty house. Mommy will have lots of time to play with you and Johnny and Elly."

Frances Beck, the woman who cared for the children, was feeding them lunch. "I don't know how you keep going, Bea," the woman told her. "You look so tired. I could never make my living that way."

"I'll do whatever I have to do to give these children a better life than I had," she answered. She met the woman's eyes. "I'm going to be rich some day, Fran."

Fran smiled and shook her head. "I don't doubt that." She sighed. "I've never met a woman so determined. Me, I'm willing to rely on Hubert. He's doing well with the supply store. I only watch the children because it gets so lonely out here with hardly any women around, except the kind folks like us wouldn't want to be seen with. Someday we're going back East, after Hubert makes enough money and the mines play out."

Bea took the little pouch from the scale. "It's the ones who furnish the prospectors with services like mine and your husband's who will get rich off this mining, Fran. Hubert has the right idea. I might go back East someday myself, as soon as I have accumulated enough money."

Fran read the hurt in her eyes. "I'm sure your husband will come soon, Bea."

Bea held her chin proudly. "Perhaps. If he doesn't, it isn't all his fault. And if he does, it will probably be more for the children than for me. He's not the best husband in the world, but he loves his children." She struggled to show she was undaunted. "Either way, it will be a while. It's already September. He could be snowed in somewhere up there and can't come down."

"I'm sure that's all it is," Fran told her. "He'll be here, come spring."

Bea did not reply. She walked back outside, determined that "come spring," she would be a wealthy woman. At a thousand dollars a month, she could be rich within a year. Maybe she would invest her money in a mine, find some way to make money that didn't involve such hard work.

When she'd run off with David Kirkland, she'd never dreamed she would end up in a tiny gold town clear out in California, scrubbing other men's dirty clothes. She could just imagine how Cynthia would sneer at her now. But someday things would be different. She would make sure of it.

She handed back three dollars in coins to the man who had left his laundry. "You're right. There is at least ten dollars in gold dust in this pouch. You can take back some of these coins. Come back tomorrow at about this time and your clothes will be ready, unless it rains."

He took the money and nodded, wondering if Bea Kirkland might be lonely. Other men had told him it had been quite a while since her husband had left her to go searching for gold, and some said he wasn't coming back. She was a hard-working woman, and he thought she might make a fine wife, a little bossy, perhaps, but a man could fix that if he set his mind to it.

The man rode off, and Bea looked up at the snowy peaks of the Sierras. At least here below the mountains, the weather was pleasant and warm. Even in winter most days were sunny. She had never lived where there was almost never any snow, where she could smell the ocean. If not for the loneliness and hard work, she could learn to like it here in San Francisco. Someday, somehow, life would be easier.

For just a moment she let herself think fondly of Kirk. She had hurt him, she knew. She also knew that he was a good man at heart, but he was a man who didn't understand what a woman like Bea needed. It had been difficult for him to change his life. He had tried, but only for her sake. Kirk didn't care about the same things she did. He could survive with nothing more than his horse and a rifle and the clothes on his back. But Bea wanted more than that—much more—especially for her children.

Little Irene came running outside, hugging her mother around the legs. Bea looked down at her little adopted daughter. She was such a lovely thing. Kirk loved his children, but she knew Irene was his pet. She touched Irene's golden hair. Yes, he would be back, for Irene, if for no other reason. But she could tell even from this distance that there were blizzards in the mountains. If he returned, it wouldn't be until spring—if he *lived* through the winter.

"Where's Daddy?" Irene asked, looking up at her with Kirk's blue eyes. She asked the same question every day.

"He's off looking for gold, darling. He'll be back," Bea promised again, hoping she was right. Her heart ached at the thought of actually losing him. She swallowed back a sudden lump in her throat, refusing to cry, as she had done so many times in her life. After all, she thought, she was accustomed to losing loved ones and being left on her own. If David Kirkland never returned, she would survive.

Ten more months passed—fourteen months since Kirk had left Bea in San Francisco. It was July of 1851 when she heard footsteps on the porch outside the cabin. Bea looked up from her ironing. Every bone in her body ached, her arms, her legs, her back. She was thin but hard-muscled from so much work.

There was a knock at the door. "Bea? You in there? It's me—Kirk."

She put a hand to her heart, setting the heavy iron on a plate. She hesitated, a myriad of emotions rushing through her. She loved him, and she hated him. She was glad he was back and was all right, and she wished he had never come back at all.

The children were sleeping. She was glad of that, wanting to see him alone first. She managed to make her legs move, suddenly realizing how frazzled she must look. Her dark hair was carelessly shoved into a bun, but pieces of it had strayed and hung limply about her face. She managed to get to the door, and opened it, almost gasping at the sight of him.

He was thinner himself, and fully bearded again. Their eyes

met, each of them surveying the other sorrowfully. "It was a hard winter, Bea. I couldn't get back." His eyes moved over her, then scanned the cabin. "I was afraid I'd come back and find you all starved to death or something." His eyes actually watered. "But I guess I should have known my Bea would find a way to survive. You're a hell of a woman, Bea. I'm sorry for all of it. I said I'd never abandon you or the kids, and I didn't. I just couldn't get back."

His voice rang with emotion. But they were like strangers again. "I'm glad you're all right," Bea told him. "I thought maybe you were . . . dead."

He shook his head. "You don't know how glad I am to find you and the children alive and well." He glanced over at the big bed in a corner of the main room, where all three children slept together. "They *are* all right, aren't they?"

She sighed, wanting to hug him, wanting to hit him. "Yes."

An awkward silence hung in the air for a moment. "Bea," he finally spoke up, "I'm going to make it up to you, just like I promised."

She looked up at him, her eyes shiny with tears. "I don't want to hear it any more, Kirk. I'm tired. I'm sick. I want to go back to St. Louis."

He smiled suddenly, his own eyes damp. "You don't understand, Bea." He had not even come all the way inside yet. He stepped farther into the room and closed the door. "I found it, Bea! I found the mother lode, and I've laid claim to it!"

She just stared at him, letting the news sink in as he removed his hat and hung it on a hook. She was so tired she couldn't think straight. She had hated him, had worked herself to exhaustion to build her savings so she could have a good life. Now here he was telling her he had actually struck it rich, something she had never truly believed could happen.

"It's . . . true?" she asked.

He took her arms, realizing she looked ready to pass out. "It's true. Come sit down, Bea." He led her to a rocker and placed her in it, then took a chair across from her, pulling it close so that he could talk softly and not wake the children.

"I know it must have been a hard winter for you, Bea, but I wasn't just sitting around up there watching the snow. I've worked hard, too, damn hard. I came near to freezing to death a couple of times. But I kept telling myself I had to find that vein—for you and the kids. I made you promises, and I meant to keep them. I had decided I wasn't coming back here without being able to tell you I'd found the mother lode. I can sell my claim for—"

"No!" She nearly startled him with the fierce reaction. "Don't sell it. That's what all the prospectors do. I've seen it happen over and over again since I've been here. Men find the gold, then sell it to developers who turn around and make a fortune. It's *ours*, Kirk. We've both been through hell these past two years. We deserve to get every penny out of that mine that we can."

He sighed, leaning back in his chair. "That takes a lot of money, Bea. I could never break enough gold out of there fast enough to make that kind of money any time soon."

She smiled proudly. "*I* have money, Kirk. I made it taking in laundry, as much as I could handle. I've worked myself nearly to death, but I've saved up twelve thousand dollars in gold coins, nuggets and gold dust. It's all buried right under this house."

His eyes widened in shock. "Twelve thousand dollars!"

"I was going to invest it in something that would mean I didn't have to work so hard, find a way to multiply the money so the children could live better. I . . . didn't know if you'd come back. I was afraid, after the way I treated you . . . maybe you had deserted us . . . or maybe you were dead."

He met her concerned gaze. "Is that all the faith you have in me?" he asked. "I told you before we married that I'd never desert you."

A tear slid down one cheek. "Sometimes a person makes promises he can't keep. You're a wandering man, David Kirkland. You were up there in the mountains, where you love to be, and when you left, I wasn't very kind to you."

Kirk shook his head. "You had good reason. That look on your face when I left, that's part of the reason I was determined not to come back until I could tell you I was a rich man. I was afraid maybe you'd pack your bags and head back to St. Louis."

She breathed deeply to keep from crying. "I thought about it. But deep inside I guess I knew you'd come, for Irene if for nothing else."

He leaned forward in his chair. "Bea, I love *all* of you. You've been a good wife. You've put up with so much. Now I can make up for it." He reached across and took her hands. "Twelve thousand dollars?" He looked down at her swollen, callused knuckles. "My God, Bea." He leaned down and kissed them. "You'll never work that hard again. That's a promise."

She pulled her hands away. Why, whenever she felt passion or wanted to cry, did she shut off her feelings? She felt so afraid of loving too much and losing it all. She rose from the rocker and began to pace the room. "We can do it, Kirk. We can work that mine ourselves. Why sell it and let someone else reap the profits?"

She turned and faced him, her eyes alight. "As soon as we get a little more ahead, we'll buy up other claims from the fools who are willing to sell too quickly. We'll develop them ourselves, build our own processing plants, stamp mills. I've learned a lot just from listening to the miners talk. I'm sure you have, too."

He listened to her, realizing sadly that the one most important thing to Bea Kirkland was being wealthy. It didn't matter so much to him, but it did to Bea, and he felt guilty for the hell he had put her through. She had married him on blind faith, and she had loved little Irene just as she had promised. If being rich was so damn important to her, he would do what he could to help her get there.

She came over and knelt in front of him. "Kirk, if we work as a team, we can have more money than we ever dreamed of! You know mining, and I have learned a lot about saving and investing. You could handle the mechanics, do more prospecting, check out other claims that are for sale. You'd know what's worth buying and what isn't. I could handle the bookwork, keep track of our earnings and such." She searched his blue eyes. "Is it true, Kirk? Is it really true?"

He grinned, happy to hear the joy in her voice. "It's true. It's a rich vein, Bea, a really big find. I haven't told too many about it yet." He touched her hair, relieved that this time she did not pull away. "You look so tired, Bea. I don't ever want you working like this again. We'll try it your way. We'll mine that gold ourselves, and you'll have that fine home I promised you. The kids will have everything."

She looked at his own work-worn hands. "I'm glad you're all right, Kirk."

He sighed deeply, kissing her forehead. "I'd like to celebrate, but I'm too damn tired, and I know you must be too. Let's just go to bed for now and get some sleep. We'll talk about all this in the morning."

She nodded, rising and walking behind the curtain that covered the doorway to their small bedroom. Kirk removed his boots, then got up and walked over to where the children slept. He watched them without a word, amazed at how they had grown. His heart ached that he'd been away from them for so long. He leaned across the bed and gave each of them a kiss—little Elly, nearly two; John, who was three and a half; and Irene, five years old now, and getting prettier all the time.

Irene woke up and yawned, looking up at her father with sleepy eyes. "Daddy," she whispered, reaching up for him. He picked her up and hugged her tightly. "Will you stay home now?" she asked him.

"Yes, baby, I'll stay home." Again he thought about her brother, wondering if the boy was still alive and healthy. He missed his Indian friends, missed the Rockies and the Great Plains. "You go back to sleep now and I'll see you in the morning."

Irene obeyed. She was an easy child, never demanding, always doing what she was told. She gave him a smile that nearly melted his heart. Kirk covered her and patted her head, thinking how good his life was turning out after all. Gold! He had found gold, and lots of it. Finally, he could give Bea what she had always wanted.

He went into the bedroom. Bea was already in bed. She looked at him strangely as he undressed. "I already took care of my horse," he told her. "I left a lot of things at the campsite. I'll have to go back up, you know."

"I know," she answered quietly, "but this time it will be for a better reason."

He climbed into bed, and she moved far over to the side of the bed. Kirk hesitated, meeting her eyes before turning out the lamp. "What's wrong?"

She swallowed. "It's been a long time, Kirk. You're . . . almost like a stranger again."

He needed his wife. He wanted to hold her, make love to her. In the fourteen months he had been gone, he had not turned to any of the whores in the mining camps. "I've been faithful to you, Bea."

She reached out and touched his hand. "I believe you, Kirk. I just . . . it's too soon. And we have to be careful. This isn't a good time to have any more children. We have a lot of work ahead of us, Kirk."

He sighed, turning out the lamp. "I know. I'll give you some time." He settled into the bed.

"Kirk," Bea spoke up in the darkness. "We can stay here now, can't we? I mean, once we get rich, we can build a big house and never have to make another long, dangerous journey. San Francisco is growing, and we can grow with it. I want to stay in one place now, Kirk."

A wolf howled in the distance, and Kirk thought about the Rockies, about a boy called Yellow Eagle. "We'll stay," he answered, a dull ache in his chest. He willed himself quickly to sleep so that he would not be tempted to pull her to him, to make her do what she wasn't ready for yet. Bea had never expressed much passion, and he realized their sex life would never be perfect. But she was a good woman, and a hard-working, faithful wife. There were certain things he would simply have to accept.

He was soon asleep, but weary as she was, Bea could not make her eyes close. Kirk had struck a mother lode! They would be rich! Her mind whirled with plans and schemes to make their money multiply. She finally fell asleep dreaming how she would word her letter to Cynthia when she wrote her cousin about her new found fortune.

CHAPTER FOUR

March 1859

Bea led Irene into the parlor of the two-story frame house Kirk had built for her. It sat high on a hill overlooking the growing city of San Francisco. A porch surrounded the entire house, and roses bloomed along the curved brick drive that graced the Kirkland's front lawn.

Kirk looked up from his favorite easy chair, where he had been smoking a pipe while he read an article about the discovery of gold in the Rockies. Irene's heart filled with joy at the sight of him, for her father was not often home. It seemed he was constantly at the mines, sometimes staying there all night. Her mother spent her days poring over ledgers and going to the bank, while the children were cared for by a servant.

"Father," Irene exclaimed, rushing up to him.

"Now, now, be careful of your new dress," Bea warned. "That's what we've come here to show your father."

Kirk grinned and set his pipe and paper aside. He reached out and gave his elder daughter a hug. "I didn't know if you would come," Irene told him.

"You didn't really think I'd forget your birthday, did you?" He rose, walking around her then as she blushed and turned in a circle for him. Kirk shook his head. "Thirteen already. And look at you. You're a young lady, Irene, not a little girl."

"She's the most beautiful young lady in San Francisco," Bea said proudly.

Irene smiled, always a little embarrassed at such remarks. Ten-year-old Elly, who had sneaked downstairs behind her mother and sister, peeked around the doorway, watching jealously. She didn't like her sister very much. Irene was prettier, and most certainly her father's pet. Because she was older, she got more privileges; and now that she was turning thirteen, their mother was having a special party for her.

Elly turned away, hating her own dark hair and eyes and her big-boned body. She was built like her mother and had her mother's coloring. Much as she loved Bea, she also resented her for her own looks, as though it was all Bea's fault her second daughter was not as pretty as her first. She wondered if her awkward body would ever fill out and take on her sister's pretty curves. It was not that she cared much for men or pretty dresses right now, but she realized someday she would consider them important. It hurt to think how often her mother's friends remarked how pretty Irene was but never had any kind words for Elly.

Elly often wondered why Irene had inherited her father's light hair and eyes. And why were there some things about her that did not resemble either parent, like her high cheekbones and slender shape? Bea and Kirk both were tall, big-boned people, and she and her brother John were built the same way. John was only eleven, going on twelve, but he looked more like fifteen.

In the parlor Kirk admired his daughter. She was indeed uncommonly beautiful, and he knew why. He had seen other children of mixed blood, and it seemed that more often than not they inherited the best features of both races. He imagined Yellow Eagle was a very handsome young man by now. "You are the most beautiful creature God ever created," he said to Irene.

"Oh, Father, you just say that because I'm your daughter," she answered.

"He says it because it's true," Bea told her. "Isn't it a lovely dress, Kirk?" She walked up to Irene, fluffing the shower of ruffles down the skirt of the soft green taffeta dress. The ruffles billowed over Irene's new hooped petticoat. "It's the latest fashion. She's going to wear it for her party this afternoon." The words seemed familiar, and suddenly Bea remembered a similar occasion thirteen years ago—the day Aunt Marlene came into the store to show off Cynthia's new dress.

Bea smiled at her victory. She and Kirk were rich now,

wealthier than her Uncle Jake could ever hope to be. She had been sure to write to her aunt and uncle in "loving concern," telling them about her new-wealth, her handsome children, the fine home Kirk had built for her in the fast-rising city of San Francisco.

Bea had already decided this home was only temporary. She was planning to build a much bigger one, a mansion that would make people stop in wonder when they passed it.

"Will you take me riding tomorrow, Father? It's been so long since we went riding together," Irene was asking.

"Of course I will." Kirk looked her over, thinking how she looked more like sixteen than thirteen, proud of how sweet and loving the girl remained, in spite of her beauty and the way Bea spoiled all the children. Elly could be greedy and jealous, but not Irene, and he knew her honest, humble nature came from the blood of Gray Bird Woman.

"Irene, you have piano lessons tomorrow," Bea reminded her. "You know it isn't ladylike to go galloping around on a horse. I've asked you over and over to give up the riding."

Irene closed her eyes and sighed. She hated upsetting her mother, but she loved riding more than anything. She loved the feel of the wind in her face, the power of a sturdy horse beneath her. Horses meant everything to her, and she had one special one called Sierra that she rode nearly every day, in spite of her mother's irritation. Sierra was an Appaloosa gelding, mostly white with gray legs, tail, and mane, and gray spots on its rump. He was three years old now. Kirk had bought the horse for Irene's twelfth birthday.

Kirk had taught Irene to ride, and it had come easy to her. Sometimes John would come riding with them, but Elly would not even consider getting on the back of a horse. She was afraid of them and haughtily agreed with her mother that riding astride a horse was unladylike.

Irene didn't care. Sometimes she felt she would rather die than not be able to ride. "Please," she begged her mother. "Father isn't home that often. We can go riding in the morning and be back in time for my lessons in the afternoon."

Bea looked at Kirk then, and Irene noticed a strange look of fear in her mother's eyes. She supposed that Bea was afraid Irene would get hurt. "You know I'm a good rider, Mother. Nothing will happen."

Bea turned and gave her a weak smile. "We'll talk about it later, Irene. You go and see that Ramona has all the party favors ready.

And tell Elly to finish dressing. Your guests will be arriving soon."

Irene smiled at her father. She knew by the look he gave her that he would make sure they could go riding. Out in the hallway Elly hurried off before Irene exited the parlor to go to the kitchen. Bea watched after Irene, making sure the hall was empty before closing the parlor doors. She faced Kirk, looking irritated. "You know what I think of her riding, especially when you let her straddle a horse like a man, and ride *bareback*, of all things!"

Kirk picked up his pipe and relit it. He had gotten used to his wife's almost constant preaching and complaining, her need not only to build their fortune, but to live a life that showed it off. Bea wanted to have the best of everything, always to do only what was "proper" for the wealthy. But no matter how rich they became, he knew he didn't belong in the elite circle. The life Bea insisted on leading forced him to associate with too many boring, stuffy people, while all he really wanted was to put on his buckskins and head into the mountains.

"She loves horses, Bea. It's the Indian in her."

"Do you think I don't know that? We have to *discourage* the Indian in her. You aren't helping me on this, Kirk. I love her like my own, and we agreed from the beginning she would be raised as our own child. It scares me when you let her experience that wild side of her nature. I'm afraid she'll wonder—that *others* will wonder."

"For God's sake, Bea, she just likes to ride. It means so much to her. There *are* other white women who like horses and riding, you know. You're letting your fears and imagination run away with you."

He turned and paced, puffing at his pipe. "Sometimes you carry all this damn wealth and putting on airs a little too far," he added. "If anybody ever suspects anything, it will be because of *you* and that look you get in your eyes sometimes, not because of Irene. You think she doesn't notice how worried and nervous you get whenever she wants to do something different? Leave the girl alone. She *is* still just a child, Bea. She'll grow out of some of these things."

Their eyes held. They respected each other but were still struggling to find the love they had hoped would come when they first married. There had been another baby, stillborn. There had been complications. A doctor told Bea she would never have any more children, and the ordeal had left her even colder sexually.

They slept together, but they seldom made love. Kirk had found relief elsewhere, occasionally visiting a prostitute when he was in the mining camps. He supposed Bea suspected, but she didn't seem to mind, as long as he was discreet, and as long as they could keep up the front of a good marriage. Especially as long as the money kept rolling in.

Their marriage had become more of a partnership. They were not the best of lovers, but they were at least good friends—two people who had made certain promises. She had kept her own promise to love Irene and be a good mother to her. Kirk in turn continued to buy up new mines and help build their fortune. He left nearly all the bookwork to Bea, who had developed a unique talent for making money grow. Now she had the fine home she had wanted, although she already talked of building a bigger house; she was one of the wealthiest women in San Francisco; the children were schooled by a private tutor; Bea and the children dressed in the latest fashions; and the Kirklands owned more mines than anyone else in the district.

But none of it seemed to be enough for Bea. Always, she wanted more. Kirk knew that deep inside she was never really satisfied, and he didn't know how to make her happy. He sensed she would never quite forgive him for the two winters she had spent in the mountains, for giving birth to Elly up there alone; especially not for the fourteen months she had spent scrubbing clothes while she waited for him. He had thought that his finding the mother lode would make up for it all, and sometimes he sensed in her a desire to reveal some hidden passion, to expose emotions she had never shown before; but always she held back.

He did not know that Bea Kirkland was simply afraid to love too much. She desperately feared losing those she loved, both her husband and her children. And she feared being poor again. She was going to make sure that never happened. In Bea's mind, Kirk was a wandering man with no mind for business and no desire to get ahead. If not for her, he would have sold that first claim for far less than it was worth and today would probably have nothing to show for it. He needed someone to give him direction, needed to be reminded of his responsibilities. She knew he would give up everything in a moment and go riding off to the mountains, if not for her and the children.

"I suppose you're right," she finally answered him aloud. "I only want what's best for her, Kirk, and I never want to see her hurt. She's so . . . so soft-hearted and generous, so trusting. She has to learn to be stronger, learn to understand people better.

Someday she'll be a rich woman in her own right. I don't want people to take advantage of her."

"They won't. She's stronger than you think, Bea. And some of those things you mentioned are good qualities that I hope never get destroyed. You push her too hard. Part of her beauty is that gentle, loving nature. You spoil her to death, but she doesn't show it because there isn't a jealous, greedy bone in her body. Just let her grow at her own pace."

Bea stiffened. "Are you calling me jealous and greedy?"

Kirk closed his eyes and sighed. He hated arguing with her. "No." He turned away and puffed the pipe for a moment, then glanced back at her, giving her a wink. "Well, a little greedy, maybe."

He gave her a teasing grin, but she eyed him narrowly. "Sometimes greed can be a good thing," she answered soberly. Bea Kirkland had no sense of humor, but she understood what Kirk meant.

She almost hated him for his ability to enjoy life and his tendency to be irresponsible, but she had learned to accept his free spirit. Considering his restless nature, he had been a good husband in most respects.

David Kirkland was still a handsome man, still big and strong and solid at thirty-eight years old. Bea had noticed how other women looked at him, sensed their jealousy, and it gave her great pleasure and pride. None of them needed to know that as lovers they left a lot to be desired. Bea knew that it was not Kirk's fault. She was simply unable, unwilling to love freely and openly.

Kirk had never mentioned divorce, and she knew that he wouldn't. It would bring her great shame and sorrow, and because of Irene and the motherly love she had given the girl, Kirk would never end the marriage, or even be cruel to her. She knew his frequent absences were mostly her fault, yet she never seemed to be able to be the supportive, attentive wife she knew he needed. Her whole world had become her children and her business.

She reasoned that Kirk was a loner at heart anyway. Surely an independent man like Kirk didn't really need her constant companionship. They led separate but amiable lives, and that was perfectly fine with her. One thing she did understand about her husband was his nature, and she could often tell by his eyes what he was thinking. At the moment there was a suspicious sparkle in those blue eyes that worried her. "What has you in such a good mood, Kirk?" she asked with a frown.

He shrugged. "It's Irene's birthday."

Bea shook her head. "It's more than that. I don't like that look. I haven't seen it since St. Louis, when you found out gold had been discovered in California."

He took the pipe from his mouth, studying her a moment, weighing the risk of telling her what he had been thinking of doing. At twenty-nine, Bea looked much older. He knew the reason, and he was sorry for it. Her grander life had encouraged her to put on weight, and combined with her dark eyes and tall stature, she appeared domineering, a battle-ax who cowed most people who dealt with her. Even the children seemed somewhat awed by her. The only person whom she could not totally subdue was Kirk himself, and he knew this was one of those moments when he would have to find a way to make Bea Kirkland submit to his will. It wouldn't be an easy task.

He sighed deeply, and the smile left his face. "I'm not happy here, Bea, and you know it," he said carefully.

He watched her stiffen, instantly on guard, as though to defend herself. "The night you came back to tell me about finding the mother lode, you promised me we would stay here," she reminded him. "No more moving around and disrupting the children."

He set the pipe aside. "I know what I promised. I also nearly died trying to find that damn vein so we could be rich—so *you* could be rich. We've done well, Bea. I know a lot of it is thanks to you and that money you saved so we could mine our own gold. But first the gold had to be found, and I found it."

He stepped closer, hesitantly taking her hands. "Bea, you're the one always wanting to expand, to make our money grow. Some of the mines are playing out. We need new investments, and you know as well as I that the quickest way to get even richer is to supply a new mining town—to go where there's more gold being discovered."

She felt the dread of disrupted lives and another hard journey. "It's that place in Kansas Territory, isn't it? I've heard the talk, Kirk, and I read the papers. Gold has been discovered near Pikes Peak, in the Rocky Mountains."

He held her eyes. "They call it Colorado now . . . figure to form their own territory before long." He began to plead with her. "You know how much I love it there, Bea. The Rockies are home to me. You have all the things you wanted to be happy. I'm only asking one thing for myself, and that's to live where I feel at home and alive. Nothing has to change. There are two towns along Cherry Creek, where they discovered the gold. One's called

Denver and the other Auraria. They'll grow, Bea, just like San Francisco is growing. We can grow with them."

She closed her eyes, turning away. "I can't say I'm totally surprised. I know you too well to have thought this could last. I had a feeling for the last several days that you wanted to talk about this." She faced him again. "You know as well as I most gold towns turn into ghost towns within a few years' time. The only thing that has kept San Francisco going is having a seaport—and the fact that the weather is good and the land is rich and makes farming ideal."

"The same thing could happen there. I mean, the settlement is right in the middle of the country, right where people have to come through to go west. People will stop there for supplies. You know the prices miners will pay for what they need. And after the miners, other settlers will come and stay, just like it happened here."

"That land can't be farmed," Bea protested. "It's worthless. Once the gold runs out, people will leave, and there we'll sit, in the middle of nowhere. And there are still a lot of Indians there. What about Irene?"

"What about her? She doesn't know she's got Indian blood. You'd sure never know it to look at her." His voice grew more persuasive. "Bea, I've got a good feeling about that area. Even if I'm not right, and the towns die out, we can still make a killing there off the miners, maybe invest in new mines in the Rockies. We don't have to give up everything we have here."

His eyes filled with a boyish excitement. "We could sell the mines here that aren't producing so much and keep one or two of the best ones, find someone to manage them. And we could keep the wholesale supply business, just expand it. We've got goods coming into port all the time, fancy spices and silks from China, food from the valley. Hell, Bea, we could order in more, have the stuff shipped to Denver and Auraria, set up new warehouses there and sell supplies to the miners. The newspaper says thousands are expected to flood into the area this summer. If we left next month, we could take a whole supply train with us. It wouldn't be like starting over, just expanding what we already have. If it all fails, we can always come back to California."

She smiled almost bitterly. "Come back, once you get back to the Rockies? I'm not a fool, Kirk. You could care less about expanding the business. That's just for me. The only reason you want to go there is to be back in your precious Rockies, no matter how much hardship it might mean for the rest of us. I should have known you wouldn't be able to keep your promise to me. You've kept so few of them."

She instantly hated herself for the remark but could not bring herself to apologize. She saw the hurt in his eyes as he turned away and picked up his pipe. "You know better, Bea," he answered. "I promised I'd never leave you, and that I'd help you have all the things you want. Those promises I *did* keep. I'm only asking for one thing for myself."

He looked more determined than ever now. "I wouldn't consider making the trip if it meant the kind of life you and the kids led when we first came out here. Things are different now. We can afford the best wagons and we can hire help. We can even take along supplies to build us a decent house to get us by until the town grows some. It would be difficult, but nothing like before."

"Kirk, you know what new mining towns are like—raw and wild and uncivilized."

He re-lit his pipe, scrambling to think of ways to convince her to go, determined to win this argument. "Sure, but people like us can help tame a town like that. And I know you better than you think. You love being queen of the roost, and in a new, struggling town, you'd be a lot more important there than you are here," he continued. "Don't you remember how you envied the big money that came to town when we were first struggling to build our own fortune here in San Francisco? You wanted to be like them, and now you are. But you came in second, came in on their heels. If we go to Denver, *we'll* be the big money coming to town. No one will look at us and remember how poor we used to be. Wouldn't you like that?"

She studied him wryly. "You're trying to manipulate me, David Kirkland."

He grinned again, trying to keep the mood light. "Is it working?"

She sighed, folding her arms. "If we go there, and I'm not saying I'll go, but *if* we do, and things work out like you think they will, which I doubt, I want to build the grandest home in the territory, and I never want to pick up roots again. *Never*."

He nodded. "Fine."

"If it doesn't work out, if this place called Denver folds, I'm coming back here, Kirk; and if you want to be near your children, you'll have to come with me. Are you sure you want to go back there and risk having to tear yourself away again?"

He came closer to her. "I won't *have* to leave it again. I'm not much for cities and civilization, Bea, but I'll do whatever I have to in order to keep the area alive and be able to stay. We'll build a city there, Bea, and we'll be one of the cornerstones. We'll make it work, with our own blood and sweat and our own money. Hell, with your brains for bookwork and investments, and my knowledge of mining, we can do anything. We've already proven that. Doesn't the challenge of it excite you? Doesn't it set your mind whirling on all the ways we can accumulate more wealth there? You'd be one of the first ladies of Denver. We could open a bank there, loan people money, charge them interest. Hell, you know more about things like that than I do."

A cynical look came into her dark eyes. "We'd be back to cold winters."

"Not as bad as farther east. I know the land, Bea. Winters aren't that bad in the valleys. You get snow, but within a day or two it's gone again. The air is too dry for it to stay long. Hell, I've seen lots of warm days in January and February out there. And the sun shines almost every day."

"Mmmm-hmmm. What about Indians?"

He shrugged. "Mostly Ute, Arapahoe and Cheyenne. I've dealt with them all my life."

She felt a jealous stab at her heart at the thought of Gray Bird Woman. "Things are different now, Kirk. There's been trouble, and it could get worse as more people begin settling in Indian country."

"It probably will, but in a settlement of several thousand people, the Indians aren't going to bother us. They'll stick to the more remote areas of the Plains. Most of them are afraid to come too near to white settlements for fear of getting white man's diseases. A case of measles can wipe out a whole tribe."

"You're ready with all the answers, aren't you?" She searched his eyes. "I mean it, Kirk. If it doesn't work out, we're not staying. I want my children to grow up in civilization, with a fine home and decent schools, someplace where there are doctors and theaters and nice dress shops and—"

"Then we'll make sure they have those things in Denver," he interrupted, "and better than that, we'll own most of them ourselves."

The remark brought a slow grin to her lips. He knew she liked the idea of being queen bee in a new settlement. "I can have the home I want?"

"Soon as we get situated. It might take a year or two, but we'll get it built."

"And we can come back if it doesn't work out?"

"I'll *make* it work, if I have to build the city with my own two hands and advertise all over the world for people to come there."

She shook her head. "I don't know. It's so beautiful here, and we're so settled. I told you once I would never leave."

He seized her shoulders. "I'm going crazy here, Bea. I want to go to Denver before I'm too old to make the journey. I'm dying here, dying on the inside."

She was startled to realize there were tears in his eyes. She knew in her heart she had been emotionally cruel to him for the better part of their married life. He was a good man, although he had no real ambitions, but she could continue to inspire him, keep him on the right path wherever they went. The thought of arriving in Denver a wealthy woman was very satisfying. She would even be closer to her aunt and uncle and Cynthia, whom she had not seen since the night she ran off to marry Kirk. Perhaps once her mansion was built, she would invite them to come and visit, to show off her wealth to the people who had hurt her the most. She could always lie about Irene's age.

"I'll consider it," she said aloud. "As long as we understand the conditions."

He thought how their whole marriage had been built on certain "conditions." Bea Kirkland was a demanding woman, but he usually found a way around her stubborn streak. Right now, just the thought of going back to the Rockies made his heart soar. He puled her close, embracing her. "Think hard on it, Bea; you'll see I'm right about this."

She breathed in his manly scent, thinking how long it had been since she had allowed her husband the simple pleasure and marital right of making love to her. To her it was a duty, although somewhere deep inside she suspected it could be an act of utmost pleasure, if she could accept her emotions and allow free reign to her desires.

"Stay home tonight, Kirk," she said quietly.

He touched her hair, realizing the remark was her roundabout way of asking him to come to bed with her. She was not a beautiful or passionate woman, but he knew she had needs that were difficult for her to admit. He had long ago given up trying to bring forth the womanly emotions she seemed intent on keeping buried. She gave him little cause to desire her, but he loved and respected her enough to know when it was important that he be a husband to her. This was one of those times. His desire for her had much to do with the fact that he had been her first and only man, and that with a woman like Bea, it took quite a man to get her to want to make love.

"I'll be here," he told her.

The parlor door suddenly opened then, and Irene gasped with embarrassment at finding her parents in an embrace. Bea quickly pulled away from Kirk, touching her hair, totally flustered at being caught.

"I'm sorry, Mother," Irene said, starting to turn away.

"It's all right, Irene," Kirk spoke up.

"You should always knock before barging into a room, Irene," Bea told her, smoothing her dress, her cheeks hot. Elly and John made an appearance behind their sister, both of them staring at their flustered mother. Elly was glad that Bea seemed a little upset with Irene. In Elly's mind, Irene was always so perfect and obedient. She enjoyed those rare moments when their mother got upset with her sister.

"Now, Bea, she's just excited about her birthday," Kirk cajoled his wife.

Yes, Elly thought. *Stick up for her like you always do, Father.*

"I—I just came to tell you Ramona has everything ready," Irene told them awkwardly. "You told me to check, Mother."

"Yes. I forgot."

"What do you children think about going to Colorado?" Kirk asked, anxious to relieve the awkward moment.

Elly frowned. "Colorado? Where is that?"

"Father east, in the Rockies," her father answered.

"I don't want to go. I want to stay here," Elly grumbled.

"Gold has been discovered there," Kirk told his daughter. "It's a great opportunity for us. If it doesn't work out, we'll come back to California."

"I think it sounds exciting," Irene spoke up, always glad to see her father happy. There had been so many times when she had sensed a distant longing and loneliness in him that she didn't understand.

Elly resented Irene for never objecting to whatever their father wanted. "I don't want to leave my friends," she said aloud, scowling. "What about our new house, Mother?"

Bea glanced at Kirk. "We haven't decided for certain yet," she answered, looking back at Elly. "But if we do go, we can build just as grand a home there as we would have had here."

Kirk looked at his son. "What do you think, John?"

The boy shrugged. "It doesn't matter to me where we live."

Kirk studied his son, frustrated by the distance between them. John was a quiet young man who didn't seem to care much about anything but building things out of pieces of wood. Kirk had hoped he and his son could be close, especially since he would never know his Indian son. But John had a withdrawn, rather cool personality, much like his mother's.

Bea was already schooling their son in how to handle money, with the idea that one day John would take over the Kirkland fortune. "He has to be ready," she would say. "As soon as he is old enough, I want him to go to college back East and study business and law. We've worked too hard for what we have to let our children squander and waste it and lose it all."

Such talk seemed too heavy a burden for young John. Kirk could tell the boy didn't care much about wealth. In that respect, he was more like Kirk, but the boy had Bea's inability to express his emotions.

"I'll need your help, John," Kirk told the boy. "If we go, I plan to take a big train of supply wagons along. We might even have to build some special wagon beds. They'll have to carry a good deal of weight. Maybe you could help with that."

The boy's eyes lit up. "Yes, sir, I'd like that."

Kirk smiled. "Good." He studied all three children then, amazed that he had ended up a settled man with a family. Taking on so much responsibility had not come easy to him, but he had always done his best. He loved his children, and they brought him joy and pride, but his marriage would never be truly happy. His life was not at all what he had planned so many years ago, but he figured the closest he could come to the life he loved most was to get back to the Rockies. For him it would be like going home.

"You'll all learn to love the area as much as I do," he said aloud. "After the party tonight I'll tell you some stories from the days when I lived and trapped in those mountains."

Irene and John's faces lit up with excitement. They loved to listen to their father's stories of bears and Indians. Elly just frowned. She was tired of her father's stupid old stories.

"Let's all finish getting ready for Irene's party," Kirk said then, walking up and kissing each of his daughters' cheeks. "I'm going upstairs to change."

Irene watched him leave the room, glad to see her father so happy. John headed outside to tinker with some wood, already wondering what could be done to make a wagon bed stronger.

Bea walked up to Elly, who still stood pouting in the doorway. "Do we *have* to go, Mother?"

"I think we probably will, Elly. I don't relish the trip, but I agree with your father that it's worth a try. Besides, Kirk loves the Rockies. He deserves that much happiness. And don't you go scowling all the way through Irene's party."

Elly wondered at her mother's statement about her father deserving some happiness. Wasn't he happy right here? "I'll bet there's nothing in Colorado but Indians and snow. We'll live in an ugly little cabin like when we were little."

"It won't be like that at all, Elly. Now quit complaining and come upstairs with me. I want to redo your hair. It's falling out of the combs."

"It's too thin and stringy." She looked up at her mother. "You think I'm ugly, don't you."

"Elly! I think no such thing! You're my pretty little Elly."

"I'm not as pretty as Irene. You think she's *beautiful*."

Bea gave her a hug. "Irene is Irene. And she is three years older. She's becoming a young lady. Such changes make a girl blossom. In a few years the same thing will happen to you. Now come upstairs with me."

Mother and daughter climbed the stairs, but Bea could hardly concentrate on the birthday party or fixing Elly's hair. Already her mind was spinning with the possibilities that could lie ahead for them in the place called Denver. She gave little thought to Elly's feelings of inadequacy, brushing it off as childish. Nor was she concerned about John's moodiness, his lack of interest in the family fortune. That would change with maturity. The important thing right now was to make sure her children had everything they wanted and needed, that they had the best life possible.

Maybe Kirk was right. Maybe Colorado was their chance to get in at the very beginning of something big. She straightened with pride as she envisioned arriving in a new mining town already rich, being envied by those who were still struggling to find their dream. She and Kirk had nearly worked themselves to death to build theirs, and she was ready to flaunt her wealth.

There would surely be more hardships, that she did not doubt. She did not relish a trip back over two mountain ranges and through the desert between them. Still, nothing could be as bad as those two winters in the Sierras, and those horrible months alone when she took in laundry. If she had survived that, she could survive anything.

"Colorado." Elly was grumpy as she sat down at her dressing table. "Someday when I'm grown up I'm coming back to California."

"If that's what you want, then you will," Bea told her, taking the combs from her hair.

PART

TWO

A great city is that which has the greatest men
  and women,
If it be a few ragged huts, it is still the greatest
  city in the whole world.

            —WALT WHITMAN,
            from "What Endures?"

CHAPTER
FIVE

Bea was appalled at what she saw as the Kirkland wagons lumbered into Denver-Auraria. "My God, Kirk, it's worse than I thought," she moaned. "Why, there is nothing here but tents and log cabins—and Indians! Indians everywhere! You said they wouldn't come near a place like this. And look how dirty they are!"

"Those are Arapaho. And they aren't dirty like you think. They just live different, that's all."

An Indian man who sat near a fire while his woman cooked for him looked up at Kirk and nodded. Kirk called a greeting to him in his own tongue, and the man smiled and answered. Some of the Indians began following the huge wagon train, curious to find out if these newcomers had anything to trade.

Kirk headed through Auraria and carefully guided his wagon through Cherry Creek onto the Denver side of the bank, while Irene, Elly, and John hung out the back of the wagon gawking at naked Indian children. Elly kept saying that they looked disgusting.

People began gathering to stare at the huge supply train as it moved along the east bank. With a sinking heart Bea studied the crude excuse for a town. She realized most of the women who came out of buildings to watch them were prostitutes. She had seen plenty of them in San Francisco, always wondering how a woman could sell her body to any man who came along. It was difficult enough for her to give herself to her own husband, who she suspected had visited such women back in San Francisco. She had long ago buried her hurt and jealousy at the thought, aware that Kirk was a man with needs she could not fulfill. She could overlook his indescretions, as long as he didn't flaunt them in front of her.

Hundreds of people began milling about, and Bea ordered the children to keep their heads inside the wagon. "Kirk, this is terrible. Every other building is a saloon!"

"What did you expect? This is a gold town, remember? You know what it's like in places like this. And look at all those hungry, eager faces. We'll make a fortune our first week here. When I send the wagons back, I'll leave orders for the men to come back with more next spring. And soon as we're settled, I'll go up in the mountains and check out the claims, buy up anything that looks promising."

She clung to his arm as though terrified. "Build our house away from all these Indians and whores. Look, to the southeast. There is a rise there. The land is higher than down here. Build our house up there."

"Wherever you want."

Crude log buildings lined the creek, with more buildings and tents scattered all the way into the foothills. Bea knew that the thousands who camped near the towns and in the mountains were only transients, people come to find gold and leave again. The stable population was probably no more than a few hundred, and it was hard to imagine this place would ever grow into a respectable town.

Horses, cows, mangy dogs, and pigs roamed everywhere, as did hundreds of small rodentlike prairie dogs. The dusty streets were littered with animal dung and trash, and it seemed that every other building was overrun by drunken men with painted women on their arms.

As they moved farther from Cherry Creek, Bea noticed a couple of supply stores, a drugstore, and a hardware store. The people who gathered looked somewhat more respectable, and a satisfied pride began to fill Bea's soul when she noticed how some of them looked at her. They knew she was wealthy, and she saw the hungry longing in the eyes of some of the women, the same look she had had in her own eyes a few years ago. She nodded to them, looking forward to selling them goods from "her" store, and loaning their husbands money from "her" bank.

Sorry sight that Denver was, at least they were here. They had come into the territory from the north, using the South Pass, northeast of Salt Lake City, to get through the Rockies. It was the same pathway they had taken to go to California, and Bea had almost gotten sick when the wagons had to stop at Fort Bridger, where she and Kirk had stayed part of the winter on that first long journey ten years ago.

This trip had been at least a little more comfortable, with more men along for protection, fine, well-equipped wagons, and plenty of supplies. But the trip had brought back too many bitter memories. Now Bea was as determined as Kirk to make it worth all the hardship, for although she would miss California, she did not relish the thought of ever making such a journey again.

From Fort Bridger they had gone east and then south, following the eastern foothills of the Rockies all the way. Kirk's excitement was so evident that Bea could have found it humorous, if not for her own doubts and dread. She was too preoccupied with worry over what lay ahead for them to appreciate the beauty of the land through which they had just traveled, to drink in the clear mountain air and enjoy the brilliant green of the foothills, the gray and purple granite of the rising peaks to the west. She had not come here because of the land or because of any youthful memories, as Kirk had. She had come here to build her fortune, and her power.

To her relief, at least one respectable-looking man wearing a neat suit approached them then, walking up to greet the lead wagon. He held out his hand to Kirk, who pulled the wagon to a halt.

"Welcome! Welcome to Denver," the man said with a wide grin. "I'm William Byers, publisher of the *Rocky Mountain News,* come here recently from Omaha with my wife and two children."

Kirk reached down and shook the man's hand. "David Kirkland, from San Francisco. I grew up in these parts, then went to California to find gold." He nodded toward the long supply train behind him. "We found it."

Young Byers surveyed the wagons, quickly realizing David Kirkland had to be a rich man, and he had brought his family with him. These were the kind of people Denver needed. "Well, I guess you did find it," he answered Kirk. "I'm happy to see a prosperous family coming to our town." He saw the sour look on Bea's face. "I know it doesn't look like much right now, but we're going to build Denver into a fine city. I hope you're planning on staying to help do just that, Mr. Kirkland."

"Most just call me Kirk." He looked around, breathing deeply, drinking in the sight of the Rockies just to the west. Bea knew her husband could hardly wait to get on a horse and ride into those mountains.

"Yes, sir, I would very much like to help this place grow, Mr. Byers. I intend to stay here. This is the land I love."

"I love it, too. The first thing we're doing is trying to convince the settlers here to merge Denver and Auraria into one city. We've got to work together if we're going to make things grow. You planning on opening a supply store with all these goods?"

"That and more," Kirk answered. "I'd like to build some warehouses and bring in a lot more goods. I'll be heading into the mountains to do a little prospecting of my own, maybe buy up some claims." He turned to Bea and introduced her. "My wife handles all the bookwork. Are there any banks in town?"

"Not yet. But we'll have banks and libraries and schools and all the other luxuries soon. I'm determined to make it happen."

"Well, my wife just might set up your first bank," Kirk told him. "What's the truth on the gold around here, Mr. Byers?"

"Call me Bill." Byers was a handsome young man, with a happy, energetic attitude.

Finding someone who shared Kirk's dream and who seemed quite proper and intelligent made Bea rest a little easier. The children poked their heads from the back of the wagon again to stare at Indians and animals.

"The gold is up there all right," Byers was saying. "We had quite a few gobacks, as we call them, for a while. I don't have much use for people who give up right away. Traitors, in my opinion. But then I didn't come out here for the gold. I came here to build a city."

The man was obviously eager to talk about "his" city. He seemed to be a forward-thinking man, and Bea liked him immediately. "Most of the gold seems to be in the Pikes Peak area," he continued. "The placer gold isn't much to brag about, but we've got some hard rock miners up at Gregory Gulch now. They've started up a steam-powered stamp mill to pulverize the ore for chemical extraction. I suppose you know all about that kind of mining."

"I do," Kirk answered. "I own several milling plants back in California . . . plan to operate more here. I'm a developer, not just a prospector."

"Wonderful! That's what we need. With families like your own settling here, it will help attract more of the kind of people we want—good, solid families. You'll want to meet General Larimer and his son. They've mapped out the town and are selling lots—really working hard to bring some organization to the area."

"Well, I'm sure my wife is relieved to know there are some dedicated, civilized people here," Kirk told the eager Byers. He hated such small talk and didn't like putting on airs for Byers. But more than anything he wanted to stay here, and he hoped such talk was giving Bea more incentive to try to make a go of it here in Denver.

"I firmly believe in development and promotion, Mrs. Kirkland," Byers was telling Bea. "I am in the ideal position to help, through my newspaper. The *News* is distributed all over the Rockies, to all the mining camps, and to several places farther east. Denver won't always be just a place for transient miners. You can see we have several businesses already, and a friend of mine, Luther Kountze, has opened an assay office. Our best carpenter is Henry Brown, a contractor from St. Louis. He'd be glad to help you get a house built as quickly as possible."

"Thank you," Bea answered. "We brought our own lumber along so we could get started right away. I want to get a roof over the children's heads." She turned and pointed. "I thought that site southeast of here, on the rise, would be a good location."

"An excellent choice. General Larimer already has a home there. He's from Pennsylvania, earned his title while in the Pennsylvania militia. He's a professional promoter, come here on the invitation of the former governor of Kansas Territory, James Denver. Larimer will be happy to sell you some land."

"If we're going to stay in Denver, we will want to invest in a good deal of land for future development," Bea told him, "not just a lot or two for a house."

Kirk breathed a little easier. After Bea's initial reaction when they arrived, he was not sure she would even give this a try.

"Well I'm sure General Larimer has plenty of land to sell to the right investor," Byers was saying. "The lots are sold through the St. Charles Company. St. Charles is what we used to call this town before we renamed it Denver. At any rate, the money you pay for the land is reinvested in improvements to our city."

In the back of the wagon, the Kirkland children paid little attention to the conversation. Elly continued to groan about what a horrible, primitive place Denver was, curling her nose at the smell of animal droppings everywhere and carrying on about how there were "wild Indians" roaming about, probably ready to scalp and torture young white girls.

Irene thought about the quiet Indian women she had seen

working over campfires at the creek. Because of her father's tales of Indians and stories of making friends with some of them, she often wondered about that wild-looking race, what their life was really like, if they were really as horrible as white people made them out to be. Her father seemed to have great respect for them, and she in turn had great respect for what her father thought was right and wrong. Her mother, on the other hand, had no use for Indians, or for people of Spanish descent.

There had been a lot of Spanish people in California, and Irene thought them very gracious and mannerly. But ever since one young Spanish boy had stolen a silver candle-stick from her, Bea preached that they were inferior and not to be trusted. "They'll smile at you and steal from you at the same time," she often told her children. "They hate us, you know, because of the Mexican war. And young white women should stay away from Spanish men. Someday you'll understand why."

The last statement always made Irene wonder. What was different about Spanish men? Did they carry some horrible disease, or were they secretly cruel and barbaric? The old Mexican who had taken care of their lawn back in San Francisco seemed friendly enough. Irene had liked him.

The wagon began moving again, and Irene, Elly, and John watched as whores and bearded, poorly dressed men roamed the streets. They knew about painted ladies. They had seen some in San Francisco, and although they didn't fully understand what they did, the fact that they were "bad" had been firmly burned into their young minds.

In the distance Irene caught sight of a young Mexican boy chasing a pig, and an older Mexican man chasing the boy and shouting something in Spanish. She was surprised, not expecting to find Spanish people here. She had always thought they only lived in California, and in that country to the south called Mexico. They heard an explosion then, somewhere in the distant foothills. Irene knew it was someone blowing away a piece of mountain in search of gold.

The trip to Colorado had been exciting, in spite of Elly's complaining and crying most of the way. This new place was certainly bustling with activity, even though life here appeared quite crude. Irene didn't mind. She knew her mother would have a nice house built for them in no time. The sad part was that she realized her father would be away much of the time. He planned to go into the mountains and look for more gold. She hated it when Kirk was gone. Life in the Kirkland household always seemed more joyful and relaxed when her father was there. Kirk knew how to laugh, but her mother almost never laughed. She seldom even smiled.

She peeked outside again, smelling fresh lumber and listening to the sound of pounding hammers and scraping saws. Apparently Mr. Byers was at least right about Denver growing. There seemed to be new buildings going up everywhere, especially in this part of town, away from the Indians. There must be hundreds, maybe thousands of men milling about as far as she could see.

She smelled fresh paint, and looked up to see a man painting a sign above a furniture store.

Another Spanish man, perhaps seventeen or eighteen years old, was standing in front of the store. He glanced up at her from the sawhorse, where he was carving a piece of wood that looked like a table leg. Suddenly, unexpectedly, their eyes met. The young man watched the wagon as it lumbered past, until Irene moved back inside and sat down, embarrassed that he had caught her staring at him.

It disturbed her that she thought him extremely handsome. The strange, new feelings she had felt when looking into his eyes made her wonder if she was being bad. She remembered her mother's warnings to stay away from young Spanish men, which surely meant it was not proper to stare at one, and most certainly not proper to feel an attraction to one.

She reddened at her own curiosity and indiscretion, glad Bea had not caught her looking; and she sat pondering what on earth was supposed to be so terrible about people of the Spanish race, or Indians, for that matter. Most of all, she wondered about her own new and changing feelings about young men. She never used to give them much thought. Her curiosity had seemed to start when she had her first time of month, and her mother, flustered and seeming embarrassed herself, explained in her own awkward way about what it all meant. She was becoming a woman now. She could have babies. She had to be more ladylike and discreet around young men.

"And you must stop that embarrassing habit of riding a horse like a man," Bea had told her.

Irene hated learning to ride side-saddle, but if it was the only way she was going to be allowed to ride, then she would do it. She didn't like angering her mother, but she had vowed not to give up Sierra and her daily rides, no matter what. Bea had wanted to sell Sierra before leaving California, and for the first and only time in her life Irene had thrown a crying fit until her mother gave in and let her bring Sierra to Colorado. The animal was tied to the back of the Kirkland wagon so that Irene could watch him and talk to him during the trip.

She looked out the back of the wagon, but the freight wagons that lumbered behind blocked her view. She could no longer see the Spanish man. She leaned out to look at the mountains then, wondering if she could persuade her mother to let her go with Kirk to the mining camps. She would much rather ride with her father and visit the mines than stay home taking sewing and piano lessons. Besides, it would be a while before they could set up the piano again. Bea had insisted on bringing the heavy instrument over the mountains. It had been hauled alone in its own special wagon because of its weight, and Kirk had fussed and complained about its burden and the danger of carrying something so heavy. But Bea had insisted, claiming it could take weeks, perhaps months to get another piano once they reached Denver.

At least it would be a while before the daily routine of schooling and lessons would resume. They had to get settled first, and that was just fine with Irene. She decided she liked this place called Colorado. She felt a strange link to this land, as though she, like her father, belonged here.

Bea Kirkland was quick to create her own form of civilization within an uncivilized town, careful to keep her daughters home, away from the unsavory characters who roamed the dirt streets of Denver, where frequent fights and even murders took place. There was still no organized law and order, and everyone seemed too busy making their fortunes to care.

Bea advertised for and found a woman to watch over the children and cook meals. Elsa Hansen's husband had been killed in the collapse of a mine. Sarah Wells, who had been a teacher back East, was hired as a tutor. Her husband had already given up prospecting and was now a busy town blacksmith. Myra Cole, a lonely, middle-aged woman who had come to Denver with her husband, leaving her grown children behind, came to work for Bea as a housekeeper. Myra's husband was gone most of the time, working in one of the hard-rock mines close to Pikes Peak.

Other towns, such as Colorado City, Boulder, and Golden, were developing, vying with Denver to be the queen city of the frontier, as Denver's promoters were calling their still-unfinished town. Kirk had helped pass the proposition to merge Denver and

Auraria into one city, and already a petition had been sent off to Washington to include Denver in a branch line of a proposed transcontinental telegraph line.

Bea was busy every day at the National Bank of Colorado, backed with Kirkland money; and she helped in the decision to establish a minting mill, in which Kirkland gold and the gold of other developers became gold coins. The federal government talked of outlawing local minting operations, but so far no action had been taken.

There was never a dull moment for Bea or Kirk, who both welcomed being too busy to worry about their own relationship. Kirk spent most of his time in mountain mining camps, and Bea, temporarily setting aside her own dreams of a great mansion, supervised the building of not only the bank and the mint, but also the warehouses, which would hold more Kirkland merchandise hauled in by wagon train in the spring of 1860. She also helped form a Ladies Union Aid Society, planning social events that could be advertised in the *Rocky Mountain News*, making Denver appear to be a growing, civilized community, in spite of trouble in the streets.

The country was on the verge of civil war, and although most of Denver stood staunchly for the Union, enough Southern sympathizers existed to make trouble, and fights became more frequent. Bea refused to let the "silly war" affect her plans. She dove into more development, hiring a contractor to build one of Denver's first hotels, a three-story structure called, of course, the Kirkland Hotel.

Seeing her last name on the sign in front of the building gave Bea great pleasure. Just as Kirk had promised, she was already known as one of the "great ladies of Denver," and the money she and Kirk had brought to town was a source of envy. "First money," Bea liked to call it. Other wealthy investors were coming to Denver, but the Kirklands were indeed a cornerstone of the city. For once Bea had to admit Kirk had been right about something involving the family business. He had also made some wise mining purchases and had set up two stamp mills, one near Pikes Peak.

Mining engineers were coming to town, using Denver as a base for their operations. More than one hundred and fifty thousand people moved in and out of Denver in the first year Bea and Kirk settled there—merchants, jewelers, assayers, doctors, realtors, surveyors, people from all walks of life. Several restaurants, two small theaters and two schools were opened, although because Bea considered the streets still too dangerous for her children, she

continued to have them privately tutored. Town lots, in which Bea
and Kirk had invested heavily, jumped in value from tens of
dollars to hundreds of dollars.

In the spring of 1860, Bea hired men to farm several acres she
had purchased south of Denver, directing them to plant potatoes.
Kirk thought the project ridiculous, but in the fall they made a
profit of thirty-five thousand dollars selling the potatoes to the
thousands of hungry miners who paid ungodly prices for everything they used or ate.

Denver's biggest problem was that everyone seemed too busy
getting rich to concentrate on law and order or to pool their ideas
into making the town more organized and civilized. Bea and Kirk
worked hard with Bill Byers to that end, but to no avail. The
general goal of most was to get rich quick, and to hell with the
city.

By the spring of 1861, Colorado had officially become a
territory. The first governor sent by the government, William
Gilpin, an aristocrat from Pennsylvania, found a treeless, dusty
town with littered streets lined with over seven hundred thousand
dollars worth of construction, a good share of them saloons. A few
lawyers had come to town, and although most people didn't trust
lawyers, Bea had the foresight to form a law firm bearing her
family's name. She hired two middle-aged attorneys from New
York to start the new enterprise. They were family men with good
reputations and proof of considerable schooling. Already, Bea
could see that the Kirkland investments were becoming more than
she could handle alone. She needed trusted men who could help
her keep track of the income and outflow.

She organized the various Kirkland businesses into one central
company called Kirkland Enterprises, appointing herself and Kirk
as co-chairmen, making sure she kept full rights to sign any and
all legal documents, since Kirk was gone most of the time. Other
businessmen soon learned to take her seriously, in spite of their
belief that the business world was no place for a woman.

It was not without some guilt that Bea realized she had
practically no time for the children. She sat down with them nearly
every night to explain what she'd been doing—all new develop-
ments in the family businesses—trying to instill in them the
importance of the responsibilities they would one day inherit. She
seldom had a word of love for any of them, or a question about
how their day had been, or an inquiry about whether or not they
were happy. There was only instructions in how to behave
properly, how to represent the Kirkland name. Bea was simply too

wrapped up in her work to see that the children neither understood nor cared about Kirkland Enterprises.

John became more withdrawn, and Elly, who was allowed anything and everything she wanted, became even more unbearable. Irene was simply lonely, missing her father. She was allowed little time for riding, Bea saw to that. But Irene never failed to sneak in a few moments every day to go out and talk to Sierra, brushing down her horse, feeding and watering him. She had begged her father several times to take her with him to the mining camps, but always the answer was no.

"Those camps are no place for a beautiful, proper young lady," Bea insisted. "You don't understand about men, Irene, especially when they've been up in the mountains alone for months at a time. And the women who live in those camps are not the kind of women you ever want to talk to or be seen with."

Her mother always glanced at Kirk when she repeated that, and Kirk always surrendered to Bea's wishes. Irene still sensed a terrible loneliness in the man, even though he had come back to this land that he loved so much. Sometimes she feared her father would ride off alone into the mountains and never come back, and she wondered if her mother had the same fears.

Bea Kirkland seemed to be working herself into a near frenzy building the Kirkland fortune, as though she was afraid someone would come along and take it all away from her, or that she might be left alone to fend for herself and the children. As Irene matured, she came to understand that things were not quite right between her parents, and she was becoming more and more confused about what love and marriage were supposed to be. Sarah Wells, their tutor, seemed very happy with her husband. She got a certain light in her eyes when she talked about him. It was a light Irene had never seen in Bea's eyes.

It was mid-1861 when Irene began to understand the seriousness of the trouble in town. Bea kept her children shielded from most of the difficulties. When it was necessary to shop, she took them to town in closed carriages under escort. One night, when the whole family was together for supper, Kirk brought up the need for law and order in Denver.

"Things are getting worse," he told Bea. "There's been trouble with the Indians—white men attacking Indian women in the camps down along the creek."

"Not in front of the children, Kirk."

"You want them to be a part of building Denver, you'd better make them understand what's going on," he answered. "The people around here have no right treating the Indians that way."

Bea glanced at Irene, fifteen years old now and getting more beautiful every day. Again Irene saw the strange fear in her mother's eyes. "The Indians should be urged to leave," Bea answered. "It's obvious the rest of us aren't going anywhere, and if they insist on lingering here, these things are going to happen."

Kirk gave her a chastising look, and Irene knew the man did not approve of her attitude toward the Indians. "You know how I feel about them."

"Yes. All too well," Bea answered, giving no further explanation. The two of them exchanged a look that only confused Irene.

Kirk sighed and broke a piece of bread in half. "It isn't just the Indians, either. It's those bummers. Charley Harrison and those Southern sympathizers of his down at the Criterion Saloon are getting bolder all the time. Harrison is nothing but a crime boss in this town. Seems he's using strong-arm tactics to take over other saloons and some of the whore—" he hesitated, "some of the questionable houses. You already know Harrison himself killed a man just for trying to sit in on his card game, and no one did a damn thing about it."

"Kirk, this kind of talk is going to get you hurt."

"I don't care. Somebody has to do something. You want this to be a civilized town, don't you?"

Bea sighed. They rarely slept together anymore, and she knew that financially she could get along quite well without him, yet the thought of something happening to Kirk pained her deeply. In spite of her independence, he remained in an inexplicable, abstract way, her strength. "Of course I do," she answered, glancing at the children then. "Kirk is right," she told them. "You should understand what is happening. This is why I don't want any of you going to town alone." She looked at Kirk. "What are you going to do?"

He leaned back, always looking uncomfortable and out of place in the hard, high-backed dining chair. "Some of us are thinking of forming a vigilante committee. Governor Gilpin isn't doing a damn thing about any of this, so we're acting on our own. The bummers have been threatening Byers for printing stories against them. We've got to take action. We're thinking of calling ourselves the Committee of Safety. With no courts or other form of law, it's the best we can do. I hope we can get rid of Gilpin and

get a better territorial governor who will help us in these things."
He looked at the children. "This conversation is just between us
right now. Understood? All three of you keep your mouths
closed." He gave Elly the longest look.

"Yes, sir," they all answered.

Bea looked at him. "Be careful, Kirk."

He grinned a little. "I've fought bears and Indians. This won't
be nearly as bad. Besides, it's not me alone. There are several
others willing to go in on this."

"Do what you think is necessary." Bea dabbed at her mouth
with a napkin. "You're right, of course. We do need some law and
order around here. Perhaps by next spring, when Irene turns
sixteen, we can have a coming-out party for her, and celebrate a
safer Denver at the same time."

Kirk nodded. "Maybe."

"I'd like to start the new house, Kirk. Maybe we can get
enough of it finished to have Irene's party in it next spring. What
do you think?"

"Oh, yes, Mother, I'm sick of this house," Elly blurted out.
"You said you would build something much finer when we came
here, but you're always too busy."

Kirk frowned at the girl's snobbish attitude, but Bea seemed to
pay no attention. "Well, I intend to keep my promise," she told
Elly. She looked back at Kirk. "I want the best carpenters, and I
want you to send some men to California to buy up silks for
draperies and some oriental rugs and vases and such. I have
already wired New York to order some Italian marble and Asian
teakwood. I need a good carpenter, to decide how much oak we'll
need, how many chandeliers, and such. And I want you to find a
good silversmith who can make us some candelabras and other
decorations from our own gold and silver."

Kirk gladly obliged. The fact that Bea was ready to build her
dream house meant she intended to stay in Denver. "I'd hire
Henry Brown to build the house," he told her. "He's got a young
Mexican man working for him who does the most beautifully
detailed carving you've ever seen. If you want fancy latticework
and detailed wood trim inside the house, he's the man to do it. I
think his name is Ramon. He's only about twenty, but he's got a
great talent with wood."

Bea sighed. "If you say so. You know how I feel about
mingling with the Mexicans."

Kirk scowled. He was always irritated by his wife's attitude
toward people of other races and nationalities, which was rubbing

off on Elly. He was happy to realize that so far Irene had not been affected by her mother's arrogant ways. "You wouldn't be 'mingling,' Bea. The man works for Brown, that's all, and he's good at his trade. He'd be an employee, not a social acquaintance. And Mexican or not, he's a fine young man. I've met him a time or two."

"I'd like to see some of his work," John spoke up. "I've carved a few things myself. I'd like to know what he thinks of them."

"You'd be better off concentrating on your studies, young man," Bea reminded him. "Carving wood won't help you make business decisions or help you get into college."

John looked down at his plate. "Maybe I don't want to go to college. Maybe I'll be a carpenter, too, some day."

Bea stiffened. "You'll go to college and learn to take care of all the things your father and I have worked hard to build for you," she answered.

John said nothing.

"Leave him alone, Bea." Kirk sighed. He excused himself and rose from the table. "I'm meeting with the committee tonight. Keep the house locked up." He looked over at John. "I'll take you to meet Ramon tomorrow," he told the boy, pleased that two of his children had inherited his tolerance.

John's face brightened, and Kirk could feel his wife's vehement reaction without looking at her. Kirk left the dining room to get a jacket from the hallway.

"Mother, aren't you going to tell him good-bye?" Irene spoke up. "He might get hurt."

Bea was still glowering at her son. "He'll be all right," she answered. "Your father can take care of himself. He's been doing it for years."

She rose from the table wondering why she couldn't run to her husband and tell him to be careful, tell him she loved him like she wanted to do. Irene quickly excused herself and hurried past her mother, running up to hug her father before he could get out the door. "Be careful, Father."

He looked down at her, thinking what a treasure she was, how she was a child of his heart. "I'll be all right. How about going for a ride tomorrow after I get back with John?"

"Oh, I'd love that! It's been such a long time."

He touched her hair. "Then we'll do it." He leaned closer. "No matter how mad it makes your mother," he whispered.

Irene smiled and watched him leave, hoping there wouldn't be trouble. She closed the door and thought about the young Mexican carver named Ramon. Could he be the handsome carpenter who had caught her eye the day they arrived in Denver two years earlier?

It had been so long ago and she had not seen him again, yet she had always remembered him. Thoughts of him made her shiver with feelings she did not yet understand. Her whole body tingled at the memory.

Bea called to her to come back and finish her dessert, and Irene was glad her mother could not read her thoughts. Their mother's accusing looks were something none of the children relished, although Elly seemed little affected by anything her mother or anyone else thought or demanded.

Elly was Elly, stubborn, determined and spoiled. Irene tried hard to love her sister, but Elly did not make it easy. Irene was closer to John, who cared as little as she did about putting on airs and impressing people.

She took a chair beside John at the table, while Bea went into the kitchen to talk to Elsa about dessert. Elly flounced after her mother to tell her she wanted an extra helping. "I'll be glad when we get a new house with more servants and a way to ring for them," she said on her way out of the room. She turned at the door. "By the way, Irene, Mother might be having a coming-out party for you next year when you're sixteen, but I'll be thirteen next year, so she'll be having a party for *me*, too."

"Of course she will," Irene answered pleasantly.

Elly sniffed and went through the door. Irene turned to John, smiling and shaking her head. "She'll be having a party for *me*, too," John mimicked his sister, twisting his mouth into a sneer. Irene laughed. "I can't stand her sometimes," John grumbled. "Hey, Irene, I wonder if that man Ramon will teach me more about carving. I'm glad Father is going to let me see his work."

"He must be very good for him to take you," Irene answered. "You must tell me what he's like, what you learned from him."

"Sure. And I'll make something just for you." He sighed. "I'm happiest when I'm working with wood, Irene. I hate my business studies, and I hate the thought of going away to college."

"It's probably best, John. When you're through with school and all grown up, you can do whatever you want, and Mother won't be able to stop you."

He looked at her seriously. "Sometimes I think she'll be telling us what to do our whole lives, maybe even from the grave."

"John! She's our mother. She means well."

Bea came back into the room, and the conversation ceased. Irene heard Kirk's horse gallop off, and her chest tightened with fear at the thought of anything happening to her father.

CHAPTER
SIX

Stories of nightly looting and killing by Harrison's bummers ran daily in the *News*, and for several nights Irene lay awake in dreadful fear for her father, who left the house after dinner, never saying where he was going or who would be with him. There were wrongs to be righted, and there was no law in Denver but the Safety Committee.

One night Irene thought she heard her father groan in pain after coming in late, heard her mother's muffled but distraught words of concern. The next morning Kirk came to the table limping. He told the family he had taken a spill from his horse, but Irene knew better. She was sure he had been shot. She approached him alone in the parlor later, tears in her eyes.

"You didn't really fall from your horse, did you?" she asked quietly. "You're too good a rider, Father."

Kirk looked up from his chair and put a finger to his lips. "Don't you tell that to anyone else."

She came closer. "I won't say anything." She knelt in front of him, putting her head on his knee. "I don't want anything to happen to you, Father."

He touched her hair, thinking how she was the only one of his three children who had come to express concern that he'd been hurt. He thought what a beautiful, loving wife she would be someday, and he hoped she would find a man worthy of her. She would be nothing like Bea. Irene would be gentle and caring. She would know how to express her love. "Nothing is going to happen," he assured her. "We're doing what we must to make the city safe. You just remember your old father here has been in a lot worse situations than this and survived them all."

The only good thing Irene could see in any of the trouble was that it kept her father home for several weeks. The whole household always seemed more happy and contented when Kirk was around; and to Irene's joy and Bea's consternation, Kirk had taken Irene riding several times.

John was happier than Irene had ever seen him. He spent every day carving objects from wood, and had presented Irene with several carved animals, which she thought looked very realistic. She kept them on a shelf in her room. John talked almost constantly about Ramon Vallejo. Kirk took John to meet with him every week. "I never saw anybody work with his hands like he can," he told Irene.

Although she had never met the man, Irene felt as though she already knew Ramon. He was twenty-one, he could read and speak good English, and his family were successful farmers and ranchers. They lived several miles south of Denver, near Colorado City. Ramon had come to Denver because he felt he could make money in the growing city using his talent for working with wood. So far the young man had managed to save a considerable amount of money, and John told Irene that Kirk had even advised Ramon on how to handle his savings.

"Father likes him," John told her, "even though he's Mexican. You'll get to meet him in the spring. The house will be finished enough by then that Ramon will have to start on the interior woodwork."

Irene felt a strange anticipation at the remark. She would finally get to meet the mysterious Ramon.

Over the winter a few men were hanged for murder, but Kirk would not discuss details. One night William Byers himself was dragged by bummers from his newspaper office and taken to the Criterion, where he was questioned and threatened before they released him. When the bummers marched to the offices of the *Rocky Mountain News* to destroy it, they were greeted with a shotgun by Byers, who wounded one of them. The newly appointed marshal shot and killed the wounded man, and the other three who had taken part in the fracas were run out of town by Kirk and the Safety Committee, men the bummers referred to as lawless vigilantes.

"Maybe we don't do everything right, but we're all Denver has right now," Kirk said one evening at the dinner table. It was January 1862, and a winter wind was roaring out of the mountains, battering the house and making the windows shake. Irene noticed her mother was unusually nervous, as she always was when the mountain winds blew. She supposed it reminded Bea of the harsh winters she had spent in the Sierras when she and Kirk first went to California.

"We try to be fair about things," Kirk was saying, unaffected by the blizzard outside. "At least we have finally convinced Gilpin we need something more. He's gotten permission from Washington to organize a regiment of volunteers, uniforms and all. With no tax base or territorial treasury, he needs some of us businessmen to put up the money. The government will reimburse us, as well as provide money to pay the volunteers."

Bea frowned. "Can we trust Gilpin to make sure we get our money back?"

"We don't have much choice," Kirk answered. "We need to do this, Bea. I want it to be safe for my wife and children to go into town. Besides, this country is at war now. Word is, the Confederates have their eye on all the gold we've got in these mountains. They just might decide to try to take over this territory. That's part of the reason we've got to keep an eye on Harrison and his bummers. They're Southerners, and if they can help from the inside, they'll do it. We've got to be extra careful now, and with most regular soldiers being pulled out of the West because of the war, all we've got left is our own volunteers. We've got to put up the money, Bea, and trust we'll get it back."

Bea sighed, always wary of any investment whose payoff seemed unreliable. "I suppose you're right. It isn't just the Confederates I worry about anyway. With hardly any regular soldiers left out here, the Indians are going to become more of a problem. Elizabeth Byers said there are rumors the Cheyenne have been moving away from treaty land down on the Arkansas River, raiding some of the outlying settlements. With no soldiers left in the territory, they aren't going to pay any attention to the Fort Wise Treaty. They'll have a heyday, once they realize we have no protection. Maybe the Volunteers will help keep them where they belong."

Kirk glanced at Irene, wondering if her brother was among the

Cheyenne who had been forced onto the small reservation in southeastern Colorado. Already people talked of totally ridding Colorado of its Indians, forcing them much farther south and east, into what was being called Indian territory. Kirk knew that land, knew that forcing the Cheyenne to live there would kill them physically and spiritually. They needed *this* land, *these* mountains.

He was gladder than ever now that he had kept Irene. If he had not, she might be dead or belong to some other Indian family, perhaps a wife to some warrior, with one or two children already. At one time he had thought nothing of the difficult life Indian women led, but now he could not bear the thought of Irene living that way, perhaps being sold as a squaw to some white trader. With her light hair and blue eyes and exquisite beauty, she would have been very valuable.

"That's the only thing I regret about the growth of this territory," he said aloud. "I don't like what it's doing to the Indians."

"They have to understand that we're here to stay," Bea said firmly. "And since they don't seem ready to live like decent people, they've got to go, Kirk. Why, just the other day some Arapaho walked right into Bela Kramer's house without any warning. They just stood there. She didn't know if they intended to beg something from her or kill her. She ordered them out, and they left, but the fact remains we can't have things like this happening. We have two young girls in this house, and I'll not put up with such things. If any Indians walk into this house, I'll shoot them."

"You'll do no such thing," he said sternly, surprising her with the sudden anger in his voice. "You want to start an uprising right here in town?" *Have you forgotten your own daughter is Indian?* he felt like asking. Bea met his eyes, looking offended. "That's just their way," Kirk continued. "There's not much privacy among the Indians. If they want to come visiting, they come visiting. There's no sense trying to explain it to you. All I'm saying is if they should happen to walk in here, it wouldn't be to bring you harm. Don't you dare grab a weapon!"

She sniffed, picking at her food, while the children watched and listened. "Well, we've managed to chase the Utes farther west. I still say something has to be done about the Cheyenne and Arapaho. They continue to camp all around us and beg. And you and your Safety Committee or Volunteers or whatever you call yourselves should do something about it . . . as well as arrest those slovenly whiskey traders who sell rotten liquor to those poor savages. There is nothing more dangerous than a drunken Indian."

Kirk said nothing. He excused himself from the table, and Bea clinked her fork against her plate nervously. "Children, I have hired a new attorney to join the others at Kirkland Enterprises. He's a fine young man, and I want him to meet the family." She moved her eyes to Irene. "Especially you, Irene. You're getting close to the age where you can receive men, and I want you to be thinking about marrying into the proper class. Chadwick Jacobs is a wonderful man, handsome and intelligent and well educated."

"Mother, I'm not sixteen yet—"

"I'm only having him for dinner," the woman interrupted. "I just want you to meet him, that's all."

Irene sighed deeply, deciding not to argue. No one liked to argue with Bea Kirkland. Her father usually made more headway than anyone else, but even he had given up tonight. Irene had noticed there always seemed to be a point where Kirk gave in to her mother. Bea would give him an odd, hurt look, a look that seemed to say, "How can you do this to me after all I've done for you?" She sometimes wondered if there was some secret to their marriage that always made her father back away from angry confrontations with his wife, but she was too young to understand everything that went on between a man and a woman. Still, she was sure that when she married, she would never treat her husband the way her mother treated her father. She would be gracious and loving, and she would allow him his pride and honor and never raise her voice to him.

She thought about meeting Chadwick Jacobs and dreaded it. She didn't mind meeting young men; and had in fact given it more thought lately than ever before. But she didn't feel ready to have one shoved on her by her mother, or to be "inspected" by someone of whom her mother "approved." She wanted to tell her mother as much, but like her father, she could see that Bea Kirkland was in no mood to be crossed.

A week passed, and so did the winter storm. Bea was elated at the temporary good weather as she lined up her children, inspecting them all to be sure they were properly attired for their guest who would arrive soon.

Jealousy burned in Elly's chest when she noticed that her mother fussed over Irene the most, retying the wide sash of her rose-colored silk and taffeta evening dress. Bea had allowed Irene to wear a dress with an off-the-shoulder neckline for the first time, and Elly knew it was because Bea wanted Irene to impress Chad Jacobs, about whom Bea had raved all week.

"Not only is he a very handsome young man, but he is so well educated," she had told them more than once, as though to be sure Irene understood what a wonderful catch he would be. "He is going to be a fine addition to Denver society. I see a great future ahead for him. And he's so friendly. He prefers to be called just Chad."

The woman repeated the words now as she fussed with Irene's sash, wanting to show off her daughter's slender waist. "Perhaps Chad will want to be your escort at your coming-out party," she was saying. The décolletage of Irene's dress was graced with delicate white lace, which only enhanced the tawny, satiny skin of Irene's lovely shoulders. The same white lace gracefully edged each tier of ruffles that cascaded down the hooped skirt.

"Mother, I feel funny with my shoulders bare," Irene complained.

"It's quite acceptable. I probably should have waited until you were sixteen, but it's only a modest cut, Irene. Nothing is showing that shouldn't be showing."

Twelve-year-old Elly wondered if and when she would fill out like Irene, wishing she could wear a bodice that dipped much lower to show off the breasts she was beginning to develop. If she were Irene, she would be complaining that the neckline was too high, not too low. She kept her hurt and hatred to herself as Bea fussed over Irene's lustrous, golden hair, making sure it was properly pinned at the back, a rose-colored lace hairpiece decorating the twisted curls. A diamond necklace sparkled at Irene's slender throat.

"There," Bea said, stepping back. She smiled, sighing deeply. "You're a picture, Irene. Chad Jacobs will be very impressed, and I know you'll like him very much." She glanced at Elly, suddenly frowning. "Elly, you know you look terrible in that color green. Put on the yellow dress like I told you."

"But I like this one better. It makes me look thinner."

"It's too tight in the waist. It only makes you look heavier because it pinches and creases right at the waistline. Wear the yellow one, and hurry up. We haven't much time." She turned to John. "You look fine, John."

He stuck a finger into the collar that felt too tight around his neck. "I hate getting dressed up."

Bea adjusted his bow tie and buttoned one button he had left open on his silk vest. "So does your father, but we want to be proper for Mr. Jacobs. And I want you to get to know him much better. Chad will benefit your career much more than that uneducated Mexican woodcarver you go on about. It's time to stop whittling away at wood and get into more serious studies, John. I want you to start spending some time at the law firm to see how things are handled. It might help you when you go off to college."

John just scowled and glanced at Irene. His sister and his father understood how he felt about wood carving. He had given up trying to make his mother understand. Bea seemed deaf when anyone in the family wanted something other than what she wanted for them. "It's stuffy up here," he grumbled, walking out of the bedroom to go downstairs.

"Our new home will be much nicer," Bea assured the girls. "Your rooms will be quite large, and you can decorate them however you like. We won't be able to move in until later in the summer, so we may have to wait until then to have your party, Irene, even though you'll be sixteen in March."

"It doesn't matter to me, Mother. I don't need a coming-out party."

"Of course you do. All proper young ladies should have one. I want to show my daughter off to all of Denver. Now come downstairs with me and we'll make sure Elsa has the appetizers ready."

Bea and Irene left, and Elly glared at the doorway, hastily and angrily removing her dress to change into the yellow one her mother wanted her to wear. It was a "little-girl's" dress, as far as she was concerned. She envisioned walking up to Irene in front of Chad Jacobs and yanking Irene's dress down to her waist, humiliating her. The thought made her laugh.

She quickly put on the yellow dress, scowling in the mirror at how it made her look. She removed the green ribbon and rebrushed her long, straight hair, then tied a yellow ribbon into it. Although she hated the dress, she agreed that yellow did look better against her olive skin and dark hair, but the dress made her look heavier. She pushed at her waist, hoping she would lose her chunky look as she got older. She studied her breasts, pleased that at least they seemed to be developing nicely. She wondered if Mr. Chad Jacobs would notice.

Someone rapped at the door downstairs, and Elly hurried out of the room, racing down the stairs just in time to see Bea and Kirk opening the door to welcome the new attorney. Elly already knew he was twenty-four, came from a prominent family in Pennsylvania, and had graduated from law school at the top of his class. What she didn't know until now was that her mother's remark about his looks had been an understatement. Her heart fluttered as she gazed upon the most handsome man her young eyes had ever beheld.

She could tell that Irene was also impressed, as her cheeks suddenly flushed at the sight of him. Elly wanted to cry when she saw how Chad, in turn, looked at Irene. Extreme delight was written all over his finely chisled face as his soft gray eyes drank in Irene's exquisite beauty. He shook hands with Kirk, then turned back to Irene, taking her hand and bowing lightly. "I'm honored and delighted to meet you, Irene," he told her. "Your mother has told me a lot about you."

Irene blushed as he turned to Bea then. "Well, Mrs. Kirkland, you do indeed have a very beautiful daughter."

Bea glowed with pride. She had a daughter much more beautiful than her cousin Cynthia could ever have hoped to be. No one had to know Irene wasn't of her own blood, and no one would ever know, as far as she was concerned. She could hardly wait until the new house was finished so she could write to Cynthia, now a married woman herself, and invite her to come for a visit.

Bea turned and introduced Elly and John. Elly stared in awe at Jacobs, whom she considered nothing short of a prince. He shook hands with John, then took Elly's hand and squeezed it. "So, this is the little sister," he commented with a gentle smile.

How Elly hated to be referred to in that way! His eyes immediately turned back to Irene. He walked beside her as they went into the dining room to sit down at an elegantly set table. Bea Kirkland had only the finest china and silverware. The huge dining table and matching chairs were a rich mahogany, and the lace tablecloth was from France.

Elly's eyes never left Chad Jacobs as they all took their places. He was more than handsome. He was beautiful—tall and well built, with thick, sandy hair; his smile showed even, white teeth, and his nose was perfect. Elly was certain there was not another man like him in all of Denver, and her heart felt crushed to think that she would never get the chance to vie for his attention. By the time she was old enough for men to notice, Chad Jacobs would most certainly be taken by someone else, and if Bea Kirkland had anything to do with it, that someone would be Irene.

Irene still felt awkward. She was not accustomed to entertaining men, and she was glad her whole family was present so she didn't have to worry about making conversation. Chad Jacobs was every bit as handsome as her mother had predicted, as well as charming and well spoken; he was, indeed, a man with a promising future. Still, there was something about him that made her uncomfortable, something she could not name. He was almost too charming, but she reasoned it didn't make much difference at the moment how she felt about him. She wouldn't even be sixteen for two months yet.

Talk turned to Kirkland Enterprises and what Chad's duties would be. It was obvious to Irene that both Bea and Elly were totally taken with Chad, but Kirk appeared somewhat wary. Irene was surprised that she felt the same way, sensing Chad was a man who could turn on the charm when needed, but that underneath there lurked a much cooler personality.

"I wanted to come west—help build a new city from the ground up," he was saying as the soup was served. "I'm very excited about being able to work for you, Mr. Kirkland."

"How about proving your loyalty to Denver first?" Kirk retorted.

Everyone looked at him in surprise. "Sir?" Chad asked. "I'm not sure what you mean."

Kirk grinned. "Just a suggestion," he told the young man. "Word is, Confederates are headed this way out of San Antonio . . . close to four thousand men."

"Kirk!" Bea paled. "Are you sure about that?"

"Byers has been getting telegraph messages for several days now. A General Sibley is marching north. He's already overtaken several Union forts. The mines up here are producing millions in gold, and the South needs it. Sibley is only a little over three hundred miles south of here, and none of us has any doubt where he's headed."

"Oh, my goodness," Bea said softly, putting a hand to her chest. "Kirk, what if they get hold of our own assets, take over the bank!"

Kirk looked at Chad. "Before you start helping Bea handle our business affairs, we have to make sure we keep our property and possessions in Kirkland hands, or there won't *be* a Kirkland Enterprises."

"If you're asking for my help, sir, you've got it," Chad offered. "I don't want Confederates running over this town any more than you do."

Kirk eyed him closely. "Good. I'm joining the First Colorado Volunteers for a march south to intercept this Sibley. You want to come along?"

The table was suddenly quiet, everyone worried, Irene concerned for her father, but Elly already concerned for Chad Jacobs. "Sure, I'll join," Chad told him. "As long as I can come back to work as soon as we do what's needed."

"Can you handle a rifle?"

"Yes, sir. I did a lot of hunting back home."

Kirk picked up a soup spoon. "Fine. I've been fighting since I was a kid, mostly Indians. Seems strange to be going up against other white men. There was a time when I never thought I'd see so much civilization in this country. I don't like it much, but I know it can't be stopped. I have a family to provide for now; so I just flow with the tide."

The words took him back to Bent's Fort. He remembered Red McKinley telling him about flowing with the tide. It had been over fifteen years since he had seen his old friend, and he wondered what had ever happened to him. What would Red think of him now—David Kirkland, a wealthy, settled man? He wanted to laugh at the thought of it.

"Well, you just tell me who to go see, and I'll pick up a uniform," Chad was saying.

Kirk swallowed a spoonful of soup. "There's a man down at the city offices by the name of Major John Chivington who's swearing in volunteers. We can go over there together tomorrow. The man is actually a Methodist minister. For some reason he got involved in all this and seems to know what he's doing. Some are calling him the 'fighting preacher.'"

Chad laughed. "And I've heard the Volunteers called Governor Gilpin's 'pet lambs.' We'll show them what we're worth when we rout out this Sibley and his men, right?"

Kirk could not help respecting Chad's readiness to volunteer, although he suspected the man's motives were mainly to impress Bea and Irene. Jacobs at least seemed to have no aversion to doing a man's job, and he certainly looked up to the task. Irene was somewhat more impressed herself, sensing her father had been testing the young man.

"I wish you would discuss these things with me before you act on them, Kirk," Bea said, trying to appear calm. "I had no idea you were joining the Volunteers."

"Well, it wasn't until today that they began asking for extra men. When I heard how close this Sibley was, I decided I couldn't just sit here waiting to see what happens. Besides, it's been a long time since I enjoyed a good fight."

"You're a businessman now. Denver needs you," Bea reminded him. "And so do we."

"That's why I'm going—to protect my family, my possessions, and Denver. But I am sorry I brought it up here at the table. Let's just eat and talk about this later."

Kirk turned the conversation to Denver itself, the mining operations, how rapidly the city had grown, and how hard he and others were working to keep the city growing, even if the gold should run out. By dessert, Chad seemed to fit right in with the family. He had turned his attention to Irene several times. Bea had made certain she was seated next to him. Chad seemed interested in her life, and she was relieved that he was not put off when she mentioned that she liked to ride.

Irene wanted to dislike him, and she didn't even know why; but he had a way of making it difficult to tear her eyes away once he caught them with his own penetrating gaze; and he made conversation easily. The rest of the evening seemed to pass swiftly. Kirk lit the fireplace in the parlor, and Bea urged Irene and Chad to sit together on a satin love seat. Elly sat in a chair near them, continually interrupting their conversation with her own questions. She struggled to get Chad's attention, but he had eyes only for Irene. Just being near him made Elly feel shaky and warm, and she felt like crying at the thought of Chad Jacobs's joining the Volunteers.

The evening wore on, and Chad had to leave. Kirk and Irene walked him to the door, and he asked if he might talk to Irene alone for a moment. Irene reddened, feeling awkward and embarrassed. Kirk frowned, eyeing his beautiful daughter, unable to blame Jacobs for being interested but wary of any young man getting close to Irene. She was not only beautiful and rich, but trusting and innocent as well. He was not going to let her be hurt. "Two minutes," he told Chad with a wink.

He left them at the door, and Chad looked down at Irene, placing a finger lightly under her chin to turn her face toward his. "I'd like to see more of you, Irene," he told her, "once I get back. Your mother tells me you're turning sixteen soon. I think your parents would let me begin seeing you more then, if you'll allow it."

Irene was not sure how she felt. She reasoned any young woman would be flattered and eager to be courted by this seemingly near-perfect man. This was something her mother wanted very much, and she decided she didn't know enough about men to be so wary of this one, certainly not before even getting to know him better. There couldn't be any harm in that.

"It's fine with me," she answered, wondering if her face was as red as it felt.

He gave her his most unnerving smile. "Thank you." He took her hand and leaned down to kiss the back of it. "We'll take care of those rebels and be back in no time."

"Be careful, Chad," she told him. "And watch out for my father, will you?"

He grinned more. "I have a feeling he's not the kind of man who needs looking after. But I'll keep an eye out." He took his tweed frock coat from a rack near the door, putting it on and adjusting the silk serge collar. He donned his silk hat and held Irene's eyes a moment longer, sensing her doubts, realizing she was quite the innocent. He imagined with aching ecstasy what it would be like bringing out the woman in this object of utter beauty.

"Good-bye, Irene," he told her softly, wondering how long it would take to break down her girlish resistance. She told him good-bye, and he left, his body burning with desire for Irene Kirkland. Not only was she more beautiful than her mother had described, but she was rich. His own parents were not doing so well anymore. He needed new resources. Bea Kirkland was paying him well, but he wanted more, and Irene could be his pathway to a lifetime of luxury. How delightful to find a rich girl who was also pretty. That made it all that much easier to marry a woman just for the money.

He considered the fact that marriage meant only one woman in his bed. To Chad Jacobs, the conquest of women had been a thrilling hobby for years. It mattered little whether they were virgins, married women, or widows. The thrill of victory was always the same, and it came easy for him. Just the right smile, the right words, the right touch, was all they needed. He had killer looks, and he knew it. He had perfected his talent in seducing women to the point where he could probably get any woman he wanted into his bed.

Except, perhaps, Bea Kirkland, he thought. She was a rare breed. He sensed right off that no man got through to that stalwart queen. She was a shrewd woman. He had to be careful with her, or she would catch on to him, and his plans for her daughter would be ruined. The way to that woman's heart was not through charm and passion, but through hard work and dollar signs. He would charm her with his knowledge, his devotion to Kirkland Enterprises, of which he intended to own a part someday, through Irene.

As far as David Kirkland was concerned, he would be even harder to fool. But he had made a good start at winning the man's confidence by quickly agreeing to join the Volunteers, much as he detested the idea.

He realized that for the time being he would have to give up chasing after other women. He had to appear devoted to Irene now. Still, a man had needs. He headed for Denver's red light district. No red-blooded young man could be blamed for visiting the whores once in a while. He needed the whores—using them and other women to get back at his mother . . . his slutty, cruel mother. God, how he hated her!

From an upstairs window Elly watched him go. She hated her mother for making her come upstairs early, and she hated Irene for being able to stay up until Chad Jacobs left. "I'll pray for you, Chad," she whispered. She was not thirteen yet, but she was in love, of that she was sure. It had taken only one evening with Chad Jacobs to develop an aching crush that brought pain to her chest.

CHAPTER
SEVEN

Early March of 1862 brought a chinook wind that warmed the valley to a delightful, if not deceitful, early spring, although there was still a lot of snow at higher elevations. Irene put on her riding habit and a cape and headed out to the stables to saddle Sierra. She was worried about her father, who had been gone over three weeks, and she was getting restless sitting around the house reading and embroidering. She needed to get out into the warm, fresh air and vent her anxiety in a good ride.

Bea had taken advantage of the weather to make a trip farther south to visit her farming project, to ensure the planting of another crop of potatoes. "With growing Indian trouble, there could be a food shortage," she had told Irene. "If the Indians should cut off our supply lines, the Kirklands will have potatoes and other items stored up for sale, and we'll be able to charge whatever we want."

Irene's feelings for her mother were mixed. She loved Bea, but there were times when the woman seemed a true hypocrite. Bea often talked of the wealthier women of Denver doing something to help the growing indigent population, yet turned around and talked about charging outrageous prices to hungry people in case of a food shortage. Irene knew that no matter how wealthy she became, she could never take advantage of anyone. For her mother, money came first. It was never wasted and certainly never given away; but Irene always felt a little guilty having so much, when there were so many homeless women and children in Denver. Men were often killed in mining accidents; others disappeared into the mountains to prospect and never returned, leaving families abandoned.

Irene mounted up, still detesting the sidesaddle; but she was at least used to it now. She was glad her mother was gone for a couple of days. It gave her more freedom. She always found it easy to talk Elsa into letting her go riding, as long as she promised to go only as far as the new house or around a fenced pasture nearby.

She gazed across the sprawling town of Denver, which lay stretched out in a conglomeration of simple log huts and grander two- and three-story buildings. She could spot the Kirkland Hotel from here, as well as the bank, and it gave her an odd feeling to realize she would one day own a good share of her parents' growing businesses. Kirk's two biggest-producing mines, the Elly May and the Irene Louise, named after his daughters, showed no signs yet of playing out. The Johnny Boy was not doing quite as well but was still profitable.

She moved her eyes along the foothills and up to the snow-covered Rockies. Someday she was going to talk her father into taking her up there to visit the mines. She had loved coming through the Sierras, had been enthralled by the Rockies through which they had passed farther to the north when coming to Denver. She had no fonder memory than that of sitting by a campfire at night in the mountains, listening to her father tell stories of the "old days."

She remembered an abundance of wildflowers in those mountains, life blooming in a thousand colors, proving there was a spring even after a harsh mountain winter. She had picked paintbrush and daisies nearly every day, preferring to walk and enjoy the sunshine, rather than ride in the wagon with a complaining Elly. She liked the pungent smell of pine and sage, enjoyed watching the green and silver leaves of the aspens flutter in the wind.

She was disappointed that since arriving in Denver there had been no time to go back into those mountains with Kirk. He was always so busy, and he still refused to take her into the mining camps. She tried to imagine what they must be like—wild, noisy, dangerous, dirty. She didn't care. She would be with her father, and she would be safe.

She turned her horse, spotting a herd of elk ambling across open land to the south. Kirk had complained about how rare a sight wild game was becoming. "People kill them off like flies," he had grumbled once to Bea. "There ought to be some kind of control or there will be no meat left someday. Same with the buffalo. There was a time when the buffalo roamed these plains in herds so big and thick you could practically walk across their backs . . . couldn't see the end of them. Not any more. They won't come around places like this, and out in the open valleys men are killing them off for their hides, leaving the carcasses. I tell you, it must make the Indians sick to their stomachs to see that kind of waste."

"I've heard some say it's a good way to get rid of the Indians," Bea had answered. "Kill off the buffalo, and you take away their strength—their food, clothing, practically everything they need to subsist. It seems like a reasonable way to get them onto reservations. If they have to depend on the government to feed them, they'll stop making trouble soon enough."

Irene had been standing near the doorway to her parents' bedroom when she overheard the remarks. There had been an odd silence, and then she heard her father's voice, surprisingly low and threatening. "I never want to hear that kind of talk again," he had told Bea.

"Kirk, I didn't mean—"

"I know what you meant," he had said. "Give some thought to whom you're talking about, and to whom you're *telling* it. They're human beings, Bea. They love and they hate and they hurt. When their bellies are empty, they get the cramps same as we do. Maybe you've forgotten how that feels!"

"I'll *never* forget," her mother had nearly spat at him.

"Won't you? I think you've forgotten a lot of things now that life is good. And another thing. I don't like living this lie. Someday it's going to come back at us, and you know who is going to be hurt the worst."

Just then Irene had been unable to hold back a sneeze. The conversation stopped, and Irene casually walked past the bedroom doorway. Bea had called out to her, asking her how long she had been standing in the hallway. Irene would never forget the pale look on both her parents' faces. "I wasn't," she had answered. "I just came upstairs."

Bea had turned away, looking ready to pass out. Her father had smiled and told her to get to bed. Irene had never discovered what her father meant by living a lie. Did he mean that they didn't love each other? She had always suspected their marriage was not extremely happy, although she could not imagine why. Her father was a handsome man and a good provider, a generous man with a strong belief in what was right and wrong. It hurt to think he might not be happy, but she was helpless to do anything about it.

She kept her horse still and watched the elk until they were nearly out of sight. She looked up at the mountains again. "High country," her father called it, saying the words with near reverence. "When I die, I want to be buried up there." She had already made a personal vow that she would make sure he got his wish. She would not let her mother bury him in the city cemetary.

She turned Sierra and headed up the hill toward the new Kirkland mansion. What a mansion it was—three stories high, walls of stone and concrete, a castlelike tower at one corner. The inside of that tower was open and contained a circular-shaped bench as part of the seating area in the third-floor ballroom. The house was not finished yet, but already it was obvious it would be the grandest house in Denver. A circular brick drive graced the front lawn, which was not yet fully landscaped, and a natural spring fed the primary lawn decoration, a marble water fountain sporting two cherubs with wings, holding hands and posed as though dancing.

She could hear the pounding hammers and scraping saws. The carpenters were taking full advantage of the good weather, anxiously hurrying to meet certain deadlines given them by Bea Kirkland. Bea had wanted the house ready in time for Irene's sixteenth birthday, which was only two weeks away. But there wasn't enough time to ship in all the material required. Her "coming-out" party would have to be postponed, which was fine with Irene. She wouldn't want a party anyway unless her father was home safe and sound. In fact, she didn't want the party at all. It seemed frivolous, and she would feel embarrassed by all the fuss.

She gazed at the ostentatious building, deciding she preferred the coziness of the home they already lived in. This new one seemed domineering and cold, and she realized with a sad heart that it did, indeed, fit her mother's personality.

She rode closer, spotting John walking toward her. "Irene, come over here and see what I'm doing."

Irene headed Sierra toward him, thinking how tall and handsome her brother was getting. John told her to come inside. She dismounted and tied the horse to a hitching post shaped like an elk.

"I don't want to stay long," she told John as she followed him through the heavy oak front doors and through a marble-floored entranceway over which hung a French chandelier. Most of the furnishings, draperies and more chandeliers would not arrive for several weeks yet, since they were being hauled out from eastern ports. Special silks for bed clothing and bedroom draperies were coming from their own warehouses in San Francisco, as well as rugs from India and Chinese vases and other oriental accessories.

The greater share of the interior was finished, including polished wood floors and rich green wallpaper in the huge central room of the house, where guests would be wined and dined someday soon. Oak beams in the central room graced the ceiling in a spokelike fashion, all meeting at the center, where another candlelight chandelier was to be hung.

"See the tiny carved flowers at the base and tips of those beams," John said as he pointed them out to her. "Ramon did them."

Irene walked closer, gazing up at the design in wonder. Her first thought was that it took a gentle, caring man to do such intricate, beautiful work—a man of great passion and dedication. "It's lovely," she told her brother.

"Come into Father's smoking room," he told her excitedly. "The fireplaces are all going to be Italian marble. It hasn't got here yet, but Ramon is already working on carving the oak trim and mantels for them. Ramon is working here at the house now. He has the oak beams laid out to work on them, and he's letting me do one. Come and watch him work, Irene. I want you to meet him."

He hurried through the next huge room, which would be the dining room, then into a room to the left of that. Irene hesitated for a moment. The mysterious Ramon was in that room. To this day she had not met him, and she had wondered about him for so long. Ramon Vallejo had done most of his carving in one of his boss's little shops in town, where Kirk had taken John to visit him. The carved wood was then brought to the house for installation.

But today . . . today he was here at her house! She had not expected this. "Come on," John called out to her from the smoking room. She moved on shaky legs toward the doorway, wondering why in the world she was so nervous. She entered the room, blushing when a dark, handsome young man looked up at her from where he stood bent over a piece of wood.

The moment was suddenly tense and embarrassing for both of them. Ramon Vallejo was indeed the same young man she had seen that first day she'd come to Denver. Why she remembered him so vividly, she could not understand. She met his dark eyes, seeing there the same passion and gentleness she had seen in his work. He was just as handsome as Chad Jacobs, only in a dark, compelling way, more intriguing, perhaps, because he was different, forbidden.

"Ramon, this is my sister, Irene," John said.

Ramon's dark eyes moved over her. He did not usually allow his gaze to linger too long on a *gringa*. It usually meant trouble. But this Irene Kirkland was the most beautiful creature he had ever beheld. "*Buenos días, señorita,*" he said aloud.

She nodded. "Hello, Ramon. John has told me a lot about you." She wondered how she had managed to find her voice. "I'm very glad to meet you."

He flashed a smile that made her feel weak. "*Gracias.* I am also glad to meet John's sister, of whom he often speaks."

You are most beautiful, he wanted to tell her, but he was afraid the remark would offend her, coming from a Mexican. He was well aware of how most whites in the area felt about his people, even though they rightfully belonged here. After all, this had been Spanish territory long before these white intruders claimed it.

Irene swallowed, thinking how the day seemed even warmer than she had realized. "I saw some of your work in the great room and dining room," she told him. "It's very beautiful."

Ramon glanced down, appearing embarrassed. He ran a dark, strong hand over the gentle curve of a piece of wood, and she was shocked at herself for suddenly wondering how it might feel to be touched by such a man. "*Gracias,*" he said again. "I love working with the wood. Someday I plan to have my own carpentry business. I already own many of my own tools."

"Irene, come and look at this mantelpiece. I carved it myself," John told his sister, too young and too involved in his own excitement to notice the attraction between his sister and Ramon.

Irene had difficulty tearing her eyes from Ramon's. She stepped over lumber and carpenter's tools to go and stand beside her brother, then lightly touched the carved flowers on the heavy strip of wood. "John! This is the best thing I've seen you do yet!"

The boy grinned with pride. "You really think so?"

"Of course I do." She looked up at Ramon, who had turned to watch her. "You're a good teacher, Ramon."

He shrugged. "He is easy to teach."

Irene wondered if there was any imperfection in Ramon Vallejo. Her mother would say that being Spanish was imperfection enough, but Irene still did not understand what was supposed to be so terrible about the race. He was not just a handsome, well-built man, but there was an inner beauty to him that shone through his dark eyes. She sensed he would be capable of great love and total devotion.

His skin was a sun-browned copper color, his dark eyes wide-set, outlined with dark lashes and a prominent brow line. His nose was straight and handsome, his lips full and well-defined, his cheekbones set high. His nearly black hair hung in gentle waves to the collar of his blue calico shirt.

Irene hoped he couldn't read her thoughts, for they embarrassed and confused her. She looked back down at the carving. "How do you get all this detail, John?"

"Mostly with a lot of patience," he answered, laughing.

"This tool helps," Ramon added, coming closer and showing her a small instrument with a sharp, rounded blade. He picked up a smaller piece of wood and quickly carved the end of it into the shape of petals. Irene watched in fascination, astounded at how fast he whittled away at the wood and still kept an amazing perfection to his work. She could understand why his hands looked so strong, for he apparently worked with them long hours every day. "There, you see," he told her, as he held out the small carving for her to take. "A flower for my friend's sister."

She reached out, surprised at how dark Ramon's hand was compared to her own tawny brown one. She took the flower, feeling strangely light-headed when his hand brushed her fingers. "Thank you," she told him. "Will you be working here at the house from now on, until it's finished?"

He nodded. "*Si, señorita.* Do you . . . come here every day?" he asked hesitantly, wondering if the question sounded too forward.

"Not every day, but I come as often as I can, usually when I go riding." She felt suddenly self-conscious. How did she look today? She had worn her dark green velvet riding habit, with a full, draped skirt and a close-fitting jacket and plumed hat. It was her nicest one, and she was glad she had chosen to wear it.

"Your brother told me about your horse, Sierra."

"Come and see him, Ramon," John told the man, walking around the pieces of wood. "He's tied out front." The boy hurried out, and Irene and Ramon stood alone in the room for a moment, feeling an awkward silence. Their eyes met again, both wanting to say words they were afraid to speak.

"You don't have to come and see the horse if you don't want to," Irene told him. "You must be very busy."

He smiled gently. "I would like to see him. I like to ride, too. On our ranch to the south, my father and grandfather have many horses. They have to watch them closely. Sometimes the prospectors try to steal them."

"That's terrible!"

He shrugged again. "They think it is all right to steal from Mexicans." A hint of anger came into his normally gentle eyes, mixed with a fierce pride. "They do not know that my grandfather comes from a wealthy, powerful Spanish family in Mexico, descendants of a branch of the family of King Charles the First of Spain, who conquered Mexico three hundred years ago."

Irene's eyebrows arched. "Really?"

Ramon seemed to stand a little taller. "*Sí.* Then in Mexico's war for independence, our family was attacked because they were descendants of the king. They fled north, with no time to bring many of their belongings. They lost everything and had to start over, so now life is harder. But my grandfather is strong and determined, and we still have our pride. Someday we will return to Mexico, when we are sure it is safe. In the meantime, I have plans to be a wealthy man again when that time comes. My grandfather told me I should come to Denver, where there is much building, and where wealthy mining people will pay much money for my skills."

She felt disappointed at the thought that he would one day go back to Mexico. "I see." She walked past him, afraid if she stood too close and let him read her eyes too long, he would see what she was thinking. "Well, your grandfather was probably right. I hope you realize your dream, Ramon." She toyed nervously with her gloves.

"Do you have dreams, *señorita*?"

She let out a little gasp of surprise at the question. "I—I guess I haven't given my future much thought. I mean . . . my mother seems to have all of our futures laid out for us. I suppose I'm expected to help take over the family business some day. I . . . and whoever I might marry."

He studied her exquisite form, longing to touch her golden hair, feeling an odd possessiveness and a jealousy at the thought of another man touching her, disgusted with himself for having thoughts he had no business considering.

"I am sorry for the question. It is not my business."

They both heard John outside calling for them to come out. Irene glanced back at Ramon, and he grinned. "I think we had better go out there," Ramon spoke up. "I must get back to work soon or my *patrona* will be angry with me."

She headed through the doorway, feeling him behind her. "I know what *patrona* means," she said, turning to watch him again as he came up beside her. "We had a Spanish man who worked for us in California. He called my father *patron*. It means boss . . . employer. You say *patrona* because your boss is a woman, my mother."

"*Si*. Do you know much more Spanish?"

"Not a lot," she answered bashfully, walking to the front doors.

"I have been teaching a little to your brother. *Es un amigo sincero*. That means he is a true friend."

They walked down the wide, brick steps. "John is a good person. I'll miss him when he goes off to college."

"He has told me he does not want to go."

She laughed. "You don't know my mother. Believe me, he'll go."

Ramon laughed, too, and walked with her to Sierra. He reached up and patted the horse's neck. "Ah, he is a fine gelding," he told her. He ran his hand along the animal's body, kneeling to inspect its legs. "He is worth much money, *señorita*."

"My father gave him to me when I was twelve. He was two years old then."

He glanced up at her. "And how old are you now?"

"I'll be sixteen soon."

He rose, patting the horse's rump. "A fine animal. My own grandfather would be proud to have this one in his pasture."

"Thank you." Irene touched the horse's head and he nuzzled at her neck, whinnying softly.

"He loves you, and you love him," Ramon told her.

Their eyes met, both of them feeling a deeper meaning to the words. "Yes," she answered, hardly aware of her brother's presence.

"You have a way with horses that I have never seen in a *gringa*," he told her. "Only in my own people, and the Indians. I have only known you a few minutes, but I can see it."

She smiled nervously. "Well, I don't know where I get it, but I do love Sierra. I love all animals."

His eyes swept the horizon. "And do you love this land? Your brother tells me his other sister hates it. She wants to go back to California."

"Elly hates everything," John put in. "That's just Elly."

They all laughed then. "Yes, I like it here very much," Irene answered. "I want to go up into the mountains, if I can ever convince my mother to let my father take me."

"*Sí*, it is beautiful." He backed away slightly. "I must get back to work now. I am very glad to have met you, Señorita Kirkland."

"And I'm very glad to have met you." Irene turned and climbed up onto Sierra sidesaddle. John untied the animal and handed up the reins. "Good-bye, Ramon," Irene told him.

Their eyes held a moment longer. "*Vaya con Dios, señorita*. Go with God."

The words and his eyes made her feel warm and safe. She reluctantly turned Sierra and rode off at a trot, back toward the current Kirkland home farther down the hill. She looked across the foothills, imagining riding at a hard gallop, Ramon at her side, both of them heading into prettier country west of Denver, exploring streams and mountain pathways. She felt a sudden pain in her stomach then, realizing what a forbidden thought that was.

She forced herself not to look back. She knew Ramon was still watching her, and she didn't want to appear flirtatious or too forward.

"Pretty, isn't she," John was asking Ramon.

Ramon watched her ride away, every manly desire deeply stirred by the *patrona*'s daughter. "*Sí, mi amigo*. Your sister is very beautiful." He looked at John. "And you should never tell her or anyone else that I said so, or you will get Ramon in deep trouble. You told me yourself what your mother tells her daughters about Spanish men."

"My mother is a snob. Irene isn't."

Ramon grinned. "I can see that in the few minutes we talked. She is not like the others." He put a hand on John's shoulder. "Just do what I tell you and say nothing. I am glad to have met her. That is the end of it. We had better get back to work. There is much to do."

They went back inside. Ramon almost wished he had never met the pretty Irene. It was not wise to have fond thoughts for a woman he could never have. Besides, there was Elena to think about. She was waiting for him at Hacienda del Sur. It was understood between his family and her own that he and Elena would one day marry. The union had been arranged many years ago between his and Elena's grandfathers. To go against a family promise would be a disgrace, and an insult to Elena. He wondered why the thought had even come to mind, and he began working vigorously with a cornice plane, venting his anger and disgust with himself through concentrating on molding another piece of wood.

Kirk and Chad rode with four hundred other men under Major Chivington, the eager Methodist minister-turned-fighter. Most of the Colorado Volunteers were hard-rock miners, come down out of the mountains to protect Denver gold, unruly men who were not easy to order around. But Chivington had a way of taking command. For the most part, the men obeyed his orders, although they were all now itching for a good fight.

Chivington had been given orders by Colonel John Slough to skirt around to the rear of the Confederate contingent from Texas that was marching for Denver. He and his men were not to instigate a battle but were simply supposed to harrass the enemy, deliberately driving them north toward Slough's waiting Volunteers. Slough would attack with the several hundred men heading south to intercept the Confederates.

"I'll be glad when this is over," Chad told Kirk. "All this riding and camping without any action is getting boring. I'd just as soon be back there with Slough and run head-on into Sibley and his bunch."

"I know what you mean," Kirk answered. "I've got a lot of things to get back to. I hope the family is all right."

"So do I—especially Irene, if you don't mind my saying so. Your daughter is beautiful and charming, Kirk."

The two men had gotten on a first-name basis, and Kirk found Chad likable enough, if not a little too eager to make an impression. The man was obviously romantically interested in Irene, and he certainly had a promising future; but Kirk was still wary of him, and considering Irene's young age, he had told Chad he would have to wait until Irene's sixteenth birthday to begin seeing her.

Her birthday had passed two weeks earlier, and Kirk felt bad that he had missed his daughter's birthday for the first time since the year he spent in the Sierras looking for gold. He argued with himself that he had no good reason for being skeptical of Chad Jacobs, except that he was naturally wary of all the young men who wanted to court his daughters, since they were rich. But Chad had mentioned more than once that he was wealthy in his own right. He certainly looked as though he came from wealth. The way he dressed, his manners, his education, all spoke of good breeding. At least that was what Bea would call it.

For Kirk, though, there were certain things that were more important than good breeding, like whether or not his daughter's husband would be kind to her, faithful to her, would love her just for who she was, not because she had money. He and Bea had married for all the wrong reasons, and deep inside he had never been happy. He didn't want that for his daughters, or his son.

Kirk's thoughts were interrupted when they moved into a narrow canyon dubbed Glorieta Pass. Chivington suddenly raised up in his saddle, pulling his sword and pointing it. "Ride hard, boys," he shouted. "Enemy ahead!"

Chivington, anxious to make a name for himself, charged ahead, and his troops followed. Kirk could barely tell what Chivington had seen. He had spotted only three men, and he surmised they were Confederate scouts. Men shouted war cries and rode hard after them, and they scattered. One scout was shot and captured, and Kirk was almost disappointed that the fight had been so short-lived that he had not even had a chance to shoot his rifle.

The wounded scout informed Chivington that Sibley's main force was not far ahead and still moving north. The next morning, Chivington led his men north to flank the Confederate troops, the eager leader on fire with a desire for conquest. Kirk suspected the man had just seen his chance for glory, and that he probably hoped to run across the Confederates before Slough and his men could steal the battle.

Kirk and Chad rode hard, choking on dust from horses ahead of them. They both realized things were finally getting serious, neither one doubting that they would see battle this time. By the time they came across Sibley's troops later in the day, the Confederates were already in a heated battle with Slough. Chivington, wanting some of the glory for himself, ordered his troops to charge ahead. "We'll cut off their supplies, men," he shouted. "That will turn them back quicker than Slough's bullets!"

They moved into Sibley's camp, and Chivington grabbed a burning stick from a fire and threw it into a Confederate supply wagon. His men followed suit, setting fire to tents and more wagons. Kirk rode up close to a cook wagon and held his gun close to an oil lamp that hung against the canvas. He fired, and the flame that spit from the gun barrel caused the lamp to explode. In seconds the canvas was engulfed in flames.

He turned his horse, letting out a warwhoop not unlike an Indian, but he quickly sobered when he saw Chad raise his rifle. The young man sat facing him, and for a split second Kirk thought

Chad was going to shoot him. Chad did fire, but the bullet whizzed past Kirk. Kirk heard someone cry out, and he whirled his horse to see a Confederate falling from the front of the wagon, a rifle in his hand.

Kirk looked back at Chad. "He was fixing to shoot you," Chad told him.

Kirk looked at the dead body, while farther ahead the fighting raged. There was no time for thank-yous. Chad and Kirk joined the melee farther ahead, but Kirk held back when he saw Chivington begin bayoneting the Confederate horses and mules. Anger raged in his soul at the sight. Chad fixed his bayonet on the end of his rifle, and Kirk grabbed the bridle of Chad's horse. "Don't do it," he growled. "Not the animals."

Chad saw no reason not to kill the animals, but he didn't want to get on the bad side of David Kirkland. He backed off, watching the bloody massacre with disinterest, while Kirk was regretting being a part of bringing Chivington in as an officer for the Volunteers. The man was a fighter, of that there was no doubt. But in that one moment of raging, bloody butchering, Kirk saw something akin to evil in the supposed man of God.

"There's no need for that," he told Chad. "We could have just scattered them, captured some of them. Come on."

Kirk rode farther ahead, joining in more combat. He shot one man, then cried out with pain when the bayonet of another jabbed his leg. He whirled and smashed the barrel of his rifle across the side of the man's head. It was then he heard a bugle sound retreat, and the Confederates began to flee. Both Chivington and Slough, along with the rough and unorganized Colorado Volunteers, pursued them for several miles. They finally realized Sibley and his men meant to keep going all the way back to Texas. With nearly all their supplies, mules and horses totally destroyed, they would have to abandon their plans to capture Denver and her gold.

Cries of victory filled the air. Denver was saved! Kirk looked down at his painful, bleeding thigh and pulled a bandana from a pocket of his buckskin jacket. He tied it around his leg.

"Kirk! You're hurt," Chad exclaimed, riding up to him. "You'd better see the medic right away."

Kirk grimaced, turning his horse. "I will." He looked at Chad. "You saved my life back there at that wagon," he told him.

Chad grinned. "Well, I wanted to be able to shoot at something. I guess I got my wish."

Kirk grabbed his hand. "Thank you, Chad. What else can I say?"

Chad thought how he could have had no better good fortune than to have had the chance to save David Kirkland's life. Irene Kirkland was as good as his. "Nothing, sir," he answered. "Just allow me permission to come and visit your daughter often."

Kirk grinned. "Anytime, as long as you mind yourself. She's pretty young to be seeing anyone yet."

Chad nodded. "Yes, sir. But I might as well tell you I'm totally taken with her after one visit. I realize how much she means to you, though. I would never be anything but a gentleman."

Kirk nodded. "Fine." He looked around. "I'm anxious to get home. How about you?"

"Well, sir, I *have* begun to think of Denver as home. I'm anxious, too, especially to dig into my work for Kirkland Enterprises. I hate the thought of your wife having to handle things alone."

Kirk raised his eyebrows, grinning slightly in spite of his pain. "Bea? Don't ever worry about Mrs. Kirkland handling anything alone. She can outwork ten men, let me tell you."

Chad laughed, and both men rejoined the celebrating. They would return to Denver heroic conquerors. Gilpin's "pet lambs" had proved their worth, in spite of their motley, unorganized condition. But Kirk was not proud of some of Chivington's tactics. He had seen the bloodthirsty expression on the man's face when he butchered the Confederate horses, and he wondered if the man could be trusted to continue to represent Denver with honor.

The *Rocky Mountain News* was splattered with headlines of victory at Glorietta Pass well before Kirk and Chad and the others managed to get back to Denver. People celebrated in saloons and in the streets. Chivington, it was said, was the true hero of the day for mounting an attack from the rear and destroying the Confederate supplies.

Red McKinley joined in the celebrating. Having just arrived in Denver, he really didn't care much one way or the other about the reasons for the dancing in the streets. He was simply having a good time joining in the fun and drinking liquor that others were buying for him.

Red moved from one saloon to the next, getting a feel for this new and growing city he had heard so much about, hoping that maybe here he could find some kind of solid work and settle down. He was getting older. It was getting harder to stay in a saddle from dawn to dark leading wagon trains, and the pay was not that good. Besides, there was talk of bringing the railroad all the way across the country, just as he had once predicted would happen. That would mean work such as his would become nearly extinct.

He looked up at the signs around town: *Kirkland Hotel, Kirkland Supply, Kirkland Bootery.* "Kirkland," he said aloud. He frowned, turning and grabbing hold of a man who was walking past him. "Hey, mister, you wouldn't happen to know the Kirkland whose name is on all these signs, would you?" he asked with his Irish accent. "Might it be David Kirkland? A big man with light hair? About my age?"

"That description fits David Kirkland, all right."

Red grinned. "No fooling?"

"No fooling. The Kirklands own half of Denver—mines, warehouses, a bank, a hotel . . . hell, you name it, they own it."

Red let go of him, looking across the street at the hotel. "Well, I'll be damned," he muttered. How long had it been since he had last seen Kirk. Back in forty-six, wasn't it? Sixteen years! He could hardly believe what he had just seen and heard. David Kirkland, a wealthy man! It was difficult to imagine. "Guess I'll have to look up my old friend," he muttered. He wondered what had ever happened to the little half-breed Indian girl Kirk had taken from Bent's Fort.

CHAPTER
EIGHT

Irene could not resist the chance to see Ramon again, even though her mother would disapprove vehemently of her seeing him alone. She had visited with him often over the last several weeks, but always with John and other workers around, and even then, only when her mother was gone. Although she knew it was probably wrong and pointless, she seemed unable to fight the attraction she felt for the strong, kind, and talented man.

The Colorado Volunteers were expected back in Denver today, and Bea was in town helping to prepare a grand welcome. She would not be back to pick up her daughters until later in the day. Against his wishes, Bea had taken John with her so he could spend the morning at Kirkland Enterprises. The young man had left with a scowl and near tears in his eyes, and Irene knew he would rather come up to the new house and work with Ramon. She was sorry for him, but could not help being glad that finally, for the first time since meeting Ramon, she had a chance to be alone with him.

Back at the main house, Elly was primping as though she were going to a ball rather than to a parade. The girl carried on about how she hoped Father and Chad were all right. Irene prayed for the same, and she was excited that her father would finally be home again; but she was not especially overjoyed that Chad was coming back, although she did hope he had not been harmed. Now that Chad Jacobs was coming home, her mother would be pressuring her to receive the man regularly, but all Irene could think about was Ramon.

She trotted Sierra toward the new house, which sat on land that was now being called Kirkland Bluffs. Denver's elite had begun building their homes up there, away from the city's "undesirables."

Irene felt daring and excited as she came closer to the mansion. Ramon was here! She had seen him ride up earlier. Her emotions were a torrent of what she felt sure was love, mixed with a feeling of hopelessness. Ramon had never voiced his feelings, but she was sure she had seen in his dark eyes the same intense emotion she felt for him. Every time she was around him, she felt more deeply impressed, not just with his dark, handsome looks and his artistic skills, but with the fine qualities he possessed.

She came near the house and dismounted, tying Sierra with hands that were suddenly shaking. Was she being too forward? Her mother would be in a rage if she knew she was here. Yet this time the thought of her mother's disapproval was not enough to deter her. She climbed the steps and walked through the double doors.

The builders had accomplished a lot in the past few weeks, but things had slowed now, since most of what was left could not be finished until the goods arrived from San Francisco and New York. Today the rest of the builders were in town, already getting drunk in preparation for greeting the troops—all except Ramon. She knew he preferred to work alone anyway. For Ramon, the news of the victory at Glorietta Pass meant little. In his mind, this land should still belong to Spain.

"Ramon," she called out. Her voice echoed through the huge, open great room. She heard footsteps, and Ramon appeared at the top of the wide stairway to her left. He stood on the first landing, looking down at her in surprise.

"Irene! What are you doing here? Aren't you going into town?"

"Not until later this afternoon."

He looked around, appearing hesitant. "You are alone?"

She felt her cheeks growing hotter. "Yes. I—I got a little bored waiting for this afternoon, so I thought I'd come up here and talk to you."

He slowly descended the stairs, his heart racing, arguments against his own feelings raging in his soul. "It—it is not right for you to be here," he warned, unable to take his eyes from hers as he moved to the bottom of the stairs.

"I don't see why not," Irene answered, trying to look brave. "You're a good friend to John and me both."

She studied him as he came closer, feeling new, forbidden, womanly desires at the sight of him in tight-fitting denim pants and a red calico shirt with rolled sleeves. Today he wore a red bandanna around his forehead, making him look more Indian than Mexican. She wondered who in his royal ancestry had been tall, for Ramon was taller than most Mexicans she had known. He carried himself with great pride, a pride she knew came from the blood of kings.

Her heart pounded harder now that he stood only two feet away, a passion in his eyes that even Irene, innocent as she was, could recognize. She felt weak and warm. "But this time . . . we are alone," he told her. He closed his eyes and swallowed. "Irene, you know what I mean."

She tossed her head, turning away from him. "I like you, Ramon. I have the right to spend my time visiting a friend, whether he's Mexican or even an Indian." She faced him again. "If you think I feel the same way toward you and your people as my mother, then you aren't as smart as I thought. You know how John and I both feel."

This time it was Ramon who looked embarrassed. He smiled slightly, warning himself to be careful. Perhaps it was possible they could remain friends, but anything more than that was another story. Yet that was all he had been able to think about lately. When he should be thinking about Elena, he was thinking of Irene. When he considered marriage, he imagined Irene in a wedding dress, not Elena. What a fool he was to have such thoughts!

"Do you want to go riding?" Irene asked.

He looked at her in surprise. "What?"

"Your horse is here, and so is mine. We could go riding if we wanted, just for a little while."

He sighed deeply, glancing around as though he thought he was being watched. "I don't know."

"Oh, Ramon, where is the harm? Besides, maybe my mother wouldn't approve, but my father likes you very much. He wouldn't mind." She told herself that somehow these wonderful, passionate feelings meant that everything was going to be all right, that somehow God would see to it that she could be more than just friends with Ramon.

She stepped closer and took his hand, stunned and on fire at its strength and warmth the moment they touched. He squeezed her hand lightly, and in that one touch she was sure that this special, unspoken feeling they shared would lead to the forbidden happiness she wanted to share with him.

"Come on," she said, putting on a smile that tore at his heart. "Just one short ride."

Ramon had always prided himself in being strong, but when he was around this young woman, he felt helpless to resist her. He loved the feel of her soft hand, had dreamed about touching other soft places, wondered how her mouth tasted. She was beautiful, sweet and clean and pure. She was nothing like the painted whores in town. Irene Kirkland needed no paint to be beautiful, no low-cut, gawdy dress to display her perfect form.

Today she wore a deep rose-colored velvet riding habit with a waist-length jacket, a matching plumed hat perched slightly to the side of her head. It seemed everything about her was always perfect, from her beautiful face and body to her golden hair and her lovely, expensive clothing. She should have been cold and unfriendly to him, like other rich *gringas*. But she was always warm and vibrant, attentive and concerned. He had never known anyone like her, looking so untouchable, yet seemingly asking to be touched.

Against all reason, he followed her outside, his whole body literally aching. They both mounted their horses, and Irene led Sierra off at a modest lope before Ramon could do any more objecting. Ramon followed, and Irene suddenly turned to him, laughing.

"I'll race you," she told him. Before he could agree or disagree, she was off, heading Sierra at a full gallop into an open valley to the south of Kirkland Bluffs.

Irene rode Sierra hard, but she heard Ramon's sleek black mare coming closer. Neither of them noticed three men who had already been riding in their direction from the west. Soon Ramon was beside her, and Irene thought how grand he looked on the horse, which was bigger and more muscular than Sierra. She imagined him as a valiant Spanish soldier in a dashing uniform, imagined him living in a king's palace.

Ramon's horse began to pass hers, and she rode Sierra harder, enjoying the feel of the wind in her face. She nearly caught up with Ramon but was afraid of exhausting Sierra. She drew back on his reins. "You win," she shouted, laughing. Ramon slowed his own horse and turned, trotting back toward Irene as she approached him from the other direction. He joined in her laughter.

"I would have beat you a lot worse if you had not had a head start on me, *muchacha bonita*."

Irene laughed more, leaning down to pet Sierra's neck. "Let's walk them for a while." She looked at Ramon. "What did you call me a minute ago? A cheat?"

He grinned. "No señorita. I called you *muchacha bonita*, a pretty girl."

Her smile faded slightly and she turned away from his gaze. "*Gracias*, Ramon," she answered. "Did I say it right?"

"*Sí, señorita*, you said it just right."

They rode on in silence for a few minutes, enjoying the scenery and the warm, pretty April day, each on fire for the other, yet both of them afraid to admit it. "Do you—do you have a girl, Ramon?" Irene asked hesitantly, realizing how suggestive and bold the statement sounded, yet unable to bear another moment without knowing. Her heart tightened when he did not answer right away.

"There is a girl down at Hacienda del Sur who is waiting for me," he finally answered, deciding the best thing to do was discourage Irene Kirkland as much as possible, for he sensed *un fuego bajo su piel*, a fire under her skin, a fire he longed to build into a raging inferno. But he had no right . . . no right at all. "Her name is Elena Baca," he continued, feeling her hurt and disappointment. "It is something that was arranged by our families many years ago. I am expected to marry her when I go back home. She is eighteen now."

Irene struggled against tears, feeling like a fool. All the joy had left her heart. "I see," she answered, forcing herself to sound bright. "Is she pretty?" She turned to meet his eyes, somewhat relieved to notice there the same passion she had seen and felt earlier.

"*Sí*," he answered. "But not as pretty as you."

She blushed and turned away again. "Do you love her?"

He sighed deeply. "It does not matter. I will learn to love her, and she will learn to love me. That is the way it is with such marriages. She is sweet and good. She will be a good wife."

Jealousy instantly raged in Irene's soul, with such force that she almost felt sick. An awkward silence hung in the air, and they were so lost in the moment that they did not see the three men coming closer.

"What about you, señorita?" he asked. "Is there someone special for you?"

She looked down at Sierra's mane and patted the horse's neck again. "Not really. There is one man—Chad Jacobs is his name.

My mother recently hired him as one of our lawyers. He's quite handsome," she said, hoping to hurt him as much as his remark had hurt her. "I know my mother has hopes for the two of us, but I hardly know him yet." She swallowed back a lump in her throat and turned her horse. "We had better go back."

"Irene—" Ramon suddenly could not bear the hurt in her eyes, could not fight his feelings or be as wise about all of this as he should. To think of another man touching her was torture, but before he could tell her so, the three strangers coming up behind them now were much closer. Ramon sensed danger. "Get back to the house, quickly," he told her quietly.

"I'm sure they don't mean any harm," she told him, keeping her horse beside him. "They're probably just some miners. Maybe they even know Father."

"I have seen them in town. They are no good. They used to run with that troublemaker Harrison before he was run out of town."

Irene's heart quickened, but she refused to look afraid. "Let's just head back. What can they do about it?" She kicked her horse into motion, and Ramon followed, knowing before it happened that the three men would cut them off. They sped up their horses to catch Irene, circling her, one of them grabbing her horse's bridle. Ramon was instantly angry with himself for being so lost in her that he had allowed her to stray too far from home.

"Well, you pretty thing, what you doin' out here with a Mexican boy, huh?" one of them asked.

Irene considered announcing who she was, but she wisely decided against it, sensing that would only make matters worse. "Let go of my horse," she warned.

"Let go of my horse," one of them mocked in a girlish tone. They all laughed, and the one holding her horse looked her over hungrily. "I'd say any pretty white girl who's caught alone with a Mexican boy is fair game, wouldn't you, boys?"

Ramon rode closer, unexpectedly and quickly drawing his rifle from its boot. "All of you, get away from her," he warned. "Her father is a powerful man. If you bring her harm, he will see that all of you die!"

One of them straightened, riding closer to Ramon, and Irene was afraid for him. "If she's so important, what's she doin' cavortin' out here with the likes of you?"

"I am a builder. She was showing me where her father is thinking of putting up a barn."

"She was, was she?" The man snickered. "I think you're lyin', boy. And I think you had better remember what happens to

Mexicans around here who get into trouble with white men. You shoot that rifle, you'll be hangin' from the rafters."

Ramon held the man's eyes steadily. "Perhaps I will. But you will not be around to watch, will you?" The man stiffened, trying to look brave, but visibly paling. "Get moving," Ramon warned again. "I do not like the idea of hanging, but if that is what it takes to protect this woman, then I will hang. At least I will have the satisfaction of the memory of seeing you fly off that horse with a hole in your face."

The man watched Ramon's eyes, deciding this Mexican man meant every word he said. He scowled at Ramon while he spoke. "Let's go, boys."

"You gonna let that greaser back you down, Hank?" one of the others asked. "We could have us some fun with this pretty young thing. She looks pretty damn good after bein' with those ugly whores in town."

The one called Hank kept his eyes on Ramon. "I said let's go," he repeated. "If I see you in town," he told Ramon, "you'll pay for this."

"You would be wise to stay out of Denver now," Ramon answered. "The Volunteers are coming back. The Confederates have been defeated, and people know who you are. You will not be welcome in Denver, and I think you know it. I think you were already running."

The man jerked his head up, as though to show pride and bravery. "Well, you thought wrong," he lied, irritated at this Mexican man's arrogance. "Keep your eyes open, brown boy." He turned his horse and rode off, and the other two men waited hesitantly, one of them still holding Irene's bridle. The other rode closer to Ramon, looking down his nose at the barrel of his rifle as though unafraid.

"No greaser orders me around," he sneered.

In an instant, Ramon whipped the rifle barrel across the side of the man's head, knocking him from his horse. He swung around as the man fell, aiming the rifle at the remaining offender. "Pick up your friend and get out of here!"

The second man let go of Irene's horse and rode to where his friend lay groaning on the ground. He glowered at Ramon but said nothing as he dismounted. Ramon whirled his horse and kicked Sierra in the rump. "Ride, Irene," he shouted.

Irene did not wait to ask questions. Her heart was pounding so hard with fear for Ramon and fear of what the men intended to do to her that she needed no added encouragement to flee. She and

Ramon took off at a hard gallop, charging across the open land and toward the hill where the new house sat, quickly leaving their antagonizers far behind them.

They reached the house, Irene gasping with a combination of fear and excitement as they thundered up to the front lawn. Ramon had put his rifle back in its boot and he quickly dismounted, tying his horse and going around Sierra to help Irene down.

"Oh, Ramon, I was so afraid for you," she said, feeling breathless. Her hair had come partially undone, and part of it fell in a beautiful, golden cascade over her shoulder. Ramon was enraptured. "What a brave thing you did," she added. "They might have killed you. They were right, you know. If you had shot one of them, you would have been hanged."

He tied her horse for her. "It would have been worth it."

He looked up at her, and she was overwhelmed with what she was sure was love. He had risked his life for her! She slowly climbed down, her legs shaking so that she nearly fell. Ramon grabbed her, and she grasped his strong arms for support. She raised her face to meet his dark eyes, her chest still heaving in quick breaths from the excitement of the moment.

She was suddenly vulnerable. Ramon imagined her looking at him this way, breathing hard from ecstasy rather than fear. With no thought to the consequences, he leaned down and met her mouth, unable to resist the full, sensual lips, slightly parted for him.

Irene had no time to resist, but she knew she would not have anyway. Ramon's mouth covered her own, and his strong arms embraced her, crushing her virgin breasts against his broad chest. What a bold and daring thing she was allowing him to do, and yet she didn't mind at all! Her arms reached up around his neck as naturally as breathing, and she whimpered when his tongue flicked suggestively at the edges of her lips.

It was her first kiss, one she was sure she would remember the rest of her life. This was much more wonderful than she had ever imagined, and she discovered it was easy to return the kiss with equal passion. She had always wondered what she would do when a man kissed her, wondered if she would find it at first offensive. But there was nothing offensive about Ramon's gentleness, or how sweet his mouth tasted, or in the love she knew he felt for her.

He finally tore his mouth from hers, grasping her hair so that her plumed hat fell off. She rested her head on his shoulder, breathing in his masculine scent. "I could not let them touch you," he said, his voice low with desire. "I want to be the one to touch you, Irene."

The words brought a fire to her blood she had never experienced before. She rubbed her face against his chest lovingly. "What are we going to do, Ramon?" she whispered. "What about Elena, and your family's promise? What about my mother?"

He put a hand to the side of her face, making her look up at him. "We will find a way, *mi querida*. Perhaps it is wrong, Irene, but I love you." He kept her close, their bodies meshed, and Irene knew in that moment that giving herself to a man would not be the humiliating, frightening thing she had thought, not if he was as loving and gentle as Ramon.

"I love you, too, Ramon," she said softly. "It scares me, but it feels wonderful, too."

He smiled softly. "We must be careful, go slowly. This will not be easy."

"I know, Ramon, but I'm not afraid."

He searched her blue eyes, wondering at his own daring, unable to think clearly when she was here in his arms this way. He worried about how this would hurt his grandfather, perhaps bring shame to the family. Already he felt his loyalties being ripped apart, but here she was, soft and warm in his arms, such an angel, so trusting. He shivered with the thought of lying naked beside her. He leaned down to kiss her once more, a deep, hungry kiss that told him that once she was introduced to womanhood, she would be sweet and responsive to him. Sudden, painful desire made him leave her lips and gently push her away.

"We cannot let anyone see us this way, not for a while yet," he told her then, letting go of her reluctantly. "There are many things to think about, and we must see more of each other first. Somehow we will find a way to be together. My work here at the house will be finished soon. It will be harder then to see you."

"Oh, Ramon, I can hardly stand to go one day *without* seeing you."

He took her hands. "Do not worry, *mi querida*. I will find a way." He looked past her then, noticing a buggy approach the Kirkland residence farther down the hill. "You must go," he said quickly. He ducked around his horse and to the other side of the iron railing of the brick steps that led to the front doors. "Go home, Irene," he repeated.

She stood there wanting to cry. How painful having to part so quickly after finally being able to admit to their feelings. She looked down the hill to see the buggy, recognizing it as her mother's. With great reluctance she turned and mounted Sierra. She guided the horse around the side of the steps where Ramon stood. "I love you, Ramon."

His eyes seemed to tear. "*Yo te quiero,*" he replied. She knew without asking that it meant "I love you."

"I'm sorry we didn't have more time."

"Just go," he urged. "Everyone must be told at the right time and in the right way. They cannot just catch us together. It will make them more angry. We will see each other again, Irene."

She sniffed, wiping at a tear. "Thank you, Ramon, for what you did out there. I'll never forget it. My Ramon is not just handsome and skilled. He is brave—a conquistador." She reached down and grasped his hand once more. He squeezed it lightly and smiled for her, trying to boost her own hope and courage. She turned Sierra and rode off, and Ramon watched after her, his heart heavy with the impossibility of his love for the *gringa*. Her wealth meant nothing to him, but he knew no one in her family would believe it. They would only see this poor Mexican man, caring not that his family had once been wealthy, that they were descendants of a king.

"What have I done?" he muttered, every bone, nerve and muscle of his body crying out for her. He waited until she was nearly down the hill before walking around his horse and up the steps to the front doors, which stood open to air out the smells of paint. He stepped inside, then stopped short, feeling a strange dread when he saw a dark-haired girl standing just inside the doorway. His mind raced with surprise and worry. Had she seen? "Who are you?" he asked aloud.

She was rather plain, but her hairdo and her clothes spoke of wealth. She eyed him with a dark, narrow look, the hint of a victorious grin about her mouth. "I'm Elly," she answered, "Irene's sister. I came up here to find Irene and tell her it was time to get ready to go into town. She went riding, against Mother's wishes, and I thought maybe she came here." Her eyes moved over him scathingly. "Did she?"

Ramon knew about this one, knew John all but hated her. Irene simply put up with her, always making excuses for her sister's behavior, unable to hate her the way John did. There was not an ounce of malice in Irene's countenance, but he saw plenty of it in this Kirkland daughter. She bore no resemblance to her sister, either in looks, or, he was sure, in personality. They just stared at each other for a moment, Ramon not sure what to do or say.

"She was here," he said carefully. "As soon as she realized no one else was about, she left and went riding. I just went outside to dump some wood shavings, and I saw her ride past."

Elly smiled more. "You must be Ramon, the Mexican man Father told us about. I know John comes up here to work with you sometimes. I could tell on him, but I really don't care what John does, as long as he leaves me alone." She looked around the great room. "I didn't know you'd be up here at the house alone today. I thought all the workers were in town." She suppressed an urge to laugh, perfectly aware that he was wondering if she had seen him kiss Irene. She decided to let him wonder. Irene—so perfect and proper—kissing a greaser! There would be no end to her mother's wrath! "I don't remember seeing your horse outside when I first got here."

Ramon watched her eyes. "I often leave him loose to let him graze."

"I see." Her eyes moved over him curiously. He was indeed handsome, in spite of his race. She suddenly wondered if he was dangerous. After all, she was thirteen now, and developing nicely. Surely he had noticed. Maybe it wasn't just Irene he was interested in. Maybe Mexican men liked all *gringas*. Wasn't that what her mother had told her? She shouldn't be here alone with him. What if her mother came up and found them? Oh, how she wished her mother had seen what she had moments ago!

Ramon watched her warily, waiting for her to do the talking, realizing that to say too much about Irene stopping at the house would seem too defensive. Perhaps she had been exploring inside the new house and had seen nothing after all.

Elly shivered as she moved past Ramon to leave, actually thinking he might grab her and do something bad to her; yet the shiver was not out of fear. It came from thinking about being raked over by this dark stranger. She had been keenly aware of men lately, ever since meeting Chad. Her curiosity was enormous, and she had daringly studied her own breasts a few times in the mirror, wondering what it felt like to let a man touch them.

She glanced back at Ramon. She certainly didn't want him to be that man. She had only considered the thought out of girlish curiosity, and because it would be a wonderful way to get the man in trouble. There was only one man for Elly, one man she wanted, and that was Chad. He was the one she dreamed about, the one she would save herself for. She hoped by the time Irene was old enough to be married, she could find a way to steal Chad away from her. She longed to be thought of as pretty, to be desired the way she had seen both Chad and Ramon desire Irene. She ached for the same love and attention that Irene received.

"Good-bye, Ramon," she said, giving him a flirtatious look, experimenting with newly awakening womanly charms.

To Ramon she looked silly, but he had no desire to laugh at the moment. He sensed that to do so would bring him trouble. He nodded to her, feeling a keen desire to shake her. He watched her leave, following her outside and standing at the top of the steps while she walked back down the hill. He wondered if she would make trouble for him. He had heard too much about this Elly to think she would keep it a secret if she had seen him kissing Irene. He felt suddenly helpless, and he hated himself for giving Irene such hope, and for thinking he had the right to kiss her that way.

He ran a hand through his dark hair, wishing he could think better. He couldn't let anything keep him and Irene apart, but he was well aware of all the obstacles. Elly had brought them to mind all too quickly.

He sighed, looking around the Kirkland mansion. His own work here would be done in a week or so. Perhaps he would go home then and speak to his grandfather about his feelings. Once he broke the news to his family, he would do the honorable thing and go and see David Kirkland. He would face the man squarely and admit his love for his daughter. Kirkland was an understanding man, and he liked Ramon.

Ramon only wished he could say as much for Señora Kirkland. He realized then who Elly reminded him of. Beatrice Kirkland had come often to inspect the progress on her new house. She was a sour-faced woman with dark hair and eyes and a penetrating look that cowed most of the men who worked for her. Ramon had treated her with respect, but he didn't like her. He knew the woman would be the biggest barrier to his love for Irene.

He walked out and closed the doors, then mounted his horse. After kissing Irene, it would be impossible today to concentrate on his work. He decided he would go into town and watch the welcome of the Colorado Volunteers. Maybe he could at least catch another glimpse of Irene there.

Back at the house Irene led Sierra into his stable. A hired hand offered to unsaddle the animal for her, and Irene agreed, telling him to be sure to brush him down and give him oats and water. "Wait a little while on that," she told him. "I ran him a little hard today. Let him cool down."

"Yes, ma'am," the man answered.

Irene hurried out of the stables and to the house, where the buggy sat empty. Her mother was already here. Until today, Irene had never dreaded seeing her mother; but even though Bea knew nothing, she felt somewhat guilty about her secret. She considered bursting into the house and telling her mother flat out the wonderful revelation she had discovered today—that she was in love with Ramon Vallejo. But she knew Bea Kirkland well enough to realize that would be the wrong approach. Besides, Ramon had said to wait. She had to let him do this his way, and now she worried when she would get to see him again.

She walked inside, and Bea called to her from the top of the stairs. "You've been riding again, haven't you?" she said, sounding very irritated. Irene realized more than ever that this was not the time to bring up Ramon.

"Yes, Mother."

"I'm going to have a talk with Elsa. She is too soft with you." The woman came marching down the stairs. "Look at you, all flushed and undone. I expected you and Elly both to be ready when I came back."

"You're back sooner than you said you would be."

"Well, get upstairs and get ready. Have you forgotten you'll see your father today?"

"No, Mother. You know how much I look forward to that."

Bea hid the slight hurt. She loved Irene, but she knew Irene was more fond of Kirk. Just as Kirk's absence and transgressions were her own fault, so was the growing wall between herself and her children. She simply didn't know how to show her love, other than to be sure they had the best of everything. "Get upstairs then, and hurry. John is waiting in town."

"Yes, ma'am." Irene started past her, and Bea touched her arm.

"Irene, you must start thinking about your future. Be sure to give Chad Jacobs a friendly welcome today. I expect he'll be calling on you, now that you're sixteen. As soon as the house is done later this summer, I'll have your coming-out party. Chad would be a wonderful escort."

But I love Ramon Vallejo, she wanted to answer. *I don't care about Chad.* "I suppose he would," she answered aloud, her heart aching. She headed up the stairs, and just then Elly came inside, flushed and out of breath.

"And where have *you* been?" Bea asked her second daughter.

Elly looked up at Irene, and Irene felt a hint of alarm. "Just walking," she answered.

"Looks more like you have been running," her mother said, now even more irritated.

"I was trying to catch a butterfly, but it kept getting away from me," Elly lied. The tasty bit of news she had to tell her mother could wait. Bea was too preoccupied right now with Kirk coming home. Besides, she had already made up her mind to tell her mother when they were alone. She didn't want Irene to realize that she knew, or that she was the one who'd told on her. She would simply deliver the information and wait to see what happened, loving the look of longing and heartache on her sister's face, as well as enjoying the utter scorn Irene would suffer from her mother.

Irene breathed a sigh of relief. For a moment, she thought perhaps Elly had sneaked up to the new house, perhaps had seen her with Ramon. If she had, she would surely blurt it out to their mother like the tattletale that she was. Her sister held no fondness for her, but Irene did not realize just how much Elly could hate.

CHAPTER NINE

 The huge contingent of Volunteers approached one end of Sixteenth Street, and Denver's citizens crowded both sides of the dusty street, cheering for their heroes, welcoming them home. There was no more talk of Gilpin's Lambs, only cheers for the victors. The Colorado Volunteers had proved themselves.

This was a day when whores mixed with merchants, drunks with preachers, Indians and Mexicans with Denver's elite. Everyone seemed to be happy. Bea Kirkland herded her three children to a roped-off platform, where they would join other prominent citizens, including Governor Gilpin himself. John and Irene would have preferred to mingle with the rest of the crowd, among people who interested and excited them, but only the governor's platform was good enough for the Kirkland family, as far as Bea was concerned.

The woman left them a moment to say hello to Governor Gilpin, and John leaned close to Irene. "Did you see Ramon today?" he asked.

She reddened, wondering if her brother knew how she really felt about Ramon. "Yes. We went riding."

"You what!" John looked at her in surprise, and Irene put a finger to her lips. She looked to see her mother still hustling about in her black taffeta dress, making sure the governor was comfortable, hovering over him like a mother hen. Elly was sauntering around the platform, twirling her parasol. She stopped to make conversation with Elizabeth Byers, who sat right next to the governor. It was obvious Elly was enjoying the way people in the crowd stared at her.

Irene took John aside. "We went riding," she repeated. "And you'll never guess what happened! Some men came along and tried to give us trouble. Ramon sent them running. He even hit one of them so hard with his rifle barrel that he knocked him from his horse!"

"Ramon?"

"Yes." She sobered. "He did it for me, John. If he had shot one of them, he could have been hanged. But he told me he would rather die than let anything happen to me. I wish you could have been there and seen it!"

"So do I. You shouldn't have gone riding alone with him though, Irene. Mother would be furious."

"I don't care what she thinks."

"Sure you do." He searched her eyes, seeing the near agony in them. "Irene, you don't . . . well, you don't want to be something more than friends with Ramon, do you?"

Her eyes glistened. "Yes. I do."

"Does Ramon feel the same way?"

"Yes. But don't say anything to anyone, John. Promise me. Ramon and I have to work this out ourselves, at the right time."

His eyes widened, making him look more like a little boy than the man he was becoming. "God, Irene, that's crazy. I like Ramon, too, but anything more than friendship between you is going to cause real trouble."

"It doesn't have to be that way." She closed her eyes and sighed. "I—"

"Children! Children, get over here up front. Your father and Chad are coming," Bea interrupted, rushing over to hurry them to the front of the platform. There was no more time to talk of Ramon. Colonel Slough and Major Chivington were passing the stand now.

A band made up of hometown citizens and a few miners struck up "The Liberty Song," and for the first time all day Irene's thoughts strayed for a moment from Ramon. She watched the passing Colorado Volunteers closely, searching for Kirk.

Come join hand in hand, brave Americans all, a good share of the crowd started singing.
And rouse your bold hearts at fair Liberty's call.

No tyrannous acts shall suppress your just claim,
  Irene joined in.
Or stain with dishonor America's name.
In freedom we're born and in freedom we'll live;
Our purses are ready,
Steady, friends, steady,
Not as slaves, but as freemen, our money we'll give.
Tears came to her eyes, and she was surprised to see
  tears in her mother's eyes also. It was a rare sight.
Then join hand in hand, brave Americans all,
By uniting we stand, by dividing we fall, they continued
  to sing.

Chivington waved to the crowd, sitting tall and proud, holding
an American flag in one hand. Irene thought he had a very stern
appearance, a look in his dark eyes that gave her shivers for no
reason she could name. She finally spotted her father, who sat
taller than most of the others, wearing the buckskin clothing he
loved best. He had refused a uniform, since funds for them were
coming from Denver citizens and needed to be used sparingly.

"There he is, Mother," Irene pointed out.

Bea put a hand to her heart. "Kirk," she said quietly. Irene
turned to see more tears in the woman's eyes. She continued to be
confused as to how much her father and mother really loved each
other. At that moment she saw love in Bea Kirkland's eyes, but so
often she saw animosity and irritation when it came to her
mother's feelings for her father, and there was seldom any sign of
affection between them. The last time she had seen them embrace
was the day she had caught them in the parlor back in California,
when Kirk had announced they were going to Colorado. That was
more than three years ago.

Chad Jacobs rode beside Kirk, wearing a uniform. Irene noticed
he seemed to be relishing the attention of the young ladies, bowing
to them as he passed, giving them his most charming smile,
sometimes reaching out and touching their hands. Elly cheered for
Chad, watching him with tear-filled eyes, her heart aching so that
she thought she might die. He looked so handsome in his uniform,
and now he had been a part of a great Union victory! She
wondered if anyone could love someone as much as she loved
Chad Jacobs.

Irene did not notice her sister's longing gaze. She was too
engrossed in keeping an eye on her father to make sure he was all
right. She thought he looked thinner, paler. He did not have the

same ruddy color as usual, nor quite the same robust countenance.

"Mother, he doesn't look right," she told Bea, whom she noticed was also watching with concern. People began moving into the thick of the Volunteers, loved ones greeting their husbands and sons.

"I agree," Bea answered. "You stay here with your brother and sister." She climbed down the platform steps and moved into the crowd, going over to greet Kirk while Irene and John watched their father, Elly having eyes only for Chad.

Chad dismounted and said something to Bea, then reached up for Kirk, who waved him off and shook his head. Irene could not hear what was being said, but to her amazement, Bea climbed onto Chad's horse, straddling it in exactly the unladylike way she had preached at Irene not to do, and rode off toward home with Kirk. None of them noticed a red-haired man shouting at Kirk from the crowd, trying to get his attention before he was gone.

Irene's heart tightened. She knew something was very wrong for her mother to do something so unusual, let alone leaving the governor and other prominent Denverites behind. Chad walked over to the platform, and Elly was crushed to see he had eyes only for Irene as he climbed up and embraced her. Irene was surprised, and she almost hated him for it. He had no right holding her close as though he were some long-lost lover come home.

"You look beautiful, Irene. I'm so glad you came," he told her.

I'm the one who came for you, Elly wanted to shout. *You should be embracing me, not Irene. She hasn't even been true to you! She kissed a Mexican boy today!*

From the midst of the crowd below, Ramon watched, seething with jealousy over the handsome *gringo* who had the audacity to walk up to Irene and hug her as though she belonged to him. *So, this must be the one called Chad Jacobs,* he thought, hating the man, yet knowing deep inside he was probably the right man for Irene, just as Elena was truly the right woman for him.

"People must stay with their own kind," his grandfather had told him more than once. "There are too many problems when you stray from your own people."

Ramon wondered where love and emotions fit into that statement. The heart did not always take the logical pathway. Seeing Chad Jacobs with Irene brought a sharp pain to his chest. He knew he could do nothing about the situation at the moment, and before Irene could catch sight of him, he disappeared into the crowd.

"Your father is hurt," Chad told the Kirkland children as he stood with his arm still around Irene's waist.

Irene gasped, pulling away to look up at him. "How badly?"

"He took a bayonet wound in his right thigh. The wound itself wasn't life-threatening, but it got pretty badly infected. The company doctor had to burn out the infection. It left a pretty good hole in his leg, and I expect he'll walk with a limp from now on. At any rate, it took a lot out of him. He was pretty sick. Your mother is taking him straight home. I'm to take the rest of you in the buggy and send for a doctor."

"Father should have gone home in the buggy," Irene protested.

"Your mother and I tried to talk him into it, but he's a proud man. He wanted to ride all the way home in his saddle, not go limping away like a wounded animal. You know how he is."

Irene turned and took John's arm. "We should go home right away," she said, heading down the platform. The others quickly followed, climbing into the two-seater buggy. Chad climbed in beside Irene, and Elly made a point to squeeze in on the other side of Chad, when she could have sat in the other seat with John.

"I'm so glad you're back, Chad," she told him, "and that you weren't hurt."

Chad put an arm around Irene, glancing at Elly. "Thank you, Elly. Say, why don't you sit across from us next to your brother? It will give us a little more room."

Elly's hatred knew no bounds at that moment, not for Chad, but for Irene. She kept her mouth tightly closed to keep from crying, feeling humiliated and embarrassed. She moved into the facing seat as the driver got the buggy into motion, but it was slow going as he guided the two horses that pulled the carriage through the crowded street. People were still cheering and singing and greeting loved ones, and no one was in any particular hurry to get out of the way.

"Move over there! Look out," the driver shouted.

"This is why your mother went on ahead on horseback," Chad was telling Irene. "She knew it would be quicker." He squeezed her shoulder. "Did you ever see such excitement?"

"I don't think so," she answered, trying to be friendly. She realized she should be flattered and proud to be sitting next to the handsome, dashing Chad Jacobs, but she only searched the crowd for Ramon. He was nowhere to be seen. She wondered if she was crazy to turn her affection to a man she could probably never have, when a very eligible, desirable man sat right beside her; and she wondered if anything ever made sense when it came to love.

The buggy finally made its way out of the worst of the crowd, and the driver urged the horses to go faster.

"It was quite a battle." Chad was telling the story of their victory. "What really did the trick was destroying their supplies. We were with Major Chivington. We had circled around, chasing off some Confederate scouts in Glorietta Pass. We headed north, right into the main camp. While the Texans were fighting it out with Slough and his men, we destroyed all their supplies, tents, wagons, food—even slaughtered their horses and mules. We made it impossible for them to keep going, even if they had won their fight against Slough, which they didn't."

"That's so brave and exciting," Elly told him.

"You killed the horses and mules," Irene asked. "Why?"

Chad shrugged. "We had to stop the man, Irene. In war, you have to do things you couldn't ordinarily do, although I have to tell you your father refused to kill any of the animals, so I abstained myself."

She breathed a sigh of relief. At least her father had not been a part of the slaughter. David Kirkland would never murder horses, not for any reason. She suspected, though, that if not for Kirk's presence, Chad would have taken part in the massacre.

They reached the house just after Bea and Kirk did. Chad quickly exited the carriage when he noticed Kirk dismounting. He hurried to his side, and to Irene's dismay, her father nearly fell. The man leaned on Chad, in obvious pain, his face pale and perspiring. She had never seen her father this way, not even when he had been shot during the bummer raids.

Bea fussed and clucked as Chad helped a protesting Kirk inside and up the stairs to his bedroom, and the children all followed. Kirk grabbed one of the four bedposts and lowered himself onto the mattress, breathing deeply for a moment before looking up at his children.

"You all look mighty good," he told them. "Come here and give your old dad a kiss before he gets some rest."

Irene rushed forward right away, kissing his cheek and hugging him. "You'll be all right, won't you, Father?"

"I'm fine, girl. I sure hate coming home acting like a weak old man, but some things can't be helped. I'll be back to normal in a few days." He patted her shoulder, finding it hard to believe she actually seemed to have grown even prettier in the seven weeks he had been gone.

Irene stepped back, wondering when her father would be well enough that she could talk to him about Ramon. John gave his father a quick hug, as did Elly, who then turned to Chad and took his arm. "Thank you for watching out for him," she said, batting her eyes at the man.

"He saved my life," Kirk put in. "If not for Chad there, I'd be lying back at Glorietta Pass with a bullet in my back."

They all looked at Chad, who reddened slightly, secretly exuberant that he had had the opportunity to make such an indelible impression on the Kirkland family. "It was just one of those things," he said, "being in the right place at the right time."

"We were burning Confederate wagons," Kirk explained. "One of them still had a man inside, only I didn't know it. I turned my back, and he was fixing to make daylight between my shoulders when Chad got off a shot and killed the man. Later we got into thicker fighting. That's when I took the bayonet wound."

Bea stepped up to Chad, taking his hand. "What can I say? We're all indebted to you," she told him. "You'll start right out as a senior partner in the law firm, Chad, with a good raise in pay."

It seemed to Irene that her mother always had a way of putting things into terms of money and prestige. How could anyone put a price on what Chad had done? Still, the fact that he had saved her father caused her to look at the young man in a different light. It was not so much that now she thought she could love him, or trust his sincerity. Her heart ached only for Ramon. But she could at least like Chad better now. He was apparently brave and skilled when the situation required it.

"Thank you, Chad," Elly was saying, hugging him.

"Yes, thank you," Irene added.

"None of it is necessary," he answered, putting on a good show of humility. He patted Elly's shoulder and moved his eyes to Bea. "Including making me a senior partner," he added. "I'm probably not ready for that yet, Mrs. Kirkland."

"Call me Bea. And I will decide when you're ready. As soon as you're rested up from this campaign, I want you to get started at Kirkland Enterprises, and I want John to come with you. I'd like him to spend some time every day at the firm now, learning right along with you. It's time he took a bigger role in family affairs and learned something more before he goes off to college."

"But, Mother—"

"No arguments." Bea looked from her son to Chad. "Would you please fetch Dr. Aimes for us, Chad? I want him to take a look at Kirk. I don't trust those army doctors. I have my doubts sometimes that they are doctors at all."

"Yes, ma'am. I'll go right away." Chad welcomed the chance to push Elly away gently. The girl had continued to hug him longer than necessary. He knew enough about women, and even girls Elly's age, to know when one had a crush on him, and Elly was entirely smitten. He thought it quite humorous, and would even have considered taking advantage of her tender virginity, if she were not a Kirkland. Trouble with Elly could spoil everything—cause him to lose his new job and rob him of his chance at marrying into the family.

"You stay here for supper tonight," Bea told him. "I will not take no for an answer. As far as living quarters are concerned, I know you were staying in a boarding house before you left. I want you to move into the best room at the Kirkland Hotel, on the house. We're already building a bigger and better hotel. When it is finished, you can stay in one of the better suites." She watched him carefully. "For as long as you wish, or until you marry and have a home of your own."

Their eyes met, and Chad felt like letting out a cheer. He knew exactly what the woman meant. He had passed the biggest hurdle to making Irene his wife. He would get no objections from Bea Kirkland.

Irene felt sick to her stomach at the way things were happening so fast, and without her consent. When she saw how Bea looked at Chad Jacobs, the thought of bringing up her love for Ramon made her head ache. If only she could be with Ramon right now, taste his lips again, feel his strong, reassuring arms around her. Oh, how it hurt to think of it, to want him so badly.

Chad left, and Bea immediately shooed the children out of the room so she could help Kirk into bed. "I don't need any help," he was protesting as they left.

The evening became one of confusion and worry, and Irene felt an odd change in the air, something she could not quite name. She knew it was brought on partly by the realization that their father was not infallible, something none of them had considered because David Kirkland was so big and strong and energetic. Recognizing that he was just human and was getting older had brought a hush to the household. The doctor stayed with him longer than Irene thought necessary for just a checkup, and after much begging, Irene was allowed to see Kirk after the doctor left. "Just a couple of minutes," Bea warned. She knew how special Irene was to her husband, and hoped she would help Kirk get back to his old self.

The room smelled like medicine when Irene entered and approached the huge bed. Medicine was not a familiar smell around a man like Kirk. She told herself he was only forty-one.

That was not so old, was it? At her age, it did seem old, but lots of people lived to their fifties and sixties, even older. Kirk smiled and reached out a hand, and Irene took it, sitting down on the edge of the bed.

"You're going to be all right, aren't you, Father?"

"I told you before that I would be. It's just the long ride back here after being so sick that got to me. The doc gave me some damn tonic, but all I need is to get back to the mountains. Bea can't understand that, but I'll bet you can."

She smiled for him. "I think I can. When are you going to take me with you?"

He sighed. "Now, girl, you got an eyeful of the mountains coming here from California."

"I know. But I want to go with you—just you and me alone. And I want to go up in the Rockies west of here, where you like it best."

"Well, maybe we can work something out." He squeezed her hand. "It's just that there is always so much to do, and you've got your schooling and you're getting to the age where you're a woman now, Irene, and you've got a woman's things to tend to. Your mother has big plans for you—and for your brother and sister. John will be spending more time at the offices in town, and you and your sister have to help with the new house. Your mother is anxious to have your coming-out party there before the summer is over."

"I don't care about a party," she told him, pouting slightly. *I'm in love, Father, with Ramon Vallejo. What should I do?* she wanted to add.

"Well, it's important to Bea, and for reasons you couldn't understand, I like to keep your mother happy, although that isn't always easy."

Irene frowned, meeting his eyes. "Why isn't she happy? She has everything."

He rubbed the back of her hand with his thumb. "Oh, it's kind of complicated. Some of it comes from not being loved much when she was younger, being treated bad by a rich uncle. I guess that's why she worries about money so much. In the back of her mind maybe she's trying to prove something to herself, and to her aunt and uncle. We all have reasons for what we do later in life, Irene, and we all were young once, just like you."

Irene considered what he'd told her. She had never given it much thought, and it helped her think of her mother's sour countenance with more sympathy.

"Some of her unhappiness is from the hard life she had when she first married me, Irene," Kirk went on, his voice subdued. His eyes looked tired, dark circles accenting the gauntness in his face. "I've never quite forgiven myself for that, and I guess I'm always trying to make up for it, so I tend not to put my foot down sometimes when I should. Bea's a good woman at heart, and she loves all of you very much. She's just a woman who has trouble expressing those kinds of feelings."

Irene wanted to ask him what the secret was that he and Bea kept from the children. The night she had overheard them talking, Kirk had said they were living with a lie. What was it?

"I was afraid when the doctor stayed so long," she told her father. "I just wanted to see you. You're telling the truth when you say you'll be all right, aren't you?"

He gave her a wink. "I am, child. Just don't get all worried if I seem to get up sooner than I'm supposed to and head into the mountains. Bea will have a fit, but that's the best medicine for me. Don't you fret one bit over it, because I'll come back a happier, healthier man."

"I won't worry," she said with a smile.

He managed a light laugh, but looked sleepy. "Meantime, don't you and the others be giving Bea a hard time. She has a lot on her mind, Irene, and that woman is what keeps all this going. Without her I think the Kirkland empire would crumble, so we don't want anything happening to her and we don't want to be upsetting her. You'll help there, won't you?"

She wanted to cry. When would she be able to tell her parents about Ramon? This was certainly not the right time, and it looked as though that time might never come. She was alone with this aching passion and desperate love. "I'll help," she said aloud.

"You're a good girl, Irene. Don't tell the others I said it, but you're a little bit special. You aren't spoiled like Elly, or always brooding like John. You have a goodness and a sweetness about you that is a joy to come home to." His words became slightly slurred from exhaustion. "Don't . . . ever change, Irene. Don't let life's heartaches . . . turn you into a bitter, unhappy woman."

She knew he meant he did not want her to become like her mother, and she felt sorry for him; but she felt sorry for her mother, too, who had been through so much hardship. Now Irene herself was experiencing her first true heartache and disappointment, in not being able to shout her love for Ramon to the world.

She understood now why it was called heartache, because her heart truly did hurt her.

"Always keep that loving, generous nature, Irene," Kirk was saying. His eyes closed for a moment. "I love you, Irene."

She squeezed his hand. "I love you, too, Father." She quietly left the room, and Kirk fell asleep thinking about Yellow Eagle. He would be sixteen now, too, a young warrior probably itching to show his worth. That was the way with young Indian men—cocky, eager to show their skill and bravery. Indian trouble was mounting, and he knew that as the War Between the States raged on, things would only get worse out here with the Indians. Chivington was already talking about diverting the mission of the Colorado Volunteers to the Indians, now that trouble with the Confederates was over. Was Yellow Eagle somewhere in Colorado?

Kirk had already decided he would never join in any Indian campaigns. He did not relish the thought of going up against his own son.

Chad seemed a little more subdued at supper, somewhat more sincere in countenance. Irene couldn't help wondering if he realized she was put off by his gushing charm, for she actually found herself liking him better this evening. Perhaps it was only because she knew he had saved her father's life. She had been faced with how devastating it would be to lose her father, and knowing Chad was responsible for Kirk's coming home safe and sound made her a little more open to him.

Elly peppered him with questions about the entire campaign, hanging on every word he spoke, and Irene was beginning to suspect her sister had a crush on the man. She thought it sadly humorous—humorous because the girl was making herself so obvious, and sad because Irene understood the aching feeling of loving someone she could not have.

Elly was not an easy person to love, but Irene couldn't help feeling sorry for her at times, not just because Elly seemed enamored with Chad. It was more than that. In all humility she knew Elly would never be a raving beauty. She was built like Bea and had nearly all her mother's features, and sometimes Irene felt guilty when Bea raved over her and practically ignored Elly. It was unfair to Elly, but whenever Irene tried to make up for it in some way, Elly only came back at her with a cruel remark. There were times when she was sure Elly wanted to hit her, and it made

Irene sad to think she would never be close to her sister. They could have shared so much, but Elly didn't seem inclined to share anything.

Now, because of Chad, the gap between them would widen even more, and Irene still wasn't sure of her feelings. Chad gave nearly all his attention to Irene whenever he was around, something Irene couldn't help and didn't even want, and she suspected that it made Elly furious. She considered talking to her sister about it, but she knew how Elly would react. She would deny everything, and she would say something to hurt and humiliate her.

Dessert was served, and Bea turned the talk to the family business, telling Chad about the progress of the new hotel she was building. She also wanted to open a second bank, and new warehouses were being built down on Wazee Street. "We have to keep them locked up good," she was saying. "They're bringing in more and more of those Chinese to work in the mines. They live down in that area, and they can't be trusted any more than the Mexicans or the Indians."

The remark cut deep. Again Irene wondered why her mother insisted there always had to be something terrible about other races. She thought that the Chinese must be very confused and afraid, living in an unfamiliar country, not speaking the language. At least the Mexicans and Indians were from this land and knew it well. She felt sick at the remark about Mexicans, and she did not see the smirk of satisfied vengeance on Elly's face. Elly knew well and good how talk about Mexicans must make her sister feel.

"Speaking of Mexicans, John has been going to see that one who works up at our new house," Elly spoke up. "That wood carver called Ramon."

John glowered at her. "You shut up, Elly."

"That is enough," Bea spoke up sharply, while Elly watched Irene come close to tears. "I will not tolerate arguing at the table." The woman looked flustered and embarrassed, and she apologized to Chad.

"Oh, I know how children can be," the man replied. The remark made Elly furious with herself for being such a tattletale in front of him. She didn't mind telling on her siblings, but she was suddenly embarrassed that she had done it in front of Chad, making her look even more childish.

"John won't be seeing so much of Ramon anymore," Bea went on. "He'll be down at Kirkland Enterprises every day from now on."

"But, Mother—"

"We have already been over this, John. If you have so much time to waste going up there and whittling on wood, you might as well be putting yourself to good use. Besides, Ramon will be done with his work in a week or two."

Irene felt as if she were going to be sick. Her stomach burned and ached. She had not wanted to acknowledge just how enraged her mother would be if she knew about Ramon, but now it hit her full in the face. After talking with Kirk, she knew her mother's dreams and goals for her children meant everything to her. How could she throw it all back at her? But how could she stop loving Ramon? She could never go to him and tell him they could not be together. The moment she was near him again, she knew how she would feel. Never had she been so alone, felt so helpless.

Bea looked around the table. "I want all of you to realize that I need you now," she said. "You're all getting old enough to start taking a more active role in the family businesses. And since you will some day inherit what your father and I have worked to build, it is important that you cooperate now, not just with me and your father, but with each other. Is that clear?"

They all nodded. Dessert was served, but Irene could not eat hers. She excused herself early, giving her apologies to Chad and saying she didn't feel well. "I think it's just the worry over Father," she said. Bea allowed her to go, and Irene fled upstairs. Elly smiled, sure Irene had gone to her room to have a good cry over her precious Ramon.

Once they had all finished their meal, Chad left. Bea retired to her sewing room, where she often went to be alone. She had few domestic gifts anymore, but she still liked to sew and embroider. One domestic chore she had long ago decided she would never do again was wash and iron clothes, even if she had to wear her clothes until they rotted and fell off. Now she had servants who did those things, and she intended to keep it that way, which meant guarding the Kirkland fortune with her life.

She turned up an oil lamp and sat down in front of a large wooden frame on which a linen dresser cloth was stretched. She was embroidering flowers onto the cloth. She took up needle and thread and continued the design where she had left off last, which had been several days ago. She looked up in surprise then when Elly walked into the room.

"There is something I think you should know, Mother," the girl spoke up hesitantly.

Bea finished a couple of stitches. "Close the door and come and tell me."

Elly obeyed, her heart pounding with glee. She kept a sober face, coming to sit down across from her mother.

"Well," the woman said. "I'm waiting. And don't be telling me something just to be a tattletale. And don't be making anything up."

"I'm not making it up, Mother, I swear on the Bible. And it's . . . it's kind of like being a tattletale, but it's for the good of the family, and so I have to tell you. You would *want* me to tell you."

"Then tell me," Bea said, sounding irritated.

"It's about Irene . . . and that Mexican man, Ramon Vallejo."

In spite of her dark complexion, Bea paled visibly. The woman moved the embroidery frame aside so that she could see Elly better, and her dark eyes drilled into her daughter's. "What about them?" she asked, her voice husky with anger. "And don't you be making this up, Eleanor May Kirkland! You're my daughter, and I love you dearly, but I know you are jealous of your sister. You shouldn't be, you know. Irene loves you."

"I love her, too, Mother," Elly lied. "I know I don't show it, but that's just the way sisters are. If I didn't love her, I wouldn't be telling you this. Besides, it's partly for the whole family. You wouldn't want a Mexican man sharing our fortune, would you? And think of the humiliation to the Kirkland name if one of us took up with a greaser?"

"I speak against them, Elly, but I don't use those names. I'll not have you using them either. And what makes you think Irene has 'taken up,' as you put it, with Ramon Vallejo?"

Elly sighed, looking at her lap and pretending to feel bad about having to tell her mother the story. "Irene rode up to the new house today. She knew he would be there alone. I didn't realize it myself until I walked up there to tell her it was time to get ready for the parade. She wasn't anywhere about."

She looked over at her mother then. "Then I heard horses. I saw them coming—Irene and Ramon. They had been riding together."

Bea closed her eyes, looking as if she might faint.

"I couldn't believe it myself," Elly went on. "I waited just inside the door to see for sure. They had been riding hard. I think there had been trouble. Irene said something to him about how he had risked his life for her, and how brave he was. Then he helped her down from Sierra, and then . . . then he kissed her."

Bea's eyes flashed open. "What!"

"He kissed her . . . full on the mouth . . . a real long kiss. He held her real close, and she let him. And he didn't kiss her just once, but twice. She put her arms around his neck, and they said they loved each other and that somehow they would figure out how they could be together."

Bea grasped Elly's hands so tightly that Elly grimaced with pain. "Don't you be lying about this, Elly!"

"I'm not, Mother, I swear. Talk to Ramon, or Irene. You'll know by the look in their eyes that I'm telling the truth."

Bea let go of Elly's hands and covered her face. "This is what comes from me being so busy. I have neglected you children, left you in the care of others too long." She seemed to sob, but Elly couldn't see her eyes because her hands were still over her face.

"What are you going to do, Mother?"

Bea breathed deeply, throwing back her head and quickly wiping tears away. "I don't know. I have to think about this." She rested her red, swollen eyes on Elly. "This is just between the two of us, do you understand?" Elly nodded. "You are *not* to tell your father, or John, or any of your friends, and certainly not Chad Jacobs. If you do, you will be severely punished."

Elly knew how far she could push her mother. This was one time she would not disobey the woman's wishes. "I won't say a word. And please, Mother, if you go to Irene with it, don't tell her I'm the one who told. She wouldn't understand that I did it for her own good."

Inside she wanted to shout with glee. She knew it was hopeless to think Chad Jacobs would ever look at her with love and desire. She would have to live with this terrible longing for him that made her stomach hurt most of the time. She wanted Irene to suffer the pain, to know how it felt not to be able to have the man she loved. Even pretty Irene could not always have what she wanted.

"I won't let on who told me," Bea answered. "You go up to bed now. I have to decide what to do about this."

Elly gave her a kiss on the cheek and left, and Bea leaned back in her rocker, closing her eyes. Irene! Her beautiful, precious Irene. It was the Indian in her, that must be what it was! Indian women were loose and too open with their affection. Irene was too generous and loving for her own good, and Bea had to nip this in the bud. One thing was certain. There would be no more horse-back riding. She would put a stop to that once and for all.

And as for Ramon . . . she shuddered at the thought of Irene allowing a Mexican man to kiss her. This had to end immediately, but she was wise enough to realize the worst way to discourage Irene was to face her with it and order her never to see the young man again. She might rebel and run off with him. Sometimes young women in love did foolish things. She had seen it happen all around her, although she had never felt that kind of insane passion. Her reasons for running off with Kirk had been entirely different.

There had to be a better way to end this ridiculous romance, a way to get Ramon out of Irene's system without her daughter ever knowing her mother had anything to do with it. It had to be Ramon himself who discouraged her.

Yes, that was it. She would take care of this through Ramon, not through Irene. She would go and have a talk with the young man, tomorrow, and Irene would learn the cruel truth about men like Ramon. It would hurt for a while, but Chad Jacobs would help her get over it.

CHAPTER TEN

Ramon carefully finished the last leaf in the wood-work that would frame the fireplace in one of the guest bedrooms. He stood back to study it, satisfied that it was perfect. He took a deep breath, looking around the room and thinking what a grand house this was going to be, wondering if and how he would ever manage to be accepted by the kind of people who owned places like this.

He walked to a window, staring out across the open land where he and Irene had ridden yesterday, wishing now that they had just kept going. Maybe they should have just run away right then and there, gotten married and consummated that marriage quickly so that nothing could be done about it.

The thought of making love with Irene made him shiver with desire. He would be so good to her, so gentle with her. He knew when he held her yesterday and tasted her mouth that they belonged together. It had felt so right, and he believed they could be happy. He loved her for the sweet and loving woman she was, and he knew without asking that if she had to give up her family's money to be with him, she would do it.

Had he been wrong not to run off with her? Wrong to think this could be done the right way? He still had his grandfather to face, and then the Kirklands. How was he going to convince them that he was the right man for Irene, that he was not marrying her for her money? He intended to be as wealthy as any man someday. He would work himself to death to provide for his beautiful Irene, to show her family that he could do it.

He had hoped Irene would find a way to come and see him today. There was still time. It was not noon yet. But he feared she would be unable to come. One of the workers had said he heard her father had been wounded at Glorietta Pass. It was possible Irene intended to stay with her father today, and he could not blame her; but he longed to see her again, hold her again, breathe in her lovely scent, feel her breasts crushed against his chest.

He sighed, turning to pick up a broom and sweep up wood shavings from the floor. He heard a woman's voice below then, heard one of the workers greet "Mrs. Kirkland." His heart rushed. Mrs.? Maybe he had heard wrong. Maybe it was Miss. He smiled, setting the broom aside and hurrying out the door and to the top of the stairway. His smile faded when he saw Beatrice Kirkland coming up the stairs, skirts hitched, a definite purpose to her steps.

Somehow he knew without asking that she was coming to see him, and his mind immediately went back to yesterday, and Elly. Had she seen more than she let on? He scrambled to think straight. He was not prepared for this. He had intended to give it some time, to approach the Kirklands on his own terms.

He quickly reentered the room where he had been working, picking up a carving tool and hoping the Kirkland matriarch would pass his room. Perhaps she had only come for another inspection on the progress of the house.

His whole body tingled with alarm and self-defense when he heard the skirts of her brown taffeta dress rustle into the room. He turned to face her, trying to look casual, determined that whatever happened, she would not make him grovel. He sensed Beatrice Kirkland enjoyed flaunting her power, and she glared at him now with those penetrating dark eyes, looking ready to fly into a tirade.

"*Buenos días*, Señora Kirkland," he spoke up calmly, squarely meeting her eyes.

She looked him over with the same scathing look he had seen in Elly's eyes yesterday. She turned and closed the door to the room, and he was certain then why she had come. He stood waiting for her to speak first, as she flounced across the room to inspect the fireplace frame. She touched the carving with hands almost too muscular to belong to a woman, then turned to face Ramon. She stood nearly as tall as he did.

"You do fine work, Mr. Vallejo," she said coolly. "And you

apparently have taught John well, although I totally disapprove of him coming here so often. Since there is so little left, I believe I'll let John finish what needs finishing. If it isn't quite the same quality, that will be my problem. You're finished with your work here, Mr. Vallejo."

He held her eyes, his own smoldering. "I know why you are here, Señora Kirkland. Apparently your daughter Elly—"

"Leave Elly out of this! This is between you and me now."

"I love Irene," he said boldly. "I would die for her. I would never bring her harm or—"

"I don't want to hear it, Mr. Vallejo. If you *truly* love Irene, then you should want what is best for her. Perhaps she thinks she loves you, but she is only sixteen, and in time, she will understand what a foolish thing she has done. I am doing everything in my power to be sure that you and I and Irene are the only ones who know about this, Mr. Vallejo. I want it to go no further, for Irene's sake."

"Irene's sake? Perhaps you are only thinking of yourself and the precious Kirkland name," he answered, keeping his voice low and calm, but there was fire in his eyes. "Perhaps that name and your money mean more to you than your daughter's happiness!"

"And perhaps the name and the money mean a great deal to you, too."

"They mean *nothing* to me! *I* have a name, too, señora, and there is royal blood in my family. My grandfather owns the biggest hacienda north of Mexico, and he would be much wealthier even than you if not for the Mexican Revolution. My family lost much, but we retain our dignity and our royal bloodlines. As for me, I intend to be a wealthy man in my own right some day. I am working hard toward this goal. I have lined up enough customers on my own to go into business for myself."

"Fine. I hope you do well, Mr. Vallejo. But none of it has anything to do with my daughter. You cannot convince me you aren't attracted to the Kirkland money, and even if you aren't, I will not have her cavorting with a Mexican. She will marry properly."

He drew in his breath, imagining how pleasant it would be to plant his hands around her throat. "It might interest you to know, Señora Kirkland, that my love for Irene will bring the same reaction from my grandfather as it has from you. He would think *I* was marrying below my station if I took a *gringa* for a wife. He would think *Irene* was not good enough for *me*!"

This time it was Bea who stiffened. The audacity of his

statement was beyond her belief. Her eyes narrowed, and she stepped closer. "Let me make you understand, Mr. Vallejo. To begin with, if you really love Irene, you will end this, here and now. Do you want to see her suffer humiliation and gossip? Do you want her to have to go without until you're able to give her all the things she is used to having? I've been through that, Mr. Vallejo. My husband couldn't properly provide for me either, in the beginning. The hardships I suffered left a permanent wall between us, left a bitterness inside me that has never died. Is that what you want for Irene?"

"It would not be that way for us."

"Wouldn't it? Think about what you are doing! Why put her through all of that when you could quickly end it, while she is still young? Why not end it now, before the commitment becomes so deep that neither of you can back out? If it is a white woman you're panting after, Mr. Vallejo, there are others out there who might be willing to take the risks of marrying a poor Mexican. Go and find yourself another!"

Bea thought for a moment that the man was going to hit her. She almost wished that he would. It would give her plenty of reasons to have him kicked out of Denver. She saw a certain pride in his eyes she had not expected. He was not afraid to face her and admit his love, and he was indeed handsome. It was too bad he was a poor carpenter, but even that was not as bad as the fact that he was Mexican.

"Is that what you think, that I just love her white skin?" His jaw flexed in anger. "There are others with skin much whiter, Señora Kirkland. And there are plenty of white girls who look at me with lust in their eyes. My love for your daughter has nothing to do with her race or her money or her beauty. It has to do with the kind of person she is. Irene is much more beautiful on the inside even than the outside. And when I look at you and listen to your cruel words of hate and prejudice, I wonder how in the world you produced such a sweet, loving daughter. I can hardly believe your blood runs in her veins!"

She started to slap him, but he caught her wrist. He barely squeezed, but Bea felt his power. "You can hit me with your words, Señora Kirkland, but I am a man, and you will not humiliate me by physically touching me." He let go of her wrist, giving her arm a light shove as he did so. Their eyes held in challenge for several seconds, until finally Bea sighed and turned away, rubbing at her wrist. She walked to a window, realizing that Kirk would probably like this man's spunk and pride. She had to get rid of Ramon before Kirk knew what was happening and had a say in it.

"I came here to try to reason with you, Mr. Vallejo," she told him, looking out a window. "But I can see you are not about to listen to the logical reasons why this thing with Irene must end." She faced him then. "So, I must resort to methods I did not want to use. You leave me no choice."

He frowned, waiting for her to continue.

"You say you have customers lined up, that you intend to get rich through your own carpentry business. I think you are aware that I could put an end to that business before you even get started. I have the power, Mr. Vallejo. People in this town listen to me, and if I ask them not to do business with you, they won't."

How he hated her! He planted his hands on his hips, glaring at her. "Denver is not the only city in this country, Señora Kirkland. I can take Irene and go someplace else."

"Yes, I suppose you could. But you have already built a reputation here, so going someplace new would slow you down considerably, and you're talking about dragging Irene around while you look for work like a beggar. Perhaps you could still make it work, but in the meantime, you would have the burden of guilt on your shoulders for knowing you were responsible for displacing your family and reducing them to wandering nomads. Since they lost so much in Mexico, I doubt they have the money to buy up enough land to run the kind of ranch they are running down around Colorado City. Am I right?"

Ramon frowned. "I do not understand."

A sly smile made one side of Bea's mouth curve. "Your grandfather, and whoever else in your family lives south of here on the grand hacienda you brag about, are nothing more than squatters, Mr. Vallejo. They do not legally own that land. They came up here from Mexico and picked out a place to settle—land that has since come into the hands of the United States. Have you heard of the Homestead Act, Mr. Vallejo?"

He watched her carefully, alarmed now, but refusing to show it. "I have heard of it."

"Well, we who are promoting Denver and Colorado expect it to be passed soon, and we think it is a wonderful way to attract new settlers—people who will be more permanent and reliable than the transient mine workers. That land your grandfather ranches will likely be opened up to settlement, and there isn't a thing he can do about it." She folded her arms. "Of course, your grandfather could lay claim to his hundred and sixty acres under the act, but

I highly doubt that is enough land if a man wants to have a ranch. In the meantime, others will claim pieces of land all around it."

She walked past him, then turned to face him again. "I can put on quite an advertising campaign to promote that area, Mr. Vallejo. I can also pay people who would be very glad to harass your family and make sure they vacate that land completely. I also have enough pull to claim it for myself—all of it. I've been thinking that it might be a good area in which to invest, since it is closer to Pikes Peak. Colorado City is growing, and the land to the south could become good farmland. I already own land to the south, and I need more, Mr. Vallejo. Denver is too dependent on outside resources for its food. We've got to start growing more of our own, and I intend to expand my farming project." Her face became brighter as she saw the dread move into his eyes. "Of course, what I could do is buy up all that land and let your family stay on as hired help. How would your grandfather feel about working as my farmhand? Is he just a rancher, or does he like to dig in the dirt and carry water?"

Ramon felt a lump in his throat that made it ache. He wished he could destroy her. He could defeat this woman in every way— except when it came to power and money. "You are a cruel woman, Señora Kirkland," he said, his voice gruff with hatred.

She held his eyes boldly. "When it comes to what is best for my children, yes, I can be *very* cruel, Mr. Vallejo. I don't mind the label. Out here a person *has* to be tough, and sometimes cruel, to survive. I want you to stay away from my daughter, Mr. Vallejo. I want you to go back to your hacienda for a few months. Let Irene think this was all just a passing fancy. As long as it hasn't gone too far, she'll get over it. She has everything she needs, and she has plenty of love and support. She'll be all right. She doesn't know it yet, but later this fall I am sending her to a finishing school in Chicago. She will be gone until next spring. By then you will be out of her blood, and she will be out of yours."

Ramon shook his head. "How little you understand. Perhaps it is because you have never truly loved that you cannot realize Irene will never be out of my blood, or out of my heart."

"What do you know about my ability to love, Mr. Vallejo? There is a lot you don't understand, and I don't intend to explain it to the likes of you. In any case, you are young and handsome, and Irene is even younger, and very beautiful. Both of you will easily find another to love and return your love. Both of you have many years ahead of you, but not together, Mr. Vallejo. Leave my daughter alone, and leave Denver for a while, or I will see that your family is left homeless. I am sure your grandfather must love his hacienda very much. Do you want to be responsible for making him a wandering beggar in his old age, for taking away what pride he has left? You said yourself he would consider marriage to a white woman a disgrace to the family. Marry into your own race, Mr. Vallejo, for your grandfather's sake. It will save a lot of people a lot of heartache."

"And what about Irene? What is she to think? I have a right to at least speak with her once more."

"You have *no* rights, Mr. Vallejo. If you try to see her again, or if you ever let on to her that we had this conversation and turn my daughter against me, I will make good on my threats. I think you know I can and will do it."

He slowly nodded his head "*Sí*, I suppose you can, but I will make *you* a promise, Señora Kirkland. Someday Ramon Vallejo will be a wealthy man, perhaps even as wealthy as the Kirklands. Someday my name will be just as important within Denver society. You have only given me more incentive than I have ever had before. And nothing you have done or said here today will change the way I feel about *mi querida* Irene. Perhaps I will marry another, and perhaps she will do the same. But the love we feel will always be there. Time and circumstance will not erase it."

She hated him for being capable of such love. She wondered for a moment if she was against this just because it was wrong for Irene, or because she was so jealous of their young, devoted love, their ability to express that love with such passion. She saw a sincerity in Ramon's eyes that told her he truly did love Irene for herself, that he wanted nothing to do with her money. She found it incredible and decided he must be a very foolish and reckless man. But then Mexican men were supposed to be hot-blooded, putting their lust and desires before practical necessities.

"Perhaps you will always love her, which I doubt," she answered. "But you will never have her. Good-bye, Mr. Vallejo. I will explain to your *patrón* that your grandfather is sick and you have to go back to the hacienda right away."

"I will do my *own* explaining," he told her. "Do not worry. I will be gone before the sun sets."

Bea felt his bitter hatred. "Very well," she answered. She started for the door, then turned. "By the way, was there some kind of trouble yesterday when you and Irene went riding?"

He frowned. "Why do you think there was?"

"Just answer my question, Mr. Vallejo."

He held her eyes. "Three men—drifters. They tried to make

trouble for Irene. I chased them off. One of them probably has a very bad headache today, perhaps a dent across the side of his head where my rifle barrel landed on him."

"I see." She began rummaging in her purse. "Well, you must have made quite an impression on Irene, being her valiant savior and all. I am sure that is what motivated her to let you kiss her. She'll realize her folly, in time." She pulled out a wad of bills. "This paper money won't buy as much as gold, Mr. Vallejo, but it does have purchasing power. Here is two hundred dollars for coming to Irene's aid, although I must add that you had no business letting her ride that far in the first place, no business riding with her at all."

"She asked me to," he told her. This time it was Ramon whose eyes were hostile. "I don't want your money, Señora Kirkland. I am sorry that you do not understand there are other things more important than gold and power. You must be a very unhappy woman. I only hope Irene does not end up bitter and hateful like her mother. It would be a shameful loss."

Bea stiffened, shoving the money back into her handbag. Without another word she turned and left, and Ramon stared at the doorway, a fierce pain in his gut that made him grasp his stomach. The worst part about this whole thing was that he was not going to have the chance to explain. If he told Irene the truth, Bea Kirkland would make good on her threats, and he could not do that to his grandfather and the rest of the family. But just to leave, to say nothing—Irene would think he had used her, toyed with her heart, grabbed the opportunity to kiss a rich *gringa*. She would hate him.

Tears filled his eyes and he turned away. Of course she would hate him, and Bea Kirkland knew it! That was the plan. Without having to say a word to Irene, she had managed to put an end to their love, and the only one who would look bad was Ramon Vallejo.

Irene could hardly eat for thinking of Ramon, wondering how and when they could be together again. Bea had asked her to take care of Kirk all day while Bea was away on business. There had been no opportunity to go up to the new house. Because John had stayed in town all day, she could not even ask her brother if he had talked to Ramon. She swallowed a piece of meat, but it felt like lead. She wondered if people ever died from loving too much, especially if they couldn't have the one they loved.

"Irene, you take a tray up to your father when we're finished," Bea told her, interrupting her thoughts.

"Yes, ma'am," she answered quietly.

"I think he'll do much better now that he's getting some decent food. Men on the march don't eat nearly as well as they should."

"Father says he'll feel better when he goes to the mountains again," Irene put in.

Bea scowled. "Him and his mountains. They'll kill him one of these days, that's what." She glanced at John. "John, I have a project for you that might surprise you."

John looked at his mother curiously. "What do you mean?"

"Well," Bea answered, gauging her words. She hated to hurt Irene, but it had to be done and over with. "It seems that Mexican fellow—Ramon Vallejo, isn't that his name?"

John nodded, glancing at Irene, whose stomach began to ache more.

"Well, the man has just up and left us flat, without finishing his work." Bea dished herself a second helping of potatoes, refusing to look at Irene. "That's how it is with these Mexicans—totally unreliable. He was nearly finished. Henry Brown isn't sure why he left. He said something about going back to his own people, where he belongs, something about missing his home—lives someplace south of us, I'm told."

"Ramon? He wouldn't just leave without finishing a job," John told her. "And I know he'd tell me good-bye first."

Bea cocked her eyebrows. "Well, now you know what I've been telling you all along. You simply can't count on people like that. Who knows the real reason he left? I remember Mr. Brown telling me once that there is some woman down near Colorado City that Ramon is supposed to marry. Perhaps Ramon missed her and decided to go home to be with her. Whatever the reason, it's probably best that he's gone. I didn't like him being around Elly and Irene when they were up there. Mexican men can be very charming. I've known more than one instance where pretty young girls were taken advantage of by men like that, just for a chance to touch or kiss what they call *gringa*."

She kept the conversation casual, as though completely innocent of any knowledge of the reason Ramon might have left, giving no thought to the fact that she was teaching Elly a good lesson in deceit.

"So, John," Bea continued, "since you love carving so much, I thought you might want to try your hand at finishing what little is left."

"Me?" John's eyes lit up. "But I'm not as good as Ramon, Mother."

"You're good enough. We'll call it a temporary reprieve. I know it's hard for you to concentrate on the family business, but you must understand that is how it must be, John. I'll let you finish the work up at the house if you promise not to put up a fuss when I send you back to Kirkland Enterprises."

"I won't. Thank you, Mother." He shook his head. "I can't figure out why Ramon left, though. I wish he'd said good-bye."

Irene suddenly scooted back her chair. "I feel sick again, Mother," she said, her voice strained. "May I be excused?"

Bea looked at her in concern, her heart torn at the look in Irene's eyes. She reminded herself this was for Irene's own good. "Irene, you have said you were sick two nights in a row. I think the doctor should see you."

"I—I don't need a doctor," she answered, struggling not to break into tears.

"Well, if this keeps happening, I'll have Dr. Aimes look at you the next time he comes to see Kirk. Run upstairs then, and get yourself to bed."

Irene quickly left, and Elly, who was certain she knew the reason Ramon had left, smiled inwardly. She knew her mother had gone up to the house this morning. Oh, how she wished she could have heard what Bea had told Ramon! Whatever it was, he was gone, and now Irene knew how it felt to love someone and not be able to have him.

Irene hurried to her room, closing the door and breaking into a torrent of tears that racked her body violently. Ramon! What had happened! Why had he gone? Was it true what her mother had said about Mexican men? Had Ramon just used his dark, handsome looks and charm to get a kiss from her? Would he go home and laugh with his friends about it?

The tears poured forth uncontrollably. She felt totally alone and deserted, in spite of having her family around her. After what her mother had said, how could she go to Bea and tell her about this terrible hurt? Elly would only laugh at her and tell on her, and her father was too sick to be upset with something he probably would never understand anyway.

She cried until she thought she might be sick. She felt weak and spent, with barely the strength to sit up when she heard someone knock at the door. "You in there, Irene?" She recognized John's voice. "Yes," she answered in a voice that sounded small and far away.

John cautiously came inside, closing the door. He came over to the bed and sat down beside her. "I'm sorry . . . about Ramon."

His words brought back the hurt again, and she broke into a new fit of tears. "I . . . don't believe it, John. It can't be true . . . that he just left like that. Something happened. He wouldn't just . . . leave . . . without talking to us."

"I know what you mean. We were good friends."

She turned a puffy, tear-stained face to his. "Do you think it's true . . . what Mother said about Mexican men? Ramon . . . kissed me, John. You're . . . the only one who knows." Her chest jerked in a sob as her brother stared at her, surprised. "Do you think . . . he just used me . . . that he would laugh at me?"

John shook his head. "I don't know, Irene. I don't know much about stuff like that." He put his arm around her shoulders, feeling sorry for his older sister. "Maybe he just knew the best thing to do was go back to his people, Irene. Maybe he did it for you, even though he knew it would hurt your feelings. Maybe he just didn't want to make trouble for anybody. You know Ramon. He's kind of quiet, and he's pretty close to his family. Maybe he thought it was all for the best. But that wouldn't mean he didn't really love you. Maybe he did it *because* he loves you."

She sniffed, wiping at her eyes with a handkerchief that was already soaked with her tears. "Do you . . . really think so?"

"It's the only thing I can think of. Ramon is an honorable man. I don't think he'd hurt you on purpose. And maybe he left without even seeing me because he was afraid he'd see you again, too, and then he'd lose his courage to do what was right."

"Maybe." She blew her nose. "And maybe he'll come back, John."

The boy sighed deeply. "The way he left, I bet he won't. He must be pretty determined. He'll probably marry that Mexican girl, Irene. He told me about her a couple of times."

Irene gripped her stomach, a raging jealousy tearing through her with relentless pain. "But . . . . *I* want to be his wife."

He squeezed her shoulders. "You can't be, Irene. Even *I* understand that. But you've got your memories of him. We both do. And we know most of what Mother says about Mexicans isn't true, and it probably isn't true about the Indians or the Chinese either. Let her think what she wants. We don't have to be like her."

Irene straightened. "No," she answered, remembering her

father's words. *Don't ever change, Irene. Don't let life's heart-aches turn you into a bitter, unhappy woman.* "I love Mother, John." She met his eyes again, feeling suddenly calmer. "But I don't ever want to be like her."

"Elly is like her, only worse. At least Mother has some excuse. I mean, she had a hard life in the beginning and all. When she does something we don't like, it's usually because she really thinks it's for our own good. Elly, she's just plain mean," he said.

Irene rose, going to her dresser to get out a clean handkerchief. She didn't want to think about Mother or Elly right now. She was sick with love and disappointment, and she wanted to feel the hurt, realizing that the more she hurt, the more she was sure Ramon had loved her, for surely he had done this for her, just as John said. Was Ramon hurting, too? Was he crying? She liked to think that he was. It was her only comfort.

"I'd like to wash my face and got to bed," she told John, her head beginning to ache fiercely. "Thank you for coming to talk to me, John."

He shrugged, getting up from the bed. "I feel bad, too, so I know you must feel a lot worse. Just think about Chad Jacobs, Irene. Anybody can see he likes you a lot, and he's good-looking and successful and all."

"He's all right. But he's not Ramon," she answered quietly. How could she explain to her younger brother how it felt to realize Ramon would never hold her again? That she would never feel his mouth on her own again, never be able to be a wife to him? She turned to face John. "I'll always love him, John. Always. It's our secret, isn't it?"

Her brother nodded. "I'm not a tattletale like Elly."

Elly. Irene thought about the way her sister had come in after she did yesterday, out of breath from running. Had Elly seen something and told her mother? Surely not. She would have blurted it right out and stood around to watch Bea scream and yell and give orders. She would have wanted to bask in Irene's punishment, and Bea would have dragged Ramon to the house and ordered both of them never to see each other again. But Bea didn't seem to know anything about it. In fact, she seemed upset with Ramon for leaving without notice, before his work was finished.

Irene and John hugged. John wished he could do or say something to make Irene feel better. He loved his older sister. In the whole family Irene was the only one he could talk to, the only one with whom he felt comfortable.

He knew his father wanted to be closer to him, but there was something about Kirk that made it difficult for John to talk to his father. Maybe it was because Kirk was such a man of the world, had done so many exciting things in his life. His father was big and strong, a mountain man who knew how to survive difficult situations. John always felt inadequate around the man, wondering if he would ever live up to his father's image.

He headed for his own room, unaware that Elly had come up the stairs in time to see him come out of Irene's room. Elly's heart filled with jealousy over the fact that her brother and Irene had always been close. She stuck out her tongue at John, then tiptoed to the door to Irene's room, listening carefully. She stifled a snicker when she heard Irene sobbing. She felt victorious, and the knowledge that Chad could never belong to her was easier to bear. Even the prettiest girls didn't always get what they wanted.

CHAPTER ELEVEN

"This is a near disaster," Bea fumed as she fluffed Kirk's pillow for him. "Gilpin should be tarred and feathered!"

Kirk quelled an urge to laugh. Whenever Bea Kirkland's money was threatened, she became as nervous and defensive as a she-bear protecting her cubs. "Bea, I'm sure the man thought the government would make good on those drafts."

"Well, he wasn't sure enough, was he!" She straightened. "I don't think you realize the seriousness of this, Kirk. Denver's businessmen, including you, I might add, invested thousands of dollars in the Volunteers, on the promise we would be paid back by the government. How could those men in Washington be so ungrateful as not to make good on their promise? Don't they realize what the Volunteers did? They saved Denver's gold for the Union! And this is the thanks we get? We'll be a long time recovering from this, not just Denver, but *us*! We will have to be very careful about spending for a while, and right when we're finishing the new house!"

"Somehow I imagine you'll find a way around this," he answered, picking up a piece of bacon from the tray Bea had brought for him.

"We'll find a way, I suppose. But the city is going to suffer. Our first remedy is to get rid of Governor Gilpin and get someone more responsible in here! Bill Byers is already working on it."

"I expect he is, seeing as how he's never been too fond of Gilpin."

"And with good reason." She folded her arms. "The man had the audacity to give most of the government printing contracts to other papers instead of the *News*, after all Bill has done for this area." She walked to a window and opened the curtains.

"Open them good and wide so I can see the mountains," Kirk told her.

"You and your mountains. I wish you would pay more attention to matters close at hand." She turned to face him. "We've already petitioned President Lincoln to appoint a new governor," she went on. "We have suggested Bill Larimer. After all he's done for this area, he's the logical choice. He knows Colorado, knows what we need and want."

Kirk ran a hand through his hair. "Well, it doesn't matter much to me. I've never seen a whole lot of difference in any of these government men. They all make promises they can't keep. We're better off each man watching after his own interests."

"Now that is the kind of attitude that will stifle Denver. We have to keep working together under some kind of leadership."

He laughed. "*You're* the one who ought to be governor."

She held her chin a little higher, stood a little straighter. "I could do it."

He laughed harder, shaking his head. "Oh, I have no doubt about that. Too bad they don't let women hold offices like that."

Bea wanted to smile and laugh with him, but she was too worried about losing ten thousand dollars of their own money that they had invested in the Colorado Volunteers, money the government had promised to pay back. She wished she could take such news as lightly as her husband, but to her it was a disaster, and Kirk's attitude irritated her.

"Yes, it *is* too bad," she answered, eyeing him narrowly. "But it's a good thing some women can assume the leadership at home, or some men wouldn't be worth much, would they?"

He sobered slightly. "Now, Bea, if I didn't lend a little humor to this household, things would be like a tomb around here. You've got to learn how to relax." He sipped some coffee. "By the way, how is Irene? Did the doc have a look at her yesterday?"

"Yes." She turned away so that he couldn't see her eyes. "He says she seems to be fine, says perhaps she caught something the day we went into town to view the parade. He gave her a tonic."

"You shouldn't tell her she can't ride anymore, Bea."

"I don't think it's good for her."

"It's the best thing for her. *That's* her tonic, just like mine is going to the mountains. I don't often go against your wishes, Bea, but I'm telling you now that I want you to tell her she can keep riding Sierra—if not every day, then at least every other day. I mean it."

The woman sighed. Knowing how deeply Irene had been hurt because of Ramon, she decided perhaps she could lift her ban on riding. At the moment, Irene needed something to cheer her up. She had taken the news about Ramon much harder than Bea had anticipated. She was worried about her daughter's despondency. "All right. I'll tell her she can ride." She wished she could explain to Kirk what the real problem was, but Irene was too special to him. He might go along with the girl's ridiculous infatuation with Ramon Vallejo and give her permission to see the man.

"Good," he said. "Later today I want to have a talk with her myself."

Bea felt alarm, worried Irene would tell her father about Ramon, and that somehow Kirk would figure out the truth about the whole incident. She wanted it to be done with.

"Has Chad Jacobs been to see her?" Kirk was asking.

She brightened. "Yes. He brought her flowers yesterday. Oh, Kirk, I hope this all leads to something. I am so fond of Chad."

"He seems like a good man—saved my life and all. I'm indebted to him. But I also want Irene to be happy."

"How could she not be happy with a man like Chad?"

Kirk just glanced at her, wondering what she would know about being happy with *any* man. He decided not to bother answering her question. He set his tray aside and moved his legs over the side of the bed. "Get me some clean pants and a shirt, will you? I want to get outside and get some fresh air. It's being cooped up in this house that's keeping me from getting any energy back."

"You should stay right in that bed."

"To hell with that. Get my pants."

Someone knocked at the door then, and Bea opened it to find her housekeeper, Myra. "There is a man downstairs come to visit with Mr. Kirkland," the woman told Bea. "Says his name is Red McKinley."

"Red McKinley!" Kirk stood up, not caring that he wore only his long johns. "Get me those clothes, Bea. I'm not going to let Red McKinley see me laid up in bed." He looked past her at Myra. "Show Red to the smoking room, will you, Myra? Tell him

I'll be right down." The woman nodded, her face red from seeing David Kirkland in his underwear. She hurriedly left, and Bea turned to her husband.

"Honestly, Kirk, sometimes you seem to revert back to the days of the rendezvous, and you treat everyone else as though they're there with you. Do you realize Myra saw you in your long johns?"

He waved her off. "She's got a husband. She's seen a half-dressed man a time or two."

She put her hands on her hips. "Who is Red McKinley?"

"An old, old friend, from my trapping days," he answered, looking more animated than Bea had seen him in a long time. Her heart fell. She hated it when Kirk talked about the "old days." Heaven only knew what this Red McKinley wanted. She moved to a dresser and took out some clothes.

"You just remember that leg and keep in mind the doctor has ordered another week of bed rest," she told him, handing him the shirt and pants.

Kirk took them eagerly. "I know better than he does what I need. Go down and introduce yourself to Red. I'll be right there."

She sighed with frustration, leaving him and going downstairs to the smoking room, which was off the parlor, with double doors so the room could be closed off. This smoking room was much smaller than the one Kirk would have in the new mansion, which would have much higher ceilings and a good deal more room, big enough for a pool table, which had already been ordered from San Francisco.

Still, as she watched Kirk's visitor gaze around the room, his back to her, Bea realized he was quite impressed. One wall was covered with bookshelves. The most prominent piece of furniture was a huge oak desk and leather desk chair. Two more leather chairs and a leather couch, all in dark green, filled out the room.

Bea hesitated at the doorway, noticing Red McKinley wore buckskins, which he apparently had had for quite some time, since the elbows were rubbed to shiny thinness. He wore knee-high moccasins and was indeed quite a spectacle of a mountain man, just the kind of "old friend" Bea would prefer Kirk never see again. She was having a hard enough time keeping Kirk civil and presentable as it was.

The man turned then at the sound of her rustling skirts. She stared at his fairly handsome face, but his skin was somewhat freckled and had a leathery look from years of living in the open. His eyes were a sharp blue, surrounded by red lashes, red eyebrows, and his face was framed with red hair, his upper lip decorated with a thick, curled, red mustache. No one needed to ask where he got his nickname. He gave her a faint smile.

"Hello, ma'am. And who might you be?"

She caught the Irish accent, folding her arms self-consciously as his eyes took inventory of her tall frame. "I might be Beatrice Kirkland," she answered. "Welcome, Mr. McKinley. Kirk says you are old friends."

"That we are. Kirk saved my life once, fought off a bunch of Crow Indians for me—nursed a bad wound." Red felt suddenly awkward under the woman's glare, wondering how on earth Kirk ended up with such a big, stern-looking woman. He knew it was a little early to be judging anyone, but there was something about this woman he already didn't like. "You're his wife then?"

"I am. I hope you won't keep Kirk too long, Mr. McKinley. He was hurt at Glorietta Pass and he became quite ill. He's still recovering."

"Well, ma'am, sometimes seeing an old friend can do a lot toward fixing something like that. Me and Kirk go way back. I haven't seen him since, oh, back in forty-five or forty-six I think it was. We were—" He hesitated, wondering how things had turned out with the Indian baby. Some people were touchy about adoption and such. Had he married this woman simply because she had agreed to raise little Morning Star? Did she know about Yellow Eagle?

He decided he had better not bring up the subject until he talked to Kirk. "We, uh, we had a drink together at a trading post," he went on. "He went his way, and I went mine, both of us knowing we had to find some other way to make a living because of the way things were changing." He noticed how she glanced at his hat, and he quickly removed it. "I just got into Denver a few days ago, came here because I'd heard so much about how the place was growing and all. I saw the Kirkland name on just about every other building, got to wondering if the man who owned half of Denver was my old friend."

Bea watched him warily, suspicious that he had come to Kirk for a handout. She detested beggars. She studied the worn buckskins derisively, and a deep dislike began to grow in Red's gut for this haughty woman Kirk had married. He read the look in her eyes, and personal pride made him stand a little straighter.

"And what do you do for a living, Mr. McKinley?" she asked.

He felt his cheeks getting hot and knew his fair skin was giving away his secret contempt and the Irish temper he was trying to hide. "Spent most of the past few years scouting for wagon trains. I—"

He did not have time to finish. Kirk was calling his name. "Excuse me, ma'am." Red gladly moved past Bea and into the parlor to greet Kirk, who came toward him using a cane. "Kirk, you big, worthless Swede, what are you doing leaning on that thing?"

Before Kirk could answer, the two men embraced, laughing, slapping each other on the back. Red was a broad-shouldered, hardy-looking man, but next to Kirk he looked small. Bea watched them warily, convinced she had to keep a closer eye on Kirk for a while, afraid she could not trust his common sense when he was around a man like Red McKinley, whom she dearly wished had never come.

"Took a damn bayonet in the leg," Kirk was saying as they let go of each other. "I'll be getting rid of this cane soon, though, you can count on that. Seeing you sure helps. How in hell have you been, Red, and *where* have you been? My God, man, it's been sixteen years or better."

"That it has, my friend." Red let Kirk lean on his shoulders as they both walked toward the smoking room. Bea stood in the doorway.

"Irene is sleeping, so keep your voices down," she told them. "Elly is with the tutor, and I'm taking John to town, Kirk. I will be gone for a while, but apparently you won't need me around anyway."

"I take it the two of you have met," Kirk asked.

Bea forced a weak smile. "Yes." She held Red's eyes. "Don't keep him too long, Mr. McKinley. He needs his rest. It's been nice meeting you."

He nodded. "Same here," he lied.

Bea moved past them, closing her eyes with disgust when she heard Kirk tell Red he could stay as long as he wanted, stay for supper, if he liked. The two men entered the smoking room, and Kirk closed the double doors, moving behind his desk and lowering himself into the leather chair, a grimace of pain on his face. Red took a seat opposite him, studying Kirk's silk shirt and having already noticed his well-tailored pants.

"So, my friend, how in hell did you end up like this?" he asked Kirk. "This is not the David Kirkland I left back at Bent's Fort. And whatever happened to that little Indian girl you took away with you?"

Kirk sobered. "She's all grown up, Red—sixteen years old. Her name is Irene, and she's the most beautiful creature you would ever want to set eyes on, let me tell you." He leaned forward.

"She doesn't know she's part Indian, and neither she nor my wife know about the brother. I hope you didn't say anything to Bea."

Red shook his head. "It's not right, not telling the girl," he warned. "That's going to come back at you, Kirk, like a gun that misfires. You know how much that burns."

Kirk sobered more. "I know. But sometimes you put things off so long that you can't fix them anymore." He opened a gold-plated box and offered Red an expensive cigar. Both men took cigars and lit them, and Kirk leaned back again, going through the entire story of how he had landed in Denver a rich man. Red listened in disbelief, finding it incredible that Kirk's attempt at providing a home for little Morning Star had led to all of this. He shook his head, leaning forward and flicking ashes into an ashtray from the cigar, which had burned halfway down while they talked.

"I never would have believed it," he told Kirk. "I never thought a kid would mean that much to you."

"I didn't either, till I held her. Now I've got another daughter and a son." He sighed. "All this money might seem pretty good to somebody who doesn't have any, but it's not all what you think, Red. I mean, this isn't the kind of life for a man like me. I only do what I do for the family's sake. I've got a lot to make up for to Bea, and I have three children to support. I also want to stay right here in the Rockies, so I do everything I can to keep Denver alive and keep our investments lucrative. Actually, Bea has a remarkable mind for business. She handles almost all the book-work and the investing, runs the two banks we own, oversees new construction, orders, all the things I hate. I spend most of my time in the mountains, keeping an eye on the mines, buying up new claims, overseeing the stamp mills, things like that."

Red just kept shaking his head. "Never thought I'd see the day. I'd sure like to meet that daughter, Kirk."

"You will—tonight at supper. I insist you stay and eat with us. You just remember she thinks she's ours—mine and Bea's. She doesn't know anything about her heritage, or even that Bea isn't her real mother."

Red took another puff of the cigar. "I hope you don't regret that decision, Kirk. You ever think about the fact that she's going to have children of her own someday, and one of them could come out looking like he ought to be wearing eagle feathers in his hair?"

Kirk paled slightly. "I try *not* to think about it, and I pray it just won't happen. If she marries a white man, a child would be three-quarters white—not too likely to give away an Indian background."

"You can't be sure."

"This is the way Bea wants it. We struck a bargain a long time ago, and that's how it is." Kirk leaned forward. "Red, I need to get out of here—get back up into the mountains. I've been away from the mines way too long, what with going out on that campaign against the Texans and all. I keep telling Bea the best remedy for me is to get out in the fresh mountain air again. How about you coming with me? You don't have any particular plans, do you?" He let out a sigh of disgust with himself. "My God, I haven't even asked what brings you here—what you've been doing with yourself."

Red shrugged. "Not much. I came here to see if I could find work, settle some. I've been scouting for wagon trains, but it's getting so I have a hard time staying in the saddle all day. These old bones can't take it like they used to."

Kirk laughed. "I know what you mean. Hell, I can put you to work anyplace you choose. I'll even float you a loan if you want to get into some kind of business of your own."

Red's heart warmed at his old friend's generosity. "Thank you, Kirk. I didn't come here for that. We'll give it some time, think on things before I go taking money from you. I just wanted to see you again, find out how in hell you ended up owning half of Denver."

"Not half. Only about a third."

Both men laughed. "Hell, I'd love to go up in the mountains with you, friend," Red said. "You're right. I don't have any other plans at the moment."

A longing look came into Kirk's eyes. "I envy you a little, Red."

"*You* envy *me*? Who's the one sitting here with millions in his pockets?"

Kirk shrugged. "Not quite millions yet. I just mean I envy the fact that you're still free. You're not tied down to anyone or anything. It's been a long time since I lived that way."

Red suspected Kirk was not at all happy with his sour-faced wife, who apparently ruled the roost. He knew Kirk was too soft-hearted to go up against the woman's wishes most of the time; and he suspected Bea Kirkland was not exactly warm and attentive in bed. But he decided that was too delicate a subject for him to bring up, especially after seeing Kirk for the first time in sixteen years.

"Well," he answered, "a man can't live that way forever. It's time for me to be taking on some responsibilities myself. Just be glad you didn't wait till my age just to get started. A forty-year-old man ought to have a family and be all settled in, not still roaming around like an Indian."

"I'll help all I can, Red. Come on. Let's walk outside. I need some fresh air."

The two men rose, and Red helped Kirk walk out of the room, wondering how Bea Kirkland would feel about his staying for dinner. He had no doubts that the woman wished he had never shown up at all.

Ramon knelt in the small Catholic chapel nestled in the foothills of Pikes Peak. In the sweeping valley below the chapel lay Hacienda del Sur. It had felt good to come home, had brought him at least a little comfort to see the beautiful ranch land he had preserved for his grandfather by giving up the only woman he would ever truly love.

"Holy Mary, Mother of God," he prayed, "help my heart to heal. Help me get over the pain of it, and to love Elena as a man should love his wife. Tomorrow Elena will be mine, but my heart cries out for another."

A tear slipped down his cheek, and he could not continue. He heard footsteps behind him, turning to see his grandfather standing in the aisle. The chapel was empty except for them, and its double doors of rich, dark wood of Spanish design stood open because of the pleasantly warm day. Ramon quickly wiped at the tear. "*Abuelo*! What are you doing here?"

Miguel Vallejo walked closer, always standing straight and tall. He was still a handsome man, in spite of the wrinkles in his aging face. His hair was still thick and dark, except for a blaze of white at the temples. His dark eyes showed life and energy, but for the moment they also expressed concern as the old man approached Ramon.

He held out a hand that displayed two gold rings, remnants of his past wealth. He touched Ramon's arm. "Come and sit down, *mi nieto*. I wish to talk to you."

Ramon followed the man to a pew, where they sat down on the cool, polished wooden seat. Always dressed immaculately, Miguel today wore black cotton pants with a white shirt that sported bloused sleeves and was decorated with colorful embroidered designs. The old man turned to his grandson, putting one arm on the back of the pew.

"I want the truth, Ramon," the old man told him. "You said in your last letter that you would not be back from Denver until the end of the summer—that you had a lot of business there with your carving and that you might even go into business on your own.

Suddenly you show up here, and I see a terrible unhappiness in your eyes. Suddenly you want to marry Elena right now and not wait a moment longer, but I do not see love and desire in your eyes when you tell me this. I see a troubled man. I followed you today, and I saw you come here to pray. Why, *mi nieto*? What happened in Denver to send you home unexpectedly, and to put such sorrow in your eyes?"

Ramon looked away. "I cannot tell you, *abuelo*. It would only make you ashamed of me."

Miguel smiled sorrowfully, aching for his grandson's unhappiness. "Nothing you could ever do would make me ashamed of you, Ramon."

Ramon leaned forward, resting his elbows on his knees and hanging his head. "This would."

Miguel put a hand on his shoulder. "Let me tell you what I think it is. I think you found another woman."

Ramon looked at him in surprise, and Miguel knew he was right. Ramon turned away again, and Miguel rubbed at his shoulders. "There is only one thing that puts the kind of pain in a young man's eyes that I see in yours, *mi nieto*. I am not so old that I have forgotten such feelings. You only made it more obvious by being so anxious to marry Elena, as though marrying her would make you forget."

"It will help."

"Perhaps. But you must not take it out on Elena and be unkind to her. You must remember that she truly does love you, and that she has not been with a man. Do not release your frustrations on her and frighten her, Ramon."

Ramon sighed, resting his head in his hands, feeling insane with the want of Irene. "I won't," he answered quietly.

"There is something else I am thinking," Miguel spoke up. "I am thinking that because you did not tell me about this other woman, that perhaps she was a *gringa*. Am I right?"

Ramon kept his head in his hands. After a long silence he answered. "Her name is Irene Kirkland. She is the daughter of the people who were building a new home where I worked." He sighed deeply. "I know this upsets you, *abuelo*, but she was unlike any *gringa* I have known. She was . . . sweet and good . . . generous and loving. She loved me just for me. She had no prejudice against a Mexican man. She is practically incapable of unkindness and bad thoughts."

"If she was so good, and you loved her so much, why are you here without her? Why did you not bring her here and insist the family accept her? Did you give all this up just because you are promised to Elena, a woman you apparently do not love the same?"

Ramon straightened, rising and walking a few feet away. "I had no choice. Her family is very wealthy. Her mother found out about us." He faced his grandfather. "She threatened to take away our land, to destroy Hacienda del Sur. She can do it, *abuelo*, and she will, if I don't stay away from Irene." He ran a hand through his dark hair, waiting for his grandfather's tirade.

The old man sighed. "I am sorry for you, Ramon. I know how love hurts at your age. I was afraid such a thing would happen if you went to that big town. What about the girl? What does she say about all of it?"

Ramon shook his head. "I don't know. I never got to see her again. I don't think she even knows her mother talked to me. By now she"—the ache returned to his throat—"she probably thinks I abandoned her, that I was just toying with her . . . a dirty Mexican out to grab a kiss from a pretty white girl. That is how her mother will make her see it."

Miguel sighed deeply, rising and standing close to his grandson, reaching out and grasping his arms. "Ramon, you should have known it could not work. It is a difficult thing you have had to do, and I love and respect you for giving away a piece of your heart for the sake of the family. I am proud of you, *mi nieto*. I must assure you that after a time, the hurt will ease, and you will realize it was all for the best. I have told you many times you should marry a good Catholic girl of your own race, a girl who understands a man like yourself, believes the same as you. This saves much heartache over the years, Ramon. And I think that once you marry Elena and share her bed, you will discover what a good wife she can be, and you will be loved just as much as the *gringa* would have loved you—perhaps more, because the white woman comes from a different world, Ramon. The difference between you would one day have caused problems."

Ramon shook his head and turned away. "Not with Irene. If you knew her, you would know what I mean." He put his head back, looking up at a crucifix. "It does not matter now. I will not shame the family and cause you again to be sent running and wandering. Now that I am here, it is a little easier. I know I must forget Irene, or at least set her aside in my heart and make room for Elena."

Miguel touched his arm. "You are not the first Vallejo to marry on a promise, *mi nieto*. My marriage to your grandmother was arranged, and we had fifty happy years together. I learned to love her more than my own life, especially when she gave me sons and daughters. It will be this way for you and Elena."

Ramon turned to face him. "You are not angry with me?"

Miguel smiled. "No. A little disappointed, perhaps; but you have learned a good lesson, Ramon, and you have proven your family pride and loyalty, proven what a strong man you are to be able to turn away from this great desire for the sake of the family, and for Elena's sake. She would be heartbroken if she knew, Ramon, as heartbroken as you feel right now. You must never tell her about this other woman."

The old man reached out and embraced his grandson. "I will not tell her," Ramon said quietly. They remained in an embrace for several seconds, Miguel patting Ramon's back.

Finally Ramon pulled away, his eyes wet with tears of determination and hurt pride. "I am going back to Denver after we are married, *abuelo*."

Miguel looked alarmed. "Why, Ramon? It will only make this harder for you."

Ramon shook his head, turning to pace. "I am going back. I have something to prove now, to myself and to Irene's mother. I have seen and felt the power of wealth, and I will never again let someone threaten me the way Beatrice Kirkland threatened me." He faced his grandfather again. "I am going back to finish what I started, *abuelo*. I am going to build my own business, and one day I will be as wealthy as the Kirklands! No *gringa* will look down on me again and think of me as a 'poor Mexican.'" He spoke the words with bitter resolve, and Miguel saw a new fire in his grandson's eyes.

"Be careful, *mi nieto*. *Un gringo rico* can be dangerous. To try to move into their world will not be easy."

"Nothing could be more difficult than giving up Irene Kirkland. Her mother thinks she has discouraged me, but she has only made me more determined!"

Miguel searched his grandson's dark, proud eyes. "Do it the right way, Ramon, with honor. Do not stoop to the ways of the *gringo*, cheating and lying to get what you want."

Ramon breathed deeply. "Do not worry, *abuelo*. I do not need to resort to such things to prove the worth of a Vallejo."

Miguel smiled. "Of course you don't. Come back to Hacienda del Sur with me now. We have wedding plans to make. Tonight you will drink much wine and think only about Elena and the fact that tomorrow she will become your wife. We will have a grand fiesta! She is so beautiful, Ramon. She will help you forget. Soon you will desire only Elena."

They both turned, kneeling and making the sign of the cross. "Good-bye, *mi querida,*" Ramon said silently, feeling as though someone was squeezing his heart in a vise. "*Yo te amo. Para siempre.*" He would be saying these words tomorrow to Elena, vowing to love her forever; but only he and his grandfather would know he had already said them to someone else, and even his grandfather did not understand that Irene Kirkland would always remain first in his heart. He left the chapel, wondering if he had made a decision he would regret for the rest of his life.

Irene walked to a window, looking to the higher bluffs where the new house sat. Now that Ramon was gone, the house meant nothing to her. She didn't even want to move into it, because every time she looked at the beautifully carved beams and fireplace frames and mantels, she would think of Ramon.

Someone knocked at the door, and she pulled her robe closer and retied it before opening the door to see her father standing there. Ever since his friend Red McKinley had come to visit two days ago, Kirk had improved with astounding rapidity.

"How are you feeling, honey?" Kirk asked, coming into the room. It tore at his heart to see the circles under her eyes and to notice she had lost weight.

"Better," she answered. "I . . . don't know what happened. I must have had some kind of influenza. It's just taking time for me to get over it."

"Well, I have an idea," Kirk told her, taking her hands. His blue eyes sparkled as they always did when he was preparing to go back into the mountains. Irene knew he and his friend were leaving the next day, against Bea's wishes. "I'm thinking maybe that mountain air would be good for you like it is for me. You've begged me for years to take you with me to the mines. So what do you think? You want to come along?"

He saw a light in her eyes that he had not seen since she was younger and went riding with him. "Father! Do you mean it?"

He winked. "You bet I do. With Red coming along, you'll have all the protection you need."

She smiled, and it felt good. "What about Mother? Won't she be angry?"

"Since when do I let that bother me?"

Irene laughed and hugged him. "Actually, for some strange

reason, your mother didn't object," Kirk told her. "I guess she's getting tired of arguing with me, and she's a little worried about you. She knows how much you've wanted to do this, so I guess she agreed it might be a good way to get you back to your old self."

"Oh, I have to go and thank her," Irene said, little realizing her mother was allowing the trip only to soothe her own guilty conscience. She had secretly but deliberately hurt Irene, and she had not liked doing it. But it was done now, and she could hardly bear the girl's obvious and utter sorrow.

"Just this one time," she had told Kirk. "Chad is anxious to begin calling on her more often, and in a few weeks I'll be having her party."

Bea appeared at the doorway then, feeling a secret relief at Irene's joy. Irene embraced her. "Thank you for letting me go, Mother."

Bea felt a lump in her throat as she managed to hug the girl in return. "Well, I don't totally approve, but then again one other person in the family ought to become familiar with the mines and how they're operated. If it makes you happier, then that's all that matters."

Elly listened outside the door, seething with a new jealousy. John and Irene were both getting more involved in the family businesses, but because she was still considered too young, she once more felt left out. It was bad enough that she was being slighted, but again her father was showing everyone that Irene was his favorite. She stomped off to her room while Irene turned to hug her father again. "Oh, I have to get ready!"

"Myra and I will get everything packed that you need, and your father will see to packing the right gear on Sierra," Bea told her. "You, child, will rest one more day. This will not be an easy trip for you after being so sick."

"Oh, I feel much better already," Irene answered as her mother herded her back to bed. She climbed in, and Bea leaned down to kiss her cheek, a rare affectionate gesture that made Irene wonder again at the strange looks Bea often gave her, as though she felt almost guilty about something. "I'll have Elsa bring up some lunch," she told Irene.

"Thank you," her daughter answered, blowing a kiss to her father as Kirk left the room. Bea went out behind him, and Irene closed her eyes, breathing deeply with joy. Nothing anyone did could have helped ease her sorrow the way this news had. She realized she must try to get over Ramon, and it would help to get out of the house and do something new and exciting. To ride Sierra into the mountains alongside her father was to her the most wonderful adventure she could ever imagine.

She turned on her side, thinking about Ramon, wondering if he had truly gone back to Hacienda del Sur. Would he marry Elena? The ache of it was getting only slightly easier to bear. She could not hate him, for she was sure it was just as John had said. Ramon must have thought he was doing the right thing. It was her only consolation.

She had no idea Ramon was also lying in bed at the same moment, studying the bare shoulders of his new wife. She had given herself to him with such utter abandon, had allowed him to bring her pain when he took her virgin body the night before, all the while not realizing that in his heart and mind he was kissing another woman, cupping another woman's breasts in his hands, invading another woman's body. He wondered if God would forgive him for his adulterous thoughts, and he decided he had better go to confession.

Elena awakened and turned, meeting his eyes with love and trust in her own. She smiled, touching his hair. "My handsome Ramon. It is hard to believe you are my husband. *Yo te amo, querido.*"

Ramon smiled, leaning to kiss her mouth tenderly. "*Mi querida Elena.*" He moved on top of her, loving her for her innocent trust and utter devotion. He would make love to her again, and this time, for Elena, he would think only of her, see only her, be one only with Elena. A good Catholic husband did not cheat on his wife. He had not done so physically, but in his mind and heart he had, and he vowed it would not happen again. Elena was his wife now. It was done.

PART

THREE

The mountains rise to protect me,
> To hold me fast.
They surround me like a fortress;
Their valleys and canyon floors cradle me.
Their bright colors comfort me, and
Their wildlife sings to me.
> I belong here.
My soul comes from these mountains;
And someday, when death claims me,
I will become a part of their glory—
>> Howling with the wolves,
>> Singing with the birds,
>> Smiling with the wildflowers.
>> I belong here.

CHAPTER
TWELVE

Irene had never felt more alive, more at home. Here in these mountains she found a new strength. It was easier now to understand why her father preferred to be here rather than in the increasingly congested city, with all its constant movement and business and pressures, the litter and the noise.

There was a kind of peace here, perhaps because one felt closer to God when at elevations so high they sometimes rode through clouds. This was different from traveling through the Sierras and northern Rockies to get to Denver from California. Because of her mother's fussing and Elly's eternal complaining, let alone the worry over accidents and the noise involved in hauling the huge freight wagons, there had been little time to truly enjoy the mountains, to sit quietly beside a campfire and listen to the night sounds that would frighten her if her father and Red McKinley were not beside her.

Irene enjoyed nothing more than sitting beside those nightly fires listening to Kirk and Red talk about the old days, rehashing some of their adventures. Irene developed a new respect for her father when she realized just how skilled and brave a man he must have been back then, especially when Red told her about how Kirk had fought off Crow Indians to save his life.

Irene had heard many of the stories before, but Red, who liked to brag much more than Kirk, revealed details that Kirk had left out. Where Kirk had simply said he once fought several Crow Indians at once to save a friend, Red offered the exciting details, describing how Kirk had landed a rifle butt into one brave, turned it and fired into the next man's "brisket," which she now knew meant his belly, and rammed a hunting knife into another. Kirk would just sit quietly shaking his head, embarrassed, begging Red not to go into the gory details. But Irene wanted to hear those details, and she sat enraptured, for Red McKinley was indeed a good storyteller.

Sometimes when she lay back in her bedroll, as she did now, the fire dimmed and her father and Red sleeping, Irene thought how easy it would be to always live this way. She wondered sometimes why she should have such feelings, for she had been raised to lead a pampered life with all the comforts the daughter of wealthy parents was expected to have. Yet she felt as natural living out here in the wild as the animals . . . or the Indians. She could understand better now why they loved this land so much, why they did not want to give up the land or the kind of life they had led for centuries.

Everything seemed so much clearer up here. It was as though the mountain air made her senses more alert, made many things easier to understand. Her father had mentioned more than once that moving the Indians to the hotter, drier land to the southeast would kill them just as surely as putting a gun to their heads. Now she understood why, and she felt truly sorry for them and a little guilty for being one of the many who were settling on their land, covering it with offices and houses and shops, bringing in thousands of whites and forcing the Indians out. It was no wonder they tried to retaliate.

She pulled her blankets closer around her face against the chilly mountain air. She had enjoyed another night of storytelling, her belly pleasantly full of rabbit cooked over an open fire, her blood warm from hot coffee. She listened to the night sounds: an owl, then the lonesome wail of a wolf, soon answered by another.

Other than the occasional sounds of night roamers and the soft hum of a light wind moving through the pines, this was the quietest place she had ever been. Down in the city there was always noise—dogs barking, pigs squealing, horses whinnying, wagons rattling, people milling about. It seemed as though every week more people came to Denver, not just prospectors now, but refugees from a battered South who had lost homes and farms and loved ones because of the war. It was sad to see. Because she lived in the West, and especially up in the mountains, the Civil War seemed so far away, as though it wasn't really happening to her own country. But then she remembered that her own father had come close to dying because of that war.

She was glad to be away from all that now, glad to see the life coming back into her father's eyes. Yes, this was where men such as David Kirkland belonged. She wondered why on earth he had decided to marry her mother and settle down to have a family. Realizing how much he apparently loved his freedom, it seemed strange that he had given it all up to live a life totally contrary to what he had always known. Had he loved her mother that much? If he had, why didn't she treat him better than she did? Would she be angry with him forever for those first couple of hard winters in the Sierras?

She sighed deeply, deciding she would probably never understand, afraid to ask her father personal questions. But she was tormented by his comment to her mother about living a lie. What lie? She couldn't ask, because she didn't want him to know she had heard.

Secrets. Maybe most people had secrets. After all, she had her own. She had secretly loved a Mexican man. The adventure of coming to the mountains had helped ease the hurt of it, but she knew it would never go away completely. Every time she closed her eyes she remembered that kiss, remembered the feel of Ramon's soft lips gently searching her mouth so that she burned for him, felt totally at his mercy, unable to think, to resist.

She knew now it would not be difficult to give herself to such a man. She wondered if it had been that way for her parents once, but it embarrassed her to think about it. She knew what people did to get babies, but she could not picture her mother and father doing that. She had so many questions about love and sex and marriage, but there was no one to ask. Was it this way for all women? Did they all simply learn about such things on their wedding nights?

She watched the stars, thinking of Ramon again. With Ramon she would have feared nothing on her wedding night. A tear slipped down the side of her face. She rubbed at it. Was Ramon thinking of her tonight? She swallowed back a lump in her throat, deciding she must learn to stop thinking about him. She had probably been crazy to think there ever could have been anything between them. Ramon knew it. That was why he had left, it had to be. If only he had talked to her about it first, at least told her good-bye and that he would always love her the way she was sure she would always love him.

A wolf gave out another long howl that moved through the mountains as a spirit might. Its call reminded her of how lonesome she felt—crying out, but there was no one to listen. She closed her eyes, deciding she must learn to be stronger, like her parents. Both of them were very strong in their own ways.

She wished she were older. It seemed that adults were better able to accept things they could not change, able to handle heartaches and setbacks. She turned her thoughts to Chad and the way he had embraced her for a moment when they were alone, just before she left with her father. He had seemed sincerely sorry to see her go, sincerely worried that she would be all right. He had kissed her cheek, and when she looked into his eyes she saw a very handsome man who had saved her father's life. Chad was everything a woman was supposed to want, and she told herself that as time passed and she got over Ramon, she would surely begin to feel the same passion and desire for Chad as she had felt for Ramon.

She closed her eyes, trying to concentrate on Chad, but always another face came to mind: dark eyes, dark hair, a man of gentle voice and gentle touch, a man she loved but could not have.

If ever a place could be called God's country, Irene decided, this was it. They followed a constantly climbing pathway that zigzagged along the side of a mountain, heading toward Central City, where Kirk owned several mines. They were following a train of supply wagons belonging to the Pikes Peak Express Company, which was the primary freighting company for most of the mountain mining towns, as well as their connection to Denver and the rest of the world.

Up here, Irene thought, it seemed there was no "rest of the world." She could see how easy it might be for a man to come up here and almost forget everything and everyone he left behind, and she still worried sometimes that Kirk might come up here and never return. Perhaps that was why her mother was so intent on making sure the family holdings remained intact, in case she was ever left alone again to care for her children. But Irene had come to know her father better on this trip, had come to realize he was more wonderful even than she had already thought. She wondered why her mother could not seem to see that. The whole family could have been so much happier if Bea would learn to be more like Kirk, to enjoy her life.

"Hold back a little, Irene," Kirk told her then, pulling up his horse. "Let that last wagon get through there first."

She watched, her heart tight with apprehension, as the last of the long line of freight wagons passed over one of the narrowest sections of the road, if it could be called a road. It was really nothing more than a pathway hacked out of the side of a mountain, parts of it natural, most of it man-made. This particular section had a gouge that cut into the outer edge of the road, creating a narrower path, barely wide enough for the wagons.

"Had a rock slide in here last year," Kirk explained. "One big boulder landed there, breaking away the road. I hired some men to come back down here and cut into the mountain more to widen it in the other direction, but I guess they haven't made it yet. I'll have to check into it."

Irene breathed a sigh of relief when the last wagon made it through. She looked down into a canyon that seemed a thousand feet deep. A river raged at the bottom, its torrent echoing in a rumble up through the canyon to those above. Irene realized that if a wagon went over here, nothing and no one would survive. They had already passed an area where the remnants of another wagon could be spotted on a rocky shelf several hundred feet below.

This was wild, dangerous country, but the most beautiful country Irene had ever seen. Brilliant, billowing waterfalls cascaded over rocks worn smooth from the water's beating. The misty spray from the raging waters often created rainbows when the sun shone on them just right. The air was filled with the smell of sweet pine, and silvery aspen leaves waved and glittered in the wind. She had seen bear, elk, deer, moose, and even a mountain lion, as well as an abundance of smaller animals. She had seen eagles soar, and her heart had soared with them. How she longed to live as they did, high in rocky peaks, free and wild, in total control.

Nature answered to no one. Nature did as it pleased. Animals roamed at will, and rocks came tumbling from precarious perches. She found it incredible that some of the overhanging rocks remained stationary. They looked ready to let loose at any moment, and sometimes they did. Rocks were everywhere, from immense boulders to tiny stones. Here and there a scraggly pine seemed to grow right out of rock.

Wildflowers amid an array of red, gray, pink, and white rocks turned mountainsides into a kaleidoscope of color. Surrounding mountains rose in purple and gray granite walls to snow-capped peaks that sparkled against a deep blue sky. The land was a shower of colors, a grand collection of sights and sounds unlike anything she had ever seen. For once she could quietly enjoy these mountains, take time to really see and listen and touch.

Irene was not afraid of the dangerous pathways. After all, she was with Kirk, and he had moved among these mountains nearly all his life. He knew what to watch for, sensed when a rock above them might give way, could smell danger. He sniffed out wild game to kill for their suppers, knew what swollen streams to stay away from, knew caves where a person could hole up when weather was bad.

"I love it up here, Father," she spoke up as he took hold of Sierra's bridle and led her past the narrow cutaway over which the last wagon had just passed.

"I knew you would," he answered, glancing at Red. Both men knew why Irene Kirkland loved the mountains, loved nature and felt at home up here. Part of her should be living free and wild, as did the Indian brother she would never know. The same old agony tore through Kirk's gut again. He felt like a traitor to his own daughter, wondered if he was doing her a disservice but afraid it was far too late to hit her with the truth now. At her tender age it could be devastating.

"I hope I get to come back again," she was saying.

"Well, your mother has a lot of things planned for you over the next couple of years," Kirk answered. "But maybe we can work something out. You need to see and understand all this, Irene, but you also need to be learning the business end of it, like John is doing, and someday Elly. And your mother wants you to be educated in the proper social etiquette, and all that. I don't much care about those things, but your mother does, and you're sure enough the most beautiful, gracious young lady in all of Denver, I'll grant that."

She blushed a little, embarrassed because of Red's presence. She liked Red McKinley and his sing-song Irish accent. He was entertaining, humorous, good-natured; she liked him most of all because he was her father's good friend.

"Someday they'll bring the railroad to Denver, Kirk," the man was saying, "and the next thing you know they'll find a way to bring trains into these mountains and do away with those freight wagons."

"You and your railroads," Kirk answered, shaking his head. "You told me that years ago, and I still don't see anybody laying tracks into Denver. As far as the mountains, that's impossible. They'll never lay track into country like this."

"Ah, nothing is impossible, my friend. You should know that by now. And they're already laying track across Kansas. You mark my words, David Kirkland. Buy up some land anywhere that you think a railroad might come through, and you won't go wrong. It will be right valuable when they bring the trains through."

Kirk just laughed. "I'll think about that."

"Think hard, my friend. I see Denver already has a foundry, and another factory making shot and shell, as well as a candle factory, and a soap factory. And there you are with all those warehouses full of fine goods from the west coast. Just think. If the railroad came to Denver, you could end up shipping your fancy things from China and such places by land all the way to places like Chicago and St. Louis. You wouldn't have to depend on ships to take them all the way around Cape Horn, or pay those high freighting costs by wagon, with no guarantee your goods will get there. The railroad is fast and safe."

Kirk frowned. "By God, you have a point there, Red."

"You see? I predict there will be a railroad coming all the way across the country some day—coast to coast. Think what *that* would do for your business, and for Denver."

Kirk glanced back at the man. "Red, I never thought you had a head for business. When did you start thinking about all this?"

"Why, I've thought about it for years."

Kirk turned around to keep his eyes on the steep road ahead, slowing his horse again and telling Irene to stop for a minute. "That one section around the next curve is a real steep climb," he explained. "Wait till the wagons get through. There's always a danger one will break loose. If we stay around the bend here, it won't come plowing into us and send us into eternity."

Irene smiled, holding up her horse and drinking in the scenery below. She could see the winding road and its hairpin turns below her, feeling a chill at being able to look down and see where they had just been. The road formed a ribbonlike curl, making its way ever upward.

Kirk took a thin cigar from his coat pocket and lit it. "Red, you're a forward-thinking man. If you want to set up a business in Denver, I'll gladly back you. I'd like you to stay around. What do you say?"

"I told you once I didn't come here for a loan. Hell, Kirk, I didn't even know you were *in* Denver when I first got here."

"Doesn't matter. Fact remains, you seem ready to settle in some, and I like having you around. I don't want you working for me. You can do better than that. And don't tell me you haven't thought about this. That's why you're telling me all these wonderful stories about how the railroad is going to come through and Denver is going to grow. What's on your mind?"

Red grinned, looking a little embarrassed. "Well, actually I was thinking about starting up a lumber mill. I worked for a while for a logging company in Oregon, got to know how a lumber mill operates. With all the building that's going on in Denver, how can I go wrong? I could lumber out pine from the foothills, and I could ship in raw hardwood from Oregon, Minnesota, Wisconsin, Michigan, places like that. It's cheaper if you just order in the logs and do the milling and cutting locally. That way, people who are in a hurry to build this or that don't have to wait for an order of finished wood from back East. Half the time a shipment comes in cut all wrong anyway. I could cut lumber to their specifications right there in Denver and get it to them right away."

Kirk shook his head. "I'm impressed, Red. It amazes me that you had all this in mind."

"Hell, I just never cared before. I've reached the point now where I *have* to care."

Kirk took a puff on the cigar. "Well, I agree about the lumber mill. I don't see how you could go wrong myself."

Red removed his hat, running a hand through his thinning red hair. "It will take some cash, Kirk. I'll need steam-powered cutting saws, carpenter tools, a building to work in, hired help—"

Kirk waved him off. "How much, Red?"

Red rubbed at his chin. "You figuring on me borrowing through your bank? I'm not sure your wife would approve of that. I've got no collateral, Kirk."

"No bank loan. You'd have to pay a high interest rate. I'll make you a personal loan, at only two percent interest. And I'll give you time to get into operation before you have to pay anything back. And don't worry about my wife. I'll take care of that end of it."

Irene wondered how the man was going to do that. She knew her mother well enough to know she would be furious with Kirk for this. She almost felt sorry for her father, knowing how Bea would react. She loved the man for he understood some things were more important than money; she knew her mother had no such philosophy. She remembered when she was very small, back in California, when Bea worked such long hours she hardly ever got to see her. She remembered Bea bringing in more gold to hide under the floorboard. She handled that gold almost as if it were sacred.

"I'd need a good ten thousand dollars just to get started," Red was telling Kirk.

"I'll make it fifteen," Kirk answered. "I have a separate account Bea keeps open to be used to invest in new mines and such. I'll take it out of that."

Red shook his head. "I don't know. I don't want to make trouble between you and your wife. You ought to talk to her about it first."

"Not when it comes to my personal friends. Besides, it's left up to me to decide what to do with that money. My wife handles the bookwork, but only because I'm up here most of the time. I still have the last word. Fact is, I thought about the logging business back in California, but I knew I didn't want to stay there, so I never got involved. Since we've been here, we've had our hands in so many other pots there hasn't been time to think about a lumber mill. I'll just call it an investment." He maneuvered his horse back to Red and put out his hand. "A deal?"

Red's eyes showed his gratefulness. He took Kirk's hand. "Only if you agree to take a percentage of the profits over and above my payments to you, until the debt is paid back in full."

"Forget it. It's all the same thing," Kirk answered, squeezing the man's hand. "Just pay it back as fast as you can without jeopardizing the business."

"I don't feel completely right about this, Kirk."

Kirk released his hand and took the cigar from his mouth. "What sense is there in being rich if you can't share it with your friends?" he answered. "Just think of it as doing something for me, instead of the other way around. It always bothers me a little to be rolling around in this money without sharing it with people who need help."

Red did not doubt that Beatrice Kirkland did *not* share her husband's outlook on friends and money. "Well, you have your lawyers draw up the right papers and all—"

"To hell with that," Kirk answered, sticking the cigar back between his teeth. "Your word is good enough. Let's get going. Those wagons ought to be over that steep climb by now. We've got to make Central City by nightfall."

Red sighed, putting his hat back on. Irene was almost sure she saw tears in his eyes. She looked away so that she would not embarrass the man, and she rode up beside her father. "Mother won't like what you did," she said quietly.

Kirk laughed, almost bitterly. "I do a lot of things your mother doesn't like." He looked over at her, realizing that on this trip he would not be able to visit the whores because of Irene. It didn't really matter. He was proud and happy to have his daughter with him. "You remember what happened here, Irene. There's nothing wrong with having money, and I expect the way things are growing, you and your brother and sister will be even wealthier than we are now, if you handle things right. Just don't be stingy with it, Irene. If you can't use it to help somebody who needs it, there's no sense having it at all."

"I'll remember," she told him.

He gave her a smile that told her how much he loved her. "I expect I didn't have to tell you that," he answered. "You're a good woman, Irene, and I'm real proud to have you with me."

"I'm proud to *be* with you," she answered.

He gave her a wink. "Let's get to Central City," he said then. "If we're going to be giving money away, we have to be *making* money, right? With those new gold discoveries in Idaho and Montana, we can't let investors and the like forget we've got plenty of gold right here. We've got to keep the mines operating and do what we can to find new veins. Follow me, child, and I'll show you the source of most of the Kirkland money."

Irene smiled, heading around the frighteningly steep curve, wondering if there really was an end to this pathway to the clouds.

Never had Irene had such an adventure. For the rest of her life she would remember the wild and raucous mining towns of Colorado's endless mountains. Before the trip was over, she had seen Boulder, Canon City, Black Hawk, Nevada City, Idaho Springs, Georgetown, and Empire City. The biggest city she had seen besides Denver itself was Central City, which Kirk told her was always in competition with Denver but was too high in the mountains to hope to grow as fast. "Too many transportation problems," Kirk told her.

Problems or not, Central City was a bustling town with nearly as many buildings and people as Denver. Some of the richest gold mines were there, and Irene discovered the Kirklands owned several of the businesses in Central City in addition to the Elly May and Johnny Boy mines.

Every town they visited was a conglomeration of shacks and cabins, tents and stores, with nearly every other sign reading Saloon. They were not much different from those in Denver, except that they were smaller and even less refined. The streets were filled with speculators, surveyors, gamblers, whores, thieves, merchants, and prospectors. Kirk kept her close, and seldom did she see a church or a man of the cloth, and in most cases, very few women, except for the painted ones who hung around every boardwalk. A few called out to her father. It embarrassed Irene, but she asked no questions.

"You spend much time in these mining towns, everybody begins to know your name," Kirk tried to explain once, "even those fancy women. Don't be getting ideas, Irene. Everybody knows who I am, that's all."

"I wasn't thinking anything, Father," she lied. Somewhere deep inside she suspected it was more than that. The thought hurt, yet she could not totally blame her father. She knew how the man was treated at home, suspected her parents' bedroom life was not what she guessed it should be between a man and his wife.

Her mind whirled with questions and confusion. She wanted to understand these things. What did it take to please a man, or did it even matter? She thought of Ramon again. She knew in her heart a man like Ramon would never visit painted women once he was married, but then he surely had a way of bringing out great love and passion in a woman. Her father was wonderful, too. In her mind he was so easy to love. Why was her mother so cold toward him? Maybe if she treated him differently, he wouldn't be so familiar with these painted women. What happened to married people that caused them to go their separate ways?

The noisy towns were a stark contrast to the peaceful mountains that surrounded them. The mines were even noisier. Kirk took her to the Elly May, where she visited the mining shaft house. A steam-driven hoist rumbled as the cable it supported raised and lowered cages carrying men to incredible depths and brought both men and ore back to the surface. Irene begged to be allowed to go down into one of the mines, but Kirk would not hear of it.

"If something happened to you down there, your mother would take a shotgun to me. Maybe when you're older."

The shaft house seemed quiet compared to the processing mill, where huge steam-driven crushers broke the rough ore into smaller pieces, which in turn were mixed with water and smashed under half-ton stamps. Irene had to plug her ears against the noise. The mixture of water and crushed ore was sifted through screens and dropped onto wide belts called vanners, which oscillated the mixture, winnowing out lead and leaving only gold and even some silver. This, Kirk explained, was dumped into amalgamating pans and cooked with mercury and other chemicals for at least eight hours, then transferred to settling tanks.

For the first time Irene understood the complexities of mining. She had envisioned men shoveling gold out of the mountains' depths but had given no thought to the complicated process of gleaning pure gold from the ore that was mined.

"It's placer mining that gives you the pure stuff," Kirk explained. "Nature does the filtering and processing for you. But a man can spend his life sifting dirt from a streambed and never make enough to live on. Once you find gold in a stream, it's the richer vein where it's coming from that you want to look for. And the real key then is to have enough money to process it yourself. That's where your mother helped back in the beginning in California. It was the money she earned taking in wash that helped us to be able to mine out our own gold."

"Shouldn't Mother come up here and see all this?" Irene asked.

Kirk shook his head. "I've tried to get her to come, but she wants nothing to do with this end of it, especially nothing to do with coming into the mountains. She leaves all of it to me, says as long as the mines are producing, that's all she cares about. And she's smart enough to know these mines aren't going to hold out forever. You remember that. It's wise to invest in other things that will tide you over when the mines play out."

Kirk was literally yelling the words in order to be heard above the machinery. He led Irene outside, and she thought how sad it was that her mother refused to share this part of her father's life.

It seemed everywhere they went, everyone knew and liked David Kirkland. It felt strange to Irene to realize most of the men she met worked for her father, which meant someday they would work for her. "Remember to keep the men who work for you happy, Irene," Kirk told her. "These are hard men who won't be put upon. I expect good labor, and they expect to get treated right in return. I listen to complaints, hire the best cooks, and I try not to make them work too many hours at a time. It can get to a man being down under the earth most of the day."

Red took in the vast Kirkland empire in awe, overwhelmed at what Kirk had ammassed but sure it was mostly due to his wife. This was not Kirk. He wondered if Irene realized how much the man must love her, for all of this came from the day Gray Bird Woman had placed a baby girl in Kirk's arms.

"We'll head south now," Kirk was telling her. "You up to a couple more weeks of this?"

"I could stay up here forever," she answered.

Kirk grinned, mounting his horse. "Well, before I take you back, you ought to see the mine named after you. It's down near

Pikes Peak. I'll show you Colorado City, but it's a pretty wild place, so you stick by me and Red, like always."

Kirk had not missed the looks Irene got from men. His heart swelled with pride at her beauty, and he was constantly alert for her welfare, putting her up in the best hotels when they were in mining towns, taking turns with Red keeping guard when they were camped away from towns. He realized that most who knew him would never think of harming his daughter, but in such wild places there were plenty of men with no respect for anyone's honor. He knew that in one sense Bea had been right to hide the girl's true heritage. For some men her Indian blood would only mean she was beneath respect.

"Next year I'll bring John up here," he said aloud.

"Yes, you should," Irene answered, but her mind was not on John. Her heart raced with the realization they were headed south—toward Pikes Peak. Hacienda del Sur lay somewhere in that area. Just to be in the same vicinity would bring back the heartache.

More and more, in her own heart she realized perhaps it could not have worked after all. She had been awakened to the tremendous responsibilities that would one day be put on her shoulders, and in spite of the hurt, she realized that not burdening her parents with news of her love for Ramon was probably the right thing to do.

She saw the bigger picture now, knew what was expected of her; and she realized that wealth brought certain expectations, certain rules and responsibilities that she and John and Elly were expected to take upon themselves. She did not really care that much for riches, but neither did she have the heart to disappoint her parents by turning away from all they had worked to build—for their children—and she realized almost grimly that perhaps it would not be possible to live her life totally as she wished. Apparently Ramon had already realized that.

She wanted to cry. She did not want to leave these mountains and go back to the pressures of life back home. She glanced at her father. Yes, she understood more and more why he came to these mountains. He had the freedom to run away from things that hurt him, from leading a life he probably hated. Was that how it would be for her, too?

She headed Sierra back down the steep, winding road that had brought them here, feeling driven by wheels of fate that she could not control.

• • •

It was warmer and drier in the Pikes Peak area, but as always, much cooler in the higher elevations where the Irene Louise mine was located. Irene could not get over the uncanny feeling that this was where she belonged, that she had actually walked this land before.

From the mine site she could look across a sea of swelling mountain peaks, with the Sangre de Cristo mountain range stretched out far to the southwest. When one was in these mountains, it was difficult to believe there could be an end to them. From every mining town she had seen nothing but endless peaks spread out in all directions, and she wondered how on earth her father had lived in these mountains without getting lost or killed.

Her heart swelled with awe at the majesty and beauty of Colorado. California and the Sierras had also been beautiful, but her constant feeling of belonging here made this land seem more beautiful to her; and she vowed to find a way to come into the mountains more often. She felt a certain peace and comfort here she found nowhere else. She knew she would go back a stronger person, now able to bear the painful loss of Ramon.

They moved out of the mountains into a sprawling, scrub-covered valley east of Pikes Peak. Irene wondered just where Hacienda del Sur was located but was afraid to ask.

"Your mother has talked about investing in more land this way," Kirk told Irene. "But a lot of people don't think it will ever be worth much, and I don't like the idea of displacing the Mexicans who are settled in through here. 'Course, considering your mother's nose for good investments, she's probably right about this area being valuable someday. We'll visit the potato farm. She's figuring on expanding that."

They rode on, and Irene felt like a tiny speck in the middle of such an immense land. She realized how much this land fit her father, for just like David Kirkland, everything about Colorado was big. A herd of deer skitted across the sage- and rock-covered land ahead of them. They rode east of the Rockies which lay in one long, dark, endless range to the west. When Irene looked at them, it was difficult to realize she had actually been in those mountains, in places so high she thought she should have been able to see God.

When leaving Pikes Peak to come into the grassland, they had moved through some of the most beautiful country she had ever seen, a feast of color and red-rock formations for the eyes to behold, contrasted with deep green, pine-covered foothills that led into the wide-open spaces of eastern Colorado. It actually hurt to have to leave any of it. Although the land was just as beautiful around Denver, she hated the thought of going back in that noisy, dirty town with its dusty streets and too many people. Most of all, she hated returning to everyday life, to making decisions she didn't want to make, to being the woman she was expected to be now.

Kirk slowed his horse as he saw a herd of cattle approaching from the north, several men whistling and shouting to keep the animals together. As they came closer, one of them nodded to Kirk and Red, calling out "Hello there!"

Irene stared in fascination. She had never seen anyone quite like him. He wore high leather boots and some kind of leather protection over the front of his pant legs. She had no idea what they were, but she suspected their purpose was to protect the man's pants from the scrubby brush scattered everywhere in this particular part of Colorado. He was tall and well built, his skin tanned dark from long exposure to the sun, and his features were honed hard and lean. He sported a wide, brilliant smile, as he put his hand out to Kirk. His handsome face and thick, dark hair were framed by a wide-brimmed hat.

Kirk shook the man's hand. "Hank Loring's the name," the man told him. He glanced at Irene, and she was stunned by soft green eyes that awakened womanly instincts deep inside her with almost as much force as Ramon's brown ones had. She instinctively sensed he was impressed with what he saw, but he quickly looked away again. "I don't think I've seen you folks around here," he told Kirk. "I bring some of my cattle out this way to graze on government land, and some of them stray a little too far."

"I'm David Kirkland," Kirk answered. "This here is my friend Red McKinley and my daughter Irene. I own a mine named after her up around Pikes Peak—brought Irene here to see it. We're headed out to take a look at a potato farm we own a little farther north."

Loring pushed back his hat. "So, you're *that* Kirkland!" He shook his head. "Well, I'll be damned. I know where the potato farm is. I've heard all about the Kirklands. I expect I'm talking to the richest man in Colorado."

Kirk laughed. "I don't know about that. Your ranch near the potato farm?"

"A few miles this way of it, more in the foothills." Irene watched him as he talked, instantly liking this Hank Loring, whose friendliness was unmistakably genuine. She thought for a moment what a solid, honest man he seemed to be, much like her father. "We've filed legal claim to the land," he was saying, "seeing as how there's all this talk about the Homestead Act and all. I don't want to get run over by newcomers. The cattle industry is growing, you know. I figure it's going to move into a real boom once the war is over, especially when they bring in the railroad."

Kirk glanced at Red, who laughed and said, "What did I tell you?"

"Well, you're probably right," Kirk answered Loring, looking back at the man. "Nice to meet you. If my wife has her way, you'll probably find yourself surrounded by Kirkland land some day."

"Long as you leave *me* enough," the man answered.

"Father," Irene spoke up, unable to control her curiosity. "Remember Ramon Vallejo? Isn't his grandfather's hacienda somewhere around here? John might ask me if we saw it."

"Oh, Hacienda del Sur is a little south of Pikes Peak, nestled in the foothills there," Loring answered. "Beautiful area. I know the grandfather, Miguel Vallejo. A fine man. Fact is, my wife and I attended quite a fiesta there a few weeks ago. Ramon got married. Beautiful girl. They made quite a handsome couple."

Irene struggled to keep a smile on her face, but the remark had hit her so unexpectedly that she felt faint. Ramon, married! She had suspected it, but to hear it so bluntly, to know for certain. . . .

"How nice for him," she answered. "He . . . he did some work for us at a new house we're having built in Denver."

"Oh, Ramon has a great talent, doesn't he? I think he said something about returning to Denver to start his own business." He looked ahead where his men were herding the cattle farther south. "I'd better catch up. Nice meeting all of you," he said, nodding to Kirk then. "You folks ever settle this way, let me know if you need anything. My ranch is the Lazy L. Most folks around here know where it is and know me."

The man moved his eyes to Irene again, and for a moment she felt he knew her agony, somehow sensed her unhappiness, although he surely couldn't know why. Their eyes held for a moment. Irene had no idea that Hank Loring thought her the most beautiful woman he had ever set eyes on, in spite of the fact that he was married and loved his wife very much.

"Thank you," Irene told him.

He looked back at Kirk and Red, giving them a wave and riding off.

"That there is an example of a new breed of man that's taking over," Kirk told Irene, oblivious to the heartbreak she was suffering over Ramon. "First we had the mountain men and the scouts. Now it's the cowboy. I wouldn't put it past your mother to look into cattle ranching, once she suspects there's money in it." He turned his horse. "Let's get going, Irene. We've got to find the farm and get you back home. We've already been gone a week longer than planned. Your mother is probably having fits by now."

The two men rode off, and Irene took a moment to glance back at Hank Loring. To her surprise, he also turned to look. She waved, and he answered with his own wave, and she felt the oddest sensation that she would see him again. She turned and rode after her father, thinking how strange and different she had felt in the mountains and here in the foothills and plains, almost removed from the real Irene, the one who would have to find herself again when she got back to Denver.

One thing was sure. She must stop thinking about Ramon and get on with her life. There would never be anything more than that one lovely day, that glorious ride, that heroic deed, that warm kiss that had awakened a whole new world of womanly desires. She could not imagine that any man could make her feel quite the same way again. She glanced back once more, but Hank Loring was just a small dot on the vast horizon.

CHAPTER THIRTEEN

 "We can move into the house in another month," Bea told Kirk. "There will still be a few things to finish, but it's done enough that we can have Irene's party by mid-August. I've written to Cynthia again and invited her."

"She won't answer, Bea. She never answers."

"Maybe she will this time."

Kirk sighed. "Why can't you let it go, Bea?"

They lay in bed together, Kirk's first night back from the trip into the mountains. He did not want to talk about the new house or business. He wanted to tell his wife about his trip and Irene's experiences—all she had learned.

"I *can't* let it go," Bea answered bitterly.

"It's been over sixteen years. They've never written back or tried to see you."

"They're just jealous, and that's fine with me. I'll keep inviting them, to show how gracious I can be."

Kirk almost laughed, but he knew what a delicate subject it was with her. "Well, I'm glad you're finally able to move into your new house."

"*Our* house."

"Yours. I never wanted all that fancy stuff."

"You have to learn how important you are now, Kirk. People

expect men like you to live in houses like that. I'd like to have a welcoming ball for the new governor, too. John Evans is a wonderful choice, except that we would rather have had General Larimer. I think he was very disappointed. At any rate, Evans is a widower—such a tragic story. Lost his wife and three children when he was only twenty-three. He was a doctor then but gave it up, probably because he couldn't save his own family."

"Who told you all this?"

"We have to know everything about our new governor, Kirk. There are ways of finding out. At any rate, he went into real estate and is also quite involved with the railroad. That's good for Colorado. Everyone says the railroad will eventually come all the way to Denver."

Kirk laughed. "You, too?"

"What do you mean?"

"Red keeps harping about the railroad. He told me years ago he thought it would come all the way west some day. I didn't believe him then, but I do now, seeing as how it's already halfway through Kansas." He turned to her, moving one arm across her breasts, hoping to get no resistance.

Bea stiffened, sure the only reason he was being amorous was because on this trip he had been unable to sleep with the whores because of Irene. Still, it had been weeks since they had made love, and each time her husband needed her, she hoped this time she could respond as she should. Why did she always suddenly freeze at his touch? Would she never get over the shock and surprise of that first night? He had been kind and gentle, yet she could still feel the humiliation, the pain. Perhaps if she had been passionately in love instead of just wanting to consummate her marriage quickly, it would have been different for her.

"How are things at the mines?" she asked, leaving his arm where it was.

He settled his head on her pillow. "The Johnny Boy isn't yielding what it was, but it's still workable. I'm thinking of buying the Eagle and the Merry Widow mines down at Pikes Peak. I don't think the owners are getting the maximum out of those mines, and I've got a hunch they both have richer veins that haven't been found yet. I talked privately with some of the workers and they feel the same way."

"Do what you think best, but I think you ought to start paying those men in greenbacks instead of gold, Kirk. For every dollar in our own gold we pay out, we have to match from our own supply; but every dollar in paper money only costs us about ninety cents in gold, and the ratio is expected to widen even more. The dollar could go all the way down to fifty cents in gold or less."

"I won't pay those men in greenbacks. Most of them know good and well paper money is worth less. They'll have less buying power with greenbacks. I won't do that to them."

"Kirk, the war is creating a lot of inflation. We'll need as much pure gold for our own use as we can get. It will buy us a lot more to the dollar, and at the same time we'd be saving on the other end by paying the miners in greenbacks."

"I said I won't do it." Kirk pulled his arm away, disgusted that even at this intimate moment, lying in bed with her husband just home from a long absence, Bea Kirkland could talk about nothing but money. "Those men trust me," he told her. "And they're good workers. I'm not going to turn on them like that, and that's how they would look at it. It's important to have good, trustworthy men working those mines, Bea, and it's important to keep them happy. They get paid in gold and that's that."

"Some of the other mine owners are turning to paper money."

"And some of their workers talk about striking. I don't intend to get into a mess like that. Strikes can get pretty ugly. I usually go along with you on your decisions, but not this one. They get paid in gold."

She sighed resignedly, irritated by what she considered his stupidity. Kirk rubbed his eyes. "If you're worried about how to watch your dollar, I'd advise you to invest in more of that land to the south, long as you don't dislocate some of the Mexicans who have been settled there for years. I met a man by the name of Hank Loring, a rancher. He says the cattle industry is growing by leaps and bounds, and I believe him. If the railroad comes all the way through Kansas to Colorado, beef can be shipped east by train. Apparently people are acquiring a taste for it. Not much choice, what with buffalo and deer and other game getting harder to find every year. I hate to say it, but wild game is becoming a thing of the past. We've got to turn to tame meat, and there's no better land than out here for raising cattle. There isn't any place east of us with as much good grazing land."

She turned on her side to face him. "Are you sure it's not a risk?"

"I've been thinking on it all the way back from Pikes Peak. It takes lots of land, Bea, but this Loring thinks the demand for beef will go sky-high, especially after the war. Might not be a bad idea to lay claim to as much of that land south of here as we can. You've always said we have to keep branching out our investments for the day when the mines play out. And I see a lot of growth down around Colorado City."

She lay back into her pillow. "The Byers and a few of our friends have talked about how some of that area could be set up as a kind of resort area, since it's a little warmer and drier in the winter."

"It's real pretty country, Bea, but Colorado City is no place for proper ladies. It's a pretty wild town."

"Well then, maybe we can form our own little vacation community there. As for the cattle idea, you could be right. I'll look into it. I've been wanting to expand the farm, too. I'll have to get busy on it right away, now that the Homestead Act has been passed. Maybe with this new law, Denver can get rid of some of its vagrants. Every day new refugees come here, mostly homeless people from the South with hardly more than the clothes on their backs."

Kirk wondered when she had lost her understanding and sympathy for such people, if she ever had any. After all, she had been poor and homeless once herself.

"They can't help what happened to them."

"They shouldn't have started the war and seceded from the Union."

"That was all political. You can't blame individuals for that. Most of these people didn't want the war."

"Be that as it may, they're flooding Denver, just when we're managing to get rid of the vagrant Indians and Mexicans." She sniffed. "Maybe we could strike some kind of deal with this Hank Loring. If he knows about raising cattle, maybe he would consider overseeing a ranch for us for part of the profits, something like that. And your friend Red is right about the value of land rising if the railroad comes through, although I'm amazed a man like that thinks beyond the next five minutes."

She turned to face him, putting a hand on his arm. "I'll look into it. I may have to use part of the special fund I set aside for the investments you make in the mines. There should be plenty, even if you buy the Eagle and the Merry Widow."

Kirk moved away from her, sitting up and putting his feet over the side of the bed. He hadn't wanted to bring up the subject of Red's loan just yet, but now Bea had done it for him. "You'll have to dip into something else," he said carefully. "I loaned some of that money to Red McKinley. We stopped down at Kirkland Enterprises today before we got here and sealed the agreement."

She was silent for a moment, but he could feel her wrath hanging heavy in the air. He was glad it was dark so he didn't have to see

the look in her eyes. He remained on the edge of the bed, his back
to her, and he felt her move to sit up.

"You actually loaned money to that vagrant?"

"He's not a vagrant. He's a good man, and an old friend."

"My God," she muttered, moving off the bed. He heard her
pulling on her robe, and she turned up an oil lamp, coming around
to stand at the foot of the bed, her hand on the huge mahogany
bedpost. "How much? And what for?"

He looked up at her, then slowly rose. "Fifteen thousand, for a
lumber mill."

She literally paled, and her eyes widened with fury. "Fifteen
thousand! For God's sake, Kirk, we already lost ten thousand
when we invested in those government drafts for the Volunteers!
And you turn around and literally give away another fifteen, when
you *know* we have to be extra careful for a while!"

"I didn't *give* anything away. The man is a friend and he needs
a start. It's a personal loan at two percent interest, and he doesn't
have to start paying it back until he's making a profit. He couldn't
have gotten a loan like that from a bank."

"Certainly not from *my* bank," she almost shouted.

"Keep your voice down," he warned. "I don't want the kids
hearing the way you talk."

"The way I talk! What about the way their father wastes money
that will be *theirs* someday? Red McKinley is a drifter, a
worthless mountain man who will throw that money away with the
wind! You know how men like that are!"

Their eyes met, and she instantly regretted the remark, but she
was not about to admit it. "I *am* that kind of man," Kirk growled,
his eyes on fire with anger and hurt. "But I still think I've done
pretty damn well by you, Bea Kirkland!"

"Only because of my common sense about how to handle
money! I set up that fund with full confidence that you would use
it wisely, and you always have. You have no right giving out such
a loan without my approval."

He stepped closer, tempted to hit her. "I'll remind you it's *our*
money, not just yours, woman! I've always given you free reign,
and you've by God got the head for handling it. But if I want to
do something for a friend, I'll not let greed get in the way."

She stiffened. "It isn't greed. It's common sense! I do not intend
to ever be poor and dependent again, David Kirkland, and that
means we cannot be handing out money to every beggar who
comes along!"

"Red's no beggar! I had to practically talk him into it. He's a proud man, Bea, and he'll pay it back. He's got a good head on his shoulders, and his idea for the lumber mill happens to make a lot of sense."

She turned away. "I don't want to hear it, not right now. I can't believe you've done this."

"And I can't believe how you've changed."

"I haven't changed. I told you exactly what I wanted before I married you." She walked farther away, folding her arms and keeping her back to him. "The word is survival, Kirk, nothing more, nothing less. How many men have we seen strike it rich only to lose it all through careless spending? We can't let that happen to us." She turned to face him. "Thanks to you, within two months we've washed twenty-five thousand dollars down the drain! You're the one who advised investing in those government drafts, and now this! Don't you ever give the children any consideration in all of this? Don't you realize you're jeopardizing their futures?"

"We have plenty to fall back on, and you know it. Those draft notes aren't my fault. Plenty of other businessmen in this town invested in them and lost their asses. That's water over the dam, Bea. This loan is nothing like that. Red will pay it back."

She closed her eyes and sighed. "You're such a dreamer, Kirk. So impractical, too wild and reckless."

He walked to a chair over which his pants were draped and picked them up, pulling them on. "And you wish you could be the same way sometimes," he answered.

"What?"

He pulled on a shirt and began buttoning it. "You heard me." He turned to face her, tucking in the shirt. "You want to let go, to be free and easy, but you don't know how. You're so wrapped up in your goddamn need to have money that you're obsessed with it, Bea, and you're going to end up destroying this family because of it."

"That's absurd!"

"Is it?" He buckled his belt and pulled on his boots, then grabbed his jacket.

"Where are you going?"

He pulled on his jacket and stepped closer. "Out to find a woman who is all the things you can't let yourself be," he told her. He saw the hurt in her eyes, but at the moment he didn't care. "I've never said it out like this, Bea, but you've known for years. What the hell else is a man supposed to do? I try to feel sorry for you, but sometimes I can't. This is our first night together in weeks, and I was actually glad to be back, actually thinking about making love to my wife; and you're all worked up about *money*!"

He turned and she grabbed his arm as though to stop him. He met her eyes, seeing the tears in them. "If only . . . if only you hadn't given him that loan," she said weakly. "It just . . . it upsets me, Kirk."

He pulled his arm away. "To say the least. I'll see you in the morning. I'll be back in time for breakfast. And don't worry. I won't do anything to embarrass the precious Kirkland name. The women I see know how to keep their mouths shut!"

He left, and Bea thought of running after him, begging him to stay; but when she pictured him handing over fifteen thousand dollars to Red McKinley, her fury knew no bounds. She climbed into bed, and moments later she heard a horse galloping away from the house. She tried to sleep but could not. She quickly pushed aside thoughts of Kirk with a prostitute. That was the least of her worries. Her biggest problem was figuring out how to make up her twenty-five-thousand-dollar loss.

The summer of 1862 became one of busy chaos. The second Kirkland hotel was finished, a four-story brick structure with an expensive restaurant on the ground floor, complete with rich wood floors, elegant velvet-flocked soft green wallpaper, and chandeliers. Pictures and paintings with gold-plated frames hung on the walls, and food was served on the finest china by waitresses wearing crisp white aprons over dark blue uniforms. The kitchen utilized the latest in coal-burning stoves with two ovens and eight burners.

Besides the hotel, the house was also completed. Amid finishing touches on the new mansion, Bea worked hard making sure the hotel, called the Denver Inn, was quickly filled so she could being making a profit as soon as possible. At the mansion chandeliers were hung, carpeting was laid, and curtains covered the tall windows.

Chad began calling on Irene, and because of her hurt over Ramon's marrying so quickly, she allowed the visits. They played checkers in the parlor or went for buggy rides, sometimes visiting Kirkland Enterprises, where John worked every day now. Irene could see the unhappiness in his eyes, and without a word each of them knew the other missed Ramon, and longed for those precious days when the three of them shared time together at the mansion.

Chad was amiable and honorable, always treating Irene with complete respect. She felt herself being drawn into a kind of invisible web of wanting to please her mother, wanting to erase the hurt of Ramon, wanting to honor the Kirkland name by seeing only the "proper" kind of young man.

Still, though she grew to like Chad more and they became friends, she did not feel the same passion for him, in spite of his striking good looks, as she had felt for Ramon, or feel the quick pull at her insides Ramon had caused. It was more than obvious the effect Chad Jacobs had on other women. Irene could read it in their eyes. They all but gawked at his handsomeness, swooned beneath his charm. Sometimes Irene wondered if there was something wrong with her for not feeling the same way. She supposed it was only because she was still not quite over Ramon, and she blamed herself for that. Maybe more time was all she needed. Surely not every relationship started out with such intense passion.

That summer also brought a variety of troubles. Drought and grasshoppers destroyed most farm crops, including the Kirkland potatoes. The vines and leaves were eaten up before they could blossom, which meant no potatoes would grow under the earth. What the grasshoppers did not destroy, lack of rain did. Still, Bea Kirkland, ever ready, had food shipped in from California, via the family's own freighting line and packed amid chunks of ice from the Sierras. Bea tripled the prices of potatoes and vegetables that made it through the journey without perishing, but Kirk insisted on handing some out free to the indigent and homeless, much to Bea's consternation.

The biggest problem that summer was Indians. Governor Evans and other Coloradans urged that all Colorado Indians be forced onto the small tract of land in eastern Colorado given to the southern Cheyenne under the Treaty of Fort Wise. The Ute were finally given land west of the Rockies, but the problem with the Cheyenne was not solved. The situation grew worse when word reached Denver of terrible raids and murders of whites by Sioux Indians in Minnesota.

People began to panic. With hardly any soldiers left to guard the frontier, the Colorado Volunteers were again called into action. This time it was the Second Colorado Volunteers, under Colonel Jesse Leavenworth, who rode out to deal with Brule Sioux who were raiding along the southern Platte River. The Volunteers chased them to the upper Republican River, but that still left a problem for the southern Cheyenne. Coloradans wanted them out of their territory all together, but it had been the Sioux and northern Cheyenne who were making trouble, including cutting telegraph lines and raiding supply wagon trains and causing a constant shortage of nearly everything in Denver.

The whole matter was a source of an almost constant rift between Kirk and Bea, since Kirk insisted the southern Cheyenne should not be blamed.

"An Indian is an Indian," Bea would say. "As long as they're anywhere around, there is going to be trouble, and it's costing us."

"The southern Cheyenne are staying where they belong," Kirk would argue. "If the government would stick to its end of the bargain and get promised provisions to them when they're supposed to, there wouldn't be any trouble at all. The only reason they stray from the reservation is to hunt. Sometimes they steal cattle, but damn it, Bea, they're hungry. I believe if you think hard enough, you'll remember that feeling yourself. I know the Cheyenne, and I'm sure the ones to the south aren't causing the trouble."

Their eyes met in that same, strange look Irene had seen so often. "Yes, you certainly *do* know them, don't you?" Bea had answered. "Have you ever stopped to think the Indians might be a lot different now than they were when you practically lived among them?" Bea asked then. "They're more hostile now, Kirk, and probably with good reason. But that can't be helped. Life goes on, people progress, land gets settled. They have to adjust or leave, or Colorado and Denver will never realize their full potential."

The argument was always the same, with the added hard feelings over Kirk's loan to Red McKinley. Irene wished many times that she could take her father and ride back into the mountains. There had been many nights when she heard her father ride off after everyone else was in bed, and she suspected why. It frightened and confused her, and sometimes she felt that it was somehow all her fault, even though she had no reason to think such a thing.

Through all the turmoil Elly remained aloof and uncaring. She was concerned only with being able to move into the new house, which they finally did the second week of August. Bea immediately began laying plans for Irene's party, inviting only Denver's most elite, including Governor Evans. For the next three weeks Bea dragged Irene to various stores and dressmakers to find just the right material, plan just the right design for the dress Irene would wear. Irene did not mind the constant shopping, since it kept her out of the new house, which held too many poignant memories. Whenever she saw one of the Ramon's carvings, her heart filled with a mixture of love and jealousy, the terrible pain of imagining another woman in Ramon's bed, loving him, pleasing him. Why she could imagine doing such things with Ramon, but not with Chad, confused her.

John had heard Ramon was back in Denver, taking on jobs, even doing some work for Red McKinley. It was three days before Irene's party when John came to Irene's room to tell her he had seen Ramon when he went with Kirk to visit Red's lumber mill.

Irene's heart raced painfully, and she was irritated with herself for letting the very mention of his name bring such fire to her blood.

"Did he have anything to say about leaving so suddenly?" she asked John casually.

"Not much. He told me he was sorry, but that it was necessary. He acted real strange, as if he didn't want to talk to me too much. He pretended he was too busy. He almost acted mad about something. I asked him if it was true he got married, and he said yes. He told me his wife is expecting a baby."

Irene felt a sick pain in the pit of her stomach. Ramon's wife, having a baby! Did she really think that he had not consummated his marriage? Had he taken the woman the first night? Was it so easy, then, for a man to bed a woman, *any* woman?

She slowly rose from her bed, fighting tears. "Did he . . . ask about me?"

John sighed in sympathy. "No. But . . . Father was standing right there. He probably thought it was best not to bring up your name."

"Yes. I suppose." She walked to a window. "How did he look?"

John shrugged. "All right. I mean, he just looked like Ramon."

"That's not what I meant. Did he seem happy?"

"I don't know. I didn't think about that. I mean, he was real busy at the time, and there wasn't time to talk." He swallowed before continuing, hating to see her unhappy. "He said he was working in consert with Red McKinley. Red cuts lumber for new buildings, and Red advertises for Ramon's finishing work at the same time—gets more jobs for Ramon. Ramon is looking in turn for men to work under him. Eventually he'll be in business on his own."

Irene faced him, her eyes misty. "I'll bet you'd like to work for him."

John smiled bitterly. "Can you imagine Mother letting me do that?"

Their eyes met. "No. But maybe it's better anyway. I might be forced to see Ramon sometimes if you worked with him, and I don't want that." She touched his arm. "Besides, John, I learned a lot when I went up in the mountains with Father—a lot about our responsibilities to the family. I guess until we're older and wiser, we'll have to do what Mother and Father think is best for us."

"I suppose," he answered. He searched her eyes. "You shouldn't get all upset over Ramon, Irene. It's done now, and you've got Chad. I mean, you've been seeing a lot of him. You like him, don't you?"

How could she make him understand her feelings? What did he know of a woman's emotions? "Yes, I like him," she answered. *But I don't love him.* She turned back to the window. "What do you think of him? You work with him every day."

"I like him all right. He's real smart, and friendly. All he does is talk about you. He told me he loves you."

Why didn't the words bring her the joy they had brought when Ramon had told her he loved her? Still, they brought a slight flutter; and Chad was everything a woman could want . . . Ramon was not only married now, but an expectant father. Again the burning pain grabbed at her middle. "He hasn't told me yet."

"Well, don't tell him I told you first. And you'd better not make him wait around too long, Irene. I've seen how other women look at him. Oh, I forgot. I came up here to tell you Mother wants to see you. She's down in the sewing room."

Irene blinked back tears and breathed deeply. She didn't want Bea asking her questions about her watery eyes. She turned to John. "Thanks for telling me about seeing Ramon. At least I know he must be happy."

She left the room and made her way down the stairs to the sewing room. She didn't want to talk to her mother now. She wanted to cry. More than anything she just wanted to see Ramon. She was sure if she could just talk to him once alone, she could find out some hidden truth that would better explain what he had done. She wanted to hear from his own lips that it had all been for her, that she had not imagined the depth of his feelings for her.

She hoped tears were no longer evident in her eyes when she entered the sewing room where Bea sat, still working on the flowered dresser cloth that never seemed to get finished. This new sewing room was much larger than the one at the old house, decorated with oriental rugs and Chinese vases and huge plants. Bea looked up at her daughter and told her to sit down. Irene obeyed.

"Irene, I've decided that after your party, I'm sending you to a finishing school in Chicago," Bea told her matter-of-factly. "You'll have full escort all the way to Abilene, Kansas, where you can catch a train, so you don't need to worry about Indians. Even after you board the train you'll have both a male and a female escort."

Irene frowned, a tumble of emotions rushing through her. No one had mentioned this before or discussed it with her first. "But . . . I want to stay here," she protested. "And what about Chad?"

"Chad will understand. He knows these things are necessary in proper society." Bea hated doing this, but she had heard Ramon Vallejo was back in Denver. Married or not, she thought it best to make sure Irene did not set eyes on the young man for several months, to make sure he was completely out of her system. Besides, now that she was seeing more of Chad, perhaps absence from him would make her miss him and long for him more, so that by the time she returned, she would think of no one but Chad. A winter away from home, with nothing but love letters from Chad to keep her going, ought to do the job of erasing Ramon Vallejo from her daughter's young, too-tender heart.

Bea set the embroidery aside. "I know this is a surprise to you, Irene, but an opening came up at a special girl's school in Chicago, and it's a wonderful opportunity for you. You've been to the mountains with Kirk. Now it's time to polish your etiquette, study some languages, learn how to conduct yourself in high society. Why, I wish I could go myself. You'll come back much more the refined lady than I could ever be. I came into this life with no background for it. I want more than that for my daughters."

She reached out and took Irene's hands. "Chad will wait for you," she assured her. "He loves you. Anyone can see that. He'll be busy here working with John at Kirkland Enterprises. It's only until April, Irene. And you'll get to see a city much bigger and more civilized than Denver. Maybe you can bring home some new ideas for Kirk and me to help build this city."

Irene's heart rushed with an aching loneliness. She would rather go back to the mountains, rather be with Ramon, but she knew one couldn't happen for a long time, and the other was impossible now. Perhaps, if she was to take on her duties properly as a

Kirkland, it *was* best that she go to this finishing school. At least she wouldn't be in this house, where so much of Ramon's spirit could be felt; and she wouldn't have to worry about seeing him in town.

Again came the terribly frightening feeling of being led through life with no control over her fate. She was living her mother's dreams, not her own. Still, maybe that was the way it was supposed to be. Her mother had had a hard life. Surely she knew what was best for her daughters. One day it would be Elly's turn to go off to finishing school. And, after all, it was a great opportunity.

"What about Sierra? He's used to seeing me every day. He'll be heartbroken."

"He's only a horse, Irene. Your father will see to Sierra. He knows how much the animal means to you."

She didn't want to be a baby, didn't want to disappoint her mother, especially after Bea had allowed her to go the mountains. It had been such a wonderful trip, one she would never forget. She would never be that happy again. It all seemed more and more like a dream.

"All right," she answered. "If it's what you want, I'll go," she told her mother.

"I knew you'd understand how important it is. The more you think about it, the more excited you'll be, Irene. And Chad will wait for you. Absence makes the heart grow fonder, you know."

Irene wondered at the statement. Kirk's absences didn't seem to make her mother's heart grow fonder for the poor man.

A maid came to the doorway, carrying a letter. Bea had hired three more servants since moving into the new house: two Spanish women, Isabelle Valdez and Esther Sanchez, and a young, homeless woman named Jenny Porter. It was Isabelle who brought the message, and every time Irene looked at the pretty young Spanish woman, she wondered what Ramon's wife was like.

"A letter for you, Señora Kirkland," the woman said, bringing it to Bea.

The woman left, and Bea looked at the envelope. "It's from my cousin Cynthia," she said, looking suddenly as excited as a schoolgirl. "Maybe she's finally coming to visit! I invited her to your party."

She tore open the envelope and quickly read the short letter. Irene watched the woman's joy leave her, watched her cheeks color slightly. To Irene's dismay, Bea's eyes suddenly teared. "Mother? Is she all right?"

Bea stiffened, folding the letter and shoving it into a pocket of her dress. "She's fine," she answered. She swallowed and blinked rapidly. "She, uh, she's not coming. Family responsibilities, something like that."

"I'm sorry, Mother. I know it meant a lot to you."

Bea met her eyes, the old, hard Bea back again. "You'll never know, Irene, and I wouldn't want you to know. I would never want you to hurt like that."

But I am hurting, Mother.

Bea rose. "Well, maybe another time. You'd best get upstairs to bed now, Irene. I'll be along to say good night soon."

Irene touched her arm. "Good night, Mother." She leaned up and kissed the woman's cheek, then turned to leave. At the doorway she looked back just before exiting to see her mother turned away. The woman had her head in her hands, and her shoulders were shaking as she sobbed quietly. Irene considered going back and trying to comfort her, but she suspected her mother would rather be alone.

She left the room, thinking how certain sorrows simply could not be shared with anyone else. They were just there to torment and tear at a person's heart, and only that person knew the true ache of it. That was how it would be for her forever, whenever she thought about Ramon Vallejo.

CHAPTER FOURTEEN

In the third-floor ballroom the men of the small orchestra began tuning their instruments, while extra maids and a butler on the main floor scurried about making sure party food and drinks were ready and everything in the grand new Kirkland home was properly prepared for guests, who would include the new governor of Colorado Territory.

Bea, wearing a deep blue taffeta ball dress cut low off the shoulders, now fussed with Irene, with the help of two young girls she had hired as personal servants, one girl straining to button the last in a row of forty tiny buttons at the back of Irene's dress. Bea's dark hair was twisted tightly at the back and decorated with a diamond-studded comb. Expensive rings decorated her plump, work-worn hands, which would never again be soft and slender; and a diamond necklace graced her neck. She was not a woman to wear much color, but she insisted Irene wear lovely, soft colors that enhanced her beauty.

Irene's dress was secured, and Bea stepped back, literally gasping at what she saw. "Oh, Irene, I have never been more proud."

Irene felt almost embarrassed. She never cared for flaunting her beauty, which she felt was the only reason for this coming-out party. She would much rather be riding Sierra, exploring the mountains with her father. She glanced in the mirror, and her only wish was that Ramon could be here to see her, that he could be her escort tonight. How handsome they would look together!

She reminded herself then that she must no longer give any thought to Ramon. Chad was going to be here tonight. Chad had been good to her. He had told John that he loved her. He had saved her father's life. He was a wonderfully handsome, intelligent man, and tonight he would be her escort.

"Mother, I'm nervous. I feel silly making the grand entrance you want me to make."

"Nonsense. That's what this is all about. As soon as all the guests arrive and are assembled in the great room, you will come down the stairs and they'll all meet our beautiful daughter. Then we will dine and go upstairs to the ballroom for dancing."

The woman breathed deeply and with pride, rechecking Irene's hair. The golden tresses were swept up into a tumble of curls, a diamond tiara nestled into the crown of her head. Tiny ruby earrings decorated Irene's ears, and a matching ruby necklace graced her slender throat. Her dress, dropped low off the shoulders and revealing an enticing peek at full, firm breasts, was a lovely blue that matched her eyes perfectly. The bodice was draped in white lace that hung to the elbows. The tightly-fitted waistline led to a deeply gathered full skirt of blue tulle, trimmed in white lace and draped diagonally across an underskirt of blue silk puffings, which were gathered and tied with bands of deeper blue velvet. The same darker blue trimmed the hem of the dress in a quilled border design.

"You are so beautiful, Miss Kirkland," Rose Boles spoke up, careful not to call Irene by her first name. Bea had forbidden it.

Rose was Irene's personal maid, a homeless young girl Bea had hired for mixed reasons. Bea told herself she was doing the Christian thing by giving the seventeen-year-old girl a home; but she was also able to pay Rose far less than the average. Rose was so happy just to have a roof over her head and so ignorant of the going rate for servants, that Bea had been able to hire her cheap. She was a plain, quiet, obedient young lady, very subservient—all that Bea demanded in her help.

Oh, how Bea wished her cousin had decided to come! Cynthia would see that her cousin now had a grander home and many more servants than Jake and Marlene Ritter could ever have hoped to have!

Bea's own personal maid, Elizabeth Thomas, agreed with Rose, as both women studied Irene. Liz, as Bea called the woman, was a mining widow whose only child had died of consumption a year ago. The woman was homeless and penniless, as were so many in Denver. Again, Bea had gotten her cheap, but she relieved her guilty conscience by reminding herself she had given these women a lovely room to share in the basement servants' quarters, and they had plenty of food to eat.

Bea urged Irene into the carpeted hallway, then called for Kirk, who appeared from his bedroom, his eyes lighting up when he saw Irene. Since moving into the new house, Bea and Kirk had taken separate bedrooms. "It's what all the wealthy do," Bea had explained to the children. "When you get older, it's difficult to sleep with someone else. Old bones ache and sleep does not come as easily. Besides, I like my room arranged a certain way, and your father likes things *his* own way. Now I won't have to smell the smoke of his infernal pipes and cigars."

Irene suspected there was more to it than doing the fashionable thing or worrying about getting enough sleep. Still, Kirk had been gone so many nights over the years, what difference did separate bedrooms make? She still didn't feel that it was the way marriage was supposed to be, but there was no one to whom she could talk about such things.

Kirk approached her, looking at her lovingly. "Aren't you the most beautiful creature who ever graced the Rockies," he said. He glanced at Bea, and Irene caught the look again, the hint of something secret. Again she felt oddly responsible for her parents' strained relationship. "Turn around for me, girl," Kirk told her then.

Irene obeyed, feeling her cheeks redden. "I must say you picked just the right dress," Kirk told Bea.

"The color matches her eyes so perfectly," Bea replied. Already they could hear guests arriving downstairs, and Bea urged Irene back into her room to wait for her entrance. Bea turned to Kirk, tears in her eyes, following him back into his bedroom. "Kirk," she spoke up, "I want these hard feelings between us to end."

He looked in a mirror and straightened the bow tie at his neck, hating his stiff shirt and tight collar. He turned to face her, and she could not help being struck with pride at how handsome her husband still was. She knew how women would look at him tonight. After all, he was the richest man in Denver. He smiled, but she saw the pain behind the smile. "You know I'm not a man to stay angry," he told her.

"I still wish you would have consulted me about the loan," she told him. "Our agreement from the beginning was that I would handle such things. That special fund was strictly for new mines and mining equipment. I have never argued with you on those matters."

He sighed, pulling on a silk waistcoat. "Bea, it's done. I want to enjoy myself tonight. Can't we ever get through one day without talking about money?"

She swallowed, turning away. "That isn't why I brought it up. I only wanted to tell you that tonight I'm—I'm very proud to be able to present Irene as my daughter, and to be able to call you my husband. I realize this marriage started with only a bargain, but I do love Irene, and I'm doing this for her. In spite of our differences we have three lovely children, and everything I do is for their welfare. I hope you understand that."

"Of course I understand it. And I haven't forgotten the fact that you have kept your promises, Bea. But I have a certain pride. I'm still the man of this family, and I don't need you insulting my intelligence."

She shook her head, turning to face him, her eyes misted. "Kirk, it has nothing to do with intelligence. My God, we wouldn't be in control of so many producing mines without that intelligence, without your wonderful ability to work with those men up there, your nose for the mother lodes. It's your *nature* that could cause us to lose it all. God knows I wish I could be more like you sometimes, but you need me to hold you in check. If not for me you would give away all of it. You're a drifter at heart, a man who could easily live off the land and nothing more. Can you understand the fear I live with, knowing you never wanted any of this? You're like a wild animal straining at the leash, and I'm trying to hang on to you. It's so hard sometimes."

He came closer, touching her arm. "We want different things. I understand what you want, Bea, and I promised you'd have it. I'm not going to do anything to take it away from you. You should know that." A tear slipped down her cheek. "Don't worry abut things so much." He sighed, pulling her into his arms. "I'm sorry that your cousin refused to come."

She broke into tears at the words. "Stay home for a while, Kirk," she sobbed. "Please just stay home."

He patted a soft, round shoulder. At times like this she was so much still the frightened, reserved young girl he had married. He wished he could understand her better, wished he could find a way to reach the responsive woman who lay beneath all that determination and pride. But he had long ago quit trying. "I'll be around for a while."

She pulled away, taking a handkerchief from his top dresser

drawer and blowing her nose. "There won't be anyone here tonight who . . . I mean, anyone from town . . . you've been with, will there? I hate gossip, Kirk. I know how women talk . . . and I know how women look at you."

He sat down on the bed to button his shoes. "I wouldn't hurt the children by causing gossip."

She turned to face him. "Who is she, Kirk?" He looked up at her in surprise. "I've never minded the flings with the whores with no name," she continued. "Some men even expect that of each other, and no one would think much of it. I know what you do when you visit the mines, and God knows I can't blame you. But you're different lately. There's one special woman, isn't there?"

He looked back down at his shoes. "You don't need to know who it is. She's a madam, and she's extremely discreet. You don't need to worry about the Kirkland name."

She watched him quietly for a moment, her heart aching, wishing she knew how to be a complete woman, to fulfill his needs—and her own. "Do you love her?"

He lowered his foot and slowly rose, facing her. "Does it really matter, Bea?"

She dropped her eyes, wishing she could fling herself at him, beg him, seduce him, let loose all her passion. "I suppose not," she answered. "If nothing else, we can be good friends, can't we? We can share our good fortune and enjoy it. You do like the challenge, don't you, of seeing just how big an empire you can build?"

He smiled sadly. "You've done that much for me. For you it's the money, for me it's the challenge. I don't break promises, Bea."

Their eyes met. "No, you don't. I'm deeply sorry I'm not the kind of woman you need, but I'm here, and I . . . sometimes *I* need you. I don't suppose your friend would mind sharing you with your own wife occasionally."

He saw the rare desire in her eyes, sensed she wanted to say she loved him but could not get the words out. He walked closer, leaning down to kiss her cheek. He put an arm around her shoulders then. "Let's go greet our guests, Mrs. Kirkland."

The elegantly dressed elite of Denver discussed their city's problems and progress over glasses of expensive wine, while they waited to get a look at Irene Kirkland. Many already knew her; a few, including the new governor, did not. Chad waited with the others, looking exceedingly handsome in a gray silk suit with a double-breasted waistcoat. Women in the crowd, married or not, stole glances at him, aroused by his dashing looks and virile stance.

Bea and Kirk greeted everyone, Bea taking a new Methodist minister and his family under her wing. She had met them only days earlier at a meeting of Denver's wealthier women who were campaigning to raise funds for more churches. She led the Reverend Will Stanner through the crowd, amid talk of Indian trouble, high prices, polluted water, and even boxing. Bill Byers was adamantly voicing his opinion to a Denver businessman that boxing was a barbarous sport that should not be allowed in Denver, although one of Denver's own, a blacksmith named Con Orem, had already been hailed the boxing champion of Colorado, after a bloody duel that had lasted 109 rounds.

Denver now had two theaters and its own baseball team. Other sports, such as horse racing, fishing, and billiards were also popular, and Denver boosters touted their city as being up to date in all areas, in spite of the fact that the most popular sport continued to be gambling, bringing with it the raucous music, bloody brawls, saloons, and whores that Denver would rather be rid of.

Mr. Stanner represented a wave of ministers and missionaries who had come to Colorado, mostly Presbyterian, Baptist, and Methodist. Bea and her women friends were working diligently with new ministers to urge the expansion of missionary work in the mountain mining towns, where men went for weeks and months without ever hearing the word of God.

Bea led Mr. Stanner and his wife and children over to Chad. She introduced him, saying "This is attorney Chadwich Jacobs, who works for Kirkland Enterprises. Chad is Irene's escort this evening."

Chad gave the new minister, and especially the man's wife, his best smile, knowing full well the woman was struck by his looks. He moved his eyes to the minister's seventeen-year-old daughter, Susan, who was literally gawking at him, her mouth half open. "Very nice to meet you, Susan," he told her.

Immediately, Chad's instincts and secret passion for women was awakened. Susan Stanner was no Irene in looks, but she was pleasant looking, and being a minister's daughter, she was the kind of challenge Chad liked. He even considered how delightful it would be to master the minister's wife with his charm, thinking what a victory that would be.

He was getting restless, putting on this loyalty act for Irene's sake. It was obvious he was not going to get anything out of Irene until he married her, and in spite of her provocative beauty, he wondered if she was incapable of passion, for he had never sensed a great deal of desire when he was with her. That confused and frustrated him. Sometimes he even thought there might be someone else, but as far as he knew, he was the only man Irene had ever seen regularly or shown any interest in. He had decided some young women just took longer to break down; at any rate, he knew he had to tread lightly with Irene, since she was the one he intended to marry. He was not about to scare her away or lose out on all that money by moving too fast.

Susan Stanner was another matter. He cared nothing about hurting her or losing her. In her he saw the possibility of another conquest, and he had contained himself far longer than he had in years. Perhaps he could find a way to seduce this one quietly. He could see the passion in her brown eyes, sensed she was totally taken by his handsome appearance. He took her hand and kissed it, rubbing his thumb over the back of her hand lightly before letting go of it. She was so struck by his looks that all she could muster was a nervous smile.

Elly stood near the stairway, watching Chad, feeling a little better about Chad and Irene. Not only had she spoiled things for Irene and Ramon, but she sensed Chad liked all women, not just Irene. He might marry her, but he would not be true to her. She wanted nothing more than for Irene to hurt inside for the rest of her life, just as Elly was going to hurt. How she wished Chad would look at her the way he looked at Irene . . . the way he was looking at Susan Stanner now.

She looked down at her dress, quickly pushing up her breasts to be sure they were temptingly exposed in the low-cut bodice. She had screamed and begged and argued with her mother for a week until she was finally allowed to wear it. She was still only thirteen, but her big build made her seem older, and her sexual drive had awakened early. She had dreamed of being Chad's wife, had studied herself in the mirror, had touched herself in ways that were sinfully delightful, pretending it was Chad who was touching her. Perhaps someday, when she knew all she could about men, when she was older and prettier, she would find away to make Chad *want* to touch her that way.

Bea did not seem to notice Chad's eye for women. Elly wondered if it was just because the woman didn't *want* to notice, or if her mother was simply so cold to men that she didn't understand their desires and passions. Somehow Elly already did understand, and she found it exciting and challenging. She noticed then that her mother seemed irritated, disgusted. Elly looked in the direction of the woman's gaze to see Red McKinley standing near a fireplace, talking to Governor Evans himself!

Dr. John Evans, a stately, handsome widower with a neatly manicured beard and earnest eyes, had been appointed governor by President Lincoln through pressure from the Methodist church. Elly had learned through careful listening to her parents' conversations that Evans was himself a staunch Methodist who had helped build Northwestern University in Illinois, and had helped get Lincoln into the presidency. Methodists had been lobbying for more representation in the West, and Lincoln owed Evans a favor. Thus did Evans become governor of Colorado Territory.

Favor for favor. Elly understood that kind of thinking already. That was how a person survived in this life, taking advantage of opportunities, guarding one's backside, having lots of money and never giving any of it away. Everything had its price. Already Bill Byers had made himself a close ally of Evans's, to make sure some of his personal projects got attention from the new governor. The two men were working hard at attracting more people to Denver, including farmers, stressing again the need for Colorado to produce its own food.

"What is he doing here?" she heard Bea grumble to Kirk, referring to Red McKinley. She had led Kirk away from the Stanners before lighting into him about Red's presence. "He's barely gotten started in that lumber business of his. He's certainly not a part of the circle of successful businessmen of Denver!"

"I invited him," Kirk answered, looking irritated. "I couldn't have a big party like this and leave out my old friend."

"Well, he doesn't *belong* here. Look at him, standing there talking to Governor Evans as though he were a rich, important man!"

"Someday he *will* be rich and important," Kirk told her, keeping his voice down, neither of them noticing Elly standing close by and listening. "I invited him, and that's that."

Elly moved her eyes to Red McKinley. She found him fascinating, if somewhat crude and unpolished. Something about his rugged looks and all that red hair intrigued her, and she realized that all men were beginning to stir her curiosity, as well as desires she was sure must be uncommon for someone her age. But she did not fight them; she enjoyed them.

There was no more time for her parents to argue about Red's

presence. "It's seven o'clock," Kirk was telling Bea. "I've got to go and get Irene now." He ascended the stairs, and moments later he appeared at the stairway landing. "Ladies and gentlemen," he announced. People quieted and looked up. "I would like to present my daughter, Irene Louise," Kirk told them, holding Irene's arm as she descended the wide, carpeted stairs with her father.

People oohed and aahed, smiled and clapped, and the hurt ran deep when Elly looked at her mother and saw how the woman watched Irene with tears of pride in her eyes. Elly's thirteenth birthday party had been held only a week ago, not nearly the extravagant party that was being held now for Irene. She knew she would have just as fine a coming-out party as Irene, but that was three years away, and her young, jealous heart could not think about that now. Hatred for Irene and love for Chad had blurred her ability to reason, and her stomach burned with intense jealousy as complimentary remarks about Irene's beauty swept the room.

Elly glanced at Chad, and the look in his eyes was all she needed to make her turn and weave her way through the crowd to the kitchen and outside, where she kicked at rocks, secretly hating her mother more for bringing Chad and Irene together, for seeming to love Irene more than herself, and most of all for bestowing upon Elly, albeit not intentionally, her tall, big-boned build and plain, dark looks.

Inside, John watched proudly as Irene came down the stairs. He sipped on a small glass of wine, the first alcohol his father had let him drink, and he liked its taste. More than that, he liked the way a few more sips soothed his inner heartache and frustration over having to work at Kirkland Enterprises and eventually go off to college, instead of doing what he really wanted to do, simply to be left alone to work on his wood carvings. Wine, he was discovering, made a person feel better. It could even make a sad person feel happy. It made all his troubles less important somehow, and as a maid walked by with another tray of filled wineglasses, he took his third helping.

Susan Stanner looked on with a flicker of envy as Chad watched Irene descend and begin greeting guests. She knew it was sinful to be jealous, but Irene Kirkland was indeed a beautiful young woman, the kind a man like Chad Jacobs would certainly desire, compared to a plain, simply dressed minister's daughter. She wondered at all the wealth she saw represented here, wondered how rich Chad Jacobs might be, wished sometimes she could live this kind of life. Immediately she said a secret prayer, asking God to forgive her lust and greed.

Bea led Irene to the Stanners then, introducing them. Susan was amazed at how warm and friendly Irene was. She wanted very much to like her, but when Chad Jacobs slipped an arm around her, his face glowing with what appeared to be love and desire, she felt a surprising dislike that disturbed her. She decided Chad Jacobs must surely be possessed of the devil to arouse such sinful feelings in her soul, for within seconds of her first prayer for forgiveness, she found herself whispering another.

The Kirklands led everyone to an immense, marble-topped table, its huge supporting legs and the matching high-backed chairs made of mahogany. Governor Evans sat at one end of the table and Kirk at the other, with Bea just to the right of the governor, Irene to his left, and Chad next to Irene. Bill Byers and his family sat to Bea's right, and the Stanners next to them. John sat beside the Stanners' son, Sam; and the chair beside John was empty. It was Elly's chair. Bea ordered one of the maids to go and quickly find Elly and tell her to get herself to the table.

Across from the Stanners and the Byers, and next to Chad, sat the other two attorneys from Kirkland Enterprises, Robert Slade and his wife Betsy, and Sigmund Brown and his wife Ramona. Beside them sat Henry Brown, Denver's most successful contractor, and the man who had built the new Kirkland mansion. Four more of the most prominent men of Denver and their wives sat next to him; and, much to Bea's chagrin, Red McKinley sat to Kirk's immediate right, completing the large table.

Bea cast Elly a look of chastisement as the girl arrived at the table late. She ordered that the food be served, feeling the secret pride of being exactly what Kirk had said they would be when they first came here—one of the first families of Denver, "old money" in the eyes of nearly everyone at the table. At the moment she had the grandest home in the foothills of the Rockies, and she doubted anyone would build anything comparable anytime soon. The streets of Denver might still be unruly and dirty, but someday it would be as important as Chicago and New York. People like herself and those who sat at this table would be recognized as Denver's founders.

Servants brought out a feast of soup, roast, ham, potatoes, an array of vegetable dishes and warm breads, served from gold and silver bowls and platters, dished onto fine china and eaten with silver forks and spoons. Just when people were almost painfully full, a variety of puddings and pies were served. The most heated topic of conversation continued to be Indians.

Red cast Kirk a look that Kirk understood well. Here he was presenting his half-Indian daughter to a group of people who would like nothing better than to see the Indians wiped off the face of the earth, or at least off the face of Colorado Territory. At that very moment Governor Evans was talking to Billy Byers about ways to make sure the southern Cheyenne stayed on reservation land, and plans he had in mind to get that reservation moved completely out of Colorado. "Settlers out on the plains are terrified," the man was saying. "We've gotten rid of the Ute. Now it's time to do something about the Cheyenne. They're getting way out of hand, and I'm getting a lot of pressure from our constituents who live away from Denver and are less protected. What I'm worried about is Denver being cut off from the East, losing telegraph communication, supply lines being cut."

Others joined in the conversation, every remark against the Indians. Kirk and Red did not share the opinions of the others, but both knew that in this group it was useless to voice their feelings or try to explain the Indian point of view. Red knew that Kirk's own concern was not just that he was hiding his own daughter's identity, but that somewhere out there his own son could be part of the Indian uprising. What would people at this table think if they knew?

Kirk glanced at Bea, who spoke against the Indians right along with the others. Sometimes he wondered if she had loved and mothered Irene with such devotion that she had actually forgotten the girl was half Indian.

After the meal, the men retired to the smoking room and the women to the parlor to visit more and rest full stomachs before climbing a carpeted, circular staircase, first to the second floor, across a balcony and up another circular stairway to the ballroom, where a six-piece orchestra struck up a waltz.

Chad started the dancing by sweeping Irene onto the hardwood floor, her blue silk dress flowing elegantly with their whirling steps. Susan Stanner watched with feelings of envy and and yet a thrill at the romance of it; Elly watched with pure hatred. The Byers joined in the dance, and Governor Evans asked permission from Kirk to dance with Bea. Kirk readily obliged, hating all the pretending, but going along with what was expected of him. This was not the life he would have chosen, but he *had* chosen this place, this land, and he was not about to leave it. Much as he hated to admit it, he liked thinking of Denver as "his" town, Colorado as "his" territory, the mountains as "his" domain. Here he was closer to the old life, closer to the son he had never known. Bea had been right about one thing. He liked the challenge of increasing his empire, and he wondered if some of her thinking had rubbed off on him more than he realized.

Sometimes he felt as if he were two different men, one who wanted to roam the mountains unencumbered, the other enjoying being Denver's most prominent citizen. One man lived with this family he had created, the other loved a prostitute named Mary O'Day. He could put up with being constantly torn between two worlds—put up with it for Irene's sake. He figured he could handle anything, except Irene's being hurt. He could not forget Red's words about how it was wrong to keep Irene's identity from her, and as he watched her float around the dance floor with Chad, he saw in her all innocence. How he would hate to see that destroyed. He wished he had never struck the bargain with Bea to raise her as Bea's daughter, but it was too late now to reveal the truth.

Indian. He could just imagine how the people watching her dance now would react if they knew Irene was half Cheyenne, the very Indians Coloradans hated most.

"You look beautiful tonight, Irene," Chad told her softly. "More beautiful than I've ever seen you."

His eyes dropped to the silken mounds of her breasts that were revealed by the low neckline of her dress, and Irene felt her cheeks going crimson. She was still unsure of her feelings for Chad, but he had a way about him that sometimes made her feel the way she had felt with Ramon. Perhaps this was how love was supposed to be, a slowly building feeling, rather than the sudden passion she had felt for Ramon.

The dance ended, and Chad led her through French doors to a third-floor balcony and cooler air, while the music started again and others began to dance. Chad led Irene away from the doors where no one could see them, and before she realized what was happening, he had pulled her close and covered her mouth in a slow, searching kiss.

She half-heartedly tried to pull away, but he pressed her closer, refusing to release her mouth until he felt her relax in his arms. One thing Chad Jacobs knew how to do well was kiss, and one thing he did not understand was that any woman might not *want* that kiss. None had ever refused, and he was not about to ruin his record with Irene Kirkland, for he intended to make her his wife, and that was that.

Irene felt somewhat stiff and awkward at first, then began to relax, thinking how this kiss did not fully awaken her desires the way Ramon's had but realizing she had to give Chad Jacobs a chance. Certain desires were aroused simply from Chad's expertise at how to bring the best out of a woman. He quickly ran his tongue inside her mouth, while he crushed her breasts against his chest and touched her bare back gently with his strong hand.

He left her mouth then, alive with desire at the sweet taste of her full lips. "I love you, Irene," he whispered gruffly. "I might as well say it out." He kissed at her neck, and Irene felt a tingle rush through her. She was not sure if it was love or just curiosity and awakened needs she did not know how to handle. He was not giving her time to think.

"I love you," he repeated, "and I hate the thought of you going away for so long." He kissed her neck, making her wonder what it might be like to let a man kiss her breasts, instantly thinking how much more thrilling this would be if it was Ramon, then hating herself for the thought. Here was the most eligible man in all of Denver telling her he loved her, desired her, that he would miss her. She felt like a fool and a traitor.

He kissed her eyes, met her lips again in a groaning kiss, then moved his lips to nibble at her ear. "I just want you to know I'll wait for you, Irene. I'll write, every day if you want. You'll write back, won't you?"

"Yes," she whispered, for the moment somewhat swept off her feet. He was so sincere she almost felt sorry for him. Were those tears she saw in his eyes? He really *did* love her, and this was surely the right match for her. She had grown accustomed to his company, and she realized she really would miss him when she was gone. "I love you, too, Chad," she found herself saying.

There were his tender lips again, searching her mouth. There were those gray eyes hypnotizing her with their sincerity. His hands touched her so gently, so lovingly. His breath was sweet, and he smelled wonderful. There was not one thing about Chad Jacobs that wouldn't excite any woman. "We've had so little time together, and now you're going away," he was saying. "I just don't want you to forget me." He pulled away slightly, searching her eyes. "My God, I'm sorry, Irene. I had no right—"

"It's all right. I—I haven't been sure how I felt about you, Chad, but I must say, you've helped me know. I wasn't sure your own feelings were this strong."

"How could you not be sure?" he almost pleaded. "I've loved you from the first moment I set eyes on you. You're beautiful, you're warm, you're sweet. A man couldn't ask for more in a woman than the lady I hold in my arms right now." He kept rubbing a hand over her back, and she thought how gentle and knowledgeable he must be in bed. Perhaps this was the way it was supposed to be—a woman learned to love and desire her husband, letting him make all the first moves, letting him awaken her desires by the right touch, the right kiss. Maybe there was something sinfully wrong with wanting a man almost from the first meeting, the way she had wanted Ramon.

She was a woman now, a Kirkland woman. Her mother had practically chosen Chad for her, and she remembered again that she had certain responsibilities. Ramon's marriage had been arranged, and maybe that was best after all. Who knew better what was best for her than her own mother? And, after all, she was going away. Poor Chad.

"It will be a long winter, Chad. I'll write often, and I'll miss you. I'll come back as soon as possible."

He smiled the melting smile that had fooled so many. "God, you're beautiful," he almost moaned. "I'll miss you so. When you come back, we'll see a lot of each other. Maybe . . ." He sighed deeply, pulling farther away, longing to rip away the bodice of her dress and reveal the virgin nipples that lay beneath the lace. "It's too soon to speak of marriage, but that thought has already come to mind, Irene. Forgive me for being so forward."

She took his hands. "It's all right. I'm honored that you would think of it so soon. We need time to think, Chad. Maybe it *is* good that I'm leaving for a while."

He sighed deeply. "Maybe. And maybe I could have one more kiss before we go back into the ballroom."

She thought of Ramon, and the hurt. He had left without a word, married someone else, with whom he was sharing these things. He had taken another woman to his bed, and made love to her, planted a baby in her belly. He had probably forgotten by now the silly *gringa* out of whom he had enticed a kiss. Should she deny herself this seemingly perfect husband because of a love she could never have?

Ramon had hurt her, whether it was for her own good or not. She would not forget how she felt the day Hank Loring had told her Ramon was happily married. It was time to forget Ramon and turn her full attention to Chad Jacobs.

"Yes," she answered. "You can have another kiss."

He smiled again, crushing her close first, running his lips tenderly along her shoulder, then across her neck, her cheek, meeting her lips again. Irene told herself this could not be so bad. If women were expected to marry, she couldn't do any better than Chad Jacobs, could she? She returned the kiss, wanting to show him she could be a responsive woman. After all, he had most surely been with other women, knew all about sex. He would surely be a gentle teacher when the time came.

She opened her eyes then to see Elly standing there staring at them. She quickly pulled away from Chad, touching her lips. "Elly! What are you doing out here!" She shivered then at the look of near hatred in her sister's eyes.

"Mother is looking for you," Elly answered. "You'd better cool your cheeks and get back in there."

Irene looked at Chad, who gave her a wink. "Maybe you'd better." He touched her cheek. "We'll go for a ride tomorrow. I want to see plenty of you before you go away."

She nodded. "Will you come back in and dance with me?"

He smiled. "You know I will."

Irene glanced at Elly again, irritated with her little sister sneaking up on her the way she had. She touched her cheeks and then straightened her dress, going back inside. Elly stood there staring at Chad, her eyes strangely unreadable. She walked closer to him then, folding her arms in front of her so that her breasts were forced together, making them appear bigger. "Will you dance once with me, Chad?" she asked.

Chad, who was an expert on young girls, grinned, telling himself to beware. This one wanted him, and he would like nothing better than to grant her wish. But Elly Kirkland spelled trouble, and he had made too much progress now with Irene to let anything spoil it. He walked closer, touching her arm. "Not tonight. Irene is going away, and I want to dance every dance I can with her." He gave her a wink, squeezing her arm. "Maybe another time, Elly, when you're a little older."

He walked back inside, and Elly struggled not to faint. Chad Jacobs had touched her, and he had glanced down at her breasts. She had seen the desire in his eyes, and she felt crazy with love for him. Someday, somehow, she would find a way to make him belong only to her. It would be her lifelong goal.

She walked to the French doors, gazing into the ballroom to see Irene dancing with her father, and Chad Jacobs dancing with Susan Stanner.

CHAPTER
FIFTEEN

1863

Chad timed it all carefully. To show any interest in Susan too soon after Irene left would make Susan suspicious. He had to wait long enough for Susan to believe he was losing interest in Irene, that he was getting lonely, that he was struggling to do the honorable thing by being true to Irene in spite of being attracted to Susan.

Four months—that was certainly long enough. In those four months he had discreetly glanced at her every week in church, while he sat with the Kirklands, and Susan sat in the choir. He knew how to give a look that accomplished a number of his goals: charmed her, but appeared merely friendly; seduced her; made him appear lonely. There had never been a touch or more than a few friendly words exchanged after work, or where he might run into her, or during an occasional game of cards or checkers with Susan, John, and Elly at the Kirkland household.

Chad Jacobs had not done one thing that would make anyone think he had an interest in Susan Stanner. But he knew that Susan interpreted his looks and movements differently. She was infatuated with him, probably secretly in love with him. He knew she would grasp any eye contact or exchanged words as meaning he was interested in her, because she so desperately wanted it to be true. Elly Kirkland held the same desperate feelings, but Elly was deceitful and conniving, and Chad knew if he ever touched her she would find a way to hold it over his head and possibly keep him from marrying Irene.

Susan was different. She was sweet and trusting, a lot like Irene. But unlike Irene, he sensed that all it would take was one kiss, one touch, to enjoy the exquisite pleasure of stealing her virginity. Where Irene was somewhat apprehensive and tentative, Susan would explode with passion.

He approached the Kirkland home, where he had been invited for supper. He gazed at the mansion, feeling extreme satisfaction in realizing that it was only a matter of time before he would be a part of this wealthy family. He had at least gotten more kisses out of Irene before she left for Chicago, had awakened some of the passion he suspected lay beneath that reserved exterior. It still irritated him that Irene had not responded to him the way other women did, and he was anxious for their wedding night. He would, by God, show her how a woman was supposed to feel, supposed to react to Chad Jacobs.

In the meantime, Irene was not here, but Susan was; and he had abstained from his flings with women long enough. Why not one more, before he was tied to just one? Already he had been contemplating the ways a man could cheat on his wife, but Irene Kirkland would be too valuable a wife to take too big a risk. He would have to be more careful than ever once he was married.

He rode his horse through a thick January snow, reaching the front entrance of the Kirkland mansion, where a buggy already sat. It was the Stanner buggy. They were also dining with the Kirklands tonight. Chad decided it was the perfect opportunity to begin moving in on Susan Stanner. He dismounted and tied his horse to a fancy hitching post, then hurried up the steps to the heavy oak doors, feeling almost giddy as he knocked.

The maid Jenny Porter let him in, giving him the same look most women gave him. He returned the look with a wink as he handed her his hat, and the woman laughed lightly, turning red, and thinking what a handsome, charming man Irene Kirkland would one day marry. What a lucky young lady she was! She took his coat and led Chad to the parlor, where the Stanners sat visiting with Bea Kirkland. Kirk himself was gone again, back in the mountains, this time with John.

The timing was excellent. Although he was good friends with Kirk now, he suspected the man was not so easily fooled. He had to be extra careful around him. Bea, on the other hand, thought he could do no wrong. There were no watchdogs now, and no Irene in the way. The only one he had to be careful of was Elly, who seemed to watch his every move.

He was warmly welcomed by Bea, and just as he expected, when he sat down in a love seat, Elly immediately moved to sit down beside him. He moved his eyes to Susan, again giving her a look in which he knew she took great hope. He watched her redden, watched her drop her eyes, watched her young, full breasts move as she began to breathe a little harder.

She wanted him. He could even see the outline of her nipples through her dress and camisole, ripe nipples that had grown taut with an ache to be touched the moment she met his eyes. He casually entered the conversation, carefully avoided looking at Susan again until they were guided into the dining room and Susan was seated across from him. Again he gave her the look, and he took great pleasure in noticing she could hardly eat.

How he loved these games! He was getting much deeper into the contest now, and his game plan was working exceedingly well. The conversation turned to how Irene liked to ride horseback, and Susan told Bea that she also liked to ride.

"I go riding every morning," she told the woman, glancing at Chad then, "down along the ravine behind the church. There are no Indians or Chinese there, so it's safe. And it's so pretty, even in winter."

Bea went on to say how she hated the cold, how nice the winters had been in California. "But Kirk loves it here, and I've grown to love it, too," she was saying. Chad and Susan hardly heard her. Their eyes met for a moment, and Chad knew Susan's admission of where she liked to ride was an open invitation for him to join her. "I still don't like Irene doing so much riding," Bea was saying. "Oh, it's fine to like to ride, Susan, but young ladies like yourself and Irene have to be thinking of other things."

Susan turned at the sound of her name, not even sure what Bea had told her. "Yes, ma'am," she answered.

Talk turned to church, and Bea's plans to win more members and work to raise money to build a much bigger, fancier church than the simple wooden structure that had been quickly erected for the Reverend Stanner to conduct services in.

After the meal, Chad asked to use the smoking room, as he liked a thin cigar after eating. Will Stanner and his family returned to the parlor, where Bea said she would join them shortly for games of checkers and chess. She followed Chad to the smoking room, closing the door. Chad pulled out a thin cigar and held it up as though to question if he could light it.

"Be my guest," Bea told him. "I wanted to see you alone for a minute, Chad, to talk business."

He lit the cigar, taking a puff before sitting down at Kirk's desk, enjoying the accepted familiarity he had with this family now. "What is it, Bea?" he asked, now on a first-name basis with the woman.

"I want to recoup some of the money Kirk loaned to that Red McKinley. We both know it will be a cold day in hell before the man begins to pay any of it back. We also lost heavily on those government drafts we purchased to support the Volunteers."

Chad leaned back in the leather chair. "There's plenty of money coming in from the other businesses and most of the mines yet."

"That's true. But there is also plenty of money going out. This house cost more than I had planned. And with the new gold strikes in Montana and Idaho, we've lost some of our outside investors, let alone the way things have slowed at the banks. Some people can't pay back their loans, loans made on claims that turned out to be worthless. Some people took out loans to build houses to stay in Denver, then ran off to Montana. We have to recoup some of that money, Chad. I want you to find someone to get those houses sold. As far as the worthless claims, I have another idea that could net us enough to make up for all our losses."

Bea moved closer, pulling a chair up to the desk and sitting down directly across from Chad. "It involves a bit of deceit, Chad. I don't want Kirk to know. From time to time I will ask you to do things that I won't want Kirk to know about. He's too generous and almost too honest for his own good. I believe in honesty, Chad, but in business, sometimes a person has to be ruthless and practical, and Kirk is incapable of either. I have a feeling you would understand what I'm saying, understand what is needed to survive in business."

Chad watched her carefully, elated that she had so much confidence in him that she would actually ask him to do something behind Kirk's back. He had won her over by a bigger margin than even he had anticipated. "I understand completely," he answered, puffing on the cigar once more. "I don't like being ruthless, mind you, any more than I suspect you do. But we're talking about protecting our own here. If it will help protect Irene's future, I'm all for it."

Bea grinned. "I knew you would be. What I want to do is sell off some of the worthless claims, as well as a couple of our own mines that have nearly stopped producing. I was talking with a realtor today who told me people back East are investing ridiculous amounts of money in worthless mines. Some other business-men and I have advertised heavily in eastern newspapers, touting how the only truly endless supply of gold is right here in Colorado. The man with whom I spoke tells me eastern investors are swallowing the stories, buying up every hole in the ground for ridiculous prices. Kirk would never go along with such a scheme, but we have to protect Colorado, Chad, keep Denver alive, keep the money right here. I'm told the Gregory Lode is suddenly selling for four hundred dollars a foot, with some investors paying up to two thousand dollars!"

Chad frowned. "I've heard some of the same, but I wasn't sure you'd go for something like that."

"I'll do anything to protect what I've worked so hard to build." Bea sat a little straighter, breathing deeply, suddenly looking to Chad as if she were a warrior ready to do battle. "I want you to send an agent east to sell stock in some of the more worthless claims, as well as in the California Girl and Red Valley mines. I want you to set up a bogus company. Leave the Kirkland name out of it. The money will go into our own banks, and when the investors get out here and discover the mines in which they bought shares are worthless, they will have nowhere to turn. The company who sold them the shares will have folded. We will draw up papers to show we bought out the company, and since we supposedly did so at a great loss, we are refunding nothing. They will be out their money, and we will have made a tremendous profit."

Chad slowly smiled. "Ma'am, I have to say you are the shrewdest businesswoman I have ever met. You could give the most successful man a run for his money."

"Can you do it . . . keep it all looking perfectly legal?"

"Sure I can, but what about all those investors who will be out their money?"

She rose, holding her chin proudly. "What about them? If a man is foolish enough to throw his money to the wind without seeing which direction it's blowing in, it's his problem, not mine. I'm careful with *my* investments, as anyone should be. If others are careless with theirs, they have to expect to suffer the consequences."

Chad nodded. "I fully agree. We think a lot alike, Bea."

She smiled. "I know. That's why I think you'll be good for Irene. She tends to be too much like her father, too kind hearted and generous. How are things between you, Chad? Have you heard from her lately?"

"I hear from her often, and I write her at least twice a week."
He rose from the chair. "I love her, Bea, and I miss her. She
sounds pretty lonely in her letters. I hope you won't send her back
next year. In fact"—he tamped out the cigar—"I ought to tell you
I want to marry her. I'm sure you know that. I just have to give her
a little more time when she gets back."

Bea sighed, touching his arm. "Kirk is insistent she wait until
she's eighteen, but that's only a little over a year. You know you
have my full blessing, Chad. I do want Irene to be happy, and I
know you can do that for her."

"Yes, ma'am. I'll try."

"I have to join our guests now."

"I'll be right along. And don't worry about this little discussion.
I'll get the job done." Bea patted his arm and nodded. Chad
watched her leave, wanting to jump up and down at his victories.
To win over a woman like Bea Kirkland was a major accomplishment. He knew exactly how to handle her. Money was her
religion, her first love. That was all he had to remember.

He looked at himself in a huge, gold-framed mirror that hung
over the marble fireplace in the smoking room, and smoothed back
his thick, sandy-colored hair, grinning at his good looks. He glanced
at the intricate carving of the woodwork around the fireplace,
touching it lightly, wondering for a moment about the wood-carver
called Ramon, the one John had told him about. Maybe one day
when he built his own mansion for himself and Irene, he would hire
Ramon Vallejo to do some work for him.

Irene sat down to write another letter to Chad. Over her lonely
months away from home, she had begun to feel closer to him and
relied on his letters full of love and even some humor to keep her
going. She could see his bright smile and dancing gray eyes as she
read, realizing how he must love her by his long letters, which
must take a considerable amount of time to write, in spite of the
long hours her mother must require of him.

She no longer doubted Chad's love for her, and she loved him,
too. She felt very mature now in realizing her love for Chad was
simply different from what she had held for Ramon. Her love for
Chad had taken longer to grow, and thus must be more solid. Chad
was of her own race, a Protestant, a businessman who understood
the immense responsibility that came with being a part of the
Kirkland empire.

Yes, she was growing up. She understood these things better

now. It had been a childlike Irene who had loved Ramon. Now she was becoming a woman, learning some of the finer rules of etiquette and social amenities, even studying French. She had wanted to study Spanish, since it could be used in Colorado, but for some reason her mother had directed the school that she should study French instead.

She put pen to paper, telling Chad about how dreary the winters in Chicago were compared to those in Colorado.

"I think it's the weather that makes me even more lonely. The sun hardly ever shines here in winter, and the air is so damp. Half the time the snow we get is more like slush, a mixture of snow and rain, and it is always windy. Even now, I look out my window and see only gray clouds and a cold rain.

"Chicago is much bigger than Denver, for it is on Lake Michigan and is a shipping port. I cannot begin to tell you how big Lake Michigan is, but then, since you are from Pennsylvania, I suppose you have seen Lake Erie, and perhaps you saw Lake Michigan on your way west. Chicago is also a center for railroads that come in from every direction. Mother would faint if she could see how many warehouses and docks there are here. I can already see that we must work hard at bringing the railroads west to Denver, if we ever want to have a truly profitable link to the East."

She frowned, leaning back in her chair and realizing she was starting to think a little more like her mother. She reminded herself to be careful, that money should not be so important that she would hurt her husband because of it, the way Bea had hurt Kirk.

She didn't want that kind of marriage. With an educated attorney like Chad for a husband, she could let him take care of business matters. She could concentrate on being a homemaker, tending to her children, giving them the attention Bea had never been able to give her own children. She understood it was different for Bea and Kirk. Kirk was a wandering man who cared little for money, and they both had started out the hard way. She didn't totally blame her mother for her actions and behavior. It was simply that she didn't want it to be that way for herself.

She thought about Chad's sweet kisses, the way he had so gently held her before she left, making her realize she actually loved him and would miss him. Still, there was a special place in a corner of her heart for Ramon Vallejo, her first love, foolish as it had been. To her chagrin, she had not forgotten Ramon's kiss, the unbridled passion it had aroused in her, a passion not even Chad had been able to unleash. Why it had been different with Ramon, she would never know for certain. He belonged to someone else now. At least she had managed to get over the hurt of it and get on with her life.

She gazed out the window again, wondering what was happening in Colorado, hating being away from home in spite of the friends she had made at the school. The teachers here were pleasant but stern; the room she shared with another girl was bright and neat, and the food was good. But this was not home. She missed her brother, missed her father. Most of all she missed the mountains. The only thing that soothed her homesickness was thinking of her trip into the mountains with Kirk, of the peace and strength she had found there.

She continued her letter.

> "I will be home in about four months. Right now that sounds like forever, for I miss you and I miss Colorado so. I even miss Sierra, and looking at the mountains. I hope you are remembering to exercise Sierra for me. . . ."

Susan rode her horse through the soft snow, enjoying the odd Colorado weather—thick snow on the ground, but a warm sun shining. Soon the snow would be gone, but it would remain heavy in the mountains to the west. She loved looking at those purple and gray bastions with their brilliant snowcapped peaks.

She wondered what it was like in the mountains. Coming from Illinois, she had never seen such country, never lived where it could snow so fast and furiously, only to disappear within a day or two under warm sunshine. Colorado was the only place where a person could go out in only a light sweater and throw snowballs.

She liked these rides alone, her chance to dream about Chad Jacobs, her chance to pretend he was here with her, telling her he loved her, not Irene Kirkland. It was a foolish, fairy-tale dream; but sometimes when Chad looked at her, she wondered if it could come true. She saw such loneliness in his eyes, saw a desire there that he must think he was forbidden to act on. She could not forget how he had looked at her when she mentioned going riding alone, and ever since that night she had almost expected him to come and join her.

But a whole week had passed, and there had been no Chad. Sometimes she thought she might die from loving and wanting him so much. Her dreams were totally hopeless and had made her so sick, so unable to eat, that she had actually lost weight. She knew that somehow she had to get over these feelings, and she had even prayed to God to help her, to forgive her for wanting someone who was pledged to another. She told herself she was young. There would be other men. Time would take care of the hurt. Still, over four months had passed, and her heart continued to ache for Chad Jacobs.

She reached her favorite spot, near an old, abandoned cabin, where the creek danced over smooth rocks, never freezing because it was always moving, now slightly swollen from a mild mountain runoff. She wondered how much deeper the creek would become in the spring. She had yet to experience her first springtime in Colorado, but she had heard about how much higher the rivers and creeks became when the snow melted in the Rockies.

She knelt and touched the water, gasping at how cold it was. She stood up, keeping hold of her horse's reins as the animal took a drink from the icy stream. Susan turned to gaze at a growing Denver in the distance, then noticed someone riding in her direction. Immediately her heartbeat quickened, and she felt every nerve end come alive when she thought maybe, by some miracle, it could be Chad Jacobs. She told herself it was a foolish hope until the figure came closer, riding Irene's horse, Sierra. She knew the horse, knew Chad rode it often to exercise the animal for Irene, knew no one else but Chad would be on that horse.

She stood frozen as he came closer, her eyes wide, her throat dry, a cold sweat moving from her neck down to her feet. He rode up close then, giving her that look that made her feel faint. He halted Sierra, holding her eyes for a moment, looking a little sad. "I was hoping I'd find the right place," he told her, dismounting then and leading Sierra to the stream.

Susan swallowed. "Hello, Chad. What—what on earth brings you out here? Is something wrong? Is my father looking for me?"

He met her eyes, moving his own over her in a way that made her feel naked and on fire. "No," he answered, appearing a little nervous. "I just—" Chad sighed, looking away, appearing apprehensive and despondent. "*I* was looking for you, Susan," he told her, feigning a tone of guilt in the words.

He turned and met her eyes again. "My God, this is as wrong as can be, but I couldn't help myself." He stepped closer, making sure to hold her eyes in his own hypnotic gaze. "For months I've been trying to think of a way we could be alone, so that I could tell you what I have no right telling you. I've fought these feelings for so long, Susan, prayed about them, searched my soul." His eyes actually teared. "When you mentioned the other night how you like to go riding alone, I just . . . I felt you were telling me something, Susan . . . telling me to come out here so we could talk."

She closed her eyes, turning away, wondering if she might pass out. She kept hold of the reins, shivering, trembling, trying to think straight. Was she misinterpreting what she had seen in those handsome eyes? "About . . . what?" she squeaked, finally managing to find her voice.

She felt his hand on her shoulder then. "You know what, Susan. We've read it in each other's eyes for months, almost from the first day I met you. I'm all but promised to another, but the whole thing was practically arranged. I don't have the kind of feelings for Irene that I have for you, and I don't know what to do about it. I couldn't go on this way any longer. I need to know, Susan, if you have the same feelings for me that I have for you."

The touch of his hand brought forth such passion, such wicked desires, that she thought again how this man must be an instrument of the devil. But then again, perhaps not. Perhaps he could really love her! Perhaps God *meant* for them to be together! Why else would Chad Jacobs risk losing out on marrying the richest woman in Denver by coming here to meet with the daughter of a poor church minister?

She turned to face him, her chest heaving in near gasps. "And what are those feelings, Chad?" she asked.

He touched her face with his hand, rubbing a thumb over her cheek. "God forgive me," he said softly, "but I think I'm in love with you."

She closed her eyes and fell against his chest, and Chad moved his arms around her. "I've watched you," he told her, rubbing his hands over her back, "talked with you, socialized with you. I've seen how good and sweet you are, what a wonderful wife you would make. Everyone thinks I should marry someone from my own so called class. I though the same way myself. I even thought I loved Irene, but now she's written to tell me she's found someone else. It hurts, Susan. It hurts so much. You're the first one I thought of when I got Irene's letter."

"Oh, Chad, I can hardly believe this is happening." She looked up at him, tears in her eyes. "I do love you so much. But you were promised to Irene, and I never dreamed anything could come of these feelings. I'm so sorry, so sorry she hurt you."

He allowed a tear to slip down his own cheek before he leaned down to meet her mouth in a deep, lingering kiss that told him all he needed to know. She was young and spontaneous and bursting with love and passion, eager to please him quickly and make sure she hung onto this miraculous new love. He could feel the heat from her body, feel the fire in the kiss she returned with amazing hunger, considering her innocence.

He knew exactly how to handle such young, urgent love. He forced her lips apart, moving a hand to lightly grasp at her bottom, doing things he knew were totally new to her, things that would quickly unravel any inhibitions she might have. He slaked his tongue into her mouth, groaning lightly, pressing her against his hardness to show her how much he desired her.

Susan was totally lost in a dizzy frenzy of love and desire and exquisite joy in realizing Chad Jacobs actually loved and wanted her. Irene had hurt him, turned him away. She was gone, had found a new love. Poor Chad was all alone and heartbroken. And oh, how she loved him!

He left her mouth, licking and kissing at her cheek, her neck. "I don't understand this," he groaned. "I only know I want you, Susan. I only know the hurt will never go away until I can touch you."

He bent over more, forcing her head back, moving his face toward her breasts, flinging back her cape and kissing at the full, firm mounds through her dress. She grasped his thick hair, knocking off his hat, panting his name. He picked her up in his arms then, and she looked into his tear-filled eyes. "I love you, Susan," he told her. "I love you, and it feels good to say it. This is right. I know it is. Somehow we'll find a way to be together forever, but for now, all we have is this moment."

She touched his handsome face, wondered if any woman had ever known such ecstasy. She trusted in his words of love, for how many men actually wept out of their desire and devotion? "It's all right," she told him, her voice sounding far away.

He searched her eyes. "Will you reach up there and untie the blanket from my horse?" he asked.

Almost painful urges swept through her insides in great waves of ecstasy, and she obeyed. He carried her to the deserted cabin. She knew what he wanted, but was too young and innocent to understand completely what might happen. She was not afraid, for he loved her, and she loved him, and God meant for them to be together. Once inside the cabin he set her on her feet and spread out the blanket, then removed his jacket. "I'm so sorry, Susan. This isn't a very good place."

"I don't care," she told him, removing her cape. She felt on fire, was oblivious to the chilly air. "Oh, Chad, I love you so much. I've dreamed of nothing but you for months. I can't believe this is happening."

He came closer, unbuttoning the front of her dress. "Believe it," he told her softly. "I want to look at you, Susan, touch you, taste you." he whispered. He met her mouth again, reaching inside her dress to grasp at a soft, full breast, rubbing a thumb over the taut nipple. He felt her shudder, thinking how this was going to be almost too easy. He gently pushed her dress off one shoulder, exposing a breast, then left her mouth, bending her gently backward, urging her down to the blanket.

His lips trailed down her throat to the ripe, pink nipple that ached to be tasted. He flicked at it with his tongue, making her cry out, then took the tip of her breast into his warm mouth.

Susan Stanner needed no more persuasion. She was totally at his mercy, willing to submit to anything Chad Jacobs wanted and needed in order to soothe his broken heart and show him how much she loved him.

For the first few weeks they met often and secretly at the abandoned cabin, a place that became special to Susan, one she often went to alone just to sit and think about Chad, about the special, passionate love they shared. In her mind, what she shared with Chad was not sinful. It was beautiful and right. Never had she known such ecstasy. Never had her heart soared to such heights. She could not think of their affair as sin, for soon, very soon, Chad would announce their love to everyone.

She did not fully understand his reason for not being open about their love, but Chad was so intelligent, so worldly, that he surely knew best. Perhaps he was right that they should wait until Irene's return. He wanted to break the news to Irene gently, to do this the respectful way.

Susan didn't care, as long as she knew Chad loved and wanted her. She even began planning with him times that they could meet secretly in his hotel room, where things were warmer and more comfortable, where she allowed him to do things to her she never dreamed a man could do to a woman. In his arms she was as brazen as a harlot, but she loved pleasing him, loved the way his gray eyes drank in her nakedness, loved the feel of him inside her, knowing she was pleasing her man.

And what a man he was, with the body of a god, brawny shoulders and soft hairs on his chest, eyes and a smile that could melt the coldest heart. He seemed to know just the right ways to bring out feelings akin to pure lust in her, so that she had totally abandoned all teachings of right and wrong. Besides, how could it be wrong to want to please the man that she loved, the man she intended to marry? She loved him totally, physically, emotionally, spiritually.

The reality of their trysts did not set in with her until she finally slowed her dizzying passion long enough to realize she had missed a period, then two, then three. She knew what missing periods meant, and her reaction was a mixture of terror and great joy. It was a disgrace to be pregnant and unmarried, yet this was Chad's baby she was carrying. It certainly wasn't his fault this had happened too soon, or hers, for that matter. It had just happened, and now Chad would simply have to decide what he was going to do about Irene.

There was no time now to wait for her return. Two more weeks passed, during which she hesitated telling Chad her suspicions, afraid she would disappoint him by being ignorant of ways to keep from getting pregnant. She was sure there must *be* ways. She just wasn't sure what they were. She knew Chad would be happy and want the baby if they were already married, sure he did want to marry her. Her only fear was that he might feel pushed or tricked.

No, not Chad. He loved her. He would understand he had to do the right thing, that he could no longer wait for Irene. She met him in his room as planned again, deciding to say nothing until he was through making love to her. She didn't want to spoil anything by telling him first. She gave herself to him in total abandon, arching up to him in an effort to take him deep, to please him the way a whore might, for she never wanted him to go to that kind of women. He touched, kissed, tasted every part of her, brought the shuddering climaxes that left her feeling weak and spent. She felt sorry for all other women who would never know this kind of love and passion, would never know what it was like to be touched by Chad Jacobs.

Chad looked at the clock then and moved off her, sitting naked on the edge of the bed and lighting a thin cigar. "It's time for you to leave." He turned to look at her, touching her face. "We won't have to meet this way much longer, Susan."

She turned away, rising and walking to the bowl and pitcher on his wash table and washing herself, not caring that he watched. She pulled on her drawers and her camisole, then came to sit down beside him in her underwear. She swallowed hard for courage. "I need to tell you something, Chad." She looked at him, studying the handsome face, the gentle gray eyes. "I'm so sorry. I didn't mean for it to happen, but we're going to be married anyway, so it isn't the end of the world."

He frowned. "What are you talking about?"

She looked at her lap. "I think I'm pregnant. I mean . . . I'm sure of it."

His blood chilled, and he scrambled to think. He had planned simply to drop her when Irene returned, to express complete ignorance of any relationship with her. If she should go into fits and tell her parents, he planned to accuse her of fantasizing and wishful thinking. After all, who would believe the love-struck child of a poor minister over a prominent attorney, the kind of man who wouldn't think of having anything to do with a plain, unrefined thing like Susan Stanner?

He cleared his throat. "How long has it been?"

"Over three months." She toyed with the lace on her drawers. "This morning I felt movement." She looked at him with pleading eyes. "He's ours, Chad. Our baby. We have to tell my parents now."

He nodded. "Yes, I suppose." He rose, telling himself to stay calm. He couldn't just turn her away this moment. She might feel desperate and create a scene. People might come running, see her in his room or leaving it. As long as no one saw, there was no one to corroborate her story of having an affair with him. He could say she pestered him, that she hounded and annoyed him, that perhaps she had turned to some other man just for spite, to try to make him jealous. He could drag her name through the mud, and people would believe it. Even Bea would believe it. He could do no wrong in her eyes. He loved her daughter. She would never believe he would have an affair with the young daughter of a minister. Not Chad Jacobs!

He came back over to her, touching her shoulders. "You get dressed and go home for now. Give me a day or two to think about this, Susan. I'll need to talk to Mrs. Kirkland, write to Irene."

She smiled. "I knew it would be all right." She hugged him. "I love you, Chad. I'll go home and wait for you." She pulled away. "You can come there, sit down with my parents, and tell them you love me and want to marry me. We don't even need to tell them about the baby until after we're married. They'll forgive us, because we'll already be married."

He nodded, kissing her lightly. "Sure they will. You get going now, and remember, don't say a word to your parents until I come. I don't want you handling it alone. It's my place to tell them. Promise?"

"I promise." She hugged him again. "Oh, I'm so relieved, Chad. I was afraid you'd be angry."

"I'm not angry. I'm happy," he told her, pulling away and urging her to her feet. "Hurry now. I have to get back to the office."

He pulled on his long johns while she finished dressing. She brushed her hair and pinned it, then put on her hat and cape. It was nearly the end of March, and a chinook wind had brought a gentle warmth to the plains. It was spring, and Susan's heart filled with love and joy. She was going to be Chad's wife, have his baby. She came over to him and hugged him once more, gave him a hungry kiss, then went to the door and checked to be sure no one was about before leaving.

Chad pulled on his pants, then walked to a window and looked down to watch Susan cross the street. "Good-bye, little Susan," he muttered. "I enjoyed it while it lasted."

CHAPTER
SIXTEEN

Seventeen-year-old Yellow Eagle stood watching the tribal priest pierce the flesh of his friends who were taking part in the sun dance. None of them cried out as skewers were placed through their breasts, the calves of their legs, the backs of their shoulders. Some already looked close to passing out, trembling and sweating, but they forced themselves to stand, for to give in to the pain too soon was a disgrace.

Strings of rawhide were tied from the skewers to the top of the central pole of the sun dance lodge. To show their bravery, the young warriors were expected to lean away from the central pole as they walked around it, so that the skewers pulled at their flesh until finally the skin gave way. Heavy buffalo skulls were tied to the skewers at their calves, so that when they began walking in their agonizing circle, they dragged the weight with them.

It was Yellow Eagle's turn next. He held the bone whistle tightly between his lips, ready to blow on it when the pain came. His uncle Fast Runner had made the whistle for him to use during the ceremony so that he would not cry out.

"When the pain is bad," his uncle had told him, "breathe deeply and blow hard on the whistle. It will help."

This was the Cheyenne test of manhood, and his own sacrifice to the Great Spirit. He must suffer, have his vision, learn what animal's spirit would guide him through life. He must find his strength, test his courage, for not only was he ready to ride as a warrior, but he had something to prove to himself and to those who doubted his right to be here, just because he carried white blood and had blue eyes.

He closed his eyes, forcing himself to think of other things when the priest shoved the first skewer through his breast. His legs felt weak from several days of fasting. He concentrated on how he hated the white eyes, hated the white blood that ran in his veins. He could not help his heritage, but he most certainly could prove now that he was all Cheyenne in spirit. When he rode with the other warriors, the whites who were stealing more and more game and land would suffer the wrath of the northern Cheyenne and the Sioux. The southern Cheyenne had grown weak. They no longer fought for what was rightfully theirs. That was why he had left his mother and her husband and his three half brothers on the reservation in the south and had come here to the Black Hills, to join Red Cloud and others who were still willing to fight.

The second skewer was placed, and Yellow Eagle concentrated on the mysterious white father he would never know. His feelings about the man called David Kirkland were mixed. His mother had no idea what had ever happened to the man or to Yellow Eagle's twin sister, who, if she was still alive, lived among the whites.

"You did not look exactly alike," his mother had told him. "You were darker. Your hair is not black like the Cheyenne, but it is much darker than was Morning Star's. As a baby her hair was almost white. But your eyes—your eyes are the same."

Yellow Eagle stood taller and broader than his red brothers, thanks to his white father's build. His mother had told him David Kirkland had been a big man, a good man, in spite of being a *Wasicus*.

Yellow Eagle was aware that the young Sioux and Cheyenne women found him exceedingly attractive, and there was one in particular he was hoping to impress today—a young Sioux girl named Dancing Waters. She was watching. She would be proud when she saw that he did not cry out or even flinch.

A skewer pierced his shoulder, and he concentrated on trying to imagine what his sister might look like today, what kind of life she might lead. Did she even know she had Indian blood?

Drums beat rhythmically and women chanted as the last skewer was placed and tied. Yellow Eagle blew hard on the whistle as he began walking in a circle around the central ceremonial pole inside the huge tipi erected specifically for the celebration. The sacred ritual was being held early this season so that the young warriors would be prepared for a summer of warfare against the white settlers. Many had already left the plains in fear. With most of the bluecoats gone fighting a war in the East, the Indians had enjoyed much more freedom, and Red Cloud had practically shut down the road to the white man's gold fields in the north. There was more to be done, and Yellow Eagle planned to be a part of ridding sacred Indian lands of the hated white eyes.

It was not long before two of the other young warriors collapsed, the skewers tearing their skin as they fell. Yellow Eagle kept going, determined to be the last to fall, determined to prove that having white blood did not make him any weaker than the others. More than that, he wanted to show Dancing Waters what a strong, brave man he was. He would take many scalps, steal many horses, once he rode the warpath. One way or another he would win her hand and marry her, for many young braves yearned for the pretty Dancing Waters, and he was not about to let any of them own her. One day she would belong only to Yellow Eagle, but her father would never allow it unless he proved his manhood now at the Sun Dance.

Dancing Waters watched the half-breed Yellow Eagle. There was not a young warrior more handsome in all of the Sioux and Northern Cheyenne tribes. What intrigued her the most was his blue eyes. Against his sun-darkened skin they seemed even bluer than the sky, and she dreamed of the time when he would make her his wife and lie naked next to her. Her blood ran hot at the thought of it, and she watched proudly as all the others fell away. Only Yellow Eagle was left, and she wept at the sight of his blood, at knowing the pain he must be suffering.

Finally he fell, but he had proven his worth. The half-breed Yellow Eagle would no longer be looked upon as half *Wasicus*. He was all Cheyenne now, a full-fledged warrior who would ride with his brothers against the whites. There would be no reservations for men like Yellow Eagle, and already Dancing Waters determined that where Yellow Eagle went, she would be at his side.

Susan Stanner waited in the alley beside Kirkland Enterprises, her heart pounding with dread at what she did not want to believe might be true. She had waited faithfully at home, two days, three days, five days. Chad had not come as promised, had not spoken with her parents about marriage. When she had gone to his room to talk to him, he was not there. She was afraid to go to his office, afraid for some reason he would be angry she had shown up to meet him publicly. Surely there was some reason he had not spoken to her parents yet, and until she knew for certain, she had to do as he had always told her and not be seen with him.

She did not want to believe there could be any reason for his failure to contact her other than something that might have gone wrong with the Kirklands. After all, he loved her, and he knew how much she loved him, knew she was carrying his baby. Surely he would make a move soon, but yesterday in church, he had not once met her eyes. She could no longer bear the heartache. She missed him so much that she thought she might die. She longed to be in his arms again, longed to share his bed again, to stand beside him before a minister and vow her love for eternity.

She peeked around the building again, finally seeing him exit onto the boardwalk. She waited until he passed the alley, then called out to him. Chad turned, looking irritated. At first she thought he was going to keep walking, but he looked around to be sure he was not seen, then hurried into the alley, carrying a briefcase. He came closer, and she felt almost sick at the strange look on his face.

"What do you want, Susan?" he asked.

She struggled to find her voice, her throat so tight she wondered how she managed to breathe. "I . . . my God, Chad, you know what I want. Where have you been? I've been waiting and waiting for you to come."

He frowned. "Come where?"

Her eyes widened. "To the house! To talk to my parents about getting married!"

He snickered, looking her over as though she were little more than dirt under his boots. "What the hell are you talking about? You know I'm to marry Irene Kirkland. Have you gone mad or something?"

She began to tremble visibly. She reached out and touched his arm. "Chad . . . I . . . don't understand. Please, don't do this. We . . . love each other. I'm carrying your *baby*!"

He stepped back. "You don't get it, do you," he said in almost a sneer. "There is nothing between us, Susan, and never has been. This is all some kind of fantasy of yours, and it has to stop. If you've gotten yourself in a bad way by hitching your skirts for some poor slob in a barn, that's your problem. You'd better find a way to explain it to your parents. Just don't drag me into it, or your name will be more muddied than the most notorious harlot of Denver, I can promise you that. As far as I'm concerned, you're a poor, demented young thing who has pestered me to death with your confounded fantasies about loving me. Just stay away from me."

He turned and left, and Susan stared after him in total shock. She was immediately deaf to all the noise of the city, barely aware of her surroundings as she half stumbled to her horse, which was tied farther back in the alley. She stopped beside it, bending over to vomit, her chest so pained she could barely breathe.

Chad! Her beautiful, beloved Chad! How could this be happening? How could anyone be that cruel? How could he have fooled her so perfectly? His eyes had held such sincerity when he told her he loved her, would come for her. He had made love to her with such utter passion and devotion. She cried out at the thought of what she had let him do to her, and she vomited again.

The horrible reality set in. He had used her in the worst way! In a sense he had raped her, over and over, for if she had known he didn't really love her at all, she never would have given herself to him. He had lied to her with a smile on his face, had raked over her naked body in pure lust, as if she were a whore! Now Irene was coming home, and he was done with her. She was left with his baby in her belly, left to disgrace her family, the daughter of a minister, soon to be walking around with a swollen stomach and no husband.

She managed to climb onto her horse and lead it out of town to open land, galloping for the deserted cabin where it had all begun, the place where she had thought she had found the love of her life. When she reached it, the reality of what she had done, what she had lost, overwhelmed her, so that she half fell from her horse. She crouched on the ground, heaving in great, bitter sobs, wanting nothing more now than to die.

Among Denver's upper class, those struggling to bring Christianity and civility to that still-wild gold town, the suicide of Susan Stanner was a great blow, especially to Bea Kirkland, who had been personally responsible for bringing the Reverend Will Stanner to town. Bea considered it an immense scandal, but she was close enough to the Stanners to feel their intense grief.

No one knew why Susan had done what she did. After she had been missing for several hours, her father rode out to the trail she used to frequent. He had found her inside an abandoned cabin, hanging from a rafter by a piece of rope off her own horse. There had been no sign of foul play, no sign of a struggle. His daughter's body had not been beaten or abused in any way. An old table had been dragged to the spot as though the girl had deliberately and willingly climbed up on it in order to tie the rope over the rafter. The table was overturned, as if she had kicked it away. Officials could draw no conclusion but suicide, and the Stanners' grief was beyond comforting.

The funeral was widely attended. Most felt deeply sorry for the Stanners; some judged the Reverend Stanner as apparently an unfit father to have had a daughter who would do such a thing, and therefore perhaps he was unfit to minister to them. Others had come out of mere curiosity, and the town was ablaze with gossip over the reasons the poor Stanner girl might have hanged herself.

At the funeral Bea wept bitterly, thinking of Irene and Elly, hoping they would never be so despondent as to do something so drastic. She thought especially of Irene, how sick and depressed she had been after Bea had secretly caused Ramon to leave town and marry someone else. Had Irene considered taking her own life? Had Susan's suicide been over a man? It was beyond Bea's comprehension that any man could mean that much to a woman, or that any woman could be so weak. But then Susan was not a woman yet. She was still so young, just as Irene was.

While she wept into her handkerchief, Bea was grateful that at least Irene had Chad, a solid, dependable man who would never allow Irene to be hurt. Kirk was still in the mountains with John. Bea had no one to cling to but Chad, who kept his arm around her.

Elly watched Chad out of the corner of her eye, suspecting he knew something about Susan's death that he wasn't telling anyone. She had not missed the way Chad had looked at the girl and the way Susan looked back at him. Something was very wrong.

Chad watched the casket being lowered into the ground with a look more of shock on his face than sorrow. Elly had no idea what was really going through his mind. Chad found it incredible that any girl would go to such lengths over a simple affair. She could have told her parents about the baby, could have made something up. She could have gone off and had the thing and given it away. Other women had been known to do such things, and it wasn't the end of the world

His stomach tightened at a thousand emotions. He was sorry for Susan, but he didn't really blame himself. She was young and apparently much weaker than he had thought; and, after all, a girl ought to know how to keep from getting pregnant. If she wanted to sleep around and believe everything a man told her, that was her problem. Still, he had apparently underestimated how much she had truly loved him, underestimated his own power over women. He supposed some of this was his fault, and he breathed a secret sigh of relief that Susan had not left behind an incriminating note. No one but he knew the real reason for the girl's death, and it gave him a strange feeling of guilt. He was not used to feeling guilty for anything, and he supposed he would get over it eventually. After all, it was not as though he had taken her to that cabin and killed her with his own two hands. At least now there would be no accusations, no explaining to do.

Bea had invited everyone to her home after the funeral, and two men had to hold onto Mary Stanner to keep her from collapsing. The woman had to be taken home shortly afterward, but Will Stanner stayed on, graciously accepting condolences from all those who came to express them. Young Sam Stanner sat crying in the corner of the parlor, speaking to no one.

When most of the people had left, Mr. Stanner asked Bea if there was a place where they could talk alone. She led him to her sewing room and closed the doors, turning red, puffy eyes to meet his own. "What is it, Reverend?" she asked.

A tall, gangly man with head and hands that seemed too big for the rest of his body, Stanner took out an already-damp handkerchief and blew his nose before turning away and lowering his head. "I must tell you something. I don't want it to go any farther than this room, Mrs. Kirkland." He turned and met her eyes. "I am taking my family and leaving Denver. You should see to getting a new minister."

Bea frowned, stepping closer to him. "Reverend, we can't always control our children. This could have happened to any one of us, I suppose. It doesn't make you any less worthy."

He shook his head. "You don't understand. Only the coroner knows, Mrs. Kirkland. Susan . . . Susan was . . . pregnant."

Bea reddened slightly, feeling a tingle through her whole body. Her first thought was of Irene again, what might have happened if she had not stopped the girl's young passion for Ramon as quickly as she had. "Oh, Reverend, how terrible for you!"

"How terrible for *Susan*. She should have felt she could come to us, but she didn't. We failed miserably as parents, Mrs. Kirkland. And considering I had a daughter who was seeing someone out of wedlock, let alone that she committed suicide, I simply cannot bring myself to go on preaching. Maybe someday, after I have had time to sort it all out, to pray about it, I will again be able to stand behind a pulpit."

"I understand. I'm so sorry, Reverend." She touched his arm.

"We'll just tell the others you're too grief-stricken to go on with your duties and that you feel a need to leave Denver for a while. No one needs to know all of it."

"Thank you. I just . . . I wish I knew who the man was who did this to her. It's a terrible thought, but I keep hoping maybe on one of those rides Susan took . . . maybe she was abducted . . . forced. Maybe she felt it was her fault and felt too guilty about it to tell us. I—I can't believe she would have willingly given herself to a man. She was so young and innocent. Horrible as being forced might be, to think it might have been that way is my only comfort."

Bea considered his theory. "Yes, perhaps she *was* forced," she said thoughtfully. A worried look came into her eyes. "I think I had better keep an extra close watch on my own daughters. Denver will never be safe as long as we still have drunken Indians and miners on the loose, let alone those Chinese and Mexicans. And now a lot of Negroes are coming here, freed slaves from the South." She shook her head. "We have to have more law and order in this town, Reverend." She sighed, touching his arm again. "There is no sense telling others, since we have no proof Susan was attacked. It would only start a panic, maybe lead to some innocent man being hanged. It's just something we'll never know for certain. I'm so terribly sorry."

Stanner nodded. "I had better get home to Mary. She—she doesn't know . . . about the pregnancy. I don't want her to know."

"I understand." Bea led him to the door. When she opened it she found Chad standing not far away, smoking a cigar and looking out a window. He looked at both of them, appearing almost worried about something.

"Is there anything I can do?" he asked quickly, curious about Stanner's reasons for talking to Bea alone. Had Susan left a note after all, naming Chad Jacobs as her lover? He was relieved to see no anger or animosity on Bea's face.

"No," Stanner answered. "There is nothing anyone can do, but thank you, Chad." The man left, and Chad looked at Bea. She read the question in his eyes.

"The reverend is leaving Denver," she told him quietly, coming closer. She dabbed at tear-filled eyes again. "It's worse than we thought, Chad. Susan was pregnant."

"What!" Chad feigned surprise. In fact, he *was* surprised, surprised that anyone else knew.

"The coroner discovered it." She took his arm and led him into the sewing room. "I am only telling you, Chad, because the reverend fears she was attacked and was afraid to tell anyone about it. That means someone in this town might have . . . might have raped her. I don't like using that word, but I want you to be alert and aware. When Irene gets back, I want you to keep a close watch on her. Don't let her go riding off on Sierra alone. Don't let her go *anywhere* alone."

"Of course I won't," Chad assured her.

Bea collapsed against him. "Oh, I'm so glad she has you, Chad. And I'm glad you're here for this. It seems Kirk is never here when I need him most."

He patted her shoulder, relieved that Stanner thought Susan might have been raped. He had not thought of that one. Such a thought could only help save him. Her parents would not be trying to find out whom she might have willingly had an affair with. They were not about to believe she would throw herself at a man with the brazenness she had shown Chad.

"Kirk will be back soon," he said aloud, "and so will Irene. Things will seem brighter then."

"Oh, I suppose." Bea pulled away. "I had better go and see to the remaining guests." She patted his arm. "What I have just told you must never leave your lips, Chad. The reverend doesn't want others to know Susan was with child."

"Of course not. I'll not breathe a word." He watched her leave, feeling almost as though he had just escaped the noose himself. He breathed a sigh of deep relief, looking down to brush some lint from his coat. He started to leave the room when Elly suddenly made an appearance, walking out from behind a grand piano. Chad caught the movement and turned to see her standing there. He frowned with irritation. "What the hell are you doing back there?" He almost hated the pesty girl for always sneaking around where she didn't belong. She was the only female who had ever made him feel uneasy.

Elly smiled, sauntering toward him in an effort to appear sexy. "I was in here when Mother and the reverend came in. I had a feeling they meant to be alone, so I decided I would hide and listen to what they had to say."

Chad stepped closer, eyeing her cautiously. "This is a very delicate matter. Your mother promised the reverend no one would know. I hope you have the sense to keep your mouth shut, young lady."

Elly folded her arms. "I'll keep my mouth shut . . . about more than Susan being pregnant."

Chad reddened slightly, suddenly hating her more. "What do you mean by that?" He found it incredible how much she resembled her mother, especially when she straightened to her full too-tall height and faced him squarely as she did now.

"It was *yours*, wasn't it?" For the first time ever, Elly saw the charm and eternal graciousness vanish from Chad Jacobs's eyes. The soft gray turned to a steely gray, and his jaw flexed with anger. She distinctly sensed he had a great longing to choke her, but she knew she was safe, and she knew she was right.

"What the hell is it you're talking about?" he hissed.

"The baby. You're the one Susan Stanner was seeing, aren't you?"

He sucked in his breath, struggling not to look guilty. He managed a sarcastic smile then. "You, little girl, are capable of great fantasies. I have better things to do than to go around destroying nice young ladies like Susan Stanner, a minister's daughter at that. I happen to be in love with your sister, Elly, something you can't stand. But it's a fact, and I am going to marry her, and I'll thank you to stop sneaking around trying to catch me at something and to stop throwing yourself at me. And you can definitely stop thinking up ridiculous lies to tell about me."

She put a hand against his chest. "I never said I'd tell. I *want* you to marry Irene, because it will keep you around. I know it's the only way I'll ever be close to you." She met his eyes boldly. "I love you, Chad, just like Susan did. I'm just not stupid enough to hang myself over it."

"Shut up," he growled, grabbing her arm.

She laughed. "I knew it!" She turned away. "It's our secret. Maybe nobody would believe me, but then again, I could make them wonder, couldn't I? Can you imagine the scandal for this family? Why, people would run you out of town tarred and feathered. And you certainly would never get to marry into the family, would you?"

Chad hurried over and closed the doors. "You're a damn liar and a foolish young girl who is so jealous and full of hatred she can't even think straight! You mention such an outrageous story to your mother, and *you* would be the one in trouble, Elly Kirkland! You know how your mother feels about me, and I am a lot smarter than you are, so you'd better think twice about such talk. No one would believe it in a million years! You'd be a laughing stock."

She pouted, stepping closer to him again. "Maybe. But I think I'm right. I can tell by the look on your face." She breathed deeply, studying his eyes, seeing the hatred there. "Someday,

Chad, I'll have you for myself. You hate me now, but you won't always hate me. I could tell on you, but I won't. That's how much I love you." She folded her arms again. "You can marry my sister. Everybody expects it, and I hate her for it. I don't care if you marry her, because I know you'll hurt her, and she deserves to be hurt, like *I* hurt. At least if you marry her, you'll still be in the family, and when you're tired of her, and when I'm older and know more about men, you'll make love to me like you did with Susan Stanner."

She daringly reached out, grasping his wrist and placing one of his hands on her full breast. "See? I'm not such a child. You'd like to do it to me right now if I wasn't Irene's sister, wouldn't you?"

He watched her eyes, gauged her intent. He could handle any woman, or girl, and this one was not going to be any different if he could help it. He gave her a smug smile, lightly squeezing her breast, totally undoing her, he could tell, with just those slight gestures. He moved his hand from her breast to touch her face, leaning down and planting a kiss smack on her lips, surprising her. He drew the kiss out until he felt the hatred and vengeance going out of her, until he knew he had her under his power. He left her mouth then, keeping his face close to hers.

"Maybe I *would* like to," he told her, his voice gruff. "But I truly do love Irene, Elly, and you're too young for me." He moved his gray eyes over her, feeling her begin to tremble. She was not as ready for this as she had thought, and he could tell he had shaken her. "You're wrong about Susan Stanner, Elly, and that's the God's truth. But you aren't wrong about me sometimes wanting you. It's just a natural manly instinct, because you're young and pretty, and I know how you feel about me. But I don't intend to act on those feelings, because I want to be part of this family, and I don't want to hurt anyone in it. It will be easier for both of us once I marry Irene and we have our own place, so I don't have to be around you so much."

He drew back, taking hold of her hands. "I'm flattered you have such strong feelings about me, Elly, but you've got to remember you aren't even fourteen yet. I'll get over these temptations, and you'll learn to love somebody else. That's the way it has to be." He squeezed her hands, leaning forward and kissing her once more, lightly. "But we'll always have this moment, won't we? It will be our special secret. If you really love me, Elly, you'll let it go at this and not bring me pain by spreading a lie about me or by telling your mother or anyone else that we just shared something so intimate."

She watched his handsome face in wide-eyed wonder, finding it wonderful and incredible that he actually did seem tempted, that he *had* thought about her after all! "Yes," she whispered. "I won't ever tell."

He gave her his best smile. "Did you think I didn't know how you felt, the way you were always trying to sit close to me, the way you looked at me? I'm honored, Elly, but it just can't be. I'm sorry."

Her eyes teared as he squeezed her hands again. "I am, too," she told him, her voice squeaky.

He let go of her, stepping away. "We had better get back out there with the others."

She nodded, all her cockiness and sureness gone. She had almost hated him when she first confronted him, but now love flooded her again. Maybe she had been wrong about Susan. But then if she was not, she could almost understand now why the girl had done what she had done. It didn't really matter. She was not about to do something so stupid. She intended to live, to learn about men, to wait for the right moment when she could steal Chad Jacobs from her sister's bed.

All that mattered now was that she had had this wonderful moment. Chad might marry Irene, but she had just shared something with him that Irene would never know about, and now she was special, too. That was all she ever really wanted to know. She felt beautiful, desired. At least now he knew she loved him. She felt a strange, flooding relief at getting it out of her system, and his kiss and the touch of his hand at her breast was suddenly enough. It had frightened her some, made her realize she really wasn't ready to be the kind of woman Chad Jacobs was used to.

She watched his eyes, and she saw only gentleness and respect there. "I'll leave first," she told him. "You'd better wait a few minutes." She leaned up and kissed his cheek, then ran out of the room.

Chad's eyes immediately glittered with hate. Oh, how he wanted to kill her for figuring it out about him and Susan! What a conniving, scheming, nosy little bitch she was! The worst part was he wanted her, not because she was pretty, for there wasn't one pretty thing about her. He only wanted her because she was ripe for a man, itching to find out what it was like. He'd like to have at the little bitch until she begged for mercy. She had a look about her, a look he'd seen in the eyes of whores. Elly Kirkland was begging for it, and he suspected that before too long she would find someone to oblige her, someone to cool the burning desire she carried for a man she couldn't have.

He sighed, relieved that for the now he had managed to keep her under control and convince her he'd had nothing to do with Susan Stanner. He had been right to deal with the girl by giving her what she wanted for the moment. He had suspected right away that it would have been more dangerous to try to go against her. Just like her mother, Elly had to be treated a certain way, for he suspected that to suffer the wrath of either Kirkland female would be an experience better avoided.

He closed his eyes, feeling satisfied he had again saved himself, deciding that for a while he would have to lay low and mind his business. But that meant staying away from other women and showing his total devotion to Irene once she returned. He was not usually so careless. From now on there would be no ministers' daughters in his bed, at least not until things had calmed down over Susan Stanner's death.

He left the room, deciding that from now on he would check every nook and cranny wherever he went in this house. Elly Kirkland was a deceitful, nosy sneak, and for the moment he wished it was she who had been buried today instead of Susan.

Chad awoke in a sweat, sitting up to get the nightmare out of his mind. He had dreamed of ghostly people standing around a grave, and then both Susan and Elly climbed out of the black hole, reaching out for him.

He rose, wiping perspiration from his brow. It had been a week since Susan's funeral, and ungodly hot for April, one of the driest springs in Colorado history. There had simply not been enough snow in the mountains the past winter to create a good runoff, nor had any spring rain fallen in any measurable amount. Everything was tinder dry, and a battering wind outside blew dust from the dirt streets below right through Chad's second-story window.

He walked over and closed it, then sat down to light a thin cigar, wondering if maybe he should go visit his favorite whore. It was obvious he was not going to get any more sleep, and Irene was due back tomorrow. Once she was home, his womanizing would have to come to an abrupt end. He leaned forward and picked up his pocket watch from a nightstand and opened it to see that it was three A.M. Not even the whores were up and about at this hour.

He puffed on the cigar, actually looking forward to seeing

Irene, hoping that having her at his side again would ease his nightmares and remove this lingering guilt over Susan. He hated her for what she had done, chastised himself for not realizing how young and stupid she had been. He wondered if any other women he had left behind had been left pregnant or had done something dumb like commit suicide over him.

He rose and studied himself in the mirror, again convincing himself it was their fault, not his own. He couldn't help it if women fell all over him. In a way, he realized suddenly that part of the reason he could think of Irene as special was because she had *not* fallen into his arms in a swoon. That fascinated him. Irene would be more of a challenge than any of the others, because for some reason he had not made her faint dead away in his arms.

Maybe it was because she was so beautiful in her own right. Or maybe it was just a certain strength she had gleaned from her powerful, determined mother that made her seem so pure and strong. There was a peace about Irene he had never felt with any other woman, and he actually looked forward to her return, even though it mean no more affairs for a while. He was curious to know if and how she had changed, if maybe now she would be more responsive to him.

The wind battered the window again, making it shake. He thought he heard a strange popping sound then, and he turned from the mirror, taking the cigar from his mouth and going to the window. He put his hand against it to look out into the darkness.

It seemed his heart literally stopped beating for a moment. A strange orange glow was rising from the vicinity of the Cherokee Hotel. Fire! "My God," he muttered. He quickly put out his cigar and pulled on his pants. In this dry, windy weather, fire could mean disaster for the whole town! He didn't stop to pull on a shirt. He only grabbed his watch and money, then charged out of his room and banged on doors. "Fire," he hollered as he ran down the stairs. "Fire! Fire! Everyone out!"

He heard a scream, then a few mumbles. Doors opened and people stuck their heads out. He yelled "Fire!" again, but kept running, heading for the lobby. His only thought for the moment was to get to Kirkland Enterprises and save whatever records he could save. He wished there was time to go and wake Kirk, who had just gotten back from the mountains, but the Kirkland home was too far. There was no time. He thought that at least its location would probably keep it safe.

He dashed outside and heard more screams. The street seemed to come alive all at once, as people began to realize what was happening. Chad ran three blocks to the Kirkland offices, which were downwind from the flames. Already he could smell the acrid smoke, feel bits of burning embers biting at his flesh. He darted inside, charging into his office and quickly lighting a lamp. With a pounding heart he yanked a drawer from his desk and shoved everything into it that was most important, including his files on eastern investors in worthless mines owned by Colorado Mining Company, the bogus company he had set up for Bea. He grabbed up land records, deeds to property and buildings, and hurried back outside.

Buildings just two blocks away were already breaking into flames, and sickening popping and cracking noises were followed by windows blowing out or sudden gushes of cinders leaping into the air. People were running everywhere now, horses whinnying, a few wagons clattering by, filled with people already fleeing the area where the fire was the worst.

Chad ran with the drawer full of files, heading away from the fire, the wind at his back. Hot ashes flicked at his skin in painful little stabs. He ran past his own hotel, the new Denver Inn, of which Bea was so proud. He ran through an alley, heading east and north, then veering in the exact direction of the fire, but keeping farther east of it so that he could get around behind it, where there was less danger.

Suddenly smoke smacked him in the face, burning his eyes, and for a moment he couldn't see or think straight. He bent over and coughed, setting the drawer down for a moment to regain his bearings. He rubbed at his eyes and looked around, noticing another building on fire that was not even in the path of the flames. Its roof had begun burning from cinders blown about in the wind. The wind was gusting in a hundred directions. There was really no way of being sure what path the fire would take.

Now the whole town had come alive with screams and shouts. A fire wagon rushed past him, but he knew it would be of no use. There was no saving Denver in this dry wind, with most buildings made of hardwood or pitch-filled pine logs, most rooftops made of split shakes. The new fire company was just that—new and disorganized.

He again picked up the drawer full of valuable records, heading out of town and toward Kirkland Bluffs. He had to alert Kirk and Bea. Maybe there was more that could be saved. The drawer seemed to get heavier and heavier as he ran, but he hung onto it. He stopped partway up the gradual but steep incline away from the city to sit down and rest for a moment, looking back on the disaster that was taking place below.

Fire seemed to be everywhere now. It looked for a moment as if the two Kirkland banks and the hotels might still be alright, but he could tell from here that the warehouses were already burning. He forced himself back to his feet and started running again, clinging to the drawer, wanting to get it to safety so he could go back to see if there was anything he and Kirk could do to save Kirkland property or help get people to safety. He wished he had a horse, but there had not been time to grab Sierra.

Sierra! He turned again. He had used Sierra yesterday, had put the animal up in the stalls used for hotel guests. Irene's treasured horse was still down there! "Damn," he growled. How could he face Irene if something happened to Sierra? He could only pray she wouldn't blame him. After all, his first thought had to be for important Kirkland records.

With an aching heart he turned and hurried on, not even thinking about how Susan Stanner's death had not affected him nearly as much as the death of Irene's horse would. He hoped the animal would survive until he could get back down to it, if he could even go near the area. He ran until he thought his chest might burst, stumbling up the steps to the house. He dropped the drawer of files and pounded on the door.

"Kirk! Everybody! Wake up in there," he shouted. He pounded again, hollering until Ester Sanchez, wearing a nightcap and a robe, opened the door and held up a lamp, embarrassed to see Chad standing there bare-chested. He pushed his way inside to greet Kirk as the man came hurrying downstairs in his underwear to see Chad standing in the great room, panting, black from smoke, small burns all over his chest, arms and back.

"Denver," he panted. "The whole town's on fire!"

CHAPTER
SEVENTEEN

Irene's blood ran cold as the Overland Stage Company coach in which she rode approached Denver. The coach made its way along Seventeenth Street, past smoldering ruins. The heart of Denver, including one of the Kirkland banks and, Irene could see even from a block away, the new Denver Inn, were gone.

"Dear God," she muttered, her heart pounding with dread. Was her family all right? And what about Chad? He lived at the Inn! Others in the coach gawked out the windows, astonished at what they saw. Everything was black, smoke still drifting from charred wood. People milled about in the streets, shaking their heads, some crying, some trying to climb amid the ruins of their homes or businesses to see if they could find anything left of value.

"This must have just happened last night," a man inside the coach spoke up. "Otherwise we would have heard about it at the last stop."

"It's been a dry spring," said another.

Irene searched frantically for signs of life as the coach passed what was left of the Denver Inn. Its brick walls still stood, but the roof was gone, and the insides were gutted. The coach slowed there, unable to go on because of debris in the dusty street. The driver climbed down, announcing the passengers would have to get off here, or he could turn around and drive them to the closest undamaged hotel.

Irene climbed out, unsure what to do. Acrid smoke stung her nose, and a pig ambled past her, snorting and nudging its nose into an overturned barrel of apples. She jumped back when two dogs came bounding toward her to chase the pig, and suddenly the air was filled with squeals and barks. The pig ran off, the dogs biting at its heels.

Everything seemed to be in chaos. Irene searched the staggering masses of people for her family, but saw no familiar faces. It appeared at least half of Denver was burned to the ground. Would her parents recover from this? Were they all right? She saw Chad running toward the coach then, his hair a tumble, his face dirty, his pants torn. She recognized the shirt he wore as her father's.

"Irene," he called out. "I've been waiting at the Overland station—" he didn't finish. He threw his arms about her waist, and she hugged him in great relief. He was all right. "What a terrible thing for you to have to come home to," he told her, kissing her hair.

She looked up at him, and he met her mouth in a gentle kiss, then pulled away, his eyes moving over her. "You look wonderful, Irene. God, I missed you."

"I missed you, too, Chad," she answered, gripping his arms. "Oh, Chad, what happened! Are my parents all right?"

"They're okay. They were up at the house when it happened." He glanced at the ruins of the Denver Inn. "Thank God I was having trouble sleeping last night," he continued, "or I might not be standing here to greet you."

"Oh, Chad," she exclaimed, hugging him around the middle, resting her head against his chest. "I'm glad you're all right."

He embraced her tightly, almost glad for the fire. The possibility of his demise had made her appreciate him more. "I managed to save most of the important papers from Kirkland Enterprises," he told her. "The offices are gone, the Inn here, and one of the warehouses. We lost one bank, but gold and paper money that was in the safe was salvaged. Your mother has already moved it to the National Bank. The Inn is a tremendous loss for her, Irene, but at least the brick walls are still standing, and the Kirkland Hotel is all right."

"This is so terrible." She wept, pulling away from him then. "Thank God none of you was hurt. What about Mother and Father? How are they handling their losses?"

"Your mother has already wired San Francisco for more goods to be shipped here as quickly as possible. With so many people in need, whatever she can get in here will bring a good deal of money. It will help a little in recovering from the financial blow." He couldn't tell her that Bea Kirkland had made a killing with her bogus mining investment company, money that would go a long way in offsetting what had happened here. "You know Bea," he added. "Always thinking ahead, diving right back into things. They'll be all right, Irene."

Irene wiped at her eyes, wondering why she had momentarily let herself worry about her parents' financial situation. If anyone could bounce back and recoup her losses, Bea Kirkland could. The woman would die before she let herself go under financially.

Chad asked the stage driver to take Irene's luggage up to the Kirkland mansion, describing where it was and handing the man a five-dollar gold piece for his trouble. "The whole family is here in town helping clean up," he told Irene, taking her arm. "They're sorry they couldn't all be here. We had planned to give you a grand reception. Bea and Kirk both missed you so much. I'll take you down to the Kirkland Hotel. Your father is there giving directions to some cleanup crews. John and Elly are at the National Bank with Bea helping set up new records. Bea is already talking about rebuilding the Inn, only bigger and grander."

Irene looked around at the pitiful ruins. One man sat crying in front of what had once been his supply store. She thought how Bea Kirkland would never cry over such a thing. She would simply get to work rebuilding.

"Bea says that after what has happened, Denver businesses had better think about rebuilding with brick," Chad was telling her as they walked slowly toward the hotel. "That could have prevented much of the damage. The wind was so bad, it just picked up all those flying embers from all the wood buildings and blew them onto rooftops, starting more fires. You should have seen this place last night, Irene. It was like a living hell."

Dogs ran everywhere, and Irene gasped when one man turned and pulled a six-gun, shooting two dogs. "Chad!"

Chad pulled her to the other side of the street. "It's a new law," he told her. "So many dogs are running loose they're forming wild packs. People are allowed to shoot any dog that isn't tied." He stopped and grasped her arms. "My God, I didn't even ask you, maybe you'd rather go to the house first."

"No. Not if everyone is here. I want to help."

His eyes moved over her. She looked ravishing in a blue-striped dress with a deep blue short velvet jacket fitted tightly at her slender waist, with darts in just the right places to accent her full bosom. Her blue velvet hat was perched on golden hair swept up in a tumble of curls. He longed for the day she would be his wife and he could forget about having to be so respectful. "You aren't even dressed for this. You can't walk around these filthy streets with these clothes on."

"It's all right. Just take me to see my father at least. Then maybe I can go home and change and come back." She studied his bloodshot eyes. "Chad, you look terrible. Have you been up all night?"

He grinned, his face looking even blacker against his white, even teeth. "Some homecoming, isn't it? Yeah, I've been awake since three or so this morning." He put an arm around her waist and continued walking with her. "I'll survive. I can't go to sleep anyway. I don't have a bed anymore. Hell, I don't even have any clothes!"

"Chad," she said softly, resting her head against his side as they walked. "You know Mother and Father will help. You can stay at our house until things get back to normal."

It did feel good to have her back. She was the calm in the storm, a rock amid the raging waters of his confused soul. He slowed his walk, turning to her again. "I'm still yours, Irene," he told her, bringing utter devotion into his eyes. "Are you still mine?"

Their eyes held. He looked so pitiful, had apparently been through hell helping save her family's possessions. And he had saved her father's life once. "Yes," she answered.

He leaned down and met her mouth again, giving her a slow, suggestive kiss. "Good," he said softly as he drew away. "I'm sorry about all this, Irene. I pictured your homecoming a lot different. There isn't even time to talk about what the school was like, or how your trip was."

She smiled, patting his chest. "The trip was fine, considering all the Indian trouble. Father hired a virtual army to ride with the coach. Once we hit Denver they spread out to see what they could do to help. As it turned out, Father didn't need to pay all those men. We saw no sign of Indians."

"Well, that's part of the reason your parents had you sent home a little early. Your father figures that in another month or two the plains won't be safe for anyone. Everybody in town figures the Cheyenne will come out this summer like a swarm of bees. Things are going to get worse, I'm afraid. This fire doesn't help, especially since we'll need a lot of supplies now." He hesitated, and his eyes seemed to tear suddenly.

"Chad, what is it? There's something you aren't telling me."

He sighed deeply, leading her to a bench in front of a building that had survived the fire. All around them people were shouting, sifting through rubble, some crying, others giving orders. And the sounds of saws and hammers were proof that these strong, resilient people had not given up. Disaster had not halted their plans for making Denver, Colorado, the biggest and finest city in the West. Nearby several men were already erecting a temporary assay office, and across the street a tent went up with a SALOON sign in front of it. Farther up the street a man held up a SUPPLIES sign, using his own freight wagon full of fresh supplies that had arrived that morning as his store.

Chad turned to Irene, grasping her shoulders. "I might as well tell you before Elly lets it slip out," he said. "She's so insensitive."

"Tell me what?"

He closed his eyes and sighed. "Sierra. I . . . had ridden him yesterday. I had him put up last night in the stalls at the Denver Inn."

She glanced in the direction of the burned-out hotel, taking a moment to realize what he was telling her. Sierra! He had died in the fire! "Oh, no," she gasped, covering her face. She leaned against his chest, and he put his arm around her shoulders.

"I'm so damn sorry, Irene. I had grown attached to him myself. I was taking really good care of him, exercising him every day. I feel like such a fool, and I wouldn't blame you if you were angry with me."

She cried for several minutes, unable to speak. Everything about the last several minutes had been such a shock. She had imagined coming home to a happy family, Chad riding to greet her on Sierra. She had wondered how Sierra would behave when he saw her again, imagined hugging him around the neck. The first thing she was going to do was go riding. Oh, how she'd missed it! But with Sierra gone, it suddenly didn't seem important anymore.

"You couldn't . . . have known," she sobbed, finally finding her voice. She took a handkerchief from her handbag.

"The fire moved so fast, Irene. When you're in the middle of an inferno, you don't think straight. I went to the offices first because I could see they would go fast. I saved what important papers I could. By then I couldn't get back to the Inn." He rubbed at her shoulders. "I didn't even have a shirt on. My back and chest and arms are giving me a lot of pain. I'm covered with little burns from hot embers."

She straightened, blowing her nose and wiping at her eyes. "Oh, Chad, I didn't know. I'm sorry. I should just be happy you're alive and unhurt. It's just . . . Sierra meant so much to me." She suddenly thought of Ramon, the day they went riding together, Sierra thundering across the open land, the wind in her face, Ramon riding at her side looking like a grand Spanish warrior. Sierra had liked running hard just as much as Irene had liked riding him that way. "I don't know if you can understand," she went on. "Sierra and I . . . we were like one spirit." The tears came again. "It isn't so much that he died, as that he died without ever seeing me again. Maybe he thought . . . I had deserted him."

He pulled her close, letting her head rest against his shoulder, almost grateful for all the grief. It seemed to draw them closer. She was warmer and more open than she had been when she left. Apparently it had been good for their relationship for her to go away. She seemed more responsive now, seemed to turn to him more lovingly.

"I think he knew you were coming back," he assured her. "I mentioned you to him every day. We, uh, we found his remains, Irene. Your father intends to use slings and pulleys to get him into a wagon so he can be buried up by the house. He figured you'd like that."

She sniffed, pulling away again. "Father would think of something like that. I'm sure Mother wouldn't care either way, but Father understands how I felt about Sierra."

"There's something else, honey," he added, using the endearment carefully, gauging her reaction. She didn't seem to mind. "Your father . . ."

She wiped at her eyes and looked at him. "He's hurt?"

"No. But . . . I don't know. He's acting kind of strange. He's short with everyone, and that's not like him. I know he's taken a great financial loss, but I think it's more than that. I caught him crying once, and he told me I might have to take over for him in a few days—that he needs to get away from all this for personal reasons."

Chad suspected what was wrong with David Kirkland. He had visited the whores often enough to hear rumors about Kirk's visits to a certain madam named Mary O'Day, and he had learned from one of the prostitutes in the street this morning that Mary had been killed in the fire. He thought it incredible that any man could fall in love with a whore, and he found it amusing that one of the most prominent men in Denver had cheated on his wife. Now Chad would not feel quite so guilty about doing the same after he married Irene. He gave no thought to what Kirk's reasons might be, but he did wonder if Bea knew.

"I just thought you should know," he told her, "so you know what to expect when we see your father."

"Maybe it's just the pressure of all this," she offered. "He never liked handling the money end of the business, and I'm sure Mother is going to harp about their losses for some time to come. It just gets to him."

"Yes, maybe that's it. At any rate, I'm damn sorry about Sierra. I wish there was something I could do or say to make it better for you."

She met his eyes and shook her head. "I can understand how terrible last night must have been. You should go home, Chad, and get some rest."

He touched her face. "I can't. I intend to work right alongside your father until *he* says to quit. This will all work out, honey. We'll be all right, and you and I will do some catching up in a few days when things quiet down."

She smiled through tears. "Yes. I'd like that."

He leaned forward, meeting her lips, irritated that they were not where he could take advantage of her momentary vulnerability. He suspected that at this moment, if they were alone, he could get more out of her than a kiss. He pulled back then, deciding she had already been hit with enough bad news that he had better not tell her just yet about Susan Stanner's suicide. He only hoped Elly would keep her mouth shut about his part in it.

Irene heard someone call her name, and she looked to see her father hurrying toward her. She rose to greet him, and in the next instant she was folded into his arms. "Irene, I'm so sorry we couldn't be there to greet you," he told her. "Thank God you made it through Indian country all right!" He pulled back then, grasping her arms. "Let me look at you."

She smiled for him, but her heart was torn over the way he looked. She struggled not to show her shock at how he had suddenly aged. Had he always had that bit of white at his temples, those lines about his eyes? Perhaps she was only just now noticing because she had been away from him for so long. Or had the strange grief he had been suffering done this to him? She noticed he at least still looked as healthy and robust as ever.

"You look so beautiful, so grown up," Kirk was telling her. He grasped her close again. "Thank God. Thank God," he muttered.

Irene nestled in his arms, feeling safer and more comforted than she did anyplace. No matter that Chad loved her, or that her mother was already busily rebuilding the Kirkland fortune. This was all she needed. The shock from seeing Denver destroyed, her sorrow over Sierra, all were relieved when she was in her father's arms. Oh, how she wished they could go back into the mountains together, but with this tragedy and all the hard work that lay ahead, she knew it would be impossible. Sometimes she wondered if she would ever get to go back.

Still, she took comfort just in knowing those mountains were there, waiting for her to return. Right now, being in her father's arms was like being in those mountains. In spite of the disaster that had taken place here, it was good to be home.

People were so busy rebuilding and salvaging that those who ran Kirkland Enterprises could not get enough help for the time being. Chad's own secretary had been killed in the fire, but business had to carry on, and Irene dived in to help, working on correspondence and other paperwork until a new secretary could be found. There were transactions to be made, records to be kept, correspondence to be handled. New shipments of supplies were on their way from San Francisco, and Bea had builders working around the clock to prepare new warehouses.

Owning supply businesses in California was a godsend to the Kirklands. While most other businesses in Denver relied on supplies from the East, which were slow in coming, especially now with so much Indian trouble, the Kirklands could haul in their own supplies and, of course, charge ridiculous prices for them. At the same time, money Bea had made off her bogus mining investment company helped offset their losses, and already she had set up temporary headquarters for Kirkland Enterprises at the rear of the National Bank. Builders who were working on the new offices insisted that every new Kirkland building be brick.

Kirk did not ask how or why there did not seem to be an unusual dent in the family funds, and Bea was not about to offer an explanation. The less he knew about the bookwork, the better. Thank God for Chad, who had saved the financial records, and thank goodness her idea about selling shares in worthless mines had panned out. Bea was glad Kirk seemed too distracted to pay close attention to their financial situation, which she and Chad knew was much better than others realized.

Bea kept as busy as possible, aware that Kirk seemed rather lost and unusually despondent after the fire. She didn't want to think about the reasons for her husband's obvious grief. She was sure it was much more than the loss of the buildings, which would not upset a man like Kirk that much. With painful jealousy and even a little sympathy, she had noticed him observe a long funeral procession that had paraded through town the day after the fire, hundreds of wild miners walking quietly behind the black, shiny hearse, paying their respects to Denver's notorious madam, Mary O'Day, who had died in the fire. Kirk had joined the procession, and Bea had said nothing about it to him later, nor had she since. There had been so much to do and no time to talk.

Irene threw herself into helping at the crowded, hectic temporary quarters of Kirkland Enterprises. She didn't mind helping, for her parents needed her, and keeping busy helped ease the loss of Sierra. Elly, however, always found some excuse for not lending a hand. John worked hard, teaching Irene more about the business. It was a good way to learn, for certain records had to be searched, files had to be put back in order, financial statements had to be resorted. She was learning about Kirkland Enterprises from the ground up.

In the brief moments she found to relax, Irene wondered about Susan Stanner, her heart heavy for the girl. Elly had told her people thought she had hanged herself over a lover, that maybe she was even carrying his baby. Irene thought it was terribly sad, in spite of how disgraceful it was. She remembered how awful she had felt those first few days after Ramon disappeared from her life, and she supposed if a woman was not strong enough on the inside, perhaps it would be easy to take her life over such a loss.

There was little time to ponder Susan's demise. The Stanners were gone now. It was odd how things were always changing. Since returning, Irene felt closer to Chad, especially when she saw how diligently he worked to help her parents, spending long hours at the temporary offices, usually arriving before sunrise and staying until after dark. His dedication impressed the whole family, including Irene. No one knew he was driven by guilt, still relieved at not being caught as Susan's lover; neither did anyone realize part of his reason for putting in the long hours was to escape Elly, who made him feel irritable and uncomfortable. The result of his hard work was a positive one for Chad, who was well aware he had totally won Bea Kirkland's respect and admiration, which only sealed the understanding that he would one day marry Irene.

For now, though, there was little time for him and Irene to be alone or to talk about marriage. The order of the day was work, and Irene insisted on doing her share. It was nearly three weeks after the fire, when she was carrying a sack of mail to Gilbert Drake's house, that a bittersweet memory was reawakened.

Drake's home served as a post office, and because of a growing Denver, the man was having a new wing built to make room for sorting the mail.

Irene approached the house full of thoughts of how much work she had yet to do this afternoon. She paid no attention at first to the man who was measuring a piece of latticework near the corner of the house. She approached the steps, then heard a man call out her name, sounding surprised. She turned, and nearly dropped the mail sack. Ramon!

She stood frozen in place, realizing in that one look that he must be able to read her thoughts, which instantly returned to the day he had kissed her, instantly rekindled all the passion and love she had felt for him. He took her by such surprise that there was no time to hide her emotions, which she quickly struggled against, reminding herself he had hurt her, reminding herself she had Chad now, reminding herself Ramon was married now.

He approached her hesitantly, still holding the latticework in one hand, a wooden measuring stick in the other. His dark eyes moved over her in a way that told her his own feelings had never changed. She literally trembled as he came closer, angry with herself for having no better control, sure her cheeks were crimson. Her head suddenly ached, and the noise in the streets dimmed.

"Hello, Irene," he said softly. "I saw you going up the steps . . . and I could not help calling out to you. It has been . . . a long time."

She swallowed to find her voice. Was he thinking of that kiss? Surely he remembered the promises he had made that day. Every nerve came alive for her. He had put on weight in all the right places, had grown even taller. He was muscular, magnificent, beautiful; but when she dropped her eyes in embarrassment at the look she must have on her face, she noticed the gold band on his left hand. She met his eyes again. "Hello, Ramon."

Now it was he who looked suddenly embarrassed, bashful, sorry, angry, a hundred looks in one pair of dark eyes. "I am surprised I have not seen you around town before now."

"I've . . . been away . . . a finishing school in Chicago. I just got back a couple of days ago."

He nodded. "It is too bad you had to come back to such a mess."

Why did she feel like crying? Should she ask him why he had never told her good-bye? Would he laugh at her? "Yes, it is. The worst part was . . . Sierra was killed in the fire."

Instant sorrow filled his eyes and he came closer. "I am sorry,

Irene. Truly I am. I know what the horse meant to you." Their eyes met, and he knew what she must be thinking. How he wished he could tell her the truth, but they could never be together now. What was the use in turning her against her own mother? And Bea Kirkland still had the power to uproot his grandfather. "I—I had my reasons, Irene. I did . . . what I thought was best for you."

She blinked back tears, hating herself for being so weak around him. "We could have talked."

"No. There are certain things . . . you do not understand . . . things I cannot tell you. I can only say . . . what I said that day was true. I did not deceive you."

Why? Why had God let her see him again? "I've learned a lot in the past year," she answered. "I realize now that your leaving was probably best after all." Why was she saying that? She didn't believe it. "I heard . . . you've married. From what John told me last year, you must have a child by now."

He smiled, sorrow mixed with pride. "*Sí*. A little son." He swallowed, looking around as though worried someone might see them talking. "I have my own business now," he said, meeting her eyes again. "I am doing very well. Soon I plan to hire men to work under me. I cannot keep up with all the orders. In some respects the fire has been a godsend for me. Everyone needs a carpenter."

She managed a smile for him. "That's good. I'm glad for you."

"And you?"

She took a deep breath. "I'm helping out with Kirkland Enterprises right now. Everything is a mess. Once things settle down, I expect to be married, within the year, I suppose. There hasn't been a formal announcement yet. I don't even have an engagement ring. It's just . . . something that's under-stood . . . a lot like you and Elena, I would suspect."

He searched her eyes, aching at the confusion he saw there. Was she only telling him about marrying to hurt him, the way he knew he had hurt her? "Chad Jacobs?" he asked.

"Yes." She stood so stiff, so defensive, but he sensed the burning passion just beneath the surface, and it was not for Chad Jacobs. It tore at his heart, teased his desires.

"I hope you will be happy," he told her, praying he was wrong in his suspicions about Chad Jacobs's character. He had seen the man around town a few times, noticed how he liked to flaunt his looks and flirt with women. He was indeed a handsome man, but Ramon suspected he was not so beautiful on the inside as he was on the outside.

"I'm sure I will be," Irene was saying. "Chad is good to me.

He's a hard worker, and he doesn't drink. He's very loyal to the family." She wondered why she was telling him such trivia. What did it matter? *I still love you Ramon,* she wanted to say. *I thought I was over you, until this moment.*

I wish I could change it all for you, he was thinking. *I have never stopped loving you, mi querida.* He sighed. "I am sorry, Irene, for the way it happened. I would not ever deliberately hurt you. I just . . . I realized our worlds are too different. If I had tried to tell you in person, it would have been too difficult for both of us to do the right thing. So I left, hoping you would learn to hate me for it so that it would be easier for you."

She dropped her eyes, blinking rapidly, desperately afraid a tear would slip out of her eye and betray her deeper emotions. "I understand," she answered. "It did hurt . . . at first. But I never hated you . . . and I never could." She swallowed. "It's all right now. Time takes care of a lot of things."

"*Sí.*"

Someone called out to Ramon then, and he turned to see Elena approaching, carrying their son, Juan, on one arm, and a basket on the other. She was bringing his lunch. He looked at Irene almost apologetically. "I did not know it was so close to lunch time. It is my wife. We live in a little frame house not far from here. Luckily it survived the fire. Elena brings me lunch every day. I am sorry, Irene."

Irene swallowed, feeling almost wet with perspiration from being so nervous in his presence. "It's all right," she told him. "I'd better take the mail inside."

"Wait," he asked, reaching out and grabbing her arm. The touch sent fire through her blood. "Perhaps you should meet her. Maybe it will help. She is a good person, Irene. She is of my religion, my people. You will see I did the right thing."

Irene waited awkwardly, wanting to run, to die. Elena came closer. She was dark and beautiful, slender, shapely. Thoughts of the woman sharing Ramon's bed ripped cruelly at Irene's heart. The woman smiled, a brilliant, genuine, friendly smile. "*Buenos días,*" she said to Irene when she reached Ramon's side.

"Hello," Irene answered. "I'm Irene Kirkland. Your husband . . . did some work for my parents about a year ago. We were just . . . saying hello."

"It is nice to meet you," Elena answered. "This is our son, Juan."

Irene smiled at the child, a handsome, round-faced, brown-skinned child who anyone could tell would probably be even more handsome than his father one day. "He's beautiful," she said, her eyes on Ramon's face. *Like you,* she wanted to say.

Elena watched them, noticed the look they exchanged. It was impossible not to notice tears in Irene Kirkland's eyes.

"I had better take this mail inside," Irene was saying. "You have work to do, and a family to tend to." She took a deep breath. "Good-bye, Ramon."

The remark had an unmistakable finality to it.

"Good-bye, Irene. It was good seeing you again. Say hello to John for me."

She nodded. "I will." She glanced at Elena again. "Take good care of him. He's a fine man," she told the woman. She turned away then, hurrying into the post office.

Elena looked up at Ramon, sadness shadowing her eyes. "So," she said quietly, "she is the one, isn't she?"

Ramon looked at her, surprised. "What?"

Elena met his gaze. "Did you think I did not suspect the reason you came home and wanted to marry me so quickly, *mi querido?* A woman knows, Ramon. There are times when you make love to only me, and times when you touch me, but you are making love to someone else in your heart. I always wondered who it was that made you run to me."

He looked away, and she had caught the sorrow in his eyes. "I love you, Elena."

"I know that. I understand, Ramon, and I do not love you less for it. I only wish you would have shared it with me."

He met her eyes. "It is over. It was just . . . so quick . . . like the wind. One kiss . . . one hopeless kiss. We both knew it could never really be. A few years from now, we will probably both smile at our youthful foolishness." He reached out and touched little Juan's cheek. "This is my future. I have a special love for you, Elena, that I could never have for another. You are my woman, the mother of my son. I do not want to speak of this again, and I do not want you to let it spoil what we have."

He leaned down and kissed her cheek. Irene glanced out a window and saw the kiss, and she felt as though someone were shoving a sword into her heart. She was anxious to get away from here, anxious to get back to Chad, to convince herself she was doing the right thing, remind herself where she belonged now.

She thanked Mr. Drake for the mail, then left, relieved Ramon had taken Elena around behind the building. She did not have to see him again, did not have to suffer a second good-bye. She hurried away, deciding she would find someone else to deliver and pick up the mail after today.

The intense pain of seeing Ramon again overwhelmed her, and she knew she could not go back to Kirkland Enterprises just yet. She ducked around the side of a building and let the tears come then. Ramon! At least they had finally been able to tell each other good-bye, but she felt so much had been left unsaid; and in this moment of remembering, she understood more clearly why Susan Stanner had ended her life.

Kirk laid a rose on Mary O'Day's grave, kneeling beside it then. "I'll miss you, Mary," he said, his voice choking. It had been a whole month since the fire, and things were slowly getting back to normal. This was the first chance he had had to be alone at the grave of the woman who had loved him the way a woman ought to love a man.

"I should have been with you," he said then, his chest aching. "Maybe I could have saved you." He touched the headstone. "I had just gotten back, Mary, from the mountains. I figured I ought to be with my family, with Bea. I'm so damn sorry. We never even got to say good-bye."

Women like Mary came along only once in a man's life. If he had not already been married, Kirk imagined he would have had no reservations about marrying Denver's infamous madam, in spite of the fact that half the men of Denver had shared her bed. Things like that didn't much matter to Kirk. Mary had a good heart. She had loved him. If he had married her, he had no doubt she would have been true to him.

Their love had been quick and hard and deep, starting not long after Kirk arrived in Denver and first met the woman. That had been four years ago. He sighed, wiping at his eyes. "I'm going back to the mountains," he said quietly. "That's the only thing that's going to help me get over you."

He rose, staring at the headstone a moment longer, unaware that someone had walked up behind him. "Kirk?"

He turned in surprise to find Bea standing a few feet away. "Where did you come from?"

"I—" she glanced at the headstone and knew her hunch had been right, "I was visiting Susan Stanner's grave. And I thought I'd put some flowers on Eva West's grave. She worked hard for Kirkland Enterprises." She shifted nervously. "I thought I recognized you standing over here." She glanced at the headstone again. "She's the one, isn't she?"

He looked back at the grave, saying nothing for several long, quiet seconds. Somewhere nearby a bird chirped, and the grassy cemetery hill was alive with wildflowers. "Yes," he finally answered Bea. He sighed deeply. "I know what you think of her kind of women, but they aren't all bad, Bea. Some of them have reason to do what they do."

How she wished she could have learned to love him the right way. "I'm sorry," she said quietly, her throat aching. "I can't help wondering . . . if you'll feel near as much grief over me . . . when my time comes."

Kirk looked at her, seeing tears in her eyes. The woman always surprised him in these rare moments of open emotion. He came closer, touching her arm. "A person loves different people different ways, Bea. Mary understood me in ways you never will; but she's not the one who married me so my child would have a mother. You are. You've always known what that means to me."

The words comforted her burning heart. She embraced him, resting her head against his chest. Kirk wrapped his arms around her, and they stood there quietly beside the grave.

In town, in a saloon Mary O'Day had frequented, men held up beer mugs in a salute to a huge painting of a pretty red-haired woman, whose breasts billowed over the lacy trim of her bright pink dress. The miners of Denver would not soon forget their favorite lady of the night, and they dreaded the day when Denver just might outlaw prostitution. As far as they were concerned, it would be a great loss.

CHAPTER
EIGHTEEN

Esther Sanchez led Red McKinley into Kirk's smoking and billiards room, where, to Red's surprise, Bea Kirkland waited for him. She sat behind Kirk's magnificent oak desk, giving Esther a look that told her she was dismissed. The maid quickly left, always glad to leave Bea's presence. She closed the door behind her, and Red approached the desk, watching Bea Kirkland's dark eyes warily.

"I came here to see Kirk," he told her. "Your maid led me in here as though he was home."

"I asked her to show you in," Bea told him. "There is some trouble with possible strikes at some of the mines. Kirk has gone back to the mountains to see about it. Sit down, Mr. McKinley. I can handle anything you might have wanted to talk to Kirk about."

Red felt his defenses rising. He hardly knew this woman, but he hated her. It rankled him the way she still called him Mr. McKinley, with that grating sneer. Knowing what good friends he was with her husband, any other woman would be calling him Red by now and would certainly be friendlier. "I'd rather stand," he answered.

She leaned forward, resting her elbows on the desk. "As you wish. What can I do for you?"

Red fingered his felt hat. He was proud of what he had accomplished so far, felt like a real businessman now, thanks to Kirk. He dressed better, and he even contemplated finding a wife.

Everyone respected him, and he felt good about himself, except when he was around this woman, who had a way of looking down on everyone scathingly, as though hardly worthy to be in her presence. He held his chin proudly when he answered her.

"Actually, I came to see if I could get one more temporary loan."

Her dark eyes bore into him. "You can see I am not surprised," she answered. "I expected this." She leaned back in the leather chair. "Have you paid back one cent of the original loan, Mr. McKinley?"

He swallowed. "Five hundred dollars."

She snickered. "Five hundred dollars . . . out of fifteen thousand. And you want more?"

He reddened slightly, wishing very much that she was not Kirk's wife so that he could tell her what he really thought of her. How sad Kirk had picked this woman to marry, how sad that the man felt so indebted to her.

"The fire destroyed a good deal of my supply of raw lumber, Mrs. Kirkland," he answered. "I've been at this close to a year now, and things were just beginning to turn over into the black for me. I was prepared to start making regular payments to Kirk, like I promised, and I can still do it. All I need is a temporary loan to have a new supply of lumber shipped in. You know good and well that there is a building boom going on. I can make up the money in no time. I've got a whole list of backorders right now. All I need is the lumber. If I hadn't lost what I had in the fire, I could keep up."

Bea's eyes moved over him as if he were a bum off the street. "I know your kind, Mr. McKinley. You can pull the wool over Kirk's eyes. The man is too good-hearted and easily fooled for his own good. But you don't fool me. You came here because you heard about your old friend's good fortune, and you thought maybe you would cash in on it. For sixteen years you never bothered to find Kirk, then suddenly you appear out of nowhere, and the next thing I know my husband is lending you fifteen thousand dollars. Did you really think I couldn't see what you were doing?"

Red nearly trembled with seething anger. "That isn't true, but I can see you don't want to believe it. And I have every intention of paying Kirk back."

"Then I suggest you do it. Until then, I have no intention of loaning you one more dime. We suffered our own losses in that fire, Mr. McKinley—a warehouse and all its contents, a brand new hotel, a bank, our offices—and you dare to stand there and ask us for more *money*? We'll be a long time recovering from this. I can't be loaning money to a worthless drifter who doesn't know how to run a business properly. You should have kept a better inventory." She rose from the chair. "I never run low on anything, Mr. McKinley. Even with the fire, I had enough merchandise in our other two warehouses to help get us by. Always plan for the worst and stay one step ahead, Mr. McKinley. That's how a business should be run."

Oh, how he hated her! He felt like a damn fool, this woman standing there telling him how to run his business! What a bitch! He considered asking once more, pleading. Without the lumber he would lose a good deal of orders to another lumber company, for people were in a hurry to get back into their houses and offices.

"With that lumber I could have a bonanza in sales, Mrs. Kirkland," he said, struggling to keep his voice steady.

"Good-bye, Mr. McKinley."

His jaw flexed in anger. "I'll talk to Kirk myself."

"No, you won't," she said sternly. "If you talk to Kirk and get more money out of him, I'll make sure you don't get any business at all. I can do it, Mr. McKinley. And don't try getting a loan through one of the other banks. I suspected you might try, and I have already told them what a high risk you are."

He eyed her narrowly. "I should think it would be in your own best interest to have me succeed," he said, his voice a near hiss. "If I don't, it's more your loss than mine."

"Perhaps. But then you would be a failure, wouldn't you, Mr. McKinley? And I would be left with a lumber mill to operate, which I am sure I could probably do better than you. It wouldn't be such a great loss after all. And Kirk will have learned a good lesson about loaning money to friends on a handshake. Good-bye again, Mr. McKinley."

Red just stared at her as he slowly put on his hat. For the first time in his life he considered blackmail. He could threaten to tell all of Denver that Irene Kirkland was half Indian, knew how that would devastate and humiliate this woman. Oh, how he would love to throw that in her face! She must not realize that he knew, or she would never treat him this way. But much as he hated Bea Kirkland, he could not bring himself to hurt Irene, who was innocent in all of this. He did not doubt that if he could go to Irene for a loan, she would give it to him without hesitation.

Still, he reasoned, even if he was low enough to stoop to blackmail and hurting innocent people, he wouldn't use it as a tool just to get money. To him it was just another form of crawling and begging. He stepped closer, his blue eyes icy with hate. "One day you'll regret this," he told Bea. "A man has his pride." He headed for the door, then turned. "You've already destroyed Kirk's pride," he added. "I feel damn sorry for him, Mrs. Kirkland. He deserves better. *You're* the fool! You have all that money, a house full of valuables, but you hurt and destroy the things that are most valuable."

The man walked out, slamming the door, and Bea stood there trembling with the glowing victory she always felt when she had a chance to wield her power. Red McKinley represented everything she did not want Kirk to be. It still upset her that Kirk had been foolish enough to loan the man so much money. Red McKinley was a threat. When he was around, she did not have the same control over Kirk as she usually enjoyed. Somehow she had to get rid of the man. McKinley was a fighter, she granted him that. But so was she, and she had the Kirkland money and power. One way or another, she was determined to run him out of business . . . and out of Denver.

Irene sat playing the piano in the library, enjoying a rare day to herself. Kirk had gone to the mines again, and Elly was being tutored, while John and Bea were, as always, at the offices with Chad. After weeks of long hours that had left everyone near collapse, things had finally begun to get back to normal. New offices were finished at Blake and Fifeenth streets, and the Denver Inn was on its way to being completely rebuilt. More supplies from San Francisco were due any day, and everyone was beginning to work regular hours. Bea had insisted Irene stop "slaving away like a commoner" and begin staying home again.

"I want you to rest, and I want you and Chad to have some time together," the woman had told her just this morning. "This afternoon I will come home early, and we'll talk about school and what you learned, what Chicago is like."

Her mother had been in excellent spirits since the fire, and Irene realized the challenge of her losses actually gave the woman new energy. Bea Kirkland thrived on hard work. The Kirkland empire was her baby, something she nurtured and loved, something to which she had given much more attention than any of her own children.

Irene was sure it could never be that way for her. She would let Chad take care of those things. She would tend to home and children, except for helping out in times of disaster, such as the fire. She didn't mind learning the business, didn't mind the work, but she did not want to be another Bea Kirkland.

She played a sad tune, and unwillingly her thoughts again drifted to Ramon, and the day she had seen him at the post office. She could not forget how wonderful he looked, could not forget what she knew without a doubt had been love in those dark eyes. Yes, he still loved her. Nothing could ever come of it now, but just to know it, to know in her heart he had not just used her and made light of it, was all she needed to soothe the hurt. What they had shared would remain a bittersweet memory, a cherished secret she would carry with her to the grave.

She sighed, looking at a picture of Chad that sat on the piano. Bea had insisted he sit for his portrait so she could add it to her collection of family pictures. The woman seemed already to think of Chad as part of the family, and sometimes it seemed she treated the man better than her own son. One thing was certain—if Irene married Chad Jacobs, there would certainly be no in-law problems. Bea all but worshipped the man. Chad could do no wrong. In Bea's opinion, her first-born daughter could do no better than to marry Attorney Chad Jacobs, and hardly a day went by that Bea did not remind Irene of that very fact.

Irene studied the picture. She supposed her mother was right, and to this day she could not think of one thing wrong with Chad, one reason why any woman wouldn't fall at his feet. They had grown closer, had laughed together, worked together, shared many kisses now. Chad had more than proven his dedication to the family business, as well as having proven his skill and bravery when he saved her father's life.

Why, then, did she still have this tiny, lingering doubt about marrying him? It wasn't strong enough that she would refuse him when he gave her a ring and formally said the words. She truly did love him, and she was confident he loved her in return. How could anyone mistake the sincerity in those gray eyes? The man was handsome, gentle, and attentive. The thought of their wedding night brought a tingle to her blood, more from curiosity than desire. She was not afraid of it, for Chad surely had experience with women, and he would never hurt her. But it still bothered her that she did not feel quite the same passion for him as she had felt with Ramon. There was still something not quite right, yet she could not imagine what it was.

"Who are you?" she found herself whispering at the picture. Maybe that was it. She had known him for well over a year now, had spent a good deal of time alone with him, had shared his kisses, his touch—yet she felt sometimes that she didn't know Chad Jacobs at all. A part of him was still a stranger to her. She realized with sudden surprise that the man never talked about his parents, his life in Pennsylvania. It was as though he had dropped out of the sky into Denver with no background, except that he had papers proving he had graduated with honors from Harvard Law School. He had mentioned that his parents were well off, which she did not doubt. It took money to go to Harvard. She knew, because Bea had already talked about how expensive it was going to be to be to send John there.

She quietly fidgeted with the piano keys as she looked at Chad's picture, deciding she would have to ask him more about his family. Her thoughts were interrupted when Esther Sanchez came to the door of the library to tell her there was someone at the door who had come to see her mother. "I told him Mrs. Kirkland was not here, and he is wondering if she will be back soon," the woman told her.

Irene closed the piano. "Who is it, Esther?"

"He tells me his name is Hank Loring, and that he is from the south, near Colorado City."

Irene frowned. Hank Loring. She remembered then who he was, and she was surprised at the flutter it brought to her heart. "Oh, yes," she told Esther, getting up from the piano bench. "Show him in, Esther. I'll come down and talk to him myself."

"Yes, ma'am."

Esther left, and Irene hurried over to a mirror, glad she had thought to dress early for supper. She wore a soft pink day dress of light cotton, and only one petticoat. It was July, and the weather had turned very hot, although inside the grand Kirkland mansion it was pleasantly cool. A stone exterior, high ceilings, and lots of windows for cross drafts made it a pleasant place to be in summer.

She pinched her cheeks for color, wishing her hair was done up more fashionably. She had merely brushed it out this morning and drawn it back at the sides with two combs. It hung down her back nearly to her waist.

She scowled then, wondering why on earth she cared how she looked. Hank Loring was a near stranger, a married man at that. And why on earth did *that* matter? "What is wrong with you, Irene Kirkland?" she muttered to herself. "Just go and see what the man wants."

She hurried out, moving through the great room to the grand entryway, where a crystal chandelier tinkled from a breeze coming through a screened window. Esther stood near the front doors.

"He told me he would rather wait outside," the woman told Irene. "He is . . . well, he has been on a cattle drive, and he says he is not presentable enough to come in."

"Oh, that's silly. I'll go talk to him, although I can't imagine why he is here." Irene opened the door and walked out onto the wide, slate veranda and down the brick steps, noticing Hank Loring stood next to a beautiful, golden stallion. To her irritation her heart raced harder when the rugged, hard-honed Loring, looked up at her and grinned.

"Well, hello there," he called out.

Irene had no idea that the instant, forbidden attraction affected him as well. Hank supposed that was just life, that a man could love one woman to his very soul, the way he loved his wife, but it didn't mean he was never attracted to any other woman. And what man wouldn't notice and appreciate this woman's beauty? He remembered her from the day he had met her and her father a year ago, when they were on their way to visit their potato farm.

"Irene, isn't it?" he asked as she came closer.

"Yes," she answered. "You remembered, Mr. Loring." She put out her hand, struck by an immediate warmth and strength she felt when he took it. His own hand was rough and strong, but his handshake was gentle. "Won't you come inside? It's much cooler."

He let go of her hand and removed his hat, revealing thick, dark hair, his green eyes making her feel at once comfortable. "Ma'am, I just brought some cattle to the Denver stockyards, and you can see I'm kind of dusty and all. I would have stopped to clean up, but I'm in kind of a hurry. There's a lot of Indian trouble for the ranchers and settlers, and I don't like to be away from the family for too long. I'm heading back tonight. I got a letter from your mother, wanting to see me about a business deal, so I thought I'd come and talk to her."

He wore a blue calico shirt and tight-fitting denim pants, with a scarf tied around his neck and a gun at his hip. He was so different from any man Irene had seen around Denver, and again she found him fascinating and ruggedly handsome. "My mother spends more time at our offices in town than here. But she *did* say she would be home early today. Please do come inside. I'll have Esther get you some lemonade."

He turned to pat his horse again. "Well, I suppose I could wait a few minutes, but not too long. I have men waiting for me outside of town."

Irene, whose love of horses was still strong, could not resist reaching out and touching his horse's nose to pet it. He whinnied softly, and Loring grinned. "I was just about to tell you to be careful. Sunrise here is an ornery one with strangers." He kept a hand on the animal's mane, slightly leaning on the animal. "I can see he likes you."

"He's beautiful. I've never seen a horse like this—all golden and white."

"He's a Palomino. The Vallejos raise them down on Hacienda del Sur. I bought this stallion and a good mare from them . . . plan to raise a few of my own."

She met his eyes. "You . . . know the Vallejos well, then?"

"Pretty well. Miguel Vallejo, the old man, he's a fine, proud man. Like I told you last year, I was invited to Ramon's wedding. I'd like to see Ramon while I'm here in Denver, but he's hard to find . . . a busy man, I'm told." He frowned. "I believe you mentioned once that you knew Ramon."

Irene moved to the other side of Sunrise to pet his neck, not wanting Loring to see her eyes at the moment. "Yes. Ramon did some work on this house for us. I was just curious." She moved toward the back of the horse. "I can't get over how beautiful he is," she said, wanting to change the subject.

"Be careful walking behind him."

"My parents won't let me ride stallions," she said, stepping back a little to admire the powerful, golden horse. "They think they're too unpredictable."

"And they're right," he answered, as she came around the other side of the animal and faced him again. "Stallions can be dangerous, but I prefer them myself," he went on. "I like the challenge, and believe me, this one gives a man a run for his money. He's finally learned who's master, though." He turned and faced Sunrise head-on, patting both sides of his neck. "Haven't you, boy?"

The animal whinnied and nudged at the man's neck, and Irene could see he loved horses as much as she did. "I'd love to ride him," she told Hank.

Their eyes held for a moment. "Not many city women pretty as you care much about horses."

She smiled. "I love them. I had a very special horse of my own—Sierra. Maybe you remember him. He's the gelding I was riding when we met you last year . . . black tail and mane, black feet."

"I remember. He was a fine-looking horse."

Her smile faded. "He was killed in the fire last April."

He frowned, keeping hold of Sunrise's bridle, never trusting the animal around strangers. "I'm real sorry to hear that."

She ran her hand lovingly over Sunrise's shoulder. He was a big horse, big like Hank Loring. She wondered if she could master such an animal. "The worse part was that I had been gone all last winter, at a finishing school in Chicago. He died before I got to see him again."

"That's too bad." She met his eyes, and she could see he was sincere. She realized then how easy it had been to talk to him, felt a kinship with him even though she hardly knew him. Hank Loring was easy to like, easy to talk with, and she knew he shared her love of horses. "Maybe if your mother and I do business together, I can sell you one of Sunrise's offspring."

She smiled. "That would be nice." She heard a buggy approaching and turned to see her mother coming. "That's my mother," she said aloud. "Now you won't have to wait."

The driver headed the rig up the circular, brick drive to where Hank and Irene stood, and Bea climbed out, brightening when Irene introduced her. "Well, Mr. Loring, I was wondering if I was ever going to hear from you," the woman said, putting out her hand. Hank shook it, thinking how callused and cold it felt compared to Irene's. He saw in her demeanor a shrewd business woman when he gazed into her dark, discerning eyes. He explained his situation, again apologizing for his appearance.

"I don't like to leave the wife and kids for too long," he told her. "There are men left at the ranch, but Indian trouble has been pretty bad and I just feel better being there myself."

"I can understand," Bea told him. "The Volunteers are regrouping, Mr. Loring. We hope to conduct our own campaign against the Cheyenne who are causing the most trouble. Heaven knows, with hardly any federal soldiers left here to protect us, we've got to do something about it ourselves."

"I agree," Hank answered. The woman insisted he come inside for lemonade, urging Irene to join them. "You might as well know about this," she told her daughter.

Irene looked at Hank with raised eyebrows, and the man just shrugged. He followed the women inside, gazing at high ceilings and beautiful woodwork, walking over oriental rugs and polished wood floors. He had plans to build a bigger house for his own family, something sprawling and beautiful, perhaps a stucco, Spanish-style home. He already knew he would never want something this ornate and ostentatious. This kind of house didn't fit a rancher, but it certainly told him he was dealing with a very rich woman, and he found himself thinking how her daughter didn't seem to fit in with all of it. She was too nice, too genuine, too down-to-earth to belong amid such wealth.

Bea led him into Kirk's office and billiards room, offering him one of Kirk's cigars, which he refused. He felt out of place here, longed to get back to the ranch. He sat down in a cool leather chair, and Esther brought lemonade, which Hank took gratefully. Bea peppered him with questions about raising cattle and his thoughts on the future of the beef industry, questions Hank answered warily, understanding this was a woman with power.

Irene watched him, sensing his pride, realizing he had a good head for business by the way he answered her mother. He sat sprawled in the leather chair as though he was too big for it, placing one big, booted foot up on his knee. She noticed that although he was dusty and had earlier been sweating, he had a good, manly scent about him, like a man who normally bathed often, so that a couple of days' dirt and sweat didn't leave him smelling bad, unlike the drifters in town who probably had not bathed in weeks, maybe months. He toyed with his hat as he spoke, and Irene decided his hands were the biggest she had ever seen.

"I want to get into the business of raising beef, Mr. Loring," Bea was saying. "When you build your fortune on gold, you soon learn that to depend entirely on mining is very foolish. Mines play out. We have to be ready for that, and I have several other investments. I happen to think that the southern area is going to begin to grow rapidly. I already have plans to build a hotel down near Colorado City, but in a quieter area, a place where the wealthier people of Denver can go as a kind of vacation. I will be coming south myself before too long to get a better idea of the possibilities there."

She rested her head against the back of the chair as she spoke, and Hank thought how the woman fit the chair like a man. "At any rate," she continued, "I happen to agree with you that the cattle industry is just beginning to see its heyday. There are even foreigners interested in investing in Colorado, not just in the mines and industry, but in farming and ranching. It is through correspondence with people from England, and through my husband's interest in the southern area, that I came up with my idea."

Hank finished his lemonade. "I'm listening," he told her, as he set his glass on a tray Esther had left.

Bea leaned forward, putting her hands on the desk, her eyes

glittering with the excitement of trying a new investment. "They're experimenting with a better breed of cattle in England, Mr. Loring, called Herefords, or shorthorns. If we can raise them right here, and if you're right about a boom in the cattle industry, we can make a fortune if you're willing to work with me. These shorthorns are extremely huge, meaty animals. They carry much more beef in proportion to their bulk than the Texas longhorns the cattlemen raise now."

Irene listened in amazement at how well schooled her mother had become regarding cattle. *Whatever you are going to invest in,* the woman had told her once, *always study your subject well first. Make sure it is a wise investment.* Bea apparently heeded her own advice.

"This new breed of cattle is mature and ready for the market in only two years," Bea went on. "I'm told it takes at least four years for Texas longhorns to mature."

Hank nodded. "Yes, ma'am. If what you're saying is true, that new breed of cattle could bring twice the money."

"Maybe more than that. Those who raise them in England believe the breed would do quite well on the southern Colorado plains, where the winters are not as harsh as farther north. At any rate, I want to have some shipped here and try raising them. I need someone who knows all about ranching and raising cattle. I'll be honest with you, Mr. Loring. I've had you investigated, and I am told you are an honest man, hard working, a man who knows the ranching business inside and out. You've done very well on your own, and I would not ask you to give up what is already yours. I am only asking if you will try raising these cattle for me. If it works out, and if I can get my hands on enough land down there, I'll have a ranch of my own, and I would want you to manage all of it—everything—hire as many men as you need, pick out good foremen, whatever is necessary."

Hank shifted in the chair. "That's a tall order, ma'am."

"And I think you can fill it."

He shook his head. "Raising cattle takes a lot of land, Mrs. Kirkland, thousands of acres, if you want to raise enough to make big money."

"I'll get the land, Mr. Loring. All I need from you is a yes or a no. Will you experiment with raising these cattle? Will you think about managing a ranch for me? I'll pay you well. You'll make enough money to expand your own ranch, build a fine home for your family."

Hank rubbed the side of his face, taking several seconds for deep thought. He leaned forward, resting his elbows on his knees. "What does your husband think of all this?"

"He is the one who suggested cattle ranching a year ago, after talking to you. Besides, my husband supports any investments I choose to make. His interest is primarily in the mines. I do nearly all other investing, and I have full power of attorney to sign any and all agreements on my husband's behalf."

Hank thought a moment longer, then slowly nodded. "All right. I'll try raising these Herefords for you. But a different breed means learning new things, maybe losing a few cattle at first, figuring out the best grazing for them, the best feed, finding out how they will adapt to a new climate, different breeding tactics, things like that. You have to realize there might be problems at first, maybe even some losses."

"I'll take the risk. I'll trust you to do the best you can."

Hank ran a hand through his hair. "Well, let's see how they work out. You pay for the cattle and for any special feed they might need, and pay me a managing fee, and I'll see what I can do with them. We'll talk about managing a ranch for you once you get enough land, but it won't be easy. A lot of people have moved in because of the Homestead Act—most of them farmers who are breaking up the land. Makes it harder for us ranchers."

"As I said, Mr. Loring, I'll take care of getting the land. If you'll come back with me to Kirkland Enterprises, I already have some papers ready for you to sign, in hopes you would respond to my letter. It won't take long, and you can be on your way."

She rose, and Hank followed suit, towering over both women. "I'd like something added to those papers, ma'am," he told Bea. "I want some kind of statement on there that says what's mine is mine, that you promise never to try to move in and take over my own land." Bea looked at him in surprise. "I've worked hard to build the Lazy L, ma'am," he explained. "Any man can see you have the money and probably the political power to take over any piece of land you want. I just don't want it to be mine."

Their eyes held in challenge for a moment, and then Bea broke into a smile. "You're a smart man, Mr. Loring. I like that. I don't blame you one bit for your concern. I know the feeling of protecting what you have worked to build. We'll add a clause to our agreement." She put out her hand. "Your land is perfectly safe. I value your knowledge of the cattle business too much to make an enemy of you."

He shook her hand again. "Fine. Then we have a deal."

Hank glanced at Irene, holding his hand out to her. "It's been nice meeting you again, Miss Kirkland." Their eyes held as she took his hand, and he closed it over hers with a gentle squeeze that seemed to have more meaning than just a casual handshake. "Remember what I told you about one of Sunrise's offspring."

"I will," Irene answered. "And I'm glad you'll be working with us, Mr. Loring."

She followed Bea and Hank outside, watching Hank mount his golden stallion with the ease of a man who fit the horse as if he'd been born on it. He tipped his hat to her and rode off alongside Bea's buggy, heading for town. Irene rubbed at her arms, thinking how strange it was the way people moved in and out of other people's lives. A casual hello while passing on the Colorado plains had led to Hank Loring working for her mother. She remembered how she had just glanced at Ramon that first day they came to Denver, and later there he was, working in her own house, riding with her, kissing her. A new, young lawyer had come to town, another total stranger, and now she would very likely marry him.

She realized that in a place like Denver, there was no "old generation," no citizens who could say their fathers and grandfathers had lived on this land. Only the Indians and Mexicans could say that. People came here from all walks of life, and all were strangers, thrown together in a common cause, heading toward a destiny none of them could predict.

She headed back inside. She had to rest and get ready for tonight. Chad was coming for dinner, and she had a feeling he was going to give her a ring. He had said he wanted tonight to be special. She turned at the door to get one last look at Hank Loring and his beautiful stallion, and just as he had that first time out on the southern plains, Hank turned and waved at her.

"Do you really think we can do it?" Chad asked Bea. It was nearly closing time at the office, and he had to get back to his room and get ready for dinner at the Kirkland's tonight; but Bea Kirkland had another scheme going, and he never walked away when Bea was talking.

"Of course we can do it," Bea answered. "We have to. You heard what Hank Loring said. I need a lot of land. Under the Homestead Act those settlers can only claim a hundred and sixty acres at a time. The government won't allow someone like me to buy up thousands of acres, so we'll do it another way. We'll pay those homesteaders twice what they would be paying for that land, have them sign papers signifying the land really belongs to us.

They just won't tell the government about it. We'll pay those homesteaders to go ahead and work the land for the time being, let them make whatever farming profit they can make, build whatever buildings they need to make it all look perfectly legal. When we need that land, we'll promise to help them settle someplace else, or they can stay on and work for Kirkland ranches. Either way, they have lost nothing, and we will have the land we need."

"What about unclaimed land?"

"I want you to find people we can trust, pay different families to claim adjoining parcels under the act in their own names, only it will all really be ours. You can even file claims for us under fictitious names."

"It all sounds illegal."

"It *is* illegal," she answered, folding her arms. "It wouldn't be the first illegal thing you have done for me, Chad."

He grinned. "I guess not."

"Remember what I said about survival. And remember that no one is being hurt by it. I wouldn't do it if it meant displacing families, but they'll all be better off. You pay a man enough, he'll do whatever you ask. And I want you to go and talk to the homesteaders personally."

"*Me!* I have my work here."

"Slade and Brown and I can take care of things here, and I might hire another man. This project in the south is very important, Chad. Someday we'll have so many holdings down there I'll need someone to run everything for me permanently, and that man could be you. I want you to go south and get a feel for the land. Besides, for what I want to do, I need someone to approach those homesteaders who is capable of talking a fish out of water. I can think of no one more charming and convincing than you. You're the ideal businessman—one who understands that to get ahead in this world, we sometimes have to skirt the legalities, and one who can make a person believe anything he says just by smiling at them."

Chad laughed. "Well, thank you for your confidence." He rose. "But I don't relish being away from Irene. We haven't had a lot of time together since she got back, Bea. I had plans tonight to ask her to marry me. I already discussed it with Kirk before he left because I wasn't sure how long he would be gone this time. You must know I have his blessing, and I hope I have yours."

She smiled. "I can't imagine you would think I would disapprove. Of course you have my blessing. I'm sorry to take you away from Irene, but if you become engaged before you leave, you'll feel closer while you're gone, and it will give Irene something to cling to. You'll only be gone a couple of months. Then you'll have the winter together, and perhaps we can plan an April or May wedding. Irene will be eighteen in March. Things will be back to normal around here by then, and you'll have a good start on buying up land for the ranching business." Her eyes lit up. "You could even take Irene to the south for your honeymoon. I'll have a hotel finished by then. It would be a nice getaway for both of you. Irene told me once how pretty it was down there. She'd like that."

Chad gave her a wink. "Then that's what we'll do."

Bea patted his arm. "Good. You go on now and get ready for dinner. I'll expect you at seven."

Chad took his silk hat from a hook and donned it, giving her a nod and a winning smile before he left. He realized with great pleasure that a trip south might not be a bad idea after all. While he was down in Colorado City, there would be no one to spy on him, no one to care what he did. He'd heard Colorado City was a wild town full of loose women. He could have himself one grand time before he came back to Denver to feign loyalty once again to one woman. He had not had a good romp with a woman ever since Susan killed herself; the mild guilt he had felt over that had left him, and he was getting restless again.

CHAPTER NINETEEN

August 1863

Chad led Irene up the stairs to the third floor and through the ballroom to the balcony outside. It was a beautiful, still summer night, a full moon lighting the distant mountain peaks. They could hear the occasional howl of a wolf far off in the foothills, while a few voices, mingled with the barking of dogs came from the direction of the city in the distance, where street lanterns glowed in the darkness.

"I like this spot," Chad spoke up, keeping an arm around Irene's waist and leading her to a white wrought-iron bench to sit down. "Maybe it's because it's where we first kissed."

Irene smiled, thinking how he looked even more handsome in the moonlight. "Did you have places that were special to you as a child, Chad?"

"Special?"

"You know. Some secret place, like a tree you liked to climb, or a place you used to hide."

He looked away. *The closet,* he wanted to tell her. *Anyplace where I could hide from my father's curses and my mother's lovers. There is nothing memorable about where I used to hide.*

"Well, our house in Pennsylvania is on the Allegheny River," he said aloud, "near Pittsburgh. I used to sit at my bedroom window upstairs and watch the steamboats go by. Sometimes I'd sit on the windowsill, with my legs hanging out and a plate in my hands, and I'd pretend that plate was a ship's wheel, and I was a captain, steering that steamboat down the river, watching for snags and other boats." He grinned, meeting her eyes again. "You don't want to hear silly things like that."

She smiled and moved closer, resting her head on his shoulder. "Yes, I do," she told him. "I was just thinking today how little I know about you. You never talk about your childhood, Chad." She moved her face to kiss his cheek. "I want to know you better, to know about your family."

You don't want to know my family, he thought, the hurt and bitterness returning to his soul. "There isn't a lot to know," he said aloud. "I mean, there was just me—no brothers and sisters. My father owns an iron mill in Pittsburgh. He's done well. I always had a nice home, everything I needed. My mother didn't go out and work like Bea does." *She was usually home in bed with some other man,* he could have added. *My father had his share of lovers himself. None of that would have been so bad if my mother hadn't let one of her male friends come after me and—*

Chad suddenly rose, taking off his jacket. "It's hotter tonight than I expected. It usually cools off better than this once the sun goes down." *Why didn't my father believe me when I told him what that man did? Because he never loved me, that's why; because he didn't think I was even his own son. But why didn't my mother defend me? Were her lovers so important to her that she didn't care what they did to me?*

Irene noticed Chad seemed suddenly upset, but she couldn't imagine why. "Do you have much contact with your parents?" she asked. "Do you think they'll come out here to visit you sometime? I'd like to meet them."

He smiled, surprising Irene by looking nervous. He ran a hand through his hair and walked to the railing of the balcony. "Well, they're pretty busy. I write them and they write me, and I've told them all about you," he lied. He had not contacted them since leaving Harvard, and he couldn't care less if he never saw either of his parents again. "They'd like to meet you someday, but my father's mill is getting a little slow." *Probably because he's too drunk to go in most of the time.* How he hated drunks! His father always swore at him the worst when he had been drinking, reminding him he was the bastard son of one of his mother's lovers.

To this day Chad seldom touched liquor. He thought it ironic that he had so many other vices but refused to drink. "He's pretty tied up keeping the business above water, and my mother is afraid to come out here to what she calls the wild West," he continued. "And as busy as your mother keeps me, I don't see much chance of your meeting my folks anytime soon. But I've always been independent of them, and they trust my judgment."

He turned to look at her, studying her trusting eyes. Yes, he had other vices, but a man had to protect himself. Or was it the little boy in him wanting to protect and be protected? He sometimes wondered at his own insatiable appetite for women, for money and power. The women helped assure his confused soul that he was indeed a man, that what his mother's lover had done to him that night did not make him some kind of freak. Then again he sometimes thought of his mother when he was with other women, hated her, wanted to get back at her. Sometimes it felt good to hurt a woman as he had hurt Susan Stanner, as his mother had hurt him by refusing to protect him from that stranger, and as she had hurt him by sleeping with so many men.

The thought made him turn away from Irene. He stared out at the distant peaks, wondering, as he had wondered most of his life, which one of those men his mother took to her bed had been his real father. "The boy is a bastard," his father used to rage at his mother. "You think I don't know that? You think that sandy hair and those gray eyes came from either one of us?"

"Chad?" Irene approached him, touching his arm, realizing he was lost in thought. "Is something wrong?"

He met her eyes, at first looking almost angry; but the look vanished, and he smiled. "Not when I'm with you," he told her, pulling her close. He reminded himself to be careful. She must not know the truth about his parents, or she might realize he was marrying her simply because marrying someone so sweet and innocent made him feel better about his sordid past. She didn't need to know his father had disowned him, had left Chad out of his will because he did not consider Chad his son. She didn't need to know he longed for the money and power of a Kirkland because it was his way of protecting himself so that no one could ever again abuse him or take advantage of him. He had to stay on top, stay in control. He needed the Kirkland money, the high-paying position Bea had given him. He needed a woman like Irene on his arm to ensure no one ever knew about what that man did to him when he was a little boy; needed all the other women to prove he was as normal as the next man.

He had one thing to thank his unknown father for, and that was his looks. He had worked hard creating a charm to go with those looks, then using both to attain his goal of being his own man, of being wealthy and independent in his own right, of being in total control.

Irene gave him a feeling of stability he had never known before. She wasn't like all the others. Most women he had known were just like his mother—easy, secretly panting after men like bitches in heat. He didn't mind obliging their whims, since every time he did, he knew he was a man. He blamed both his parents for instilling in him sexual needs that were not easily satisfied. But he could at least thank his mother for his good looks, and thank his father for teaching him how to lie with a smile on his face.

Now he would marry Irene, a woman who could give him everything he needed, a woman who was innocent and unspoiled. She had not gone down easy, as Susan had. She didn't look at him with the eyes of a whore, his mother's eyes, the look he had seen in Elly's eyes and the eyes of so many other women. He could have the others and still have this one special one for himself, this one woman who gave him a feeling of security he had never gotten from his mother.

"You do love me, don't you, Irene?" he asked quietly.

There was a strange urgency to the words that made him sound like a little boy. Irene sensed a sudden vulnerability she had never noticed before. Chad Jacobs exuded such confidence, brashness, and sense of humor, it always made her forget her doubts about marrying him. Now that he'd shared with her the tiny bit about his past, telling about his childhood pretending, she felt he needed her, and she was all the more sure that she loved him.

"Of course I love you," she said, looking up at him. "Why would you need to ask?"

He searched her eyes. "I love you, too, Irene." So often he wished that he understood what love was supposed to be. His father's many affairs could not possibly have been love. What his parents shared was not love; what his mother did with other men was not love. Irene made him feel safe. Maybe that was love. He was sure she wouldn't be unfaithful as other women were. He only wished he could promise the same fidelity, but he knew he could not.

He covered her mouth with his lips, still intrigued that he had never gone further than this with her. He felt her respond, begin to kiss him back, and he felt his power over women return. He needed to know women responded to him, found him virile and desirable. When he was enjoying a woman, he was not a cowering little boy at the mercy of a stranger. He was a man in total control, behaving the way a man was supposed to behave. When he broke a woman's heart, he was breaking his mother's heart, and it was a good feeling.

He ended the kiss by pulling her tightly against him. "Enough about my family," he told her. "I had a very dull, ordinary childhood." He whirled her around. "I came up here for other reasons."

Irene laughed as he set her on her feet. He kissed her again, more suggestively this time, experimenting with her mouth, her emotions, her responses. She was so proper it made him laugh even while he was kissing her, and she pulled away. "What's so funny, Chad Jacobs?"

"Never mind. Just tell me you'll marry me. We've both known that's what is supposed to happen ever since your mother first invited me here for supper over a year ago. I don't know why your father insists on waiting until you're eighteen. You're all of a woman right now, from what I can see . . . and feel," he added, pressing her closer again and making her blush. "If I have to wait, then I will. But we can at least spend the next few months planning a wedding."

He reluctantly let got of her and walked to where he had laid his jacket. He took a small black box from the pocket and placed it in her hand. "Will you marry me, Irene?"

She trembled a little and felt warm inside as she took the box. At that moment she had never been more sure she loved him. Ramon could never be a part of her life now. That dream was done. She had responsibilities now, and there could be no more perfect man to welcome into the Kirkland empire than Chad Jacobs. If she allowed her unspoken doubts to keep her from this man, there were probably a thousand other women in Colorado alone who would gladly take her place.

She opened the box, and the huge diamond inside sparkled in the moonlight. "Oh, Chad, it's beautiful. But it must have been so expensive."

"Not nearly big or beautiful enough for you, but if I spent any more I wouldn't have enough to take us away for a honeymoon. I don't intend to sit back and let your parents support us, Irene. I think I've proven that by how hard I've been working since the fire. The money I have is money I've rightfully earned, and that's the way I intend to keep it. I bought that ring with money I saved from my regular salary."

She sighed, taking the ring from the box and sliding it onto her left hand. "It's the most beautiful ring I've ever seen." She looked up at him. "Yes, I'll marry you. I love you, Chad."

He smiled then, a smile that had led Susan Stanner to a tragic destiny. "And I love you, Irene Kirkland. I'll admit I knew your mother was just trying to set me up at first, but I didn't need any prompting when I saw how lovely you were. When I realized how sweet and loving you were on top of it, I knew I'd be a fool to let you slip through my fingers."

He pulled her back into his arms, kissing her hungrily, lifting her off her feet and making her laugh again. "What do you think of Europe?"

"Europe?"

"Your mother wants us to go south for our honeymoon, take care of a little business at the same time. But after that, I say we take a nice, long voyage to Europe. What do you say?"

Her eyes lit up. "Oh, Chad, it sounds wonderful!"

"Then we'll do it. Let's go and show your mother the ring."

"One more kiss," she begged.

Her eyes met his, and Chad gladly obliged. He was surprised how happy he felt, that he did want to marry her. He reasoned that taking a wife was just one more bit of proof that he was a real man. He already had the satisfaction of knowing he had gotten Susan Stanner pregnant. What better proof of manhood was there than that? Now Irene would have his children—his legal children—and he would openly prove that his seed was strong.

He whisked her up in his arms and carried her off the balcony, stopping to grab up his jacket but keeping her in his arms as he walked through the ballroom and down the stairs. Irene was laughing the whole way. "Don't drop me," she pleaded, wrapping her arms tightly around his neck as he joined in her laughter.

"Do you think I want to answer to your mother for dropping you down these stairs?" he answered. "Can't you just picture the look on her face? I'd be run out of Denver."

Chad carried her to the parlor, while Esther Sanchez and Jenny Porter watched from where they were still cleaning the grand dining table. They looked at each other and giggled, both greatly envying Irene Kirkland for landing the handsomest, most eligible bachelor in the Territory. He carried Irene into the parlor and set her on her feet, and she rushed to show her mother the ring. Bea beamed in an unusually warm smile as she studied it, congratulating them both, embracing her daughter.

"We'll have a party announcing the engagement," she told them, always delighted to do something that would make the society column of the *Rocky Mountain News*. "Come and let's show John and Elly. They're up in their rooms." She took Irene's arm and led her to the door. "Chad, I have some business to talk about with you later. Why don't you just stay the night here? You can use the guest room you used after the fire. Besides, all this Indian trouble worries me a little. I'll be glad when Kirk gets back."

"Sure. I'll stay," he answered Bea. He looked lovingly at Irene. "The ring isn't too heavy for your hand, is it?"

She laughed and shook her head, turning to go out with her mother. Chad watched, feeling a moment of unusual peace, a peace only Irene gave him. It lasted only until he heard them greet Elly in the hallway. Irene exclaimed over the ring, and he heard Elly say it was beautiful; but there was no enthusiasm in her voice, and only Chad knew why. Much as he enjoyed cavorting with women, Elly was one young lady he wished had no interest in him.

She appeared at the doorway to the parlor then, giving him an irritating look that told him she knew too much. "Well, you finally asked her," she said, sauntering closer. "Congratulations, Chad. I hope you'll both be *very* happy."

"I'm sure we will be," he answered, his momentary happiness leaving him. She came closer and instantly aroused all the worst in him. "I'll never forget what we said, Chad, or the way you touched me that day we talked in the sewing room," she whispered. "I still love you, but I know we can't be together . . . at least not now."

He wasn't sure what she meant by "not now," and he was not about to ask.

She toyed with the ruffles of his shirt. "Did you hear Susan Stanner isn't really dead at all. Her parents just said she was because she was pregnant and they wanted to get her out of Denver?"

Chad visibly paled. "What!"

Elly broke into laughter and whirled around, lifting her skirt as she did so. "I was just joking." She laughed again, then came closer, and Chad wrestled with a strong desire to knock the smile off her face. He realized with sudden clarity that she reminded him of his own mother. It wasn't her looks, but those eyes, her teasing ways. A whore at heart. He could spot one a mile away. But Elly remained dangerous, and he had to humor her.

"You're quite a tease, aren't you?" He grabbed her arms and leaned down to kiss her cheek. "Now leave me alone, Miss Kirkland. This is a happy night for me."

"And you're staying *all* night?"

He read her eyes warily, then lightly pushed her away. "I'm going to find Irene and John." He quickly left the room, hating her with great passion, wanting her with equal passion. There was not one thing physically attractive about the girl, but she represented another conquest, another victory he could not resist.

Elly's heart beat wildly as she approached the door to Chad's room. The house was dead quiet, everyone asleep, even the servants. She knew the only person who might have heard her steps would have been her father, a man accustomed to listening even when asleep, senses still alert from his days of living the dangerous life of a trapper.

But David Kirkland was not here, and she knew this might be her only chance to realize a wonderful "first" on her sister. Irene was older. She got to have her thirteenth birthday party first, was first to wear a low-cut dress and have a coming-out party, first to go to finishing school. She was first in her father and mother's hearts, and she had been chosen to be the one allowed to marry Chad Jacobs. Irene was beautiful, perfect, special, worshipped.

Elly was determined to have the last laugh on her sister. She knew something about Chad Irene didn't know. She also knew something about Irene that *Chad* didn't know—that Irene had loved and kissed a Mexican man. Such secret knowledge gave her a wonderful feeling of power. She could use either secret to worm her way out of trouble if the hurt she brought either Chad or Irene came back at her. Neither of them could threaten her, because she could threaten them right back.

She was determined now that if she could not have Chad for herself, she would at least share his body before Irene did. She quietly opened the door, glad it did not squeak, already wondering what other marvelous secrets she could discover to build her power. Between her cleverness, and the money she would one day inherit, it was Elly Kirkland who would one day be the first lady of Denver, much more powerful than her mother, she was sure. And someday, somehow, she would bring Irene down from her exalted throne. She needed something much more destructive than her sister's girlish passion for Ramon. Perhaps once Irene married Chad, and Chad continued his sordid affairs, which Elly had no doubt he would, maybe then she would find a way to malign Irene, make her sister appear to be a bad wife somehow, a disappointment to her handsome, caring, loving husband.

Elly approached the four-poster bed, where Chad slept quietly.

She dropped her robe, then carefully lifted the covers, her heart pounding so hard she was sure it would awaken someone. She slid her young, naked body under the covers, moving close to Chad and wondering what to expect, if it would hurt. It didn't matter. What mattered was that she did it.

He groaned slightly and shifted, and she daringly reached out, realizing with shock and utter ecstasy that he slept naked. She touched that part of a man that fascinated her. She had sneaked a peek at her brother more than once, out of curiosity, and she wondered how that soft thing could get inside a woman to make a baby. It took only seconds to understand. She was surprised and at first frightened when she felt the sudden swelling in her hand.

Chad jumped awake, grasping her arm. "What the—" At first he thought that by some miracle it might be Irene who had come to his bed. Someone planted her mouth over his and moved her hand back to his privates, arousing him in his sleepy state almost to the point of no return. She left his mouth and moved her lips to his ear.

"I want it to be me, Chad," she whispered. "Let me be first."

All his senses came alert then, and he grasped her shoulders, pushing her back and rolling on top of her. "Elly?"

"Please, Chad. I won't ever, ever tell, because I might want to come back to your bed again sometime when the time is right. I swear to God I won't tell, but I will if you turn me away. I'll make a fuss and say you lured me in here."

She felt him stiffen. "You reckless bitch," he hissed.

She reached up and touched his face. "You said you loved me, that sometimes you wanted me. Feel me, Chad. You'll see I'm a woman. I'm fourteen. I'm old enough."

"For God's sake, Elly, you're Irene's *sister*!"

Now that his eyes were adjusted to the dark room, he could see her smiling. "Does that really matter to a man like you? I think you're the one who ruined Susan Stanner, and she was a preacher's daughter. That didn't stop you." She felt his privates again, astonished at the magnificent swelling there. She had seen horses mate once, and realized now the same thing happened to a man. "I'll tell, Chad. I swear I'll tell if you don't make love to me. Please? If I can't have you for a husband, then at least let me have you this way *before* Irene. I want to be a woman, Chad, and I don't want anybody else to be my first."

They spoke in whispers. The dark room, her hand gently massaging that part of him so easily aroused was more than he could fight. She was a whore hungering a man, just like his mother, just like all the others. There was nothing wrong with a married man having his flings. Even David Kirkland had loved a whore. And, after all, he was not a husband yet.

He grasped Elly's face in his hands. "If you ever let this out, you'll never see me again, Elly Kirkland," he swore.

"I would never want that. I won't tell."

He drew in his breath. He could no longer resist her lustful desire, and he met her mouth, suddenly, hungrily, brutally. He took her hand from himself and moved his own hand between her legs, bringing a soft whimper to her throat as his fingers found the hot moistness that told him this young girl was as eager for him as Susan had been. He used his fingers expertly, and she drew a pillow over her face to stifle her pants of passion, while he moved his lips to devour the taut dark nipple of her full breast, breasts too big for such a young girl.

He moved between her legs. If she wanted this, she would get it. She was begging for it, just as the others had. He hated them all but gladly obliged them. He pushed hard, and Elly Kirkland was no longer a child.

Ramon opened the door, stunned to see it was Chad Jacobs who'd knocked. Why would this man who was to marry Irene be at his door—he must have found out about Ramon and Irene! Was he here to order him out of Denver? Put him out of business?

"Yes?" he asked quietly.

To his further amazement, Chad gave him a most charming smile and offered his hand. "Ramon Vallejo?"

Ramon watched him warily but took the man's hand. "*Sí.* What can I do for you, Señor Jacobs?"

"You know who I am?"

Ramon thought of the day of the parade, after the victory at Glorietta Pass, when he had seen Chad run up and hug Irene. "*Sí,* señor. I have seen you around. You are a popular man, a right-hand man to Señora Kirkland. I read the article in the *News,* that you are to marry Señorita Irene Kirkland. I . . . have met her."

"Well, then, I don't need to introduce myself. May I come in?"

Ramon, still confused, stepped aside, allowing Chad inside his home. Chad studied the beautiful Mexican woman who looked up at him from the table where she sat holding a child of perhaps eight or nine months of age and feeding him soft potatoes. He nodded to her, recalling the grand time he'd had in bed once with a Mexican whore who was so hot for him he could hardly keep up with her. This one, though, seemed quite proper. He didn't see any lust in her eyes when she greeted him.

"This is my wife, Elena," Ramon told Chad. Ramon asked Elena to get Chad some coffee, but Chad refused.

"I don't mean to stay long. Actually, I came here to talk business," Chad told Ramon.

Ramon led Chad into his office, a small addition to his stucco house. Everywhere Chad looked he saw Spanish rugs and paintings, vases painted in Spanish design, Spanish-style furniture. In Ramon's office a poncho hung on a coatrack, and Spanish-style boots sat in a corner, decorated with silver conchos.

Ramon sat down behind a teakwood desk with a beautifully designed border and legs, a spray of flowers carved into its back where customers could see the work. "Your desk is magnificent," Chad told him. "Did you carve it yourself?"

"*Sí.* It is my work. I did it for advertising. When customers come in they see what I can do."

Chad grinned, shaking his head and sitting down. It was obvious Ramon was doing well and would probably do even better in time. "Well, it's damn good advertising."

Ramon remained wary. He didn't like this man at all, but he did not have much choice but to be friendly to him. Ramon could understand why women probably came easy to this man. He doubted there were many who could resist him, and it tore at his heart that Irene probably trusted him implicitly. He would hurt her. Ramon was sure of it. He wondered if he could keep from killing the man if he destroyed Irene's lovely personality and delicate trust. More than that, his insides burned with jealousy at the thought of Chad Jacobs making love to Irene, being her first man. That was a privilege he had once dreamed would be his own. He hoped the man would be gentle and understanding with her.

"What can I do for you, Señor Jacobs?"

Chad sat down across from him. "Well, Miss Kirkland and I are getting married next spring. After that, we're going south for our honeymoon, then to Europe. When we return, I'd like to have a home of our own ready to move into. I figure one could be completed between now and then. It wouldn't be anything as huge or grand as the Kirkland mansion, but I want it damn nice. You've got a reputation for being the best carpenter in Denver. I already know Irene loves your work, and I've seen the carving you did at the Kirkland mansion. I'd like you to build our house for us."

Ramon stared at him in near shock, struggling to hide his

emotions. How little the man realized what a difficult task such a thing would be for him, to build the home his beloved Irene would share with another man! How could he explain such a thing to Chad Jacobs? He searched for his voice, while he glanced down at some work on his desk to hide his eyes. "I am a very busy man, señor. I am booked up for weeks."

"Come on, Ramon. Refer them to someone else. I really want you to do this. What better advertising could there be than to be the man hired to build a new house for the Kirkland's newly wed daughter and her attorney husband? Hell, I'll pay you twice the asking price. You'll make a fortune, and you'll build your business besides."

Ramon met Chad's eyes. Did the man know? Was he doing this just to be cruel? No. He would know it by Chad Jacobs's eyes, and he saw only genuine friendliness there. He reasoned the man would be easy to like, if he was not the cad Ramon suspected he was—and if he was not the man who would be sharing Irene's bed.

"Does Señorita Kirkland know about this?" he asked.

"Irene? No. I want to surprise her. She loves your work, and I'm building the house as a wedding present."

Oh, she will most certainly be surprised, Ramon thought. *Cruelly surprised.* "What about her mother?" Ramon asked then. "She is not fond of Mexicans."

Chad waved him off. "Don't worry about Bea. She goes along with anything I want to do. Besides, she let you do the carving work at her own home, didn't she?"

Ramon realized Bea had kept her word, had never told a soul about what had happened between him and Irene, or about her talk with him. He could think of only one good reason to do this job, and that was to imagine the look on Bea Kirkland's face when Chad Jacobs told his future mother-in-law who would be building his and Irene's new home. The woman would be in shock, but she would have no valid excuse for telling Chad not to hire Ramon, unless she wanted to tell Chad the truth, which Ramon knew now she would never do. Bea wanted this marriage.

The only drawback was that it would be hard on Irene—and hard on his own emotions. Still, his goal was to become as rich and powerful as he could—and someday give Bea Kirkland a run for her money. He would be important enough in Denver society that he could not be ignored by Denver's highest circles. He wanted to make Bea Kirkland eat crow. This job could do wonders for his business. And even though it would be a strain on both him and Irene, it would give him a chance to be near her, to keep an eye on her happiness.

Still, was that any longer any of his business? "I will need a day or two to think about this," he told Chad. "There are other customers I will have to disappoint. I do not want to turn down too many. If I take the job, I would rather work extra hours and finish some others already promised. I would not be able to start until at least October or November, but I would try very hard to finish by the time you are back and ready to move in. I need to know what kind of house you want so that I can go ahead and order some of the things I will need."

"Fine. I'll talk to Irene and we'll let you know."

"The only thing that might slow me up is the Indian trouble. Sometimes it is hard to get supplies through."

"Then we'll order as much as we can through Kirkland Supplies, out of San Francisco, rather than from the East. That will help."

Ramon thought of how utterly irritating and frustrating that would be for Bea Kirkland. "*Sí*, we could do that. I will give you my decision the day after tomorrow."

"Good. I hope you'll do it." Chad rose, putting out his hand again.

Ramon shook it, gauging the man's strength. "Thank you for thinking of me, señor. It is true this job would help my business a great deal."

"After Irene and I get back, we'll have a housewarming party, and you'll be invited. A good many of Denver's elite will be there. Some of those people will pay outrageous prices for what they want. You can drum up even more business and start catering to people who will make you a rich man."

No, Ramon thought, this man surely didn't know about him and Irene, or he would not be doing all this for him. How sad that he could never like the man. "That would be a great advantage. Thank you again, Chad."

Ramon led him back into the main house and to the door. After closing it he turned to look at Elena. She gazed at him with tear-filled eyes. "You left the door open," she told him. "I heard. Will you do it?"

He looked at her lovingly. "I will do whatever *you* want me to do."

She sighed, kissing little Juan's dark hair. "She will be another man's wife. Nothing can be done about that, and I know that you love me, Ramon. It is a great opportunity for you. This one job could help you realize all your dreams. You cannot turn it down."

He left the doorway and came around to kneel in front of her. "I suppose not." He leaned up and kissed her lightly.

"It will be hard on you, building the home she will share with another man," Elena told him.

He reached up and touched her face. "But every night I will have you to come home to." He leaned up and met her mouth again, this time harder, more demanding. "Come to bed, Elena. Suddenly I need you." He kissed her throat, kissed at her full breasts, then rose, helping her up. She carried little Juan to a playpen Ramon had built for the boy, a place where they could put him to play without having to worry about him crawling away. She followed Ramon into their bedroom, and he took her into his arms, kissing her hungrily and pulling her dress from her shoulders.

She knew what was going through his mind—knew this would be one of those times when it was not Elena Vallejo in his arms. He was making love to Irene Kirkland. As long as he could not physically realize that need, she could bear the pain of it, for it was her body he used, her bed he slept in.

CHAPTER TWENTY

January 1864

Chad and Irene took advantage of an unusually warm winter day to drive the Kirkland buggy to the site of their new home, only three hundred yards from the Kirkland mansion. It would be a much more modest house than the mansion was, but elegant in its own right. The two-story structure was already framed up, brick layers finishing the outer walls.

With great apprehension Irene disembarked the buggy. She did not relish having to face Ramon at all, let alone with Chad on her arm. When Chad had told her that he had hired Ramon to build their house, it had been difficult to hide her shock. It was true Ramon was probably the best man for the job, and she was more than happy to help his business, but a more ironic situation could not possibly exist for her. She felt sorry for Ramon, who must have accepted the offer with painful misgivings.

There was nothing Irene could say against the plan that would make sense, and she knew it had been the same for poor Ramon. Chad carried on elatedly about how quickly and beautifully their new home was taking shape. "You can decorate any way you want, Irene," he told her. "I want you to have everything exactly to your own taste. I know you like lots of pretty woodwork. That's why I hired Ramon." He led her to the double oak doors, their stained-glass windows adding to the rich, elegant appearance of the house.

"I have already been talking to Mother about it," Irene answered. She often wondered why Bea always seemed so nervous when they discussed the new house. Her mother should have been thrilled at Chad's wedding gift, glad they would have a home of their own to come back to after their honeymoon. But she did not seem very enthusiastic. Irene decided Bea was just disappointed that Irene and Chad would not be living at the Kirkland mansion. She was losing a daughter, and that upset her. Besides that, the woman had no use for Mexicans, especially Ramon.

They walked inside, admiring the huge central great room, which would be two stories high at its center, with a magnificent chandelier hanging from its peak. All other rooms were off to the sides, with an open, circular staircase leading to the upper bedrooms, which opened outward to a circular balcony that was visible from the great room. The marble flooring of the central room had not yet been laid, but the polished, honey-colored primavera wood banister that graced the entire stairway and balcony was in place. The delicately grooved banister was enhanced at intervals by beautifully carved support posts. After entering the great room, visitors could see a magnificent stair landing that was crowned by a ten-foot-wide stained-glass window.

Irene thought the stairway was one of the most beautiful features of the house, as well as the Primavera wood that trimmed every room. She had strived for a house that would be warmer and more homey than the castlelike Kirkland mansion. She liked this house much better, and had secretly admired Ramon's lovely, personal touches. She had not had to bear seeing and talking to Ramon yet, always being sure to visit the house when he was not there. But today Chad had come home early, and he was eager to do some inspecting. Irene knew Ramon would still be here working, and in spite of wearing an engagement ring, she was thrilled at the thought of seeing Ramon.

They found him bent over one of the railing posts on the landing, sanding a rough edge. He looked down when Chad called out to him, and his smile quickly faded when he saw Irene. She could see him struggle to keep his composure as he nodded to Chad. "So, you bring the señorita with you," he said, slowly coming down the stairs to shake Chad's hand.

Irene caught the look in Ramon's eyes, knew how he must feel about Chad, the same burning jealousy she felt over Elena. They gripped hands firmly. "Yes," Chad was saying. "With everything framed up and partly finished, Irene can get a better feel for how she wants to decorate. Irene"—he put a hand to Irene's waist—"I think you already know Ramon."

Their eyes met, and she wanted to cry, hating herself for this instant rekindling of old feelings when she was standing beside the man she was supposed to marry. "Yes," she answered, putting out her hand. "It's . . . been a long time, Ramon."

He took her hand hesitantly, squeezing it gently, and she knew in that one touch he wanted to do much more. A rush of desire swept through her that made her lower her eyes. "*Sí*, señorita." He released her hand reluctantly. "Congratulations on your coming marriage."

The conversation turned to progress on the house. Irene could not help nóticing Ramon's dark, muscular arms as he lifted a piece of wood that would be a fireplace mantel. He had rolled up the sleeves of his shirt, finding the work inside unusually warm today. The recurrent chinook wind had made the January day seem more like a spring one. Was Ramon really so much bigger and stronger, so much more handsome, or did it only seem that way because she had not seen him in so long, and because she still wanted him so?

He explained how he would design the particular piece of wood he was holding, then set it aside. "I am afraid this is going to cost more than we thought," he was telling Chad. "You know yourself how high prices are going, and it is hard to get the wood, especially the imported primavera from South America. And now the carpenters and brick layers are forming unions, demanding higher fees."

"Don't worry about it, Ramon. I'll cover any costs you didn't plan on. I want you to make good money on this. And like I said when I hired you, we want you to come to our housewarming, don't we, honey?" He turned to Irene, who had trouble finding her voice.

Ramon realized her agony, felt sorry for her in this awkward situation.

"Yes, of course," she answered. "And you must bring your wife."

Ramon smiled softly for her before moving his eyes to Chad. "We will think about it when the time comes. Right now I have to work at finishing, or you will have no reason for a housewarming."

Chad laughed, and Ramon wondered if Irene knew how her fiancé flirted with women in town.

Irene could no longer take the strain. "Chad, I'm going outside to look at the front doors again. They're so beautiful, prettier than Mother's, don't you think?"

"Much prettier," he answered. "Come right back. I'm going to have a look at the den." He turned to Ramon as Irene hurried away. "Beautiful, isn't she?"

Ramon watched her a moment, then forced his eyes back to Chad. "*Sí*, señor," he answered. "She is most beautiful." He hoped his deep feelings did not show in his words.

As she exited the double front doors, Irene saw her mother coming up the steps. She walked down to greet her. "Mother! What are you doing here? I thought you were at the offices this morning."

The woman appeared upset. "I came back to the house for something, and Elly told me you and Chad had come up here together." She glanced around, as though looking for someone. "I—I thought I'd come, too . . . see how things were going. Is that fellow Ramon Vallejo here?"

"Yes. He's doing a magnificent job, Mother. I hope you aren't going to be nasty about his leaving the work on your house. That was . . . a long time ago. I'm sure he had good reason. He's very good at what he does, Mother, and we want to help his business grow."

Bea gazed at her oddly. "Yes. I suppose you do." She sniffed. "Well, I wouldn't give that Mexican the time of day, but Chad seems to like him well enough." She studied the fine work on the outside of the house. "He does seem to know his business." She looked at Irene again. "Have you talked to him?"

"Of course. Chad is still with him."

Bea watched her daughter's eyes. If she still had feelings for Ramon Vallejo, it was difficult to tell. She was furious with Chad for hiring the carpenter, but she dared not voice her feelings. If Chad knew about Ramon and Irene, he might lose his respect for Irene and not marry her. And, after all, Ramon was married now. Still, he was one of those hot-blooded Mexicans. He could not be trusted. Thank goodness Irene had not come here alone.

Bea took Irene's arm. "Come inside with me, and show me around."

Irene felt her mother tense when they approached Ramon. Ramon gave her mother a strange, venomous look, and Irene began to wonder if her mother had somehow insulted him at one time. Maybe that was why Ramon had not finished his work at the mansion. "How do you do, Señora Kirkland?" he said, putting out his hand. "We meet again."

Bea had no choice but to take his hand. He squeezed hers nearly to the point of pain, but she made no sound. "Yes," she answered. "I trust you will finish this job and not run out on it before you're through."

He let go of her hand, glancing at Irene, then back at her witch of a mother.

"I was younger then, señora. And in love." He watched her eyes, felt Irene's hurt. He knew Bea Kirkland knew what he meant by being in love. "I decided I did not want to wait any longer to marry my Elena." He glanced at Irene again, hoping she understood he had to be careful what he said. At the same time he saw the slight relief in Bea's eyes. "Besides, I was not running my own business then. Now I am," he reminded her, a note of victory in his voice. "I finish what I start, Señora Kirkland. Already many of Denver's most prominent people have been asking me to do work for them. I have your future son-in-law to thank for that."

He smiled, wanting to laugh at her chagrin. He had won his first small victory over Bea Kirkland, and it felt good.

"What's this about not finishing a job?" Chad asked, coming out of the den.

Ramon met his eyes, thinking that no matter how much he disliked the man, he could never hate Chad Jacobs as vehemently as he hated Bea Kirkland. "I am afraid I left my work at the Kirkland mansion before it was finished. I went back to Hacienda del Sur to get married."

Chad laughed. "Well, I can understand that. The want of a woman can make a man do some crazy things."

Irene saw Ramon tense. His dark eyes moved to meet her blue ones. "*Sí*," he answered. "This is true." He looked back at Bea and smiled, sure she would never understand such a feeling. "I must get back to my work now. Look around all you want," he told Chad then. "Just be careful with the señorita. There are a lot of tools and some lumber lying around. I would not want her to get hurt."

Chad took Irene's arm and led her to the den. Bea remained with Ramon, and after a moment, spoke. "If you do anything to hurt Irene, or her marriage, I'll see you dead," the woman told him flatly.

Ramon's dark eyes blazed with hatred. "You have already hurt her more than I ever could," he warned. "And she will be hurt more by that womanizer you are allowing her to marry."

"Chad Jacobs is a fine man, the perfect husband for Irene."

Ramon turned away and began sanding the wood again. "Believe what you want. It is no longer my concern." He faced Bea. "I love my wife and son, Señora Kirkland. Irene will always be important to me, only in that I wish her to be happy. Do not worry about your precious daughter. I have no evil plans for her. My only goal now is to be a wealthy man, and I am going to make it!" He leaned closer, gritting his teeth, actually frightening her with his powerful frame and fiery eyes. "And *you* will not *stop* me, or I *will* tell Chad Jacobs the truth about me and Irene! Now get out of my sight, *bruja!*"

Bea had no idea what *bruja* meant, but he terrified her with his fierceness. She sucked in her breath, holding her chin high as she marched away, going down the stairs to find Chad and Irene. Ramon turned away, shaking with murderous emotion.

Spring came, and wedding plans were made. It was not the best time for a wedding, but then Bea decided the people of Denver needed a grand society event to help them forget their mounting woes. The war, as well as months of Indian ravages, had brought dangerous shortages, especially in food, since Coloradans still depended on outside sources for most of their staples. Prices had risen so dramatically that people were starving. Flour went from twelve to twenty dollars for five pounds. Twenty-five cent haircuts now coast a dollar each.

Even doing business cost more, since a ream of paper jumped from five dollars to twenty. Bea gave strict instructions to those at Kirkland Enterprises that anything that could be handled orally should be, to avoid unnecessary paperwork. After months of fund-raising, with Bea Kirkland at the helm, a Methodist seminary had opened, but closed again due to lack of funds. Early spring rains, unusually heavy, were inundating the plains, ruining spring plantings. Already Coloradans knew this would be another bad year for farming. What the sun had dried up last year, the rain would drown this year.

There was also unrest at the gold mines, where those miners being paid with paper money were forming unions. It took two dollars and forty cents now to buy one dollar's worth of gold, and the extreme gap forced even Kirk to begin paying his own men in greenbacks, the last thing he wanted to do.

Even other kinds of workers were forming unions—bricklayers, tailors, carpenters—forcing prices higher because of demands for higher pay. Men now wanted eight-hour workdays and shorter workweeks. Bea was beside herself with concern over the cost to Kirkland Enterprises. "Those uneducated drifters think they can get away with robbing people like us who have worked hard for everything we have. They might as well come in with guns and steal right out of our safes and jewelry boxes," she would complain.

Still, gold stocks continued to soar, and those with money in Kirkland mines enjoyed high dividends. But on April eighteenth, less than a month before Irene and Chad were to wed, everything came crashing down. The price of gold fell, based on the discovery that certain claims were worthless. Bea had made a killing selling shares in just such claims, but now the legitimate gold mines would suffer.

Times were hard, but investments in warehousing and supplies, hotels, the banks, and an iron mill helped carry the Kirklands through the worst. There came a cry for statehood, led by Bill Byers, Bea, and other prominent citizens who thought it was the only thing that would save Denver and Colorado. They promised better organization, more recognition from the federal government. But there were plenty who opposed statehood, voicing a fear of high taxes—county, city, school, road, license, income, and postage taxes. Their cries were voiced in a rival newspaper, along with those of the Spanish-Mexicans, who feared they would lose considerable rights to land they held in southern Colorado if it became a state.

Ramon was one of those who led an antistatehood movement, concerned for his grandfather's land in the south. His actions only made Bea hate him more, and she secretly vowed, now that Irene was marrying someone else and Ramon could no longer try to steal her away, that she would find a way to claim Hacienda del Sur and banish the Vallejos. She surmised that Ramon loved Irene too much to hurt her by going to Chad with the truth. He might have threatened to do so, but Bea was certain he would not. She needed his grandfather's land for her new venture in cattle ranching, and she was determined to get it. She'd have the last laugh on Ramon Vallejo.

Amid all the turmoil of political and financial upheaval, Bea insisted her daughter's wedding go on as planned. Now that Irene had been exposed to Ramon again, the sooner she was married to Chad, the better. Irene wondered at her mother's strange urgency over her marriage, as though it meant more to Bea than it did to Chad and Irene. The wedding would be held at the Kirkland mansion on May eighth, and promised to be the society event of the year for Denver.

Elly would be Irene's maid of honor, something she didn't mind doing, now that she secretly knew Chad Jacobs had been hers first. She had shared Chad's bed twice more since that first night at the Kirkland mansion, wonderful liaisons that had awakened every form of lust in her soul. Chad did terrible, wonderful, naughty things with her that only made her hunger for more. Since she could not have him with her always, she had decided she would find other ways to satisfy her insatiable sexual appetite. She felt beautiful and victorious in her seductions, not only of Chad, but of the boy who cleaned the Kirkland stables, and Tommy Slade, the twenty-year-old son of Robert Slade, one of the Kirkland attorneys. She had seduced Tommy in a back room of the new Kirkland offices, while her own mother worked out front. It was a terribly daring and exciting experience.

Chad had awakened a great need in Elly Kirkland—a need for male attention, a need to make up for what she considered her father's neglect. Mostly she needed and wanted Chad Jacobs, but as long as she couldn't have him permanently, she decided she would take him when she could get him, and satisfy the delicious passion he had aroused in her through other men.

A friend with whom Irene had shared a room in Chicago came to visit that spring, and stayed on to be one of Irene's bridesmaids. Charlene Simms came from a wealthy family in St. Louis, and the young woman raved over Chad, envious of Irene for her prize "catch."

Two other young ladies from the Methodist church to which the Kirklands now belonged would serve as the other bridesmaids. In spite of bad times, Bea had managed to raise money to build a new, much grander church than the original small building in which Reverend Stanner had preached. The new minister was older, with grown children and grandchildren.

Because Irene had led such a sheltered life, she had few close friends from whom to choose her attendants. The two young ladies from church were merely the daughters of close acquaintances of Bea's. Irene knew them, had talked with them several times at church meetings, but as she made her wedding plans, she realized she had never had much chance to develop intimate friendships.

She often wished she did have closer friends, or at least one very close woman friend with whom she could talk about her

upcoming marriage and what to expect. Charlene was too giddy
and childish, and since it had been a year since Irene had left the
girl's company, they were not close enough anymore to share such
intimate feelings.

It embarrassed her to think of talking about sex with her mother,
and she wondered how much help the woman would be anyway,
considering Bea's cold relationship with Kirk. Sometimes Irene
considered talking to Rose, her personal maid. Rose was nearly
the same age as Irene, but this poor orphan, pulled off Denver's
streets, came from such a different world, Irene was not sure how
to talk to her. Besides, would Rose understand that Irene might
have problems, that she had once loved someone else, that she
was a little bit afraid of her wedding night? Once a woman was
betrothed to a man like Chad Jacobs, who would have eyes for
anyone else? Who would be anything but thrilled about the
prospect of spending her wedding night with such a romantic,
handsome, nearly heroic figure?

Irene suffered her fears and doubts alone. Her only relief came
in trusting Chad, in believing he knew what to do, how to treat a
woman. He was not a cruel man, he didn't drink, he had always
been a gentleman. Chad was her best friend now, she reasoned.
He was all she needed.

The long-awaited wedding day finally came. Kirk was home, as
excited as everyone else over his daughter's marriage. Convinced
this was what Irene wanted, he was confident that Chad Jacobs
would be a loving, hard-working, devoted husband.

Chad had invited Ramon to the wedding, but for reasons only
Irene understood, the man had declined, insisting that if Chad
wanted their new home completely ready when they got back from
their honeymoon, he could not take any time off. "Weddings are
for family and close friends anyway," he had protested. When
Chad insisted, Ramon had politely told him that because he was
Catholic, he could not go to a Protestant wedding. Irene doubted
that was true, but Chad seemed to believe the excuse, and Irene
was relieved she would not have to walk down the stairway on her
wedding day and see Ramon watching her from the crowd.

She chastised herself for thinking it would matter. This should
be the happiest day of her life. She loved Chad, and after today
there would never be another man in her life.

After a great deal of fussing and hours of getting fitted into her
wedding gown, the time was at hand. An organ had been brought

into the house just for this occasion. People were waiting downstairs, waiting for Irene to descend the circular staircase to the great room, where she and Chad would speak their vows. Afterward there would be a grand reception in the ballroom, and then she and Chad would go to the newly rebuilt Denver Inn for their wedding night. The next morning a Kirkland carriage would take them on their journey south, where they would spend two weeks at another new Kirkland hotel in a new town near old Colorado City. The new town, called Colorado Springs, was where Denver's wealthier class now went to "get away." It was a cleaner, more respectable town than Colorado City, although still very small and undeveloped.

From there Chad and Irene would leave for St. Louis, then take a steamboat to the Gulf of Mexico and board a bigger ship for Europe. Everything was planned, but as far as Irene was concerned, it was happening too fast. Her heart pounded when she heard the organ begin to play. Her father came for her, his eyes bright with tears at the sight of her.

There she stood, the little half-breed baby girl he had taken from Gray Bird Woman's arms, now a grown woman of eighteen herself, and the most beautiful creature he had ever seen. She wore a white, low-cut silk dress with long sleeves dropped off the shoulder, the area between the low bodice and her neck filled with a chemisette of delicate white lace. Her tawny, velvety skin showed through the lace just enough to be deliciously enticing to her husband-to-be, and the tight-fitting bodice accented her slender waist and led to a full skirt graced with tiers of hundreds of silk puffs. The puffs were tied with white satin ribbons, and the brocade hemline was decorated with more white satin ribbon, and with pearls. A wreath of orange blossom graced her golden hair, which was swept up into a cascade of waves and curls, and from the circlet of flowers fell a white veil that covered her face. A train of lace-edged silk trailed out behind her for several feet.

"My beautiful Irene," Kirk said, taking her hands. "I hope you'll be happy, sweetheart. That man had better treat you right, or he'll answer to me."

"He's good to me, Father. I'm sure that won't change." How she wished she could ask him what had gone wrong with his own marriage. At the same time he was wishing he could tell her the truth about her heritage, dreading the possibility she could have an Indian baby. Whatever happened, he would love her, protect her. He would not let Chad or anyone else hurt her. How he wished he could have found a wife who would have been as good to him as he knew Irene would be to her husband. How Bea had managed to raise such a charming, gracious, genuinely caring daughter, he would never understand. Perhaps her gentle nature was inborn, inherited from her Cheyenne mother.

"I love you, Irene. I don't say such things often, but . . . you'll never know how special you are."

Does it have something to do with the secret you carry, Father, she wanted to ask. *Why do you always look at me that way? Why am I so special?* "Do you think we'll ever get to go back to the mountains?" she asked him.

He smiled sadly. "You'll be busy with a new husband and a new home. Before you know it, there will be children to look after." He leaned down and lifted her veil to kiss her cheek. "But maybe . . . someday."

She knew "someday" would be a long time coming. He lowered the veil and stepped back to look at her once more. "Ready?"

"I think so."

He looked out into the hall, signaling the procession to begin. Bea was escorted down the stairway by her attorney, Robert Slade. Chad's parents had not come. "My father can't leave the mill," Chad had told Irene. "And like I said, my mother won't come out here." He had presented Irene with a diamond necklace, telling her it was a gift from his parents and that they sent their love. She had no idea that Chad had never contacted them, that he was ashamed of them, that he hated his mother. He had bought the necklace himself.

Chad's best man was Irene's brother, John, who escorted Elly down the carpeted stairway as the organist filled the Kirkland home with the beautiful music of the wedding march. John was sixteen now, soon to go off to college. Somewhere in the last two years he had finally surrendered his dream of carving and working with wood, drowned it in a newfound love of liquor. So far he'd managed to hide his drinking from his parents.

The rest of the wedding party followed John and Elly down the long staircase. Then it was time for the bride to make her entrance.

Gasps of pleasure and admiration came from the crowd below when Kirk appeared at the top of the stairs with Irene on his arm. Chad watched with equal appreciation, every nerve end coming alive. Finally! Tonight she would have no more excuses. Tonight she would be his legal wedded wife, and he would know the pleasures of Irene Kirkland's beautiful body. He knew Elly was watching jealously, but he didn't care. Today he had eyes only for Irene, who came down the stairs watching him lovingly.

Music filled the magnificent Kirkland mansion as Irene descended. Kirk wished Red was here for this moment, but the man had refused to come. He had acted strangely aloof lately, and Kirk decided it must be because the man's business had not done well the last few months. Red had lost a lot of raw material in the Denver fire and was having trouble getting in new supplies. Kirk had offered to help but Red had flatly and angrily refused, saying he would make it on his own. "You'll get your money, one way or another," he had nearly growled. Kirk had explained it didn't matter, but Red was adamant, apologizing for not being able to pay off the loan as quickly as he had planned, swearing he would be on his feet again soon.

Kirk was concerned over Red's behavior and valued the man's friendship. But he decided he could not worry about Red today. Today was special.

They reached the landing, and Irene let her eyes stray from Chad for a moment, noticing that Hank Loring was there with a pretty woman standing beside him and a little girl in his arms. Bea had told her Hank was doing so well with the new breed of cattle she'd shipped in from England, that she now had him breeding them. He was well on the way to developing a whole herd.

Hank smiled, and Irene smiled in return, startled that seeing him still brought an odd flutter to her heart. She reasoned the woman beside him must be his wife.

She turned her eyes back to Chad. She must not think about Indians or money problems or her father's secrets today. She must not wonder about men like Hank Loring or worry that she had caught John with a half-emptied bottle of whiskey the other night. She must not wonder when she would go to the mountains again or worry why her parents' marriage was not perfect. Most of all, she must not think about Ramon.

This was *her* marriage, and she would make sure this one *was* perfect. She would give her husband and children all the attention her own father and his children had never gotten. She would put hearth and home above all things. She was marrying a handsome, successful, hard-working, gentle man—a man any woman would love to have for her own. Irene watched the glitter in Chad's gray eyes as she approached him then, saw the love there. No. She would not be afraid.

Chad walked over and took her arm, and the minister asked, "Who gives this woman to be wed to this man?"

"Her mother and I," Kirk answered, his voice choked up.

Irene felt a lump rise in her throat, and she blinked back tears. She looked at Chad, and he gave her that smile that always made her feel loved and cherished. They moved through their wedding vows, Irene hardly aware of anyone or anything around her now. Chad slipped the gold band on her finger, and she slipped one on his. He belonged to her now. No other woman could have him. And it was the same for her.

It's done, Ramon, she thought as the minister pronounced them man and wife. Chad lifted her veil and touched her mouth in a warm, delicious kiss that made her want him.

"I present to you Mr. and Mrs. Chadwick Jacobs," the minister announced.

They turned to greet the guests, and people broke into cheers and claps, some throwing rice as the organ played on. Bea wept, Kirk's arm around her shoulders. Elly watched with a strange look of victory in her eyes, but a hot pain in her stomach. John congratulated his sister and hurried off to find the whiskey.

Irene looked up at Chad with tears in her eyes. "I love you, Mr. Jacobs."

"And I love you, *Mrs*. Jacobs," he answered, anxious for the reception to be over, anxious to see how easily he could bring out the wanton passion he was sure lay just beneath that beautiful, satiny skin. Perhaps he had to swear off other women for a while, but with one like this in his bed, what did it matter? If and when he tired of her, he would find a way to be with the others.

Irene picked up her train, and Chad kept his arm around her as he led her up the stairs, inviting everyone to follow them up to the ballroom. Hank watched Irene, secretly admiring her beauty. He put an arm around his wife and leaned down to kiss her cheek before he led her up the stairs.

At the same time Ramon stood on the second-floor balcony of the new house Irene and Chad would soon move into. He could hear the organ music, recognized the recessional that marked the ceremony's end. "So," he said softly, "you belong to another now. May God be with you, *mi querida*."

CHAPTER
TWENTY-ONE

Rain came down in torrents, and Irene wondered vaguely if it was some kind of omen that it should rain so hard on her wedding night. It was late, and after a grand reception, she and Chad were finally alone at the Denver Inn. There had been little time to think or even breathe, and once the door was closed, Chad continued the whirlwind, drowning her in his kisses the way the rain was drowning everything outside.

She was not sure what to expect, but Chad was gentle, cajoling, tender. She wanted so much to please him, wondered if he understood her fear and apprehension of the unknown. Should she ask him to slow down? No. He was her husband now. He deserved to have his pleasure, and how could she not take pleasure in return with such a handsome, experienced man? She reasoned she had only to let him take control, and everything would be all right.

He worked his mouth and hands and body in such a way that she wanted him, in spite of her fear of what was to come, in spite of the tiny, lingering misgivings over marrying him at all. She felt her dress coming off, gasped when he was suddenly tasting at her breasts, then kneeling to remove her underwear. She felt herself lifted and laid on his bed, the bed she could not know he had shared with poor Susan Stanner, and twice with Elly.

She could hardly believe she was doing this, and in spite of

Chad's expert ways, something still did not seem right. Was it that in her heart she knew she would be responding much more passionately if this were Ramon? Oh, how she hated herself for thinking such a thing!

He slipped her shoes and silk stockings off, then kissed her lightly a dozen times, before pulling the covers over her. "Are you all right?" he asked.

How kind of him, she thought. "Yes," she answered, her voice sounding small and far away.

"You're the most beautiful woman I've ever set eyes on," he told her. "I want you to be just mine, Irene. You'll never let another man touch you, will you?"

She thought the question a peculiar one, especially on their wedding night. "Of course not, Chad. Why would I? I'm your wife."

He looked at her strangely, then stood up and undressed to his long johns. She reddened as she watched him, studying his broad, naked chest, seeing him intimately for the first time. He unbuttoned his underwear. "Don't be afraid, Irene." He removed the underwear and she looked away.

In the next moment he turned down the lamp and climbed into bed with her. She felt frozen in time. He was pulling her into his arms, his naked body against hers. It was frightening, yet thrilling. Inside, she wanted to respond with great passion, but outwardly she felt herself freezing up. What was wrong? She loved him, didn't she? She was his wife now. The poor man expected to get his pleasure tonight, and she had vowed to be the loving, attentive wife her mother had never been. The last thing she wanted was for her husband to have to go running to the whores. How devastating that would be! And babies—she wanted babies. There was only one way to get them.

She reasoned that once it was over the first time, it all must surely come easier. She just had to relax and let it happen, and everything would be all right. He smothered her with kisses, pressed her naked breasts against his firm chest, moved a hand over her bottom, then around between her legs. It was a startling touch—too soon! This man was touching her in intimate places, awakening desires she had never before been aware of.

She was embarrassed, yet excited. It seemed wrong, yet why should it be? Chad was her husband now. Still, if this were Ramon . . . Ramon. The thought of him touching her this way made her respond suddenly. She returned Chad's kisses, then concentrated her thoughts on Chad, where they belonged. He trailed his lips down her neck, then lower, gently taking a breast into his mouth. The gesture, combined with the way he used his fingers, made her gasp his name.

Yes, he knew just what to do. She was glad, except that now she felt a sudden jealousy of all the other women who might have shared such things with him. She forced back thoughts of Ramon and decided that once and for all she must never allow them again, not in moments like this. It was wrong. Chad was being so gentle, so loving. He had chosen her for his wife. She was precious to him. From now on she would be his only woman.

"We might as well get it done, honey," he whispered, moving on top of her. He licked and kissed at her neck, her ear, her cheek, met her mouth with lips that nibbled and teased. "It will hurt at first, but it gets better," he told her then. "I promise you. It gets much better."

She was lost in another kiss, her stomach tight and on fire, her body suddenly rigid again. She felt so vulnerable, helpless, lying there with his weight on top of her, her legs spread open to him, at his mercy. Something about their lovemaking still didn't feel right, but she wanted to get over the initial pain of it and learn to enjoy this.

She felt him press against her groin, felt the panic rise in her. He reached down to position himself, and suddenly pushed hard.

Never in her life had Irene known such pain. She screamed out for him to stop, but how could a man stop when he had gone this far? Chad pushed again and again, and to his horror, amid Irene's screams, he realized he wasn't penetrating her more than an inch or two. Never had he had this problem, and it confused Chad as much as Irene. For the first time in his life he panicked while with a woman. He put a hand over her mouth to smother her screams, and he shoved again, still getting nowhere. Finally her cries and tears destroyed his desire, and he pulled an aching penis from inside her, totally frustrated, at a loss to know what had gone wrong.

Irene rolled to her side, curling up and weeping. Chad turned up the lamp to see he had blood on himself. He cursed again, getting up to wash and pulling on his long johns, while Irene continued to cry. His mind raced with misgivings. This had never happened to him before.

She had rejected him! His own wife, the one woman he thought he could love. No, she had not rejected him—he had *failed* her! That was it. And now he had lost his erection. This was unbelievable. Was he so incapable of love that when he did feel something special for a woman, he couldn't perform? Did he have to hate them first, the way he hated Elly and all the others?

He didn't know how to handle this. His wife lay practically writhing in pain, weeping—on their wedding night! He walked over to the bed, bending over her. "What the hell is wrong, Irene?"

"I . . . don't know. It was . . . so painful."

"If you'd just let me get it done—"

"No! Something is wrong! Oh, god, Chad, I'm so sorry! I'm so sorry! I don't know what to do!"

He began dressing nervously. "I'll leave you alone for a while."

"No. I don't want to be alone. Not on our wedding night."

He came back over, bending down to kiss her cheek. "I'm sorry I hurt you. You rest. I'll figure out what we can do. Maybe I can find a doctor."

"No! I don't want a doctor looking at me!"

"Well, we sure as hell have to do *something*, now, don't we?"

She shivered at his anger and frustration, and she wanted to die. He finished dressing. "I'll be back in a while."

He was suddenly out the door, and Irene stared at it, astounded that he had left her at such a terrifying moment. She needed him with her. She just wanted him to hold her in his arms and tell her everything would be all right. Ramon would have. He would have been willing to be patient, to give her some time, to try once more and then let her see her own doctor if it didn't work. Most of all, he would still love her just as much. It was not love she had seen in Chad's eyes when he left. He looked as if he were an angry, stubborn, betrayed little boy.

Chad stood in the hallway, considered going back inside, then decided against it. He needed to know right way that he was still all right. He knew a couple of whores who would keep quiet. They would understand that sometimes a man's wedding night was disastrous because his wife was such a prissy virgin. He would go see them, prove he was just as much a man as ever. Maybe in turn they could recommend a doctor who knew about these things, someone who could get over here and discreetly fix whatever was wrong with his wife.

He headed down the back stairs, making sure no one saw him.

Irene had never known such pain and humiliation, nor would she ever forget the terror her husband put her through that first night. After she lay there alone and confused for two hours, Chad finally returned, bringing with him a doctor she had never met. She well knew Denver had its share of quacks, with people of all walks of life coming to the gold town. She begged Chad to wait until morning and get her own family doctor, but Chad refused.

"I can trust this man not to say anything. I don't want others knowing I couldn't break in my own wife on her wedding night!"

The words had stung, and she felt like a miserable failure. She was sure she smelled cheap perfume on her husband. Had she frustrated him so that he had gone to a whore on their *wedding* night? Was this doctor a man who administered to such women? Chad made her drink something that made the room spin. His face became a blur. She felt the horror and humiliation of being exposed to the strange doctor, yet she felt lifeless, unable to speak or resist. The pain he caused her then was beyond description, and she passed out.

She awoke to a gray morning. Rain continued to fall, and Irene began to shiver. She felt cold, too cold for a warm spring morning. She felt a hand on her shoulder then. "How do you feel, honey?"

She pulled away. "Don't touch me," she answered, wanting to vomit. "What did that man do to me?"

She heard a deep sigh, felt Chad sitting up. "He said some women just can't . . . there's a kind of wall there a man has to break through. With some women it's just a little more difficult, that's all. It has to be done with an instrument."

She curled up more tightly. "How dare you let him do that to me?" she groaned.

He reached over and picked up a thin cigar, lighting it. "Irene, it had to be done. You want to be a wife to me, don't you? I only did it to help you."

"You visited a whore last night after you left me, didn't you?"

He puffed on the cigar. "There are things you have to understand about men, Irene. One is that you can't take a man halfway. It's almost painful. I had to get some relief, that's all. I only did it because I didn't want to hurt you. It was obvious I wasn't going to be able—" He sighed again and rose. "Once you're healed, everything will be fine."

Just like that, she thought. *Everything will be fine. You weren't man enough to stay with me when I needed you most, to hold me when I needed holding, to be a little more unselfish about your own needs. You couldn't have waited one or two days, let me see my own doctor.*

How she wanted to spit it all out to him. But her marriage was so new, and she wondered if he was right about a man's needs. What did she know about such things? Maybe he really thought he had done the right thing. But she could not imagine that Ramon would have reacted the same way. Even after what she had just been through, she could still think of Ramon, knew that she would have let him make love to her, even though such a thing seemed revolting at the moment.

Chad came around to her side of the bed, kneeling beside her. "I'm sorry for what you went through, Irene." She closed her eyes, and he touched her face. This time, to his relief, she did not pull away. How could he explain what her rejection had done to him? He could never explain it, because to do so would be to tell her about his mother's lovers, about his brutal childhood. He thought she would be disgusted, scared by what he'd seen and known. "I promise," he continued. "Once the pain and bleeding subside, you'll feel just fine, and then we can try it again." He moved to take one of her hands. It felt cold and clammy, and he hoped she was not going to get sick because of this. How would he explain it? "Just promise me you won't . . . you won't tell anyone," he asked. "It would be very embarrassing for me."

"What about me? I feel like a failure," she said weakly.

He set his cigar aside. "Maybe we both failed each other a little last night."

But I didn't do anything wrong, she wanted to argue. *I couldn't help it*. "Why couldn't you just have stayed with me, Chad?"

He squeezed her hand. "Believe me, honey, it's best to get these things done and over with. It's hard for me, too, you know. I mean, a man wants to be the first, you know? He doesn't want his wife's virginity taken by some doctor."

She groaned at the words, grasping her stomach, loathing the memory, wondering now if she could ever enjoy making love. The thought of letting him try again was horrifying, yet she knew that she must, or her marriage would end up just like her mother and father's. She did not want a marriage on paper only, with her husband running off to the whores.

"I'm sorry . . . the way it happened," she told him, swallowing her pride, deciding that with her marriage so new, she must work quickly to patch up the hard feelings, try to get things off to a better start. "Please be patient with me, Chad. Don't go running off to those other women."

"Never again," he lied. "You rest, and I'll have breakfast sent up. Later today we'll load up and head south. I'll bet it's not raining there. You'll feel better soon, Irene—with the warm sunshine, in the country you love."

Her eyes teared. She needed to cry, needed someone to talk to, but there was no one. "Yes," she answered. "That does sound good."

He patted her hand and rose to dress. The rest of the day was agony for Irene. She felt nauseated, and she bled heavily. She forced herself to get up and wash and dress, forced down a little food, forced a look of happiness when her parents came to see them off. Her mother hugged her, asking if she was "all right." Irene knew what she meant. How could she tell the woman what had happened? And she certainly couldn't tell her father. She would have to suffer the horrifying memory in silence. Who would understand anyway?

She gave her father an extra hug, suddenly longing to stay with him, to go back to the mountains. She knew she would not see him for a long time. He was leaving right away for Georgetown, where silver had been discovered. He intended to check out the silver strikes for himself, do some investing. Silver was the new hope for Colorado's sagging economy. From Georgetown, Kirk would head for San Francisco, to take care of some business and sell the remaining Kirkland mines there. Business had grown to such an extent in Denver that it was becoming increasingly difficult to continue to manage all the Kirkland holdings still in San Francisco.

At that moment Irene wished she could go with her father, wished she was a little girl again, living in a little shack in the Sierras, back in a time when, in spite of poverty, her life was carefree and full of adventure.

With great effort she managed to climb into the carriage, waving good-bye to everyone. Once their baggage was loaded up, they were off, headed for Colorado Springs. Irene could feel the heavy bleeding, prayed nothing would show. The pain was still with her, and she made the long journey nearly unconscious on Chad's shoulder. She told herself she had to get through this, had to rise above it. After all, she was a married woman now. Nothing could be changed. There was no going back.

The rain continued to pour, and snow in the higher elevations continued to melt at an unusually rapid rate. Colorado's Front Range was deluged, the hills around the headwaters of Cherry Creek were saturated. People who had lived around Cherry Creek for several years had never known it to swell dangerously beyond its banks, so no one was overly worried about the unusually wet weather. A few people who lived on the edge of the creek evacuated, but it was only an annual spring precaution.

Like most others, Ramon also was not worried. He lay in bed late in May, thinking about things forbidden, wondering about Irene. Had Chad been good to her on their wedding night? Had he been gentle, considerate? It could not have been easy for someone as innocent as Irene. He knew, because he remembered the fear in Elena's eyes, remembered the pain he had brought her. He had even offered to wait, but Elena had wanted it done. He felt there was a fragility about such things for a woman; sensed that the wrong move, the wrong words that first night with Elena could have affected all the rest of their nights together.

He sighed and turned onto his side, feeling tense, angry. He had felt this way ever since Irene's wedding day. Night after night he was tortured with the vision of Chad Jacobs taking what Ramon still felt should rightfully belong to him. He wondered if he would ever get over this feeling, hated himself for it. He wondered sometimes if he should just leave Denver, perhaps go to Cheyenne, another growing town to the north. Or he could go someplace like San Francisco, or farther east, to St. Louis.

It would be best, yet he knew he would not go, because to remain in Denver meant being near Irene, even though he could not have her or even express his feelings in any way. She belonged to another man now, and he belonged to another woman. Such sacred relationships were not to be soiled, and he had often confessed his sinful thoughts, lighting candles, asking the local priest at the Catholic church he attended to pray for his soul. These feelings must end once and for all.

He heard a rumbling sound then, frowned, strained to listen. He had never before heard anything like it. The ground seemed actually to shake, and he thought at first perhaps the area had been hit by a rare earthquake. The rumbling grew louder, and at the very instant he realized what was happening, the house literally exploded.

He was at once engulfed in cold water. The bed was swept out from under him. He grasped for Elena, but she was gone. He thought at first he was going to drown, as he struggled in dark waters, trying to get air. At last his head bobbed above water, and he gasped for breath. "Elena," he screamed. "Elena! Juan! Where are you!"

He realized he was in the open air, being washed along with

pieces of buildings and logs. A huge boulder smashed into his side, and he cried out from the pain of broken ribs. He tried to see in the darkness. Where was Elena! And where was little Juan! He could hear screams, cries of agony, and the rumble of the rushing water was deafening. Buildings creaked and snapped, and his own house had been completely swept away by some sudden surge of flooding water. He figured it must have taken the route of Cherry Creek.

He moved in a kind of strange dream world. Nothing was real. People were screaming for their families and loved ones, and rain poured out of the dark night sky. He was cold, so cold. He could feel he was naked, his long johns swept right off him by the torrent. Every breath brought excruciating pain from his broken ribs. He grabbed out at things to keep from sinking, finally catching a tree branch that kept him afloat. "Elena," he shouted, the tears coming then. "My God, Elena, where are you! Juan! Juan!"

Was this his punishment for lying in bed and thinking about Irene? The woman who loved him, who had given him a child—the woman who should have been first in his heart—might be dead. And his son, his little Juan! How could he bear such a loss! He could only pray that somehow both of them had survived.

Irene basked in the warm sun, her only comfort. She sat in a lounge chair outside the new Colorado Springs branch of the Kirkland Hotel. She and Chad had been in the new resort town for nearly two weeks now, Chad busily taking care of business matters for Bea while there. For the first week after their disastrous wedding night Irene's pain and bleeding had continued. Chad seemed anxious and frustrated. As far as Irene could tell, he had not gone to see any prostitutes, but after that first night she felt she could never fully trust him again.

Chad's inability to understand what she was going through was a great disappointment. The fun and friendship they had shared before they got married had suddenly vanished, and Irene convinced herself that it was her own attitude that was the problem. She had to get over this, had to get this marriage quickly back to where it should be, or it would be finished before it began. She refused to let it be a failure, to bring shame and embarrassment to the rest of the family.

She had finally managed to dredge up the courage to allow Chad his husbandly rights. On that second try at mating with his new wife, he was not gentle. She had sensed his anger, and was hurt by it. Perhaps he was still upset that he had technically not been the one to "break her in," as he had so crudely put it. He had shoved hard, brought more of the terrible pain, but she had gritted her teeth and had not cried out. She wanted so desperately to be a proper wife. Chad had ravaged her, made her feel used, as if she were a whore.

After that first time he had wanted her every night, and she wondered if most men were that way. He at least seemed to soften toward her, to lose some of the anger. He became gentler, prompting her, touching her in ways that ignited at least some desire on her part. But she was so tired and still in pain. She didn't want to make love so often, but she kept quiet about it, convinced it was a wife's duty to submit to her husband's needs.

She had imagined it all so differently. She hoped that maybe once they were home in their own house, and especially if she could get pregnant and give Chad a child, things would get better. After all, he did love her. He had told her so night after night; and he certainly seemed to enjoy making love to her, even if she didn't experience the same satisfaction. Maybe a woman wasn't supposed to like it, maybe even the whores didn't like it, just did it for the money.

But now, lying here in the warm sun, with Chad gone off on business, she felt her thoughts turn again to Ramon. She knew love was not supposed to be like this at all. It would all have been different with Ramon. But it had not been Ramon who put the wedding band on her finger, and it was not Ramon who shared her bed.

Her eyes stung with tears. She loved Chad, and she knew the main problem was her inability to forgive him for that first night. It still gave her nightmares. The memory of it made it difficult to want to give Chad any pleasure at all. She told herself she must forgive him, forget what had happened. They would soon set off for Europe. This was supposed to be the most exciting time of her life. But she was tired, so tired. She had been unable to eat and had lost weight, and when she looked in the mirror she saw a face too pale.

She closed her eyes, enjoying the peace and quiet. Moments later her temporary peace was interrupted when she heard the clatter of a carriage approaching at nearly breakneck speed. She opened her eyes to see it was Chad. He ordered the driver to stop and climbed down. "We've got to get packed," he said, rushing up to her. "We'll load the carriage and head back home." His eyes were wide with concern.

"Chad, what is it?"

He helped her up. "There's been a terrible flood in Denver. The wire came in while I was at the post office. We've got to get back there!"

"A flood! In Denver? There's only little Cherry Creek—"

"That's what flooded. It came unexpectedly, a literal wall of water, they say, in the middle of the night. So many people are dead, Irene. Half the town was washed away!"

"Oh, dear God," she murmured, hurrying with him up to their room. She tried to remember just what buildings were closest to the creek, and she wondered if the offices of the *Rocky Mountain News* had been lost. What else was near the creek? She hastily threw some clothes into a carpetbag, then felt a rush of cold through her veins. Ramon lived near the creek. The flood had hit during the night, when people were sleeping. So many must have died. Could Ramon have been one of them?

Sick fear filled her heart. Please, not Ramon! In spite of the fact that they could never be together, just knowing Ramon existed had been a comfort to her. To think he could be dead brought a great empty, lonely feeling to her soul.

CHAPTER
TWENTY-TWO

Most of downtown Denver was washed away. Again, the city suffered tremendous devastation, and again its people pulled themselves up by the bootstraps and determined they would not let this latest disaster make them give up or leave. They had overcome the fire; they would overcome the flood. They had been sorely tested, tempered and honed hard by fire and water—but they were fighters. They dug in and began cleaning up and rebuilding.

This time the Denver Inn had been spared, but another Kirkland warehouse had been washed away, as well as a Kirkland supply store. The store had literally vanished without a trace. The same fate was suffered by Bill Byers and the offices of the *Rocky Mountain News*. A three-thousand-pound steampowered printing press Byers had imported from the East was nowhere to be seen.

By the time Irene and Chad arrived, people were still milling about in shock, astonished at the power of water. Bea welcomed Chad and her daughter, too distraught to notice Irene's loss of weight, the circles under her eyes, her pale skin. Irene reasoned that if her mother did notice, she probably thought it was due to Irene's worries over the flood.

"You two should have gone on to Europe as planned," Bea fussed. They stood outside the new offices of Kirkland Enterprises, which had been spared. "Oh, I wish you had already been on your way when this happened. I hate to see your honeymoon ruined!"

"Bea, you know we wouldn't leave you to handle this alone, especially with Kirk gone." Chad patted her arm and she quickly embraced him, then embraced Irene.

"I've wired Kirk that we can handle things here. As long as he's already in Georgetown, he might as well go on to California," she told them. "There is so much there to be done. He'll have some supplies sent in from the coast."

"How bad are our losses?" Chad asked.

"Bad enough, considering the fire, then all the rising prices and the bottoming out of mining investments. We have so much to talk about, Chad. I want to know how things are going in the south. It's more important than ever." She quickly kissed Irene's cheek. "Have the driver take you to the house, Irene. John is still there. He'll be coming down soon. I'd like to borrow Chad for a while, if it's all right."

"Yes, Mother," Irene answered quietly. *I need to talk to you,* she wished she could say. *I'm so unhappy, and I don't know what to do.* Chad leaned down and kissed her lightly.

"Go home and get some rest," he told her. "I'll be along."

Irene entered the carriage, feeling numb. A honeymoon to Europe was not likely now, and she didn't even mind. She reasoned since she was home, she would feel better, especially once they could move into their own house. One thing she did love was her house, the warmth of the rich wood floors and paneled walls, the beautiful stained-glass windows. Being in that house, surrounded by Ramon's work, would be like having Ramon near her, watching over her. Wrong as it was, ever since the horror of her wedding night, she had thought more about Ramon. Now, wondering if he might have been killed in the flood, those thoughts were stronger than ever.

She stared sadly at the devastation as the carriage clattered away, and once out of sight she ordered the driver to take her past the street where Ramon lived. When they reached the spot where his house used to stand, she saw nothing but rocks and silt, flattened grass and uprooted cottonwood trees. "Dear God," she whispered, then told the driver to continue on. When they arrived, Irene hurried inside, where she met John coming down the stairs.

"Irene! What the hell are you doing here?"

"We heard about the flood. John, I need you to do something for me."

He came closer, looking her over. "You're supposed to look radiant and happy. You look terrible. What's the matter?"

She reddened slightly. "I'm . . . I've been a little ill," she explained. "All that rain before we left, I suppose. I'm all right now. Chad is in town with Mother. She's waiting for you, but I want you to do something for me as soon as you get the chance."

"Sure. What do you want?"

She smelled whiskey on his breath but said nothing. "Ramon," she said, stepping closer and keeping her voice down. "His house was swept away, John. Please find out what happened to Ramon."

He frowned. "My God, Irene, do you still think about Ramon? You just got married!"

"Don't make me explain, John, and don't ask questions. We've always been good friends. Please, will you do it?"

He sighed deeply, moving to put an arm around her. "I already know," he answered. "Ramon sent a messenger here to tell us it would be a while before he could get back to finishing your house." He led her to a satin-covered bench at the foot of the stairs and made her sit down. "His wife and son were killed in the flood, Irene."

The pain of it hit her as though someone very close to her had died. She knew how devastating such a loss would be to someone as tender-hearted as Ramon. His beautiful little boy! "Oh, no," she groaned, putting her hands to her face. "Poor Ramon."

John put his arm around her shoulders. "I know. I felt terrible when I heard about it. If it makes you feel any better, I went looking for Ramon. I found him at his church, lighting candles for his wife and kid. Catholics believe in lighting candles for the dead, that it helps get them to heaven or something like that. I told him how sorry I was, but he was devastated. I'm not sure he even realized I was there. He's pretty broken up."

The shock and trauma of the past two weeks overwhelmed Irene. She burst into pitiful sobbing. Everything was so wrong, so out of place. Ramon had loved her but married another. She had done the same. Now Ramon was alone again, and she was wed to a man she was not sure was capable of love.

"Irene, you'd better let me take you up to bed." John helped her up the stairs to her old room, and made her sit down on the bed.

"You've got to . . . find him again, John," she told him. "Tell him . . . how sorry I am . . . that if there is anything any of us can do . . . he should tell us."

"I will. But it might take a while. I think he went back to Hacienda del Sur. He said something about needing to get away for a while." He pulled back the covers of her bed. "You'd better lie down and get some rest. You don't look too good, Irene. I'm glad you're back, but it's too bad you missed going to Europe. Is everything okay with Chad?"

"Yes," she lied, "everything is fine. Just try to find Ramon and make sure he's all right." John took a clean handkerchief from the pocket of his jacket, handing it to her. Irene took it gratefully, wiping at her eyes. "I can't help feeling sorry for him, John. He's such a good man."

"I know." He helped unpin her hat, surprised she had been so concerned about Ramon. "He'll be all right," he assured her. "Ramon is a strong man, and he's still young. He'll find another wife and be happy again."

Her heart tightened at the words. "Yes. I suppose he will."

"You sure you're all right, Irene? I mean, is something more wrong than the flood and Ramon's loss? You really do look terrible."

"I'll be all right."

John wished his father was there. He had never been very close to him, but he knew Kirk had special feelings for Irene, and would not like the way she looked. "Maybe I should get a doctor—"

"No! I don't need any doctor," she told him, terrified now of any doctor, even her own. Besides, maybe the family doctor would figure out what was wrong with her, and Chad would be upset. Others would find out, and she would be gossiped about. "Whatever I had, I'm better now. Just let me rest, John."

He sighed and rose from the bed. "Okay. I'll let you know if I find Ramon." She took off her shoes and lay down, and John covered her with a quilt, then left, ordering the servants to let her rest.

Irene turned on her side, letting the tears come, exhaustion from the trip and weakness from her ordeal bringing a heaviness to her eyelids. She cried until blessed sleep began to take over, unaware that Elly had walked quietly into her room. The girl noticed how sick and pale Irene looked, and that she seemed terribly distraught.

"Irene?"

Irene, nearly asleep, opened bloodshot eyes to see her sister standing and grinning strangely.

"You came back because of the flood?"

"Yes," Irene answered weakly.

"Terrible, wasn't it?" Elly said, sobering then. "Bill Byers's office got swept completely away, but people say he'll buy out the *Commonwealth* and open up again. He's a lot like Mother— nothing gets him down. I'm going to town myself pretty soon to help out. Is Chad there?"

"Yes. I . . . really don't want . . . to talk right now, Elly. I don't feel well."

Elly shrugged. "All right. But . . . how was your honeymoon? You'll have to tell me all about it so I'll know what to expect when *I* get married."

"Don't be . . . in any rush," Irene answered, so worn out that she hardly knew what she was saying. She didn't see Elly smile. Her sister's mind was awhirl with what the statement could mean. Had the honeymoon been some kind of disappointment? Surely not with a man like Chad! Maybe it was *Irene* who was the disappointment! If she was, Chad would not be a happy man.

"This is our chance," Bea told Chad. "I'm sorry you had to come back, son, but now that you're here, I have to tell you this flood was a godsend."

Even Chad was astonished at the statement. He closed the door to his private office and turned to her. "How do you mean?"

"The city hall was washed away, along with all records, including records of land titles."

Their eyes met, and Chad grinned. "And all we need is proof on our end of what we own."

"Yes. This is our chance to lay claim to more land in the south, including land the Mexicans are squatting on. There is one particular piece of land I am interested in. It's called Hacienda del Sur, and it's prime land. Hank Loring can put it to good use. I am also glad to report that Red McKinley's sawmill was destroyed—nearly all his equipment. The man is totally bankrupt, although he hasn't come to me yet. He will, soon enough. Go ahead and draw up papers claiming that site as ours. He won't be able to fight it. We'll open our own sawmill, and Red McKinley will be on his way, which is just fine with me. I'm glad Kirk wasn't here for this. He might want to help the man again, but we've lost enough to that drifter. He'll be gone by the time Kirk comes back."

Chad rubbed at his chin. "I'll get started on things, but doesn't that hacienda belong to Ramon Vallejo's family? I've heard him mention it."

"I know you like Ramon, Chad, but his family is squatting illegally on that land. Remember never to let friendship interfere with a good business deal, Chad. We need that land. Claim it under a fictitious name for now, if you want. Ramon doesn't have to know. In fact, I would prefer that he didn't."

Chad felt a hint of guilt, but after all this was Bea Kirkland talking. He was not about to do anything to undermine her confidence in him. He shrugged. "If that's what you want, I'll take care of it."

Bea smiled. "That's my Chad. Besides, it isn't wise to get too close to Ramon, Chad. I know you like his work, but he is Mexican. A man of your standing shouldn't be seen with men of a lower class. You're part of the Kirkland family now."

He nodded. "I understand."

Bea sighed. "I do have some bad news. Finishing your house will take a little longer than expected. Ramon lost his wife and son in the flood."

Chad looked at her with genuine concern. "That's terrible."

"Yes, isn't it?" Bea seemed to shift uncomfortably, and Chad wondered at her anxious demeanor every time Ramon Vallejo's name came into their conversation.

"We have to get as much taken care of as we can this summer," Bea went on. "We'll be losing John's help in a couple of months. I'm sending him off to college. He's a little young, but I think he's well schooled enough to manage. He may have to take some preparatory courses at a boarding school first. We'll see how he does on his entrance exam." She watched Chad closely, folding her arms. "How are things with Irene? Is the marriage all right? Is she happy?"

Chad flashed his usual smile. "Of course she is. You don't think I'd let my wife be *un*happy, do you?"

Bea smiled with relief. With a man like Chad at Irene's side, she shouldn't worry about Ramon being left a widower. From everything she had seen, it appeared the silly crush Irene had had on that Mexican man was long over. Her daughter was a married woman now, with a wonderful, successful, attentive husband.

"No, I can't imagine you making her unhappy," she answered. "It's just that Irene looked a little peaked."

"She's just tired from the trip back, and she was a little out of sorts for a few days. I had a doctor tend to her. She's fine. It might be better that we *did* come home, where she can be around familiar things. She'll rest better that way." He sighed. "I really love her, Bea. I'm a very happy man, and with any luck, in another year you'll be a grandmother. We're working on it."

Bea reddened slightly at the remark, but she glowed with happiness at the statement's meaning. Perhaps Irene had learned how to please her man in ways Bea had never understood. She wanted so much for her daughter to be happy in that way, for Irene's marriage to be better, closer, than hers had been. At least she and Chad had married for the right reasons—out of love and desire—not out of necessity.

"Nothing would thrill me more than to have a grandchild," she told Chad. "I'm so happy for both of you. Maybe once we get over this present crisis, you and Irene can still take that trip. I'm so sorry it didn't work out."

"I am, too. But Irene understands. As long as we can be together, that's all that matters. Europe can wait. First things first, and you need help." He felt the inner victory he always felt when he won this woman's confidence. This was one woman who could not be controlled sexually, but he had found a different means of keeping Bea Kirkland on his side. He intended to remain indispensable to her, continue to build her full confidence in his legal skills. He was a part of the Kirkland empire now, and he intended to keep it that way.

Red McKinley stormed into Kirkland Enterprises, shoving aside Robert Slade when the man tried to stop Red from barging into Bea's private office. "Look, Mr. McKinley, you can't do this," Slade argued.

Red whirled around and glared at the older man. He was bigger than Slade, certainly more rugged, and, as anyone could tell, more experienced when it came to fighting another man. "You really think you can stop me," he growled, his face red with anger, making everything else about him appear even redder.

"It's all right, Bob," Bea Kirkland called. "Let him come in."

"*Let* me come in?" Red stepped through the door and slammed it shut. "I'll come in when I damn well please," he told her gruffly. He stepped closer to Bea's desk, thinking how much he'd like to kill Bea Kirkland, woman or not—if only he wouldn't be caught. "What's this about what's left of my holdings being in Kirkland hands? I could have at least sold what was left and paid a little something! Maybe I could even have started over!"

Bea glared at him. "Started over? With what? You had no capital, no inventory left, and half your equipment was washed away. You still owed my husband over thirteen thousand dollars! I had every right to take over that mill, Mr. McKinley, and you know it."

"You move fast when Kirk isn't around, don't you! It's only been two weeks since the flood, and I find out through another bank that I no longer even own the land where my sawmill was—land bought and *paid* for—land that I never signed off!"

"You signed that land off when you failed to make payments on it," Bea said flatly. "It was bought with *Kirkland* money—hard-earned money, I might add, something you wouldn't know much about! I'm protecting my own. God knows our losses over the past year have been phenomenal. Your reckless use of the money Kirk loaned you certainly did not help. When Kirk gets back, he'll understand the mistake he made. You are *through* in Denver, Mr. McKinley!"

Chad barged in then, looking upset. "What's going on here? Slade told me you might have some trouble here, Bea."

"It's all right, Chad. Leave us alone," Bea answered.

Chad glowered at Red McKinley. "You watch yourself."

"Don't threaten me, kid! I've gone a few rounds with Indians and outlaws and bears! I'm not afraid of the likes of you!"

Chad looked at Bea. She nodded for him to leave. He did so reluctantly. Red turned hate-filled eyes to Bea, trembling with anger. He stepped even closer, leaning over Bea's desk. "I might be through in Denver, lady, but I'm not through *with* Denver! And maybe, just maybe, I'm not through with *you*!"

Bea frowned. "What is that supposed to mean? There is nothing you can do to me *or* to Denver. You're a penniless drifter and a failure!"

Red straightened. "There are other forms of power, Mrs. Kirkland. You have your money, your political clout, your underhanded lawyers. But I'm one up on you, because I knew Kirk before you did. I would think you might have figured out by now that I know about *Irene*!"

He watched her turn visibly pale, and he took great delight in her obvious, sudden panic. "Yes," he said with a sneer. "All this time I was doing you and Kirk a favor by keeping my mouth shut. You know what? I still won't say anything, for one reason only—for Irene herself. How in hell a woman like you raised such a beautiful, gracious daughter, I will *never* understand! It must be her Indian blood that makes her so naturally sweet, in spite of being raised by the biggest *bitch* in Colorado!"

"How dare you!" She started to rise.

"How dare *you?*" Red answered. "Knowing what I know, and you treat me this way. Well, I'll tell you something more that I know, *Mrs.* Kirkland." His stance was so threatening that she sat back down. Red leaned closer, keeping his voice low. "Something I'll bet even *you* don't know! Your precious Irene had a twin brother," he told her, almost laughing at the shock on her face. "The Cheyenne kept the boy and gave Kirk the girl. Kirk never told you that, did he? Your daughter has a half-breed brother running around out there with the murdering Cheyenne. I've even heard his name come up, as one of the young leaders among the Cheyenne raiders."

Bea trembled. "You're lying," she said. Her chest heaved in great gasps of shock, and Red realized telling her about Irene's brother had given him more satisfaction than hitting her ever could.

"Don't you wish I was," he sneered. "Just ask Kirk when he gets back. The boy's name is Yellow Eagle. Remember it!"

He donned his hat and turned away. "Where are you going?" Bea managed to gasp. Red turned and looked back at her.

"I don't even know yet, but you'll be happy to know I'm leaving Denver for now. Like I said, I'm not through with this town—or you."

He turned away, smiling when she called out to him once more. "Wait. Maybe . . . maybe we can work something out."

Red snickered, meeting her dark eyes again. "No, ma'am. I'll not beg, borrow, or steal from the likes of you, and I make no bargains. I'm going to pay back what I owe Kirk. I'll find a way. And I'll make it big on my own. The whole world doesn't revolve around Kirkland Enterprises, Mrs. Kirkland, in case you didn't realize that."

She rose and came around from behind her desk, her eyes glistening with tears. "Is it true—about this Yellow Eagle?"

He grinned. "It's true."

She met his gaze. "I don't mind for myself, Mr. McKinley. But I don't want my children hurt, least of all Irene. We raised her as our own, and I love her as much as if she came from my own body. She is very trusting. To find out we have lied to her all these years would be devastating to her, let alone to find out she has *Indian* blood."

He shook his head. "You should have thought of that back in the beginning. And you'd better pray she has white babies." He put his hand on the doorknob. "Don't worry. I don't want Irene hurt either, or Kirk, for that matter. But if I can ever find a way to hurt *you*, lady, I'll do it! I'll be back someday. That you can count on, Mrs. Kirkland."

He turned and left, and Bea actually felt faint. She closed the door and staggered to her desk, collapsing into her chair. He knew! Red McKinley knew about Irene—and more! There was a brother, a legal heir to the Kirkland empire—and an *Indian*! What if their friends knew that a son of David Kirkland's was among the hated Cheyenne who were giving Coloradans so much trouble? Why had Kirk never told her! She hated him at this moment more than she could say.

She realized now she should have known that Red knew about Irene. Kirk had never mentioned it. Had he been afraid it would upset her and she would want Red out of Denver? She didn't feel so guilty now about the secrets she kept from her husband about Ramon, and about how she ran the business. David Kirkland had been keeping some secrets of his own.

A son! A full-blood brother to Irene! If she ever found out—Bea quickly rose, brushing aside any concern over Red McKinley. He was leaving Denver, and his threats of revenge were nothing more than that, just threats. The man had nothing and never would. He could do no real harm, except for what he knew, and she suspected he valued Kirk's friendship and admired Irene too much ever to reveal the truth.

The important thing now was to go talk to Governor Evans and find out what was going to be done about the Indians. Denver's woes had only been increased by the raiding in outlying areas. Supply trains were constantly being attacked and destroyed. Food and other supplies had been slow in coming or had not come at all. It was time to make some tough decisions about the Cheyenne, time to run them out of Colorado completely, or annihilate them. And, at the same time, she hoped, kill off one Indian in particular named Yellow Eagle.

Elly appeared at the doorway to Chad's office. It had been a month since the flood, and she had not had a chance to talk to Chad alone. She came into the room and closed the door, smiling at the irritated look on Chad's face.

"Everyone is gone, left early for some meeting about the Indians," she told him, trying to make her voice sultry. "I told Mother I wanted to help you finish up. She said you can bring me home. Wasn't that nice of her?"

Chad reddened slightly, closing a file and leaning-back in his chair. "What do you want?"

She laughed. "The same thing you want. You don't have a room at the inn anymore; you live at our house. But since you're sleeping with my sister now, I can't come to you there, either. We'll have more trouble finding opportunities, but where there's a will, there's a way."

"Here?"

She came closer, leaning over his desk. "Tommy Slade didn't mind."

She saw surprise and even a hint of jealousy in his eyes. "Tommy Slade? You've been with him?"

"You'd be surprised who I've been with. Don't tell me you, of all people, are *jealous*?"

"Of what?" How could he explain he was not at all jealous of whom she lifted her skirts for, that his only concern was whether they might satisfy her more than he did. He needed to know he was the best she ever had, that he was not lacking in some way. Irene had certainly not helped feed his hungry ego, his burning need to prove his masculinity to himself. When he made love to her she lay there as if she were a piece of wood. He was failing with Irene, and it tore at his self-confidence.

"Oh, I don't know," Elly was saying. "I just get the impression married life doesn't suit you. Neither you nor Irene act like the blushing, happy newlywed couple who can hardly stay out of bed." She came around the desk, kneeling in front of him and brushing her hands along his thighs. "What went wrong, Chad? Did you find out the beautiful, perfect Irene Kirkland is a disappointment between the sheets?" She met his eyes, leaning up and touching his privates. "I may not be as pretty, but I'll bet you've had a lot better time with me than with her. Wish you would have waited and married me?"

He grasped her wrist, glancing at the door. "Irene had a few physical problems. She's all right now."

"And a complete priss in bed, I'll bet." She touched his face with her other hand. "If she's left you feeling dissatisfied, I can help you. You know I can, and you know how I feel about you. The other men are just substitutes, for when I can't have you."

He watched her eyes, thinking that except for the expensive clothes and expert attempts to do her hair and makeup, she would be close to ugly. He could just picture her hanging out in the red-light district with the other young whores, stringy hair, that distant, hungry look in their eyes—his mother's look. Fourteen. She was only fourteen. But her big build and knowing look made her seem so much older.

It frustrated him that she had it all figured out about him and Irene, frustrated him more that he knew how good this one was in bed. Why couldn't Irene respond to him the way Elly did? How he would love to see wanton desire in her eyes. He had seen it a few times before they married, but somehow he had botched it all.

He needed to know, needed to boost his self-confidence. Since returning from Colorado Springs he had been too busy, and Irene remained too sick for him to have intercourse with her as often as he would like. He was afraid Bea would hear her cries of pain. And in these delicate, early weeks of marriage, while they were still at the Kirkland mansion, he had had to be very careful. He had to show Bea how much he loved Irene, had to be home every night.

But here sat a whore he could trust not to breathe a word, and they were alone. "You're a little bitch, you know that," he said, before leaning forward and seizing her mouth.

Elly only laughed, wrapping her arms around his neck and pulling him to the floor.

John came into the parlor, where Irene sat, softly playing the piano, a distant look in her eyes. He hated to see his sister looking so sad, knew she was not happy with Chad, although he didn't quite understand why. He came and sat down beside her on the piano bench, putting an arm around her waist. "You're the only one I'll miss when I go to college," he told her.

Irene stopped playing, turned to him, and smiled. "I wish you didn't feel that way, but thank you anyway. I'll miss you, too, John, very much." She smelled whiskey on his breath, and she frowned. "John, you've been drinking again."

He shrugged, taking his arm away and toying with the piano keys. "I found out I like it. Did you know that a couple of drinks can just about erase all your troubles? You ought to try it."

"You're too young to be drinking so much, John. Besides, a couple of drinks might make you feel better about things, but when you sober up, all your problems are still there. You would have to drink constantly to keep them away forever, and you know what that would make you."

He grinned nervously. "I'm not in that bad shape yet. I can handle it. Besides, who but you gives a damn if I'm drunk or sober? Who gives a damn if I'm happy? Mother sure doesn't. All she cares about is the Kirkland name, the Kirkland money, the Kirkland prestige. Her son *must* go to college and study law. He *must* be able to take over the Kirkland empire."

Irene sighed. "You'll probably like college once you're there, John. Chad says some of his best memories are from college. You'll make new friends, see cities much more advanced and refined than Denver, more so even than Chicago, where I was. Maybe it will be good for you to get away from here."

He blinked back tears, not wanting her to see them. He was going on seventeen now. Men his age didn't cry. "Maybe," he answered. He took a deep breath and put on a smile. "You look a little better since you got back. How are things with you and Chad?"

Now it was Irene who looked away and toyed with the piano keys. "All right. I've just . . . had a little trouble adjusting to being married." She reddened a little, and he suspected it had something to do with sex. He couldn't very well ask her about something so intimate, but he reasoned a man like Chad certainly ought to know how to handle such a thing. He put a hand back around her waist.

"Everything will work out, Irene. Chad's a pretty good guy."

He turned to a whore on our wedding night, she wanted to tell him. *He brought a strange doctor back with him who did a terrible thing to me. I'll never forget it. Never!* "Yes, he's been good to me," she answered aloud. She decided John had enough trouble with having to go off to college and with his drinking. He didn't need to know his sister was so unhappy. She faced him again. "I really will miss you a lot, John. You've been a sweet brother, caring and understanding. Thank you for never letting on to anyone about Ramon."

He watched her eyes, wishing he understood about love and marriage, why people loved one person and then married somebody else. He liked Chad, couldn't quite understand why Irene wasn't blissfully happy. One thing he was sure of—Irene had loved Ramon. Maybe she still did. "Ramon is the reason I came in here," he told her. "I told you about his leaving Denver and going back to Hacienda del Sur. He's back now. I just saw him up at the new house. He's there alone, Irene, if you want to talk to him."

Her eyes lit up. "Oh, yes, I want very much to talk to him," she said. "Where are Mother, and Chad and everyone else?"

"Mother's at some kind of meeting about the Indians, and Chad is still in town. Elly stayed on to help him."

"Good." She hurried toward the door, then turned. "Thank you for telling me, John. After what Ramon has suffered—you understand why I have to talk to him, don't you? We were all good friends once. The least we can do is extend our sympathy, give him our support."

He nodded. "I understand." *I understand you still love him,* he wanted to add. "That's why I told you he's up there. I know you've been worried about him. Just don't look shocked when you see him, Irene. He looks pretty bad."

She nodded. "If Chad comes back, just tell him I got bored and lonely and walked up to the new house to see how things were coming." She turned and hurried out, and John tinkered with the piano a moment longer, wondering at how wrong everything seemed to be, wishing his father had never found that gold in California. He closed the piano and left, heading for the liquor cabinet.

With a pounding heart Irene approached the new house, already tired from the walk. She still had not fully recovered from the ordeal on her wedding night, and had occasional spotting and pain. She worried the doctor had done something wrong, afraid she had developed an infection that had kept her from recovering properly. She wished she could make Chad understand how much it still hurt to have intercourse, but her fear of his turning to someone else, her fear of being the cause of an early failed marriage kept her from saying anything to him.

She stopped at the doorway, wondering if she had been right in coming here, yet unable to stop herself. She could not help being concerned for poor Ramon, and she argued with herself that it had nothing to do with whether or not she might still love him. She was only here out of the sweet friendship they once had shared.

She opened the door and went inside, stopping short when she saw Ramon sitting at the bottom of the stairway just ahead of her. He glanced up at her in surprise, and Irene understood John's warning about how he looked. Ramon was much thinner. At the moment he looked years older than twenty-three. She had no idea he was thinking the same of her. His first thought was to wonder why she was so thin and pale, to wonder what had happened to the beautiful, glowing Irene he had known before her wedding.

She stepped closer, and at first neither of them said a word. Ramon thought how pitiful and vulnerable she looked. She stood there in a yellow linen day dress that had apparently fit her a few weeks ago but now hung on her too-slender body.

"Hello, Ramon," she finally spoke softly. "I . . . John told me you were here. I wanted to tell you . . . how terribly sorry I am . . . about Elena . . . and your little son. I wish there was something I could do."

He slowly stood up, and in spite of his loss of weight, she was still struck by his grand physique, still moved by his firm chest revealed by his open shirt. He wore a crucifix around his neck. Again their eyes held for a long time, saying a thousand things, even though neither of them spoke for several quiet seconds.

"There is nothing anyone can do," he told her then, his voice dull. "I will tell you the worst part, *mi querida*." His use of Spanish for "my darling" stabbed at her heart. Why had he called her that? She turned away. "The worst part is that I did not give Elena the love she deserved. We were happy together, and we both loved our Juan so much." His voice began to break. "But . . . she knew she was not . . . the only one in my heart."

"Don't say it, Ramon."

"Why not? What does it matter any more? My grief is not so much for my own loss, but for what I never gave Elena when she was alive. The very night she died, I had just made love to her." He watched her stiffen. "And then I turned around and lay there in that bed, thinking of someone else. I received a proper punishment for my infidelity, did I not?"

"I didn't come here for this, Ramon."

"Didn't you? You have wondered if I still love you, and I could not say it before because of Elena. Now I see it was all for nothing. All I did was hurt a woman who loved me very much . . . and now she is gone. Now I am free to love you, but it is too late . . . for both of us. Life can be so ironic, can't it? Now you belong to another man, but John tells me he does not think you are very happy. Look at me, Irene."

She swallowed back a lump in her throat, her eyes misty as she turned to face him. His eyes moved over her, too knowingly. "I think John must be right," he told her. "You do not look like the happy, glowing bride." He stepped closer. "Elena never looked the way you look. What has that man done to you?"

She reddened. "I'd better go. I can see you don't appreciate my coming here."

"Wait." He touched her arm. "Forgive me, Irene. I tell myself it is not my business, but I cannot help it. I am just as concerned for you as you are for me."

His touch brought on all the old needs and desires. Right now she only wanted to be held by a strong man who truly cared for her, sympathized with her. She turned and nearly collapsed against his chest, and he wrapped his arms around her. "Irene," he said softly, *"mi vida."*

She could not help sobbing then. She needed to let it out, all the pent-up horror of the strange doctor, her disappointment in Chad's callousness to her needs, the cruel fact of Ramon's being married when she was free, and now that she was married, Ramon was free. Yes, she still loved him. What did it matter that he knew? He had already admitted the same to her. And where was the harm in letting him hold her? It certainly wasn't as terrible as what Chad had done on their wedding night.

"My poor Irene," he told her as she wept. She found it ironic, after his own losses, that he should be so concerned about her.

"I came here . . . to express my sympathy," she sobbed. "You're the one who needs consoling, not me."

"Perhaps it is something we both need," he answered, kissing her hair. "We have quietly loved each other, *mi querida,* and we have both suffered. It tears at my heart to think you are unhappy. Tell me what is wrong."

She pulled away, taking a handkerchief from the pocket of her dress. "I can't." How could she tell him something so intimate, especially when she knew he still loved her? The important thing was that she still believed it could be good with a man, knew instinctively that if it was Ramon Vallejo making love to her, she would not feel the pain, or at least she would not mind it. Ramon would have understood, would have been patient.

"It doesn't matter now," she added then. "What good would it do to tell you, Ramon? I'm a married woman now. I spoke my vows before God, and I meant them." She wiped at her eyes and faced him. "Chad is basically good to me. He's not a drinker or a wife beater or any of those things."

"There are other kinds of abuse." He reached out and touched her face. "You are not well, Irene. He forced you too quickly, didn't he? Perhaps he has already cheated on you."

"Stop it, Ramon!" She grasped his hand, her face crimson.

Ramon studied her with an aching heart. How he longed to show her how beautiful it could be to love a man. But that was impossible. His heart was too full of grief now over Elena and his little son to truly express the feelings he still held for her. He squeezed her hand. "I have overstepped my bounds."

"All we need to comfort each other's heartache is to know we love each other, Ramon, that we care. Perhaps we can never be together, but we can know we love each other, and take comfort in that. I don't understand all the reasons you left, but at the time you thought it was the right thing to do, and I eventually came to believe that, too. We'll learn to live our lives apart, because this is how it has to be now." She let go of his hand and wiped at her eyes again. "What's done is done."

He watched her sadly. *"Sí,"* he said quietly. "Life plays cruel tricks sometimes." He stepped back. "You had better go now. I will have your home finished soon. Perhaps things will be better for your marriage once you are moved into this lovely place."

She swallowed back more tears. "Perhaps. What will you do then, Ramon? How much did you lose in the flood—financially, I mean?"

He turned away, looking around the great room. "Most of my money was in a bank that was untouched, and most of my tools were in another building—many of them right here. I will survive. It has been hard getting over the shock of it. In one swift second Elena and my son were swept away from me. Their bodies were not found until two days later."

She closed her eyes at the horror of it.

"A man does not easily get over losing his son, Irene. I feel . . . numb and cold. To make things worse, the grief of it killed my grandfather. While I was at Hacienda del Sur, he died, adding to my loss." *Another twist of fate,* he thought. *I let you go to protect my grandfather's land, and now he is dead. It was all for nothing.* "Before I left, authorities came and told the rest of my family that they had to leave," he continued aloud, "that someone else had laid claim to our land and had papers to prove it. They would not say who it was, and we had nothing legal to prove we owned any of the land. The rest of my family has gone back to Mexico. Everything is gone now, even my old home and my grandfather."

"Oh, Ramon, how terrible for you!" Her chest tightened. "Will you . . . will you go to Mexico, too?"

He turned to look at her, wondering if her mother had anything to do with taking over Hacienda del Sur. He had been unable to discover who had filed the papers, but it smelled of Bea Kirkland. Still, he had more reason than ever not to tell Irene the truth. She was hurting and lonely. She needed her family. Why burden her with the truth of her own mother's treachery? Why add to her heartache? She would have enough problems trying to find some happiness for herself with Chad Jacobs.

"No," he answered. *I have some unfinished business right here in Denver with your mother.* He had not forgotten his long-term goals. He would simply approach them now with much more determination, much more ruthlessness. Elena and his son were dead, and his heart was hard and bitter. He could concentrate on building his money and position without worrying about hurting anyone. Even his grandfather could no longer be hurt. He was alone now, alone against a society that refused to accept him. He would *make* them accept him, and the bastard Irene had married would help him. It gave Ramon at least a little satisfaction to know that Chad had unwittingly been helping a man who loved his wife.

"I will stay in Denver," he told her. "My business is growing, and I love Colorado. There is no place else I want to go. Do not worry, though. You will see little of me. I will be sure to stay out of your life, but I will be watching, Irene. If you need me, I will be around."

She shook her head. "It can't be that way, Ramon. This has to be the end of it. After today, if I see you socially, I will have to treat you as I would treat any other casual acquaintance, and you have to do the same. This is the last time I will seek you out alone. It's too hard for both of us."

"*Sí, mi querida.*" He stepped closer again. "I am glad that you came, though. Glad we could speak our feelings."

Her eyes filled with tears again. "I'm just so sorry that you're alone now, Ramon. It isn't fair."

He brushed her cheek with the back of his fingers. "Nor is it fair that a woman so beautiful and loving should be married to a man who does not appreciate her goodness."

She knew in that one touch how it ought to be with a man. She closed her eyes, taking his hand and kissing his palm. "I will always love you, Ramon. I can't give you any more than that. And knowing you love me gives me the strength I need." She pressed his strong hand against the side of her face. "This is the end of it, Ramon. We have no choice."

"I understand. I will pray for you."

"And I for you. Our religions are different, but we pray to the same God, don't we?"

He nodded, smiling sadly. "*Dios le bendiga, mi querida.* Thank you for coming."

Their eyes held, and Irene felt suddenly stronger. "*Adiós, mi amigo,*" she told him. "Did I say it right?"

He smiled at her use of Spanish. "*Sí, mi muchacha bonita.*"

She leaned up and kissed his cheek, and before she could pull away he grasped the back of her neck, meeting her mouth in a kiss that told her how different things might have been with the right man. Oh, what a long time it had been since that first kiss! Chad had never kissed her this way, had never brought out these needs and desires, had never quieted her fear of sex the way Ramon did. He slowly released her. "*Vaya con Dios, mi querida,*" he whispered.

Irene pulled away. *"Vaya con Dios."* She turned and hurried away, realizing with a shock that for one brief moment she had been tempted to do the unthinkable. Ramon's kiss burned at her lips, and her heart. But she belonged to another man—to Chad. She had made vows before God, and she intended to keep them. She resolved she must work harder at making a happy marriage, at least as happy as possible. Being with Ramon had given her a certain strength, in spite of the heartache.

She half ran back to her mother's house, needing to get away quickly before she betrayed her husband and her vows. She was suddenly almost anxious for Chad to get home, so she could welcome him and reassure herself that she had been true to him. She wondered what was keeping him and Elly so long at the office.

Ramon stood in the doorway, watching her, feeling the vast, sickening loneliness that the loss of his wife and son had created. Knowing he could never have Irene only made it worse. He turned back inside and closed the door, looking around the house Irene would be sharing with Chad Jacobs. He picked up a hammer and threw it across the room, then sank down to the stairs and wept.

CHAPTER
TWENTY-THREE

September 1864

 Bea stretched her arms, tired from a long morning that had started at five o'clock. She put away some papers, preparing to go to lunch, when she looked up to see her husband standing in the doorway of her office.

"Figured this was where I'd find you," he told her, walking in and plunking down two saddlebags full of papers on her desk. "I haven't even gone home yet." His smile faded when he noticed a look of malice in her eyes. Considering he was just back from San Francisco, he had expected a warmer welcome.

He stood in his buckskins, and Bea thought how he looked hardly different from the night he first visited her back in Kansas. She wondered sometimes if part of her resentment toward him was due to the fact that he had hardly changed physically or in personality, while she had changed a great deal. At the moment it was that old Kirk who made it impossible to give him a merry welcome. She was still too full of fury over the news of Irene's brother.

"There in those saddlebags is everything you need," he said. "I got rid of a lot of mediocre mines and other holdings, like you wanted. We're down to one mine and the shipping business." He looked around the office. "Well, thank goodness we didn't get washed out with the rest of the town. I'm glad everybody is all right. I see a lot of rebuilding—"

He hesitated, frowning as he removed his hat, irritated that she still had said nothing. "It would be nice to get a smile or a 'welcome back' or some kind of reaction from my wife. I've been gone four months."

She sighed and rubbed at her forehead. "Close the door and sit down, Kirk."

He set his hat aside, turning to close the door and coming back to her desk. "What's wrong? The children all right?"

Her dark eyes studied him. He hated it when she behaved this way, so condescending and judgmental. She finally nodded.

"Yes. They're fine. Irene was a little ill the first couple of weeks after the wedding—too much excitement, I suppose. And becoming a wife isn't always easy for a young girl." She closed her eyes briefly, remembering her own wedding night. "But Chad is good to her. They're in their new house now, but with Chad working so much Irene got lonely. She wanted to open a ladies' clothing store to keep herself busy, and I decided it was a good idea. If anyone can sell clothes, Irene can, just by wearing them. She makes anything look beautiful."

Kirk smiled nervously. "That she does. But I'm surprised. Before they married, she talked of wanting to stay home and letting Chad be the breadwinner."

"She had more of a mind for business than she realizes. But you know Irene—once she's with child, she'll stay home. She wants children very badly. Heaven knows, with her gentle nature she'll make a good mother."

Their eyes met, and she knew Kirk was thinking Irene would surely be a better mother than Bea ever was. Bea looked suddenly weary. "Oh, Kirk, why do you always have to make it so hard to love you," she asked then, surprising him with the question.

He sat down and put one moccasined foot up on a knee. "Maybe if you told me what happened while I was gone, I could answer the question."

She had gotten over the shock of it, but not the bitter disappointment. She told herself she couldn't scream and yell, or others in the office might hear. This was something no one must ever know. "Why didn't you ever tell me Irene had a brother?"

His face darkened. "Who the hell told you that?" he asked, his gaze full of fury.

She leaned back in her chair. "Your dear, trusted friend, Red McKinley."

Kirk quickly rose. "I'll go talk to the son-of-bitch—"

"Kirk, he's gone. He's left Denver."

He frowned. "Left? Why? What the hell went on here while I was gone?"

Bea's face reddened slightly with her own anger. "My God, Kirk, you should have *told* me! It might have made a difference. You left me open and vulnerable to that man, and I don't like to be in that kind of position! Not telling me could have destroyed Irene—*and* her marriage!"

"Get to the point, Bea." He leaned over her desk. "What happened between you and Red? I know the man. He never would have told you about Yellow Eagle unless he was damn mad."

She slowly rose to face him. "Then it's true—about the son."

He closed his eyes and sighed. "It's true. It's been hell for me all these eighteen years, knowing I have another son out there. By now he's too wild to be brought here to be civilized."

She gasped. "Don't even *suggest* such a thing! If you ever try to give part of the Kirkland money to that savage, I'll take you to court, no matter the publicity!"

He stared at her, astonished at how far her bitterness and greed had taken her. "He's as much a Kirkland as Irene."

She whirled. "I mean it, Kirk! Haven't you heard? This has been a terrible summer—settlers raped and murdered, telegraph lines cut, supply wagons attacked. Denver has been threatened and harassed and cut off from the rest of the world by those savages. And guess whose name keeps popping up in the headlines as one of the ringleaders of the *worst* of them?"

Kirk's eyebrows arched. "Yellow Eagle?"

"Yes! Can you imagine the horror for Irene—first, to learn she is part Indian, then to learn her own *brother* is one of the worst of the raiding murderers? My God, Kirk, it hurts bad enough—you not telling me about the son, let alone the destruction keeping it from me might cause. If I had known Red McKinley knew all of this, I would have handled things differently."

"What do you mean—handled them differently? What happened between you and Red?"

She closed her eyes and turned away again. "Most of his sawmill was washed away in the flood. He wanted more money. I refused. I told him I was taking over what was left of the mill and property. I've bought out Hansen's mill, eliminating the competition, and I've hired Hansen to take over all of it, put him in charge of rebuilding Red's mill."

There was a long silence. She finally turned, meeting her

husband's angry eyes. "Damn you, Bea," he spat out. "Don't you have *any* respect for me and what *I* might want? I told you how I felt about Red McKinley. You could have at least helped him out until I got back and we talked about this. I can just imagine how he felt, because I know what you can do to a man's pride! He had to hate you an awful lot to tell you about Yellow Eagle! He knew I never wanted anybody to know!"

"He only told me to upset me. He likes you and Irene too much to go blabbing it to anyone else."

"And you're real sure of that, I suppose."

"He told me in his own words."

"Well, the man hasn't had time to let it settle yet! Who knows what he's up to? You've turned my best friend into an enemy! Did he say where he would go, what he would do?"

"No. He just said he didn't know himself where he would go. He said he respected Irene very much, that if it wasn't for her . . . and you . . ."

"Well, you had by God better hope he doesn't change his mind!"

"Don't go blaming this on me, David Kirkland," she said then, her dark eyes blazing. "You should have *told* me! Do you have any idea how I felt, what a shock it was! If I had known, I would have known how to handle the man!"

"I thought I was sparing you," he growled back at her, struggling to keep his voice down. "It was enough to ask you to take Irene in as your own. It just didn't seem right to tell you in the beginning, and the longer I went without telling you, the harder it got."

"Does Yellow Eagle know who his father is?"

"I expect Gray Bird Woman told him. I imagine he asked questions when he got older. He's half white—had blue eyes, they told me. I never got to see him myself, and it's eaten away at me all these years!"

"That savage could come here and try to claim an inheritance!"

He just glared at her a moment, then let out a long sigh of disgust, shaking his head. "That's all you're concerned about, isn't it, that he might get his hands on some Kirkland money! My God! You don't even give a damn what I've gone through all these years. You don't give a damn that Irene's own brother is out there somewhere struggling to survive. You can't even *begin* to understand the Indians' side of this." He picked up his hat and walked toward the door. "Don't worry about your precious money, Bea. I know Indians well enough to know that they don't give a damn about things like that. What would a warrior like Yellow Eagle want with the Kirkland fortune? He'd rather have his land back, plenty of game roaming the plains again. He'd rather be left alone to live the free life of following the seasons and the buffalo. He'll never come here asking for his white father's money. He would consider that shameful. They *do* have their pride, Bea. You don't seem to understand that about people. The only thing you understand is money in the bank." He put his hand on the doorknob.

"Where are you going?"

"Do you really care? Would it matter to you if I walked out of here and never came back?"

He saw her tremble slightly, in spite of her rigid stance. "I care, Kirk. It's just that . . . you keep making me so angry with you."

"Well, you do a pretty good job of that yourself, don't you? We just seem to keep butting heads. If it weren't for the children—" He sighed. "I guess we're both in too deep now, aren't we? No matter how we feel about each other, we have to keep all this together for the kids. They're all still too young to understand."

"Yes," she answered. "We have to work together to protect Irene. We've gone this far, Kirk. I want your promise that if, God forbid, Irene should find out she's part Indian, you won't ever tell her about her brother. With the reputation this Yellow Eagle is gaining, it would all but destroy her to know it's her own brother committing these acts of depravity."

He held her eyes. "We can only take a day at a time and handle whatever we have to when the occasion arises, and pray you're right about Red valuing our friendship and Irene's reputation more than his own wounded pride."

"What do you think he'll do?"

He let out a sarcastic snicker. "Well, now, I don't really know. I'm not a mind reader, Bea. And I don't know what all was said, although I can just imagine. All we can do is wait and see. Right now I'm going into town for a couple of drinks. I want to hear what people are saying about Yellow Eagle."

She turned away. "I'm not sorry the way it happened, Kirk. It isn't really my fault. You should have told me."

"I don't care if you're sorry or not, Bea, because all the times you *have* been sorry for something, you've always been too late with your apologies. Don't expect me home too early tonight. I'll talk to the children in the morning. Maybe I'll go look up Irene now. Where's her shop?"

"Two blocks up on Fifteenth Street." She turned to face him.

"You should spend a little time with John the next few days. He's leaving in a week for Harvard."

"Then I'll be home early after all."

He walked out, and Bea went to the door, resting her head against it, wondering which one of them was most responsible for always ruining Kirk's home-comings.

Irene dressed a mannequin in the window of her elegant new shop, which catered to Denver's wealthier women. She covered the form in a deep blue velvet day dress, and over that she put a short sealskin jacket, which was the latest fashion for winter wear. It was time for women to be thinking about cold weather.

Unlike her mother, Irene had not opened the shop with the thought of how much more money she could bring herself and Kirkland Enterprises. It was true that the markup on her clothes was high, but many women in Denver gladly paid ridiculous prices just to wear the latest fashions. And Irene had not forgotten Denver's countless homeless women and children. Without her mother's knowledge, she had decided to contribute a good share of her personal profits to a shelter for widows and orphans. She and Bea both belonged to the women's committee that had founded the shelter, but Bea just did it to make an impression. Irene was more concerned about sharing her wealth with those who had so little. It didn't seem right just giving money to the charity. She wanted to give something from her own resources, and much to Bea's chagrin, she had also begun donating some of her own time to working at the shelter.

She pinned the jacket from behind to make it fit the mannequin better. She had decided that keeping busy was better than sitting around her new house with only servants for company, thinking about Ramon, thinking about her own unhappiness. Since she had opened the store and begun working at the shelter, she was too busy and too tired to dwell on her unhappy marriage to an unfaithful husband who, on several occasions, had not come home at all, or who claimed too often to work late.

When he was home, Chad was always loving and attentive, pretending nothing was wrong, but Irene knew better. Their marriage was only four months old, but her husband was already cheating on her. In part she blamed herself. Her dreams of what a marriage should be were already shattered, in spite of the fact that her husband did not drink or abuse her. Still, she remembered

Ramon's remark that there were other forms of abuse besides physical ones, and she knew he was right.

Dealt the blow of ironic fate that had trapped her in a loveless marriage, she refused to believe nothing could be done about it. She was trying very hard, never turned Chad away from her bed. She prayed for a baby, hoping Chad would settle more, love her more, if she could give him a child. She was in this marriage to stay, and she wanted to find a way to make it work, a way to be at least a little bit happy.

She glanced out the window then to see a familiar figure, and she dropped a hat and hurried to the door. "Father!" In the next moment she was in Kirk's strong arms. There came a flurry of hugs and kisses and welcomes. Then Kirk stood back and studied his daughter, who he thought looked too thin and pale.

"Your mother says you've been ill."

She wished she could tell him the truth. "I was, but I'm all right now," she answered slowly.

He frowned, studying her closely. "You happy, Irene? Is Chad treating you right?"

She reddened slightly. "Yes. I just don't get to see a lot of him. Mother keeps him working long hours. It's been a long haul, rebuilding and getting finances back in order after the flood. It was so terrible. Chad and I never got to go to Europe." She shrugged, trying to appear cheerful, turning and waving an arm in a sweeping gesture. "With Chad gone so much, I got a little lonely, so I opened this store. Isn't it nice?"

Kirk looked around at shelves of elegant materials, fashionably dressed mannequins, stands that sported extravagant hats. Irene herself wore a yellow silk dress with cashmere trim. The hem was looped up slightly to reveal the bottom of her white petticoats, which were short enough to see her delicate feet in shiny, high-buttoned shoes. She noticed him glancing at her petticoats and exposed feet, and she laughed. "It's the latest fashion," she assured him.

He shook his head. "Well, whatever the fashion, you always make it look good." He gave her another hug. "All I really care about is that you're happy."

How she wished she could explain, but her soured marriage embarrassed her, and she believed it was mostly her fault. "I am, Father." She leaned back and looked up at him. "Don't tell Mother, but most of my own profits go to the new shelter for homeless women. She would never understand that, but I know you do."

He grinned and winked. "I see success hasn't spoiled you."

They both laughed. "So how was your trip?" she asked. "Have you been to see Mother yet?" She noticed a change in his eyes, a look of sorrow.

"Yes. That's how I knew you were here." He quickly brightened. "Everything went real fine. I—"

There was no time to finish. A commotion arose in the street outside, and people began running and shouting, crowding around and following someone. Kirk let go of Irene. "Now what?" he muttered. "You stay right here. I'll go see what's going on."

Irene walked to the door and watched curiously, as Kirk left and moved into the crowd. More people gathered, beginning to shout obscenities about the "damn, dirty Cheyenne." "Murderers! Rapists!" people yelled, fists raised. "It's time to do something about this! Somebody ought to get hold of Governor Evans right away," another man shouted.

Irene told her assistant to watch the store. She moved into the crowd, asking one man what was going on.

"It's those damn savages," the man raged. "They've been on a rampage, raping, murdering, burning homes and crops, stealing horses. Some settlers just rode in to show us the kind of horror those damn Indians can commit—brought the bodies of a whole family, massacred! You'd best stay inside, ma'am. You don't want to see this."

The man left her, and curiosity goaded Irene on. Her father had always tried to explain to her the Indian point of view. She wanted to understand, wondered why there had to be so much fighting and bloodshed. Considering the hell the Indians had visited upon Denver this past summer, it was difficult even for Irene to sympathize with them.

She moved through the crowd, now pushed along by rough, angry men. Lately people had been worked up and fighting in the streets over the subject of statehood for Colorado. A recent vote to admit Colorado to the Union had failed, and those who had wanted statehood were angry. Besides that, the Civil War was fast coming to a head now. The South was being ripped apart, and Denver was overflowing with bitter, angry refugees from that ravaged area. Now with the Indian problem, Denver seemed ready to explode.

Someone shoved Irene, and she suddenly found herself in front of the unruly mob, staring at stripped, mutilated, bloated body parts of what had been a man, his wife, and two young girls. They were being laid out in the street. The man who had brought them raised his arms for the crowd to quiet.

"This is what's left of the Hungate family," he announced. "Innocent people, hard-working settlers and a loving family—man, wife, two daughters—raped, murdered, cut to pieces by the murdering Cheyenne! This is the work of Yellow Eagle and his young warriors!"

The crowd broke into an uproar, fists raised, shouts for the Colorado Volunteers to get into action. "Get the Cheyenne out of Colorado," they yelled. "Kill them all—women and children—like they do to us!"

Irene felt she would be ill from the gruesome sight. She looked across the way to see her father in some kind of heated argument, and she knew he was arguing that they couldn't be sure which Indians had done this. Nearby a fight broke out when one man shouted at another that this was the fault of those who had voted against statehood. "If we were a state, we'd get more help from the federal government," the man insisted.

"If we were a state, you'd be bled dry through taxes," the other man returned. "We can take care of the Indians ourselves!"

"Well, we haven't so far, have we," the first man roared. "Why don't you try taking care of *me*!" He proceeded to land a fist on the second man's jaw, and Irene jumped back as a brawl broke out. Soon more joined in, and Irene couldn't see her father anymore. Was he fighting, too? Her mother would be outraged if Kirk got into a common street brawl. She put a hand to her stomach, still sick at the sight of the mutilated bodies, while some men tried to quiet the crowd. Suddenly a strong arm came around her waist.

"Irene, get out of here," someone said. She looked up at Chad, who hurriedly whisked her away, keeping hold of her, actually ducking over her protectively as he guided her out of the worst of the crowd. He led her up onto a boardwalk. "What on earth were you doing in that bunch?" he asked her.

"I just . . . I wanted to see what all the commotion was about." She looked up at him. "Oh, Chad, did you see those horrible, mutilated bodies!"

The street was still in an uproar, and he hurried her back toward her shop. "I saw," he was telling her. "You get inside here and stay put, you hear? I'm going to see what's going on."

"Chad, Father is back. He's in that awful ruckus out there."

He led her inside her shop and closed the door. "I'll go see if I can find him. You all right?" There were times, like this one, when she actually believed she saw true love and concern in

Chad's eyes. It would be so much easier if she always saw it there, if she knew he was faithful to her. She couldn't know his tender concern was inspired by a guilty conscience. He had just come from the Kirkland mansion, where he had gone to pick up some papers for Bea, and had ended up making love to Elly on the couch in Bea's study.

"I'm fine," she told him. "Be careful, Chad."

He leaned down and kissed her lightly. "I might as well tell you Bea just got a wire from Colorado Springs. Hank Loring's ranch was attacked. His wife and daughter were killed."

"Oh, no! The poor man!"

"Yes. All hell is breaking loose. Something has to be done, Irene. We'll talk about it tonight. Don't leave here until I come for you."

He left and closed the door, disappearing into the wild crowd. Irene wondered what would come of all this Indian hatred, wondered what it was like on the other side of the conflict. The Indians were losing all that was precious to them. But in turn, innocent people like Hank's family were suffering. Her heart grieved for the man, who had always seemed to be so devoted to his family.

Her thoughts were awhirl with how wrong and unfair life could be: her unhappiness with Chad, the Indian massacres, the fire, then the flood, those poor mutilated souls in the street, Hank Loring's terrible loss . . . and Ramon—who was always there in the back of her mind. He had come to the housewarming, but they had been cool and formal with each other, all the time wanting to hold and be held. It had been an evening of hell for both of them, Chad dragging Ramon around to introduce him to Denver's elite, Bea acting upset and nervous about his presence there.

Chad came back inside the store. "Things are getting rough out there. You'd better close up for today and send your help home. We'll all go out the back way." He locked the door and pulled the shade. "Let's go."

Irene followed him, asking no questions for the moment, thinking again about the murdered settlers. Were there enough Indians lurking just beyond Denver to come and attack the whole city?

The *Rocky Mountain News* was filled with lurid details of Indian massacres. Meetings were held. Governor Evans called upon citizens to do their patriotic duty and join the Volunteers, who under Major John Chivington would soon go on a campaign to put an end to the Indian attacks. People were being murdered, homesteads burned, women taken captive, stage stations attacked, telegraph wires cut. The citizens of Boulder hastily built a fort, where people in nearby areas could come for safety. Women began carrying small supplies of strychnine to swallow in case they were captured, preferring to die rather than be raped and tortured by Indians.

Bea was beside herself with rage over lost income, but Kirk was strangely quiet, often sitting alone in his study. Direct links to the States were cut off, and mail had to be delivered by a southern route to San Francisco, then brought overland into Denver from the west, a terrible inconvenience that brought important correspondence many weeks too late. Prices rose out of sight, and paper became almost nonexistent. Badly needed mining machinery could not be delivered. Farming nearly came to a halt, as settlers left their farms and moved into bigger communities for safety. Stages stopped running, and easterners stopped investing in Colorado businesses and mines because it was impossible to get through to the endangered area. The rumor spread that more than ten thousand Indians were preparing to attack Denver, most of them gathering in southeast Colorado. Kirk found the fear ridiculous beyond measure.

"There aren't even close to ten thousand Indians in this whole Territory and beyond," he told his family one evening when Irene and Chad joined them for dinner. "It's the Sioux and northern Cheyenne doing most of this, not the southern Cheyenne at the reservation. What's going to happen is innocent Indians are going to suffer for this, and that will just make the rest of them even angrier."

"There is no such thing as an innocent Indian," Bea had argued.

The political atmosphere in Colorado became volatile, each faction blaming another for the current problems, people screaming at Governor Evans to do something. Evans declared martial law and campaigned harder to build the Third Colorado Volunteers.

Many answered the call, including a good share of miners. Chad also joined, prompted by Bea, but warned by Kirk not to join Chivington. "I don't trust the man. He's out to make a name for himself, feeding on everyone's hysteria," he told Chad. "This is going to lead to real trouble."

As usual, Bea won. Chad found it easier to go against Kirk than against his mother-in-law. He left in mid-October with the Third Colorado to put an end to the Indian problem. Kirk closed himself in his office and spoke to no one, suffering his own secret hell at the thought that his own son was out there . . . somewhere.

A cold rain beat against the windows, making Irene shiver. She was glad she had taken today off so she didn't have to go out in the wet weather. She sat in Chad's study, counting money donated during a special fund-raising drive for the new shelter.

Even at home she wanted to keep busy, especially now that Chad was gone. In spite of their rocky marriage, she was worried about him. He had been gone a month now, and she worried he could be horribly wounded or murdered by the Cheyenne, let alone that he was out on the open plains in this terrible weather. She was haunted by the memory of the mutilated bodies of the Hungate family, and she prayed every day that her husband would come home alive and in one piece.

She looked up then as Jenny Porter came into the room, carrying a package. When she moved into her new home, Irene had brought her maid, Rose Boles, and Jenny from Bea's home. With John off at college and Irene gone, Bea could manage without the two extra women; and Irene felt close enough to Rose now that she didn't want to lose her. Once in the new house her first order to both women was that they should call her Irene, not Mrs. Jacobs. Her gentle nature made them extremely loyal, and both women were relieved to be out from under Bea Kirkland's rule.

Jenny handed the package to Irene with a smile. "A messenger brought this," she told her.

Irene took the brown paper-wrapped package curiously, noticing it was addressed to her and was marked Personal. Jenny left, and Irene quickly opened the package, gasping at its contents, her eyes filling with tears. She knew who the sender had to be when she withdrew a magnificent carving of a horse, accurate in every detail, shaped and pointed to look like Sierra.

"Ramon," she whispered. The carving was at least twenty inches long and perfectly porportioned in height. She carefully set it on her desk, her heart torn with gentle memories that quieted her worry over Chad. She quickly opened the letter accompanying it, blinking back tears so that she could see to read it.

My darling Irene, I know your husband is away, so I took the chance on writing this letter, which you can destroy after you read it. I hope you like the horse. You can tell everyone it is a belated housewarming gift from your contractor, but you and I both know it has a deeper meaning.

This is my farewell gift to you, *mi querida*. I am going away for two, maybe three years."

Her heart tightened with dread.

"We both know it is best. We must not see each other for a long time, and perhaps then the pain of what we cannot have will subside. A Catholic priest here in Denver has recommended me to supervise the building of a great cathedral in Los Angeles, California. It is a very honorable appointment, and I will personally carve a great wooden crucifix that will hang at the front of the church. I will receive a great deal of money for this project, enough to one day come back to Denver a rich man.

I cannot promise, however, that I will come back to Denver at all. It is possible I will stay in Los Angeles to start a new life. Although I love Colorado as the place where I grew up, we both know why it might be better if I stay away.

Whatever I do, I want you to remember always you were my first love, and that I will always cherish you in my heart. You will forever be in my thoughts and prayers. I know you understand why I must do this. I would come in person to tell you good-bye, but I am afraid with you there alone, it would be unwise. I cannot trust my emotions, and you are an honorable woman who wishes to be true to her vows, as well you should. I can only hope your husband realizes he is married to the most wonderful woman in Denver, and that he will try harder to make you happy.

Adiós, mi querida. Vaya con Dios.

Ramon

Irene read the letter once more, stopping often to wipe tears from her cheeks. She wadded the letter up in her hand. Gasping with tears, she walked over and threw it into the fire. *"Vaya con Dios, mi querido,"* she sobbed.

In spite of the December cold, Denver citizens turned out by the thousands to cheer the returning, victorious Third Colorado regiment and John Chivington. Kirk watched with an aching heart from his office window, realizing some people didn't even realize that the "souvenirs" some of the soldiers carried on bayonets and wooden poles were women's body parts.

Black Kettle's band of southern Cheyenne near Sand Creek had been attacked by Chivington and nearly wiped out. The headlines were filled with the "great victory," but Kirk suspected it was nothing more than a massacre of peaceful Indians. He could not help wondering if Gray Bird Woman was still alive, and if she had been a part of the slaughter, and if Yellow Eagle had been involved. He knew from experience that what had happened at Sand Creek would only make matters worse. Black Kettle had been peacefully camped, waiting for instructions about where the U.S. government wanted him and his people to go. The rest of the Cheyenne would be furious over the unneccessary killing.

The Volunteers paraded through Denver, receiving praise and cheers from the crowd in the streets. Irene watched for Chad, finally spotting him not far away. Elly watched also, calling out to him, but as soon as he caught sight of Irene, he headed straight for her. Elly pouted and stormed back to the Kirkland offices.

Irene was astonished at the gaunt look on Chad's face. To her surprise, he reached down and hoisted her up onto his horse in front of him, riding off with her. He headed out of town, through a fresh, deep snow and up toward their house, saying nothing. He finally stopped when they were well away from the people and the noise, but before they reached the house.

He dismounted, helping her down, and Irene pulled a fur cape closer around her. "Chad, what is it? You look terrible. Were you wounded?"

Their eyes met, and he suddenly embraced her. "It was awful, Irene," he said hoarsely. "I couldn't be a part of that parade any longer, letting people cheer us as if we were great conquerors."

She leaned back and looked up at him, astonished to see tears in his eyes. "Chad, what is it?"

A bitter smile crossed his mouth. "That was no victory. It was a *slaughter*. Chivington just wanted to be able to say he had found some Indians and destroyed them, for his own political gain. They were *peaceful*, Irene. That village was made up mostly of women and *children*."

He turned away. In spite of his own immoral deeds, even Chad Jacobs could not condone what had happened at Sand Creek. He shook his head, a December wind blowing at his sandy hair. "The explosions, the gunshots, the screams . . . they'll echo in my head for a long time, Irene. I've never seen anything like it. I shot two warriors myself, and I feel bad enough about that. We attacked in the early morning. They were peacefully camped, still sleeping. The two men I shot were half naked, barely awake, unarmed."

He wiped at his eyes with a shaking hand. "I drew back right away. Then I saw some of the other men raping the Indian women. Others cut off arms, cut out women's privates while they were still alive, murdered little children."

"Chad! My God!"

He swallowed. "It was like . . . like being in hell. Black Kettle had an American flag flying over his tipi. He even tried at first to plead with us to stop, showed us his peace medal from the President. I think he got away, but not many did. The worst part . . . was when they just . . . kept at it . . . riding into a ravine where women and children were trying to hide . . . raping, murdering, running bayonets through babies' heads."

The last words were spoken in a near whisper, and he closed his eyes, real tears trickling down his cheeks. "Denver can cheer now, but this is going to haunt them, Irene . . . forever. We're supposed to be civilized, a step above the savages. But those men . . . proved they're no different from the Indians. It makes me sick that I was a part of it."

He broke into tears, and Irene embraced him. For now, at least, Chad had turned to her, had shown a side of himself rarely displayed. For the moment his cocky arrogance had left him, and he truly seemed to need her. His sudden vulnerability made her pity him, even made it easier to love him. Maybe after being away from her, and after the horrible experience that made him turn to her, he would try harder to love her and be true to her. Her husband was home, and he needed her. Surely they would be happier now.

She could only take hope in the moment. Chad wrapped his arms around her and wept. "It was all for nothing," he sobbed. "The one called Yellow Eagle wasn't even . . . caught or killed. Women . . . children . . . all for nothing. All that blood-shed . . . for nothing."

PART

FOUR

An old friendship is like an old piece of china. It is precious only just so long as it is perfect. Once it is broken, no matter how cleverly you mend it, it is good for nothing but to put on a shelf in a corner where it won't be too closely looked at.

AMELIA B. EDWARDS
The New Joy of Words.

CHAPTER
TWENTY-FOUR

August 1866

Bea stood watching the street below, proud of how Denver was growing, in spite of the mounting sewer problems. She was helping form a campaign committee to urge people not to litter the streets, and wild dogs were less a problem since the law was passed allowing citizens to shoot them. Still, litter and roaming animals were common, and she frowned with disgust when she saw a man spit tobacco on a boardwalk.

But there had definitely been progress. Most of the streets were dirt, but some were being bricked, and just below her window men were laying rails for horse-drawn trolley cars. She and Kirk were both founders of the Denver Horse and Railway Company, which by 1867 would be in full operation, hauling visitors and shoppers to their destinations by trolley car and helping limit the number of animals and thus the amount of smelly dung they left in the streets. The trolley line would also help reduce the number of accidents, with fewer wagons, horses, and pedestrians.

Soon, Bea thought, there would be other rails coming to Denver—the Union Pacific! It had been announced that the government was building a transcontinental railroad, and she could not imagine that it would come west without linking up with the West's Queen City. Denver's, indeed, all of Colorado's, importance would rise dramatically then. Eventually this Territory would be a state. She was determined to see that happen.

She was also determined that the Mexicans in the south would not secede from the Territory and link up with New Mexico, as they were threatening to do. She was glad so many others shared her own prejudice and hatred for the Mexicans. Again it proved she was right not to trust them, even if her resentment of them was personal. Thank God Ramon Vallejo had left town. He was no longer a threat to Irene's marriage. She hoped wherever he had gone, he had failed miserably; and she took great pleasure in thinking he had left because he could not be successful in Bea Kirkland's town. He had been gone two years now. It was obvious he was not coming back.

She smiled at the thought, going back to sit down at her desk. Yes, things were coming along nicely. Irene and Chad seemed happy, although Irene still had not been able to conceive. She owned two clothing stores now, and was proving herself a very adept businesswoman. It was hard to believe Irene was twenty already, but not hard to believe she had grown even more beautiful.

The only thing that irritated Bea was her daughter's generosity. As far as Bea was concerned, Irene devoted far too much time to the shelter for widows and orphans, associated too much with women of a lower class. After all, Kirkland Enterprises gave a great deal of money to charity. That should be enough. Irene should be giving more time to Chad. Bea blamed Irene's loss of her normally open, happy personality on being around "those women" too much. She was not the same Irene she had been two years ago—still loving and generous, but too somber, as though she were unhappy, when she should be the happiest woman in Denver. She had everything—beauty, money, power, a dashing and attentive husband. What more could her daughter want?

She leaned over a ledger, studying the latest financial figures for Kirkland Enterprises. Hank Loring was doing well with the cattle business, which was becoming quite profitable. Hank had survived great tragedy, and kept going. She liked that in a person.

A third Kirkland-owned bank had been opened, and the new lumber mill was doing well. Red McKinley's idea had been a good one, and now that it was in Kirkland hands, it was going strong. She breathed a deep sigh of satisfaction. Kirk seemed to have gotten over the incident with Red. No one had heard from the man, and Bea was becoming more confident that they never would.

The only trouble was, she knew Kirk would never quite forgive her for what had happened, nor would he forgive her support for Chivington's attack on the Cheyenne at Sand Creek. Kirk had withdrawn to the mountains for six months afterward. It was not that he didn't realize something needed to be done about the Indian problem; he simply disagreed vehemently with how John Chivington had handled the situation, calling the man a warmonger and an opportunist.

Even Chad had been despondent after Sand Creek. She had tried to assure him he had done the right thing. She hated seeing the loss of his normally charming, buoyant personality. He had finally recovered his old self, and Denver was slowly getting over what most in the nation considered a shameful incident.

Now that the Union Pacific and Kansas Pacific were both coming west, it would not be too much longer before the demise of most of the Indians, anyway. Buffalo were being killed off by the thousands, and the roaming range of the Indians had been cut back severely. Kirk had always said the Indians could not survive without the buffalo and without being able to follow the migration of that animal and other wild game. Their days were numbered. The West would be settled, and Denver would be the greatest city between Chicago and San Francisco!

Bea looked up then as Kirk walked in, carrying an envelope and looking somber. Because of Red McKinley, and their disagreement over the Indians and Mexicans, her relationship with her husband had deteriorated dramatically over the last two years. Kirk no longer came to her bedroom at night, not even once or twice a month as he used to do. They had once at least shared a friendship, but even that was strained now, although they continued to put on a good front for their friends.

They were more like business partners now, their only common interest protecting Irene and protecting the Kirkland fortune for the children. She knew Kirk took pride in helping Denver grow to prominence, knew how much he loved the area. And she knew she could count on his never leaving her, because he would never leave Colorado, or the city that displayed his name on several buildings. He would never bring shame and disgrace to his children by divorcing the woman who had been a mother to Irene.

He threw the envelope on her desk. "There's something that should interest you."

She slowly picked it up. "What is it?"

"Open it up. There's a valid draft in there for sixteen thousand dollars, from Red McKinley."

"What!" She looked inside and pulled out the check, which bore the insignia of the Union Pacific. "This money is from the *railroad*," she corrected him.

"And look who signed it."

She noticed Red's signature at the bottom. "I don't understand."

Kirk was obviously upset as he spoke. "You're supposed to be the one with the brains, Bea. You ought to be able to figure it out if I could. There's a letter in there. Red is working for the UP now. He's a railroad manager working directly under Tom Durant. You know the kind of money we're talking about when that name is mentioned, enough to make us look like *paupers*. That money is to pay off Red's debt to us plus more interest than necessary, which means he's cut a hell of a deal with the railroad. He also says he's coming here to Denver with some other railroad representatives to talk about the Union Pacific."

"Well, good. Who cares if he works for the railroad, as long as he's paid off his debt? Apparently you were right about McKinley being a man of his word, so I offer my apologies for not believing he would. And there can be no doubt why he's coming to Denver. Don't you see? He wants to bring the UP through Denver, and he's buttering up Denver's most important citizens." She smiled smugly. "He probably wants to buy up some land as cheap as he can get it."

Kirk snickered. "I figured you to be smarter, Bea."

She glanced at him in surprise. "What do you mean? It's all quite obvious."

He shook his head. "You remember what I said about wounding a man's pride. He's up to something. I guarantee it. I know men like Red better than you ever will!"

Bea sobered slightly, remembering Red's parting words. "If I can ever find a way to hurt you, lady, I'll do it. . . . I'm not through with Denver . . . I'll be back someday." "Well," she spoke up, "if the man is out for some kind of revenge, paying us sixteen thousand dollars is a strange way of showing it."

Kirk leaned over the desk. "You'd better understand, Bea, that sixteen thousand dollars is a drop in the bucket for men like Tom Durant! Red is setting us up for something. You can count on it. You'd better call a meeting of Denver's best and be prepared to wine and dine these railroad men, and you'd better pray Red is coming here for the reason you think he is. If that railroad doesn't come through Denver, this city might suffer a loss from which it will *never* recover!"

Bea rose. "We've survived fire and flood, disease, inflation, financial ruin, drought, and Indian troubles. Nothing is going to destroy Denver, Kirk, certainly not one uneducated mountain man. Besides, Denver is much too important to the rest of the country now. There is no way the UP would *think* of coming west without stopping here. They know we already have engineers working to plan the best route through the mountains."

"Well, I know the mountains better than anybody, and the best route is the South Pass, way north of here, out of Colorado Territory. You'd better consider the fact that it's Red McKinley coming here, and remember the mood he was in when he left. You decide when and where to meet with them, and you send back a letter. Then you pray Red values the friendship he once shared with me more than his desire to hurt *you!*"

He abruptly turned and left, and Bea's heart pounded with dread. She felt relieved when she read Red's letter, finding no malice in anything he wrote. She called in her secretary and immediately dictated a letter of reply, telling Red that all of Denver welcomed the UP executives to their fine city, and she and Kirk would be glad to have Red and his associates to their home for dinner, to discuss their plans. It irritated her that she was reduced to welcoming a man she hated, but she was willing to put Denver above her own whims. And she couldn't forget that Red knew about Irene and Yellow Eagle.

As she dictated the letter, her resentment toward Kirk was rekindled. She hated being put in a beggar's position, having to cater to Red McKinley. The man would probably gloat and strut his fine, new position with the railroad; but he and his associates would soon see where the *real* power lay when they came to Denver.

"I'll miss you, Chad," Elly cooed, kissing his bare chest. They lay in Chad and Irene's bed. It was the servants' day off, and Rose and Jenny had both gone to town. Irene was at her clothing store, and Chad had supposedly come home to pick up some papers. Seventeen-year-old Elly, home packing for her trip to finishing school, had hurried over to meet him as planned, and they had enjoyed an hour of heated lovemaking.

"I'm sure you'll find some male companionship in Chicago," Chad told her with a grin, fingering her breast.

Elly lay back, stretching her arms over her head. "I suppose," she answered, kicking away the blankets so that she lay sprawled

completely naked beside him. She was already nearly as big as
Bea, but slightly more slender, more youthful looking. It was
obvious she would be built exactly like her mother as the years
progressed. Chad still found nothing attractive about her except
her voracious sexual appetite. One thing was sure—she knew how
to make a man feel good, a far cry from her older sister. "And
what will *you* do for comfort while I'm gone?" she asked Chad.

He rolled on top of her, tasting at her breasts. "I'll make do."

Elly laughed, ruffling his hair. "You won't find any women
better than me, I'll bet." How she loved the power she had over
this man! More than that, she loved knowing she pleased him
more than Irene did. Irene might wear his wedding ring, but Elly
possessed him. It was a delicious victory for Elly. She considered
her affair with Chad just recompense for all the years people had
gaped over Irene's beauty while hardly paying any attention to
Elly, a proper consolation for her father's favoritism, her mother's
pride in her eldest daughter.

Now that John and Irene were gone from home, Elly got less
attention than ever. When she came back from finishing school,
she would be a full-fledged proper lady, ready to take on Denver's
social and business worlds. But her outward victories would never
compare to the inner victory of stealing Irene's husband, sleeping
in her sister's own bed with the man she had wanted since she was
thirteen years old. She might never own Chad legally, and there
would be other men in her life; but Chad Jacobs would always be
her first and only real love.

Chad moved to the edge of the bed and got up to wash. "We'd
better get back to where we're supposed to be," he told her.
"Make sure there aren't any stains on the sheets, and make the bed
so it doesn't look slept in." This was the part she hated, the cold,
practical side of it. "You sure you're being careful?" he asked.

"I learned all about it from my personal servant, Jesse Tibbs.
She has five grown children." Elly put a towel between her legs
and moved to sit on the edge of the bed. "I cried to her one day,
told her I didn't understand about men and babies and that Mother
wouldn't explain such things to me. Jesse said that if a woman
waits until just before or just after her period, she can't get
pregnant."

"Well, I hope you're right." Chad washed and pulled on his
underwear and pants. He came back over to where she sat, leaning
down and kissing her savagely. He knelt then to relish a last taste
of each breast, while Elly smiled. "That will have to tide you over

for the next year or two," he told her. "At least from me. I'm sure you won't go without while you're gone."

Elly laughed lightly, then sobered as she watched him dress. "Will you write me, Chad? Please do. I promise to destroy the letters."

"Sure, I'll write you if you want. Just don't write back, at least not directly to me. You can tell me all about the men you seduce there when you get back."

She watched the movement of his beautiful muscles as he reached for a shirt. "None of them will compare to you, Chad," she told him.

He grinned with great personal pleasure at the remark. "Why, thank you, little sister." She scowled at the term he knew she hated, and he smiled. "I'll see you tonight at your farewell dinner. Now hurry up and get dressed and get this bed in shape. We can't always count on Irene not showing up. I've got to get back to the office before they begin wondering what's taking me so long." He buttoned and tucked in his shirt, then went to a mirror to adjust the small bow tie around the piccadilly collar of his shirt.

Elly quickly hurried to the washroom to clean herself, careful not to leave behind any signs of her presence. The washrooms of both the Kirkland mansion and Irene's home had gravity-forced running water that came from tanks on the upper floors, which were kept filled by the servants. Normally servants brought hot water to the washrooms every morning and every night, or on demand, as needed for washing and bathing. Today Elly had to make do with cold water, and she shivered as she washed. She threw the towels down the laundry chute so Irene would not find them.

By the time she finished and came into the bedroom, still stark naked, Chad was fully dressed and ready to leave. "Remember what I said about the bed," he told her.

"I will." Her eyes were suddenly moist. "Good-bye, Chad. Can't I have one more hug?"

He gave her his best smile and walked over to embrace her. "The time will go faster than you think," he told her, "especially once you're there and find out how much fun it is." He pulled back, kissing her once more. "Don't forget me."

"I could never forget you," she answered, touching his hand-some face. Chad made her feel pretty, wanted. She knew he didn't really love her, but she owned him just the same. She didn't worry about whether he would still want her when she got back, because he was afraid *not* to want her. She knew too much. She had Chad under her thumb, her mother and Irene totally fooled. The magnitude of her transgressions sometimes almost overwhelmed her, not with guilt but with great pleasure.

Chad left, secretly relieved he would have a year, maybe two, without Elly around to pester him, although he would miss their romps in bed.

The *Rocky Mountain News* could not find enough words to describe properly the importance of the meeting to be held between the Union Pacific officials and Denver's powerful backers. The city's very life depended upon the outcome of the meeting taking place at the Kirkland mansion this night.

Irene sat at her dressing table helping Rose put a few finishing touches to her hair while Chad donned the jacket of his best suit. "Is this good enough to impress the men of the UP?" he asked, coming to stand in front of Irene.

Rose looked up, and he winked at her. She reddened slightly, always somewhat stunned by Irene's husband's handsomeness, but also not trusting him. He had never made advances toward her, but she suspected it was only because she was so close to Irene. And if someone so rich and handsome, with a wife as utterly beautiful and sweet as Irene, would fool around with the servants, who else might he fool around with? She kept her suspicions to herself. It was not her business, she supposed, and Chad was always kind and gracious to her. Besides, she liked her job and did not intend to lose it.

"You look wonderful, as always," Irene told him.

"I'll go see to cleaning your shoes," Rose told Irene, quickly leaving. She found it embarrassing to be in the bedroom when Irene and Chad were both there, and she had long ago vowed that if Chad Jacobs ever made advances toward her, she would turn him away. She loved and respected Irene too much to sleep with the poor woman's wolf of a husband.

"And you, as always, are beautiful," Chad told Irene. He looked in her mirror to adjust his tie. Irene watched him, wishing she could trust him but knowing she couldn't. He never offered explanations for the frequent nights he came home much too late, often smelling of cheap perfume; and Irene continued to wonder where she had gone wrong. She wanted so much to love him totally, to feel he loved her the same way, but there was a strange emptiness about Chad Jacobs. Physically he was as much man as any woman could want. But emotionally he seemed cold; unreachable. The closest he had come to showing any true feelings had been after Sand Creek. But once he got over that, he had returned to his usual carefree, devilish nature, always clamming up whenever she wanted to talk about anything serious, always avoiding her questions about his family.

If only he would talk to her, she thought, truly talk to her, it might be easier. They had come to live a life of let's pretend: pretending to be a happily married couple, pretending he did not see other women, pretending she worked at her stores and the shelter because she liked being busy, when she only kept herself busy to keep from thinking about how unhappy she was.

She continued to struggle to be a good wife, searching for ways to get through to her husband, letting him make love to her because she feared he would stray even more if she didn't, praying she would get pregnant, but still she had not conceived.

Somehow she had to survive this marriage, wait things out. Why did Chad want other women? Why did he leave her so emotionally starved? She had never dreamed that two years into a marriage to the most desired man in Denver she could be this unhappy. They shared their bodies, but she had never been able to see into his soul.

"I'm ready if you are," he said, donning a top hat.

Irene adjusted her own silk-and-straw bonnet, and Rose came back with her shoes, helping her get them on. "Is the buggy ready?" Irene asked.

"Yes." Chad was looking in her mirror again. She suddenly realized that Chad Jacobs was probably more in love with himself than anyone else. He turned his head different ways to see how he looked in the hat. "This is an important night, Irene. Your mother has worked hard pleading our case to the Union Pacific. We need that railroad."

"I know. It's odd that Red McKinley holds such a high position with them now. I'm glad for him, though. I always liked Red."

"Hmmm." He turned to look at her. "For some reason your mother didn't—thought he was a bad influence on your father, I guess." He did not tell her exactly how Bea had taken the mill from under Red and left him broke.

"I know she didn't like Father loaning Red that money, but Mother said it got paid back. I think that's wonderful. I knew Father could count on Red."

"Well, don't be so sure of that. The man works for the railroad now, and that kind of power and money can often make a man push friendship aside. I'm not sure what is going to happen tonight." He looked her over, putting out his arm. "This could be a very interesting evening, Mrs. Jacobs."

She smiled at him, taking his arm, wondering how a man could be so tender and considerate sometimes, yet so difficult to love.

Bea and Kirk welcomed the top echelon of Denver into their home, Irene and Chad standing beside them. After most of the invited guests had arrived, the railroad executives made their appearance—four men, arriving in a fancy, polished carriage. They came to the door of the Kirkland mansion, eyes unreadable, led by none other than Red McKinley, who smiled and nodded at the servant who took his silk top hat and gloves.

With a sting of jealousy at the man's apparent success with the railroad, Bea noticed Red wore a dark silk suit with velvet-trimmed lapels, the jacket short-waisted at the front but with knee-length tails at the back. A silk brocade vest could be seen beneath the open jacket front, a gold watch chain hanging from a pocket. A silk tie graced the piccadilly collar of his shirt. His hair was cut more neatly than Bea remembered, and he had shaved his red beard, leaving only a fine-looking mustache.

Bea watched him with a smile on her face but bitter hatred in her heart as he and his associates approached the Kirklands. She knew instantly by the look in his blue eyes that Kirk was right. Red McKinley had not forgotten his wounded pride, and Bea began to worry. Red approached Kirk first, taking his hand, both men almost glaring at each other. Kirk was sorry about what had happened, but he was not about to let Red ruin Denver or Irene and the Kirkland family over it. Bea could see they were gripping hands more tightly than necessary, longing for open warfare.

"Welcome back, Red," Kirk said stoically. "Congratulations on the fine position you're found with the railroad. I'm sorry for any hard feelings you might have had when you left Denver, and I mean that."

"I'm sure you do, old friend. But some things run deeper than friendship, don't they?" The man glanced at Bea, then back to Kirk. "The railroad is a great business, Kirk. It can make a poor man rich in no time at all. I trust you got your money."

"The extra wasn't necessary. If I had been here—"

"If you had been here, I might never have landed my position with the railroad." He glanced at Bea again. "So, I suppose I should thank your wife for that," he said dryly. He quickly turned and began introducing his cohorts, deliberately leaving Bea out of the introductions, passing her by then and going directly to Irene, leaving Bea to introduce herself awkwardly.

Bea raged inside at the affront. The man was trying to show he was more important than she was! She watched in near terror as he talked to Irene and Chad, but she saw only genuine friendliness in his eyes as he held Irene's hand. Irene congratulated him on his new position with the railroad, telling him how sorry she was that the flood over two years ago had ruined him. Red knew that she meant it, was sure she didn't know the truth about how her mother had all but kicked him out of Denver. He squeezed her hand. No, he wouldn't destroy this innocent, beautiful woman. But he would do some damage to Denver, and to Bea Kirkland's pride before this night was over.

He glanced at Bea, watching her practically grovel at the feet of his associates, and knew she was sure the reason for the meeting was to discuss bringing the railroad through Denver. He smiled and turned back to Irene. "I kind of fell into the job because of my scouting skills," he told her. "I helped map out the best route, then was chosen to manage some of the land deals," he explained. "I'll say one thing about the railroad business, Irene—it's one of great opportunity, where a nobody can be a somebody in no time at all if he plays his cards right. It's a very lucrative business too—big money, almost as big as gold."

"I'm sure it must be, considering the importance to the whole country a transcontinental railroad will have," Irene answered. "And building a railroad must take considerable investment—bonds, land purchases, government loans, private investments . . ."

His eyebrows arched. "You've become quite the business-woman since last I knew you."

She smiled, and he saw the genuine sweetness still in her eyes. "I'm a Kirkland, Red. We end up knowing the ins and outs of business whether we like it or not."

He leaned closer and winked, while Bea glanced at them again, hating the man for having power over her simply because he knew the Kirkland secret. "And I'll bet you *don't* like it," he told Irene. "I'll bet sometimes you'd rather leave it all and go to the mountains, just like your father."

The memory of their trip together always brought a soft glow to Irene's heart. Would she ever get to go back? "Yes," she answered. "You know me too well, Red."

A sadness seemed to come into his eyes then. "Oh, yes, child." He glanced at Bea to make sure she was listening. "I know you better than you think," he finished. He turned to Chad and spoke a few words. Servants brought out drinks and appetizers while a small orchestra played soft music. There was a lot of talk about the coming railroad, but none of the UP officials were giving any indication it would not come through Denver.

A nervous Bea stayed unusually close to her husband, hating him for creating all this tension, but aware that Red's fondness for Kirk and Irene was the only chance Denver had of not being all but destroyed financially. Red's pompous attitude grated on her nerves, and she was beside herself with jealousy and anger at his new importance. She never dreamed he would ever amount to anything once he left Denver, and now here he was, in a position to make or break the Queen City!

The railroad officials were served the finest wines and an elegant dinner of lobster, steaks, or prime rib at the huge dining table. "The beef is from our own ranch in southern Colorado," Bea informed them. "We have several thousand acres now, and are raising English Herefords—the best beef you'll ever eat. When the railroad comes to Denver, the cattle market will triple."

The railroad men said nothing. Everyone expressed pleasure at the grand meal, which included a variety of potatoes and vegetables, fruits and salads, followed by chocolate pie and ice cream, the newest craze in desserts. Once the meal was finished, Red, who sat at one end of the table with Kirk at the other, cleared his throat and rose, quieting everyone at the table. Denver's founders watched the man with great anticipation, full of pride and enthusiasm at what the railroad would do for Denver.

"Ladies and gentlemen, it is with mixed feelings that we come here to meet with you," Red announced. Immediately Bea's heart began to sink as Red's eyes moved to meet hers. "You have been very gracious to us, and the whole country recognizes Denver's contribution to progress in what men like myself and David Kirkland remember as wild, untamed country. Twenty years ago we never would have dreamed the West could grow so quickly, or that a group of tent dwellers could, in seven or eight years' time, turn a little settlement along a creek into a major city, one with few rivals."

He sipped his wine, the room nearly dead silent. Bea studied Red, while Kirk glanced at the other railroad men, noticing they all wore the same smug look.

"But, alas," Red continued, "Denver *does* have its rivals. Other cities have also made their mark in the West." He paused. "We are here, as you know, to let you know our decision regarding the best route for the Union Pacific." His eyes moved to Kirk. "My old friend David Kirkland, an experienced mountain man, knows there is only one reasonably easy way over the Rockies. What would you say that route is, Kirk?"

Kirk glared at him, reddening slightly. "Why don't you tell me?"

Red smiled. "All right. The only reasonable route over the Rockies is the South Pass, near Fort Bridger in Wyoming." Bea remembered the place well, remembered again that whole, horrible first trip west. "Then on through the Nevada desert," Red continued. "Now, ladies and gentlement, the UP has to be practical. A transcontinental railroad is no small undertaking, and the cost will be phenomenal. So, we have to cut costs wherever possible, which means taking the most direct route possible. Using the South Pass as our point through the mountains leaves us no choice—and I tell you this with extreme regret—but to stay to the north and take the railroad through Cheyenne."

"This is an outrage," one man spoke up. "It's a deliberate insult to Denver!"

"We'll *die* without the railroad," another put in. "Businesses will pull out on us!"

"What about Colorado's cattle industry?" said another. "Who made this decision?"

Red looked at Bea, half smiling, watching her face redden with her own unexpressed rage. He enjoyed the fact that there was absolutely nothing she could say. She couldn't very well rise up and accuse him of making this a personal vendetta. After all, to do so would mean she would have to admit how she had treated him. Everyone would know what a crook she was. And if she insulted him too badly in public, she had to worry whether he would tell the world that Kirk's own son was the hated Cheyenne warrior responsible for some of the worst of the raids.

"A lot of thought was given to this decision," Red said. "The final decision was Doctor Durant's, and he sent us to express our regrets."

"My God, we're finished," one man mumbled. "I've got to get home and start making plans right now to pull out. It's Cheyenne that will grow now, not Denver."

"Don't be so hasty," Kirk spoke up. He rose, glaring at Red. "We'll find a way around this, McKinley. The people of Denver have survived a lot of things. They'll survive this."

"Kirk, without the railroad—"

"I said we'd find a way around this," Kirk interrupted the man who had spoken. "Right now I'm calling a meeting, so I guess our guests will have to leave. We have business to tend to. There will be no dancing and refreshments in the ballroom." He met Red's eyes. "When you wound Denver, you wound me," he told Red. "I take it personally. You deliberately let us wine and dine you, let us make fools of ourselves. This friendship is over, Red. Get out of my house!"

Bea was surprised, but pleased, at Kirk's treatment of his old friend and the way he had suddenly taken charge.

"Father, I'm sure he tried—"

"Don't say it, Irene," Kirk told his daughter. "Let the snake slither out the way he came."

Both men's eyes held a challenge, but Red's expression was victorious. "Well, gentlemen," he said to his colleagues, "we are apparently being asked to leave." He looked around the table. "I'm sorry about the misunderstanding. But then you're all businessmen"—he moved his eyes to Bea—"and women," he added. "You understand practical economics. It's called cutting costs in order to reap the most profit." He nodded to Bea, then glanced at Irene, sobering. "I'm very sorry," he said, sounding sincere. He turned and asked for his hat, and the other railroad men followed suit.

"What was that all about," Chad asked Irene, "looking at you and saying he's sorry?"

"I have no idea," Irene answered.

Bea, totally shaken, blinked back tears as she looked at Kirk. "What are we going to do?" she said brokenly. "This could turn Denver into a ghost town."

Kirk put a hand on her arm. He found himself suddenly feeling sorry for her, realizing how hard she had worked for Denver, that she had done it because he had brought her here and wanted to stay. "There's no sense laying the blame on us or Red," he told her quietly. "This decision probably would have been made even without Red being in the picture. I have a feeling he asked to be the one to come and tell us, for his personal satisfaction. But we're not going to take this lying down, Bea. You're the one who told me Denver could survive anything. Don't back out on me now."

She was heartened by his sudden, surprising need of her. "No . . . I won't," she told him.

"Father, what can we do?" Irene asked. "I want to help."

"Yes, we'll do whatever's necessary," Chad said.

"We've got to start laying plans right away," Kirk told them.

"Plans for what?" Chad asked.

"I don't know yet. Maybe our own railroad, a link to the UP at Cheyenne."

"Our own railroad! Do you know the kind of money that would take?"

"We'll raise it," Kirk answered. "Somehow we'll rally Denver's citizens together and raise the money through bonds. If we work fast enough, we could be ready at the same time the transcontinental is completed. We could even build a connection south to the Kansas-Pacific. Most of our cattle shipments could go that route."

Chad grinned. "By God, maybe we *could* do it at that."

"It will be a horrendous project," Bea said.

"We just have to get enough people together on it," Kirk answered.

"You'd better move fast," Chad told him. "Hunter over there is already talking about pulling up stakes. As soon as this hits the *News*, all hell will break loose around here. People will head north."

"Then we'll just head them off," Kirk answered.

Irene listened in total confusion. None of it made sense. She could understand the railroad's decision, but she could not understand the animosity she had seen between Red and her parents, especially between Red and Kirk. What had happened to the warm friendship they once shared? She knew Red had paid back the money he had borrowed from Kirk, knew her father well enough to know Kirk never would have demanded that money.

She glanced at Bea. There were few times that her mother looked totally shaken, but this was one of them. Had her mother done something to offend Red McKinley? The sawmill bore the Kirkland name now. Irene had always thought Red had given up the mill willingly, but perhaps he had not. Chad had already said Bea all but hated the man. Why?

Kirk was ordering Chad and another man to go out and gather together certain builders, engineers, a few other men with power and money, calling a meeting for that very night. Something had to be done, and quickly. Other communities had to be contacted, to let them know this was important not just to Denver but to all of Colorado. The Union Pacific would not come through Denver! Such an affront would not be tolerated by the Queen City.

CHAPTER
TWENTY-FIVE

Elly lay in severe pain, but decided what she had done was worth the discomfort. How could she have explained her pregnancy to her mother? She would have lost faith with the family, maybe even have been disinherited. Besides, her baby might have looked just like Chad, for Chad most certainly had to be the father. If the family found out, everything would be ruined. Chad would hate her for giving away their secret. Irene would leave him, and Chad might in turn leave Denver, and she would never see him again.

She grasped her pillow tighter, looking around her room, wondering how long she had lain passed out after the operation. What day was this? Was she going to live? If she did, she had already decided that the first thing she was going to do when she got back home was fire Jesse for telling her there were certain times she couldn't get pregnant. Now that she knew that was not true, she wasn't sure what she was going to do about her sexual adventures. She was not about to stop seeing Chad, or other men, for that matter.

She lay in a state of confusion and remorse, not over getting rid of her baby, but over the pregnancy itself and near panic at realizing it could happen again. Why her? Irene was the one who wanted a baby. A child was the last thing Elly *ever* wanted.

She curled up as another cramp rocked her. She had gone out

into the streets of Chicago and found a woman who, for a fee, had taken her to a doctor who got rid of babies. The trouble was, the man had all but killed her. The violent sickness and bleeding that had followed the abortion had alarmed the school president, who had no idea what was wrong with her. A doctor had been called in, and that was about all Elly remembered. The doctor had performed some kind of operation on her. She wasn't even sure yet what had been done to her, but now the president of the school knew she had had an abortion in some hideous back-alley room, an abortion she had hoped to keep secret. It surely wouldn't be long now before Miss Oxford told her family.

She fell into a light sleep, then opened her eyes when she heard the door open. Miss Oxford and the doctor came into her room, Miss Oxford looking pale and shaken. She approached Elly, touching her hair. "How do you feel, child?"

"Terrible," Elly answered. "You didn't . . . you didn't tell anyone, did you—the other girls, I mean?"

The woman took a chair near her. "No. I've told no one." She looked at the doctor. "This is Dr. Morrow. You were so sick when I brought him to see you, I wasn't sure you would even remember him. He's come to check on you, and to talk to you about something very serious, Elly." The woman's eyes began to tear. "Oh, Elly, why did you do this? Don't you understand your mother's power? She'll have this school closed for good, and I'll lose everything I have ever worked for."

The woman sniffled, and Elly frowned. She hated sobbing women. "You didn't do anything," she told Miss Oxford. "I'm the one who had the abortion."

"But you were out there in the streets without our knowledge. It makes us look bad, Elly, makes it look as though we don't keep a good watch on our girls. And to think you almost died, let alone—" She glanced up at Dr. Morrow. "There is something you have to know, Elly. We had to make a decision on our own, without yours or your mother's permission. When you learn the truth, it will go bad for the school, I'm afraid."

Elly looked at the doctor. "Learn what truth? What's wrong? Am I going to die?"

"No, Elly, you won't die," the doctor assured her. Miss Oxford watched Elly as the doctor talked, thinking how different the girl was from her sweet and beautiful older sister who had been there three years ago. Elly was belligerent, demanding, and snobbish, always rubbing it in to the other girls about how wealthy she was. She did not have many friends here except among those whose wealth matched or surpassed her own, and in four months she had managed to cause arguments among some of the others. Elly Kirkland was a clever schemer who knew how to create friction among the other girls while looking completely innocent herself.

"I am afraid we had no choice, Elly," the doctor was saying. He cleared his throat, looking nervous. "Whoever performed the abortion did a very messy job. He or she damaged the womb—the uterus, it is called. I removed it vaginally. It is a very rare operation, and you're lucky the school called me, because I am an expert in this field. If I had not done what I did, you would have most certainly died. However, I am afraid you . . . well, my dear, you can never have children now."

Miss Oxford broke into more tears, and Elly just stared at the doctor, letting the words sink in. Never have children? She couldn't get pregnant? She quickly surmised they expected this news to break her heart. She could think of no better news, but she put on a look of horror and dismay. "No babies?" she whimpered.

"I'm sorry," the doctor told her. "I had no choice, and there was no time to try to contact your parents first. Even if we had, the decision would have had to be the same, in order to save your life." The man ran a hand through his hair as he walked over to get another chair and bring it closer to her bed. He sat down and leaned forward, his elbows on his knees. "You won't have any more periods, Elly. I hate to talk so bluntly, but considering the fact you were pregnant in the first place, such talk should not be a total shock to you, and I want you to understand what has happened. It was an internal operation, so you will have no scars."

No scars! No one would even have to know! She could hardly contain her joy at the news.

"You do still have your ovaries," the doctor was explaining. "So there will be no interruption of your hormones. You will hardly know the difference, except for the awful realization you can never have children. I'm very sorry. It may not seem that terrible at the moment, but when you're a little older, more mature, marry a proper man, you'll want children. It will be up to you whether or not you tell the poor man that you can never give him any."

Elly managed a few tears, not from disappointment, but from her own pain, and the remembered horror of the abortion. "Can I—I mean—can I be a normal wife someday to a good man? Can I have . . . normal relations with him?"

"Yes," the doctor answered gently. "The operation in no way will affect your ability to—uh—to please your husband sexually. It only means you can't give him children."

"How terrible for him," Elly answered, a note of sadness in her voice.

"It's just too bad a good man will have to suffer one day for what some rogue did to you," Miss Oxford spoke up between sobs. "It doesn't matter to us personally who the father was, Elly, or who the horrible doctor was who nearly killed you. It will be up to you if you want to give your parents such information. The biggest problem for us is the fact that you sneaked out of here and went to see that quack, and that we have had to make such a dramatic decision about your entire future. I can only hope when we tell your family that they somehow understand we did our best." She stopped to wipe at her eyes, a new wave of tears coming. "Something like this has never happened here before!"

Elly's mind whirled with the sudden information. She couldn't get pregnant! She was completely free to have sex whenever she wanted! She didn't even have any scars. No one even needed to know! She kept a sober look on her face as she spoke to Miss Oxford. "You mean, you haven't contacted my family yet? You and Dr. Morrow are the only ones who know about this?"

Miss Oxford nodded. Elly reached out and took her hand. "Miss Oxford, I don't want the school to go under because of me. And I'd like to stay here and finish my schooling like Mother wanted me to." She let a tear slip down her face. "Please, Miss Oxford, if you won't tell, I won't tell. My mother will send me any amount of money I ask for, so I can pay the doctor myself. I'll even pay you something extra not to tell. I'll make up some excuse to my mother for why I need the money."

Miss Oxford glanced at the doctor and back to Elly. "You mean . . . you don't want your parents to know? You aren't angry with us?"

Elly turned on her back, staring up at the ceiling. "How can I be? It's all my fault, not yours. Dr. Morrow did what he had to do. I'm the one who sinned, Miss Oxford, and I'm the one who tried to get rid of the baby." She turned her head to look at the woman. "I brought this on myself. You shouldn't be held responsible. As long as I don't have any scars, I'd like to be allowed to decide on my own when and if I tell anyone. When the day comes that I meet the right man, it will be up to me whether or not I tell him I can't"—she managed a sob—"give him children."

Miss Oxford rose, leaning over the girl. "Elly, are you sure? I wouldn't want this to come out later."

Elly wiped at her eyes. "If I wait a few years, I don't even have to tell when or where it happened. For now it will be just our secret—my own secret when I get home. Please, Miss Oxford. Please don't tell. By the time I go home next year, I'll be just fine. No one needs to know. I'd—I'd be too ashamed. I don't want to hurt my mother. I promise to be a better student and to stay out of trouble. Just please don't tell my parents about this."

Miss Oxford looked at the doctor, who looked relieved. "You know how I feel about it," he told her. "I have a well-established practice, Miss Oxford. I don't want to lose my license. From what I hear, this Kirkland family has enough money and power to put us both out of business."

Miss Oxford sighed deeply, looking back at Elly. "You've been through so much, you poor child. We'll do whatever you want."

"What I want is for no one to know. And . . . I'd like to be alone for a little while, please?" She looked at Dr. Morrow. "Can't you come back a little later? I'm so tired. I want to sleep a little more."

He smiled and nodded. "You're a brave young lady," he told her. "Foolish and too trusting, though, I'll wager, and apparently you trusted some scoundrel who doesn't deserve you. I'm just sorry you had to learn such a hard, cruel lesson from it. Thank you for understanding I only did what I had to do."

"I do understand." Elly closed her eyes, wanting them to leave. Miss Oxford and the doctor looked at each other in secret relief, turning to leave the room quietly. As soon as they were gone, Elly wiped away the remaining tears and grinned in spite of her pain. Her worry over children and getting pregnant was gone! Without even knowing it, Dr. Morrow had done her a great favor! If she could just get well now, keep this secret from her family, everything would be perfect! The doctor and Miss Oxford would never tell. She could see it in their eyes. They were too afraid of losing their jobs. Even here in Chicago she could wield the Kirkland power!

She put a hand to her stomach. No scars! Soon she would be well. She would go back to Denver a new woman, more free than she had ever been—free to be with Chad whenever she wanted!

Eighteen sixty-seven and 1868 were years of turmoil and hasty decisions for Denver and Colorado. A few faint-hearted citizens quickly headed north, but Kirk and other Denver power figures worked with Byers through the newspaper to help calm the panic caused by the news about the Union Pacific. Meeting after meeting was held. It was agreed a new rail line must be built from

Denver to Cheyenne, and the Denver Pacific Railroad Company was soon organized.

Letters were sent to Washington, and Kirk was delegated to go to Washington and plead Denver's case, resulting in a federal land grant that opened the route north. Bea and a number of Denver businessmen negotiated a series of complicated and intricate financial deals, raising over five hundred thousand dollars in bonds. To Bea's personal delight, Denver even managed to acquire additional capital from none other than the Union Pacific, by agreeing to allow the railroad to use their tracks to come to Denver. Eventually the Denver Pacific would link up with the Kansas Pacific, and a virtual circular connection with the East and South would be accomplished.

What appeared to be a tragedy had actually led to great progress for Denver. The city's citizens, and those of outlying communities, had proven to themselves that by working together they could overcome great obstacles. Building the railroad line that would connect them to the rest of the country was proof that Denver would never fold as had so many other gold towns. They had been tempered now by fire and water, had come together, in spite of their differences, to fight toward one goal—the preservation of the Queen City of the West. And now that the Civil War was over, even the Indian problem had improved. More federal soldiers were sent west, and more forts had been erected. New campaigns were being waged against the Sioux and Cheyenne, and Denver citizens took hope that soon there would be no more threat from the "savages" of the plains.

The hard work involved in seeing Denver's railroad dreams realized kept Chad busier than ever, and working so closely with Bea and Kirk kept him closer to home. Irene actually felt a new hope that their marriage would improve and survive, and that hope was encouraged by their working together for the common cause bringing her own parents closer. Even Kirk had stayed home much longer than he ever had before, working night and day with her mother on the tremendous project of building a railroad. Anyone could see Bea and Kirk had been drawn closer, that there was a new energy in their marriage, a new light in Bea's eyes. For the first time in years, Kirk was putting all his energy into the business and into saving Denver. Irene was not sure of all the reasons. What had seemed to spark him was the break in his friendship with Red McKinley. It was almost as though her mother and father shared some secret, as though they were working to protect something—something more than just Denver and Kirkland Enterprises.

Irene was saddened that Red McKinley had become an enemy, for reasons she supposed she would never understand. But she was happy to see her parents were closer than they had been in years. Kirk was turning to Bea for help in handling the financial aspects of the railroad. Bea was in turn looking to Kirk for strength and energy, and depending on his likable nature to create the enthusiasm necessary to raise money. It was Kirk who talked to individual businessmen, convincing them the railroad could be built and encouraging them not to abandon Denver. It was Bea who managed the money, making sure the entire project was so well handled that those who had invested the most heavily, including themselves, would eventually realize tremendous profits from the railroad connection.

December of 1868 was a Christmas of celebration. To Irene's great joy, her doctor told her that she was three months' pregnant. The railroad was progressing rapidly, her parents were getting along famously, and Chad, who as far as Irene could tell, had not strayed in weeks, appeared to be delighted over the coming baby. She was sure that at last her marriage was on the right track, that the child would create a new bond between her and Chad, perhaps even help draw out his hidden emotions and make it easier for him to express his feelings. She had almost forgiven him for their wedding night, and his other women, for he had planted the seed in her womb that would give her the child she so longed to have.

On Christmas Eve there was a warmth in the Kirkland mansion that Irene had never felt before. Denver was on the rebound, Irene was pregnant, and life was very good. After they attended Christmas Eve church services, and ate a late Christmas meal, Bea read a letter from Elly, who had decided to stay another year at the finishing school. Unlike Irene, Elly was determined to gain as much schooling as possible, planning to move into management of some aspect of Kirkland Enterprises as soon as she came back home. She explained in the letter that all she wanted was to be a knowledgeable businesswoman when she came home, to be able to contribute as much as Chad and her mother to the family business.

Bea glowed with pride at the letter, and only Irene suspected it was Elly's way of winning her mother's confidence and attention. She mentioned to Chad that night that she was sorry for Elly, who she suspected had always felt a little neglected. She would never know the twinge of guilt the statement brought to her husband, who just the day before had written to Elly to tell her how much he missed their liaisons. Irene still had no idea her husband had slept many times with her own sister in their bed. Nor did she know that the reason Chad had been home more at nights was because his latest affair was with his secretary, Milicent Delaney, who gladly obliged him in the back room of Kirkland Enterprises. He didn't worry that Milicent would give away their secret. After all, she had a husband and three children of her own. She wanted their affair to remain secret as much as Chad did.

Chad felt smugly satisfied. He had found a replacement for Elly, while putting on a show of the happy father-to-be. At least this was a baby he could acknowledge and take credit for, and Irene's pregnancy was proof to the outside world that they had a happy marriage.

The only dark spot for Irene on that Christmas of 1868 was that no one had heard from John in months. He was twenty now and had been gone four years, choosing to stay at school year-round so that he could finish sooner. "I can't come home," he had written Irene once. "I hate it here in the East, hate the weather, hate what I'm doing. If I come home, I'll never come back and finish, and dear old Mother wouldn't like that, would she?"

Progress reports from Harvard showed John was doing well scholastically, but the few letters Irene had received showed a despondent young man who was not living the life he would have chosen, and she worried about his drinking. Six months ago the letters had stopped completely, and Bea had said she would "check into it," complaining that John had never been a very grateful son.

Irene tried not to fret over John, not wanting to let herself get too upset. She wanted to stay happy and calm, to take no chances with her pregnancy. She wanted this child more than she had ever wanted anything in her life. She was sure the baby would change everything for her marriage. Chad seemed so happy, was so much more attentive. With a baby to hold and love and nurture, she was sure she could at last find the happiness that had so far eluded her.

Winter of 1868 passed into spring of 1869, and because the rest of the family was busy with the new railroad company, Irene took over the projects closer to home, one of which was the building of yet another new Methodist church. The family's chosen church had again outgrown its capacity, and a much bigger, grander building was being planned. They had come a long way from the little log building in which the Reverend Stanner had preached. Irene offered to head the committee to raise funds and take bids for the project, and in March of 1869, a meeting was called to talk to various contractors.

In spite of her growing belly, Irene felt good, and she took on the project with enthusiasm, hoping to have her baby christened in the new church. She sat at the front of the current church with the other members of the committee, while members and bidders filed inside for the meeting. She opened the meeting herself, explaining what the church wanted to do, apologizing for the absence of her parents and husband.

She looked up when the door opened to allow yet another member of the public inside, and her words stuck in her throat when she saw who had just entered. She stared at him in such surprise that others turned to look, deciding Mrs. Jacobs's sudden speechlessness was due to the fact that a Mexican man, most likely a Catholic, had entered the building.

Ramon Vallejo looked back at Irene with equal surprise. He had not known this was her church, or that she was on the planning committee for the building project in which he was interested. He had been back in Denver only a few days. He had become good friends with Jack Scotland, a wealthy Irish-Catholic who attended mass at the grand cathedral he had built in Los Angeles and who had contacted several of Denver's elite to suggest that Ramon Vallejo was the best man for any major building project. It was an excellent connection that promised to secure Ramon a permanent niche among Denver's upper echelon.

Ramon had returned a rich man. Irene stared at a tall, dark, even more handsome man than the one who had left. He wore a dark silk suit and a white ruffled front shirt. He had changed, his physique more manly now, and his skin even darker from the California sun.

Their eyes met and held for a moment, both of them in near shock. Irene had not expected ever to see him again, and Ramon had not expected to encounter her so soon after returning, or to see her heavy with child—Chad Jacobs's child. He was almost stunned at the stab of jealousy the sight brought to his soul. He had been so sure, after being gone four years, that he had finally gotten over her, that it was safe to come back to Denver—safe for his heart.

Now, here she stood, as beautiful as ever, but pregnant with another man's baby. So, the marriage must be improving, he thought. That was good—for Irene. He moved into a pew and sat down, feeling the stares of others. Irene somehow managed to find her voice and finish her talk. Questions were raised and answered, and bids were made. Suddenly Ramon wanted the job more than ever, just because this was Irene's church. It didn't matter to him that it was a Protestant church. He would do as beautiful a job as possible, because it would be Irene's place of worship, the place where she found the faith and the hope and the courage she must need to be a wife to Chad Jacobs.

The bidding began, and Ramon deliberately bid lower than any of the others. One of the wealthier men of the church stood up and spoke in favor of Ramon, describing the letter he'd received from Jack Scotland, who vouched for Ramon's excellent skills. "I even have pictures of the cathedral Mr. Vallejo built in Los Angeles," the man said. "If I had known he was going to be here tonight, I would have brought them with me. The work the man did on that church is beyond description in beauty and design. He even carved a huge, twenty-foot crucifix, and we all know how difficult it has to be to carve a human face."

"That's just the point," another man said, rising. "The man is Mexican. He's Catholic. We can't have a Catholic man building a Protestant church."

"I don't think God cares about his race or religion," one woman said. "He might be Catholic, but he worships the same God as we do. And we all know that it is about time, as Christians, that we accept people of other races. After all, the Mexicans were here first. Unlike the Indians, they have never caused us trouble, not here, anyway."

Arguments flew back and forth. Finally one man asked Ramon directly if he was such a skilled builder, why was he bidding so low? Ramon glanced at Irene, and she knew the real reason. Her heart rushed with awakened memories, with an old love she now, more than ever, must not show. She was carrying Chad's child, had been another man's wife for four years.

Ramon turned to the man who had questioned him. "My reasons are personal," he said. "I could ask much more, and I would deserve it. However, in this case, I wish to do the Christian thing. This is a church, not a place of business. This will be God's house. Besides that, I feel I owe it to Denver. This is my home, and I am happy to be back here where my roots are deep. I am making this offer as a gesture of affection for Denver and for Colorado." He looked around at the others. "I can assure you, I will do as fine a job for your Protestant church as I did for the Catholic cathedral in Los Angeles. The only thing I ask to make up for my low price is that if you are as pleased with my work as I think you will be, you all will give me your support and recommendations for other building projects in the city." He looked at Irene again. "I have come back to Denver to stay, and I will be opening my own contracting business here."

As he sat back down, he gave her a gentle smile. She wondered if he had found a wife in Los Angeles, or if he was still single. She told herself it didn't matter. When the vote was taken, the room was divided. The deciding vote was Irene's.

"Mr. Vallejo did a lot of work on my parents' mansion," she said, "and he built my present home. I can vouch for his expertise. Considering the fact that we must always watch our budget because of Denver's constantly unpredictable economy, I feel we must take the lowest bid, especially when it comes from someone I feel could rightfully ask the most money. He is indeed worth every penny. My vote is for Mr. Vallejo."

People began filing out once the meeting ended. Some stopped to shake Ramon's hand; others shied away from him, still not certain that a Catholic man should build their Methodist church. Irene waited her turn, feeling overheated, in spite of the chilly, wet March night. She felt a little uncomfortable in her condition, finding pregnancy, as did many other women, somewhat embarrassing proof that she had been with a man, even though it was her own husband. Somehow it was even more embarrassing in front of Ramon.

She wondered how he felt now, if everything had changed. Of course it had. He had been gone four years. They had both matured. She was twenty-two years old, and Ramon must be at least twenty-six now. It had been six years since . . . since that stolen kiss. They were practically children then, weren't they?

Suddenly she was in front of him. He took her hand, squeezing it warmly, his gentle, handsome smile still able to melt her heart. "Thank you for your vote, Mrs. Jacobs," he told her, aware there were people around them.

"You're welcome, Mr. Vallejo," she answered, angry that her eyes were damp with tears.

Ramon could feel her trembling slightly. He squeezed her hand more firmly in a kind of reassurance that everything was all right. "I will do a good job for you," he told her.

"I'm sure you will," she replied.

He reluctantly let go of her hand, talking to a few others, finding excuses, as Irene did, to linger, until at last he and Irene were the only ones left. She pulled her shawl around her shoulders self-consciously, letting it hang over her belly as though to hide it.

"So," he said, his eyes moving over her, "you are with child. Is it your first?"

"Yes," she answered, dropping her eyes. "We've . . . tried for a long time. I was beginning to wonder if something was wrong." She felt her face grow hot with embarrassment.

"I am glad for you," he said gently. "You must be happy then."

How could she tell him that this baby was her only hope for happiness, that she prayed it would bring the closeness she and Chad had never had, that her husband was a notorious womanizer? What business was it of his anymore? What right did she have talking about her marriage to this man who was supposed to be out of her life now?

"Yes," she lied.

Ramon sensed a strain. He knew she was probably lying, but did he have any right to question her further about it?

"Irene," he said softly, "I did not know you were on this committee."

"It's all right," she answered, putting on a confident smile. "I'm glad you're back in Denver, and that you're here to stay. I'm equally glad to have you building this church. Chad and I will help you get started any other way we can, just as Chad promised before you left."

She was trying to be so strong, so nonchalant about his return. He looked at her lovingly. "I did not come here to make trouble, or to upset anyone," he assured her. "I missed Colorado." *And I missed you,* he wished he could add. But there must be no more such talk. They both sensed that. "Irene, I just want to tell you—we will both always hold fond memories. No one else needs to know about our . . . special secret. But I do not want you to feel uncomfortable or embarrassed about it. I would like to be able to be friends."

"Yes, I want that too. Considering my activity in the community, and that you will be involved in other building projects, we have to find some kind of happy compromise, don't we? After all, we might end up working together again."

He nodded, longing to hold her, to kiss her again, wondering if she was longing for the same. He put out his hand. "Friends?"

She took it, her own hand trembling. As soon as he wrapped his hand around hers, she felt a strength, a warming comfort. He would do his best not to cause her undue pain, she was sure. Ramon was back, and they could at least be friends. "*Amigos,*" she answered with a smile. She detected tears in his eyes, but neither of them would say anything more about their feelings. It was forbidden now more than ever. "You look wonderful, Ramon. California must have been good for you."

He nodded. "I did a lot of healing there. I found a new strength when I was working on the crucifix, and I know in my heart that I am forgiven for . . . for the hurt I caused Elena. I learned to live with the pain of losing my son, who is at least with his mother and will not suffer the heartaches and pain we who live are often doomed to suffer."

She folded her arms, self-conscious of her belly and her ballooning breasts. "Have you remarried? You should, you know."

A sadness filled his eyes. "I had little time in Los Angeles to think about women." He smiled briefly, and both of them reddened slightly, realizing there was only one woman he had ever really wanted. "Perhaps, in time, I will think about it again. But no, right now there is no one special."

Why was she glad of that? He deserved happiness, and she had no right wishing that he stay single. What did it matter to her now? The man should find love again, should have companionship, children to take little Juan's place in his heart, if that was possible.

"Thank you so much for the horse. I have it sitting on a fireplace mantel," she told him. "I will always cherish it—and the words of your letter. I . . . destroyed the letter."

He nodded. "It is best. I am glad you like the horse."

Chad came inside then, having come to pick up Irene. He was surprised to see Ramon, and he thought at first that Irene and Ramon were looking at each other rather intimately. But he brushed away the notion, realizing they were, after all, old friends. He greeted Ramon warmly, shaking his hand vigorously and asking about his work in Los Angeles. He wondered how Ramon would feel if he knew Bea Kirkland was the one who had stolen Hacienda del Sur from under his grandfather's feet, that Chad had handled the illegal paperwork. Still, he liked Ramon, and he echoed Irene's promise to help Ramon's business grow.

The three of them exited the church together, and Chad helped Irene into the waiting carriage. Ramon was glad to see the man seemed to be doting on her and appeared to be very happy that he would soon be a father. Chad turned to Ramon before the buggy drove off. "I can't wait to tell my mother-in-law who has been chosen to build the new church. Bea will be in a dither over this one, but I'm glad to have you aboard, Ramon."

Chad tipped his hat and entered the carriage, quickly driving

off. Ramon smiled at another secret victory. Yes, he had offered
to do this project for far lower than its worth—only for Irene's
sake, once he realized it was her church. But he was getting a
bonus, and it wasn't just good advertising. This was Bea Kirkland's church. He was getting an unexpected payment from this
job. This would stick in her craw even more than the fact that he
had built Irene's home.

Ramon Vallejo was back in Denver to stay. He had money and
prestige now, and good backing. The day was fast arriving when
Bea Kirkland would no longer be able to look down her nose at
him. He imagined her reaction when she heard the news about the
church. His little victories over Bea Kirkland made the pain of
returning and having to face Irene again more bearable. If he could
not put his energy into loving Irene, he would put it into his very
pleasurable revenge against her mother.

"She will be in a 'dither,' all right," he muttered, watching the
carriage clatter off into the darkness, wondering if Irene had
looked back at him. He could not see her.

CHAPTER
TWENTY-SIX

May 1869

Cattle had become big business in the state, with three hundred thousand head of beef now rambling over the vast, rolling hills of eastern and southern Colorado. The B&K Ranch was one of the biggest and best managed, thanks to Hank Loring. With cattle selling for twenty dollars a head, Bea was realizing tremendous profits.

The Overland Stage Company had sold out to Wells Fargo, which was now one of the biggest transportation companies in the West—and one in which Bea was an important stockholder. The company was competing with the railroad, but continued to do well by running connections into mining towns and other places where the railroad still could not go.

A rival newspaper to Bill Byers's *Rocky Mountain News,* called the *Denver Tribune,* opened its offices in Denver. The Denver Horse and Railway Company would soon complete its tracks and hoped to be in business by 1870. More industry had moved into Denver, and farmers were learning how to use Colorado's unique soil to the best advantage, producing more food and decreasing the state's reliance on outside sources.

The city of Denver remained in many ways a rough prairie town, yet it had theaters now, a library, churches, and schools. The Kirkland mansion sat stalwartly among other elaborate but less ostentatious houses on Kirkland Hills, overlooking an amalgamation of office buildings and shacks. The city was a grand mixture, a crude mining town still struggling for prestige and respect, as well as a place of beauty and opportunity, where gold in the nearby mountains was still plentiful. The city's tills were enriched by foreign investment, due to heavy advertising abroad as the fastest-growing city in the West. Bea contemplated making a trip to Europe as a city representative, to look for even more foreign backing. She kept close watch on the New York Stock Exchange, upon which Kirkland Enterprises had begun selling shares. However, to protect the business in case of a stock market crash, Bea kept seventy percent of the company holdings in the family. She still did not fully trust the stock market, could not bring herself to put "her" company into the hands of thousands of stockholders who were strangers to her.

She moved cautiously when it came to stocks, preferring to keep her own investments right in Denver. K-E had expanded its offices, which now took up half a city block, and Bea had hired six more men. She had begun helping other businesses make investments, opening her own brokerage firm so that she could keep a close eye on New York. Seventeenth Street, in Denver, where the K-E offices were located, had been nicknamed the Wall Street of the West.

The biggest drawback to getting too involved in the real Wall Street was the current administration under President Grant. Grant was showing himself to be a weak president who did not know how to control Congress. His administration seemed totally untrustworthy. Nearly every day the newspapers carried stories of scandal. The value of paper money fluctuated dramatically. Bribes and payoffs by large corporations, and especially the railroad, to men in government were rumored, and Bea did not doubt the stories. Durant and his Union Pacific were the supreme example of monopoly and corruption. After the insult the UP had handed Denver, Bea would forever consider them an enemy, in spite of the Denver Pacific's deal with the UP to use their lines.

Bea never saw her own underhanded dealings as wrong, just as necessary to protect the family. It was the other big businesses who were the scoundrels, and the most notorious was the railroad, of whose power Bea was almost jealous. It made her furious that the railroad could make or break a community through freight rates; yet she encouraged such threatening tactics within the Denver Pacific to wheel and deal with Denver politicians and businesses. The railroad had almost omnipotent power because of their monopoly over freighting, especially in the West, where people and businesses were dependent on them. Bea did not doubt that Tom Durant and other railroad magnates were reaping incredible profits and paying off the right people to hold their powerful monopoly together. She did not consider the fact that in Denver she had her own monopoly. K-E was at the helm of so many banks and businesses that few other businesses or municipal agencies could make a move without her permission or without affecting K-E.

The latest K-E venture was an investment in a water project that would bring fresh water from the mountains to Denver. The Platte River and Cherry Creek were becoming badly polluted, with few sanitary laws in effect. Most of Denver's elite were still too intent on getting rich to worry about the more common concerns, like water pollution, littered streets, industrial waste, and the like. But already the city's new hospital had too many cases of sickness and disease from poor sanitation, and Bea could see the growing need for water, not just clean water, but *enough* water, period, to supply Denver's burgeoning population. She was now the biggest investor in K-E Water Company, in which she had encouraged others to invest, and engineers now worked in the mountains to bring water to Denver. As soon as the Denver Pacific was completed and the celebrations were over, Kirk would be going to the mountains to oversee the project, which would include a series of dams. It would be a magnificent undertaking, one that would require considerable outside investment in the long run, but one that would surely prove as profitable as would the Denver Pacific.

Work was also progressing on steam-powered, pumped water throughout the city, most of it coming from the Platte. Knowledgeable men, hired from universities across the country, were working on ways to clean up the drinking water. Foreign investments were helping with the costs of the project. A municipally owned and operated gas company was also in the works, and plans were laid to light Denver's streets with gas lights by 1871.

Bea leaned back in her chair, looking across the long, now empty oak table in the K-E boardroom. She had just ended a board meeting to discuss the many branches of the company, and she felt the warm glow of accomplishment. All of this had come from those months of scrubbing clothes in the foothills of the Sierras. She studied her hands, which would never be beautiful, and she thought what a long way she and Kirk had come since first agreeing to marry. They had had some very bad times, had never had a really loving marriage, but the Denver Pacific and Denver's fight not to be defeated by the UP had brought new life to her marriage, and she had gleaned a new respect for her husband.

They had been too long separate sexually to come together that way now. Perhaps they never would again. At thirty-nine, with gray at the temples and even more weight on her heavy frame, she doubted she was much inspiration to him. Kirk, on the other hand, had remained hard and strong and handsome. Sometimes she actually wanted him again, but she was afraid to tell him so.

She thought how at least Chad and Irene were happy. Irene's baby was due in another month, and Bea could hardly wait to be a grandmother.

The only shadow on all the good things that were happening was that Ramon Vallejo was back in Denver. Bea was certain the man could no longer interfere with Irene's happiness. It had been six years since her silly crush on him.

Still, it annoyed her that Ramon was back at all, and a rich man, no less. He was certainly far less wealthy than the Kirklands and could probably never hope to come close to such wealth, but he was a fast-rising businessman, backed by people with a good deal of money, and she had been forced to sell him lumber from her own mill.

It infuriated her that it was Ramon who was building the new Methodist church, but she could not publicly do a thing about it without causing suspicion, and Ramon knew it. It worried her a little that Irene had been instrumental in hiring him. She was sure it was only out of old friendships, and because Ramon was a talented builder (much as Bea hated to admit it), but there was a little nagging worry that Irene had given the deciding vote for deeper reasons. Bea had never quite gotten over the faint guilt of shattering her daughter's heart years ago when she sent Ramon away. She realized that such unrequited love could sometimes be dangerous.

Such thoughts were foolish. Irene had Chad, and a new baby coming. Nothing could keep a woman's heart where it belonged more than that. Chad was so wonderful, and Irene was so excited about the baby. Bea decided her fears were unjustified, and attributed them to her own jealousy and chagrin that Ramon had managed to amount to something. She had hoped to be permanently rid of him, and now he was back in Denver, pricking at her like a burr under a saddle. She had to stop thinking about him and get back to the business at hand. The UP was expected to be connected any day now at Promontory Point, Utah, with great ceremony, and at the same time the Denver Pacific would also be completed. Denver had its own celebrations planned. The UP had not defeated the Queen City. If anything, Denver was stronger than ever.

Irene left the meeting of the Ladies Union Aid Society early. Chad had told her he had to work late tonight, and she hated the thought of going home to an empty house. There was too much excitement in the air over the coming celebrations. She wondered if perhaps Chad would like to go out to eat at the Denver Inn. She could help him finish his paperwork at the office, so he could get out early, and they could have a quiet, elegant dinner out.

Life had been so much better lately. She had more confidence than ever in her marriage, and it had even been easier to be near Ramon on the several occasions they'd had to work together on the church project. The old feelings might never go away, but the pain was made more bearable by having a husband who seemed to have become what she had always wanted. And now there was the baby. She had only one month to go, and she felt good. There had been no complications.

She ordered her driver to take the carriage to the K-E offices, where she disembarked, noticing the lamps were not lit in the main lobby. She had her own key to the building, and she quietly let herself in, closing and locking the door behind her. Denver might be progressing rapidly, but the streets were still not safe at night. The many saloons were always busy, and a number of poor, homeless people roamed the streets. Muggings and robberies were common. Bea gave strict instructions that if anyone worked late, he or she must always lock the main door to the building.

Irene made her way up the stairs to the door to Chad's office, where she thought she heard voices. She frowned, listening closer, hearing a woman's laughter, then a shuddering sigh. A sick feeling began to invade her stomach. She wanted to be wrong, needed to be sure, for she had been so happy these past several months.

She opened the door, horror immediately engulfing her when she caught her husband in the throes of lovemaking with Milicent Delaney, his secretary, both of them stark naked. Chad looked up in surprise, and Milicent gasped, leaping up and grabbing her dress to cover herself. "Irene," Chad said weakly.

Irene turned and ran out. "Wait," she heard Chad call out. She did not stop. She staggered to the top of the stairs, the ugly picture blazing in her mind. Chad! Why was she so surprised? She had known there had been others, but somehow thinking they were only one-night stands with whores seemed to make it easier to accept. But this . . . this had probably been going on for a long time. This was probably the only reason Chad had been home more—he had a more convenient lover!

She felt she would be sick. Milicent! The woman was married and had three children! She and Chad had even invited them to their home for dinner once—Chad and Milicent had acted as though everything was strictly business between them. Seeing it with her own eyes made it all so ugly, so unbearable.

"Irene," she heard Chad call again. He appeared at the doorway, still fumbling at the buttons of his pants. "Irene, you don't understand it all."

She turned to look at him. "I understand everything, Chad. Everything."

He came closer, and at the moment she could not bear the thought of him touching her. She stepped back, in her horror and humiliation forgetting where she was standing. Her heel slipped over the top step of the wooden stairway, and the next thing she knew she was falling, screaming, pain ripping through her as she rolled and tumbled down the stairs. In her awkward condition, she could do nothing to stop herself. Her head slammed against something as she landed at the bottom of the stairs, and everything went blessedly black.

Irene stirred, and immediately every part of her hurt, especially her head. She tried to think, to say something, then remembered the horrible picture of Chad and Milicent's naked bodies. "Chad," she muttered.

Bea leaned over her daughter, thinking she was calling for her husband out of pain and need. "Irene! Thank God you're conscious," her mother told her. "I'll get Chad. He's been beside himself with worry."

Irene tried to object. She did not want to see her husband, not for a long, long time. The next thing she knew he was standing over her, leaning close. They were alone in the white hospital room. She turned her face away.

"Irene," he said quietly. "You've got to let me explain. There are things about me you don't understand."

"I hate you," she groaned, at the moment meaning every word. How strange that she had never hated anyone in her life, and now she was saying those cruel words to her own husband, the man she had vowed to love forever. "Go away, Chad."

"Irene—" She could tell he was crying. "My God, Irene, I was happy about the baby. I swear to God I was. I just . . . I wanted to be sure everything went all right. I couldn't make love to you because of the baby."

He couldn't even abstain because of the baby, she thought. *He couldn't go without for a few weeks. What kind of animal have I married?*

"It wasn't . . . just the baby," he told her. "When you're better, Irene, we'll talk. I'm sorry, Irene. At least . . . at least you don't have any broken bones—just a lot of bad bruises, and a slight concussion." She heard him sniff. "Damn it, Irene, a man is just a man . . . he has needs . . . it had nothing to do with how I feel about you . . . or how I felt about the baby."

A horrible suspicion began to creep into her veins because of the way he kept mentioning the baby. The baby! That was all she had now, but . . . vague memories flooded her muddled mind now. She had been unconscious, yet aware of something—a terrible pain, much worse than the pain in her bones from the fall. It was a deep, ripping pain. . . . She slowly put a hand to her stomach, realizing then with horror that it was nearly back to its normal size. She had given birth!

She opened bloodshot eyes to see Chad's blurred face leaning over her. "Where's . . . my baby?" she asked.

Real tears slipped out of his eyes, as he grasped her hands. "You . . . you lost it," he said, practically sobbing. "It came early, because of the fall. It couldn't live, Irene. It was still too small. It was . . . a little girl."

She just stared at him, letting the gruesome reality sink into her confused mind. The baby! Gone, just like that, like a puff of wind. All those months of carrying it, being so careful, feeling her baby move inside her womb, dreaming of bringing her child home to the beautiful nursery she and Chad had designed. She thought for an instant how this reminded her of her wedding night, of the horror her husband had brought her. Now he was doing it again. Again he had brought pain, and an ugly memory that would last a lifetime. The first time was forgivable. This time was not.

She pulled her hands away, covering her face, breaking into pitiful, deep sobs that racked her sore body.

"My God, Irene, I'm so sorry. I wish . . . I wish there was some way I could make up for it—"

"Get out," she groaned. "Just get out." Her baby! Her precious baby! How long ago had it happened? Was it already buried? She would never even get to see it! The tears came so hard then that she could barely catch her breath between sobs, and her chest felt on fire. She heard other voices then, as more people came into the room—heard her mother fussing, heard Kirk's voice.

"It's going to be all right, Irene," she heard Kirk saying then. She felt his strong hands on her arms. "You'll have more children. The doctor says there is no reason why you can't."

First I have to have a husband who loves me—a man whose seed I want to carry. "Hold me, Father," she sobbed. Kirk thought it strange she should turn to him and not her husband, but he decided she was in such a bad state she could not think straight. He leaned down and put his arms around her, and it was her father who brought her the only slight comfort she knew for the moment.

Chad watched with horrible dread, expecting that any minute Irene would spill the truth, but she said nothing. He prayed she was too ashamed. Although he hated the idea of her being ashamed of him, the thought of everyone knowing the truth was much worse. The last person he wanted to face with the truth was Bea Kirkland. "Maybe the doctor should give her something to make her sleep now," he spoke up. He hoped to keep her quiet until she was more stable and he could reason with her.

Bea patted her daughter's hair and looked at the doctor. "Can you give her anything more to put her out of her pain?" she asked the man.

"Perhaps a little more laudanum, but not too much."

Bea leaned down and kissed Irene's cheek. "We'll be right here the rest of the night, Irene. Oh why, oh why, didn't you just go straight home last night? You shouldn't even have been at that Ladies Society meeting in the first place. Oh, this is so terrible, and just when we had so much to celebrate."

Last night. So, it had been at least twenty-four hours.

"She probably was figuring on surprising me," she heard Chad saying. "It could have been such a wonderful night for us. But I've told her and told her not to come to the office and climb those stairs in her condition."

Now she knew why he had wanted her to stay away from the office. She thought how smoothly he lied, imagined how cleverly he had gotten out of any blame for this. Had he hurriedly sent Milicent scurrying out a back door before he fetched a doctor? Had he let her lie helpless while he dressed himself properly before anyone could see him?

Chad! The nausea came to her stomach again at the ugly

memory: the naked bodies; Milicent, lying there on the floor with her legs spread for another woman's husband, while the woman's own husband sat home with her children waiting for her.

"I want to go to the mountains, Father," she said weakly, feeling as vulnerable as the young woman who had made that trip, wanting to be that girl again, wanting to start over. "Take me to the mountains."

"She's getting delirious," she heard Bea saying, "Oh, Chad, you poor darling." She heard the woman sobbing then. A man was crying. Chad. Was he crying because he was sorry, because he had lost a child? Or was he crying because he had been caught, because he was scared to death Irene would tell on him? He could be strong and intelligent and even brave, but now she saw him only as weak and stupid and cowardly. He suddenly wasn't even handsome any more.

Someone gave her something bitter to drink, and soon the blessed blackness returned, that floating, other world where she didn't have to think about what hurt, or think about the baby that would never be.

Irene could hear the celebrating in the streets, here and there a gunshot and a rowdy, rebel yell. The transcontinental railroad had been completed, and now the Denver Pacific.

"We have to be there," Bea had told her of the party planned at the mansion. "We've had this planned for so long, darling. But I'll be back tomorrow."

It had been three days since losing the baby, three days of hell and pain. She wanted her family with her, but, after all, there were other things to tend to. She knew they all loved and sympathized with her, but they didn't really understand the magnitude of her grief, for it was grossly enhanced by the memory of what had caused her to lose the baby. Everyone thought she was despondent because of her loss, that her injuries had only made her even weaker. No one knew the secret grief she suffered.

Chad came to see her only because he had to appear to be the doting, concerned husband. He even put on a good show of grief, but he very wisely did not get too close. He knew his entire future and career hung by the thread of Irene's choosing whether or not to tell the truth. She was not sure yet herself just what she would do about Chad. She was tempted to tell her parents everything, yet that seemed too childish. This was her problem, although she could not help resenting her mother for pushing so hard for the marriage in the first place.

She felt trapped. Divorce was shameful, unheard of. Most people tended to blame a soured marriage on the wife. Chad would probably come out of it untouched by the scandal. After all, her family was the one with money, and people loved to gossip about the rich. All kinds of stories would circulate, none of them good, about how the poor, hard-working Chad Jacobs had not been good enough for a Kirkland. Or perhaps his wife was a cold fish who didn't know how to please a man. Was she? She had tried so hard to love him, had never turned him away, had overlooked painful infidelities. Who would understand the agonizing memories she suffered over her wedding night? Even if she managed to tell the truth about her husband, people would smirk and whisper and maybe even pity her. Pity was to her as unbearable as vicious gossip.

Either way, she would suffer. Her family was already too much in the limelight. What would normally be simply shameful in getting a divorce would only be magnified tenfold.

Besides, there was her determination not to fail. Maybe this horrible event would set Chad on the straight and narrow at last. It would take her months, maybe years, to forgive him, if he should be repentant and stay in his own bed. But it seemed possible, if only she could believe the terrible sorrow in his eyes. She could not imagine he could have no feelings about losing the baby. He had truly seemed to be in considerable grief, had cried when he told her about the baby's funeral, how beautiful it was, what a lovely headstone he had erected at the little grave.

How much was a wife expected to put up with? She had made vows, for better or for worse. But her marriage couldn't get much worse than this. Chad had begged her forgiveness, had told her it had been only a recent affair, had admitted he had been weak, that he had let Milicent go, that it would never happen again. He had carried on about how Irene was the best thing that had ever happened to him. He had tried to explain there were certain things she had to understand about men, that many husbands strayed, but only because they didn't want to impose upon their wives, that it was hard for a proper woman to respond to a man as often as he needed her to. He had told her it was different for men than it was for women, that his infidelities had been to spare her, that he always meant to keep them discreet and would never deliberately hurt her.

It was only the very last statement that she believed—that he truly never meant to hurt her. But hurt her he had, and she could not help feeling an engulfing sorrow, that somehow she must have failed her own marriage. She felt empty, numb, sick. She had no baby feeding at her breast, nothing left to love.

Tonight everyone she knew was happy and celebrating. She could understand her parents' responsibility to be at the mansion. What hurt was she knew Chad was at that party, probably putting on a show of great sorrow, but celebrating, nonetheless, flashing his charming smile at women, winning their devoted sympathy.

Again, in her hour of real need, he was not here. Again, he had left her with another ugly memory, only to let her wrestle with it alone, in secret agony, just as on their wedding night.

The loss of a baby was something a husband and wife should share quietly, together. They should be able to draw strength from each other, but she felt nothing from Chad, and she had nothing to give in return. It was impossible to believe everything he told her. He resembled a shell, beautiful to look at from the outside, but empty inside.

The agony of her situation, and the terrible loss of the child, again brought on a wave of bitter sobbing. Life hardly seemed worth living now, and she could understand how easy suicide might be after all. Had Susan Stanner felt this desperate, this trapped, this alone?

She sensed someone come into the room then, but her back was to the door. In the next moment a hand touched her shoulder. "I hope I do not overstep my bounds by coming to see you, *mi querida*," she heard Ramon's voice say. "I wanted to tell you how sorry I am for your loss."

She turned, hardly able to see him for the tears. "Ramon," she whispered. She was in a private room, and no one else was around. He leaned down and scooped her into his arms, moving to sit on the bed while she wept against his shoulder.

Ramon was here! Always it was Ramon who gave her the comfort her husband should be giving her. He had heard of her loss, and he had come. He had lost a son. He understood.

"You must cry," he whispered. "Cry and cry and let it all go." He stroked her hair. "And then you must turn to God. Only the Christ can bring you the comfort you need. He understands all things, and when you feel unloved, He is there to love you."

She did not care if it was right or wrong. Ramon was here and Chad was not. She needed desperately to be held, to feel the strength and genuine love of a man who loved her. "Don't let go, Ramon," she sobbed. "Don't let go."

"I am here. I will not leave until you have wept away all the sorrow."

She clung to his strong arms, let him cradle her, rested against his powerful chest, drew strength and comfort from their poignant, unique friendship. Ramon was here, and although they could not speak of it, she knew he still loved her more than her husband ever could.

There was nothing more to say. He knew no other words could comfort her, just as words could not comfort him when he had lost his wife and son. He simply held her until there were no more tears to cry, listened with horror to her mumbled story of how it had happened, laid her back down, held her hands until she finally slept, stayed by her side until the break of dawn.

He quietly left her, too angry to feel the aching weariness he should be feeling. The streets were quiet, most people sleeping off a heavy drunk from the celebrations. Ramon climbed on his horse and headed for Kirkland Hills and the Jacobses' home. He had something to settle with Chad Jacobs.

CHAPTER
TWENTY-SEVEN

Chad stirred at the sound of Jenny Porter's voice. "Sir, you can't go in there! Mr. Jacobs is sleeping."

"Just show me where his room is," he heard someone answer. "Do it, or I will barge into every room until I find him!" It almost sounded like Ramon Vallejo. Chad frowned, starting to sit up as he heard the voices come closer. The door suddenly burst open, and Chad pulled a sheet over his nakedness while Jenny reddened and turned away.

"I couldn't stop him, Mr. Jacobs," she said, as Ramon stood glaring at Chad. Totally confused by Ramon's sudden animosity, Chad told her to leave and close the door. The woman obeyed, and Chad stared back at Ramon.

"What the hell is this?" he asked. "I thought we were friends, Ramon. What are you doing here this hour of the morning?"

He rubbed his eyes as Ramon stepped closer. "The question is, why are you not at the hospital with your *wife*?" Ramon answered.

Chad frowned, an odd alarm sounding in his head. He threw the sheet aside and began pulling on his long johns. Ramon almost felt sick at the thought of the man's naked body moving over Irene's, confessing love, making her pregnant, while at the same time he slept with other women.

"What the hell does it matter to you whether or not I'm with Irene?" Chad answered, rising to pull up his underwear. He faced

Ramon, his hands on his hips. "Irene has lost a baby, and she's in a pretty bad way. She asked me to leave. She *wants* to be alone."

"*No* woman wants to be alone at a time like this. Maybe you should tell me the *real* reason she does not want you there!"

Chad's face began to darken with anger, his defenses rising. "What's this all about? Matters between my wife and me are none of your damn business, Ramon!"

"I happened to be at the hospital and found out she was there. I went to see her, as an old friend. I found her crying so hard she was making herself even sicker. She was alone, alone at a time when a woman suffers such sorrow she would like to *die*! It is dangerous to leave a woman alone at such a time. She feels she has nothing left to live for."

Chad watched his eyes, man to man. One thing he knew how to read in anyone's eyes was passion, and he saw it in Ramon's eyes. He dropped his hands to his sides, forming fists. "I thought you and Irene were just casual acquaintances. What the hell are you doing here sticking your nose into our private affairs?"

"I care very much about Irene! She and John were my good friends once. Perhaps she did not tell you we were close, because I am Mexican, and she feared it would sound bad. You know how Irene is. She is open to everyone. She is not prejudiced like so many others. Last night I sat with her because she needed the company, and in her terrible sorrow she told me the truth!" He watched Chad redden. "I know the real reason why she lost the baby, and I am here to tell you that if you hurt her so badly again, I will kill you!"

Bitter anger darkened Chad's gray eyes, and he stepped closer. "It's none of your damn business," he snarled. "And Irene had no right telling you! I'm beginning to wonder about this *friendship* you supposedly shared. What the hell went on between you and Irene that I don't know about? What happened back before we met? If you fucked her—"

Chad was not allowed to finish the statement. A hard fist landed into his gut, and another blow cracked against his cheekbone and sent him sprawling back across the bed. Chad saw only a blur as Ramon leaned over him, his dark eyes on fire.

"I would expect filth like you to think the worst," he growled. "Maybe because that is where your dirty mind is always groveling! I have never touched your woman. I am not the kind of scum you are! I do not go around fucking innocent virgins and married women!" He stood up straighter, his fist aching, his breath coming in pants of anger.

Chad rolled to his side, putting a hand to his cheek, then sitting up. His steely gray eyes watched Ramon. "I might remind you that I got you a start in this town. I can finish you just as easily!"

"Your threats do not worry me," Ramon answered. "Or the threats of your mother-in-law! Do you think I don't know who was behind the takeover of Hacienda del Sur? You had better remember that I *also* have good friends in high places. I am gaining my own power. Threaten me all you want, Chad Jacobs, but if you try to ruin me in this town, everyone, including Bea Kirkland, will know the truth about you! I will make sure of it!"

Chad glared at him, hating Irene for telling Ramon, of all people, what had happened. "You bastard," he mumbled. "I called you friend. I really liked you, Ramon."

"I am not the one who changed that. *You* did. You had the chance to have the world in your hands—everything a man could ask for—and you threw it all away because you cannot keep your pants closed! You are weak, and you are too stupid to realize you have the best woman a man could ever want!"

"Irene had no right—"

"Irene has no idea I am here, and I don't even think she realized what she told me. She was practically delirious with grief. I am only here to warn you that you had better start being the husband she deserves, or it is not I who will be ruined in this town. It will be *you*, and I do not think you want to lose your position with the Kirkland empire! We both know that is the only reason you married Irene. A man like you could have had any woman he wanted!"

Chad slowly rose, still rubbing at his cheek, his stomach on fire. "Get out of my house. I won't have a Mexican coming in here ordering me around!"

"Apparently you need someone to tell you what to do! You have not done a very good job on your own!" Ramon's booted foot came up hard, landing in Chad's groin. Chad cried out and went to his knees, then rolled to his side. "*Cabrón!*" Ramon called him bastard before storming out.

Chad moved gingerly when he disembarked the buggy, a sickening ache still plaguing his groin. He could hide the inner wounds, but he couldn't hide the deepening bruise on his left cheek. He decided he would explain that he had gone off riding alone this morning, that his horse had stepped in a hole and thrown him against a fencepost. Bea would swallow the story. She believed everything he told her. Being thrown would also explain why he walked more slowly.

He entered the hospital, feelings of rage and curiosity engulfing him. Why had Irene told Ramon, of all people? What was there between them that he didn't know about? There was no doubt that Irene had been a virgin when he married her. That was a fact no one could dispute. He didn't really even doubt her loyalty since then, but now that she knew about his affair with Milicent, perhaps she would change.

She had been working closely with Ramon on the church project. He didn't like that. It was obvious the casual friendship they had once shared might be turning into something more, and he was not about to be outdone by a Mexican, not by *any* man, for that matter.

His fragile ego had been damaged, his manhood threatened. He couldn't lose Irene, for she represented respect, wealth. She was his proof that he was a fine man, a settled man, a man of honor. He needed Irene to show that he was all the things people expected him to be, and he was not about to give up the Kirkland power and prestige. If Irene left him, telling everyone the truth, he would lose everything. And if he left Irene, claiming she was in love with a Mexican man, Bea would never forgive him for dragging her name through the mud. He would still lose everything.

He had to find a way to keep the marriage together, a way to hang onto Irene. If he ever lost her, it had to be in some way that would leave him looking innocent, some way that would at least keep him on good terms with Bea and keep him employed at Kirkland Enterprises.

He climbed the stairs to Irene's room, wondering if, after all, Irene was not the perfect, unstained woman he thought she was. Maybe there was a reason she was so unresponsive in bed. Maybe it was because she had another man on the side.

Ramon? He could not imagine it. Maybe when she was younger, she had had a fancy for the man. He stopped short at the door. Of course! And he was willing to wager that Bea Kirkland knew about it. That would explain Bea's vehement dislike for Ramon. That would explain why she stole his grandfather's property, why she was always uncomfortable talking about him in front of Chad. Maybe that was why she pushed so hard for them to get married as soon as possible, why she was upset when Chad chose Ramon to build their house.

He quietly opened the door. Irene was asleep. He closed the door and watched her for a while. He could not imagine Irene being untrue to him. It just didn't fit her. No, he decided, nothing had happened . . . yet. And he was not about to *let* it happen. No Mexican was going to move in on his territory—and *no* man was going to show his wife a better time in bed than he could. Old fears of inadequacy surfaced, bringing on near panic. Was it possible he could only please a woman when sin and lust and contempt for the women he bedded were involved? He felt none of those things for Irene, and in return, his rousts in bed with her had never been satisfying—not for him, and certainly not for her. He could tell when a woman was enjoying it, and Irene had never responded the way other women did.

He stepped closer, studying her pale, sad face. The key to saving his marriage, he decided, was to get her out of Denver for a while, away from Ramon. He had to convince her he was totally repentant and would cheat on her no more—and he had to get her pregnant again. She needed a baby to take the place of the one she had lost, and he needed it to prove he was still a man, to prove that the marriage was solid.

Irene stirred, opening her eyes to see him standing there watching her. "Now you come," she said weakly. She closed her eyes and turned onto her back. "Did you have a good time celebrating, while your little girl lies in her grave?"

For a moment, flashes of his mother moved through his mind. Was it possible for Irene to be like that, to lie with other men? No, not Irene. She couldn't do that to him. "I hear you had all the company you needed," he said aloud, anger in his voice.

Irene looked at him again, noticing then the swelling bruise on his cheek. "What happened?" Her eyebrows arched. "Did *Ramon* do that to you?" She could not help feeling a secret joy, but she was afraid for the consequences this could bring Ramon. Still, Chad had to realize that if he tried to ruin Ramon, Ramon could do the same to Chad.

He stepped closer, his jaw flexing in anger. "What the hell did you think you were doing, telling Ramon our intimate problems? Just what kind of relationship do you have with that man?"

She stiffened. "If he hit you, you deserved it," she answered, her eyes suddenly cold. He had never seen such a look in her eyes. "And to answer your question, Ramon and I are just good friends. We always have been. I just never told you the extent of it because I was afraid you wouldn't understand, which I can see you don't. In your mind you think a woman can't be good friends with a man without going to *bed* with him!" She closed her eyes again. "You know good and well I've never done such a thing. Take a good look at yourself, Chad Jacobs, before you go pointing any fingers at me!"

Chad decided the conversation was not going as he'd planned. He changed the subject. "We're going away, Irene, as soon as you're well."

She watched him, saw his strange nervousness, the look of a little boy afraid of losing his favorite toy. "Going away? Where?"

"South. Your mother has been after me to go down to Colorado Springs and drum up more business. Now there's a silver strike. We have all kinds of reasons to go."

"What are you running from, Chad? Yourself? Ramon? Ramon is no threat to our marriage. You are."

His eyes flashed their anger. "I told you I was sorry, Irene. It won't happen again. We'll go to Colorado Springs, and we'll start over. Maybe you'll even get pregnant again."

"Right now I can't bear the thought of you touching me."

The words stabbed at his fear of sexual failure. "Don't say that!" He came closer and grasped her arms, and she was shocked at the obvious fear in his gray eyes. "After a while, everything will be all right. Don't turn me away, Irene. Don't do this to me."

She stared at him in disbelief. "Do *what* to you? *I'm* the one who has been hurt, Chad, not you! How can you expect me just to instantly forgive you and fall back into your arms?"

"I don't! But I'm your husband, and you're my wife. Sometimes men stray, Irene, but not wives—not unless they're *whores*!"

A sickening feeling engulfed her, along with a rage she had never felt before. "Is that what you're calling me?" she asked, sitting up slightly.

He let go of her. "I'm only saying that's what wives are who sleep with other men."

"Does Milicent Delaney know you consider her a whore?" He turned away. "How *dare* you even *use* that word around me?" she seethed. "How *dare* you talk to me of *wives* who stray! All these years I've suspected what you were doing, put up with it, did my best to be a good wife to you! You know better than to even *think* I would cheat on you! And this is what I get for it—a dead baby, filthy accusations about a wonderful friendship! If you were a proper husband, this never would have happened in the first place! I wouldn't be lying here . . . wishing I were dead!"

The last words came brokenly, and she lay back down, filled horror and grief. She needed comfort so badly, and here he was whining about her friendship with Ramon, trying to shift the blame away from himself. "I'm not sorry Ramon hit you," she said then, putting a hand to her head. "If I were capable, I would have done it myself."

Chad felt all his fears converging at once. She was colder, harder, and suddenly wiser. He didn't like this change in her, feared the loss of her naïveté. Everything had been perfect until that damn Milicent had insisted they had time for a go-round before he went home the other night. Could he help it if he was so irresistible? His mother's lover had not taken any of his masculinity from him. He had proven that over and over. He ran a hand through his hair, stepping closer. "I've told you I was sorry, and I'm not accusing you of anything, Irene. I just think we need to get out of Denver for a while, have some time alone, find a way to straighten this out. You're right in saying it's my fault, but I . . . there are certain things about me you don't understand."

"Then explain them, Chad. *Help* me understand."

He reddened slightly. "I can't. Just suffice it to say I'll try harder." He leaned closer. "I swear to God, Irene, I would never deliberately hurt you, and I would rather have died than let something happen to that baby. Surely you believe that much."

The terrible pain swept through her again, and her eyes teared. "As sorry an excuse for a man that you are, I do believe that much," she answered, little realizing how deeply the words cut him. Her voice was dull, full of disillusionment and sorrow. "We'll go south, if that's what you want. I wouldn't mind getting away myself. But you'll be busy, and I don't intend to just sit around every day waiting for you. If we're going to go, I want to build a house on the B&K. Mother has been wanting a place down there where the family can go if they want. And I want to buy some horses. I haven't had horses or been riding in a long time. I miss it."

He brightened a little. "Fine," he answered. "You can have anything you want, Irene, anything. Nothing can make up for what we've lost, but we're young, and you can have more babies. We *will* have more, Irene, I promise you that, if you can find it in your heart to forgive me, to let me be a husband to you again."

She watched him, realizing he thought it could be so easy. He expected her to forgive and forget, to take him back to her bed just because she was a woman, a submissive wife who was expected to overlook her husband's faults. It didn't seem fair that so much was expected of a wife, or that a man should be able to get away with anything he pleased. She realized that what she hated most about him was that he was bringing out all the feelings she never wanted to feel, bringing out a hardness, a bitterness she had never known before. She didn't like feeling this way about anyone, especially her own husband.

"I don't want to be a divorced woman, Chad. I just wish you would open up to me, tell me what drives you, tell me what it is that keeps you from talking to me whenever the conversation turns to you or your real feelings. You keep saying I don't understand. *What* don't I understand?"

He drew back. How could he tell her the truth? Besides, a man could have worse faults than enjoying women. Plenty of men enjoyed them. He wondered, though, if all men hated them the way he did. Still, he didn't hate Irene. She was about the *only* one he didn't hate, yet she was the one he'd hurt the most. If only he could curb this insatiable appetite for sex, this need to use women and then throw them away. He wondered what she would do if she ever found out about Susan Stanner . . . or Elly.

"I just . . . I never felt loved when I was growing up," he told her, hoping it was a legitimate excuse. After all, it was true. That should be enough. He could never bring himself to tell her about his mother, or that his father claimed he was a bastard.

"*I* loved you," Irene told him. "I've been a good wife, Chad. Why did you need to turn to others?"

He shrugged. "I don't know. It won't happen again, Irene."

Why didn't she believe him? How was it she knew instinctively that this was the rocky road she would travel the rest of her married life? Would going south really change anything? What choice did she have but to try? At least it would be a change of scenery—scenery that she loved. At least she could have horses, ride again.

"I hope you're telling the truth, Chad." A tear slipped down her cheek. "I want to forgive you. I want to try again, to have another baby. But I can't right away. Every time I look at you I see you lying naked on top of Milicent Delaney, and it makes me sick." She swallowed against the ache in her throat.

"As soon as you're well, we'll go," he told her. "I'll explain to your mother that we both need to get away. She'll understand that. And she really does need someone down in Colorado Springs who can take charge of things. We can check up on the cattle business. Maybe Hank Loring can show us around the ranch, fill us in on costs and such."

Hank Loring. Irene had not thought about the man in a long time. It had been nearly five years since he had lost his wife and daughter to the Indians. She had admired his courage in the wake of such sorrow. She took strength in the knowledge that she was not the only one who had suffered a terrible loss. At least she had not held her baby, played with her, watched her grow, only to lose her to a gruesome death.

"Fine," she said aloud. "It's settled then. We'll leave as soon as I'm able to travel."

He turned to meet her eyes, and she realized that to her he didn't look nearly as handsome as he once did. She was seeing him through different eyes now, the eyes of knowledge. She knew the inner Chad Jacobs. Everyone else knew only the outward man—the melting good looks, the fancy clothes, the intelligent, educated, hard-working man who could do no wrong. What a far cry he was from Ramon—gentle, understanding, loyal Ramon. But even knowing what Chad had done, she felt guilty thinking affectionately about another man. She was still Chad Jacobs's wife, and she had to live with the fact, had to remember her wedding vows, even if he had not.

How could her happiness have turned into such utter despair in one quick look, one wrong step, one cruel awakening to the truth? She turned on her side, and she heard his footsteps as he walked to the door. It closed quietly, and the tears came again.

Ramon stood back and studied the angle of the arched entrance to the church, which curved and then led to a rising point at the center, a cross at the tip of the point. Other men worked with a hoist that would be used to raise a steeple, and six huge bells sat stored in a Kirkland warehouse, waiting to be installed as a finishing touch. But there was a considerable amount of work to be done before the bells could be mounted.

It was difficult to concentrate on his work for thinking of Irene. He wished she was here to see his progress, wished he had not let his temper get the better of him. It was probably his fault Chad had taken her away. Now she was not where he could keep an eye on her, but then he was wrong in thinking he had the right to interfere in her life at all. He never should have gone to Chad's house, but the thought of what the man had done had made him contemplate murder. Chad deserved nothing less.

He only hoped he had not made trouble for Irene, but then how could a man who had done what Chad had done turn around and accuse his wife of anything? He was sorry he had to hate a man who had helped him. Chad Jacobs could be likable in many ways, but Ramon had always suspected his friendly nature was only a veil covering something much more evil. He regretted not telling

Irene his suspicions long ago, before she ever married Chad. But he was married to Elena then, and it all seemed pointless. Besides, he had no proof.

It had taken time for the real Chad to reveal himself, and now he had, to poor Irene's dismay. What heartache and disappointment she was being forced to live with. Every time he thought of it the anger returned, the horrible frustration of not being able to do anything about it. Now she was gone. God only knew for how long, or if Chad Jacobs would be a better husband. Poor Irene was still grieving, and she didn't even have her family to turn to.

He picked up a chisel and turned to see Red McKinley coming toward him. He remembered Red from before the flood, when he had bought lumber from Red and worked for him on a project. He had not seen the man in years, but he had heard he held an important position with the Union Pacific. From the way he was dressed, that much was obvious. He smiled, putting out his hand as Red came closer. "Señor McKinley," he spoke up. "It has been a long time."

"That it has, Ramon," the man answered, taking his hand. "I've been asking around about you and have heard nothing but good things." He glanced up at the church. "You are apparently doing a damn good business, and you deserve it. Glad to see you're coming up in the world."

They released hands. "Not as much as you, I hear," Ramon answered. "You are a rich railroad man now. I even saw your name in a newspaper clear out in Los Angeles, an article about the Union Pacific taking their tracks through Cheyenne instead of Denver." He stood back. "And you dare to step foot back in this town?" he asked with a laugh.

Red returned the laughter. "Well, now that the Denver Pacific has a connection and things are coming along smoothly, I'm not quite so hated. I was only acting on behalf of the railroad, son. Business is business, you know."

Ramon folded his arms, the chisel still in his hands. Red thought what a superbly handsome man he was. "And I'll bet you're *here* on business," Ramon was saying.

Red frowned, touching a hand to his chin. "I was just thinking what an intelligent man you are, and now you've proven it. How did you guess?"

"Ah, men like you do not just come to chat like a woman."

"No, we don't. I have a proposition for you, Ramon. It will make you even richer, and that's what every man wants, isn't it?"

Ramon watched him carefully, never fully trusting *gringo* businessmen. "That depends on the proposition."

Red took a cigar from an inside pocket of his jacket. "Well, I'm back in Denver to stay. I did well with the railroad, but that required a lot of moving around. For personal reasons, I want to stay right here. In fact, there is a Mr. Palmer from this area who is talking about a new railroad, one that will go into the mountains. I intend to lend my expertise to him if and when the occasion arises. At any rate, in the meantime, I have money, and I want to get back into the lumber business. I have some very personal reasons for doing so."

He lit the cigar and turned to look at the church again. "Now, I'm told by everyone whose opinion counts, that you're the most talented and sought-after builder in Denver, that Jack Scotland himself recommended you. I hear you built quite a cathedral in Los Angeles, that it took several years."

"Yes, sir. It was quite an undertaking. I was surprised I was asked at such a young age, but I proved that I could do it."

Red met his eyes. "Your business is going to grow fast, Ramon, I can see it already. Nearly all truly important building projects are going to be handed to you—the ones that net the most money, the ones that are most expensive."

Ramon's eyebrows arched. "And I suppose you want me to buy *your* lumber."

Red puffed on the cigar, then took it from his mouth. "I'll be sure to ship in the best, Ramon, even those exotic woods from South America. I can do it. I've got the money. I'll specialize in premium material—no cheap stuff. If you will agree to order all material only from me, and urge other builders to do the same, I'll give you a special discount. You quote the normal price to your customers and pocket the difference. It will be a little bonus to you for bringing me the business."

Ramon frowned. "I suppose you know that the only other lumber business in town is owned by the Kirklands."

Red grinned. "I am perfectly aware of that."

"They are powerful people in this town. I see something in your eyes, Mr. McKinley, that looks like revenge."

"You're an observant young man. That's exactly what it is. I have my reasons, Ramon, for going up against the Kirklands—Bea Kirkland to be more specific. Her husband and I were good friends for many years, but she cleverly put a stop to that. She ran me out of this town once, stole my business right out from under me. I've come back to do the same thing to her. Before I'm through, she'll give up her lumber business. I just figured that if I can tell people Ramon Vallejo is my top man, it would help bring more business my way, and bring down Kirkland Lumber that much sooner."

Ramon grinned slyly. "How do you know I will not go to Mrs. Kirkland with what you have just told me? This is her church I am working on, you know."

Red shrugged. "For one thing, it wouldn't make any difference. I have enough money that the Kirklands can't hurt me or stop me. For another, I know for a fact it was Irene Kirkland who hired you for this, not her mother. I always check my facts, Ramon, and my contacts. I know firsthand what Bea Kirkland is like, and she never would have hired a Mexican, let alone a Catholic, for this project. I also know you did a lot of work at the Kirkland mansion. Kirk told me about it years ago. I'm guessing you've had more than one go-round with Bea Kirkland yourself. I'll bet you took on this project only because of Irene. She's the only Kirkland who's worth knowing, isn't she?"

Ramon felt the flutter of passion, the painful memories. Their eyes held. "*Sí*, señor. Irene Jacobs is a fine woman. It is too bad she lost a child."

Red sobered, genuine concern coming into his eyes. "She did? I'm really sorry to hear that. Well, I hope Irene will be all right." Red took another puff on the cigar. "I like that young lady." He kept the cigar in his mouth. "What about my proposition, Ramon?"

Ramon faced the man again, and Red was shocked to see tears forming in the man's eyes. He had hit the jackpot without even realizing it! He had come here to see if Ramon would help him corner the contracting and lumber market, but he had thought it might take some arguing. There was something more here than he knew, something to do with Irene. Just how well did Ramon Vallejo know her?

Ramon spoke quietly. "This is just between us, Mr. McKinley, but I will tell you that I would like to run Bea Kirkland out of business myself—perhaps more than you. It is a long story. We cannot hope to touch the greater share of Kirkland Enterprises. They are too big for that. But if we can destroy even one tiny part of it, it will be a victory. With your financial backing, and my reputation as a contractor, we can do it."

Red saw eager revenge in Ramon's eyes. "Well, well," he muttered. "I have found another victim of Bea Kirkland's iron hand."

"*Sí*. She has insulted me, and she stole my grandfather's land away from him. She caused me to do something many years ago that I will regret for the rest of my life, something that will ensure I will never be a happy man. I will not say what it was. I will only say I am glad to help you. But I do not want the money under the table. We will put Bea Kirkland out of the lumber business faster if we underbid her up front. You sell me the lumber cheaper, I quote cheaper prices, we get the business. My extra money will come from a bonus you will pay me for bringing you business, and I will charge my normal labor costs, which are high. I do good work, Mr. McKinley."

Red nodded. "Fair enough. I like the idea."

"We sign nothing. I have my own contracting business. I do not wish to go into any kind of a partnership. It will just be a verbal agreement that I buy all my supplies from you."

Red grinned widely. "Fine. I'm not out to move in on your business, Ramon. In fact, after what you have told me, I hope you become the richest contractor in Colorado. Maybe you'll even get your land back someday."

Ramon grinned. "Maybe." He put out his hand and Red took it. "And maybe someday you will buy out Kirkland Lumber."

They squeezed hands. "I like the way you think, Ramon."

"When it comes to Bea Kirkland, we think alike. Open your business, Mr. McKinley, and I will start buying from you."

Red tipped his hat. "I'll be in touch. We'll have dinner together."

Ramon nodded and watched him walk away, taking deep pleasure in planning to out-do Bea Kirkland in at least one area of her vast empire. He had no doubt that between himself and Red McKinley, it could be done.

CHAPTER
TWENTY-EIGHT

September 1869

Irene knelt to plant another rosebush in the open courtyard of her nearly completed home. Resting among the green foothills of the Rockies, it was a two-hour ride south of Colorado Springs, on B&K land. Nearby was one of several bunkhouses that were scattered across the vast B&K, where the ranch hands who worked various shifts lived.

Chad had argued that it was not safe for Irene to stay there alone, had tried to get her to build their house closer to town; but Irene had insisted on this location because of its beauty. There had been no Indian trouble in years, and she was not afraid of them or outlaws. Since losing the baby and being so rudely awakened to the reality of her marriage and the prospect of a lifetime of emotional disappointment, physical danger meant nothing to her. She would gladly take the risk, if she could at least be here in this beautiful country, far from the rush of another growing city.

Here she had found peace. Here she could think and heal and feel close to God, for if any country resembled what heaven must be like, it was this part of Colorado.

She pushed dirt around the rosebush, then stood up to see how it looked. She breathed a sigh of satisfaction and gazed around the open courtyard, which was in the center of her new home, a sprawling, stucco, Spanish-style structure of only one story. It was far different from their home in Denver, certainly different from the Kirkland mansion. She wasn't sure if Bea would like this house, if and when the woman came south and used it on occasion; but that didn't matter. What mattered was that Irene liked it. She had decided she was going to be selfish for a while, indulge in whatever she wanted; most of all, be herself, and not cater to Chad Jacobs's every whim. She had tried that, and it had brought her nothing but insult and humiliation, and a lost baby.

She was tired of worrying about pleasing her mother and her husband, tired of the pressures of being the center of society in Denver. Here she could just be Irene. She didn't have to wear fancy dresses or attend social events. She didn't even want to be around Chad any more than necessary for the time being. His attempts at pretending everything was getting back to normal made her feel sick. In the four months since losing the baby, they had spent three of them in Colorado Springs while the house was being built, but they had not made love. She couldn't bring herself to let him touch her, and she wondered sometimes if she ever could again. She knew that by turning him away she was only making him more angry and frustrated, but she was tired of simply submitting to his whims because he was her husband. Their marriage had been sorely fractured, and just going to bed together was not going to heal the wound.

She kept hoping he would be a real man about it, would come to her and explain his feelings, would somehow change; but there was no change at all. The new house was not quite finished yet, but she had moved in anyway, no longer able to bear the pretending to which their marriage had returned.

Chad had promised to come home weekends, but he spent most of them in Colorado Springs, sending messengers to the ranch house to be sure she was still all right. She had thought that time alone together here in the quiet, open country would be good for them, had thought they could slowly rebuild their marriage. But Chad had quickly returned to his old ways, charming, laughing, acting as though nothing had changed, as though there had never been a baby, or an affair. At thirty-two, he sometimes seemed like a much younger man, one who had not developed the wisdom and strength a man his age should have. He remained shallow, fake, undependable. His initial sorrow and repentance over the baby had quickly vanished once he got her away from Denver, and she had no doubt that back in Colorado Springs he did not often sleep alone. She put no faith or trust in his promises of fidelity.

At least here she had found a new peace, was building her

strength, both physical and emotional. She loved having a garden right in the middle of her house. The sun shined here every day, and she spent long hours sitting in the courtyard and reading. She turned and walked inside to make herself some tea. She loved this house, loved the bit of independence she found here. She had not even brought down any servants yet. She was doing just fine on her own, enjoying the cooking, even the cleaning, with the help of one old Mexican woman named Flor Valdez, who lived in a cabin a half mile away and sometimes cooked for the ranch hands.

She walked across polished wood floors, proud of the fact that she had designed the house herself. Woven rugs of Indian and Spanish design decorated the floors, and huge ceramic pots painted with the same designs sat in every room, filled with exotic plants. The stucco walls made it cool inside, even though outside it was in the nineties. She wasn't sure why, but she loved the bright colors of Indian and Mexican designs, loved the simple style of the house. Some nights she even slept on a cot in the courtyard under the stars, where she would lie and dream about the nights spent outdoors beside a campfire with her father in the mountains.

Such a long time ago that all seemed, another time, another Irene, one who trusted in true love, who believed in happy marriages, who wanted to please everybody else and be a good daughter and a good wife.

She put a kettle of water on the cook stove, shoving some coal under the burner and lighting it. Soon everyone would be cooking with convenient gas stoves back in Denver, but piped gas would be available only in the bigger cities. Someone had yet to figure out how to provide it in the more remote areas, but she did not doubt that someone would come up with a solution.

Things seemed to change and progress so fast, with the railroad penetrating places no one could have dreamed they would come, running water and soon gas lights and cook stoves in Denver; so much progress in the mere ten years since they first arrived in Colorado and watched dogs and pigs and Indians chasing around in the muddy streets.

She sat down to wait for the water to heat, glad to be out of the rush of business for a while. Kirk was in the mountains again, helping with the dam projects. Bea had temporarily given up plans to go to Europe. She remained in Denver, working as hard as ever. Chad was now Bea's counterpart in Colorado Springs. John and Elly were both due home soon, ready to take on their roles at K-E. For now Irene wanted no part of it. She had trustworthy women watching over her clothing stores. She knew the rest of the building committee would handle the church project, and she had full confidence in Ramon's talents.

She missed Ramon. She wished she had been able to explain why she was leaving, had been able to talk once more with him. It angered her, after what Chad had done, that he had dared to accuse her of carrying on with Ramon. He had even objected to this Spanish-style house, saying she only wanted it to remind her of her Mexican "friend." "I never want his name mentioned in my presence again," he had ordered. Ever since Ramon had hit him, Chad had been more belligerent, actually turning on her at times, trying to make her feel as though losing the baby were her fault, trying to divert the blame from himself. There were moments when she had actually been afraid of Chad, and for the time being she was almost glad they were apart most of the time.

All she wanted now was peace and quiet. Later today she would take the buggy to Hank Loring's house, which was a good five miles to the northeast. The hired hands had shown her the road that led right to it, and some of the men would ride with her for protection. Her heart rushed with delight at the thought of seeing Hank's golden Palominos again, of buying several for herself and starting her own herd.

The water had not steamed yet when she heard horses approaching outside then. She went to the heavy wooden front doors and opened them, seeing a man approach. She was surprised and delighted to realize it was Hank. He had not changed, the same dark, wavy hair, the same rugged, handsome look about him. She recognized the stallion he had ridden the day he came to visit her mother, a grand animal not easily forgotten. How many years ago had that been? Five? Six? He was leading another Palomino, a mare, which was saddled. He smiled the familiar broad grin as he came closer, dressed in knee-high boots and denim pants, a red checkered shirt and a leather vest, a red bandana around his neck. A six-gun rested on his hip, a rifle sat cradled in its scabbard at the side of his saddle.

"Hello, Mrs. Jacobs," he called out. "Word came to me you were coming to my place today to look at horses." He rode up in front of her then. "Thought I'd bring my best mare here, and you can ride her back to my place . . . see how you like her."

"Hello, Mr. Loring. It's been a long time."

He dismounted, removing his hat, his exotic green eyes moving over her in that same old way that brought a tingle to her blood. "Just about five years, to be exact," he answered. "Last time I saw you was on your wedding day." He looked around. "Your husband here?"

He did not miss the sudden change in her eyes and composure. He quickly detected something was very wrong. What was she doing here, anyway? Was it true, what the men said, that her husband stayed in Colorado Springs most of the time? Why? If he had a woman like Irene Jacobs to come home to—

"No, he's not here," she answered. "We—we've come south to build on some investments here—open a bank, build another hotel, that kind of thing. I decided I needed some peace and quiet for a while, so I had this house built so I could get away from town." She walked up to the mare, petting its neck. "I came here to heal, to get over my grief, Mr. Loring. I lost a child back in Denver."

Hank sobered. "I'm real sorry to hear that. I understand that kind of loss, Mrs. Jacobs."

She could feel the hot redness of her cheeks at being so open with him so quickly. She remembered how easy he had been to talk to that day she first met him, already felt an aura of masculinity, a maturity about him that was absent in Chad. "Yes," she answered, "and your losses were so much greater. I'm so sorry about your wife and child." She looked up at him then, and saw the terrible sorrow. Here was a man who had been true to his wife, had been a loving husband and father. It didn't seem fair that God should take away the family of a man like that. It was the same with Ramon—good men who would have been true to their wives, would have made wonderful fathers.

"It's been five years," he was saying. "It happened not long after your wedding, I remember. It was Yellow Eagle and his bunch. They've still never been caught." He looked around. "You should be pretty safe here. The Sioux and Cheyenne almost never come to this area any more. And right now they're pretty well concentrated in the north."

"That's why we picked this spot." She put on a smile for him. "It's nice to see you again, Mr. Loring. I know you've been in frequent touch with my mother and that the cattle business is doing well, but we never actually get to see you."

"Well, I heard you came to Colorado Springs and were building a house in this area, but I've been gone the last few weeks since you moved in . . . been in Kansas at a cattle auction. Otherwise I would have come by a lot sooner. You finally ready to buy some horses?"

"Oh, yes." She petted the mare again. "And this one is

beautiful." She met his eyes again, feeling strange little stabs of desire only one other man had ever created in her. "I was going to come to your place later today in the buggy, but this will be so much more pleasurable. Come inside and see the house while I change into my riding clothes. I have some hot water on the stove. Would you like some tea or coffee?"

"Nothing, thanks, except maybe a drink of water." He followed her inside, thinking how she had changed so little in five years. She was prettier even than he had remembered. He had always admired her beauty and lovely personality. He thought how she was nothing like her mother, totally untainted by wealth, her personality still open and friendly, just as he remembered her. She wore a plain blue dress that gave no indication of wealth, although she carried herself with more poise and elegance than any settler's wife.

He wondered how her marriage had fared. Chad Jacobs had seemed like the almost ideal man, yet here was Irene, grieving over a lost child, living here alone in her sorrow. It didn't seem right, and something about the look in her eyes when he mentioned her marriage left him feeling sorry for her.

"By the way," he told her as he followed her into the kitchen, "considering the fact that you're technically my boss, you should be calling me Hank."

She laughed. "Well, you have your own ranch, too, and you're a very successful man in your own right. You just seem like Mr. Loring to me."

He grinned. "That isn't fair. Just because I'm probably twenty years older than you doesn't mean you have to address me like an elder."

She pumped a glass of water for him with an indoor hand pump that brought water from a tank outside the house, which was kept filled most of the time by the power of a windmill. "You can't be twenty years older. I'm twenty-three, Mr. Loring."

"Well, almost twenty years then, seventeen. That's bad enough. Please do call me Hank."

She handed him the glass, feeling the strange tingle again when his fingers touched hers. His big frame seemed to fill the room. "Then you have to call me Irene," she answered. She reddened slightly and turned away. "I'll go and change."

He nodded. "Thanks for the water."

"You'll have to be patient with me, Mr.—I mean, Hank. I haven't been riding in a long time, so go easy on me."

"I promise not to try to race you," he answered with an easy grin. He watched her leave the room, then looked around the lovely house. Kitchen cupboards were still unfinished, and outside men were working on building a barn for horses. He walked to a window to watch, thinking how strange it was that someone brought up as she had been would want to be out here in such remote country raising horses. His mind raced with questions—how had she come to lose a child? Why was she out here alone, why wasn't her husband with her, or why wasn't she in town with him? Why had she looked so sad when he mentioned her wedding day?

They would all be questions that would have to be left unanswered, since none of them were any of his business. The answers would have to come from Irene, if and when she might decide to volunteer the information. She was hurting. He could read it in those pretty blue eyes. She was hurting, and so was he. They had that much in common.

"Hello, Chad." Chad looked up to see a replica of Bea Kirkland, but with a younger face.

"Elly! By God, it's good to see you! When did you get back?" He quickly rose and Elly sauntered closer. "I was hoping you'd be as glad to see me as I am to see you."

He reddened slightly, walking over to close the door to the temporary office he had taken inside the southern branch of the Kirkland Hotel. "Of course I'm glad to see you," he told her. He walked up and embraced her firmly, realizing he had better make her believe it. Her sudden appearance had forced him to think fast. Elly was back! Now that Irene had discovered his affair with Milicent, she would be more suspicious. He had better stay on good terms with Elly Kirkland. She knew enough to destroy what little faith Irene had left in him.

"I missed you, Chad," she said softly.

He thought what an armful she was compared to Irene, but she at least at one time had appreciated him and knew how to be a woman. Already he could tell none of that had changed. "I missed you, too," he lied, realizing he didn't even have to look down at her; she stood as tall as he. The fancy, feathered hat she wore made her appear even taller.

"I'm glad," she answered. "Thank you for all the letters, Chad. I hated staying away so long, but . . . I was sick the first year . . . and then I decided to learn all I could—to outdo Irene in my education. I want to be a big part of Kirkland Enterprises. Mother is very happy with everything I learned."

Their eyes met, and he could see what she wanted. He still held her in his arms, and he leaned closer, meeting her lips in a hungry kiss, as though she had never left. He knew by her response that she was as eager for him as ever, but there was a more mature air about her—more experience? He wondered how many men she had gone down for since she left.

She ended the kiss and rested her head on his shoulder. "Oh, Chad, I was afraid it would all be different, especially when Mother said Irene lost a baby. I thought maybe you had decided to devote everything to her."

He pulled away. "Things were bad for a while. Irene needed to get away from Denver. We had a house built south of here. She stays there alone. She's gotten into raising horses. You know Irene and horses."

Elly sniffed. "Yes. I suppose she'd rather be out there shoveling manure than here with her husband, where she belongs."

"Something like that."

Elly caught the hint of guilt in his eyes. "Chad Jacobs, there is something you're not telling me. Mother said Irene fell at the office, and that's why she lost the baby. It was past working hours." She ran a hand over his chest. "You're the only witness, Chad. What really happened? I know Irene. Something bad happened to make her stay on the ranch while you're here. What happened to the sister I thought would be such a devoted wife?"

He grinned a little. "None of your business. You haven't been back long enough that I'm sure I can trust you, you little brat."

Elly laughed. "I'm not little anymore. I'm twenty years old. I suppose I am a brat, though. But I'll show you trust, Chad. I'll tell you something I would never want Mother to know." She put her arms around his neck. "I told you I was pretty sick that first year. You want to know why?"

He frowned. "You never let on in any letters you wrote home that you had been sick."

"That's because I didn't want Mother to know." She let go of him and turned to look out a window. "When I first went to Chicago, I had an abortion, Chad. You got me pregnant."

Silence filled the room. "Good God, Elly, you could have died," Chad gasped.

She turned to face him. "I almost did. Another doctor had to operate on me to stop the bleeding. The school was afraid to tell Mother about it for fear she'd have them closed down. I promised not to tell if they would promise the same. I didn't want her to know any more than they did." She moved to his desk, taking off her gloves. "The doctor removed my uterus, Chad." She set her gloves aside and met his eyes. "That's what holds the baby when a woman is pregnant, in case you don't know," she said, telling it as casually as if she had lost a fingernail. "It was the worst thing I've ever gone through, but at least now it's impossible for me to get pregnant."

Even Chad was surprised at her attitude. "You can't have children?"

"No. But who wants the messy little things anyway?"

Chad put a hand on her arm. "You sure it doesn't matter to you? This is partly my fault, Elly."

Oh, how she loved him blaming himself! Nothing had changed. She had a new hold on him. "I know. But I don't blame you, Chad. It takes two to make a baby." She looked him over. "You do seem to be good at that."

The suggestive remark stirred his neglected needs, reminded him Elly was one who always had been good at showing him he was indeed a man who could perform the way a man should, a man who could bring out the lust in any woman, except Irene. His failure with Irene ate at him, as if it were a cancer.

"Let's see now—that's three babies you've made and lost. There was Susan Stanner, and me, and now Irene. Who knows how many others?"

He felt his defenses rising. Damn her! She had always gone down easy for him, like most of the others; but he had had the upper hand with the others. If only she wasn't Irene's sister. "I never admitted to being Susan's lover, Elly. That one is all in your head."

"Oh, Chad, it was years ago. Why keep lying about it? Besides, who cares anymore?" She smiled and put her arms back around his neck. "I just wanted you to know what I went through, for you. I couldn't have that baby. What if he or she grew up to look like you?"

"I'm sorry for what you must have gone through," he told her.

"Now it's your turn." She traced a finger across his mouth. "What really happened with Irene?"

How he hated her insight. She was the only person who even came close to really understanding his character. "Where did you get all this sly wisdom?" he asked.

She grinned. "I learned at a young age to watch people, use them—just like you do. I've never been the favored one in the family, Chad. When that happens, you learn to watch out for yourself. You learn how to defend yourself, how to get what you want even when someone else has all the advantages. You're like that, too, aren't you?"

He sighed. "You've always known me too well." He folded his arms. "All right. I'll tell you the truth. Irene caught me with Milicent Delaney. She ran out, and when I tried to grab her she fell. It's going to take her a long time to get over it. She blames me for losing the baby, and I blame myself. Believe it or not, I do feel bad about it."

She put her hands on her hips. "About being *caught*, you mean."

He grinned. "Yes. But I really did want her to have that baby."

"Because it would make the marriage look better, give Irene a reason not to leave you?"

He shrugged. "I need this marriage, Elly. I like my position with K-E. You know that."

"Well, what Irene neglects to give you, I'll make up for, now that I'm back. You won't need Milicent Delaney." She burst out laughing then. "*Milicent!* Chad, you devil! She's married and has two or three children!"

He shrugged. "I had to do *something*. You weren't here, and things were getting tight. I had to put on a show of coming home every night. There wasn't time to visit the red light district. Milicent was right there handy. I always knew she wanted me. It was easy."

She came closer and ran her hand over his arms. "It's always easy for you. One look at you and a woman has a terrible desire to pull up her skirts."

Their eyes held, and he knew she was already eager to renew their affair. He met her mouth in another hot kiss. It had always been easy for him to overlook her body, her plain looks. He needed the reassurance of his manhood that Elly was always best at feeding. He left her lips and kissed at her neck. "You staying here at the hotel?"

"Yes," she almost groaned. "Mother sent me here to work with you. Isn't that delicious? Eventually she intends for me and John to take over down here and for you to go back to Denver. But John won't be here for a couple of months yet, and with Irene staying at the ranch, it's just you and me, Chad. We can go to each other's rooms every night if we want. We're free, Chad. I can't even get pregnant!"

He met her lips again, this time more savagely. Irene had not let him near her in months. The child in him could not handle the rejection. Elly knew how to soothe that little boy. It was as though she had never left.

Winter moved down the mountains and onto the plains, and Irene often awakened to a soft blanket of snow on the ground. Sometimes the buffalo grass and sage would have little caps of snow on them, but usually the snow disappeared as quickly as it came. No matter what the weather, Irene went outside every day and exercised her horses. She had five now, one good stud and four mares. Two of the mares were pregnant.

The first horse she had purchased from Hank had been the one he had brought to her. She called the mare Sunrise, and she was beginning to cherish the animal as much as she had cherished Sierra. She often helped the hired hands with cleaning stables, currying the horses, shoveling feed. She enjoyed the work, and the men who worked for her gained a new respect for the Kirkland name. They had heard stories about her tyrant of a mother, and had expected the daughter to be the same. But Irene was surprisingly different, and beautiful as well.

Irene was beginning to resign herself to the fact that her marriage would probably never be what it should be. Sometimes she went to Colorado Springs for a weekend, and sometimes Chad came home; but she still had not been able to let him make love to her, no matter how sweet he tried to be to her. As long as he refused to talk about his inner problems, refused to talk about the baby, as long as he continued to act as though nothing had changed, she found it difficult to love and forgive him, much as she wished that she could.

Her loneliness had led her to begin relying too much on her friendship with Hank. She could not help comparing Hank to Chad. He was so much more solid and dependable. She and Hank had so much in common. Hank was a good man, through and through. There was nothing vain or deceitful about him. She thought how much like Ramon he was in many ways.

She had seen a lot of Hank over the past several months. He had shown her the boundaries of the B&K, had explained the business of breeding and raising cattle, had sold her the beautiful horses that now pranced in her corral. In many ways, Hank had helped her get back to living and surviving, had helped her bear the loss of her child.

It was becoming more difficult to think of Hank as just a friend, and her feelings frightened her. She and Chad were growing farther apart, and he seldom came to the ranch. He stayed busier than ever, especially now that both Elly and John were back and needing Chad to teach them the ropes of the southern branch of K-E.

She still worried about John. He was twenty-one now, a tall, handsome young man. There was a distant loneliness in his eyes, and Irene noticed when he visited the ranch over Christmas with Bea and Kirk and Elly that John was still a heavy drinker. She knew he had never been happy and had sometimes wondered if he would ever come back home once he went off to college.

"Mother doesn't understand how much you love it here, does she?" John told Irene in the kitchen Christmas Eve. Irene had cooked the entire meal herself, Bea fuming and fussing that there was no reason for one of her daughters to be working like a "little slave." The woman had complained that Irene should have built a much bigger house, that she should come back to Denver, that she should stop working around her horses as if she were a common ranch hand, that she and Chad should be together more so that Irene would get pregnant again. The woman had no idea of the emotional pain her daughter was suffering.

Irene smiled at her brother, setting a pie on the table. "There are a lot of things most people don't understand about me," Irene answered.

"All Mother understands is making money." John slugged down a shot of whiskey. "I tried to open my own law firm back East, Irene. Did Mother tell you that? I never wrote to tell you. I wanted to wait to see if I would succeed."

She sat down at the table with him, while Bea, Elly, and Chad talked business in the dining room, and Kirk walked outside for a smoke. She could see John was already feeling his whiskey. "Mother never told me," she said.

"Probably because I failed. I lost a really important case that involved a big company. They blackballed me. On top of that, Mother sent me a letter telling me that if I didn't come back and work for K-E like her good little son, she would cut me off. Told me she didn't spend all that money sending me to school just to have me desert the family. I was ordered back home, and considering my big flop as a lawyer, I figured what the hell, I might as well come." He leaned closer. "You want to know Mother's first words when I got back home?"

She put a hand over his. "John, don't do this. Mother thinks she is doing what's best for her children. She doesn't understand—"

"'So, the prodigal son returns,'" he interrupted. "That's the first thing she said. 'How dare you squander your education on something other than this company I have built for you!'" He picked up a bottle of bourbon he had carried with him to the kitchen and poured himself another shot. "Nothing about missing me, being glad to see me back. No hug." He swallowed the drink. "But, what the hell? I'm a big boy now."

Irene squeezed his hand. "*I* love you, John. I missed you very much, and I'm *very* glad to see you back."

He smiled bitterly. "I wonder sometimes if you really have any of Mother's blood in you. You're too good to be a Kirkland. Now Elly—*there's* a Kirkland! She's going to be a worse tyrant than Mother ever was. You notice that?"

Irene could not help feeling disappointed at how Elly acted toward her. It was obvious Elly all but hated her, and she could not imagine why she should. Since coming back from school she was more haughty and bossy than ever. "Yes," she answered. "Elly has always had a problem trying to fit in, trying to win glory in Mother's eyes."

"That's where we're different. I don't really give a damn *what* Mother thinks of me. I'm just here for the ride, Irene. I'll never amount to anything on my own, so I'll tag along on the coattails of K-E."

"You shouldn't talk that way, John. You're a handsome, intelligent young man. You'll find your own way someday, but it won't happen if you don't stop the heavy drinking."

He snickered and shook his head. "Whiskey is what gets me through the day. I can handle it just fine." He sighed and rubbed at his head. "I'm real sorry about the baby, Irene."

"I know you are, and thank you. . . . I'd better get in there with the pie."

Chad came into the kitchen then, offering to help carry the pies, again putting on a show of being the doting husband. Kirk came back inside and everyone ate pie and opened presents. Chad sat next to Irene and presented her with diamond earrings, kissing her cheek when he gave them to her.

Irene wondered if he really thought that material things could make up for what he had done. She thought of Ramon's carved horse and the beautiful Indian blanket Hank had given her two days ago, gifts that held much more love and meaning than anything Chad had ever given her. Elly watched Chad hang over Irene and wanted to laugh. He was so clever at putting on the charm for others to see. She didn't mind that he paid attention only to his wife for the moment. She knew whose bed he would be sleeping in once they got back to Colorado City.

John in turn watched Elly. He had noticed a few things, certain looks Elly and Chad exchanged at times, the way they often found excuses to work late in town. He liked the Chad. He didn't want to think the worst, but he had never forgotten Irene's apparent unhappiness when she came home from her short honeymoon. Now she had lost a baby, and at a time when she and Chad should be closer than ever, they were living apart most of the time. Something was wrong somewhere, but he was too lost in his own world of whiskey and failure to get involved.

Bellies full, weary from a long day and evening, everyone retired: Elly, Bea, and Kirk to the two guest rooms, John sprawled drunk on a leather couch. Irene undressed in the bathing room, unable to bring herself to undress in front of Chad. She wondered if her aching weariness came more from a long day of cooking or from pretending—pretending to be the happy wife, pretending it had been a wonderful Christmas.

It seemed everyone was pretending things were what they were not, and most of the pretending was for Bea Kirkland's sake. Elly was trying so hard to win her mother's favor. Kirk remained the quiet, obliging man, although things did seem a little better between her parents ever since the incident with the railroad. And John, pretending his own happiness, losing himself in whiskey.

She came into the bedroom to find Chad waiting for her in their bed. He smiled. "It's time we let bygones be bygones, Irene. I've paid my dues. It's been a long time."

Their eyes held, and all she could see was his naked body groveling over Milicent Delaney. Again she reluctantly found herself comparing him to men like Ramon . . . and Hank. Hank had been on her mind a lot this Christmas. She was sorry he was spending Christmas Eve alone, knew how hard it must be for him. He still grieved for his wife. Somehow she could not imagine Chad grieving for long over her if something happened to her. When she looked at Chad she saw only a shallow little boy. She could not even see him as a man.

She pulled on her robe. "Are you trying to tell me that when you're gone for weeks at a time you're sleeping alone, Chad," she answered. "I see no change at all. You've made no effort to prove anything to me, least of all that you love me and are being faithful to me." She tied her robe and walked to the door. "Just go to sleep, Chad. I'm going to the kitchen for some tea."

She left the room, and Chad slammed a hard fist into her pillow.

CHAPTER
TWENTY-NINE

Where it began and where it would end, Irene was not sure. She only knew that when she was riding with Hank she was happy, happier than she had been in years. He filled many roles that were missing in her life—father, brother, friend—everything but lover. In spite of what Chad had done to her, she still could not allow herself to act on some of the baser feelings Hank stirred deep in her soul, emotions and desires that before now only Ramon had awakened in her, except that her feelings for Ramon were even more intense, had been more immediate, and she had loved him secretly for so long.

Now there was not even Ramon to talk to. She realized Hank had simply come into her life at a time when she felt desperately alone and disillusioned. She loved him as a friend, a good, dear friend. She loved him out of an empty need. But she loved him as secretly as she loved Ramon, for she was still a married woman, frail as that marriage might be. Hank respected her, never made a wrong move or a wrong suggestion; but she could read his provocative green eyes. She saw the desire there, felt his own loneliness.

Spring of 1870 came early, and it was roundup time on the Lazy L as well as the B&K. Irene needed the activity, and against Chad's vehement arguments, she insisted on helping with the roundup. She wanted to know everything she could about the ranch, loved every aspect of this kind of life. To the surprise of the hired help, Irene Kirkland Jacobs rode as well as any of them, learned how to herd a steer in the right direction, ate and slept in the open country right along with the best of them.

She was an expert rider and even learned how to use a rope. It was Hank who taught her everything, Hank who stood behind her and held her arms to show her the proper way to swing a rope. They saw each other nearly every day for several weeks, and Hank grew to admire Irene's courage and strength, her skillful riding, her willingness to work as hard as the men. She was everything a man like himself could want in a woman, but she was married. It tore at his guts like a knife. He knew she wasn't happy, but she had never explained in detail what was wrong.

They were becoming dangerously close, more than just friends. He knew she had to be perfectly aware he was falling in love with her, and he knew her feelings for him were mutual. It was all left unsaid, but it was there, nonetheless.

Irene felt the same helpless attraction. It had actually been there for years. Was it possible to love more than one man? She would never stop loving Ramon, never. He would always be her first love. But in her lonely, desperate state, these last few months it had been Hank Loring who had been her salvation. His attention, his efforts at keeping her busy, had helped her through the moments when she even considered taking her life.

She helped with the branding, failing to cringe the way the men thought she would. She cooked a big meal for the hired hands, using Hank's own kitchen. Hank had a lovely home, a sprawling, stucco structure much like her own. Inside, there remained remnants of another woman's decorating and furnishing, and Hank talked often about his wife and daughter, showed her their graves. When she had seen the terrible sorrow in his eyes, she had grasped his hand, and he squeezed hers in return.

They needed no words. They knew what was happening, and neither one of them did anything to try to stop it. It felt too good to both of them to find such a pleasant friendship, such a wonderful relief from the loneliness. They shared so much, especially their love of horses and riding. They found it easy to talk to each other, and Hank was beginning to realize he had loved Irene Jacobs just a little ever since the first day he set eyes on her. Now he loved her more, and he saw himself headed down a pathway of unavoidable hurt, but just as Irene was doing, he galloped ahead full speed.

• • •

Chad stretched out on his back, nearly worn out from Elly's insatiable appetite for him. Elly raised up on one elbow, her dark, waist-length hair hanging thin and straight over her shoulders as she leaned down to kiss at his chest. He thought how she reminded him of a witch, and she was indeed exactly that.

"We've got to be a little more careful," Chad told her. "John has been giving us some strange looks lately. I think he suspects something."

"John is too drunk most of the time to notice. All he cares about is where his next bottle is going to come from."

"That's too bad. He's a good kid. I've always hated drinking myself."

Elly sat up. "I've always wondered about that. Why don't you drink, Chad? I've never known a man who didn't drink."

He turned away, reaching over to pick up a cigar. "My father drank, in extreme excess. When you see enough drunken rages as a child, you learn to hate liquor."

"Chad! You never told me that before. Have you ever told Irene?"

"I don't talk about my childhood—with her or with you. Enough said."

She sighed. "You should know by now you can talk to me about anything."

"All right then. How about telling me what you know about Irene and Ramon Vallejo."

She pulled a sheet to her waist, leaving her huge bosom naked. Her mouth dropped open at his question. "*Ramon!*" She hesitated. "Why do you ask that?"

He lit the cigar. "Because while Irene was in the hospital, Ramon came storming over to my place, telling me I ought to be with my wife, telling me what a rotten husband I was. He landed a fist into my gut and a boot in my groin before I realized what was going on. It was pretty damn obvious he thinks of Irene as more than just a casual acquaintance."

She smiled, then laughed. "Ramon did that?" She laughed again. "Then he *does* still love her! I wonder if Irene loves Ramon."

Chad frowned. "She told me they were just good friends. What the hell are you saying?"

"Oh, it was before Irene met you. She was only fifteen or sixteen. One day I went up to the new house while Ramon was still working on it, and I caught him and Irene kissing."

Chad paled visibly. "Irene? And Ramon?"

"Oh, Chad, it was a long time ago. I told Mother, but don't you ever tell Irene that I did. Mother chased him off without Irene knowing what had happened. She thought Ramon ran out on her. He married a Mexican woman after that—the one who was killed in the flood. I know Irene well enough to know nothing ever happened between them once she started seeing you. Irene is too much of a priss to go cheating on a man, but I know it really hurt her when Ramon left and got married. I decided she deserved to hurt, just like I was hurting with love for you," she pouted.

All Chad could think about was his mother. Was it possible Irene wasn't the perfect woman he thought she was? The thought literally terrified him. It was one thing for him to cheat on Irene. But he had taken her for a wife, and he expected complete, perfect loyalty on her part. He had married her because she was not like his mother and the others. Had he been wrong about her after all?

"I think I'm going to have a little talk with my wife."

"Oh, Chad, don't tell me you're jealous of a *Mexican* man!"

He grabbed her arm. "She's my *wife*! She's my *property*!"

"Chad, I didn't think you cared."

"Of course I care." He got up, stark naked, and paced.

"Keep your voice down, Chad. We're in a hotel, you know."

He came closer. "Do you think Ramon still loves her?"

She shrugged. "I don't know. Maybe." She saw the anger in his eyes, and she smiled inwardly with delight. There was going to be trouble over this. She loved the thought of perfect Irene having to defend herself as the cheating wife, when Chad was sleeping with her own sister. "It isn't Ramon I would worry about," she told him, a gleam in her eyes.

He set his cigar aside. "What do you mean?"

"I'd be more worried about that Hank Loring, if I were you. She's been seeing an awful lot of him, you know . . . camping out with him, riding with him."

"She's just learning about the ranch."

"And I thought you were smarter about things like that. Didn't you see how Hank looked at her when we were all there for supper last weekend? I'd find out what's going on, if I were you. There he is, a big, strapping, handsome man, a lonely widower." She watched his eyes, delighted at the worry she saw there. It was so easy to manipulate him. She imagined Irene trying to defend herself and Hank. Anything she said would just make her look more guilty. "If I were you, I'd ask a few questions the next time you go home."

His gray eyes gleamed with fury. "Yes, I think I'll do just that."

He paced again. "You'd better get back to your room and get some sleep."

She pouted. "Oh, Chad, you aren't going to let this change things between us, are you? I don't want to go back yet." She got up and walked over to him, rubbing against him. "Just once more?"

He thought of his mother, remembered hearing her say those words to strange men. "Not tonight," he answered, pulling away from her. *Irene! She wouldn't do that, would she?*

Elly scowled and pulled on her robe. "I never should have told you about Ramon and Hank. What do you care what Irene does anyway, as long as you're free to do what you want?"

"That's different. Just go, Elly. I'll see you in the morning."

Her dark eyes flashed. "Don't send me off like just another whore, Chad. Don't forget who you're talking to."

He met her eyes, hating her for having this damn control over him. Hating her . . . hating her. That was the key for him. He walked up to her and yanked off her robe. "*Don't* go back then." He jerked her over to the bed and pushed her onto it, his hatred making him want her again. He wanted to use her, hurt her, as he had been hurt. In moments he was pushing inside her again, angry, thinking about how men had used his mother this way.

Elly took him gladly, wildly, loving it when he was savage about it. All Chad could think about was the possibility that Irene was cheating on him—like his mother, like his mother, like Elly and the others had. Not Irene! He'd go home and find out. He would show her once and for all whom she belonged to. There would be no more turning away her own husband! He pushed hard and deep, just as he would to Irene when he saw her again. She had no right turning him away! She had used the baby and his infidelities as an excuse long enough. A wife was a wife, and he would show her whose property she was! No other man was going to out-do Chad Jacobs!

"How about a little celebration picnic?" Hank suggested, as he and Irene watched the last of the newborn calves branded. "The roundup is finished and we had a good winter, more calves born than we expected. I'll be helping herd a few head of cattle to the Denver stockyards before long, be gone a few weeks. I might be out of line by saying it, but I'll miss you, Irene."

She sat on a wooden fence, unable to bring herself to meet his eyes. She almost wished the roundup had never ended. She had loved helping, loved being with Hank every day. "And I'm probably out of line telling you I'll miss you, too," she answered. She looked down to brush some dust from her suede skirt. "A picnic sounds wonderful. When do you want to go?"

He leaned next to her on the fence, standing almost as tall as she, even though she sat on the top rail. "Tomorrow?"

She nodded. "Have someone accompany me home and I'll get everything ready. You can meet me there in the morning." She finally met his eyes, both of them realizing they had no future, yet unable to act rationally. "It will be kind of nice to just go riding for the enjoyment, instead of chasing after calves and eating dust."

He gave her a wink. "You're a full-fledged cowhand now, Mrs. Jacobs. I'd hire you any day."

She laughed. "Thank you, Mr. Loring." She turned to climb down, and he grabbed her around the waist to help her. She grasped his arms, and the touch sent heated desire through both of them, painful, unspoken passion that made Irene's cheeks feel hot. He set her on her feet, and she quickly pulled away from him and mounted Sunrise. "I'll see you tomorrow morning . . . about nine?"

He nodded, holding her eyes as he shouted for two of his men to ride with her back to her house. "Look forward to it," he told her.

She smiled, her heart racing, wondering why the right men seemed always to come into her life at the wrong time. She rode off, and Hank watched after her.

You're asking for big trouble, Hank Loring, he told himself. But at the moment it didn't seem to matter. If he lost his ranch and everything dear to him, it wouldn't matter, if he could somehow have Irene Jacobs.

They rode into the foothills, enjoying the fresh smell of mountain air, the May weather still cool from snows melting in the higher elevations. Irene's heart soared at the sights and sounds and smells of this land she loved, rode Sunrise through the vast, magnificent open grassland into the rich, green foothills, longing just to keep riding right into the mountains again.

Spring roundup had taken them over the vast expanses of eastern Colorado. Now they could ride into even greener country, where streams were swollen from spring runoff, and the rich scent of pine met Irene's nostrils in a pleasant stimulus. "Someday I'm going back up there," she told Hank, nodding toward the snow-capped peaks that rose ahead of them. "The happiest memory of my life is when I went to the mountains with my father. I live right here at their feet, but life has been such a whirlwind, I've never had the chance to go back. Is there anything more splendid or more beautiful than those mountains?"

Hank did not reply, for to reply would be to betray his feelings. *Yes, there is something more splendid and beautiful, and she's sitting right next to me.*

Irene smiled, turning to look at him, admiring his rugged handsomeness, the powerful forearms beneath his rolled-up shirtsleeves. She looked at the mountains again, thinking this place, several miles from the ranch, was a delightful array of colors and smells and sounds. "Let's eat right here," she said, dismounting.

She wondered why she had done this, knew it was wrong, but had done it anyway. Hank spread out a blanket, and Irene set out the food. They ate, they talked, and both knew it was time to start being honest. Before the afternoon was over, Hank had told her the gruesome details of his wife and daughter's deaths, how he had met her in the first place, how much he had loved her, how happy they had been when their daughter was born. His voice had choked, but he knew Irene would understand it was all right for a man to weep over such a thing. He spoke of his hatred for the Indian called Yellow Eagle, but told her he could sometimes understand the frustration of the Indians.

Irene found herself spilling out the truth to Hank about how she had lost her baby. It felt good to be able to tell someone the truth. Before she knew it, she was even telling him about her love for Ramon, amazed at how easy it was to tell him such intimacies.

"I'll be damned," he said, putting a hand on her shoulder. "Remember that first day we met, back when you were with your pa and his friend? You asked about Hacienda del Sur."

It seemed like such a long time ago. "I remember," she told him. "I'd like you to take me there sometime. I'd like to see Ramon's land, although it doesn't belong to him any more."

"It's part of the B&K now."

"What?"

"Didn't you know that? Your mother took it over. I'm still not sure how she did it."

"My mother!" Did Ramon know his land belonged to Kirklands now? What was going on that she didn't know about? Why did Bea hate Ramon so much? A sickening dread moved into her heart. Had her mother somehow known all along about her and Ramon? Did she have something to do with the reason Ramon left that first time?

"I remember you asking about the Vallejo land," Hank was saying. "I got the funniest feeling that day, like there was something very special about the place for you. I remember the look on your face when I told you Ramon had married. It's strange how things work out, isn't it? Cruel is the better word."

"Yes," she said, "very cruel sometimes." She was beginning to understand how cruel her mother could be. She looked at Hank. "I still see Ramon occasionally, back in Denver. And we still . . ." She looked away. "We're good friends, a lot like you and me. Ramon is quite a successful builder now." She sighed deeply, wondering what had gone on behind her back. Poor Ramon. She was going to find out the truth the next time she saw her mother. "Do you think it's wrong, Hank, to be married to one person and love someone else? It seems to happen to so many people."

He watched her, wanting her, needing her. "No. It's not wrong. I loved my wife about as much as any man could love a woman, but every time I set eyes on you, I had thoughts I shouldn't have had."

She reddened, turning away. "I guess I felt it."

The air hung quiet for several seconds, with only the sound of the wind in the distant mountains. A hawk flew silently overhead, its shadow moving across them.

"It's even possible to love more than one person at the same time," Hank added cautiously. "There are different kinds of love, Irene. You still love Ramon. I expect maybe you always will. And then there's . . . you and me."

"Don't say it, Hank. I'm just feeling lonely, that's all." She quickly stood up. "Maybe we've let our friendship go too far. I've turned to you when I had no right. You just . . . you're so easy to talk to, and I've held all this in for so long. I'm sorry."

He stood up and came to stand behind her, putting a big hand on her arm. "Sorry for what? For bringing me the most happiness I've felt in a long time?" She started to pull away, but he kept a firm grip. "Get rid of him, Irene. After what you've told me, I can't believe you're still with him. I always knew there was something terribly wrong. Chad Jacobs is no good. He's destroying you!"

Her eyes filled with tears. "I can't give up that easily. He's my husband. I vowed to love him forever."

"And he made the same vow, but he *broke* it. *He* destroyed the marriage, Irene. Nothing that has happened has been your fault."

"But he would find a way to make it *look* like my fault. And maybe it is, at least partially. Maybe I . . . maybe there's something wrong with me. You don't know . . . I can't . . ." She covered her eyes, breaking into tears. "My God, Hank, don't make me tell you things I can't talk about."

"Like the fact that you don't desire him, that you think it's your fault he turns to other women, that you're a failure in bed?"

She jerked away. "Stop it!"

He grabbed her arms and forced her to face him. "Those are damn stupid thoughts, Irene! You've never wanted him because you've never really *loved* him. You were pushed into that marriage! If you don't love a man, you can't respond the way a woman *ought* to respond—with real passion. You've never even known what it's like to enjoy sex, have you? It's just been a *duty*."

She tried to pull away, but he pulled her closer, his power too much for her. "I can guess how you would respond to Ramon, if you felt you were free to do it. You aren't sure you love me that way, but you want me, don't you, Irene? You want me, and that scares you to death, because *sex* scares you to death. What did he do to you, Irene? What are you leaving out?"

"Just take me back, Hank."

"Not yet." He lifted her chin with a strong hand. "Not just yet." She met his eyes, and in the next moment his mouth was covering hers, his strong arms were coming around her, crushing her against his powerful chest. She started to resist, but it felt too good, too delicious. His hand moved to her bottom, pressing hard so that she felt his own urgent need while he smothered her with a groaning kiss that awakened passions she had not felt since kissing Ramon.

She wanted him! The realization almost startled her. Chad had made it all so ugly, and never once had she enjoyed just being a woman pleasing a man. She thought of Ramon . . . Ramon. If he ever touched her again this way, she would surely break the wedding vows she had so faithfully made. She hated Chad even more for putting her in this position of wanting to do something so terribly wrong.

Hank released her mouth, his breathing heavy, his grip strong. "My God, I want you so much, Irene," he groaned. "And you want me, I know it. Somebody needs to show you what it's like to be with a man out of sheer desire and passion."

"No! No, it isn't right." She put her hands against his chest. "I have to think. Take me home, Hank, please. Please help me by not touching me."

She could feel him trembling as he slowly let go of her. "It's going to happen, Irene, and there won't be one damn thing wrong about it, you hear me? Someday you're going to realize you can and should get rid of that man and let yourself be happy. I love you—enough to tell you that I don't even care if you turn to Ramon instead of me. I only know you'll never be happy the way things are now, and the longer you cling to those wedding vows, the deeper you're going to fall into a pit of sorrow you'll never be able to climb out of."

She pulled away, quickly picking up the picnic items, tears stinging her eyes, needs boiling deep inside that made turning him away almost painful. She remembered now how she had felt that first time Ramon had kissed her, and when he had kissed her at the house after his wife had died. She had wanted to respond with wild abandon, much as she imagined a whore might respond, and it surprised and almost frightened her.

She quickly tied the basket onto her horse, rolling up the blanket and throwing it over her saddle, desperately afraid that if Hank managed to get her down to that blanket, there would be no turning back. "I want to go home," she told him.

She heard a deep sigh. "Fine." He said nothing more. He mounted up, and she did the same, wearing a split riding skirt so she could ride full saddle instead of sidesaddle. The sight of her straddling the horse made Hank feel almost crazy with the want of her. He rode off ahead of her, afraid to touch her again or even look at her, for fear he would not be able to stop himself. She was in too delicate a condition for that. There could be no hint of force. It had to come from her. She had to recognize her own needs and desires and realize there was nothing wrong with wanting a man.

Irene followed him, hardly able to see for the tears. He wanted her, but she was not free for the taking, or free to give herself willingly. She had known this could happen, had let herself be led along by her own loneliness. Now she had hurt Hank. She had not wanted to do that, and she hated herself for it.

They rode in silence for several minutes. Hank turned his horse then and trotted back to ride beside her. "I'm sorry," he said. "I let myself get carried away, and I put you in a bad spot. I guess I would have been surprised if I hadn't met with some resistance. You're a good woman, Irene. I just think you're married to a stinking cad of a husband who doesn't appreciate you, and I can't stand it. I love you, and that's the hell of it. I'm not going to beat around the bush about it."

"I don't want to hurt you," she answered, blinking back tears. "I have so much to think about, Hank. I feel like my heart has been cut to little pieces. I should love my husband, but he makes it almost impossible. Then there is Ramon—" She looked over at him. "Now you. Sometimes I don't know my own mind anymore."

"And you won't until you leave Chad Jacobs. I meant it, Irene, when I said I would understand if you turned to Ramon. All I want is for you to be happy—to get rid of Chad Jacobs."

She looked ahead again. "You're a good man, Hank. I don't take lightly the fact that you love me. I guess we've both known how the other felt for a long time. We probably shouldn't have let ourselves be alone together." She quickly wiped at her eyes. "I need time to think. I can't just . . . just act on a moment of passion. I'm still a married woman."

You're just afraid, he wanted to tell her, *afraid to be a woman. You don't even know what it feels like. Passion is exactly what you should act on, for once in your life!* "I'll give you all the time you need," he told her. "I'll be leaving in a few days for Denver. You'll have time to think while I'm gone."

She swallowed back a lump in her throat, her heart torn. "I'm sorry, Hank."

"Don't be sorry for anything. You worry too much about hurting others, while you let yourself be hurt over and over again, Irene. You've got to stop it and start thinking about your own needs." He pulled closer, reaching out and grasping her shoulder to squeeze it. "I want you to think about the things I said. When I get back from Denver, we'll talk again."

She reached up and put a hand over his. There was nothing left to say for the moment.

"Let's work out the horses," she told him, kicking Sunrise into a harder run. They raced over the plains, sod flying from under horses' hooves, until reaching the last rise before coming to Irene's house. Irene slowed her Palomino and trotted to the top of the hill, drawing the horse to a halt when she saw a buggy sitting in front of the house. Hank halted his horse beside her.

"What is it?"

"That's Chad's buggy," she told him. "He's never come home in the middle of the week before. I wonder if something is wrong."

Hank frowned, feeling uneasy. "You think it's all right for me to ride in with you?"

She smiled bitterly. "After the things Chad has done? I think I have a right to go riding with a friend if I want. Besides, he knows we have been working together."

"Maybe you had better untie the picnic basket and leave it here," Hank suggested. "I'll pick it up when I leave. The basket makes it look a little personal."

She turned and looked at the basket, untying the leather cord that held it. "This seems a bit ridiculous, but maybe you're right, for now." She remembered the look in Chad's eyes when he had asked her at the hospital about Ramon, his remark about whores. She had never seen that look in his eyes before, and it had frightened her. She dropped the basket and rode forward.

Hank followed, and Chad came out to greet them when they approached the house. He called out to them, putting out his hand to Hank when they came close. Hank reached down and took his hand, thinking how he would much rather kill the man. For Irene's sake, he kept a smile on his face. He tried to read Chad's eyes and saw no anger there. Still, he felt uneasy.

"Out exercising the horses, I see," Chad told him.

"Yes," Hank answered. "Just a little ride to celebrate finishing the roundup. I'll be taking some cattle to Denver soon. Be glad when the Kansas Pacific makes it into Colorado. It will make my job easier."

"The Atchison, Topeka and Santa Fe is expected to connect at Pueblo within a couple of years," Chad replied. "That will be even closer for you. The KP is going to veer north into Denver."

"Either way, the railroad is a godsend to the cattle industry. You can tell Bea that this has been an exceptional year—a lot of new calves were born. Irene will be able to give her a firsthand report."

Chad glanced at Irene, who was petting Sunrise. "Yes," he answered, a slight hint of sarcasm in his voice. "I'm sure she will." He looked at Hank and grinned. "Well, nice seeing you again, Hank. I have some things to talk over with Irene. That's why I came home early."

Hank nodded, tipping his hat to Irene. "You've done a good job, Irene. I'll be in touch after I get back from Denver."

Their eyes held, and she knew he wanted to say much more. "Fine," she answered, giving him a smile. Hank nodded to Chad before turning his horse and riding off.

Chad watched him, saying nothing at first. He went inside and waited for Irene to take Sunrise to her stable. Irene could not help an odd, wary feeling that something was not quite right. She wondered what Chad needed to talk about. She asked one of the hired help to take care of Sunrise and headed back to the house. She had no more got inside and closed the door than a strong arm came around her from behind under her chin, cutting off her air.

"You goddamn *whore*," Chad growled. "You're just *like* her, aren't you—just like my *mother*!"

Her mind swam with confusion as she struggled against his grip, but without enough air, she quickly lost her strength. Black spots swam before her eyes as she felt herself being dragged into another room.

"How many times has Hank Loring fucked you?" Chad snarled. "You've been sleeping with him behind my back, haven't you? You probably let Ramon Vallejo under your skirts, too!"

She felt herself released, sensed they were in the bedroom. Her body was tossed, and she landed on the bed, gasping. Before she could gather her thoughts she felt her blouse being ripped away from her bosom, her skirt and bloomers being yanked away. "Chad," she groaned. "I haven't—"

A hard blow came across the side of her face, and she tasted blood. She was vaguely aware of being naked, except for her boots. A heavy body was on top of her then, pulling painfully at her hair at both sides of her head. "I thought I married a woman I could *trust*," he snarled. "I've never hurt a woman before, because I never gave a damn how much of a slut they were! They're all like my mother—bitches and whores—*all* of them! But *you*, I thought you were *different*! You're my *wife*! I'll not have my wife spreading herself for other men . . . not like her! Not like my mother!"

There came more stinging blows, before she had a chance to answer him or fight back. It had all happened too suddenly. Her head swam with his words. His mother! Now she knew why he had never talked about his childhood. What else didn't she know about him? She never dreamed Chad Jacobs was capable of this kind of violence. She felt strong hands deliberately squeezing her thighs, painfully shoving them apart. She knew instinctively that to try to fight him now would only bring more painful blows, and she was already choking on blood.

"I'll tell you something else, Irene Jacobs," he snarled. "I'm a man, understand? I'm a *man*! No woman turns me away, especially my own *wife*! I'm tired of you holding out on me, *rejecting* me! I'm the best. There's nothing wrong with me, you hear? I'm good with women. They love it, and *you* should love it, but not with Hank Loring or Ramon Vallejo, you hear? With *me*—Chad Jacobs!"

She felt him ramming himself inside her then with violent thrusts, his hands gripping her hips painfully. Everything became a blurred darkness after that. She was vaguely aware of his mouth biting at her breasts, bringing her pain, and a second violent intercourse. Finally his weight moved off her. The room was quiet, and she heard shuffling sounds as he straightened his pants and shirt. Then suddenly came the sound of someone sobbing.

"It's his fault," he wept. "*He* made me do it . . . him and my mother. She shouldn't have let him hurt me." Someone touched her hair. "Now you know who you belong to, Irene. Don't do this to me again. I can't . . . let any other man . . . be better . . . take you away from me. I didn't mean to hurt you, but . . . I can't let you be like her."

She felt a blanket come over her. "I've got to get back now. There's nothing left to talk about. It's settled now. We'll go back to Denver pretty soon. We'll have another baby, and everything will be all right."

She couldn't move or speak. Everything was a blur, and her whole body screamed with pain. She thought she heard a door close, vaguely remembered hearing a buggy clatter away.

CHAPTER
THIRTY

Hank slowed his horse. He was nearly home, but feelings of uneasiness continued to plague him. He kept seeing Chad Jacobs's smile, almost too friendly. He thought again about the way Chad had looked at Irene when he had told Chad that Irene could give a firsthand report on the ranch. Something about the tone of his voice then was what alarmed Hank and kept eating at him now.

He turned his horse. He figured he was probably going to look like a fool going back, but something told him Irene might need him. He kicked at the sides of his big stallion. "Sorry to do this to you, boy." The horse galloped off at a hard run, its mane and tail flying, Hank's hat blowing off his head and hanging around his neck by its cord.

Because of its run earlier in the day, Hank had taken it easy on the animal going home, taking nearly an hour to get there. Now he suddenly feared time was important, and in less than thirty minutes he was back at Irene's house. He noticed Chad's buggy was gone. He rode to the barn, where one of his best hands was feeding Sunrise.

"Tim, have you seen Irene?" Hank called out.

The man looked up at him. "No, sir. She brought her horse in here to be brushed down a couple of hours ago, maybe less than that. Her husband was here, but he left."

"Already? Was Irene with him?"

"I don't think so."

"Is the old Mexican woman in the house with her?"

"Flor is at her cabin, cooking our supper. Something wrong?"

"I don't know. I'm going to the house." Hank dismounted. "Unsaddle my horse and cool him down, will you? I ran him awfully hard."

"Sure thing." Tim Barnes took the stallion from Hank, wondering at the look of deep concern on his boss's face. He had worked for Hank Loring a long time, knew how deeply the man had grieved over his wife and daughter. He and most of the other men were aware of their boss's feelings for Irene Jacobs, and they feared Hank was headed for trouble.

Hank hurried to the house, getting no reply when he knocked at the door. He called out Irene's name, then tried the door, which was not locked. He stepped inside the house, calling for her again. A sick feeling began to move into his gut, a premonition that he was going to regret having left Irene alone with her husband today. He searched through the main rooms, and with a racing heart he headed for her bedroom. He cautiously entered and saw Irene lying on the bed, a blanket tossed over her bottom half. Her bare legs were partially exposed, her boots still on. Her clothes lay in a torn heap on the floor. She lay face down, and Hank could see she was naked to the waist.

"Dear God," he groaned. He slowly approached her. "Irene?" He saw a bruised arm now, touched her shoulder. She let out a groan of protest as she turned, then began hitting at him.

Hank grasped her wrists, appalled by her bruised face and a cut lip. Her arms were also covered with bruises, her breasts showing purple marks. "Jesus," he swore, pushing her arms to the bed. "Irene, it's me—Hank. It's all right now. He's gone. He's not here. He won't hurt you anymore."

She gasped, gritting her teeth, and he could see blood in her mouth. "It's me, Irene," he repeated. "It's Hank. Your husband *left*, Irene."

She just stared at him a moment, her eyes widening then as she began to tremble. "Go away," she squeaked. "Don't . . . look at me." She curled away from him, and his eyes teared. He pulled the blanket over her shoulders, leaning over her and kissing her hair. "Let me hold you, Irene. Let me help you. I'm so goddamn sorry I left. I should have known."

She put a hand over her face, breaking into trembling sobs, and he moved up onto the bed, lying down beside her. He pulled her into his arms, and at first she remained stiff and resistant, then began to realize it really was Hank, that Chad was gone. If he came back, Hank was here. He wouldn't let Chad near her again.

It didn't seem possible Chad could be capable of such violence. What had triggered it? What had he meant about his mother? She felt dirty and humiliated, and to have Hank see her this way only made the shame worse. She buried her face against his chest, sobs of near hysteria engulfing her. In spite of her embarrassment, she needed him right now, was glad he had come. She curled into his arms, feeling safe there, loved, protected.

"I'll get Flor. She can help you," he was saying.

"Don't let him come back," she sobbed.

"Don't worry about that. I'll not leave you alone with him again, Irene." Inside Hank raged at what Chad had done to her. Other men might say a man couldn't rape his own wife, but there was no other description for what had happened here. He was glad the man had left. If he saw him right now, he knew he'd kill him without an ounce of hesitation.

For three days Irene lay between pain and fitful bouts of sleep, during which the nightmare would return. Every time she woke up from the horror, strong arms came around her, a steady, loving voice spoke to her. Hank was there almost constantly, feeding her, sometimes just sitting with her. At night he slept with her, and she thought how strange and wonderful it was that she could just lie in a man's arms, knowing he loved her but knowing he expected nothing in return. He was not her husband, yet it seemed perfectly right and natural to lie with him. She had not been able to bring herself to talk about what had happened, and Hank seemed to understand that. She just needed to be held and loved.

It was five days after her attack when she finally got up and got dressed, with Flor's help. She walked on shaky legs to the main room of the house, where Hank sat at the huge mahogany, Spanish-style dining table, going over some paperwork. He looked up at her with concern, getting up right away and going to her side. "You sure you should be up?"

She put a hand on his strong arm. "I'm sure. I want to make breakfast for us."

"Flor can do that."

"No. I *want* to do it. Please let me, Hank. I've got to stop lying around thinking about it."

Hank glanced at the old Mexican woman who had cared for

Irene as if she were her own child the past few days. "I tried to reason with her, señor," the woman told Hank. "But then I think—maybe it would be good for her after all. I will go and get some of my work done, and then I will come back here and clean, *sí*? If she needs me, you come right away."

Hank sighed, taking Irene's arm. "All right. I don't know what we would have done without you, Flor. *Gracias*."

"*Por nada*, señor. I have grown to love her like my own. That husband of hers, he is a bad *hombre*." The woman patted Irene's back. "I will be back soon. Do not do too much, Señora Jacobs."

The woman left, and Hank grasped Irene's arms. "It's time we talked."

She met his soft, green eyes. "I know." She reddened slightly, realizing he had seen her naked, finding it incredible that she had allowed this man to lie beside her every night. How could one man, her own husband, be so dreadful? Yet she realized she wasn't sure she could have made it through the last few nights alone without this man, who was not her legal husband at all. How sweet and kind and patient he was. "I'll never forgive myself—"

She put her fingers to his lips. "You've said that too many times, Hank. It wasn't your fault, and I don't want to hear you blame yourself again. Let me make some breakfast. Then we'll talk."

They both heard the sound of a buggy, and he felt her stiffen with fear. "Stay right here," he told her, gently leading her to a chair. "If that's your husband, he's not getting inside the house."

She sensed his rage, and she feared for both of them. "Hank, don't do anything stupid, please," she begged.

He walked to the door, where his rifle sat propped against the wall. "You sure as hell don't want to see him, do you?"

"No. Not for a while yet." She thought of Chad's words about his mother. What was it she didn't know about him? She put a hand to her eyes. "My God, Hank, he's my husband. Don't hurt him."

"*Kill* him is what I'd *like* to do!" He opened the door, and Irene sat frozen as he stepped out onto the porch. She saw the buggy just before Hank closed the door, recognized Chad. The horror of his beating returned, and she was glad the door closed so that she did not have to look at him.

"Stay right in that rig," she heard Hank tell him, as soon as the buggy came to a halt.

"What the hell are *you* doing here?" Chad answered. Just the sound of his voice made her feel sick again.

"I could ask *you* that question, after what you did to Irene," Hank answered. "She doesn't want to see you, Jacobs, so you can go back to Colorado Springs and stay there until Irene decides what she wants to do." She heard the click of Hank's rifle being cocked. There was a moment of silence.

"You can't order me away from my own wife and my own house," Chad growled.

"I'm doing it," Hank answered. "You were wrong about Irene and me, Jacobs. Even if you had been right, you wouldn't have had any reason to go blaming her for anything she does. Whatever happens, you drove her to it, you stinking bastard! Any man who rapes his own wife is the worst kind of coward!"

"You get out of my way, Loring, or I'll see to it Bea Kirkland fires you and you lose your own ranch as well. I can ruin you!"

"Go ahead and try. I'll do whatever it takes to protect Irene from your filthy hands. Now get off this ranch!"

"You wouldn't use that on me."

"Wouldn't I? *Try* me! It wouldn't take much to put me over the edge, Jacobs! And you'd better be aware that most of the hands around here already know what you did. You push this thing too far, the gossip might spread to Colorado Springs, maybe to Denver— and your *mother*-in-law. I have a feeling that even if she thought her daughter had done something wrong, she wouldn't take kindly to what you did to her. Her father would like it even *less*. The man thinks the world of Irene. You'd better remember that!"

There was a moment of silence. "Look, I need to talk to Irene," Chad said then. "It's important. What happens between me and my wife isn't your business, Loring. I want to apologize. I need to explain something to her. We—we had this all settled. If you'd keep your nose out of it, there wouldn't be any problems. What's going on between you and Irene!"

"Nothing! You should have asked that question in the first place, before you beat and raped your wife! Now you've lost your right to talk to her at all, Jacobs! Get out!"

"Damn you! You're nothing but a cow-fucking ranch hand, Loring! You can't—"

There came the sound of some kind of blow, followed by a grunt and a scuffling sound. "Now get in that buggy and get the hell out of here," Hank growled, "or I'll have my men throw you in a pile of horse shit where you belong!"

Irene heard a coughing sound. "I'll be back," Chad spat out then. A moment later she heard his buggy clatter away. She watched anxiously as Hank came back inside, his green eyes blazing.

"That's the hardest I've ever tried to keep myself from killing a man," he told her, setting his gun aside. "One bullet, Irene, and he's out of your life forever! I wouldn't care if I hanged for it!"

She closed her eyes. "No. I don't want him dead, and I certainly don't want you dead either."

"Then you'd better pack some things. I'm taking you to my place. If we stay here, he'll be back, and I don't know if I can keep from pulling the trigger next time. You think you can ride, or do you want a buggy?"

It was an order, not a request. She realized he was probably right. Maybe it would be best to get away from the house for a few days, away from the room that held so many ugly memories now. Chad would not dream of setting foot on the Lazy T . . . not now. She rose. "I think I'd rather ride. I'm well enough."

He studied her beautiful but bruised face. The bruises were a yellowish-green now. He had not seen her other bruises since the day of her attack, but they stuck in his mind like knives in his heart—ugly finger marks on her thighs and hip bones, bruises on her ribs and around her breasts. Something else stuck in his mind, too—the memory of her beautiful body, the flat belly and full breasts. She was such a beautiful, sensitive woman to be treated so brutally. He stepped closer, putting a big hand to the side of her face. "He'll never hurt you again as long as I'm alive," he told her.

She smiled, putting a hand to his strong wrist. "I know." She dropped her eyes, wondering how it was she could actually feel this tingling desire after what Chad had done to her. Love. That was what made all the difference.

Every day they rode together, Irene letting the southern Colorado sun and fresh air warm her body, heal her outer wounds. Brilliant wildflowers and singing birds reminded her there was still beauty in life. She drew strength from sitting for long, quiet hours in Hank's arms staring at the mountains. She had been staying at his house for ten days, neither of them caring if the men talked and wondered. Hank had not touched her, and since she was better, he had stopped sleeping beside her at night.

She missed his presence, but knew why he stayed away. Now that she was healing, he could not bear to be so close to her without wanting her. What surprised and disturbed her was that she wanted him, too. They had become so close, and he was so understanding. He had sent other men on to Denver with the cattle so that he could stay with her. Irene found herself telling him everything, even what had happened on her wedding night; she had sensed his rage, knew he never would have been the animal Chad had been.

Twelve days after coming to the Lazy L they went on another ride, this time taking a picnic lunch again. They took a different direction, heading toward a sea of rolling hills south of Hank's ranch, to a place where wildflowers bloomed in abundance, and the grass grew green and thick. They found a clearing surrounded by rocks and yellow yucca bushes, where Hank spread out a blanket. Irene opened the basket lunch, and they ate fried chicken and apple pie, then just sat together watching several deer through an opening between the bushes. The animals grazed quietly in the distance, unaware of any human presence. Irene leaned against Hank's shoulder, enjoying the warm sun, the security of his presence.

"It's time to make some decisions, Irene," he told her softly.

"I know. I just haven't wanted to think about it." She met his eyes. "I don't know yet what I'm going to do about my marriage, Hank. I don't even know what to do about my feelings for Ramon. I still love him."

She saw the hurt in his eyes, and she touched his face. In that one look, that one moment, she knew what had to be, realized what she needed to know above everything else.

"You're the one here right now, Hank; and you've done so much for me." A strong shiver suddenly surged through her body, and she wondered if it was really she talking, she wanting these things. "You told me once that I had never known how it felt to take a man willingly, with passion and desire. You were right. I said I didn't know what I would do about my marriage, or my love for Ramon, Hank. But if I can give you some pleasure and happiness while you show me the way it's supposed to be with a man, then I know what I want right now, at this moment. I want you."

Their eyes held, as his own brightened with desire. "Irene . . . are you sure?"

"I've thought about it every night since you stopped coming to bed with me and holding me. I miss you in the night, Hank. I'm confused about a lot of things, but I'm not confused about how I feel about you anymore. After all that has happened, I don't care if it's right or wrong. I just . . ." Her eyes were wet. "I want you to take away what he did to me."

His look of surprise and passion told her she'd said the right thing. "Irene," he whispered. He leaned forward and kissed her forehead, put a big hand to the side of her face, moved his lips to her eyes, her nose, her mouth, lightly running his tongue along her lips as he parted them and gently laid her back onto the blanket. His lips left hers and brushed softly against her cheek. "I want you to be sure, Irene," he said softly. He raised up slightly to remove his gunbelt.

She could feel his own trembling, saw nothing but love and utter devotion in the green eyes. He was older than Chad, more weathered, yet at the moment he was a thousand times more handsome. He was fully a man in ways Chad would never be. "I've never been more sure of anything in my life," she told him, "but right now I feel as scared as if I'd never done this."

He grinned slightly. "Maybe I feel the same way."

She smiled, her eyes misty. "Somehow I don't believe you." She reached up and touched his hair. "I love you so much, Hank."

He put a hand to her ribs. "And I love you." He met her mouth again, and fire ripped through her in hot flames of need when his big, rough hand touched her breast as gently as a kitten might brush against her. She was soon lost in him, determined not to hold back this time, wanting so much just to be a woman in the fullest sense. She whimpered with ecstasy as he captured her mouth in hungry kisses while he opened her blouse.

She gasped his name as his lips trailed down her neck. He pushed her blouse open and untied her camisole. His hand slid inside the camisole, gently massaging a breast, lifting it up to meet his warm, moist lips. She grasped his hair, closing her eyes and whispering his name as he took her nipple ever so gently into his mouth.

He raised up slightly, pushing her blouse and camisole away from her breasts, leaning down to kiss lightly at every bruise, touching her almost reverently. She felt a big hand moving up her leg as his lips met her mouth again. He grasped at her hip under her riding skirt, his kisses growing hotter, his tongue running into her mouth suggestively, bringing out an almost painful passion she never dreamed could be so glorious.

There was nothing left to be said. Her response let him know that for once in her life she wanted this, needed it. He might be heading for a broken heart, but he was not going to deny her need, or his own. He turned her on her side, and she buried her face against his chest as he unbuttoned the back of her riding skirt. She watched him boldly then as he sat up and removed her boots, then gently removed the skirt and her bloomers. She drew up her knees slightly as he softly caressed her thighs, her bottom, moved his hand to her flat belly, rubbing at old bruises. He met her eyes then, and she thought she might die with the want of him.

"You're so damn beautiful, Irene," he told her. "I don't know how any man can do anything but worship you."

She grasped one of his hands. "I've never felt . . . so free and alive," she told him.

He squeezed her hand, bending down to kiss lightly at her belly, then bringing a shudder of desire when his lips pressed a kiss at the core of her womanhood. He moved up her body then, tasting at each breast, his hand moving between her legs. She was amazed at the difference between his touch and Chad's. Chad had usually tried to be gentle, in their earlier years together, but his touch had never made her feel like this. After a while he had given up on foreplay and had simply taken to smothering her with kisses and grasping at her breasts, expecting her to want him so madly that all she needed was for him to move on top of her.

This was so different. Hank was working magic with his fingers, bringing a brazenness to her soul that she had never experienced. She realized he must be right, that when a woman truly wanted a man, every aspect of lovemaking was ecstasy. She felt a wonderful explosion deep inside that made her gasp and arch against his hand. His kisses grew deeper, hotter, as he pressed his hand hard between her legs, then carefully ran it along the inside of one thigh, gently urging her legs apart.

He moved between them then. She kept her eyes closed as she felt him raise up. She knew he was freeing himself from his own clothes. Would it seem as repulsive as it had that horrible day with Chad? She grasped at Hank's arms, knew he was looking at her brazen nakedness in the Colorado sun. She had never actually wanted a man to look at her, but now she felt no shame. She only felt beautiful, wanted, revered.

She felt his weight come down on her then, felt him pressing hard against her groin. "Hank," she whispered.

He sensed her sudden apprehension. "Look at me, Irene. Don't close your eyes like a scared little girl."

She met his eyes, and in the next moment he was sliding into her, filling her with his hardness, yet moving in such a way that he drew forth all the natural moistness of a woman who wanted to mate. She drew in her breath as he pushed harder, and she was amazed and delighted that nothing hurt, that it seemed only beautiful and right. She wanted him! She wanted him to take her and take her. She arched her chin back, and he bent his head to taste lightly at her breasts while he moved rhythmically. She found herself wanting to meet his thrusts. He raised up, grasping her hips, groaning with his own shuddering desire at the glory of taking her. He gripped her hips tighter as his life spilled into her.

"Don't stop," she whimpered, amazed at her own words. "Please don't stop."

"Just lie still," he told her. He came closer again, kissing at her neck. "It's been a long time for me, Irene. It's hard for a man to hold back, especially when he wants a woman as much as I wanted you." His mouth covered her own in a savage kiss, and in moments she felt his passion returning. He began moving again, more slowly, filling her again with almost teasing thrusts. She met them with deliberate wantonness, opening her eyes again to meet his, seeing there the glazed look of a man in deep ecstasy, seeing his utter adoration.

She knew she should feel guilty, but Chad had left no room for such feelings. She knew she needed to do this or lose her sanity. There was a time when she never dreamed she would be capable of committing adultery. She had not planned her life to be like this, had thought her marriage would sustain her.

This time the rhythmic ecstasy lasted for several minutes. Hank took pride and satisfaction in realizing she was truly enjoying lovemaking for the first time in her life. He wanted it to be so good for her. Finally he could no longer hold back his own ecstasy, and his life surged into her again. He lay down beside her then, keeping her in his arms. "We're taking our chances, out here in the open," he told her.

"I don't care. It feels good to be daring and bold and free."

He laughed. "We'll do this more tonight, in a nice, comfortable bed."

She unbuttoned his shirt, opening it and kissing lightly at the hairs of his chest. She had never wanted to do this to Chad, had never really hungered for him this way. She touched at his nipples, leaned up to kiss them. There was only one other man who could make her feel so brazen and passionate—one other man who could awaken such fiery ecstasy in her soul. Somehow she would have to find a way to explain this to Ramon. She loved him, maybe more than she loved Hank. But she had needed this moment, and it was Hank who was here. She would not hurt him now. Somehow she knew Ramon would understand what had happened to her today. He knew the pain she had suffered.

"It was so beautiful, Hank. I want to stay with you forever," she told him. "I've never been so happy. It was everything you said it would be."

He kissed at her eyes. "We have a lot to talk about. It won't be easy leaving your husband, but people can talk all they want, Irene. It won't make any difference to me. I know the kind of woman you are, and I love you. I need you so much, Irene." He met her mouth again, groaning in another hungry kiss. "Thank you for this." He petted her hair. "I needed it as much as you did." He kissed at her breasts. "Let's go back to the house," he said then. "I want you in my bed. I want to lie naked next to you."

"And I want the same," she whispered.

He grasped at her thick hair. She wore her blond mane long and loose today, the way he liked it best. "I don't think I can make it back without being inside you once more before we go."

She leaned up and met his mouth, experimenting with her tongue, telling him it was fine with her if he wanted her again. He rolled on top of her again, both of them feeling brazen and wicked and alive and in love. They smiled as they kissed, and he moved inside of her, already big with desire again. He had not been so hot for a woman since his first week of being married, and he felt like a much younger man.

Irene felt another delicious climax building, although she didn't even know what to call it. Something about the way he moved against her so softly, so lovingly, something about wanting him as she had never wanted Chad, brought this exhilarating throbbing she had never known before this day.

Her breathing came in quick gasps, and Hank moved his big hands under her hips, his broad shoulders hovering over her as he pushed hard, as though he couldn't get enough of her. "Let yourself enjoy it," he whispered. She dug her nails into his strong arms, crying out with the glory of it.

Moments later he again released his passion, not caring if this was right or wrong. Nothing mattered now. She would leave Chad and they would be together. He would support her through all the pain of what was to come. His whole body shuddered with the thrill of finally mating with this beautiful creature, not just once but three times in a matter of minutes. His great need of her brought out a masculine prowess he had not felt in years.

He took a deep breath then and moved off her, getting to his feet and pulling up his long johns and pants. He walked over to his horse to get his canteen. He carried it over to her, along with a washrag and soap from his saddlebags. "I've been carrying these for a while, hoping you'd need them one of these times when we went riding," he told her with a wink. "I was beginning to think we'd never have need of them."

Irene reddened as she took them, and Hank turned away. "I'll wash and change when we get back." He buttoned his shirt. "Maybe we can even take a bath together. Is that too daring for you?"

The thought of it was delightful. "Not anymore," she answered, quickly washing herself. "I want to do everything, Hank, as long as it's with you."

She pulled on her bloomers and handed him the canteen, washcloth, and soap. He put them away and picked up the food and blanket while she finished dressing. "Let me do that," he told her, as she began buttoning her blouse. She studied his handsome face as his big fingers worked the tiny buttons with amazing agility. She felt on fire at his fingers brushing against her breasts, at the thought of how intimate they had been, and she actually wanted to jump with joy at how wonderful sex could be with the right person. No one could ever convince her it had been wrong.

He pulled her close. "I love you, Irene. I want to take care of you, want to share my life with you."

"And I want the same. We'll have it, Hank."

He leaned down and met her mouth in a warm, delicious kiss, moving his lips to her ear. "Let's get back to the house so we can continue this in bed," he told her. "We just might not get up for two or three days."

She smiled, hugging him, feeling alive and loved in ways she had never been loved before. She reluctantly pulled away from him, looking into his soft, green eyes. "I don't care if we stay there forever."

He gave her another wink. "Somebody has to tend to the cattle and horses, and we do have to eat sometime, I suppose."

"I suppose," she replied. She smiled, walking over to mount her horse. Hank climbed onto his stallion, and Irene glanced at the spot of matted grass where they had lain together. "I'll never forget this place or this day for the rest of my life," she told him, tears in her eyes.

He rode up beside her. "Neither will I. Let's get back to the house. We have some time to make up for, and a lot to talk about."

They rode off, heading north toward the Lazy L, two people set small against the vast Colorado plains, two people who thought they were alone. They moved across the grassland, rising and falling with the sea of hills, never noticing that on another hill to their right eight Indian braves lay flat on their bellies, watching them.

"Only two," one of them said to his leader.

The young Cheyenne warrior, Yellow Eagle, kept a steady eye on the man and woman, and their mounts. "Those are the same yellow horses like those we stole many years ago from the white man's ranch not far from here. I have never seen such grand horses."

"Now we will have two more, plus a woman for ransom," one of the others said.

"Aye," Yellow Eagle answered. "She has hair like the sun." He stood up. The two riders were past them now, unaware the Indians were behind them. Yellow Eagle quickly put an arrow in his bow and drew back the taut rawhide string, letting the arrow fly. He grinned when it landed square in the back of the big white man who rode the golden stallion. He heard the woman scream out "Hank!" He watched the man fall from his horse.

CHAPTER
THIRTY-ONE

Irene heard the whirring sound, the thud. It all happened in a split second, so quickly she did not realize at first what had taken place. Hank had not made a sound. He simply slumped forward and fell from his horse, an arrow in his back.

"Hank!" She whirled her horse, looking around, seeing several Indians on the rise behind them. "Oh, dear God!" Her mind raced with horror and confusion. Hank! Was he still alive? She had to know, had to protect him, protect herself. Should she try to run? But Hank! What about Hank! If she left him here alive, he might be tortured! He needed help!

She dismounted, kneeling down beside him, groaning at the sight of the ugly arrow embedded in his back. There was hardly any blood. Somewhere, sometime, she had heard that if there was no blood, a person was already dead. Bleeding stopped once the heart stopped beating. No! Not Hank! Not now! Not when she had just found this happiness!

"Hank," she screamed. "Wake up! Don't die on me, Hank!" She tried to roll him over, at the same time hearing the war whoops of the Indians. They were coming! "Hank!" She had managed to push him up on one side. Horror engulfed her when she realized he was surely dead. He was so still, and the point of the arrow protruded from the middle of his chest, pieces of flesh on the end of it. "Noooo," she screamed. "No! No! No!"

There was not even time to hold him, mourn him. The Indians were getting closer. She knew instinctively they were coming for her, that they would want her alive. She stood up and ran to Hank's horse, pulling his rifle from its boot. She had never had to use a gun before to save her life. She cocked it, turning and taking aim as the Indians came closer. She had waited too long to outrun their swift ponies, but she was not about to go down without a fight; and there was Hank's death to avenge.

She fired, and to her own surprise, one of the Indians fell from his horse. There was no time to think about the fact that she had killed a man, or to wonder why and how these Indians had come to be here. Everyone had thought this area was safe now. She fired again, but to her dismay she hit one of the Indian ponies instead of the man. The animal crashed to the ground, and the Indian went rolling off his dead mount.

She cocked the rifle again, but it jammed. She threw it to the ground, running to Hank's body and yanking his six-gun from its holster. She raised it, firing again, but the shot missed. The Indians spread out, surrounding her. She fired at another one, and the man cried out as a bloody hole opened up in his shoulder. He flew back off his horse.

Before Irene could fire again, something hard came crashing down painfully across her right shoulder, making her drop the gun. She heard a loud war cry close to her, and someone grasped her hair, yanking hard. Irene's first thought was that she was going to be scalped. How many times had she been told that Indian men loved to rape and scalp blond-haired white women? The warrior yanked her to the ground, keeping hold of her hair as he straddled her, sitting down on her belly. He placed a huge blade to her throat and began moving rhythmically on top of her, as though to hint at what he intended to do with her.

"So," he said leaning closer, surprising her when he spoke English, "the white woman is very brave, very good with a gun, huh? Maybe she is good in an Indian man's tipi. Maybe she would make a good mate," he sneered.

She was shocked to realize he had blue eyes, eyes as blue as her own. His hair was not blue-black like the others', but a dark brown, with streaks of blond in it. She had heard descriptions of Yellow Eagle more than once, the young half-breed who had wreaked so much havoc across the Colorado plains. She was at the mercy of one of the worst of the Cheyenne rebels!

"You're Yellow Eagle," she spat at him.

His eyebrows arched, and he grinned in a sneer. "And how do you know this?"

"I have heard about the half-breed snake who makes war on innocent people! Why did you have to kill him? You already made him suffer when you killed his wife and daughter six years ago!" Her eyes filled with desperate tears. Hank! Nothing mattered now that Hank was dead. How could it be that only minutes earlier she had lain in his arms, taken him inside herself? The shock was so great that she didn't even care now what Yellow Eagle did to her.

"If I killed his wife and child, I did not know they belonged to this man. No white man—or woman—means anything to me! If you had been at Sand Creek, if you had watched your mother being raped and cut open, your wife and little son butchered, you would not care either!" He pushed at the knife so that it nicked her skin, and she gasped, sure her life would end any moment. "Before that, there were all the broken promises, and there was the white man, killing off all our game while our children's bellies screamed with hunger! There are many reasons, white woman! Many reasons why my friends and I will take you to our camp and enjoy you before we sell you back to your family."

He yanked harder on her hair, making her cry out, arching her head back to the side so that it was hard to get her breath. "What are you called? Are you worth food, many guns, horses?" He pressed the knife again. "Speak, woman!"

The others with him picked up their dead comrade and grabbed hold of the two Palominos. The wounded one walked around cursing in his own tongue, telling one of the others to tie something around his shoulder.

"I am . . . Irene . . . Jacobs," Irene answered. "My father . . . is David Kirkland . . . Denver. He'll pay you . . . much more in ransom . . . if you don't hurt me. He's—a wealthy man."

Yellow Eagle's blood ran cold. The knife came away from her throat. He shoved it into its sheath at his side and grasped her hair at both sides of her head, holding her head up so that she had to look him straight in the eyes. Yes! He saw it now—in the eyes!

Irene watched the expression on his face, that of a man in near shock. He suddenly leapt off of her. "This is true? You are the daughter of David Kirkland?"

She put a hand to her throat, rolling to her knees. "Yes." She looked up at him, feeling a strange familiarity when she met his eyes again. Why was he looking at her that way? "Please let me go."

His eyes moved over her in a kind of strange reverence, and

Irene thought that, if he were not so wild and painted, he could be handsome. "I will not harm you, but I am taking your horses." He backed away. This had to be the sister. He guessed her to be his age, saw himself in her eyes. She must not know she had a brother, or she would have said so. She would have shouted right away that she was his sister so that he would not harm her.

"You are free to go," he told her. He turned and said something to the others in his own tongue, and they all looked at Irene as though she were some kind of apparition.

Irene watched in confused amazement as they mounted their horses. The man whose horse she had shot took the dead man's horse. They threw his body over the animal in front of him. Two of the other men each took the reins of the two Palominos. Yellow Eagle walked over and took a canteen from one of them, throwing it to Irene, then mounted up. "We need the horses. Ours are easily worn out from always running from the soldiers," he told her. "I leave you water."

Irene wondered why he was bothering to explain, as though he was suddenly sorry to leave her here without a horse. And why was he leaving the water? Their eyes held a moment longer, and then he turned his horse.

The Indians rode off, leaving her alone with Hank and the dead horse. Irene had no time to wonder why she was spared. She stumbled over to Hank's body, trying to roll it onto its side again. She could feel he was already getting stiff, and she recoiled, a shuddering groan of horror engulfing her, rippling through her and coming out of her in vomit.

She threw up until it seemed her own stomach would come out of her throat. She finally calmed enough that she could rinse her mouth. She got to her feet and stepped away, staring at Hank, whimpering his name over and over. How could life end so quickly? How could a man be holding her and making love to her one moment, and be dead the next? Her body shook in bitter sobs, and she stumbled away. She had to get help. She had to get men out here to pick up Hank's body before the crows and buzzards and wolves got to it.

She clung to the canteen and started walking, the hot sun beating down on her bare head. She remembered then that her hat was still tied to her horse. She felt a wetness at the collar of her dress and realized her throat must be bleeding where Yellow Eagle had cut it with his knife. She could hardly believe she had come face-to-face with the notorious warrior and had been let go with nothing more than the cut.

But Hank! Hank had not escaped! There would be no lovemaking in his bed tonight. Never again would he hold her! Never again would she hear his soothing voice or feel his big, strong hands moving over her. Never again would they go on a roundup together, go riding together.

She walked blindly toward what she hoped was the right direction. Someone had to come and get poor Hank's body. She walked for what seemed hours, the sun beating down on her, blood soaking and drying on the front of her dress, a hot dizziness overwhelming her until finally she sank to the ground.

What did it really matter? Hank was dead, and she would probably die, too. Who would care? Her mother was busy with Kirkland Enterprises, the only thing she really cared about. Chad certainly didn't care anymore. He had all his other women. Elly hated her. Hank was dead, and John was lost in his world of whiskey and self-pity.

But then there was Father. Kirk would care, and she was her father's daughter. She had to be strong, a survivor, like David Kirkland. And there was Ramon—Ramon! Yes, there was always Ramon, faithful, loving Ramon. He would understand all of this. He would not blame her. Ramon. She could see his face, see him reaching out, telling her to be strong, telling her that no matter what happened, he would always be there for her.

She got up and started walking again. Maybe, she thought, she could walk all the way to Denver and to Ramon.

The doctor came into the main room to talk to Chad and Elly and John, who had been summoned from Colorado Springs by one of Hank's men. Irene had been found lying on the ground a half mile from Hank's ranch house. That had been yesterday. She had managed to tell the man what had happened, and he had sent a man riding hard to Colorado Springs to get a doctor and Irene's family. Other men went searching for Hank's body, while Irene was taken by wagon back to her own house, where Flor took care of her until the doctor came.

The entire atmosphere among the ranch hands was one of great sorrow for a good man lost, a man deeply respected in southern Colorado. In Colorado Springs wires were sent to the various forts to request that soldiers hunt down Yellow Eagle.

John sat in a big leather chair in the corner of the room, quietly drinking, watching Chad and Elly sullenly, angry with Elly for seeming so unconcerned, still suspicious of his sister and his brother-in-law. He couldn't prove anything, but something about the way they looked at each other, the way they stood a little too close when working together, made him wonder if there was more going on than anyone knew about. He knew Elly, knew she had had a crush on Chad when she was younger, knew what a brat she had always been and how she felt about Irene.

"She's going to be all right," the doctor told Chad. "I cleaned and bandaged her throat. There might be a faint scar, but nothing dramatic. She's been through a pretty rough time. I hope you realize how lucky you are. Anyone who meets up with Yellow Eagle, especially a woman, and survives the encounter with only a cut has walked away from a sure death. Seeing Hank Loring killed before her eyes was traumatic for her. Maybe you should send her back to Denver for a while."

Chad nodded. "I'll talk to her . . . see what she wants to do."

The doctor frowned. "What I can't understand is the bruises."

"Bruises?" Chad glanced at Elly, who gave him a half smile. She knew what he had done, had delighted in the thought of Chad accusing Irene of infidelities, of Irene being beaten into submission.

"She has a lot of bruises, but not from this incident. They're old bruises. I asked her where she got them, and she just said she fell; but the bruises I saw didn't come from a simple fall." The doctor held Chad's eyes, noticing Chad's look of sudden self-defense and near threat. Flor, who had come out of the bedroom, cast hateful glances at Chad, but she said nothing. These were matters for rich people. Old Mexican women did not get involved.

"If my wife says she fell, then she fell," Chad answered. "If you're through with her, I'd like to go talk to her."

The doctor sighed. "I left some laudanum on the table beside the bed if she happens to need any for pain or to help her sleep. There really isn't anything more I can do." He put on his hat. "I'll be going back to Colorado Springs now. I just hope the soldiers find Yellow Eagle and hang him by his heels. Hank Loring was a damn good man, a *damn* good man. This just makes me sick."

"Yes. Us, too," Elly purred. "I guess we're going to have to find a new ranch manager, Chad. Mother might want to move quickly to merge the Lazy T in with the B and K. I can go back with the doctor and wire her, if you like."

John thought how like his mother Elly was—in a time of such personal horror for Irene, Elly was already thinking about the effect Hank's death would have on the business.

"Yes. It's about time we let her know what's happened here," Chad told her. "Tell Mother not to worry about Irene. Tell her I'm bringing her back to Denver to recuperate. We can't leave her here alone, and I have to get back to Colorado Springs as quickly as I can. I'll leave things to you and John for a few days."

Elly rose, walking over to get her cape. "Don't you want to see your sister first?" the doctor asked her.

"Oh, she's probably awfully upset. It won't do any good for me to go in there. She needs Chad right now." Elly glanced at Chad, giving him a half grin. "I'll see you when you get back to Colorado Springs."

Chad nodded, and John took another swallow of whiskey as Elly left with the doctor. Chad glanced at him, a look of disgust on his face. "Why don't you quit the damn liquor?" he told John. "You're ruining yourself, John, and I have to tell you I'm losing my respect for you."

John snickered. "Seems to me, brother-in-law, you should be more concerned with Irene right now. Why don't you tell me where she got those bruises? I remember one day you went home in the middle of the week, came back the same day with a bruised hand and strange-looking scratches on the side of your face."

Chad held his eyes. "Your mother wouldn't be very happy to know how bad your drinking problem is, young man."

"I don't give a damn what my mother thinks of anything. But *you* do!" John got up from his chair, his bloodshot eyes blazing. "You beat her, didn't you?"

"You're drunk," Chad sneered.

John startled him when he smashed his whiskey bottle. Flor jumped back, cringing as he held up the jagged edges of the bottle by the neck. "You ever lay a hand on her again, and I'll leave a cut on that pretty face of yours that will make women puke to look at you! That's a goddamn *promise*, Chad. You won't be able to sleep at night for fear of waking up with your nose and lips sliced off!"

Their eyes met in a challenge. Chad swallowed then, putting on a slight grin. "It was a one-time thing, John—a misunderstanding. I came back to talk to Irene about it, to make up for it if I could, but Hank wouldn't let me in the door."

"Good for Hank! I'm sorry as hell he's dead. *You're* the one who deserves to die."

Chad sighed. "Look, John, don't say anything to Irene's parents. Surely you realize this is between man and wife, that it's Irene's decision what she tells them, not yours."

"I won't say a damn thing. I'm just telling you what I'll do if you hurt her again!"

Chad nodded. "Then we have an understanding. I like you, John. I want to help you all I can. That's why I'm concerned about your drinking."

"Just go see your *beloved* wife. I don't buy your charm anymore, Chad. Irene hasn't been happy since the day she got married. I don't know what all is going on, and I know some of the talk going around about Irene and Hank, but I'm betting that if she turned to Hank, she had damn good reason! She's a good woman . . . too good for the likes of you!"

John walked to the door, going outside and slamming it shut. Chad glanced at Flor, who gave him a scathing look. He realized she must know what he had done. "You mind your own business, old woman, or you'll be off this ranch and wandering the desert." He turned and went into the bedroom, and Flor quietly began picking up the broken bottle.

Irene lay in bed, her throat bandaged, dark circles about her eyes. She looked up at Chad, her eyes filled with hatred and bitterness. "Why are you even here?" she asked. "I'm sure . . . you would have been quite happy . . . if I had died out there."

Chad sighed, bringing up a chair to sit down beside her. "No, I wouldn't have. My God, Irene, when I heard what had happened, I can only thank God you're alive, that I have this chance to tell you how sorry I am about what I did a couple of weeks ago. That's the God's truth, Irene. I've never hit a woman in my life."

"Or raped one?"

He closed his eyes, putting his head in his hands. "Never."

"You never had to. You just *charmed* them all into your bed, but you were never quite able to do that with me, were you? That's . . . what made you so angry with me."

"Partly."

"I don't care anymore, Chad. I don't care about anything, now that Hank is dead." She met his eyes. "I loved him, and I don't care if you know it. He was the kind of man you'll never be—a *real* man, who *respected* women, appreciated them. I . . . can't live this way any longer, Chad. I'm divorcing you . . . no matter what the shame."

"No!" He felt the desperation rising. She couldn't do this! He would lose everything! She would tell Bea, tell the world what he had done! He had no defense. If he tried to drag her name through the dirt, he would just be all the more ostracized. Everyone knew what a fine person she was. Bea would never believe her daughter could do any wrong. She thought the world of him, but if it came to a showdown between himself and her daughter . . . "Irene, you have to give me a chance to explain. We're still husband and wife. I did something terribly wrong, I know, but . . . men do that sometimes when they're crazy with jealousy."

"It wasn't jealousy. It was something much more, Chad . . . something from deep in your soul . . . your past . . . something that could drive you to beat me again. I can't live with that fear."

He couldn't fail! A divorce would mean he had failed as a man, as a lover; and he would fail in his career. He had no choice now but to tell her the truth. Irene was discreet. He could trust her. What did it matter if his own wife knew, if it meant he could keep the marriage together, even if it was just for appearance sake. "Irene, I—I can understand why you turned to Hank. I really can. I don't blame you for that anymore. I don't even want to know if—if you had an affair with him. God knows I drove you to it."

She watched him in surprise, mixed with deep suspicion. It was hard to believe anything he told her anymore, hard to feel anything but hatred for him. She swallowed back a painful lump in her throat. "I don't want to talk about this now, Chad," she said, a tear slipping down her cheek. "You don't know what I've been through. After what you did . . . Hank helped me . . . loved me. He was . . . a good, good man. To see him killed . . . in front of my eyes was . . . worse than losing the baby . . . worse than being beaten by my own husband. Nothing matters anymore, Chad, . . . nothing."

He thought how vulnerable she was now, how easy it would be to win her sympathy. He leaned closer. "Irene, listen to me. These things *do* matter. They matter because . . . no matter how much you hate me, I still love you. I always have . . . even when I strayed. I—I hold you in such reverence—"

"Reverence!" She turned her face away. "My God, Chad, what kind of a fool do you take me for?"

"It's true. That's why when I thought you might have been with Ramon, or with Hank, I just went crazy, Irene. I—I grew up with a mother who was nothing more than a whore, Irene. That's the God's truth. She was always bringing strange men home." He hesitated. He would not tell her what one of them had done to him. He couldn't tell her that! That was one thing he would never tell anyone! "That does something to a boy, Irene. It—it makes him afraid to trust *any* woman, makes him look at women as worthless. Can you imagine what it might be like . . . for a boy coming into manhood . . . to see his mother entertaining all kinds of men except his own father? Can you imagine what it's like to be told by your drunken father that you're a bastard, that he isn't really your father at all—to find out your father was some stranger you'll never know, some one-nighter your mother slept with?"

She looked at him then, remembering his growling words that awful day he beat her, remarks about her being like his mother. "A bastard? Your father told you you were a bastard?"

His eyes actually teared, and intuition told her the tears were genuine this time. "I have no doubt he was right," he answered, running a hand through his hair, his cheeks reddening slightly. "I saw enough to figure it had to be true." He sighed and leaned back in the chair. "My mother was a whore and my father a drunk, Irene, and that's the truth. That's why I always avoided talking about my childhood. That's why I made up reasons why they couldn't come to Colorado. The gifts I gave you from them were gifts I bought myself. I haven't seen them in years, and I don't care if I never see them again."

She closed her eyes. "You could have told me a long time ago. I would have understood."

"Maybe. It's hard for me to talk about it. When I started thinking about you and Ramon, you and Hank . . . I don't know. It all just boiled up in me, all the rage against my mother. You've always been different—special—a woman I could trust. Then I got scared maybe you were like all the others, my own wife, I couldn't stand it. That will never happen again, Irene, I swear before God. As far as the other women . . . I guess it's just my way of looking for the love I never got from my mother."

"I gave you plenty of love, Chad. You had no reason to turn to those other women. You're leaving something out."

"No. I swear I'm not. I just—I grew up totally confused about women and love and all those things. I married you because you represented all the stability I never had before—trust, loyalty . . ."

"And why did you expect those things of me but not of yourself? I can't do it all alone, Chad."

"I know." He cautiously took her hand. How could he explain that deep inside he needed the other women, that they represented proof of his abilities as a man, that they really meant nothing to him, while his marriage to her meant everything? If only she could overlook the affairs. He had to have the others, for his own peace of mind. "I want to try once more, Irene. Please give me another chance. I'll take you back to Denver. Once I get John and Elly settled into running things here, I'll be back myself. We've both had some bad experiences here. We need to go back home."

She pulled her hand away, still not able to bear his touch. She could not forget the horror of what he had done. No matter what he told her, the fact remained he had beaten her and raped her, pure and simple. "I'm sorry for your childhood, Chad. I hope you mean it about never hurting me again, but who knows when something might trigger that desperate fear in you again? I need time to think about all of it, time to mourn Hank."

She sniffed, more tears coming. "I suppose . . . it is best I go back to Denver. Right now the memories here are too painful for me to stay. I'm ready now . . . to go back and get involved in my work in Denver. I've lost everything that was dear to me here." She met his eyes. "We'll talk when you come back to Denver. I tried my best to love you, Chad, and you did nothing but hurt me in return. Such things are not easily forgotten."

He sighed. "But we *are* still husband and wife. The vows we made require us to try once more. Just give me a chance, Irene. Let me make it up to you."

She watched his eyes, gray and pleading, looking so sincere. How many other times had he looked that way, only to be lying through his teeth? "At least you have finally opened up to me, Chad. You should have done it a long time ago. After losing the baby, you came down here and got involved in your work and acted as if nothing had happened. All I have wanted is to be able to really *talk*."

He nodded. "I know. I stayed away because of my own guilt, because I figured it was my fault about the baby. Acting as if everything was all right was just my way of avoiding the truth. I didn't come home much because I couldn't stand to see the look in your eyes, to know what I had done to you. I know you think I lie about a lot of things, but I meant it when I said I was sorry about the baby. I have so many faults to work on, Irene, and I know I'm not much good in some ways. But I am sorry about that, and about . . . about what I did to you that day I came home. That's why I came back to see you, that day Hank wouldn't let me in. Maybe if he had, we would have straightened all this out, and this thing with Hank wouldn't have happened."

Hank. The mention of his name brought it all back. With Hank at her side, it could all have been so different. She would have left Chad for certain, no matter what the shame. She would have had all that much more reason. Now Hank was gone. The pain of it brought a sob to her throat. All she would ever have was the memory of those precious few hours in his arms, that one beautiful moment when she discovered the true ecstasy of being a woman.

Now that Hank was dead, she didn't want his name or his memory muddied. He would be buried beside his beloved wife and daughter. "There was never anything between us like you're thinking," she told Chad. "He took care of me after . . . after you were here. You hurt me bad, Chad. I needed help. When I think of how you left me, I'm not sure I can ever forgive you. You've done so many things that prevent me from loving you the way I could have. Right now I can't think about how or if we can ever have a decent marriage. I just want you to know there was never anything going on between me and Ramon or me and Hank. Just don't ask me to make any decisions right now."

"I won't. All I'm asking is that you wait . . . wait until you're healed, wait until I come back to Denver, before you make any drastic decisions. Will you do that much?"

She put a hand to her eyes. "Yes, mainly because I'm simply too tired and too full of grief to go through a divorce right now. God knows the pressure we would both be under once the news hit the papers. The public loves gossip about the rich. I'm not ready for that right now."

He breathed an inward sigh of relief. If he handled things right, she wouldn't divorce him at all. At least he had stalled her for a while. "Thank you, Irene, for loving me enough to give me this chance to make up for everything."

"I didn't say that I love you. You destroyed those feelings, Chad, almost from the first night of our marriage. I only said I'd wait and think things over."

"It's a start. I'm just glad you weren't killed out there." He rose, relieved that he had been able to calm her initial plans to divorce him. He could hardly wait to tell Elly that Irene was going back to Denver. "As soon as you're well enough, I'll take you back home. Your parents are going to be damn glad to see you once they find out what happened."

"Yes. I miss them. I especially miss Father."

Chad left the room, and she lay there thinking about Hank again, wondering how she was going to go on living without him. She should be able to turn to her husband, but that was impossible. Chad was trying, and she felt sorry for his childhood, but that did not erase what he had done. Nothing could. Right now all that mattered was Hank was dead. Dead! She had not even been able to tell him once more that she loved him, to tell him good-bye. She didn't even have Sunrise anymore. Yellow Eagle had stolen her precious horse, the one thing that gave her a link to Hank. The torture of it engulfed her again, and again the tears came.

John came into the room then—John, her sweet, loving brother. He smelled of whiskey, but that didn't matter right now. He took her into his arms and held her. They were not Hank's arms, but they were more comforting than her husband's. *"Don't let go,"* she remembered telling Hank once. Now he would never hold her again.

"What all really happened, Irene?" Kirk asked his daughter. They sat alone in the parlor of Irene's house in Denver. The commotion of Irene's return was over. Chad had gone back to Colorado Springs, and after fuming and fretting and mothering Irene for three days, until Kirk finally arrived, Bea was back at work.

Irene looked at her father, seeing that same, strange fear she had seen in Bea's eyes when the woman questioned her about the attack, the same look she had seen occasionally over the years when the Indians, especially Yellow Eagle, was mentioned.

"You know what happened," she told her father. She sipped on a cup of tea. "Hank and I were out exercising the horses. We were on our way back to the ranch when . . . when I heard the arrow." She stared at her tea. "In that one swift second, Hank was dead. He fell from his horse. I couldn't just ride off and leave him there. If he was still alive, the Indians might have tortured him. By the time I realized I couldn't help him, it was too late to try to run. I grabbed Hank's rifle and shot at them. I killed one of them, wounded another."

He smiled at sad, bitter smile. "So, you're not only a good ranch hand, you're an Indian fighter now, are you?"

She smiled in return, but her eyes were teary. "I guess I am."

Kirk shook his head. "Irene, do you know how lucky you are to be alive?"

She studied his eyes—so blue, blue like Yellow Eagle's. "Only because I was a Kirkland. Yellow Eagle himself attacked me, held a knife at my throat. He was ready to. . . ." She looked down at her tea again. "He asked me if I was worth much. When I told him who I was, he immediately got off me and backed away." She met his eyes again. "Why did he do that, Father?"

Kirk forced a look of confusion, while his heart raced with the joy of knowing his son was still alive and all right, mixed with the fear he would be caught by the soldiers and would give away his identity. He didn't care for himself, but Irene . . . thank God the man had not killed or raped her. If Irene discovered he was her twin brother. . . .

"I'm not sure," he answered, hating piling lie upon lie like this. "I used to be close with the Cheyenne. Maybe one of his uncles or one of his parents once knew me, talked about me. I'd like to think I still have a lot of friends among the Cheyenne."

"I suppose maybe you do. It was so strange, being right there, being touched by that wild renegade. I was sure I would lose my hair and my life. It still gives me shivers, the way he looked at me."

Kirk stood up and lit a pipe, turning away. Yellow Eagle! His son! If only he could see him just once. "What was he like? I guess I'm as curious as the next man."

"As curious as the whole city of Denver," she answered. "Bill Byers has already been over for a firsthand account for the newspaper."

You're telling them all about your own brother, he wished he could tell her.

"He was taller than most Indians," she was saying. "He could even be considered handsome. It was strange, looking at that dark skin and painted face, with blue eyes looking back at me. His hair is dark brown, not nearly as black as full-blooded Indians. He was well built, strong, but there was a viciousness in his eyes that made my blood run cold. It seemed to disappear when I told him who I was."

Kirk's back was to her. He puffed on the pipe a moment, breathing deeply to control his emotions. "Thank God the name apparently meant something to him."

"The newspaper is making you out to be an old Indian fighter, once a friend to the Cheyenne," she told him. "I don't think people will hate you for it. Most of them already know you once lived among them. They understand that was a long time ago, before they became so warlike. Actually, you're turning into a kind of hero. 'The name that saved his daughter,' they're saying. 'It was only because Irene Jacobs was a Kirkland, the daughter of our founding father David Kirkland, once a mountain man who lived among the Cheyenne, that she was spared.'"

He turned to look at her. "Well, maybe they're right—about the name, I mean," he said, smiling. He sighed, sitting down across from her again. "I have to tell you your mother says you've changed, Irene. I can see it too, in your eyes. It's something more than the Indian attack. What's been going on down there? Why were you off riding alone with Hank that day?"

She took another sip of tea. "A lot of things have happened. You have probably already noticed Chad and I aren't . . . the marriage isn't what Mother thinks. I've been terribly unhappy since losing the baby, and things just got worse." She faced him squarely. "You might as well know Hank had become . . . more than a friend." Tears welled in her eyes. "I loved him, Father."

He held her eyes, showing no surprise. "What has Chad done to you? I know you, Irene. When you spoke those wedding vows, you meant them. You loved Chad. A woman like you doesn't fall in love with some other man for just any reason."

She shook her head. "It's my problem, Father. I have to work it out with Chad."

He leaned closer. "Irene, this is no fool you're talking to. You have some faint bruises left on your face and arms. I'm an old, seasoned man who knows the age of bruises, and those aren't from your attack. They aren't new enough. What happened, Irene?"

She reddened slightly, setting her cup aside. "Please, Father. It's for me and Chad to work out."

He reached out and took her hands. "Maybe so. But no man lays a hand on my Irene, understand? I've watched Chad. I have figured for a long time he's free with women. I was hoping maybe he had straightened out. I've always wondered about the night you lost that baby. Chad wasn't just upset that night. He seemed almost scared to me—like a little boy who had stolen something and was afraid he might get caught. What happened that night, Irene? You can tell me. I don't worship him the way your mother does, even though he did save my life once."

She met his eyes. "Why do you turn to other women, Father? Is it that common for men to do that? Am I supposed to keep forgiving and forgiving?"

He looked surprised and leaned back. "So, you know that much about me, do you?"

"Father, we all know. But you're our father. It's easy to forgive your father, but not your husband."

"It's different with me and Bea," he tried to explain. *I married her so you would have a mother.* Why hadn't he just told her the truth from the beginning? "Back when we got married, people sometimes married for necessary reasons. I was ready to settle and wanted a wife. Bea was in an unhappy situation she wanted out of. I guess we married for the wrong reasons, but we learned to love each other in our own way. We still do. But you know your mother. She always wanted to be rich, and it became an obsession with her. I was just a tool to help her get there. The richer she got, the more I fell by the wayside. You know for a fact how she felt about that loan I made to Red McKinley. Things like that would make her so mad she wouldn't let me near her. Your mother can be a cold, calculating woman when she wants to be, Irene."

She thought about how Bea had taken over Ramon's land. "Yes, I'm beginning to see that."

"That doesn't mean she can't love. She loves you kids very much. Don't ever forget that. But when it comes to loving a man, Bea has never been able or even willing to let go and be a woman, or to just love me for me, without setting dollar signs on my head. A thing like that can drive a man to drink, or to other women. I chose other women, and Bea has always pretty much accepted that. You're the only person I've ever talked to about this, Irene, and I'd like to keep it that way." He puffed on the pipe again. "What I'm saying is, you're not like her at all. Any man who had a woman like you for a wife ought to worship her, shouldn't have any reason to stray at all. Chad's got some kind of problem when it comes to women, and I won't have him hurting you."

She blinked back tears. "He does have a problem. I can tell you that much. He's done some terrible things, but he says it will never happen again, and that he wants one more chance. I intend to think about it while he's down in Colorado Springs. I can't let go of this marriage easily, Father, and I don't want to bring scandal to the family."

"Don't worry about scandal. It's your happiness that matters."

She smiled through tears, thinking how strong and handsome her father still was. He sat there in buckskins, not at all resembling the wealthy man he was. "Thank you, Father. I know whatever happens, I can always turn to you."

"You bet you can. And I intend to have a little conversation with Chad when he gets back to Denver."

"No, Father. If I need you to talk to him, I'll let you know. Right now things are calmed down. I need this time to decide what to do, to get over my grief for Hank."

He set aside his pipe, leaning forward, his elbows on his knees. "What happened between you and Hank, Irene?"

She reddened, the tears coming. "Don't make me say it," she whispered. "I loved him so much, Father. Chad had . . . I can't tell you what he did . . . but Hank was the only one there to comfort me . . . my only friend in a time of terrible need. That day . . . that day he was killed—" She broke into bitter sobbing. "I am changed, Father. I've learned nothing in life is the way we plan it . . . the way we dream about it. Nothing."

He touched her hair. "My God, Irene. What can I say? How can I comfort you?"

"You can't. Just telling you helps. I just . . . I asked you about you and Mother because I wanted to be sure it wasn't my fault my marriage is so bad. I tried, Father. I tried so hard. I can only pray that when Chad comes back to Denver, there might be some way to save the marriage. I'm not sure it can be saved at all." She straightened and wiped at her eyes. "Don't say anything to Mother yet. She wouldn't understand. She thinks so much of Chad. She's lost in her own world. She can't see much beyond K-E."

"How well I know." He sighed deeply. "I'm glad you told me, Irene. You come to me from now on if you need my help."

She got up from her chair. "I will. For now I just want to get back into my social work and the clothing stores and keep busy again. But one day I'm going back to the ranch, once I feel I can bear to go back there and face the fact that Hank is gone and never coming back. I love that life, Father."

He smiled. "You always have liked roughing it, haven't you?"

"Physically, yes. But not emotionally. If I seem changed it's just because I'm more determined not to let Chad hurt me again, or to let others dictate my life."

"Don't let things that have happened destroy the love that is in you, Irene. You've always been a sweet, caring person. I told you that once, years ago. Don't lose track of the real Irene."

"In some ways I already have. Right now I'm not sure who she is. I've been *too* trusting, maybe too caring. I cared so much that I did what everyone else wanted me to do. Hank told me once I had to start thinking about my own happiness, and he was right."

Kirk nodded, rising to stand near her. "Yes, he was, as long as it doesn't turn you into something you aren't."

"I'll try not to let it. It's just that I have been rudely awakened to some amazing truths, and the dreamworld I once lived in is gone."

His chest tightened at the words. How would she react if she learned the cruelest truth of all—that she was Yellow Eagle's sister? Near panic filled his soul at the thought of losing his daughter's love and trust.

"We all get rudely awakened to the truth as we get older, Irene." He stepped closer, grasping her shoulders from behind. "Just remember one thing, that no matter what happens, no matter *what*, your father loves you more than his own life, and always will."

She smiled, turning to embrace him. "I know. Thank you for coming home."

He patted her shoulder. "After hearing what happened? I couldn't very well stay away." He pushed her slightly away. "Your mother says Chad told her your brother is drinking heavily. Is that true?"

She sighed. "I'm afraid it is. He means well, Father. He's smart, and he has so much to contribute. But he's never been happy."

She saw the concern in his eyes. "I know. We were never as close as I would have liked. He's my only . . . son." He glanced at a painting of soldiers chasing Indians that hung over the fireplace. "My only son."

Irene watched him, thinking how unfair life could be—people living with people they didn't love, with so much love to give that had to be kept frozen inside.

Kirk shook his head, still staring at the painting. "Thank God," he muttered. Irene felt an odd misgiving. Was he thankful she was alive and well, or was it something more? She glanced at the painting herself, her eyes falling to the beautiful carved horse that sat on the fireplace mantel.

Ramon. The old, sweet comfort of knowing he was near came back to soothe her aching heart. She had not seen him since the night he sat with her at the hospital, over a year ago.

CHAPTER
THIRTY-TWO

Irene climbed out of her carriage and looked at the sign over the brick and frame building that read simply Vallejo Construction. Her heart beat a little faster at the thought of seeing Ramon again, and she already felt the calming comfort his presence always gave her. She entered the double doors of the three-story structure, stepping into a marble-floored hallway. It was a beautiful building, the inner doors and their frames constructed of polished oak, lovely paintings hanging on the walls.

She breathed deeply with pride and satisfaction at Ramon's continued success. The building was owned by Ramon, had been constructed by his men, and contained the offices of several other businesses, rented from Ramon. She walked through the hall, seeing a sign on one door: James McKinley & Associates, Lumber Milling, Railroad Construction, Entrepreneurial Services.

Yes, she thought, Red McKinley was certainly an entrepreneur. She smiled at the thought of how her mother's attempt at destroying the poor man had only made him more determined to be successful. She had gotten at least some truth out of her mother a few days ago at the offices of K-E, but she was not certain she had gotten all of it.

When she had confronted the woman about Hacienda del Sur, Bea simply told her that the land had come up for government sale and was needed for grazing land for the B&K. "A lot of Mexicans were displaced back then, Irene," the woman told her, "not just the Vallejos. It's something that can't be helped, like displacing the Indians. It's called progress. You have to understand that in this business, sometimes people get hurt."

"And it had nothing to do with my friendship with Ramon?" Irene had asked. She still remembered the flushed look that came to her mother's face then.

"Of course not," Bea had answered. "I am perfectly aware you and John and Ramon were friends. I never liked the idea, but taking over the Vallejo land had nothing to do with that."

"You've always hated Ramon. Why, Mother?"

"I don't hate him at all," Bea had replied. "I just don't have a lot of use for Mexicans, and when you were younger and more easily influenced, I didn't think it was wise of you to be around a Mexican man."

Irene did not fully believe the woman, but she decided after all these years there was no sense beating the issue to death. She asked about Red McKinley, asked Bea if she had forced the man out of business after Kirk's first loan to him. Bea had looked surprised. "What has happened to you, Irene?" the woman asked her.

"I've learned a lot over the past year," Irene replied. "I don't like being left in the dark, Mother. You and Chad have made decisions about certain things that I know nothing about, and I have a feeling Father doesn't know either. I don't want to be left out of decisions any more, as if I were some helpless, frail child. I don't like learning in round-about ways how Kirkland Enterprises wields its power, and I don't like being a part of a company that hurts other people to get what it wants."

She felt sorry for hurting her mother with the remark, but not really sorry she had made it. Bea had looked hurt and shaken. "Everything I do is for you children," she told Irene. "You don't know—" The woman had hesitated, and again Irene saw the strange, fearful look in her mother's eyes.

"What don't I know, Mother?"

Bea had looked away. "You just . . . you don't know what I went through to get where we are today."

Always Irene felt a little sorry for the woman. Her intentions were good, but her tactics were in some instances deplorable. Still, Irene believed the woman actually thought she was doing the right thing.

"Are you and Chad having problems?" Bea had asked her.

Irene almost laughed at the question. Problems? She knew Bea thought Chad could do no wrong. "Yes," she had answered. "I'm not going into details, Mother. When Chad comes back to Denver, we'll just have to try to work them out ourselves."

"Oh, Irene, you make such a beautiful couple. Chad is such a wonderful man. I know losing the baby somehow changed you, but—"

"Mother, you don't know all of it. There are things you don't tell me, and things I don't tell you. When and if I think it's necessary, I'll tell you more. Right now I just want to keep busy. I have to, or I'll go crazy. You said a few days ago that the governor and his scholastic committee are planning to build a university at Fort Collins. I'd like to be on the planning committee, and I think the project should go to Ramon."

The woman stiffened. "All contractors are free to bid on it."

"With Ramon's skill and reputation, I'm sure he'll get the job."

"Ramon Vallejo and Red McKinley have just about put Kirkland Lumber out of business. You shouldn't be defending them, Irene."

"Whatever they're doing, you probably drove them to it. I love you, Mother, but I can't accept some of the things that have gone on. Be that as it may, I want to be on that planning committee, if you can swing it, no matter who builds it. I need the diversion. I—" Hank! Sometimes the thought of him and that day they had made love would slam into her brain and her heart almost like a physical blow. "I just need to keep busy. I also want to be kept informed on what happens now with the B&K."

"Hank had no immediate relatives," Bea told her. "We had an understanding that if something happened to him, the Lazy L would become part of the B and K."

"Good, Just don't . . . please don't sell anything without telling me. If you want my opinion, a ranch hand by the name of Tim Barnes would be a good candidate to take over as manager. And I want it understood that after a year or two, when I feel I can bear to go back there and face Hank's death, I might want the job myself."

"A ranch manager? Irene, you—"

"I can do it, Mother. I've spent too many years doing what everyone else wants me to do. If I want to manage the ranch, that's what I'll do. I loved it there. I was happy there. In the meantime, I'd like to be the one in charge of the books for the ranch on this end. In fact, I could relieve you of the entire project. Then you'd be free to devote your time and attention to other matters. You're always talking about how you want your children to take over K-E someday, so I'm offering to take over the cattle business, as well as building projects and of course my clothing stores."

Bea had looked at her so strangely. "You *have* changed, Irene." She had stepped closer. "You're stronger, and that's good. I'll gladly let you handle those things. There was a time when I never thought you'd want to get so heavily involved in the company."

"Things change, Mother. People change."

Bea had turned away. "Yes. How well I know that." She had sighed, facing Irene again. "Well, for you the change is good. I've always thought you were a little too sweet and trusting for this business. You need to be more assertive when you're handling something this big, Irene."

"It's one thing to be strong, Mother, even assertive. But I intend to be fair in my dealings."

"Of course. You're so much like Kirk, aren't you? You take after him in looks, you think like him; but I think you'll be wiser when it comes to business matters."

"Do you love him, Mother?" Irene had asked.

"Of course I love him. He makes me awfully angry at times, but I love him."

Irene tried to imagine her mother making love, but she could not. She could understand Kirk's reasons for turning to other women. She had never wanted to turn hard and determined as her mother had, yet she felt that very thing happening to her. The only difference was that Bea was driven from within, while she was driven by outside forces. Instead of her inner goals destroying her marriage, the marriage was forcing her to set new goals for herself. She had once imagined being the passive mother and housewife, had thought she would never get deeply involved in the business. That had all changed now. Chad had forced the change, and Hank's death had sealed up that part of her heart that longed to love and give and live a simple, happy life.

She opened the door to Red's office and was greeted by a middle-aged woman at a desk. When she announced who she was the woman quickly went into another office, and a moment later Red McKinley came out, his hair and mustache and freckles as red as ever, his sun-wrinkled face slightly flushed with joy at seeing her. He was still a strong-looking man, handsome in a rugged, weathered way, much like Hank. He put out his arms.

"Well, the famous Indian fighter is up and about," he said with a smile.

Irene smiled and allowed him to embrace her. "Is that what people are calling me?"

"Oh, yes!" The man stepped back, keeping hold of her hands. He thought how beautiful this half-breed woman was, standing there in a deep pink dress with a jacket bodice and a paler pink apron overskirt. She was the epitome of fashion, but a woman who would be stunning in a simple tunic. If she had remained with the Indians, she would have been considered a very valuable commodity. Young braves would have murdered each other over the chance to win her hand. He thought how strange fate was. If not for Gray Bird Woman's husband not wanting the girl child, Irene Kirkland Jacobs would be living in a tipi right now, maybe on a reservation, or dodging soldiers.

He studied the thin red scar still visible on her neck. "Well, not many people can say they have looked death in the face and spit right back at it."

Her smile faded. "I only wish I could say the same for Hank Loring."

Red squeezed her hands. "Yes. I read he was killed right before your eyes."

"He was one of the finest men I've ever known, Red. I'll never know why Yellow Eagle spared me. I told him who I was, and he acted as though he were looking at a ghost. Father said it was probably because some of his people knew and remembered him."

Red quickly looked away. "Yes, I suppose it could have been that." He cleared his throat. "What on earth brings you here to the enemy camp?" he said then, leading her into his office.

"I don't consider this enemy territory at all."

Red closed the door and offered her a chair. "You should. Your mother certainly does."

"I am not my mother."

He sobered as he sat down behind a huge oak desk. "No. You certainly aren't, thank God. I hope you never do become a Bea Kirkland, Irene. I'm sure you love your mother, but when it comes to business. . . ." He sighed. "Well, I'm not going to sit here and say bad things about your own mother."

She smiled sadly. "It's all right, Red. Actually, I came here to apologize for anything she might have done in the past. I didn't know at the time what was going on."

He gave her a wink. "Well, I didn't think that you did. I highly doubt Kirk even knew."

"I wish you and Father could renew your friendship, Red. I think Father would be willing, if you would."

He frowned. "I don't think so, honey. He's not about to forgive me for that fiasco over the railroad, and I don't blame him. I was very deliberate in my intentions that night. There's too much water over the dam now, and with the way I feel about your mother, I don't think the friendship could ever be the same. Things are probably best left the way they are."

"Well, I don't agree, but it's for you to decide."

"So, you came here just to apologize?"

She smiled. "Mainly. And I wanted to see Ramon's new office building, and to congratulate you and Ramon both on your success."

"Well, thank you." He leaned across his desk and called out to his secretary. "Ethel, go and get Ramon, will you? Don't tell him who's here." The woman left, and Irene felt her cheeks growing hotter, her heart racing. She had not been sure Ramon would even be in. "You and Ramon are pretty good friends, aren't you?" Red asked, watching her eyes.

Irene smiled nervously. "Yes, we are. A few years ago Ramon taught John how to carve. He was very good at it. But Mother, of course, put an end to that and sent John off to college. She considered carving a waste of time and energy."

"Yes, she would." Red saw the excitement building in her. Ramon had never told him all of it, but he was sure that at some point there had been more than friendship between him and Irene. Ramon's hatred of Bea Kirkland only made Red more certain that the man had loved Irene once. Bea had somehow found a way to put an end to it. He thought how sad that was. What a gloriously handsome couple Ramon and Irene would make. She seemed much more suited to someone like Ramon than to the cad she was married to. He had met a few people who knew Chad Jacobs and felt he was nothing but hot air with a pretty face. Ramon had told Red how much he despised the man.

"I'm sorry about your losing that baby, Irene," he spoke up. "And sorry about the hell you've been through these last few weeks. The past year hasn't been very good to you, has it?"

"No, it hasn't. But sometimes a person just has to look ahead and keep going. It hurts too much to look back."

"You ever get back up into those mountains?"

She smiled sadly then. "No. Maybe someday I—"

"Irene!"

She looked then to see Ramon coming through the outer office and into Red's. It was impossible, in her present state, not to be overwhelmingly happy to see him. Ramon! How could she resist letting him embrace her? Oh, how welcome were those strong arms! How wonderful he looked and smelled and felt. Red watched them, and there was no mistaking the love there.

"I have some things to take care of. I'll leave you two to talk alone," he told them. He quickly left, closing the door, and Irene looked up at Ramon. Neither of them could resist a soft, light kiss.

Their eyes held, and Ramon quickly stepped back from her. She studied him with tear-filled eyes. How wonderful he looked! Now that she had been with Hank—now that she knew the glory of being with a man she truly loved, she knew how beautiful it must be to lie with a man like Ramon.

"Thank God you are alive and well," Ramon told her, his dark eyes sparkling. She could see the love was still there, and it was comforting. They had reached a point where everything was understood now. They loved each other and always would, but their lives would take different directions. They took comfort in their friendship, but they could not act on their baser desires. Now there was Hank to think about. Even if she were to divorce Chad, it would be a long time before she could get into another relationship. The pain of losing Hank was still too intense.

"I have to thank my father for my life, I guess," she told him. "Yellow Eagle asked if I was worth anything, and when I told him I was a Kirkland, he let me go."

Ramon grinned. "The papers had articles about how your father used to live among the Cheyenne and the Sioux, that he knew them well before they became 'wild, ruthless savages,' as the paper put it."

Irene smiled sadly. "Well, wild and ruthless is a pretty good description, I guess. Father always told me the Indians had good reason for some of the things they have done, but when you're right there being a victim of it all, it's a little difficult to sympathize with them." She turned away. "It was horrible, Ramon, seeing Hank killed right in front of me that way."

"You were good friends? I remember Hank Loring. He was a fine man. The paper said he was the manager of your mother's ranch."

"Yes. We were very good friends." *We made love, Ramon. I almost feel as if I've betrayed you, for I always thought if I turned to another man, it would be you.* She turned to look at him. Yes, he would understand, if she explained it all, explained about Chad. But what was the use now in telling him? "Ramon, I came here to congratulate you on your wonderful success—and to . . . to apologize. I didn't know until I went down to the B and K that my own mother had taken over the Vallejo land and made it a part of the ranch. You knew, didn't you?"

He sobered, a gleam of revenge coming into his eyes. "I suspected. But that is in the past now. You should not be sorry. You were not a part of it."

"In a way I was. I think my mother suspected our feelings for each other. I tried to get the truth out of her, but she wouldn't admit it had anything to do with us. I think it did, and I'm terribly sorry."

He shook his head. "Do not ever be sorry for what we had, Irene. I am not." She had been through so much that he still could not tell her about the confrontation between himself and her mother.

His dark eyes moved over her, awakening old passions. He wore tight denim pants, with a wide leather belt and a blue calico shirt today, apparently prepared to go to a construction project and do some of his own manual labor. Like Hank, he was all man, hard, strong, not afraid to get his hands dirty. Most of all, he was a man of compassion. She realized that was the main ingredient Chad lacked—compassion. He had shown only a slight hint of it after Sand Creek, but that had lasted only as long as it had taken him to forget the incident. "I am the one who is sorry, for going to your house and hitting your husband," Ramon said. "If I had not done that, he might not have taken you away, and none of the other things would have happened to you."

But then I never would have met Hank, she thought. "It doesn't matter. For the most part I was happy, Ramon. I love the ranch, love working with horses. I even went on a roundup, learned to shoot a rifle and rope a calf. Can you believe that?"

He grinned. "Knowing you, yes, I can believe it." He searched her eyes. "What about you and Chad, Irene? How is the marriage?"

She turned away. She sensed that if she told him what Chad had done, his anger would be uncontrollable. She would not be responsible for Ramon doing something irrational that could ruin his career and reputation. She reminded herself this was not Ramon's problem. "Things aren't what they should be yet," she answered. "Chad will be back in Denver soon, and then we'll have some things to talk about, to decide."

She heard a deep sigh. "I had hoped that getting out of Denver would help. I want so much for you to be happy. And I had hoped that some of the things I told Chad would make him think." She felt him step closer. "I told him that if he ever hurt you that way again, I would kill him, and I meant it, Irene."

She shook her head, turning to face him. "Chad isn't worth your losing everything, Ramon. We decided once that we couldn't talk about these things. Please leave it at that. I only came here to see you and Red out of old friendships, and to apologize for things my mother did." She tore her eyes from his and moved away from him again, walking behind Red's desk. "And I came to tell you that the Territory is going to build a university up at Fort Collins. I wanted you and Red to have firsthand knowledge of it so you can be prepared to bid on it. I intend to join the building committee. I'm ready to get back into business."

He watched her lovingly, wanting so badly to be able to look at her as just an old friend now, but he knew he would never stop loving her, wanting her. He wondered how long he could go on living with this unrequited passion, pretending it was not there.

He had given considerable thought to acting on his attraction to the young Mexican girl who cleaned house for him. Anna Garcia was eighteen, and beautiful. He had a sprawling stucco house east of Denver now, but he was so busy he was not there often. Ramon had found Anna at the shelter for homeless women. She had come to Denver with her widowed mother to find work, and her mother had died. He hired Anna to take care of the house for him, and she was a sweet, shy girl.

He was nearly thirty now, and it had been six years since he had lost Elena and Juan. He wanted a wife and family, but he wanted so much for that wife to be Irene. How long should he wait to see if he could ever possess her? The moment he set eyes on this, his first and deepest love, it was difficult to even think about Anna.

"Well, it is too bad your personal life is still not as it should be," he told Irene. "And I thank you for letting me know about the plans for a university." He folded his arms. "Irene, if you need me, in any way—if that bastard husband of yours gives you any more trouble, you tell me. I mean it. Do not worry about what will happen to me. I can take care of myself. I am not foolish enough to lose everything over someone like Chad Jacobs."

She watched him sadly. "Thank you, Ramon, but you have your life now, and I have mine. I've been through so much, I don't want any more trouble right now. The last thing I want for you is any kind of scandal. You've done well, but there is still a lot of prejudice in this town. I just . . . I wanted to say hello, to congratulate you and tell you about the university. And I wanted to tell you how beautiful the church is, more beautiful than I imagined."

He smiled. "There is still some interior work to do, but I have other men taking care of that. I did all the carving for the pulpit and the arms of the pews, as well as the table of sacraments."

"Well, it's the most beautiful building in Denver." Their eyes held in unspoken feelings. She moved from behind the desk to the door. "Well, perhaps we'll be working together on the university project."

He came closer and nodded. "Perhaps." He took a deep breath, breathing out as though to expel feelings that should not be there. "Would you like to see my office?"

She smiled. "Yes. That would be nice."

He nodded, putting a hand to her back and leading her out and down the hall. He ushered her past his secretary's desk and into a room similar to Red's. But she felt as if she were walking into a Spanish home in Mexico. Spanish-style rugs and vases decorated both the outer office and his own office. Paintings of bulls and bullfighters, street scenes of small Mexican towns and men wearing huge sombreros, and one of Spanish soldiers decorated the walls. A huge rubber plant sat in one corner of his office, and a six-foot-tall ceramic figure of a conquistador stood in the other corner. Hand-drawn blueprints lay scattered across his desk and an extra table.

"This is beautiful," she told him, gazing around the room. Her eyes fell on the blueprints. "You're so busy, Ramon. I'm happy for you."

"I owe part of it to your mother," he told her. "She never thought I would amount to anything. She made me determined to prove her wrong."

"Well, I'm glad," she replied. "I have to get back to my own office now. There is going to be a meeting this afternoon about the university."

He nodded. "I have much work to do myself." Their eyes held. "Good-bye, Irene. Take care of yourself."

She blinked back tears. "You do the same." She tore her eyes from his and left. Ramon stared at the doorway, his whole body aching for her. He turned then, swinging an arm across his work table, sending blueprints flying, damning himself for still loving her.

Elly placed reports from the new Kirkland silver mines on Chad's desk. "It looks like my alcoholic brother is straightening up some," she told Chad. "He actually got this report done on time and it looks neat and correct."

Chad looked it over. "John's been a little better since your father came down here and talked to him." He sighed, looking up at Elly. "He gone?"

"Yes. He just left, and so has everyone else."

Chad leaned back in his chair. "Elly, when Kirk was here, he didn't talk just to John. He had a little private conversation with me, too, and those blue eyes of his held a threatening note. He knows Irene and I aren't getting along, Elly, although I don't think Irene told him the worst of it. At any rate, he warned me he didn't want her hurt. I managed to keep things civil and to smooth his ruffled feathers somewhat, but things are getting tight right now. If I'm going to manage to keep this marriage alive, I'm going to have to go home pretty quick, and I'm going to have to be more discreet than ever."

"So? Let the marriage fail." She folded her arms. "Then you and *I* can get married."

"That would never work, and you know it. You'd be disinherited, and I'd lose my position here. Besides, we both know that what makes it so good for us is that it's forbidden. If we make it legal, all the fun will go out of our sex life."

She laughed. "Maybe you're right. But I love you, Chad. I always have, and I always will. At least if you were divorced you'd be free to do what you want."

He shook his head. "You know Bea. I can't go accusing Irene of anything, and if Bea finds out I beat her . . ." He rubbed at his chin. "If I ever get divorced, Elly, it has to be something that is totally Irene's fault, something that can't be denied. In the meantime, I'm stuck with her, and you and I have to face the fact that the time is coming when we can't sleep together every night. I've got to get back to Denver soon."

Elly pouted. "I don't want to stay here alone without you."

"Well, you'd better stay here for a while at least. If you go chasing home as soon as I leave, it will look suspicious. With John not drinking so much, we can eventually let him take over, hire a couple of extra men for down here, and you can come home. After that we'll see."

He realized he had actually grown somewhat dependent on Elly, who was expert at satisfying his sexual appetite. He had the best of two worlds. His marriage to Irene gave him a kind of wholesome respect, at least to the outside world; while Elly satisfied his baser needs. The only trouble with Elly was that she was one he could not toss aside, as he had Susan Stanner. He had to be very careful with her.

"I'll miss you so much, Chad," she was telling him.

"I imagine you'll find other comfort."

She smiled wickedly. "Maybe. But they won't be you." She put her hands on her hips, walking to a window. She wore a paisley print taffeta dress, which rustled as her heavy frame moved about, and Chad thought how she always wore dark colors and rather ugly dresses, or was it her build that made them seem ugly? "Mother and Father make me so angry . . . Father coming down here and threatening you, Mother expecting you back in Denver. If it weren't for them, we wouldn't have so much to worry about. I wish they'd hurry up and die so K-E would be in our hands. You could divorce Irene and we'd all be a lot happier."

"I wouldn't go planning anything in that direction. They're both healthy as a couple of horses."

She looked at him, then sauntered around his desk and leaned down, kissing him lightly. "Well, horses get sick and die, too, you know."

He grinned. "I know."

She sat down on his lap, a bigger load for him than she realized. "I know that pretty soon we won't get to be together so much. But we'll find ways."

He grinned, meeting her mouth then, moving a hand to grasp at her breast while they kissed hungrily. She met his tongue suggestively, then left his mouth, closing her eyes and putting her head back as she sat up straighter to let him unbutton the front of her dress. He kissed at her throat as he reached inside to toy with a taut nipple, both of them quickly lost in each other while outside a light rain peppered the window. Neither of them realized John had come to stand in the doorway.

"Well, well."

Elly gasped and jumped up, fumbling to button her dress, while a red-faced Chad sat staring at John, who watched them with an ugly sneer on his face. "I suspected something like this was going on, but to see it in the, uh, flesh, so to speak, kind of makes a man want to puke, you know what I mean?"

"What are you doing here?" Elly demanded, nearly screaming the words. Her face was livid with anger.

John smiled. "I brought a telegram I happened to pick up. I decided it was important enough that Chad should read it right away."

"You deliberately sneaked in here to try to catch us," Elly fumed.

John sobered, his words turning into a near snarl. "If you'd behave like a proper *lady*, there wouldn't be anything to worry about!"

"John, listen—"

"I don't want to hear it, Chad," John said, coming closer, his own face showing his fury then. "What a pair of stinking bastards you are! My own sister! I don't know which one of you I detest the most—my sister for sleeping with her own sister's husband, or *you*, for sleeping with your own wife's *sister*! Six of one and half a dozen of the other, wouldn't you say? Any way you look at it, it smells worse than rotten eggs!" He shoved papers and ink pens off Chad's desk, leaning over and grabbing Chad by the shirt front. "You lying, cheating, wife-beating son-of-a-bitch!"

Chad brought his arms up between John's, pushing hard and quick outward to force John to let go of him. He rose from his chair, and they faced each other challengingly. "Calm down, John! There are a lot of things you don't understand here."

"Oh, I *understand*, all right! I understand my sister is a *slut*, and you're no better than a damn *gigolo*! Maybe it's not my business when it's the sluts in Old Colorado City you're with, but when it's Irene's sister, that's a little too much to take! I think I told you once what I'd do to you if you hurt Irene again!"

"I *haven't* hurt her! Not physically. I told you that wouldn't happen again. As far as Elly and me. . . ." He glanced at Elly, who stood glaring at John, looking ready to light into him. "It's only been since she got back from school," he lied. "You know Irene and I were having problems. Irene stayed down on the ranch so much, and Elly and I have been working so closely these last few months—"

"*Save* it, Chad!" John breathed deeply for self control, moving angry eyes between Chad and Elly. "The two of you are lower than the dirt under a snake's belly! I don't want to hear your excuses!" He moved his eyes to Elly. "And I don't need to tell you what our dear *mother* would think of this! You'd both be out scrubbing *privies* for a living!" He stepped back, enjoying the fear in both their eyes. He sneered. "Don't worry, dear sister and brother-in-law. I promise not to tell. But for one reason only, and that's *Irene*! I don't intend to be the one to give her the biggest hurt she's suffered yet!" His eyes began to tear with rage. "She's been through enough hell. I think I'll spare her this one."

He walked closer again, taking the telegram from his pocket

and slamming it onto Chad's desk. "Here's the reason I'm not telling Irene. She's already lost one baby. I don't intend to be responsible for making her lose another one!"

Chad frowned. "Another one?"

John laughed in disgust. "Yes, dear Chad. Your beloved wife is pregnant! That's what the telegram is about. Mother wants you home with your wife, where you belong. You can go back to Denver and play the doting husband and happy father again." He moved his eyes to Elly. "And you, my loving sister, will have to find some other man to satisfy your slutty needs." He backed away, still looking at Elly. "You're worse than the whores in the red light district. At least they're open about what they do. They take money for it. Chad's getting it for *free*! Don't sell yourself so cheap, Elly. You ought to go to Old Colorado City. Maybe you'd make more money than the allowance Mother pays you to work here!"

"Get out," Elly screamed. "Just get out of here! I hate you, John Kirkland!"

"Hate yourself, Elly. Don't turn it on me. Take a good look in the mirror someday and see who deserves hating."

"I love Chad! I've loved him for years. You don't understand! The only thing you've ever loved is in a bottle!"

He grinned sadly. "Maybe so. But at least the only one I hurt is myself." He turned and left, and Elly let out a near growl of fury and frustration, making her hands into fists and storming around the office.

"Damn him," she shouted. "Damn him! Damn him!"

Chad read the telegram in dismay. Irene was pregnant? It must have been from the night he raped her. He hadn't been near her for months before, and not at all since. Could it happen so easily, in one night? He was hardly aware of Elly's screeching, his mind racing with the possibilities. A baby could do wonders for their marriage, but a creeping dread moved through his blood. Was the child his, or had Irene lied about not having an affair with Hank Loring?

"I've got to get back to Denver. This has really done it, Elly. We've got to quit seeing each other whether we like it or not."

"I hate this family! I hate Mother and Father, Irene and John, *all* of them!" She looked at him, then ran over to him to embrace him. "Oh, Chad, I'll miss you so."

"I'll miss you, too, Elly. We'll work something out. You just lay low until I figure out what to do about this."

She rested her head against his chest while he raised the telegram and looked at it again. IRENE PREGNANT. FOUR MONTHS. LEAVE ELLY AND JOHN IN CHARGE. YOU ARE NEEDED HERE. BEA.

Four months. It had been four months since Hank's death.

CHAPTER
THIRTY-THREE

Chad checked into his office at K-E as soon as he got back to Denver, only to find Irene sitting at his desk. He stopped short at the door, surprised to see her there. After being apart for four months, he had been planning all the way home how he would approach her, what he would say to her, and now he was facing her sooner than he had planned. "What are you doing here?" he asked in surprise.

Irene's own look of surprise soon changed to one of near disgust and quick defense. "I'm a Kirkland. I work here. Now that you're back, I suppose I'll have to find another office."

"Why aren't you at home?"

She leaned back in her chair. "Why should I be? It's empty and lonely there."

He came inside and closed the door. "You're pregnant. You should be home taking care of yourself."

"Oh, Chad, how sweet of you to care," she said sarcastically.

He watched her carefully. This was a new Irene. He could see already he had not beat her into submission. He had only beaten out the sweet, trusting woman, and someone else had come to replace her. "What's going on here, Irene? Are you really pregnant? I came as soon as I got the telegram. I was worried about you."

She remembered how she felt before she married him, excited, trusting, so sure it was the right thing to do. Why hadn't she listened to that little voice so long ago, the one that told her something was not quite right, that little voice that had made her just a tiny bit afraid of him? "You know, Chad, you really missed your calling," she told him. "You should be in New York, in the theater. You wouldn't need one bit of training to be an actor."

He frowned, removing his hat and hanging it on a hat tree near the door. "What is that supposed to mean?" He came closer and took a chair across from her, putting on an air of confidence.

"It means I know what you're really after. The only thing that concerns you about this baby is whether or not it's yours."

He could hardly believe the cold look in her eyes. There was no fear anymore. He shifted in the chair, reaching over to take a cigar from a box on his desk. "Well, then? *Is* it mine?"

She smiled bitterly. More than ever she wanted to tell him no, that it was Hank's. She had had a period shortly after Chad beat her. Only Hank had touched her since then. She was glad. She did not want to think that this child could have been conceived out of that ugly day when Chad raped her. How much nicer it was to know it had come from that beautiful afternoon when she lay in Hank's arms. Now she would have Hank's child, a little remnant of the love they had shared.

Still, this child was going to call Chad father. He or she would carry his name and live in his house. Now that she was pregnant, she had to try harder than ever to make this marriage work, for the baby's sake. She wouldn't have the child born into an ugly divorce, gossipped about, called a bastard. For the time being, at least until the baby was older, she had to stay with Chad, sick as the thought made her feel. And if she was going to do that, Chad had to think this baby was his. If the man had any ability to love, perhaps he would reveal it with a child of his own. This was his last chance to prove he was capable of feelings, their last chance to do something about their marriage. She would not have her baby growing up with a father who looked at it with hate in his eyes.

She stared at Chad long and hard, going over all the reasons again before finally answering. Yes, if he could lie to her about his lurid affairs, she could certainly tell a lie to protect her precious baby. "Yes," she said aloud. "I told you after Hank was killed that there had never been anything physical between us. It's your child, Chad, and I hope to God he or she never finds out how it was conceived. What you did to me was unforgivable, but apparently God has seen fit to help us try to pick up the pieces and find some little bit of beauty in it by giving us a baby."

He watched her closely. Was she telling the truth? She certainly looked sincere. Or had she grown to be the expert at lying that he was? He only knew one thing. The baby was their only possible salvation. He had to accept it as his own and try to be a good father, or eventually she would leave him. He had been given a chance to save this marriage after all. She couldn't leave him now, not with a baby coming.

"Well, then," he said aloud. He lit the cigar. "It appears we have to make amends, if possible. I'm back to stay, Irene. Just tell me what you want."

"What I want? You make it sound so simple, Chad." She rubbed at her temples, getting a headache just looking at him. "I don't want you to be seen cavorting with the whores. I want you to believe this child is yours, because it is, and I want you to love it, if you're capable of love. While I'm pregnant, I don't want any surprises that will make me lose it, and I certainly don't ever want to feel your fist in my face again, or to see you in the same bed with me—not until after the baby is born, and even then, not for a long, long time. It will take a considerable amount of change on your part before I'll be able to be a wife to you, or be able to forget what you did, if that's even possible."

He sighed deeply. "I told you once I'll never do that again. I told you why I did it, and I've managed to resolve some of those reasons within myself. I'm going to believe you when you say the baby is mine, Irene, and I'll love him or her. But, if you're going to turn me out of our bed, maybe for months, how can you expect me to keep away from other women? A man can only take so much. Your own father is an example of that."

She stiffened. "My father is not part of this conversation. How dare you even *begin* to compare yourself to my father! He and my mother might have their problems, but he would never, *never* lay a hand on her! You and David Kirkland are on very different levels of worth and respectability!"

He rolled his eyes. "For God's sake, Irene, am I to be punished for the rest of our married life? I tried to explain to you what happened. I realize now I never should have suspected you and Hank. Even if it was true, after some of the things I did, I shouldn't have blamed you. I'm sorry, Irene. How many times do I have to say it? I want to make this marriage work, and making love is a pretty big part of marriage, wouldn't you say?"

"Yes—making love, not rape."

He let out a long sigh, running a hand through his hair. "You say you want me to love the child, that you want to patch up the marriage. That can't be done if we don't sleep together and I wind up turning to someone else for what my wife won't give me. You said yourself at least one beautiful thing came of it, and that's the baby. Doesn't that count for something? I've suffered, too, you know—when I was a child. And I've suffered a lot of remorse after what I did to you. I don't know what the hell else to do; how I can make it up to you. Just tell me. I'll do anything you ask, but don't expect me to go for months or years without a woman. The best-intentioned man can't do that."

"And what *are* your intentions, Chad?"

He kept his eyes true. "To love you. To make up for what I did. To love this baby."

She held his eyes several long seconds before replying. She leaned forward, resting her elbows on the desk. "All right. I'll make a deal with you, Chad. You stay out of our bed until the baby is born. If you have an occasional need and find a way to take care of it during that time, I don't want to know about it, as long as it isn't anyone I know and isn't flaunted on Kirkland property like Milicent Delaney was. I'll go along with you on a man having his needs, but I don't think I could let you touch me any time soon. Waiting for the baby gives us five months just to be together. To talk, to work together, to redo the nursery. I want you home every evening where you belong. I want to live the life of a normal married couple. After the baby is born, when I'm healed, I'll—" She hesitated. Could she ever really let him touch her again? She had to try. She had no choice, and he was still her husband.

"I'll let you make love to me, but only when *I'm* ready, and only if you have yourself checked out first. It's apparently a miracle you haven't contracted some hideous disease and given it to me. You're not touching me again unless I know you're all right. And if you ever try to force me again, I'll kill you, if I have to. The least I will do is divorce you and tell the world the truth about you. If we manage to find our way back to each other sexually, maybe we can make this marriage work." She held his eyes. "But once I take you back to my bed, there can be no other women, Chad. I mean it. You're very close to losing everything, and I don't think you want that. I want a normal marriage and a loyal husband. I won't turn you away again, and I never did the first years of our marriage. You had no excuse then, and you won't have one this time."

He watched her closely. She meant it. He couldn't frighten her anymore, couldn't threaten her, and he had certainly lost his ability to charm her into or out of anything. "All right," he lied.

"Once we're back together, there will be no more women." He wondered how he was going to manage it. If only she could understand his needs. He would have to find a way around this. Maybe when Elly was back. . . . "That's a promise, Irene."

"I hope you're able to keep it."

He didn't like this at all, but he was stuck with it. He had always been the one in charge, the one with all the clever moves and words and looks, the one who got his way, especially with women. Now he was not only being controlled by Elly, but by Irene.

He rose. "I'll keep it," he answered. He leaned over the desk. "Maybe once the baby is born and weaned, we can leave him or her with a nanny and take that trip to Europe we never got to take. I've always thought part of our problem was the miserable way this marriage started, Irene. What happened that first night, then me being so busy in Colorado Springs, and then the flood. We never seemed to get the chance to get on the right track, and I'm sorry about that. I loved and wanted you so bad that first night that I just got so frustrated—" He straightened, turning away. "I know you never forgave me for that, either. Either way, we deserve that trip to Europe. It would force us to be closer, away from the business here, away from everything familiar."

"We'll see. First I want to see the completion of the latest building project. I'm on the committee to build a university at Fort Collins. Once Colorado becomes a state, it will be our first state college. I'm helping work on the design of the buildings, the curriculum, appropriate tuition fees, that kind of thing."

His eyebrows arched as he turned back to face her. "You sure you want to be this busy?"

"Yes. I need to be. I'm perfectly healthy and I get plenty of rest at night. I am also now the one overseeing the ranching operation. I asked Mother to give it to me. I certainly think I'm qualified."

He looked her over, having to admire her abilities. He had married a passive, trusting child; now she was a strong-willed woman. "Yes, I suppose you are," he answered. "What about this university thing? Have they started construction? How involved is K-E?"

"Very. We've donated a good deal of money. Mother feels a university nearby will bring a good deal of prestige to Colorado. Ramon Vallejo is handling the construction plans."

She watched the color rise in his face, the anger move back into his eyes. "Ramon?"

"Yes," she told him calmly and confidently. "He's been working with the committee. He's the best builder in the area."

His jaws flexed in repressed anger. "You've been working closely with Ramon?"

She drew in her breath, meeting his eyes squarely as she rose from her chair. "Yes, I have. Just as in the past, Ramon and I are just good friends, Chad. Considering the fact that I am carrying your child, as well as the fact that Ramon has gotten engaged to another woman, I hardly think you have anything to worry about. You never did in the first place."

"Ramon is engaged?"

"Yes. Anna Garcia, a young girl he hired to take care of his house." Oh, it was so hard to think of it! Somehow knowing Ramon was single and available had always been a comfort. She knew he still loved her as much as ever, but when she had told him about the baby, about how, for the baby's sake, she had to keep her marriage alive, Ramon had soon after told her he was marrying his housekeeper.

"I am tired of being alone, Irene," he had told her. "I want a family of my own. I thought for a while perhaps. . . ." There had been the hesitation, the moment when they both almost admitted their feelings. But now there was the baby. She would not allow the nasty gossip, the name-calling. She could not allow her child or Ramon to suffer. A man couldn't wait around forever, and she couldn't selfishly expect Ramon to deny himself happiness the rest of his life just because she "might" need him someday.

"I understand," she had told him. "I want you to be happy, Ramon." Oh, but the thought of him sharing his body with another woman, giving her the same pleasure Irene had known with Hank and now realized would be so fulfilling with a man like Ramon. . . .

"They're getting married in six months," she answered Chad. "The major part of the college construction will be in full swing then."

Chad suppressed a smile of deep satisfaction at knowing Ramon was getting married. There was one man who would never cheat on his wife. Once he was married, he wouldn't be sniffing around Irene any longer. He faced Irene. "Well, I'm happy for Ramon, in spite of our differences. I always knew he would be a success in the building trade." He sighed deeply. "Well, if we're going to patch things up, how about starting with lunch? You can fill me in on all the details about the university and whatever else is going on in Denver."

"Oh, plenty is going on," she said, walking from behind the

desk. She thought how easily he could change the subject. She took her hat from the hat tree and looked into a mirror that hung near the hat rack, putting the hat on her beautifully coiffed hair and pinning it. "The clothing stores are doing fine. I think I'll have one opened in Colorado Springs. Maybe Elly can handle it for me. How are she and John doing?"

She took her cape from the hat tree, and Chad put it around her shoulders for her. "I think they can handle things all right." *If they don't kill each other first*, he felt like adding. "Elly wants to come back to Denver. She misses the conveniences of a bigger city. She calls Colorado Springs a cow town."

"She would." She turned to look at him. "I'll write her about opening a dress shop for me there, and send someone down to manage it. Have Mother send some good men down there if Elly wants to come home then. I'm not sure John can do it alone. I still don't trust his drinking. Maybe we should have him come back to Denver for a while instead of leaving him there alone."

A strange expression appeared in Chad's eyes, and he quickly looked away. "John will be all right. You know how he feels about Bea. He's better off staying in the south."

"Maybe. I worry about him. He's never been very happy."

Chad felt the dampness under his shirt. If John ever told what he had seen, it would be the end of everything. "He'll be happier being away from your mother. Let's go find her. Maybe she'd like to have lunch with us."

He had no more spoken the words than Bea came rushing toward them, her arms open. "Chad! Son, you're back! Oh, how good to see you." She embraced him, and Chad returned the hug, putting on the charm again. "Isn't it wonderful about the baby! Oh, everything will be good for both of you now, I can feel it."

"It will, Mother," Chad replied. "It's good to be back in Denver." His arm came around Irene's waist, and she felt as though she were lying in a grave, with someone shoveling dirt over her, burying her alive.

David Chadwick Jacobs was born in February 1871. Bea and Kirk were beside themselves with joy over their first grandchild.

Within four days of the news, Elly and John came home—John to see the baby, Elly insisting the same but really returning to see the baby's father. Brother and sister had barely spoken since the day John discovered Elly and Chad together. Elly would stay in Denver now, and John was glad to be rid of her, except for his worry about what she and Chad would do. He was sure that with the baby, and because of Bea's presence, it would be much more difficult for his sister and Chad to renew their ugly affair. The thought of the hurt Chad had already inflicted upon Irene made it impossible for John to tell his poor sister the truth. Now there was the baby. Maybe everything would be better for Chad and Irene. He could only hope for the best. The worst had already happened.

Chad opened the door to greet them, looking somewhat stunned at first. John gave him a look of renewed warning. "We're here to see the baby," he told Chad.

Chad let them inside, struggling to keep his composure, living with the constant fear now that John would tell people the truth. "He's, uh, he's beautiful," he told them both. "Irene was in labor nearly thirty hours, though. She's still pretty weak. I think you'd better visit her one at a time."

"Is Mother here?" Elly asked. She almost laughed at how casual Chad was trying to act.

"No. She stayed the first three days, but Irene has Rose and Jenny. Rose helps Irene with the more intimate things that need tending to. Bea had to get back to K-E, and Kirk is in meetings for the Denver and Rio Grande." He smiled at John. "You'll be glad to know that within another year a narrow gauge railroad will connect Denver with Colorado Springs. You'll be able to get to Denver a lot faster once that happens, and vice versa."

"I don't intend to come home much," John said dryly. "I'd like to see Irene." He looked around the house. "Do you realize I've never seen the inside of this place since it was finished? I left for school before you got to move in. When I first got back last year, I was at the mansion, then came to Colorado Springs." He looked around, studying the unusually beautiful primavera wood that made up the elegant stairway and framed the rich stained-glass wall of the first landing. "Ramon sure does beautiful work, doesn't he?" He ran his fingers over the curved banister.

Elly glanced at Chad. "Yes, he does," she cooed. "Wasn't it smart of Chad to hire *Ramon* to build his and Irene's house?" She laughed when Chad reddened at the remark.

John glanced at them. Did Elly know about Ramon and Irene? Had she told Chad? What a bitch she was! She was as deceitful and scheming as their mother, except that Elly had no morals. At least his mother had surely never pulled up her skirts to get what she wanted. He glared at both of them. "Don't forget my warning," he told Chad then. "Which room is Irene's?"

Chad looked up at the circular balcony, nodding to his left.

"Second door on that side. You can't miss it. It's filled with gifts from well-wishers, friends of the family. And Rose is in there fussing over her."

John stared at them both a moment longer, then turned and finished climbing the stairs, taking a small flask from his jacket pocket and drinking a quick swallow of bourbon before entering the room. Irene lay holding a tiny baby in the crook of her arm. She looked at John, her eyes lighting up. "John," she whispered, "you came!"

"Of course I came," he said quietly.

"Rose, leave us for a minute?" Irene asked the woman. Rose smiled, happy for Irene, hoping against hope that the baby would bring Irene all the happiness her cheating husband had denied her.

John moved to the side of the bed, leaning over to take a look at his new nephew. "He's beautiful, just like Chad said," he told Irene. "I'm happy for you, Irene. What about you?" He knelt beside the bed, lightly touching the sleeping baby's hand.

"This baby means everything to me, John. I'm happy he's so healthy. I need this child."

"I can imagine. How are things with Chad?"

"Better. He seems really happy about the baby." She kissed little David's soft cheek, praying he wouldn't grow to look so much like Hank that it would be a dead giveaway. Right now his hair was white-blond, and his eyes a deep blue. Bea had said he looked very much the way Irene looked as a baby. Maybe that meant he would have her coloring, and it would be difficult for anyone to tell he was not Chad's. She had a little bit of Hank with her forever now! He had given life before he died. If only he could have known he had a son! "He's such a good baby, John. I'm giving up my work for a few months while I nurse him."

"That's good. Don't ever get so involved you neglect your children, Irene. Don't do what Mother did."

She smiled, her face pale but her eyes bright. "I won't. But there are certain things I want to keep track of, like the ranch. I'd still like to go back to Colorado Springs someday. I just can't bring myself to face any of that yet."

"I know." He rubbed the little hand with his thumb, secretly wondering if this could be Hank Loring's child. He was not going to upset her by asking. He hoped it was Hank's, and not the seed of his sister's bastard husband.

Downstairs Elly pulled Chad into his study, giving him a quick, suggestive kiss. "God, Chad, I've missed you so much."

He gently pushed her away. "Not here and not now. John is too close. I told you when I left Denver you'd have to wait for me to make the first move and let you know when and where we can get together."

"I can meet you anywhere, anytime." She ran her hands over his chest and he grasped her wrists.

"Don't do that, Elly. One of the maids could come in."

She pouted. "Then close the door."

He gave her a warning look. "Elly, things are going pretty good right now. Irene and I have made a kind of pact. As soon as she's healed from the baby, we're going to try it as husband and wife again. I promised her I'd stay away from other women."

She let out a sarcastic snicker. "You don't expect me to believe you'll *keep* such a promise, do you? And what have you been up to while we've been apart?"

"I have my sources. But things are getting tougher all the time. I've got to convince Irene I'm sincere about this, Elly. In the meantime, if I'm going to get caught, it will be a lot better if I'm caught with a prostitute than with my wife's own sister. That day John walked in on us, I realized the stupid chances we've been taking. If John ever talks, or Bea finds out some other way, we'll lose everything."

She frowned. "What are you telling me?"

He grasped her arms. "I'm telling you we've got to stay away from each other, Elly, for a long time."

Her eyes began to tear. "I *can't* stay away from you, Chad."

"Do you think it's easy for me? It has to be this way, Elly. It doesn't mean we can't ever be together. It's just going to have to be more secretive than ever, which means far fewer times. Irene expects me to be home with her every minute I'm not at that office. Even Bea seems to be watching me more closely. I'm telling you, Elly, it's been a bitch ever since I got back."

He was not about to tell her he had been finding ways to meet Milicent again. He had run into her in a restaurant, and they casually had lunch as "old friends." He discovered she no longer worked, but her husband had taken a sales job, riding circuit among several towns surrounding Denver. He was gone for days at a time, and after that first meeting they began arranging times when they could begin seeing each other again.

"Bea and Irene, Bea and Irene," Elly mocked. "I'm sick of hearing their names."

"Damn it, Elly, do you want to lose everything? This has nothing to do with wanting to be with you. It just can't *be*, that's all."

"It's *you* I don't want to lose. Mother and Irene kept me from you in the beginning. Now they're doing it again. How I hate them both!"

He touched her face, putting on a look of total sincerity. "You aren't losing me, Elly. We've just both got to go our separate ways for a while. I've got to see this through, or I'll lose it all. Besides, I have a son now."

"Do you?" she asked. "How do you even know its *yours*? It's probably Hank Loring's bastard!"

He flinched almost as though he had been hit. How he hated that word! Irene wouldn't give birth to a bastard like his own mother had, would she? No! He couldn't let himself believe it. He had to make this marriage work. If he lost control and hurt her again, or let her think he didn't love the baby, it would be over. He still wondered himself, could not find the love he should have for his new son because of his deep suspicions. Still, Irene had been so adamant about not having had an affair with Hank.

"I believe it's mine, Elly, and I have a chance now to patch up this marriage. I have to do it, for your sake as well as mine. You must know that. Getting caught by John could have been a real disaster."

Her lips puckered. "It's not over between us, is it, Chad?" A tear slipped down her cheek, and he grasped her shoulders. Finally, he was getting back some of his control! He could thank John for that much.

"No," he answered. "We'll find ways, Elly. But in between I've got Irene, and there might be others, others who aren't so dangerous. And you'll have to do the same. The best thing you could do is get married. That would throw John off the scent for good. Hell, being married doesn't mean we couldn't see each other. It might even be a good idea! We could work close together and no one would think anything about it. Hell, there must be a lot of men who would *kill* to marry you, just to get their hands on Kirkland money."

"Like you did?" She stiffened and wiped at her tears. Nothing else had made her cry—not her mother's neglect, or the fact that she felt neither one of her parents loved her, not even getting rid of her and Chad's baby. But to have to let go of Chad. . . .

"Maybe I did," he was saying, "but that didn't keep me from other women's beds. And you getting married doesn't have to keep us from being together."

She turned and walked to his desk, studying a gold paper weight. Then she looked at him, holding her chin haughtily.

"Maybe I *will* get married. If I do, it will be someone who will give Mother a heart attack, someone she hates. She has denied me happiness all these years, always loved Irene more than me. It's time I paid her back."

"How do you think you're going to do that?"

"I don't know yet. I'll think of something." She grinned. "The first thing I'll do is make Mother very nervous by having a *lot* of suitors, letting her wonder what I'll do next. I'll pick young men who work for competing companies. That should ruffle her feathers-some."

Chad felt the little stab of jealousy, not because he loved and wanted her, but only because of the deep-seated fear that she might find someone who pleased her more.

She came closer, touching his face. "At least I had you for a while, didn't I? You were mine, Chad, for a lot longer than anyone knows, and in more ways than you ever belonged to Irene. In some ways you'll always be mine, won't you?"

He was relieved to see she was not going to throw a fit or make trouble. Surely she realized that she was as trapped as he was. Their knowledge of each other's stained pasts left them locked in this together. If Elly Kirkland tried to destroy him now, she would go down with him, and she damn well knew it. "You know I will," he told her. "And I'll always be the best, won't I?"

She arched her eyebrows, wanting to torture him the way it would be torture for her to let him go. "Maybe. I haven't gone man hunting since I came home."

"Stop it, Elly."

She smiled wickedly. "We can at least meet just once while Irene is laid up, can't we? Don't you have a meeting to go to, something where you can bow out early and meet me someplace?"

"Maybe. But we can't do anything until John goes back to Colorado Springs."

She breathed deeply, studying his gray eyes. "I'll never forget how it was there, Chad. We'll never again have that much freedom, being together nearly every night for almost a year. The last five months without you have been terrible."

"They have been for me, too. Now you'd better get up to see the baby before John and Irene both get suspicious."

She moved to the door to be sure no one was coming, then hurried back over to plant a warm, suggestive kiss on his mouth.

She then cast him a seductive smile before turning and running out. Chad watched after her, aching all over.

•   •   •

Irene disembarked the carriage, wearing a sealskin jacket over her deep blue velvet dress. A late April snowstorm had hit the mountains and had swept into Denver in the form of a cold rain. "Wait for me. I'll only be a few minutes, Jim. I promise not to make you sit in the rain forever," she told the driver. The elderly man, who had been driving her family's carriage for years now, nodded and smiled, thinking how Irene was the nicest member of the Kirkland family, and surely the prettiest.

Irene took a package from the carriage and ducked her head, following a bricked walkway to the double doors of Ramon's lovely, Spanish-style home. It sat on a rise with a view of the mountains, but today that view was shrouded by gray clouds. It was not the best day to be out visiting, but she wanted to do this while Chad was working, and Ramon, according to the gossip column of the *News,* had "recently returned to Fort Collins most reluctantly, to continue work on Colorado's proudest project, the new university. We say reluctantly because Mr. Vallejo left his new bride behind."

Irene's heart beat a little faster as she knocked on the heavy oak doors, on which were intricately carved scenes of trees and flowers. She studied the carvings lovingly while she waited, standing under the protection of a wide veranda. Moments later a very beautiful young girl opened the door, and Irene felt a rush of painful jealousy at the sight of her. She wanted to hate this woman, just because she had the privilege of enjoying the exquisite pleasure of sharing Ramon Vallejo's bed. She thought she was prepared for this moment, but it still hurt, in spite of the fact that she could not help being glad for Ramon's happiness.

"You must be Anna," she spoke up.

"*Sí.* May I help you?"

"I am Irene Jacobs. My father is David Kirkland. Maybe Ramon has spoken of me?"

She watched a strange sadness come into the woman's eyes, mixed with a hint of jealousy and even fear, as though she had suddenly been threatened. "*Sí,* he has spoken of you." The young woman seemed suddenly very nervous as she stood aside. "Please come in."

"*Gracias,*" Irene answered, stepping inside. She instantly thought how being inside this house must be like stepping into Mexico. She looked around in wonder and admiration. There was not one thing American about the house. It was filled with plants, Mexican-designed rugs not only on the floors but also on the walls. Everything was immaculate, and everything spoke of

Ramon. She could almost feel his arms around her just by being in this room.

She turned to Anna. "Your house is very beautiful."

"Thank you." Anna watched her expectantly, looking a little defensive, and Irene realized how awkward she must feel.

"I'll only be a minute. I . . . wanted to bring this gift for you and Ramon. I know Ramon is in Fort Collins, but I wasn't sure when I'd get another chance."

Anna looked at the gift curiously. "*Sí,*" she answered. "He took several days off after we were married, but then he had to go back. He will come home weekends. I am just glad there is the train now. It does not take him long to go back and forth."

She took the gift from Irene, and Irene struggled with the terrible torture of envisioning Ramon and this pretty girl enjoying their honeymoon. She could see in an instant that Anna Vallejo was a sweet, quiet young woman who would probably make Ramon very happy. "It was not necessary to buy us a gift," she was saying.

"Yes, it *was* necessary. Ramon is a very good friend."

Their eyes met. "He has told me so," Anna said. "If you are wondering, he told me everything, Mrs. Jacobs. He said that he kept it from his first wife, and ended up hurting her. He did not want to do the same with me."

Irene reddened a little, smiling sadly. "I see. Well, Anna, I didn't come here to upset you. I only came because I wanted to tell you I think . . . I think you're married to the most wonderful man in Denver. You're a very lucky young woman, and I hope you will make Ramon very happy. He deserves love and happiness more than anyone I can think of."

"Except for you," Anna answered.

Irene's eyes teared. "Thank you, Anna. I just . . . I wanted to bring the gift to congratulate you, and as an expression of how much I hope you will have good, long lives together. I truly mean that."

"*Gracias.*" Anna looked down at the gift, thinking how heavy it seemed. She carefully opened it, tearing off the paper and opening a flat box. She gasped at its contents. "Oh, Señora Jacobs, it is too much!"

"Nothing is too much for the two of you."

"Oh, my!" Anna's eyes teared as she lifted out a golden crucifix.

"It's real gold, Anna. I'm told that . . . well, one old Cath-olic woman told me once that if you hang a crucifix over your bed, you'll be blessed with many children." Oh, what torture those words were!

Anna smiled bashfully. "Then that is where I will put it," she said. "I want to give Ramon many—" She carefully laid the crucifix back in the box, embarrassed to finish the statement. She missed him, couldn't wait until he was home again. Ramon had shown her a whole new, wonderful world—the world of womanhood and gentle loving. She felt honored to be married to the successful builder Ramon Vallejo, who had shown Denver the worth of its Mexican race. She met Irene's eyes. "He truly is the most wonderful man. I sometimes think perhaps I am dreaming that he is my husband."

Irene blinked back tears. "It's no dream. Do you . . . do you think Ramon will like the crucifix?"

"Of course he will. He will be very touched, especially since it is from you. I love him, Señora Jacobs. But still I am sorry about the unhappiness you have suffered. Ramon is hoping the baby has helped. He has not seen you since it was born."

"You can tell him the baby has made me very happy, as happy as I can expect to be. I'm taking some time off to be with my little David, so Ramon won't see much of me the next few months, but I will be meeting with the committee again in another six weeks or so. I'll go to night meetings, but I won't be putting in full days at the office for quite some time. Just tell him I'm going to be all right. He'll understand."

"*Sí*, I will tell him. And I am glad for you. Would you like to stay and talk? I can make us some tea."

"No. I don't like leaving my little David for too long. I just wanted to bring you the wedding gift."

"It is so good of you. It is the most beautiful thing I have ever seen. We will both treasure it. It is a most generous gift."

"Nothing is too generous for Ramon and his new wife. It is Ramon who has been the generous one all these years, generous with his love and patience and his kind understanding." Her throat suddenly ached, and a tear slipped unexpectedly down her cheek. She quickly brushed it away. "Take good care of him, Anna."

"I will. I love him very much. I am honored to be his wife."

"Yes. It *is* an honor." Irene leaned forward and kissed her cheek. "*Vaya con Dios*, Anna." She turned and hurried out the door.

"*Vaya con Dios*," Anna called after her. She watched Irene run through the rain and climb into the carriage, which quickly clattered away. She looked down at the crucifix, amazed at the utterly beautiful, expensive gift.

Yes, Irene Jacobs surely did love her Ramon, but Anna did not feel threatened. She had seen the truth and honor in Irene's eyes, and she trusted her Ramon. She almost felt sad for both of them. She would try very hard to make it up to Ramon by being a good wife, and she prayed that already his life was growing in her belly. She touched the crucifix. It would seem strange to hang it over their bed, this gift from the *gringa* Ramon had loved.

Inside the closed carriage Irene wept. She had a baby now, a marriage to try to rebuild. There could never be a Ramon in her life. She had made an agreement with Chad. Perhaps it was time to adhere to her part of the bargain. Maybe, somehow, she could bear it. He had treated her better than he had since that brief period when she was so happy before the first baby. He played with David, seemed to love the boy, believed he was his. Now it was her turn. She had to face reality, and Chad was right. If she was sincere about making the marriage work, she couldn't put him off forever.

CHAPTER
THIRTY-FOUR

Like the true survivors Denver's founders were, they struggled through the panic of '73, when overproduction of goods across the country, feverish speculation, and government corruption created a drop in prices that put many companies out of business and played havoc with the stock market. New silver discoveries helped boost the economy, and Kirkland silver mines began to support K-E's basic financial structure in as important a manner as the gold mines had.

President Grant's term of service proved a boon for all sorts of crooked dealing, and big businesses began gobbling up little businesses, creating vast monopolies. Bea Kirkland took no exception to the now-established rule that it was perfectly fine to grease the palms of Territorial representatives and congressmen to urge them to support tax laws that benefited bigger companies; and she folded some parts of K-E into huge trusts, melding with other companies in the areas of manufacturing, loan companies, and municipal utilities to create a stronghold in all areas, forming a central board of trustees in charge of securities, and power.

The newspapers screamed with headlines of government corruption, the Democrats claiming it was time for a change in the administration that was on its way to bankrupting the nation. It was discovered that the government had been defrauded of millions of dollars in taxes by what was being called a "whiskey

ring," centered in St. Louis, instigated by treasury officials and
the president's own private secretary. The Indians, most of them
on reservations, were becoming the victims of unscrupulous
agents who sold most government supplies for profit and left the
intended recipients cold and hungry. Graft penetrated nearly every
area of government, even the navy.

Bea's main concern was that K-E remain strong. She complained about government corruption, while thinking nothing of
doing her own bribing. The warehousing and supply branch of
K-E grew into one of the company's biggest supports, now that the
Union Pacific went all the way to San Francisco and had a Denver
connection. The Kansas Pacific had also made its way into
Denver, and the still-growing Denver and Rio Grande Railroad
reached all the way south to Colorado Springs and Pueblo, with a
branch into the mountains to Canon City. With Chad's help, Bea
wined and dined and bribed the proper railroad officials into
keeping K-E freight rates lower than their competitors, helping
widen K-E's monopoly in the supply business.

Denver now had two Catholic churches, several Protestant
churches, and even a Jewish synagogue. Still, saloons continued
to predominate, outnumbering churches by six to one. But
Denverites were proud of their growing city, which now had
several doctors and dentists, and an abundance of shops, restaurants, banks, and hotels, as well as several schools. Immigrants
continued to swarm into Denver, hearing of its promises for a
chance for a better life and equal opportunity. People came by the
thousands, seeking new dreams—to farm, to open a new business,
or to practice their trade. Many were disappointed and left, but
many more stayed, realizing at least a modest income and
something better than what they had left behind.

But there remained an elite network of powerful founders who
held themselves above the middle and lower class, called by some
the Sacred 36 and comprised of white Protestant men. Bea
Kirkland was the exception, an anomaly in the world of big
business and the topic of many conversations among her counter-
parts. David Kirkland and Chad Jacobs were the male representatives of K-E, but everyone knew who made the decisions they
brought to the board rooms.

Denver citizens, indeed most Americans, overlooked the corruption of those in power, deciding it was a necessary evil in the
name of progress. By 1872 the Water Company was pumping
filtered water from the South Platte into Denver residences and
businesses, although most homes still used well water. Other

water projects had proved expensive and were still being explored. Trolley cars and railroads took people and goods to their destinations; gas lit and heated homes; buildings were rising higher. Sitting in the middle of a vast, open, endless plain, Denver began to rise out of the desert like an oasis, the true Queen City of the West. The time had come to bring up again a vote for statehood.

April 1874

Irene moved through the crowded room, searching for Ramon. Everyone who was anyone was here tonight, not only Denver's backers, but important dignitaries from other Colorado cities and from the various railroad companies and utilities, as well as mining representatives, cattlemen, and guests from Washington. Food and drinks were furnished by the Kirklands, owners of the Denver Inn, where the kickoff meeting for statehood was being held. Speeches had been made, a state flag proposed, a fine dinner served. Now it was time to mingle, butter up the right people.

Irene thought how fake everyone seemed, smiling, laughing, wooing. Chad was the supreme expert, laughing and talking with a congressman. He called her over, and she obliged, wanting statehood as much as her mother did but still not caring for some of Bea's methods. She suspected Bea and Chad both were still making deals behind her back, but she had become so involved with her work for the poor, as well as devoting time to her son, that she had again lost touch with the basic economics of K-E. When David got just a little older, she was determined to become more involved with the decision-making of the company.

Chad sported his most winning smile, slipping an arm around Irene and introducing her to Jay Gould, the famous, if somewhat notorious, railroad magnate. Irene joined in the conversation, her natural beauty and sincerity charming everyone she met. Others gossiped about the strikingly handsome couple Chad and Irene presented. Irene was growing used to being watched by the public.

They talked about statehood for Colorado, and all the time Chad kept a firm arm around Irene. He had played the happy husband and father for three years now, and Irene had managed to derive some little bit of pleasure in their bed, only because she knew she had to learn to love her husband all over again or go crazy. Chad remained attentive and considerate, but Irene knew deep inside he was incapable of total love and devotion. She was doomed to make the best of her marriage, and she deliberately forced back her suspicions of his continued infidelities, for little David's sake.

The boy was more than three years old now, and he bore little resemblance to Hank, with Irene's coloring and many of her features. Chad seemed to have accepted the child, showing no resentment or animosity, teasing him, playing with him, but he never hugged the boy. She had learned that her husband was simply incapable of tender, genuine love, perhaps because he had not been loved as a child. She loved David all that much more, showing him plenty of affection to make up for what his father could not give him. Chad was at least attentive and patient with him.

Talk turned to the railroad and Gould's clout in Washington, how he could help swing votes that would benefit Colorado once it became a state. Chad talked easily with the man, and Irene thought how sad it was that he was so wonderfully charming and likeable on the outside, but so empty on the inside.

Glasses tinkled and people laughed, some turning to stare at the "lucky" Mrs. Chad Jacobs, who not only had a most handsome husband, but who was a beauty herself. She wore a mint green satin straight-line dress, with a fitted waist and a slight bustle in the back. The skirt was gathered into tufts that draped down the back, meeting in a huge bow below her knees, with a short train gliding out from under the bow. Ruffles spilled down the front of the skirt, and the dropped waist and fitted bodice accented her still-slim, curved figure, the open, square neckline showing just a hint of her lovely bosom, mint green lace forming a delicate border around the neckline and the ends of her three-quarter-length sleeves.

People gossiped about what a stark contrast Irene presented to her younger sister, Elly, who paraded through the crowd in a dark blue taffeta dress, designed much like Irene's, which was the latest fashion, but looking nowhere near as pretty because of the stocky young woman who filled it. The neckline, to Bea's outrage, was cut much lower than Irene's, displaying a good portion of Elly's generous bosom.

Elly moved through the crowd, a proud representative of K-E who had demanded that her mother let her take over some facets of the company, and who had already lost a woman's millinery store because of overspending and poor bookkeeping. Bea was upset with Elly's carelessness, and that she was seeing too many men. "You should settle down, get married, act like a proper lady," Bea had often fumed, to Elly's delight.

Twenty-four-year-old Elly was not about to be told what she could and could not do. She glanced at Chad, who looked at her in return, his eyes running over her. Yes, he would meet her later tonight inside her personal carriage as planned. Her blood rushed at the thought of it. It had been weeks since she had been with Chad. She had tried to make up for her need of him through the other men she dated, enjoyed the power she had over them just by being a woman with money; her many affairs made her feel beautiful and wanted, and best of all, they upset her mother.

She spotted Red McKinley then, watched him as he talked with William Palmer, founder of the Denver and Rio Grande. Red was an important man now in Denver, and she thought how her mother detested the man. She took a glass of wine from a tray a waitress offered, and strolled in Red's direction.

"Hello, Mr. McKinley," she purred. "And it's so nice to see you here, General Palmer."

Palmer nodded a hello. "Your family has been generous, furnishing all this fine food and drink, as well as these facilities," the man told her. "I think I'll go find your mother and thank her. It's too bad Kirk can't be here."

"Oh, you know Father, always roaming around in the mountains sniffing out more gold and silver," she answered with a sly smile, glancing at Red. "Mr. McKinley knows my father very well. He used to hunt and trap with him in what Father calls the 'old days,' didn't you, Red?"

Red watched her eyes. The girl was up to something. She was so much like her mother, but perhaps more vicious. "That I did," he answered.

"Well, we'll have to talk about those exciting times, Red," Palmer told him.

The man left, and Elly gave Red McKinley her most seductive look, one an experienced man like himself did not misread. He thought how closely it resembled the looks the whores gave prospective customers who passed the doorways of their brothels. How unlike Irene this one was.

"And what brings you over here to talk to someone your mother despises?" he asked, letting his eyes rest on her abundant bosom for a moment. She might be Kirk's daughter, but she was young and certainly no innocent.

Elly took his hand, squeezing it lightly, glancing through the crowd to see Palmer talking to her mother. Bea looked in their direction, instant consternation coming into her dark eyes. Elly instantly smiled at Red, keeping hold of his hand. "It's precisely *because* my mother despises you that I intend to befriend you," she answered. "I've discovered some of the things my dear mother did to you, and I happen to be very sorry about it."

Red laughed heartily. "You don't really expect me to believe that now, Miss Kirkland, do you? You're talking to a seasoned old man."

She smiled wickedly. "I'm talking to a very handsome, gentlemanly 'older' man, but not old. You're just like my father, Red—still as strong and virile as you were in those old days you talk about."

He shook a finger at her, giving her a wink, enjoying the flirtations. "You're up to something, young lady."

She kept hold of his hand as a twelve-piece orchestra struck up a waltz. "I'm up to dancing. Will you dance with me?"

"Well, I'm accustomed to doing the asking, but I'm not going to turn down an offer from a pretty young lady." He moved out onto the dance floor with her, thinking how she wasn't pretty at all, but she was indeed young. A few more years difference, and he could be her grandfather. Still, he was only fifty-one, and by God, he *was* still strong and virile. There was no mistaking this replica of Bea Kirkland was as capable of deceit as her mother, but in a strange way she was fun, excitingly dangerous.

"Now, isn't this just delicious," she said, moving a hand to caress his neck while they moved around the floor. "Mother is watching, and she's beside herself."

Red chuckled. "I have to admit I enjoy getting her dander up."

"That was pretty obvious when I read about that dirty trick you played on the whole city of Denver over the railroad. I really wish I could have been there to see Mother's face. But, alas, I was away at finishing school in Chicago. I missed all the fun."

Red drank in her full bosom again, and Elly tingled with the excitement she always felt at the thought of bedding a new man. "Well, it was something to see, I'll tell you that."

"I'll bet it was." She toyed with the hair at the back of his neck, thinking how easy it was to manipulate men. "I've never known anyone with such red hair." She looked down at his chest and farther down, then met his eyes again suggestively. "Is it that red all over—your arms and chest, I mean?"

He watched her eyes. Yes, this one was well seasoned. In spite of who she was, he could not help a base attraction to the sultry seductress. He reddened a little, sobering, pulling her a little closer, thinking how furious her mother would be if Red McKinley started seeing her daughter. "Yes," he answered, holding her eyes. "It's red . . . all over."

She smiled, wetting her lips with her tongue. "Tell me, Red, did you know my mother and father back when they first got married?"

He frowned. "No. I saw Kirk back in, oh, forty-six, it was, just a few weeks before he met and married your mother, so I never knew her then."

"Forty-six? You must remember it wrong."

"Oh, no. I have a good memory for dates."

She continued to rub at his neck, her mind racing with a new wonder. There had always been something different about Irene, something strange about her parents' beginnings, the way Irene was so different from her and John. "But you must be wrong," she insisted. "Irene was *born* in forty-six. Mother always told us she and Father married in forty-five."

She felt him stiffen slightly. Red watched her slyly, realizing his error. This one was clever, and he had a feeling she had no lost love for her sister. He realized immediately he had made a serious mistake. "Well, I guess maybe you're right at that," he told Elly. "A man gets to be my age, he gets a little forgetful. We're talking about something that happened twenty-eight or twenty-nine years ago. That's a long time to remember."

"Yes, I suppose it is." She moved daringly close to him. "You'll have to tell me about those old days sometime, Red. I'll bet your version is different from Father's. Why don't you meet me here tomorrow evening for a quiet meal? It's hard to talk in such a big crowd, and I have to 'mingle,' as Mother puts it."

He held her eyes. "I don't think your mother would care to have you going to dinner with me."

"I do what I want."

"I'll bet you do."

"Then will you come?"

"You sure?"

"I happen to find older men very attractive. And it's time someone in this family made up for what Mother did to you years ago. That railroad thing wasn't anything you could control, I'm sure. It wasn't your fault, and now we're linked to the UP anyway, so where is the harm? You can pick me up at our house at seven."

He laughed. "You actually want me to come to the Kirkland mansion to pick up their young daughter for dinner?"

"Of course. Mother will die."

The thought of Bea Kirkland's fury brought a feeling of wonderful vengeance to Red's soul. If this young woman was the innocent she should be, he would not consider wooing one of Kirk's daughters; but he could already see this one had already been soiled. Courting Bea Kirkland's daughter would be more fun and bring him more satisfaction than he had achieved when he finally put Kirkland Lumber out of business.

"All right," he told her. "I'll be there. I just hope I'm not met at the door with a shotgun."

Elly laughed coyly, glancing at Chad, aware he was watching her. She loved making someone as handsome as Chad just a little bit jealous. He deserved to hurt a little, just as she hurt at the thought of Chad's taking to Irene's bed again. Besides, she was perfectly aware that Chad Jacobs had other women on his coattails. What was good for the goose was good for the gander. She wanted all of them to hurt—Chad, Irene, John, her mother, all of them. She held Red McKinley's eyes. What a fine fit her mother would be in if she married him. Perhaps she could win her way to the altar with this man. He was wealthy on his own, and, after all, her mother had been after her to "settle down."

"I look forward to tomorrow then," she told Red. "It will be fun, I promise you."

His eyes fell to her bosom. "I look forward to it myself."

They danced past Irene, and Elly gave her a scathing, haughty look. Irene watched in surprise, wondering what her sister was up to. Elly hardly gave her the time of day anymore, never seemed to have time to visit either Irene or little David. She was gaining a questionable reputation, and no one in the family seemed able to control her.

Irene turned away. She had long ago given up trying to have a normal relationship with Elly, and had given up trying to understand anything she did. She excused herself from Chad and Gould and continued her search for Ramon, who was now considered an important part of Denver's "upper crust." There was a time when it would have been unheard of to have a man of Mexican blood at such a function, but Ramon had more than proven his intelligence and his right to be included in major decisions that affected Denver.

Still, unlike others who reached the privileged plateau of the wealthy, Ramon had remained the same kind, sincere, caring person he had always been. Irene saw him only occasionally, running into him at meetings, seldom having a chance to talk at length. Always the old feelings were there, hidden deep in their hearts. They no longer discussed their past. Irene was aware Anna had still not given him children, and she felt sorry for the woman, sure it must break her heart that she had not conceived.

She finally spotted him through the crowd. He wore a dark, silk suit and white ruffled shirt with a black string tie. As always, he looked stunningly handsome, his skin glowing bronze against the white shirt, his black, slightly wavy hair cut neatly around the collar. Women stared at him and made a point to talk to him, even though he was Mexican, but Irene knew that Ramon would never take advantage of his looks and money the way Chad did. She forced back the madly destructive thoughts that always came when she looked at him.

He saw her then, and as always, their eyes held in that special, secret feeling they shared. He gave her a warm, welcoming smile as she came closer and asked where Anna was.

"Some women whisked her away from me to talk about some church functions," he told her, his dark eyes moving over her. "You are looking beautiful, as always."

"Thank you," she answered, blushing a little. "And you are looking very handsome." This time it was Ramon who smiled bashfully. "I came to ask you a favor," she told him.

"Anything for you. You know that."

"Good. I'm starting a drive to raise money and collect food and clothes for the underprivileged. We've had so many coloreds come to Denver, and the railroad and mining has attracted a lot of Italians and Chinese. They're being horribly discriminated against, Ramon, cut off from the rest of society, and the district around Hop Alley and along Wazee Street is in terrible shape. I want to get people interested in cleaning it up and helping those people. We need schools that can teach colored children and help the foreigners learn our language and customs. I thought maybe you would have some ideas to help me on the project. You certainly understand discrimination."

He frowned. "Very well, but I am surprised your mother lets you get involved with the so-called underclass."

"She hates it," Irene answered with a smile.

He broke into a wider grin. "Ah, then I will *definitely* help you."

Irene laughed. "I thought that would win you over. Actually, I think the only reason Mother and Chad both let me go my own way is because they know better than to argue with me about it. Besides, it keeps me from sticking my nose into K-E too deeply and finding out the crooked deals they're up to."

"That I do not doubt." He scanned the crowd beyond her, noticing Chad was watching them. He sobered, holding Chad's eyes for a moment. His hatred for the man had not changed, and he knew without asking that Irene was still not totally happy. Men like Chad Jacobs never really changed. They only pretended.

"Maybe your husband would not like the idea of us working together again. We have not really joined forces since the university was built."

"My husband has no say in it. He knows when it comes to things like this, I make my own decisions."

He met her eyes again, feeling the pain in his gut at the thought of Chad Jacobs making love to her. But he had no room for jealousy. He had Anna, and he was happy.

"Well, then, I will help however I can."

"I know you're a busy man, Ramon. I just thought maybe you could put a little pressure on your workers and your business associates to donate whatever they can. I'm going to gather some K-E people together for the same thing, as well as speak at the various churches in hopes of raising public interest—and money."

"And I will talk to my priest about it. The Catholic church has always been very generous to the poor. In fact, they have already been doing a few things to help the Hop Alley area."

"I know, and I'm grateful. I could talk all night about my feelings about this. I've hated prejudice ever since my mother started talking against Indians and Mex—" She caught herself, reddening slightly.

Ramon smiled bitterly. "You can say it. I am well aware of your mother's attitude toward my people. I am also aware that I would not be at this party if I were not already a rich man. I am Denver's token example of how even a *Mexican* man can be successful in this city if he is willing to work hard."

Her eyes misted. "Well, you *are* a fine example, for *any* race. I'm so proud of what you've done, Ramon."

"Well, I had some excellent incentives, all given me by your mother."

Irene smiled. "I wonder if she realizes how much she has helped you."

Ramon laughed, and Chad watched, his old fears returning. He was already frustrated by having to sneak around to grab his extra thrills as he could, while Elly had the time of her life sleeping with every willing man in Denver. Irene had become more satisfying in bed, but she was his wife, and she did not understand his baser wicked needs. He continued to crave the satisfaction he attained from conquering and pleasing other women, while at the same time he could not bear the thought of Irene even looking at another man.

Was she having whoring thoughts this moment for Ramon? He told himself he must always stay in control. Their relationship had become bearable, almost happy. He was even beginning to believe little David just might be his own son. He didn't dare let his imagination about Irene with another man get the better of him, or he would ruin everything he had gained.

The orchestra played another waltz, and Chad excused himself from his conversation and headed straight for Irene. A dance was a good excuse to get her away from Ramon. He came closer, holding Ramon's eyes, and Ramon turned to face him while Irene watched with a rushing heart.

"Well, Ramon, I've seen you here and there quite a bit since last we, uh, talked," Chad said. "A man of your importance has trouble keeping a low profile. Even so, I haven't had the chance to actually speak to you." He sipped on his wine, the only form of alcohol he allowed himself to drink. "Perhaps after these five or six years since then we can shake hands again." He put on a smile, but his eyes held a warning. "I owe you much more than a handshake, but I'm willing to show you I'm not a man to hold grudges." He put out his hand. "In fact, you were probably right in your opinion that day, but things have changed considerably." He looked at Irene. "Haven't they, Irene?"

Irene held his eyes. "Yes," she answered. "You two may end up working together again sometime. I would like to see you back on good terms."

Ramon grasped Chad's hand, each man squeezing hard, testing each other out.

"I suppose I do owe you something for your support when I was getting started." Ramon told him. "I am willing to put the past behind us. I am glad to know things are better between you two now."

"I suppose you are," Chad answered. The clasp lasted longer than normal, and for a moment Irene thought one of them was going to lose control. Chad finally let go, moving an arm around Irene. "I trust that this time around you aren't going to oppose statehood for Colorado, are you?" he asked Ramon.

Ramon held his eyes boldly. "No. After all, I have no more land to fight for, do I? Most of the Mexicans have been chased out of southern Colorado, by land-hungry cattle barons, one whose name I will not mention."

Chad grinned slightly. "Times change, Ramon. Times change. It's called progress. Most of the Indians understand it now, except for a few renegade Sioux in the north." He touched Ramon's arm. "But you're a wealthy businessman now. You understand those things." He held Irene a little closer. "Now, what does my wife have up her sleeve this time? Seems like whenever she talks for very long with you, you both end up on some project together."

Ramon glanced at Irene, who answered for him. "I want Ramon to help me create interest in more donations to help the Hop Alley district. I'll be talking to all the important businessmen about it, not just Ramon."

"Well, now, I know how involved you get in those projects, Irene," Chad answered, putting on a broad smile. "But I'm not sure if it's a good idea to start it right now, since I'm thinking of taking you to Europe this summer."

Irene looked at him in surprise. "This summer?"

He gave her a wink. "Yes. I've been promising you that trip since the day we got married. We got cheated out of it because of that damn flood, and we've been trying to go ever since." He set his wineglass on an empty tray and kept a firm arm around her, deliberately urging her out to the dance floor and away from Ramon, who stood watching with renewed hatred. He was well aware Chad was deliberately flaunting his marital rights in front of him. He tore his eyes from Irene and turned to Anna then, who was coming toward him from across the dance floor.

"Ramon, what is it?" she asked. "You look upset."

He looked down at his beautiful wife, who had wept many tears over the fact that she had still not given him a child. He loved her dearly. Instantly the animosity and anger left his eyes. "Nothing," he told her. "Dance with me, will you?" He urged her out to join the others, making sure to keep his eyes from Irene.

"What's that about going to Europe this summer?" Irene was asking Chad. "I have a lot of plans, Chad."

"Then change them. We owe ourselves this trip, Irene. I don't usually interfere with your activities, but I really wish this time you would hold off on any plans. We agreed a long time ago the trip would do us good, remember?" He had to get her away again, away from Ramon!

"What about all the work ahead of us in getting statehood for Colorado?"

"That's just the point. How long are we going to let things like that stop us? There comes a time when you just have to *do* it, Irene. Wouldn't you like to see London, the old castles of France and Spain? Wouldn't you like to see Paris? Rome? Athens?"

It sounded wonderful, but how could she make a man like Chad understand she would rather go to the mountains than to Europe? He was trying to surprise her, wasn't he? And this marriage needed all the repair work they could give it. She didn't want to abandon her project, but she could always resume her responsibilities when she returned. They had talked about Europe for so many years. "Can we see the mountains of Switzerland?"

"Whatever you want."

"And can we take David with us? We could take his nanny along to watch him while we go sight-seeing. I don't want to leave him for that long, Chad. I'd get so lonely for him that I wouldn't enjoy myself."

"Then he'll come with us. Besides, I would miss him, too." He whisked her around the dance floor, feeling smug about charming her into the trip and away from Ramon.

Irene glanced at Ramon as he and Anna passed them on the dance floor. She could go to his office and talk to him tomorrow. Maybe he could get a few things started without her. She had to keep her priorities, and her first priority was to continue to work at a happy marriage. She would go to Europe.

"Looks like your little sister is up to no good," Chad told her then, watching Elly with Red McKinley.

Irene glanced at them. "You never know what Elly is up to."

Chad smiled. "How true." He would ask her himself when he met her later that night.

CHAPTER
THIRTY-FIVE

July 1874

 Bea looked across the breakfast table at Elly, who still sat in her robe, her hair a tumble. "You know we always dress before eating," she chided, signaling Esther to pour her more coffee. "You should be dressed and ready to go to the office."

Elly shrugged. "I don't feel like it today."

"Because you got home so late last night?"

Elly met her mother's eyes squarely. "I'm almost twenty-five years old, Mother! What I do is my business."

Bea drew in her breath, totally exasperated with her youngest daughter. "Dating Red McKinley is *all* our business!" She set down her fork. "I want to know once and for all what you're up to, Elly. Why do you insist on continuing to see that man?"

Elly held her chin proudly. "I can see whoever I want. Red is a very nice man, and I happen to love him, and he loves me."

"You're causing gossip all over Denver! If this continues, I'll be forced to keep you out of K-E. I don't like your associating with someone who would destroy this company if he could! You'll lose the job and prestige you have here, as well as the generous amount of money I pay you!"

Elly rolled her eyes. "Mother, Red McKinley is a wealthy man in his own right. Why do you think everyone lives and breathes for K-E? Go ahead and kick me out. There is still the inheritance.

Father would never leave any of us out of that. In the meantime, Red couldn't care less about this company. You don't have to fret that he can do you any damage. You know better. K-E is much too powerful." She sipped some orange juice. "Red simply enjoys my company. I make him happy. He isn't after anything, and if I marry him, I'll lead just as comfortable a life as I do as a Kirkland."

"*Marry* him! You've actually talked of marrying?"

Elly leaned back in her chair. "Yes," she answered coldly. "You're the one who has been after me to settle down, don't forget."

"With someone like Tommy Slade, or perhaps someone in politics—"

"Oh, Mother, you can't pick our mates like you choose which stock to invest in. We're dealing with people here, not figures. I swear, you don't know the difference. At any rate, I have a feeling Red is going to pop the question any time. Just think of the juicy news it would make for the gossip columns." She smiled smugly at the look on her mother's face. "It might even show what generous people you and Father are—allowing their daughter to marry their arch-enemy. It would be a sign of peacemaking."

"At heart Red McKinley is still nothing but a crude drifter who just happened to get lucky. He never did one damn thing to earn what he has! Your father and I struggled to build K-E, while Red just came here to borrow off your father and try to make it the easy way! He *hates* us, Elly. You know that! Why are you doing this?"

"I *told* you. I love him. Besides, we'd *better* get married," she said flippantly. "I've already been to bed with him. He's amazingly agile and virile for his age. Tell me, Mother, is Father still that romantic and energetic?"

Elly watched her mother's face grow beet red, watched the anger come into those dark eyes. She enjoyed it immensely. She knew good and well her mother had probably not been with a man in years, and she wondered if the woman had ever enjoyed sex.

"Do you really hate us that much, Elly," Bea asked, "that you would shame us so?"

Esther quickly and quietly left the room. She had never liked Elly. She hoped the girl *did* marry and leave the Kirkland mansion.

Elly's eyes narrowed as they bore into her mother's. "Yes," she answered with deliberate emphasis. "All my life you have scolded me, insulted me, compared me to Irene. Father is even worse. Irene has always been his pet. He hardly knows I exist. All my life

I've come in second, Mother. I've struggled for your attention and tried to please you, and now I don't care any more."

"So, you would use Red to get back at us."

"Of course I would."

"He's using you, too. I hope you know that."

She smiled wickedly. "Then we'll have fun using each other. As long as we're both aware of it, who is going to get hurt, except maybe you and Father?"

Bea just stared at her a long, quiet moment. "You're wrong in thinking how we feel about you, Elly. We love you. Parents love all their children the same, but show it differently. It's impossible not to hurt them at times. Circumstances sometimes make it appear they love one child more than another. There are things you don't understand. If you did—" She sighed deeply. "Never mind. You're going to do what you think you have to do, and I can't stop you. If you go through with this, then so be it. Publicly we will cooperate, for appearance' sake. But privately, I do not want that man in my home, and I cannot let you keep working for K-E if you marry him. But you're right about one thing, Elly. We won't disinherit you, because we love you."

Elly sniffed. "It's a little late to try to convince me of that, Mother." She dug into a grapefruit, conducting the entire conversation as though hating her family and carrying on with Red McKinley were nothing. Bea watched her a moment, her heart heavy. She had not wept in years. She was not about to start now, not in front of this ungrateful daughter.

Elly ate some of the grapefruit, aware of the painful silence in the room and loving it. She thought about Chad in Europe with Irene, and it grated on her. What hurt even more was they had gotten word Irene was pregnant again. Oh, how she missed Chad! How she hated the thought of him giving all his attention to Irene!

"I expect Chad and Irene will come back a little sooner, now that they know Irene is pregnant," she said aloud. "I'll hold off on the wedding until they get here. I wouldn't want them to miss it." She grinned. "I want an even grander wedding than Irene's—in the new church, with a reception at the Denver Inn. Considering the fact that we'll be uniting two very big companies, I imagine half of Denver will attend. It will be the wedding of the decade." She breathed deeply. "For once, *I'll* be the center of the society page instead of Irene."

Bea just stared at her as she finished her coffee. She rose then, leaving the room without another word. She walked on weary legs to the stairway and up to her bedroom to get her hat. She wondered where she had gone wrong. All these years she had worked to build something for her children, and Elly hated her. Her son was an alcoholic, and she had no doubt he also hated her. If not for the other men she hired to help John in Colorado Springs, everything there would fold. She had left him in the job only to help boost his self-confidence, but she was horribly disappointed in him.

Even Irene was different, although she still remained the most loving and grateful of the three children. Irene was stronger, and she was the kind of child who would love her parents no matter what. She worried sometimes that Ramon might have told her the truth about the first time he left Denver, but if he had, Irene had never let on. It was something that still haunted Bea, for it was the only time she had deliberately done something that she knew would hurt one of her children.

Or had there been other times? Why were Elly and John so venomous? She had been a good mother, had given them everything they could ever want or need. She realized she was not the most affectionate person in the world, but surely they knew she loved them. Irene was the only one left who seemed to understand that.

She pinned on her hat and looked at herself in the mirror, realizing how much she had aged. She was forty-four but looked, and sometimes felt, older. Didn't anyone realize and appreciate how hard she had worked all her life? She hadn't felt well lately, didn't seem to have the energy she once had. She attributed it to her busy days, and she said nothing to anyone, wondering if any of them would even care.

She turned away, refusing to dwell on her deeper fears about Red and Elly. She had never forgotten Red McKinley's words years ago about Irene—"You'd better pray she has white babies." Irene was pregnant again, and there was always the possibility Irene could have a baby that looked very Indian. Even if she didn't, would Red someday tell Elly the truth about Irene? Elly hated her sister. She would waste no time letting Irene and all of Denver know that Irene had not only Indian blood, but a brother who was none other than Yellow Eagle.

She decided that if Red married Elly, she and Kirk would have to be as gracious as possible about it. Red McKinley could destroy them. Her only hope was that he still thought the world of Irene. She went down the stairs and outside, where her driver waited to take her to another day at the office. She had gone too far now to turn back, and she wouldn't if she could. Whether her family hated her or not, she was proud of what she had built in the Kirkland name, proud of her accomplishments. She had never meant for it to cost her her family's love, but apparently it had. She climbed into the carriage, wondering why she felt so strangely short of breath so early in the morning.

September of 1874 saw the society columns full of news about the Kirklands. Elly Kirkland was engaged to be married to James McKinley. A Christmas wedding was planned. Mr. and Mrs. Chad Jacobs were home from a trip to Europe, and a second child was expected soon after the wedding of Irene Jacobs's sister. Another article carried the story of Chad and Irene's tour of Europe.

Ramon read the article carefully, wondering if Irene was happy now. So, she was going to have another child. Perhaps she and Chad were finally truly getting along.

He set the newspaper aside, wishing poor Anna could conceive. His heart ached for her. Her barrenness was certainly not due to any lack of trying. She was sweet and wonderful in bed, and sometimes he thought maybe she tried too hard to please him. Maybe her inability to conceive was simply because she was too upset about still not giving him a child.

He got up from his desk and walked to a window, looking across a now-thriving Denver toward Kirkland Hills. Irene was back. If she was going to have a baby, it was unlikely she would soon get back into the business or into fund raising. He knew what her wishes were, though, and he had worked hard while she was gone. He and his church had organized several fund-raising events, and a school was planned for the coloreds. Food and clothing had been donated for the jobless, whose numbers were growing. He decided perhaps he would pay her a visit and let her know how much had been accomplished in her absence.

He turned then at the sound of solid footsteps and rustling skirts. He felt a strange heat come into his face and neck at the sight of Bea Kirkland standing in the doorway of his office. Their eyes locked in mutual hatred. "I usually have people announced before they come barging into my office," he told her, surprised at her presence.

Bea held his eyes squarely. "Your secretary is away from her desk." She looked around his office, obviously not caring for its Spanish decor. "I am here on business," she announced.

Ramon sighed, moving back behind his desk. Bea glanced at

the newspaper that lay there, seeing it folded to the article about Irene and Chad. She met Ramon's eyes. "I see you keep track of my daughter's personal life."

He did not flinch. "The Kirkland family life is practically a public matter," he answered. "What do you want, Senōra Kirkland?"

She stiffened. "I am here to tell you that you have won one small battle you have waged against me. If you think I don't realize you helped Red McKinley close my lumber business, you're wrong."

"Quite the contrary. I wanted very *much* for you to know I was a part of it."

She sniffed. "One lumber company cannot make or break K-E. At any rate, what I am referring to is your battle to prove you could be worth something. You have done very well, and now that you are happily married and successful on your own, I wish to congratulate you."

He let out a sarcastic snicker, sitting down in his chair. "I would like to accept your congratulations, but I know you better than to think you would come here just for that. You are no fonder of me now than the day you told me to stop seeing your daughter, so why don't you tell me the *real* reason you are here?"

She stepped closer. "All right." She looked around the office again. "I have decided to build a new home, an even bigger one than what we have now. I want the grandest mansion in Denver." She met his eyes again.

"You already *have* the biggest house in the city."

"It isn't grand enough. Denver has grown considerably since that house was built. We entertain some of the most important people in the country, and I want something that shows the wealthiest of dignitaries just how important Denver is, that this is a place in which a man can wisely invest, that Denver is a place for success and progress. Besides, our home is surrounded now by others. It doesn't stand out as much as it used to. I have chosen a site slightly away from the other houses, one that is a little higher."

"And you want *me* to design your new home?"

"Yes. I won't come crawling on hands and knees. I am a businesswoman and I understand when we have to face what is practical. You are considered the finest builder in Denver. It wouldn't look right if I asked someone else to build it. Being a Kirkland, I am expected to hire only the best. I am sure it delights you that it irks me to have to admit it, but you *are* the best, and

I am hoping you will set aside your hatred of me long enough to do the job."

He grinned slightly. "I am expensive. How do you know that in your case I won't make myself even more expensive?"

"Because you also have a reputation for being honest and fair."

He nodded, watching her closely. "Things seem to have come full circle, señora. I believe we started out this way twelve years ago."

Their eyes held. "Why didn't you ever tell Irene the truth?" she asked then.

Ramon glanced at the article, then back to Bea. "Because no matter how much I hated you, you were her mother. I loved her, which was something you never understood. I could not bring myself to tell her the kind of person her mother really is. Some things must remain sacred. Motherhood is one of them."

She quickly swallowed back the ache in her throat. "Well, for that much I thank you, and because of it, I am willing to forget the past and call a truce."

He shook his head, smiling sadly. "I will not forget, señora. You destroyed the only real happiness Irene and I could have had. She is not happy and never will be. I have a good wife, and I love her; but a part of me died when Irene married Chad Jacobs, and I will not forget. I will build your home, if something so big can be called a home. If you wish to flaunt your wealth for all of Colorado to see, it is your decision. It will give me great pleasure to take your money."

"I'm sure it will. If you will meet with me tomorrow morning at our present home, I will take you to the site I've chosen and explain what I want. You can draw up some blueprints and come up with a price."

He nodded. "I will be there at nine o'clock."

Bea clutched her handbag. "Fine. I will be expecting you." She turned and left, seeming nearly as tall and wide as the doorway. Ramon watched her leave, his heart pounding with hatred.

"I will build your castle," he muttered. "And you will walk about your empty house alone!" Every time he saw her it brought back the memory of that day. He never should have left! If it hadn't been for his grandfather . . . for his own youthful ignorance . . . He picked up the newspaper again. "Mr. and Mrs. Chad Jacobs Return from Europe," the headline read. He threw it in the wastebasket.

• • •

It was one of Denver's biggest weddings. The church was overflowing with guests, friends and associates of K-E and its many branches, as well as railroad executives who knew Red, and people from the many other businesses with which he was associated. Red and Elly had deliberately invited anyone and everyone they had ever known, both of them having reason to flaunt their marriage.

Red was reasonably happy. He was sure he had managed to tame his new young wife enough to trust her, and he knew that marrying would mean Kirk and Bea would have to eat crow.

The organ music started, and Red walked out to stand at the head of the aisle to wait for his bride. He glanced at Bea Kirkland, and the look on her face was all he needed to feel the ultimate revenge for the insult she had inflicted to his pride ten years ago. Kirk walked his daughter down the aisle, his eyes riveted on Red in a warning look.

As Elly came down the aisle, she glanced at Chad. She wanted to laugh at everyone there, to shout to them that just last night she had sneaked out of the house and met Chad in the stables for one last hour of passion before going on her honeymoon. Since Irene was big with child, poor Chad was having a time getting all the sex he needed, and he had been unusually amorous. She thought how she would miss their liaisons, which would have to be even fewer now. How she wished it was Chad who was waiting for her, waiting to slip a ring on her finger and take her home to his bed.

Still, Red was exciting, and he doted on her. He could at least openly give her all his attention, and he made her feel pretty. He was excited to be marrying someone so young, even more excited that his wife would be a Kirkland. She noticed the anxious look on Chad's face. She had assured him Red was not nearly as wonderful in bed as he, but she knew with secret delight that Chad was upset she was marrying, even though they both knew that was the best thing she could do.

She moved her eyes to Irene, who stood near the end of one of the front pews watching her. Irene could not be in the wedding party because of her swollen belly, and Elly was glad for the excuse not to have to ask her. She held her chin proudly as she approached Red, thrilled that she was having a much bigger wedding than Chad and Irene had had ten years before, when Denver was much smaller, and the Kirkland name was not as well known in the Territory and even in other parts of the country as it was today. She hoped Irene was swimming in jealousy.

She turned her attention to Red then, who beamed with pride and victory. She wondered if she would still be relatively young when the man passed on and she inherited his estate all for herself. After all, there would never be any children with whom she would have to share it.

Irene watched her sister pass. She didn't know whether to be happy for her or upset with her. It was obvious she was doing this to spite their mother, but she and Red did seem happy together. She liked Red, and was more worried about him than about her sister. She hoped the man knew what he was doing.

As soon as Elly and Kirk moved past her, she could not help glancing at Ramon, who sat on the other side of the aisle, on the side reserved for Red's friends and associates. He met her eyes, and the old pain returned. It should be them walking down the aisle, at least it should have been them ten or twelve years ago. Now it could never happen. His eyes dropped for a moment to her pregnant belly, and her cheeks felt hot. It was more obvious than ever that she was in this marriage to stay. If she could never be truly happy with Chad, she would at least have her children to love and to love her back.

She tore her eyes from Ramon's, watching the wedding party take their places in front of the church. Two of the bridesmaids were secretaries from K-E whom Elly had befriended, another the daughter of one of K-E's most prominent attorneys. The maid of honor was Mary Brown, the very plain old-maid daughter of Sigmund Brown, one of the original attorneys for K-E. Elly hardly knew Mary, and Irene wondered if she had chosen her simply because she was far from beautiful. Next to her, Elly actually looked pretty, and Irene thought that she truly was pretty today. She seemed happy. Whether it was because she was marrying Red or because she was exacting sweet revenge on her family, no one could be sure.

She glanced at Chad, thinking how ten years ago, they had done this. She had been so happy, so trusting, so in love. Chad met her eyes and cast her a smile, and she thought how he had been right about Europe being good for their marriage. For once she had had him all to herself, without the intrusion of K-E and a hundred other things that got in the way. He had been attentive and amorous, almost lovable, except that she still sensed the empty, dispassionate man who dwelled within the handsome outer body.

Still, he had at least given her the life that moved inside her now. There was no doubt this time that this was Chad's baby.

She listened to the wedding vows, keenly aware of Ramon standing across the aisle from her. She wished John had come, but he had refused, saying he could not leave the K-E southern branch right now. Irene knew he simply wanted no part of Kirkland family functions, and it broke her heart. She had no idea Elly had written to tell him she didn't want him there.

· The ceremony was soon over, and Red planted a kiss on Elly's lips. Irene thought how her sister's wedding night would not be the disaster her own had been. In fact, she suspected the two of them had already shared a bed. She was not proud of her sister's conduct since she had returned from school, and she was as glad as Bea to see Elly settle down with one man.

Everyone moved through the reception line, hugging, kissing, shaking hands. The entire procession and guests climbed into their various fine coaches and buggies and made their way to the Denver Inn for a huge sit-down dinner, to which only the most important people had been invited; and an orchestra began playing. Everyone watched the newlyweds dance, people clapping and smiling, Bea and Kirk forcing a look of delight.

"At least she seems happy." Irene tried to console them.

"You know good and well Red married her just to spite us," Kirk answered.

"It's done now, Father. We have to accept it."

The partying began then, with drinks flowing heavily. Irene watched Chad dance with several other women, realizing she was in no condition to dance. She saw how they still looked at him, how easily he could cast his spell on them. She tried to ignore it, told herself he was just being Chad and just being sociable.

Elly was also watching. Her eyes remained on Chad as one dance ended and he moved back to Irene, putting an arm around her as if he were the happy husband. Elly swallowed some more of the sweet rum drink she held, aware it was not ladylike to drink, but not caring. Red had shown her that sex could be even more exhilarating with alcohol in the blood, and tonight she would have sex with her new husband. She wanted to enjoy it to the fullest, to try not to think about Chad for one night.

She was losing him, slowly but surely. She didn't like the feeling. Chad and Irene were becoming a little too happy. She had out-done her sister in the grandeur of her wedding, had nearly taken over the spotlight in the gossip columns. But she was losing

Chad, and somehow she had to spoil what little happiness Irene had found with him. Perhaps if Irene found out the truth about Susan Stanner, it would cause new conflict and distrust in the happy Jacobs household. If that didn't work, there was always that slipup Red had made about when her mother and father were married. Maybe there was something to it. Had Irene been illegitimate?

She would have to think about it while she was away in New York on her honeymoon. Chad had been right about one thing. Sex was much more fun when it was forbidden. She remembered the first time she had seduced Red inside his enclosed carriage, how he had trembled when she pulled her low-cut dress from her shoulders and untied her camisole to offer him her generous bosom. It had been a deliciously sinful night. Now that she was married to the man, she had a feeling she was fast going to become bored with her new husband.

Red came up and kissed her then, and she suddenly realized how old he was. But he was at least robust and fun, and if she handled him right, she could bleed him for every last penny, and still have lovers on the side to bring back the excitement she would lose with her husband. Chad was one lover she would never give up; and to make sure she never lost him, she realized she had to find ways to keep his own marriage in a turmoil without looking like the culprit.

Red held up a glass then and proposed a toast to his new marriage. Everyone joined him, after which Red pulled Elly close, planting another kiss on her lips. "I might have had ulterior motives for this, but I do love you, Elly."

She smiled. "And I love you," she cooed. She glanced at Chad to be sure he was watching, then gave her new husband another embarrassingly passionate kiss.

Irene sat beside a Pembroke table in the great room, opening mail. Christmas, and Elly's wedding, were both over a week past, and she surmised Elly and Red must be in New York by now. The huge Christmas tree they had erected in the great room still stood, but Rose and a butler were in the process of taking it down now, while David, who would be four in February, played near his mother with a new set of blocks.

Irene studied one letter curiously, noticing it had no postmark or return address. There was no way to tell when or from where it had been sent. She frowned as she opened it, taking out the note inside, feeling a sick shock when she read it.

"Ask your husband about Susan Stanner," it read.

There could be no mistaking its meaning, and a tight pain gripped at her insides. "My God," she groaned.

CHAPTER
THIRTY-SIX

The baby came too soon, and was born so quickly that Irene lay in shock for two days afterward, unaware of the remarks about her new daughter.

"Why, she looks just like a little Indian," Rose had joked.

Chad had stared at his new daughter in alarm. Her skin was a deep red, her eyes a black-brown, her hair a thick shock of black strands. She bore no resemblance to either him or Irene. He reasoned that Bea, Elly, and John were dark, but even they weren't this dark.

Bea summoned Kirk from Canon City, telling him only that Irene had had her baby. When he arrived and saw his new granddaughter, his eyes showed his dread and sorrow. "My God, Bea, this is just what I was afraid of. We should have *told* her," he groaned.

"Maybe the baby will change. She's only two days old, Kirk. It's hard to tell when they're this little."

"For God's sake, Bea, I've seen my share of Indian babies! She's not going to change! All we can do is hope people think she takes after her grandmother. But if her facial features . . ." He shook his head. "What did Irene say?"

"She hasn't really seen her yet, not in a really conscious state of mind. She's been pretty sick."

"What about Chad?" Kirk asked.

Bea sighed with weary frustration. "I can see by his eyes that he's upset and confused." She put a hand to the back of her neck. "Oh, Kirk, Irene has such light hair and those blue eyes. I never thought this could really happen, especially if she married a man who was also fair."

"Nature is nature. You can't predict something like this, Bea. You always think you have so much damn control over everything. Where is Chad now?"

"He's in with Irene. She's just come around. It was such a fast birth, and she lost a lot of blood; but the doctor says she'll be all right. She just needs plenty of rest."

Kirk looked down at his little granddaughter again. She was so terribly tiny, born earlier than expected. He gently touched the soft black hairs of her head, smiling sadly. Being Irene's daughter, she would surely be a beauty, a grand mixture of Indian and white that Irene was, only with the provocative beauty of the Cheyenne coloring. What kind of life lay ahead for her—and for Irene?

Chad came into the nursery then. "Irene wants her baby," he said, the words hinting that he considered it hers and not his. There was a look of anger in his eyes, but he said nothing. "I have to go out for a while."

Bea blinked back tears, turning to pick up the infant girl. She carried her granddaughter into Irene's room, and Irene reached up for her. Bea lay her in the crook of her arm, and Irene gasped, then smiled. "Mother, she's so dark. Rose told me she looked like a little Indian, but I didn't believe her."

She kissed the baby's soft cheek, stroked the dark hair, giving no indication she thought there was anything odd about her new daughter. Kirk and Bea shared a moment of temporary relief, neither of them realizing Irene was still too upset over the news about Susan Stanner and Chad to take a really good look at her new daughter and realize just how different she truly was. She had said nothing to Chad yet about Susan. The ugly, shocking letter had brought on her labor, and for now she could only thank God that her slightly premature daughter had lived. In her weakened condition, with a brand new baby at her breast, she could not bring herself to talk about something so horrid, but she had no doubt it was true. She hated to think that the father of this beautiful new baby was capable of treating women like so much garbage, capable of seducing innocent young girls and having no feelings of remorse or guilt when they hanged themselves over him.

Outside Chad turned up the collar of his overcoat and bent his head against a winter wind, climbing into a carriage. He could not get the picture of his new daughter out of his mind. Dark . . . so dark. His jealous, suspicious mind was at work again. There was no way that baby could belong to him. He was sure of it. She even had slightly slanted eyes, like an Indian's—or more to the point, like a Mexican! Ramon! Irene must have had an affair with him before they left for Europe! He remembered how they had talked and laughed at the party for statehood, remembered how Ramon had squeezed his hand threateningly.

He slammed his fist against the side of the carriage. He would give the baby time to get over the distortions of a newborn, two months, maybe three. He would not say a word to Irene . . . not yet. But if that baby didn't change, and if Irene didn't offer him the truth on her own, there was going to be hell to pay!

He had his proof now. He had an excuse to divorce Irene, and he could drag Ramon Vallejo through the mud at the same time! They weren't going to get away with this! He wished Elly were here to talk to. She could help him decide what to do. He ordered old Jim to take him to Milicent's house. He had to take his frustrations out on someone. Milicent would understand.

Irene! He had tried to make this marriage work, and now look what she had done! Had she done it purposely to spite him? He clenched his fists. Oh, how he wanted to hurt her!

The driver pulled up in front of Milicent's house, and Chad climbed out. "Go find something to do for a while," he told Jim. "And if you say a word about where you brought me tonight, you'll lose your job and that nice room you get to live in over the stables! You'll find yourself down along Hop Alley digging in the garbage." He walked up and pounded on the door, and a woman let him inside.

Jim turned away, tears in his eyes. There was poor Mrs. Jacobs lying up at the house with their brand new little baby, and her husband was seeing another woman. He had never liked Chad much. He saw right through that white man's fake smiles. He shook his head, driving the carriage away.

John took the train home just long enough to see the baby and spend one night at Chad and Irene's. Bea and Kirk were also invited, and a strained silence hung about the table. Irene knew it was because of little two-week-old Sharron Rose, a beautiful child with creamy-soft skin and big brown eyes. She looked so different. Irene knew John noticed, but he had said nothing. He had only smiled and congratulated her, perhaps too lost in his own unhappiness to care why little Sharron was so dark. He drank himself to sleep and left the next day with a hangover.

The way visitors looked at her baby made Irene even more protective of her little girl. She held the child almost constantly, except when she shared her with young David, who liked to help take care of her. Few words had been exchanged between Chad and Irene. Chad seemed to make himself very scarce, and he had taken to sleeping in another bedroom, telling Irene he didn't want to disturb her sleep while she was still healing.

Sharron was six weeks old when Elly and Red returned from New York. They came to see the baby, Elly putting on a show of the glowing, happy bride. Her mouth dropped open when she saw Sharron. "Irene! Why, she looks like a little Indian!"

Irene noticed a strange look in Red McKinley's eyes. He leaned closer to study the baby, then looked at Irene, putting on a near sorrowful smile. "She's real pretty baby, Irene."

"But she's so dark! And look at those eyes," Elly said rudely.

"Shut up, Elly," Red barked. "You're dark, aren't you? So's your mother."

"But not *that* dark." She leaned closer, toying with the baby's hand, her mind racing. Ramon? Could this baby be part Mexican? Something was wrong here. She remembered again about Red being so sure at first that Kirk and Bea had married in '46. Red was leaving something out, and she was going to find out what it was. She glanced at Irene, seeing the hurt look in her eyes. Good, she thought. My sister has some explaining to do. She wondered if Irene ever got her note about Susan Stanner. She had bribed the man at the letter office not to mark it in any way so that Irene wouldn't know where it came from.

"Where is Chad?" she asked slyly, a suggestion of sarcasm in her voice.

"He's working," Irene answered.

Elly couldn't wait to see him and see what he thought about this baby. She hoped maybe they could find a way to meet soon. She had missed him so.

"Well, I'll have to go to K-E and see him and Mother and everyone—tell them about our trip." She slid her arm into Red's. "New York is just fabulous, Irene, but then you got to see it when you went to Europe, didn't you? Of course, you didn't really stay and see the sights, go to the theaters and all." She looked up at Red. "We're going to Europe ourselves next year. Red promised me, didn't you, darling?"

Red watched her with a frown, angry over her remark about the baby. He had quickly learned he had married a whining, demanding woman with a voracious sexual appetite that had at first been exciting but had soon grown tiresome. What irritated him most was that he really did love her.

"Yes. I promised."

"But first we're building our own mansion. I don't want to live in Red's house. It's beautiful, but it isn't *ours*. As soon as Ramon is finished with Mother's new home, I want to hire him to build ours." She looked at the baby again. Could it be? Would a man like Ramon cheat on his wife? How delicious! She tugged at Red. "Let's go, darling. We have a hundred places to go today. Congratulations on your new baby, Irene."

Their eyes held. "Thank you," Irene said coolly. She looked at Red, seeing pain there. Elly was already making him suffer, she could tell. But there was something more, as though he wanted to tell her something but was afraid.

"She is truly a beautiful baby," he said then before turning to leave with Elly. *My God,* he thought as they left. *She's a little Indian. Irene can't ignore it forever.* He had warned Bea Kirkland about this years ago. Now the worst had happened, and there would be hell to pay for it. The sad part was that the ones most innocent—Irene and little Sharron—would suffer the most.

Irene finished nursing the baby, then laid her gently in her crib. At two months she was still very small. Irene buttoned her night gown and stood watching her little daughter sleep. She leaned down to touch her soft, dark hair, realizing now that she needed some answers. She loved this child as deeply as any mother loves her own, but Sharron was different, and Irene did not like the gossip she knew was beginning to filter through Denver. Her first thought was to protect Sharron. An awful dread was beginning to move through her veins, urged on by the memory of her parents' exchanged looks of fear at times, the conversation she had heard between them years ago about living a lie. What was that lie? Why had two so obviously mismatched people gotten married in the first place?

She heard the door close downstairs, and her heart tightened. Chad was home. He had been silent these past two months, had not even asked to hold Sharron. It was obvious he had taken again to womanizing on a much grander scale. It was four A.M. He had been gone all night. She had no idea he had been with Elly while Red was out of town. Elly had gladly planted new seeds of doubt in Chad's jealous mind, had again stirred his anger and suspicions.

Irene stepped out onto the balcony and closed the nursery door. She looked over the railing to see Chad coming through the great room to the stairs. He looked up at her, a scowl on his face. Their eyes held as he came up the stairs, and Irene moved along the balcony toward him.

"Chad, we need to talk," she told him quietly.

He gave her a strange grin, and she stepped back, seeing with horror the same look in his eyes she had seen the day he beat and raped her. "About what," he sneered. "Your affair with *Ramon*?"

Her eyes widened. "Ramon!"

"I was wondering when you'd finally admit it," he told her, coming closer. "You couldn't hide it this time, Irene! His seed is lying in that nursery!"

She stepped back again. "You're wrong, Chad. We need to both go and talk to my parents. It's—it's *me*, Chad! It's something about me."

"Like hell it is! If you wanted to get back at me for my affairs, Irene, you could have at least picked a *white* man!"

"Chad, you'll wake the servants and the children."

"I don't give a damn!" She stood frozen as he came closer and suddenly grabbed her wrists. "You slept with Ramon, didn't you?" He shook her. "*Didn't* you?"

"No! You're wrong, Chad, I swear to God!"

He back-handed her hard across the side of the face and she spun around, landing against a wall before sliding to the floor. "You lying slut! I was right that first time, wasn't I? I'll bet *David* isn't even mine! He's Hank Loring's kid, isn't he? I've been fathering two children, and neither one of them *belongs* to me!"

She put a shaking hand to the side of her face, which stung painfully. She slowly rose, grasping at her gown, turning cold, blue eyes to meet his gray ones. "Let's talk about who is *really* in the wrong," she told him, her voice shaking. "Let's talk about Susan Stanner!" She watched the blood nearly drain from his face, and she knew for certain it was true.

"Who told you about Susan?" he gasped.

"It doesn't matter," she sneered, stepping back from him again. "I should have figured it out for myself." She tasted blood from a cut on the inside of her mouth. "But I was too young and ignorant and trusting. We both know who has been the unfaithful one, Chad, for many years. We both know who went to sleep with a whore while his wife lay in pain and sorrow on her *wedding* night! We both know who sleeps with every whore and willing woman in Denver, and who is capable of raping his own wife!"

He stood glowering at her, his fists clenched. "I didn't have much *choice* but to sleep with other women! I sure wasn't going to get any satisfaction out of my frigid wife, now, was I? The only way I could get my own wife into my bed was to force her!" He stepped closer, his handsome face now ugly with rage. "I don't even want you *that* way any more! I told you before that what I do with other women means nothing! But I also told you how I felt about my *wife* being with other *men*!"

"I haven't been with anyone," she screamed. "Sharron is *ours*, Chad. She's *ours*. And I'm taking her to Mother's to find out the truth!"

She ran into the nursery to wrap Sharron in two of the baby's heaviest blankets. Rose came from her room behind the kitchen, clutching at her robe and wearing a night cap. She stared up at Chad. "Mr. Jacobs! What's wrong?"

Her voice startled Chad, who had started toward the nursery door. He hesitated as Irene turned with the baby in her arms. He panted with rage. "Go ahead," he sneered. "Try to find an excuse for Ramon! I want you out of this house anyway—you and *both* your bastard kids!"

Rose hurried up the stairs, afraid for Irene. Chad glared at Irene a moment longer, his eyes dropping to little Sharron in a look of disgust. He turned and went to his room, slamming the door shut.

"Irene, what is wrong?" Rose asked.

"Get my coat, Rose, and get David up. We've got to get the children out of here."

"Don't you want to dress first?"

"There's no time. I can't trust Chad when he's in this mood. I'm going to my parents'."

"Irene, it's four o'clock in the morning!"

"I don't care. Something is wrong, Rose . . . with me. I have to find out what it is, and I have a feeling only my parents can help. I have to find out why Sharron is so dark. Chad thinks. . . ." She couldn't bring herself to say it. She would not allow Chad to drag Ramon into this when he was perfectly innocent. She had to find out the truth and find out quickly before an ugly rumor got started that could ruin Ramon's own marriage.

She hurried to David's room, where the boy was already sitting up and sniffling, confused by the shouting outside his door. Rose quickly pulled on his slippers and overcoat. David rubbed at sleepy eyes as the women took both children and hurried downstairs, where the butler stood in dismay, awakened by all the shouting. Irene handed the baby to Rose while she pulled on a coat over her nightgown and pulled on a pair of fur-lined boots.

"Is there anything I can do, ma'am?" the butler asked, feeling sorry for Irene, sorry for the children.

"No, Thurmond." Irene buttoned her coat quickly, glancing up the stairs, her heart pounding. "Yes, maybe there is. I want Rose to pack me some clothes and some things for the children. I'm going to my parents', and I may stay there a few days. When Rose has the things ready, bring them to my Mother's house."

He frowned at the ugly bruise forming at the side of her face. "Yes, ma'am."

She took the baby from Rose. "And don't listen to anything Chad says. He's half crazy when he's like this. He's beat me before." They both looked shocked. "He's making accusations that aren't true. He'll calm down after a while. Right now I have to get the children out of here." She took a still-crying David's hand, holding Sharron in her other arm, and left.

"God be with you," Rose called after her.

Irene hurried through the cold darkness toward the Kirkland mansion, glad Kirk was home and not up in the mountains. She shivered from the cold air and near shock over her confrontation with Chad. She wanted to cry, felt the hysteria building; but she forced herself to stay calm for the sake of the children. No matter what happened, she had to protect them above all else.

In minutes they were at the mansion. She pounded on the door until finally the butler came. He quickly let her inside, and Kirk was coming down the carpeted stairs, tying a satin robe. He stopped short when he saw Irene.

"My God, what happened?" he asked, hurrying toward her. He saw her bruised face then, and his eyes widened. "What has Chad done to you?" he asked, his anger rising.

She clung to the baby. "That isn't important right now, Father. What *is* important is that he thinks I've slept with Ramon and that Sharron is Ramon's daughter. I won't have a good man's name destroyed, Father, especially when what Chad thinks isn't true." She saw her mother come to the top of the stairs. "I came to learn the truth." She looked back at Kirk. "From both of you! My daughter has either Indian or Mexican blood, and I want to know how she got it!"

Kirk's eyes filled with great sorrow. He turned away, ordering the butler to take David upstairs and put him to bed in the room they now kept for the children. The man took the sleepy, confused boy with him, and Irene clung to Sharron. "I'll keep the baby with me."

Bea came down the stairs, her eyes already tearing as she approached them. Kirk rubbed at his eyes, putting a hand on Irene's shoulder. "Come into the parlor, Irene. I'll open the register and warm it up more."

Bea came closer, touching his arm. "Kirk?"

"We've got no choice now, Bea."

The woman moved her eyes to Irene. "Who . . . hit you?"

"Who do you think, Mother?" Irene answered coldly. "It's about time you understood the kind of man Chad really is. He's beat me before. He even raped me one night when he suspected that I was sleeping with other men." She watched her mother stiffen in shock. "It's Chad who has been unfaithful, Mother, many times. The night I lost that first baby I had caught him on the floor of his office with Milicent Delaney."

The woman gasped. "Irene—"

"It's *true*, Mother! Why do you think he had to let Milicent go? And I only recently learned that Chad Jacobs is the reason Susan Stanner killed herself. I'm through covering for him, Mother, through pretending this marriage can work. Tonight he called my children bastards. I won't live in the same house with a man who doesn't love his children. And I won't have him spreading it all over town that Sharron is Ramon's child! Ramon and I have never once done anything wrong, but I did love him, Mother. I still do, if you want to know the truth. And now I want the truth out of you and Father. Sharron is Chad's daughter. Why is she so dark?"

Bea's eyes teared more, and she took a handkerchief from the pocket of her robe and walked on shaking, tired legs beside Kirk as he led Irene into the parlor. Irene sat down in a plush velvet chair next to a heater, still clinging to Sharron. Bea turned away, dabbing at her eyes, while Kirk closed the door and turned up the heat.

He sighed deeply and turned to Irene. "I'll say it straight out, Irene," he began, his voice calm and resolute. He swallowed before he managed the words. "You're half Indian—Cheyenne."

Bea let out an odd groan, and Irene felt as though the life was slowly flowing out of her. She held Sharron closer. "Cheyenne!"

Kirk closed his eyes, rubbing at his forehead. "Your mother and I—that is, Bea and I—married because your Cheyenne mother had given you over to me and you needed a mother."

"I've always loved you like my own, Irene," Bea put in, her voice beginning to break. "I wanted the best for you. We thought it best you didn't know. I was so proud to call you my daughter. You were so beautiful. I wanted everyone to think you were mine . . . and I wanted *you* to think it."

Irene blinked back tears of shock, looking at Sharron, touching her black hair. "Cheyenne," she repeated. "Dear God."

"There's more, Irene," Kirk told her, deciding to get it said and over with. "The reason Yellow Eagle didn't harm you that day he attacked you is because—because he's your twin brother."

Irene stared at him in wide-eyed horror. "My *brother*!" She shivered visibly. "My God, Father, how could you not tell me such a thing! Yellow Eagle! He killed Hank! My own brother killed poor Hank!"

"Calm down, Irene—"

"Don't tell me to calm down," she nearly shouted at Bea. "I've just learned I'm half Indian! My own brother has raided and murdered and . . . he killed Hank!" She rose from the chair, clinging to Sharron, trembling with the rage of betrayal. "I'm a half-breed! Of all the things Chad has done to me, none of them equal the betrayal the two of you have committed against me! You should have told me! You should have told me!"

"My God, Irene, you don't know how hard it was for us," Kirk answered, "how we wrestled with this. We love you so much."

"Get out," she gasped, turning her back to them. "Just get out and leave me alone for a while." The stark reality of the news churned inside her, tearing at her stomach. Half Indian! In one brief moment, with just a few words, her life had changed forever.

Bea fled the room sobbing. Kirk hesitated. "We'll leave you alone for a while, but we need to talk more about this, Irene. And you need to remember how much we love you. We were just protecting you from cruel prejudice."

Seconds later she heard the door close. The reality of what she had been told gripped her like a vise. Half Indian! Now she understood the looks of fear in her parents' eyes, her father's comment about living a lie. She understood so many things—her love of the mountains and riding free on the plains, her love of horses, her slightly olive complexion, the high cheekbones. And Yellow Eagle! No wonder there was something about his eyes that had held her spellbound for that brief moment. No wonder he had let her go! But that meant he had known all along. He had been told, but she had not. He could legally claim part of the Kirkland fortune, but he had not done so. Did he love his Indian ways so much and hate the white man so much that he would turn down a chance at a fortune? Would she feel just as he did if she had been raised with him? There . . . but for the grace of God . . .

She shivered, and sank back into the chair. She had an Indian mother, but she remembered Yellow Eagle saying his mother, wife, and son had been killed at Sand Creek. Her own mother and a nephew at Sand Creek! Chad had been there. It all seemed so unreal, so impossible, yet it all made so much sense now. She realized Red must know. That was why he had looked at the baby so strangely. Maybe that was even why there had been the terrible tension between Red and Bea. Bea must have been afraid Red would tell the truth!

Her mind swam with answers to so many questions, with the horrible reality of her blood. Bea Kirkland was not her mother at all, not physically! No wonder she looked so different from Bea and Elly and John.

She leaned back in her chair, looking down at Sharron, sleeping peacefully, innocent of all the lies. Tears ran down Irene's cheeks, dripping onto the baby's blanket. She touched Sharron's tiny hand. "I'll not let you suffer for this," she sobbed. "Not you or David. We'll go away. We'll leave Denver and go someplace where we can be free, where you won't have to suffer insults and ridicule and stares." She leaned down and kissed the baby's velvety cheek. "We'll go away," she repeated. "I won't let them hurt you."

The train whistle blew, sounding the lonely agony in Irene's heart. She rode the Denver and Rio Grande south for Colorado Springs and the ranch. She knew that by now, back in Denver, the newspapers would be screaming with headlines about the half-breed daughter of David and Bea Kirkland. Chad had quickly filed for divorce on the grounds he had never been made aware of his wife's Indian blood. She had gotten out just in time, before she could be hounded by reporters and public gawkers. She refused to submit David and Sharron to the gossip and stares. If Chad wanted his divorce, he could have it. He had been looking for a good reason for a long time. Now he had it. He could send the papers to her to be signed when they were ready. She was not going to contest the divorce and let the newspapers drag her name and the children's names through the dirt.

In one respect she was shocked and saddened by what she had learned; yet in another way she felt suddenly and wonderfully free. There were no more secrets, and an anxious, unexplainable confusion she had always felt inside was suddenly gone.

Sharron lay sleeping in her arms, and David sat watching the passing scenery out the window. He turned to her then. "Is Daddy going to come and be with us?" he asked.

The question tore at her heart. Perhaps one day she would tell him who his daddy really was. "I don't think so, David. Daddy has a lot of things to do. You'll like the ranch. Wouldn't you like to learn to ride a horse?"

His face lit up. "Can I have one of my own?"

"Of course you can."

The train whistle blew again, and she looked out at wide grassland that stretched for miles, picturing golden Palominos galloping across the plains, one of them carrying a big, rugged cowboy. She looked away. Hank was gone, killed by her own brother. She had to face the reality of it, had to try to pick up the pieces of her life. Most of all, she had to protect the children. The ranch would be good for them, a life away from the public eye, away from the hustle of being involved with K-E. Rose and Jenny were coming down to join her. They would bring a tutor to continue David's lessons.

But first Irene wanted some time alone—time to put aside all that had happened and just enjoy the ranch and the children. She looked forward to seeing Tim Barnes again and some of the other men. It had been almost five years since she left. Old Flor was still alive and had been taking care of the house. She supposed little had changed . . . except that Hank was gone.

The whistle blew again, penetrating her heart, piercing the air. She saw no buffalo. They were fast being destroyed, as this once-wild land was fast being settled. Indians were almost unheard-of anywhere near the mountain towns now. In one sense she truly could understand how it must be for them—driven from this beautiful country, the buffalo that kept them alive being butchered for their hides and bones. Progress, Bea would call it.

She rested her head on the back of the seat as David excitedly watched some antelope run. She wondered what the headlines would read today . . . and what Ramon would think of her now.

PART

FIVE

They sin who tell us love can die;
With life all other passions fly,
　　All others are but vanity . . .
　　Love is indestructible,
　　Its holy flame forever burneth;
From heaven it came, to heaven
　　returneth . . .
It soweth here with toil and care,
But the harvest-time of love is there.

—ROBERT SOUTHEY
"The Curse of Kehama"

CHAPTER
THIRTY-SEVEN

June 1877

Irene helped Jenny trim the roses in the courtyard, while Rose played with six-year-old David and two-and-a-half-year-old Sharron. Irene stood up to watch the children, little Sharron's long black hair swinging with her movements, her bright, dark eyes dancing with joy as she tried to chase David. She was a beautiful child, her soft skin so dark, her smile so bright, dimples showing; the kind of child one could hardly look at without wanting to hug.

Chad had never come to see his daughter. A few months after she fled Denver she had received divorce papers to sign, which she had not hesitated to do. According to John, and what she read in the Denver papers that she received weekly from Colorado Springs, Chad Jacobs had left Denver for "parts unknown." It seemed strangely unfair that Chad could have wreaked such havoc with her life and now just be gone, as though he had never existed.

It was John who had told her the ugly truth about Chad and Elly. The news had been so shocking and abhorrent that she had never been able to bring herself to tell even her parents. It was obvious Chad had never even really cared for Elly, or he would have stayed in Denver. She realized now that Elly's hold on him was probably the threat of losing his position with K-E if his affair with Elly were exposed. But that had happened after all. After learning the true extent of his cruelty to Irene, Bea had fired Chad from K-E.

Chad apparently could not handle the disgrace, or perhaps he simply had grown tired of the women in Denver and had moved on to destroy more poor female souls elsewhere. At least he had realized little profit from his cruelty to her. Irene's interest in K-E was still under Bea and Kirk's control, which meant Chad could claim none of it. He had, however, sued to keep the house he had built for Irene, and all their savings. Irene made no objection, wanting only for the whole horrible experience to end.

Now the pretty house had been sold, and no one knew where Chad had gone. If Elly had really loved him, Irene still could not bring herself to feel sorry for her sister for losing him. All her life she had sacrificed her own true love for what she thought was the proper way to behave, only to discover Elly had thrown it all in her face.

She couldn't help feeling sorry for Red, wondering how often Elly had cheated on the poor man; and she realized now what had been going on between Elly and Chad that first year she stayed here at the ranch. To think of what Chad had done to her, while at the same time sleeping with her sister, had upset her for months, and she was glad Chad was gone now, glad she would never have to look into those handsome, gray, lying eyes again. It had not been easy trying to explain to David why his father had "gone away." The boy seemed to be adjusting well, and she tried to give him plenty of love to make up for any feelings of desertion he might be experiencing.

The past two years had been a time of great emotional upheaval for Irene. A few reporters had even traced her to the ranch to interview the "half-breed daughter" of David Kirkland, wanting the ugly details of her divorce, hounding her until she ordered some of the ranch hands to keep them away even if they had to use their guns to do it.

Irene still was not over what she considered the ultimate betrayal—her parents' decision to keep the truth from her. She had asked them to stay away from the B&K, sent regular reports to K-E about the status of the ranch, but refused to go to Denver herself. With considerable help from Tim Barnes, she managed the ranch now, and she was glad she had brought the children here and kept them away from the turmoil they would have known in Denver. They were happy, unaware of the ugly truths about their father, still not fully understanding about their Indian blood.

"Mommy! Mommy," Sharron shouted, running on chubby legs

toward her then, while David pretended not to be able to catch her. She grabbed Irene's skirts and Irene lifted her, laughing. "You got away," she praised the girl, hugging her.

Sharron hugged her back, kissing her cheek. "I run fast," she squealed, screaming and giggling then when David grabbed her foot. Irene held her up so high David couldn't reach her even when he jumped.

"I think someone is knocking at the door," Jenny shouted to Irene then.

"I'll get it," Irene answered. "It's probably Dorothy. Come with me, Rose. It's time for Sharron's nap." She looked down at David. "And you have lessons, young man. Miss Campbell will be here any minute," she said. Dorothy Campbell was the tutor she had hired from Denver. She had built a small frame house for the woman so she could live at the ranch, and Dorothy had also begun tutoring the children of some of the ranch hands. Plans were already in the making to build a school on the B&K that all the children could attend, including the children of surrounding ranchers and farmers. Irene wanted David and Sharron to be around other children their age, children from families of common, hard-working people who might not be rich, but who were good people who had been kind to her since her arrival at the ranch. She did not want her children to be isolated from the rest of society the way she and John and Elly had been.

"I want a hug, too," David told her as she turned to answer the door. She bent down and hugged him, remembering how starved she and her siblings had been for signs of affection from their mother. She wondered how different Elly might have been if Bea had been more attentive to her. "I love you," she told David, kissing his cheek. "You pay attention to Miss Campbell now and be a good boy."

Rose took Sharron from her. "Let's go to the kitchen and get out your papers," she told David. He followed her into the house, going to the kitchen while Irene headed for the door. She was still smiling at the thought of little Sharron thinking she had out-run David when she swung open the door.

Her smile quickly faded in surprise, then returned, as her startled heart rushed with a thousand emotions. "Ramon!"

"Hello, Irene." He stood in the doorway looking more handsome than ever. He held a tiny little boy, who looked nearly the same age as Sharron. The child was as dark and beautiful as his father. "May we come in?" Ramon asked.

Irene realized she had been literally staring at him, and she gasped, stepping aside. "Of course! Ramon, I never expected . . . I mean, I'm so surprised. It's wonderful to see you again."

He moved inside and she closed the door. She reached out then and touched the little boy's hand. She already knew Ramon had a son, had read in the *News* about the wife of Ramon Vallejo dying in childbirth. She had realized the agony losing a second wife must have been for Ramon, but she had not contacted him, unsure how he felt about her now, realizing he needed time to grieve. "What is his name?" she asked.

"This is Alejandro Ramon Vallejo. A *gringo* would shorten that to Alex." The boy stuck a thumb in his mouth. "He is just two years old, and right now he is tired from our long trip on the train. He fell asleep in the buggy I rented to come out here."

She smiled, almost wanting to cry at seeing him again. "Rose is putting my Sharron down for a nap. There is an extra bed in her room if you think he would go to sleep there."

Their eyes met, and she was sure she saw the same look of love and adoration she had always seen in his eyes. "That would be fine."

There was a moment of commotion then as Miss Campbell arrived and introductions were made. Irene showed the woman to the kitchen, then took Sharron from Rose and brought her back with her to Ramon. He smiled, and his eyes lit up when he saw her. "So, this is the little girl who caused such a stir in Denver," he said, looking her over. "Irene, she is a most beautiful child."

Irene kissed her cheek. "Thank you. I brought her here to keep her away from the cruel gossip and stares I knew she'd get in Denver. Follow me and I'll take you to Sharron's room." She turned and walked through the sprawling central room of the house, leading him to a hall and into a bedroom decorated in pink. Ramon studied her beautiful form as she walked, thinking how little she had changed, sorry for the emotional horror she had suffered over the last two years. He laid his son on a small bed, touching his hair and soothing him to sleep, while Irene closed the shutters to darken the room. She put Sharron down for her nap, and the girl curled up with her favorite stuffed animal. Irene turned then, facing Ramon in the darkened room.

"I did not know if I should come," he said softly. "You have been through so much—the gossip, the ugly divorce." He stepped closer. "When I first heard, Irene, I wanted to come to you—to help you, comfort you, to tell you you must not let the knowledge of your Indian blood make you ashamed, for it is *not* something to be ashamed of. When the news first hit the papers, you were already on your way here, and my Anna was finally pregnant, after so many years of trying. I did not want to do anything that might upset her, so I stayed in Denver."

She smiled softly. "I understand. I'm so sorry, Ramon, about her death. It must have been so terrible for you, after losing Elena and your first son."

He sighed deeply, his eyes suddenly misting. "She had a choice. The doctor said he could kill the baby and take it from her, and she would live. She had been trying so long to give me a child. She would not let the baby die." He turned away. "It was a terrible way for her to die. Afterward, it just . . . it took me a long time to get over it. For a while I could not think of you, or my business, or even my son. I almost hated him at first, but I realize now he is my gift from Anna, and he is innocent of all of it." He leaned over and patted the boy's bottom. "He is my son, and I love him. I hired a woman to nurse him the first several weeks, then hired a nanny to feed him by bottle and care for him. I have slowly learned to accept Anna's death, learned I must keep going, for Alex's sake."

He breathed deeply as he straightened and met her eyes again. His gaze moved over her appreciatively, and in the darkened room a hundred notions of passion suddenly rushed through Irene's blood. It was as though both of them suddenly realized that for the first time since that first kiss fifteen years ago, they were actually free to act on their emotions. For Irene it was an almost startling realization. Was that why he was here? What were his feelings now, after being through so much? She wasn't even sure of her own feelings anymore, except that there was no mistaking how hard her heart was pounding at this moment, no mistaking the warmth that rushed through her blood.

"I'm glad you came, Ramon," she told him. "It's been a long time since I've seen anyone from Denver." She dropped her eyes. "I haven't even seen my parents. I just . . . haven't been able to bring myself to go back there, and I have asked them not to come here."

He shook his head. "Irene, part of the reason I am here is because I have been afraid you are not letting yourself face the truth. You cannot hide down here forever. And you should not keep blaming your mother and father. They must have thought they were doing the right thing."

She met his eyes again. "*You're* sticking up for *my* mother?"

He smiled softly. "She talked to me about you once. She knew how I felt about you, and she was not very kind. I have not much use for Bea Kirkland, but I will say that in spite of her behavior, her love for you was very real, Irene. Whatever she has done, I believe she thought she was protecting you. And anyone could tell how much your father has always adored you. It is not good for the soul to turn your back on your parents, Irene. Think how it would break your heart if one of your children did the same to you."

She sighed deeply and turned, going to the door. "Did one of them send you here, thinking you might be the only one who could reason with me?"

He grinned, following her out of the room. "No. I have not even seen them. It is just that you have been on my mind for many months now, and Anna's death made me think more deeply about a lot of things." He looked down at her, touching her arm hesitantly. "Mostly it made me think about how much mothers are willing to sacrifice for their children. Anna gave her life for Alex. Your mother risked losing your love in order to do what she thought was right for you."

Again she felt the old passions returning. How quickly he could stir her most basic womanly needs. "I know what you're trying to say, Ramon. Part of the reason I came here was to protect the children, but also to give myself time to think, to reckon with the truth about myself. I haven't abandoned my parents. I just need time away from all things familiar."

He nodded. "I have had such needs." He reluctantly let go of her, and she wondered how a man could get so much more handsome as he got older. She was thirty-one now, so Ramon must be at least thirty-five, she reasoned. There was still no hint of gray in his thick, dark hair. A few added pounds had landed in all the right places, making him look even more robust and virile. He wore dark denim pants and an expensive black silk suit jacket over an open-neck shirt that revealed some of his firm chest. A silver and turquoise necklace graced his neck, accenting the dark skin.

She smiled softly. "Come out to the courtyard with me, Ramon. I'll have Jenny get us some lemonade, or would you prefer wine or tea or something else?"

"Lemonade is fine. It is a hot day."

Irene turned, wondering if the day only seemed hotter because of Ramon's presence. Ramon was wondering the same, thinking how beautiful she looked in the simple white shirt and the riding skirt she wore. Her still full, firm breasts filled out the shirt nicely, and her slender hips swayed in perfect proportion to the rest of her supple body as she led him to the courtyard. As they walked through the big, sprawling living room, he noticed his carved horse on her fireplace mantel. So, she had brought it from Denver. Yes, she still cared. "I see you chose a Spanish-style home," he told her. "It is very beautiful, Irene."

"Thank you." They walked into the sunshine. "Your people had the right idea, Ramon, building stucco houses. They're much cooler."

Irene asked Jenny to get the drinks, and she offered Ramon one of the white, wrought-iron patio chairs that decorated the courtyard. She bent down and picked a rose, then took another chair across from him, holding the rose in her hand. "So, tell me, Ramon, how are things in Denver, now that Colorado is finally a state?"

He leaned forward and removed his jacket, rolling up his sleeves as he talked. "There was a grand celebration in Denver. The capitol building is nearly completed. It is quite beautiful, with a golden dome."

She smiled. Of course it would be golden. The term was being applied to the whole new state of Colorado.

"Now there is a new man in town as wealthy as the Kirklands, it seems. He has built an opera house, and has brought in builders from the East to design and build a grand hotel that will have real elevators and a ballroom that hangs on cables so that the floor will bounce properly for the dancers."

"Ramon! Can that be done?"

He shrugged. "Anything can be done if a man sets his mind to it. There is a lot of big money in Denver now besides Kirkland money, Irene. More mansions are going up on Kirkland Hills. I am kept so busy that I do not mind the competition from other builders who have come in. Lawrence Phipps has moved into town. He has become wealthy producing steel. He is having a pipe organ built into his house. That big real estate man—Kitteredge—has hired me to build a house for him, with a dining room big enough for a table that will seat a hundred people at once."

She shook her head. "I can't believe it. What about Mother's new house?"

He grinned. "Oh, it gives stiff competition to the others. It is the biggest showpiece in Denver—four stories, a ballroom on the third floor that is much bigger than the one in the original house, servants' quarters on the fourth floor instead of off the kitchen, several bathing rooms, running water, gold door knobs. She even had me order a twenty-five-thousand-dollar stained glass window from Tiffany's in London. And she is first on the list to have one of those new contraptions installed; they're called telephones. Can you believe a device has been invented so that one person can actually speak to another person across town?"

She frowned, "You mean, you can hear each other's *voices*?"

"*Sí*. It is most amazing. I have not seen one yet, but I have read much about them, and they are already being used in the East. I am sure it will not be long before we will have them in Denver, and they say that someday people will be able to talk to each other clear across the continent, from New York to San Francisco. You can imagine what that would do for business dealings. I am sure your mother is thinking the same thing."

Irene sniffed at the rose, leaning back in her chair and thinking about her mother. Her heart ached with confusion. She still loved her parents, but she had not quite been able to forgive them. "Yes, I can just imagine. I've learned to accept Mother's near passion for K-E with a grain of humor."

"Sometimes that is the best way to face things that are painful," he told her.

There was so much to say, but they were so afraid to say it. "Do you see much of Red? I worry about him. I know what my sister is like."

Ramon shook his head. "Things are not so good for Red. I am afraid your sister is gaining quite a reputation in Denver, and it is not a good one. It is rumored . . ." He hesitated.

"You can tell me, Ramon. I've learned Elly and Chad were having an affair behind my back for years."

His eyes widened in shock. "My God, Irene! She is your *sister*!"

"She has always hated me because I've always had what she wanted. Elly is a selfish, confused young woman, Ramon. I should hate her, but I can only feel sorry for her."

Ramon shook his head. "The rumors are that Elly sleeps with Red's clients to help make deals. I am afraid she is not just breaking Red's heart, but she is bleeding him dry financially. Now they are building another house. It is as though she is trying to keep up with her mother, to show she can build her own fortune now that she gets nothing from K-E. Red is a rich man, but he does not have the kind of money the big moguls like your parents and the others have."

"Poor Red. I'm so sorry."

He leaned forward, his elbows on his knees. "It must have been a horrible thing for you to learn about your sister and Chad."

The sick feeling moved into her gut again at recalling the day John told her. "It was," she answered. "It hurt terribly to think my own sister would do such a thing. As far as Chad was concerned, I wasn't surprised." She held his eyes. "I had already learned Chad was the one who had been carrying on with Susan Stanner before she hanged herself, Ramon."

He sighed deeply. "My God," he said softly.

"You know about Chad and Milicent Delaney, that night I lost the baby. But Chad's affairs aren't the worst of it. That first time we came down here to live for a year, he—he showed me his jealous side. I know now that Elly probably planted the ideas in his head. He came home one day accusing me of carrying on with Hank Loring. He beat me until I was barely conscious, and he—" she reddened slightly, "he proceeded to show me to whom I belonged. He was so cruel in ways no one else knew about."

He clenched his fists, rising from the chair to pace. She could sense his anger. "If I had known—"

"I knew exactly what you would do. That's why I never told you. Now it doesn't matter anymore. I'm rid of the man. It tears at my heart to be a divorced woman, but I couldn't stay with him—not that he wanted me anyway once he found out I had Indian blood. For a few years after David was born, things were fairly decent between us—until Sharron was born. As soon as he saw her—" She stopped, waiting for Jenny, who brought the lemonade and quickly left again.

"Chad accused me of having an affair with you," Irene continued, "because little Sharron was so dark. I was not about to let him drag your name into the gossip columns when you were perfectly innocent, so I went to my parents and demanded to know the truth. You know the rest."

He turned, his hands on his hips, his dark eyes holding her own. "It could have been true, you know, about you and me—not then, because of Anna—but many other times over the years."

She smiled nervously, her eyes suddenly tearing. "It's all water over the dam now, Ramon. So much has happened to both of us."

He came closer, kneeling in front of her. "*Sí*. We have both suffered through many trials and heartaches, Irene; but we know where our strength came from, what kept us going."

Did he still love her? Had he come here then to try to recapture what they once had shared so briefly when she was only sixteen? Had there been too much hurt in between ever to find that love again? "Ramon, there is something you should know." A tear slipped down her cheek. He reached up and brushed it away, and his touch made her shiver.

"And what is that?"

She swallowed. How could a woman feel as though she had betrayed a man who had never been her husband, had never had any kind of claim on her? She felt worse about her affair with Hank for Ramon's sake than her own husband's.

"I told you Chad beat me because . . . he thought I was having an affair with Hank Loring."

He smiled gently, taking her hand. "And your son was fathered by Hank, not by Chad Jacobs," he said, making it a statement rather than a question.

Her eyebrows arched in amazement. "You . . . knew?"

"I suspected. You forget that I knew the kind of man Chad was, knew how a woman with so much to give would feel starved by a man like that. I also knew Hank, the kind of man he was. I knew the terrible loneliness of being a widower, and how easy you are to love. When you came back to Denver after Hank's death, and I saw the look on your face when you talked about it, I needed no further explanation." He squeezed her hand. "If nothing else, we have always been the best of friends, Irene. Did you really think I would not understand what you went through during that time? I was not there for you, but Hank was, and I am glad that he was. If you had ended up marrying him, I would have been happy for you, because all that really mattered to me was that *you* should be happy, and away from that bastard Chad Jacobs."

"I felt like I had somehow betrayed you," she murmured, trying to hold back tears.

"I had no claim on you."

"Yes, you did," she answered quietly. "You . . . owned my heart, Ramon. You always have."

Everything seemed suddenly quiet, as though they were in a small room together, rather than being outside. There was only the faint buzzing of a bee that landed on a nearby rosebush.

"Do I still?" he asked hesitantly.

Why was she crumbling so quickly? He had come here for a simple visit. Too many years had passed, hadn't they? This should be a casual conversation for now. She should not have let it get away from her like this. She was surely making a fool of herself in front of him. Still, the look in his dark eyes told her he held the same fears about himself, that he had never meant for this to happen. Surely he still loved her to be talking this way. And what did she have to lose now? Her heart had been shattered a hundred times over. She had lived a life of lies and pretending, and she was not going to keep it up.

"Yes," she answered.

His own eyes suddenly teared. "And *you* have always owned *my* heart."

"This isn't right, Ramon."

He reached up and touched her hair, which she wore long and loose. "After all these years and all we have been through to get to each other, you say it isn't right? To continue to deny what we have always felt, *mi querida, that* would be wrong. I am not saying we have to do anything more than admit how we still feel. I am only saying we no longer have to deny it. If what we have always felt for each other should now finally grow, we are free to let it. We both deserve some happiness, Irene."

"I wasn't sure . . . I mean . . . I'm older now."

"And I am not? You are as beautiful to me today as when I first held you."

She shook her head. "This is all too soon. We shouldn't be talking this way."

"You are right. We shouldn't be talking at all. We should be holding each other."

She searched his eyes and saw the old sparkle of love there. "I do need to be held," she whispered.

He grinned. "I will tell you a secret, *mi querida*. I also need to be held."

She studied the handsome face, the need in his eyes. He was still the same Ramon she had always known and loved. She reached around his neck, and his arms came around her as he stood up, pulling her up with him. She burst into tears of vented love and need and hurt, deciding it felt good to let someone else be strong for her, to let herself openly feel her real emotions, to be honest about them and not to have to pretend anymore.

"Don't let go, Ramon," she wept. "Don't ever let go. I'm so tired of pretending." Where had she heard those words before? She had said them to Hank. Now she realized Hank had just been a gift from God, to be there for her when Ramon could not. Perhaps all along God had meant for them to be together, and they had been too young and too afraid to act on what should have been.

"I will never let go," he said softly, kissing her hair. "In my mind and in my heart I have held you this way so many times, *mi vida*. It feels so good to be able to do it freely."

"It feels so wonderful, Ramon," she sobbed. "I love you so.

I've always, always loved you. For fifteen years, I've lived a life of lies. . . . I've been so miserable. And now . . . I wasn't sure what you . . . would think of me because of my Indian blood."

"Hush, *mi querida*." He put a strong hand to the back of her head, holding it tightly but gently against his shoulder, wrapping his fingers in her golden hair. "Why would your Indian blood matter to me? I understand prejudice firsthand, Irene."

"I'm so sorry . . . so sorry for how my mother treated you—"

"That is all behind us now. Now we have each other, and nothing can come between us—nothing, Irene."

She raised her face to look into his eyes, but he was a blur through her tears. She only knew that his face was close, and that in the next moment his mouth was covering hers in the kiss they had both needed to enjoy for so many years. He groaned as he met her mouth almost savagely; his tongue searching deep, hinting at a much more pleasurable way in which he would like to invade her.

It felt so right, tasted so good. He released the kiss, but instantly smothered her with more, many lighter but searching kisses, as though savoring a delicious fruit. A thousand pent-up needs were unleashed in her soul, and she knew in that one embrace that even Hank had not brought out the total woman in her. That was for Ramon to do.

He shuddered, gently and reluctantly leaving her mouth but keeping her close. "We cannot do this yet," he told her, his voice gruff with desire. He tangled his hand in her hair and she could feel him trembling. "Much as I would like to, Irene, we have waited so long. I want it to be a splendid event, something celebrated, something done when the time is just right. I love you so much, Irene. And if you still want me after all these years, I want you to be my wife."

She touched his chest. "That's all I've ever wanted since I was sixteen years old. Are we crazy to be talking this way so suddenly?"

"Suddenly? You just said yourself you have loved me since you were sixteen." He grasped her arms and looked down at her. "For fifteen years we have denied ourselves so that we would do what we thought was proper. We have both suffered terrible heartache and loss on this long road to finding each other again. There is nothing sudden about this, Irene, maybe to others, but not to us."

She smiled through tears, her heart feeling as though it might explode with love and happiness. "Then, yes, I want to be your wife. I'll become a Catholic if it's necessary. I'll do whatever I have to do."

He pulled her close again, kissing the top of her head. "It is true I would want to be married in the Catholic church. But there is something more that must be done first, Irene, something you have to settle within yourself."

She raised her eyes to meet his. "I don't understand."

He kissed her forehead. "I want so much to take you off right now and make love to you, to make you my wife and have it done. But I said earlier I think you are hiding down here, Irene. You said you were tired of pretending, but you continue to pretend when it comes to the truth about your heritage." He felt her stiffen in his arms, and he refused to let go of her. "You must face the truth, Irene, and not just within yourself. Before we marry I want you to be a whole person, and that means accepting your Indian blood and being proud of it. It also means facing your brother."

She frowned. "What!"

"He is your *brother*, Irene."

"He was probably at the Little Big Horn. He probably took part in that terrible massacre of Custer and his men last year!"

"Perhaps he was. But most of them have been hunted down and are now on reservations in the Dakotas. I think you should try to find Yellow Eagle."

She shook her head, pulling away from him. "I can't—"

"Yes, you can. I want you to be a whole person, Irene, to be truly free. You will not be until you find him and recognize him as your brother. He is a closer brother to you even than John, because he is a full-blood brother."

She thought of the day of the attack, how Yellow Eagle had looked at her. "He killed Hank."

"He did not know who you were until it was too late. And you have never let yourself understand the reasons for some of the things they have done, Irene. You know only the bad things about Indians. You must learn to understand the good things, the heart of the Indian. Some of the things they have done have not been because they are savages, but because they thought they were protecting their own, their land, their children, their sources of survival. A man is capable of many things when he thinks he is doing them to protect his loved ones. I have seen your father, Irene, and I know that his heart is broken over all of this. Not only is it killing him to have you turn your back on him, but he also longs to meet and know his Indian son. I think you should go to

Denver and talk to him, ask him to take you to the Dakotas to find Yellow Eagle. Your soul will never be at peace until you do. It is the same for your father."

Yellow Eagle! He was her brother. She had tried to ignore that fact, but she knew Ramon was right to say she was hiding here at the ranch not just for the children's sake, but to run away from the truth about herself. "I couldn't leave the children—"

"They have all the care they need. Rose and Jenny love them, I am sure. And maybe it would be good for your mother to see her grandchildren, have them with her for a while. I am told she is not well, Irene. Would you want her to die with things the way they are, or to have Yellow Eagle die without your ever seeing him?"

She met his eyes in alarm. "Mother is ill?"

"You know I hold no fond feelings for her, but no one deserves to die with hard feelings still in the heart of their loved ones. I got the news through Red, who was told by business associates that your mother has not been coming to work the way she used to, that sometimes when they take papers for her to sign, they find her in bed."

"Mother?" She looked away. "She's always seemed so . . . so strong . . . the rock of the family."

"You are the rock, Irene, not her and not your father. At any rate I could not just come down here and sweep you away and marry you and just let you keep hiding down here." He moved behind her, touching her shoulders. "Someday I am going to make love to you, *mi querida,* and it will be the most wonderful thing either of us has ever known. It is torture for me now to do nothing more than just kiss you. But it will not be right for you if you continue to be plagued by ghosts from your childhood, or by the guilt I know you will carry if something happens to your mother before you have a chance to make amends. You have to go back to Denver and face them, Irene, and you have to learn to be proud, learn that you don't have to run away from these things. When I marry you and take you to my bed, I do not want just part of you. I want all of you, with no more secrets, no more shame, no more hard feelings that block out the kind of love I know you are capable of giving."

She reached up and put a hand over his own. "Will you come with me?"

"To Denver? Yes. But I think meeting Yellow Eagle is just for you and your father. I will stay in Denver and spend time with your children so that they get to know me and Alex better. I will love them as my own, Irene. That is a promise. And when the time is right, we will marry. We will have many more children of our own."

He moved his arms around her from behind, crossing them over her breasts. She leaned her head against his firm chest, on fire for him, wanting him as she had never wanted a man before, yet knowing he was right. How comforting it was to realize he was willing to wait, that he was not the groping animal Chad had always been. How wonderfully understanding he would have been on that horrible wedding night. How kind of him to care about and sense her frailties.

"I need to think," she told him, grasping his strong forearms. "I'd like to go riding. Would you ride with me?"

"Like we used to do?" He grinned, kissing her hair. "It has been many years. Yes. I would like that very much."

She turned in his arms. "Let's ride to your old hacienda. The house is still there, Ramon. I went there one day, just to think about you. Another Spanish couple lives there. They work that end of the ranch for us."

He sighed deeply. "I would love to go."

"You can tell me about your grandfather and how it used to be there. And when we're married, it will be yours again. Mother couldn't keep it from you after all, could she?"

He smiled sadly. "No more than she could stop me from loving you."

He leaned down and kissed her again, and she realized she could stand the wait, simply because she knew how much he loved her, that he would always be here for her. How much sweeter it was all going to be when she had settled other things that still burdened her heart.

"I'll go to Denver," she told him. "And I'll go with Father to find Yellow Eagle. I'll do whatever I have to do to be your wife. Besides, after all we've been through, I think a grand wedding right in Denver would be fitting, don't you? Let's give the *News* something to write about. I've always loved you, and now I want them all to know it."

He grinned. "We will have whatever kind of wedding you want, as long as we just do it. All I care about is what comes afterward."

The words sent arrows of passion ripping through her whole being at the thought of being in Ramon Vallejo's bed . . . at last. She raised her face to his for another kiss, but he only touched her lips with his fingers. "We had better go for that ride before I change my mind," he told her.

She smiled wryly. "You're teasing me, Ramon."

He ran his fingers lightly over her lips. "I intend to tease you. I want you to think about what is to come, to want it so badly that our wedding night will be the most beautiful experience of your life. I have a feeling your wedding night with Chad Jacobs was something better forgotten." He watched the hurt come into her eyes. "Someday you can tell me. I only want you to know that it will be different this time. I will make up for it, Irene."

She watched his eyes, so dark, so true. They were eyes she could trust, and it felt so wonderful to know that.

He gently pulled away from her, keeping hold of her hand as he picked up his lemonade and drank it down. "Let's go saddle some horses. And go easy on me. Something tells me you are a much better rider now. You have been practicing while I have been pounding nails and digging pictures in wood."

She laughed as he pulled her toward the door. She felt sixteen again, and in love, so much in love. She could feel the chains of lies and pretending being unloosed. She could see the road to freedom now, and Ramon would lead her down it. She would do anything to reach its end and be with him.

CHAPTER
THIRTY-EIGHT

A tight feeling grabbed Irene's stomach as she and Kirk rode onto the Cheyenne River Reservation in the Dakotas. They had taken a train to Cheyenne, Wyoming, hauling their horses along. Then they rode northeast to Fort Robinson, Nebraska, and afterward with two soldiers in escort, they rode even farther north, a three-week journey by horseback.

It seemed unreal to Irene that these were really her people. Hundreds of tipis were sprawled in various circles across a vast expanse of open land, many of them perched along the Cheyenne River, others farther in the distance camped along the Missouri River. Irene gazed at the scene with a mixture of apprehension and sorrow, realizing how easily she could have been living among these people, a weathered, work-worn Indian woman with several children by now, forced to live in squalor and to wait for handouts from the government.

Smoke from several campfires filled the air, and dogs ran about freely. Little children played, so many of them looking just like little Sharron, except they ran naked and looked hungry. She felt strangely guilty riding her fine Palomino through the camps, wearing an expensive riding habit, free to travel wherever she pleased. Before she discovered she was half Indian, she had thought it seemed perfectly proper to put Indians on these reservations. Now that she saw what life here was really like for them, she realized these people must feel as though they were in jail.

They had been told that Yellow Eagle was on this reservation, allowed to live here, even though it was a Sioux reservation, because his second wife had been an Oglala Sioux. She had since died, leaving behind a small son. Irene's heart rushed with a mixture of anticipation and some fear at what they might find. Would Yellow Eagle even agree to see them?

One of the soldiers who accompanied them, a Captain Zimmer, pointed to an old woman who lay on a blanket looking shriveled and nearly dead. "Several of these people die every day," he told them. "They contract white man's diseases, die in childbirth, a lot of reasons. But mostly, it seems, they're dying from broken hearts—literally—especially the old ones. Their pride can't bear being forced to live in restricted areas, to beg for rations from the 'Great White Father' in Washington, rations that never come on time. It's a pretty sad state of affairs. We try to teach them to farm, but the men say farming is woman's work, and most of them can't stand tearing up the ground. They say it's like tearing the heart out of Mother Earth."

"You won't change their way of living in a few days or a few weeks, Captain," Kirk answered. "I could have told Washington that years ago. You'll be lucky to do it in one or two generations. There's a certain spirit among the Indians that can't be changed—a need to be free, to provide for themselves from nature. They don't want Washington's damn handouts. They want to hunt and dig roots and pick berries. They need to follow the seasons and the buffalo—except that there are hardly any buffalo left."

Irene could sense Kirk's frustration and anger. Everything they had seen and heard so far had only upset him more. Near the train station at Cheyenne they had seen several box wagons loaded with buffalo bones, picked up off the prairie by scavengers called bonepickers. They were paid by the ton for the bones, which were used for fertilizer, buttons, combs, and other things by eastern manufacturers. The bones were what had been left behind by hide hunters, who for years had been slaughtering buffalo by the millions, leaving the entire carcass for the buzzards and taking only the hides.

"And they call that progress," Kirk had fumed. "The Indians never wasted one part of the buffalo. Nearly everything the Indian needed to subsist came from that one animal, and it didn't cost the government one cent! Now they'll spend thousands, probably millions, over the years keeping the Indian on reservations providing their food and everything else. It's ridiculous!"

Irene had to agree. "Look at them," Kirk was saying now. "Their pride is gone, Irene, their happy spirit has vanished. When I knew these people, they smiled and welcomed me. Now they look at us with frowns and suspicion and sadness in their eyes. These aren't the Indians I knew. Look at that one over there, slugging down rot-gut whiskey. He's so drunk he's hardly aware of where he is."

"Most of them drink heavily," the captain told him. "We try to keep the whiskey traders off the reservation, but this is a lot of territory to cover."

"They drink because it's the only way they can feel good about themselves," Kirk told him. "They feel ashamed, Captain, and I can tell you right now that the men are bored to death. This is no way for them to live! There's going to be more trouble yet." He looked at Irene as they headed for reservation headquarters. "When I lived among the Sioux and Cheyenne they roamed this land from Canada to Texas, lived in the mountains in summers and anywhere they pleased out on the plains in winter. They were proud, so proud. That's what I see missing here more than anything else—that fierce pride."

"Some of the younger warriors still have it, and you're right, Mr. Kirkland. Our troubles aren't over yet."

Irene gazed at some of the old women, suspecting a lot of them were not nearly as old as they looked, wondering what her Indian mother would be like if she were still alive. She realized now that Ramon was right. She could not ignore this side of herself. These were her people, too, and she had to face that, in spite of how the public felt about them. She was beginning to understand some of the misconceptions about the Indian, beginning to understand why they retaliated against white intruders who had stolen so much from them, "white eyes," who had brought diseases that killed them by the thousands and who murdered by the millions their primary source of survival.

They reined in their horses at headquarters, and Captain Zimmer spoke with the agent who had come outside to meet the strangers. The agent looked too well-dressed for these parts, and his big belly portrayed a man who ate well. He was a stark contrast to the starved-looking Indians they had seen on the way in, and Irene felt her anger rising. Perhaps the Indians were not getting their proper rations, but this agent most certainly was.

"Yellow Eagle," the man repeated after the captain's inquiry. "Yes, he's here. He's at the farthest village, up on the Missouri, if he's not already dead."

"Dead!" Irene could see the fear and agony in her father's eyes, and her own heart tightened with dread. "What are you talking about? My son is only thirty-one."

"Your son?" The man looked him over in astonishment, then moved his eyes to Irene. He frowned slightly. "What's a fancy woman like you doing here?"

"Yellow Eagle is my twin brother," Irene answered proudly, suddenly angry at the sight of the man's big belly. "I've come to see him." It was all so clear to her now, why the Indians had become so belligerent. This man was an example of the government's lies and broken promises. She imagined herself in moccasins and a tunic, struggling to find ways to boost the spirit of her once-proud husband, who now sat around with nothing to do all day, his children hungry because he could no longer hunt.

"Your brother!" The man looked her over, the respect in his eyes suddenly leaving. "Well, if you had grown up among them, you sure would have been one valuable squaw."

"Watch your mouth, mister," Kirk told him. "She's my daughter, and by God, I'm not too old to answer any insults."

The man frowned, deciding he'd better not say anything more about the woman. This Kirkland fellow looked as if he'd been a few rounds in his life. He was a big, powerful-looking man, in spite of his age. He sat there in buckskins, well-armed, probably to protect his daughter. "Kirkland," he said aloud. "There's a real wealthy family from Denver by that name, isn't there?"

"One and the same," Kirkland answered. "Now what's this about Yellow Eagle dying?"

Respect moved back into the man's eyes. "Well! I'm honored to meet you, Mr. Kirkland." He glanced at the daughter once more, wondering how Denver felt about one of their wealthiest citizens being half Indian. He tugged on his vest to put on a better appearance before answering. "Well, sir, I'm sorry to tell you, but Yellow Eagle hurt his foot pretty bad on a plow. We make all the men try to learn a little farming, but they aren't very willing. The fools would rather be out riding over people's farms and ranches trying to chase down wild game." He chuckled, but Kirk just glared at him and his smile faded. "Well, uh, at any rate, Yellow Eagle cut his foot and it got infected. He's refused to let a white doctor look at it, and now he's in pretty bad shape. We told him he'd live if he'd let the doctor take the leg off, but he won't hear of it. He says if he's supposed to die, he'll die. Won't let a white man touch him."

"Damn," Kirk swore. "Let's get over there." He turned his horse, and Irene followed, her heart aching as much for her father as for Yellow Eagle. So, her brother would die, not in glorious battle, but a slow, miserable death on a squalid reservation. In all his battles with soldiers and settlers, and even surviving Sand Creek, he would still be defeated by the white man in a much more shameful way—a stupid cut from trying to learn how to farm. She had not lived the Indian way, but she sensed a man like Yellow Eagle would much rather have died in battle.

After much searching and questioning, they found Yellow Eagle's tipi. It had not been easy. No one seemed to trust them, and few were willing to volunteer any information. An old man sat outside the tipi where Yellow Eagle was supposed to be dwelling, and Kirk studied him closely as he dismounted. The old man's eyes seemed to light up a little, and he spoke a word of greeting in the Cheyenne tongue.

"Fast Runner," Kirk asked, saying the name in Cheyenne. The old man grinned and nodded, slowly getting to his feet. They studied each other, Kirk realizing this was Gray Bird Woman's brother. "It's me, Kirk," he told the old man. "Yellow Eagle's father."

"Kirk," the man repeated. "It has been many, many years since last I saw you down at old Bent's Fort." He spoke in his own tongue.

"Thirty-one winters," Kirk answered. He turned to Irene, who had come to stand beside him, and Irene saw tears in her father's eyes. "This is Fast Runner, Irene, your uncle. He is Gray Bird Woman's brother." He turned to Fast Runner and explained who Irene was, and the old man's eyes grew misty. He nodded, reaching out hesitantly to touch her arm.

"Morning Star," he said in Cheyenne.

Irene asked her father to tell her what he had said, and he explained. "That was your Indian name."

Irene felt suddenly guilty for having lived such a comfortable life compared to the one she would have lived if her father had not chosen to raise her. Kirk conversed more with Fast Runner, who kept nodding and quickly wiped at a tear that slipped out of his eye.

"He says it's true that your Indian mother was killed at Sand Creek," Kirk told Irene then. "As well as Yellow Eagle's first wife and son. Yellow Eagle remarried, but his second wife died in childbirth. He has another little boy, Jumping Bear. The child is inside the tipi." He grasped her arms. "Are you sure you are up to this, Irene?"

Her eyes met his. Over the past weeks they had grown much

closer again. Irene understood her father had done what he thought was best, except that he had disagreed for years over telling Irene the truth. She knew how insistent Bea could be, realized the torture her father had lived with all these years, never knowing his Indian son. This was a great moment for her father. "I want to see him, Father, and my nephew."

He turned to Fast Runner, telling the old man to go inside the tipi and tell Yellow Eagle they had come to see him. Kirk paced with worry that Yellow Eagle would refuse, deciding he would go inside anyway if he did. He had not come this far to leave without seeing his first-born son.

Fast Runner finally emerged, smiling sadly and signaling them to come inside. Irene took a deep breath and followed her father, ducking down to clear the tipi entrance. She was surprised at how clean and roomy it was inside, but for the moment she did not take time to study the contents of the dwelling.

A man sat up against a pile of robes and blankets, one of his legs covered with a blanket. He wore a wolfskin jacket, apparently cold in spite of the summer heat, a sign the infection was ravaging his body. His blue eyes moved to Irene's, eyes she had seen once before, eyes of the man who had killed Hank. She wondered now why she didn't see the resemblance that day. They were her eyes, Kirk's eyes.

Yellow Eagle. She could hardly believe she was in the same dwelling with such a notorious man, and that he was her own brother. A little boy sat beside him who looked nearly the same age as little Sharron. Yellow Eagle quietly moved his eyes from Irene to Kirk, watching both of them warily.

Kirk knelt in front of him then. "I am David Kirkland," he spoke up in English. "I'm your—"

"I know who you are," Yellow Eagle interrupted in English. His eyes moved to Irene. "I remember her—my sister." He looked back at Kirk. "I can see by your eyes that you are the white father I have never known." His features remained rigid as a stone. "Why do you choose to come now, after all these years, now, when I am a dying man?"

Kirk sighed. "It's a long story, Yellow Eagle. I can only say I've always wondered about you, worried about you. If your mother had just let me have you back when you were born, I would have raised you like my own."

"And now you wish to see your son before he dies a shameful death." He sat up straighter. "I was not always weak like this! I was a great warrior! I bear the scars of the Sun Dance! I am *Cheyenne*! I do not recognize my white blood."

Kirk removed his hat, and Irene kept glancing at the little boy, who stared back at her with wide, brown eyes. "I didn't know you were dying, Yellow Eagle. I've told Irene here who she is, that you're her brother. She wanted to see you again."

Yellow Eagle glanced at Irene, his eyes moving over her. "Why would you want to see me? I killed your man."

She was so nervous her legs felt weak. "He wasn't my man. He was a very good friend."

He looked away. "I did not know who you were, or I would have spared the man's life."

"I believe you," Irene told him, kneeling down beside her father. "I've hated you for seven years, Yellow Eagle, actually longer, because of the terrible things you did to other settlers over the years. But I think I understand more now. I understand why you did some of those things. I wish there was some way to make up for it all, but there isn't. And I wish we could have been raised together, but we had no control over our different lives. Let us help you now, Yellow Eagle. Father is a wealthy man. He can get you the best doctors—"

"No!" He threw aside the blanket and Irene gasped, feeling ill. Kirk closed his eyes as though in pain. The leg was swollen to twice its size, and was nearly black. An ugly odor drifted into the air. "No doctor can help this," Yellow Eagle sneered. "And no white man will touch me! No one is going to cut off my leg and send me to the Other World only half a man!" He pulled the blanket back over his leg, and Irene realized the rest of his coloring was more of a sick gray than a healthy brown. His face looked thin, and he seemed to be perspiring. "I wanted to die in battle, but this is how I die—in disgrace!"

"Yellow Eagle, I can help you—"

"I said no," the man told Kirk. "For many years I have known you were a man with great power among the whites. But I have wanted *nothing* from your world. It stands for everything that I am against! Now your people have put us on this stinking reservation, and our rations do not come on time. Our braves sit around with nothing to do but drink and be sick! Our women no longer respect their men because they are not allowed to ride free and make war and bring back food and do all the things a man is supposed to do! Our women sell themselves to white men to get the money to buy the whiskey that makes their men sicker and lazier. Our children are taken away from us to school, where their hair is cut off and they are forced to wear white man's clothes, where they die of broken hearts. I want nothing to do with a world that destroys the earth and the buffalo, a people who steal land from others and then tear it up and destroy the trees and make the water unfit to drink! Compared to the way we once lived, I see nothing better about your world!"

He shivered then, obviously trying not to show his pain. "In two more days I will no longer be on this earth. You can stop worrying about me then, my white father. Worry about yourself, and what you are doing to the earth."

Kirk sighed deeply. "I've never liked some of the things that have gone on myself, Yellow Eagle. But in spite of my wealth, I was not powerful enough to stop it. Some things *can't* be stopped—and they can't be changed. I've only come to tell you that I'm sorry I didn't try to find you sooner. I'll go to my grave regretting it, son. I just wish I could have kept you with me when I took Irene."

"I do not. I am *glad* I was left with the Cheyenne. You think I had a bad life, but I did not. It was good, a life of freedom and hunting and following the seasons. It is those I leave behind for whom my heart carries great sorrow. Life will not be the same for my children and their children."

He stiffened for a moment, grimacing with pain. He seemed to relax again, then reached over and pulled his little son next to him. "It is for this child that my heart grieves, not my own death. He has nothing to look forward to but the filth and boredom of this reservation. He will never ride free on the plains and learn to be a proud warrior."

"Yes, he can," Irene spoke up, surprising them both. "You can let *me* have him. You saw with your own eyes the golden horses I raise on our ranch in southern Colorado. You prized them so much that you killed for them. I still live on that ranch a good share of the time, Yellow Eagle, and I still raise the golden Palominos. I am getting married soon, and my future husband is a man who loves and honors the land just like you do. If you let me take your son, he will grow up in the sunshine, in the land in which his ancestors were born and lived and hunted. He will ride the golden Palominos and he'll be free to do whatever he chooses. He'll never be able to live the life his people once led, but he'll at least be free, Yellow Eagle. He'll be able to go where he pleases and hunt all he wants. I would teach him about his people and never let him feel ashamed. Please tell the reservation agent you are giving your son to us. We can give him a good life. I promise he would be free and happy, and he would never be hungry."

He studied them both, keeping an arm around the boy. His eyes suddenly filled with tears. "Jumping Bear is all I have left," he said quietly then.

"Which is all the more reason to let me take him, Yellow Eagle," Irene urged. "I'm his aunt. I have children of my own, who would be his cousins. I want to care for my Indian brother's son. Here he could die. With me, he'll live and be happy and free!" She wondered how it had been so easy to make such a decision, how the idea had come to her so quickly. It seemed so logical, so right. She had her own children, and when she married Ramon there would be little Alejandro. What was one more? She suddenly could not bear the thought of going home and leaving little Jumping Bear behind. His only other close relative was Fast Runner, and he was getting too old to be of much use to the little boy.

Yellow Eagle looked down at his little son, touching his hair, taking several minutes to reply. "I do not like the thought of him living in the white man's world," he finally said, moving his eyes to meet Irene's again. "But I see a truth in your eyes that makes me trust you. You have a good heart—our mother's heart—and you are my sister. We share the same blood, and now you are my son's closest relative. For this reason alone, and because he can be with his cousins, I will let you take him. But he must always be taught about the Cheyenne."

"Father will help me. He knows the Cheyenne ways as well as he knows his own people."

Yellow Eagle breathed deeply. "Do not take him—" his voice choked, "until I am gone." He trembled and closed his eyes for a moment. "You do not have long . . . to wait."

Irene's eyes teared as she sat down fully near him. "I'm sorry, Yellow Eagle, so sorry for all of it—for what has happened to the Cheyenne and the Sioux and all the rest."

"You had no part in it. One day my people will be strong again. One day . . . you will see." He laid his head back and closed his eyes, pulling the wolfskin jacket closer around himself in spite of the summer heat. "It is the time of the Heat Moon, yet it feels more like the Moon of Strong Cold."

Kirk hung his head. "My son," he groaned. He suddenly rose and left the tipi. Irene moved cautiously closer to Yellow Eagle, ignoring the smell of his leg, thinking what a grand, strong, handsome man he once was and still would be if not for the wound. She picked up a blanket that lay nearby and she put it over him, seeing that he was still shivering. Little Jumping Bear watched her, his brown eyes as big as saucers. He seemed to know what was happening, as he scooted against his father's side and rested his head on the man's shoulder, patting his chest with a chubby, brown hand. Irene saw in that moment that the Indians were as capable of loving as any whites, that they were not the savage animals she had once believed. They were human. They had fought for what they thought belonged to them, fought for their loved ones, just as any white man would do.

Yellow Eagle opened his eyes a moment, watching her quietly. "Stay," he said then, surprising her with the statement.

Her throat ached with a need to cry. "I will," she answered. All the hatred and bitterness toward him for killing Hank left her then.

Irene held a sleeping Jumping Bear on her lap as the Denver-Pacific chugged its way south from Cheyenne. Jumping Bear, whom Irene had already decided to rename Samuel John, had taken to her as though he understood who she was. He was a quiet boy, who Irene knew for now must be very confused, traveling with strange people on the noisy train.

The whistle blew and the boy jumped, snuggling closer to her breast for protection. He had cried when first boarding, but soon apparently decided that the train was not some monster that was going to eat him alive. Irene patted his bottom, as she leaned back and watched the mountains to the west. She tried to imagine the land so black with buffalo that "a man could almost walk across their backs," as Kirk had once put it. She suspected it was not such a great exaggeration. She understood so much about herself now, her love of the land, her yearning to ride free across the plains, her appreciation of bright colors and Indian and Mexican designs. She loved Ramon all the more for urging her to do this, for she felt more at peace than she had in years.

Her heart still ached at the memory of Yellow Eagle's slow, painful death. Near the end she had held his head in her lap, sponging the perspiration from his face, assuring him little Jumping Bear would have a good, happy life, that the boy would be well schooled in the Cheyenne way. She had attended the burial, had watched Yellow Eagle's body raised to a platform, high enough to keep the wolves away, high enough to send him well on his way to reaching *Ekutsihimmiyo*, the Hanging Road that leads to a place where the buffalo are plentiful, and where one can be with loved ones who have gone on before.

She pictured Indians riding free now, chasing the buffalo, claiming all this land for themselves. Such a beautiful land it was! It was no wonder they had fought so hard for it. But, as Bea would say, progress cannot be stopped. The Indians were finally outnumbered, and the white man's appetite for gold and land was insatiable. The Great West offered both. There was no going back and changing any of it.

She no longer felt any shame. She felt only pride in being directly related to the grand history of this land. She stood to inherit a great deal of it, along with a good deal of power, and she suddenly realized how fitting that would be, for her and Ramon both.

She looked at her father, who sat next to her, and she reached over and took his hand. He looked at her sadly, and she knew that Yellow Eagle's death had deeply affected him. He would never be quite the same. "You've told me about the Cheyenne belief in the circle of life, Father," she told him. "I think this is an example of things coming full circle." She squeezed his hand. "You couldn't have Yellow Eagle, but you had me, and now you have Yellow Eagle's son, and he and I will win back some of this land through our inheritance. It's all going to work out."

He smiled and sighed, blinking back tears. "I'm not sure I could have survived all these years without you, Irene. You were the rock that kept me going, and you didn't even know it. It wasn't Bea or the business or the gold mines—none of those things. It's all been for you. Thank you for offering to raise Jumping Bear."

She smiled and kissed the boy's hair. "Ramon won't mind one bit. He'll be happy and proud to raise him as our own." She laughed. "What a grand mixture we have! David is one-quarter Indian and looks white, while Sharron is also one-quarter Indian but looks like a full-blood. Then there is Alejandro, who is Mexican; and now little Sam, three-quarters Indian. Ramon and I are starting off with a ready-made family that is quite a mixture. We'll have a time explaining it to the children."

Kirk smiled, quickly wiping at a tear. "I'm glad you're marrying Ramon, Irene. He's a damn good man. Your mother will have some adjusting to do, but Bea deserves to eat a little crow once in a while. She'll get over it."

"How do you think she'll react to Sam? We're bringing home an Indian grandson she doesn't know anything about."

He chuckled. "Well, I've sprung things on her before. I think she's getting used to it." He sobered slightly. "I'd like him to carry my name, Irene. Do you think Ramon would mind?"

"Kirkland?"

He looked at her. "I'd be grateful. I'm not sure John will ever marry, and he's slowly killing himself with drink. There might not be anyone left to carry on my name. It just seems fitting that the son of my first-born should do it."

Their eyes held. "All right," she told him. "He'll be Samuel John Kirkland. I hope you realize you're only adding to the confusion that is going to pervade the Vallejo household."

He smiled through tears. "It's going to be a happy household, Irene, I can tell. I'm glad you're finally going to be married to a man you really love, and I'm sorry about the years of hell you went through so silently. You never should have kept it so hidden."

She looked down at little Sam. "I thought it was my duty. The first few years I thought everything that happened was my fault." She closed her eyes. "It's over now. Chad is gone from my life, and I don't want to think about him anymore. I just want to think about Ramon and what lies ahead. I just wish Yellow Eagle didn't have to die that way. I'm sorry, Father."

"There's really no one to blame for it. The Indian is in for a bad time of it, and there isn't a damn thing that can be done about it. It makes me sick to think of it. In a way I suppose it's men like me who unintentionally started it—coming out here to hunt and trap, befriending the Indians, living among them, leading them to believe they could trust all white men." He sighed deeply. "What's done is done. This land is never going to be the same."

"Next stop—Denver," a conductor shouted.

Denver, Irene thought, remembering what a tiny, dirty, log-cabin town it was when her family first arrived. Yes, the land would truly never be the same, but one thing had not changed, and that was Ramon. He would be waiting for her at the station. She sat up straighter, buttoning the little jacket she had purchased for Sam in Cheyenne. "Time to wake up, son," she told him. "You're going to meet your new daddy."

Her heart rushed at the realization that the waiting was over. Now that she had found Yellow Eagle and was truly at peace with herself, she and Ramon could be married. At last she would lie with the man who had first awakened all her womanly needs and emotions, the man she had loved for what seemed most of her life.

The train rumbled toward Union Station, and high brick buildings blocked the view of the mountains. She thought what a contrast Denver was to the sorry Indian villages on the reservations, and she realized the contrast would be even more startling for little Sam. The train whistle blew again, and Sam hugged her tightly around the neck.

September 1877

Organ music filled the grand cathedral, as Irene began her walk up the aisle. Her heart soared with the music, and she wondered how she was going to get through the ceremony without breaking down into tears of great joy. This was like a strange dream that at one time she never thought possible. Ramon stood waiting at the end of the aisle, wearing a silver-gray silk suit and white ruffled shirt, looking as royal as his ancestors, standing tall and dark and handsome.

This was their moment, and she thought how both of them deserved this happiness. The church was filled with friends and business associates of both bride and groom. Some had come out of genuine happiness for the couple, others out of curiosity, wanting to see the half-breed daughter of Bea and David Kirkland marry the Mexican contractor. Irene knew a hundred different rumors had probably been spread about her divorce and now her marriage to Ramon. They mattered little to her. People could think what they wanted. She only knew that at last she was marrying the only man she had truly loved, totally loved, from the very beginning.

Red stood beside Ramon as best man. He watched her with a smile of genuine happiness, but Irene noticed how much thinner and older he looked. Elly had made the poor man's life hell for him. The day before he had apologized to Ramon for coming to the wedding alone. Elly refused to attend. She wanted no part of her half-breed sister's marriage to a Mexican. Irene was not surprised at the affront, and she was not about to let it disturb her. She had not seen Elly since first coming back to Denver, and she was sure Elly had dreamed up a way of blaming her for Chad's departure.

John stood next to Red. He had managed to stay away from liquor for twenty-four hours, having promised Irene he would not show up drunk at her wedding. He looked a little pale, and she knew he was anxious to break out the whiskey at the reception. Irene loved him in spite of his weaknesses, and she wished he would find a good woman and marry, but he seemed to be interested only in drinking and carousing in Old Colorado City.

She told herself she must not think about that now. She must think only of what a happy day this was. She glanced at Rose, who smiled warmly. To their surprise and delight, Irene had asked Rose and Jenny to be maid of honor and bridesmaid, respectively. Both had remained faithful, trusted servants and had come back with her from Colorado Springs to live in the Kirkland mansion and help Bea tend to the children while Irene went to find Yellow Eagle. In all these years Rose had never married. She was a plain, plump woman who seemed to enjoy waiting on others, never complaining about her status in life. Jenny was now seeing a man who delivered ice at the mansion once a week, and Irene suspected she would lose the woman to marriage soon.

Little Sharron skipped down the aisle ahead of her mother, throwing flowers from a basket. People looked and whispered, most of them smiling and commenting on the child's exquisite beauty, which no one could deny. At the end of the aisle stood the three "sons" in jackets and short pants: handsome, six-year-old David; little Alejandro, almost two; and two-and-one-half-year-old Sam Kirkland, his hair hanging past his shoulders and a headband around his forehead. Irene had promised Yellow Eagle she would not cut his son's hair until the boy was older and able to decide for himself whether he wanted it short or long.

Irene could not imagine a happier moment in any woman's life. Her only worry now was Bea. She glanced at her mother, who stood at the front of the aisle wearing a deep green taffeta dress of the latest fashion. She held herself tall and erect as she always had, but she was noticeably thinner and grayer. She had accepted this marriage with cool resignation, realizing she could no longer do anything to stop it. Irene suspected the woman was sicker than she let on. Bea had probably made no vehement objections to the marriage because she was simply too tired to do so; perhaps because she suspected she would not be on this earth much longer, and she didn't want to leave it with bad feelings between herself and her children. She had tried in vain to make some kind of amends with Elly, but the girl would have nothing to do with the family. John had also been distant. For Irene's sake alone he had agreed to come to Denver for the wedding and be civil to his mother, but Irene suspected her brother would feel no great loss when something happened to Bea. It was a source of great sadness for her, and she knew it was for Bea.

She moved her eyes back to the front of the church. She must not think of sad things today. This was her day, hers and Ramon's. After the wedding there would be a grand fiesta-style reception held on the lawn of the Kirkland mansion, with catered food and drinks, Mexican music, and even a piñata for the children. Bea was in a stew over not having the reception in her grand new ballroom, with a violin orchestra. Irene had learned to take her mother's fits with a grain of salt. She was marrying a proud man descended from Spanish royalty, and their reception would have all the flavor of that heritage, whether Bea liked it or not.

She approached the wedding party, people staring in awe at the beautiful Irene Kirkland, who seemed unaffected by the years. Some whispered that her beauty was owed to her mixed blood. Irene wore a white satin sheathlike dress, the front skirt a tumble of satin tufts, each one inset with tiny red rubies. The dropped waist accented her slender form, and the gentle cut of the lace-trimmed bodice provocatively displayed just enough silken, tawny-colored bosom to put fire into Ramon's blood as she came closer. A train of lace into which real roses had been sewn spread out for six feet behind her.

Irene shivered from the majesty of the organ music and the way it penetrated the domed ceiling of the cathedral. She and the children had been baptised into the church and Irene had completed her catechism. She was now Catholic, gladly accepting her new religion in spite of her mother's objections.

She came closer and Kirk left her to go and sit with Bea. From then on no one existed for Irene and Ramon but each other. Irene had trouble getting through her vows. Her voice kept breaking, and tears kept wanting to come. Ramon held her hand tightly in reassurance as she managed to complete her promises, and his own eyes were misty when he returned the vows. Irene clung to his arm for fear of collapsing. How she managed to get through the long ceremony, she was not certain. She floated through the receiving line, hardly aware of the faces that smiled at her, kissed her, congratulated her. She climbed into the wedding carriage with her new husband, falling into his arms and weeping with relieved joy as the carriage made its way to the reception.

"Nothing can drive us apart again, can it, Ramon?" she said tearfully.

"No, *mi vida*. We will never be apart again."

The reception became an evening of laughter and dancing, food and games, Ramon teaching Irene a slow Spanish dance, their eyes holding in the building heat of long-starved desires. She was glad now they had waited, for the anticipation would make their union even more intense and satisfying. They cut the cake, took time to visit with well-wishers, danced with the children.

Everyone drank and grew happier. The children were blindfolded and given sticks to hit at the piñata to try to break it. Watching them brought hearty laughter to the rest of the crowd. The children screamed and banged at the colorful paper donkey until it finally broke and showered them with candy. As they laughed and squealed and scrambled to pick it up, Ramon's arm suddenly came around Irene from behind, and he pulled her away from the crowd.

"*Vamos, mi querida,*" he said softly, whisking her back to the wedding carriage. A few people spotted them, running after them and throwing flowers and rice as they climbed into the carriage that would take them to the most elegant suite at the Denver Inn, where their clothes had already been delivered. Because of the children, and her mother's delicate health, Irene had decided against a trip away from Denver for the time being. Until her mother seemed better, they would stay in Denver for a while, living at Ramon's house.

She rested her head against Ramon's shoulder, and his strong arm came around her. He touched her chin to make her look at him, and his mouth met hers in a delicious kiss, one hand moving to touch her breast lightly. The touch sent a fire roaring through her veins, a fire that would only be quenched when Ramon Vallejo consummated their marriage. Old Jim drove the carriage through the gas-lit streets of a now-thriving Denver, a broad smile on his face. For once "Miss Irene" was a truly happy lady.

CHAPTER
THIRTY-NINE

Irene felt sixteen again, but this time she was not afraid. How long had she and Ramon had to live with this intense desire without being able to do anything about it? Now, at last, they could physically share the love they had been so long denied. Ramon kept his arm around her as they climbed the stairs, stopping at each landing and pulling her into his arms for another hungry kiss. When they reached the floor where their suite was, he whisked her up into his strong arms.

Irene laughed. "I feel like a silly girl," she told him.

"And I am a boy again," he answered, kissing her again. He stopped outside the door, and Irene's smile faded.

"I'm nervous, Ramon." She closed her eyes and put her head on his shoulder. "I want so much to please you."

He kissed at her hair. "If you think you would not please me, you are a foolish woman. Besides, it is the love and desire that make it pleasing, Irene. You have never known how it should be with a man."

He opened the door and carried her inside, setting her on her feet and grasping her face in his hands. "You had only that one moment with a man you truly loved, and even that was not totally free and right like this is. We are husband and wife now. Nothing can stop us from taking all the pleasure we want in each other."

He kissed her lightly and moved to close the door, then turned to take the headpiece and veil from her hair. She stood still as he unpinned her hair. Her breathing deepened, her heart pounded, every nerve end alive with anticipation and desire. Her hair fell in golden waves nearly to her waist. Ramon led her to the bed, setting her down on it and kneeling to remove her shoes. "You are to do nothing but enjoy, *mi querida*," he told her. "I will do it all."

She felt a flush come to her cheeks as he pushed up her dress and undid the stockings from her garter belt, peeling each one down and tossing it aside. He rose then, taking off his jacket and tie, his shoes and stockings, his shirt. Irene watched him, breathing deeply at the sight of his muscular, brown body. He removed his pants, leaving his long johns, and she shivered with need at the sight of him.

He knelt down in front of her then, and she touched his hair as he unbuttoned the front of her wedding dress, opening it and pulling it from her shoulders, revealing her camisole and corset. He pulled her to her feet, pulling her dress and slips away, then unlaced the corset and let it fall. He unhooked her garter belt, leaving her standing there in only her camisole and drawers.

Ramon struggled to keep himself in control, refusing to ravish her the way he would like to do, wanting it all to be good and sweet. He moved his fingers under the straps of her camisole, pulling them off her shoulders while their eyes filled with heated desire. He untied the camisole, and Irene closed her eyes and sucked in her breath as Ramon Vallejo gazed upon her breasts for the first time.

"*Que mujer más hermoso,*" he whispered. "*Yo te quiero, mi querida.*" His lips covered her mouth then in a warm, passionate, searching kiss, as he moved a thumb over her taught nipple. The touch sent fire through her veins, and she moved her arms around his neck, returning the kiss with the passion of a young girl in love for the first time. He crushed her breasts against his bare chest, moving a hand to her hips and pressing his hardness against her.

"*Siento el fuego bajo tu piel,*" he whispered, running his hand over her bare back. She knew he had said something about the fire under her skin, and she could feel the fire under his own.

He picked her up and laid her on the bed, not even bothering to turn down the covers. Neither of them wanted to take the time. He moved on top of her, and Irene closed her eyes as his lips trailed down her neck, moving to her breasts. She gasped with the glory of his warm lips and tongue gently savoring their pink fruits. She grasped his hair and pushed herself toward him, suddenly feeling as though she could not give him enough.

From then on neither of them could move slowly and take their time as planned. The need was too strong. They had waited too many years for this. Ramon groaned with great need as he tasted her breasts, but oh, so gently, not painfully the way Chad had done. Irene gasped his name as his lips moved downward, kissing at her belly as he removed the last of her clothing. He pulled them off, and she wondered if she would faint at the ecstasy of lying naked before him. He kissed at the golden hairs that hid that part of her he wanted most to invade.

Never before had Irene wanted to be so bold before a man. Never before had she felt she could not give enough, or felt so daring that she wanted to reveal and offer up every part of herself. His hands moved gently to her inner thighs, urging them apart, and she cried out at the ecstasy of allowing him his pleasure, reaching up and grasping the bed rails as his tongue explored, sending her into a realm of ecstasy she had never known before. Not even Hank had made her feel like this, and in moments she was crying out Ramon's name as the wonderful climax engulfed her. His lips trailed back over her belly, and in the next moment he covered her mouth in a hot, urgent kiss, while he removed his long johns.

She could taste her own juices on his lips as he explored her mouth. She felt his naked power then when at last he slid into her, filling her full and deep. At last they were one! Irene knew if she died this night she could never have lived long enough ever to know such happiness and ecstasy again. In moments his life poured into her in swelling throbs, but he did not stop his rhythmic movements. He whispered to her in Spanish, words she did not understand, but she sensed their meaning.

In moments she felt the swelling again, as their heated bodies pressed against each other. He raised up then, grasping her under the hips and raising them with strong arms, looking down on her naked body as he moved in rhythmic, circular motions that made her feel wild and free and wanton. She grasped his forearms, thinking how he looked like a conqueror and she was his willing captive. She arched up to him in total abandon, never dreaming she could want a man so badly that it was almost painful.

Again his life surged into her as he shuddered and groaned, and again he did not pull away from her. He only leaned down, moving his arms under her shoulders and resting on his elbows as he kissed and licked at her mouth. "I meant to go slower, *mi vida*," he said softly. "But I cannot get enough of you."

"I don't care," she answered, her words coming in whispered pants. "Do whatever you want with me, Ramon."

He kissed her almost savagely, and she didn't even mind. "It is the same for you," he told her then. "You must do whatever you want with *me*. You have never enjoyed a man before, never allowed the true woman in you to be released. I am as much yours as you are mine." He kissed her again. "I want you to learn there is nothing wrong with allowing your passion to decide your moves, *mi querida*." He kissed at her eyes. "I have tasted you, and I will do it again and again, and you will taste me. For my people, there are no lines drawn when it comes to making love. Nothing we think to do can be wrong, because we belong to each other. God has given us to each other, to enjoy however we choose."

The night became a series of more than heated couplings. Irene learned to enjoy man, savoring Ramon in the same bold way he had savored her, doing things she never dreamed she was capable or brave enough to do. Sometimes she became the aggressor, exploring his maleness in near wonder, tasting him, moving on top of him in glorious union, riding him in splendid boldness. She never realized there could be so many positions, or that two people could want to make love over and over this way until by morning they were finally spent.

Dawn was breaking when he finally gathered her into his arms and pulled the blankets over them to sleep. Never in her life had Irene felt so gloriously worn out, or so safe, so loved. She was painfully jealous of the other women who had shared this man, yet wanted to cry with relief at the knowledge that from now on he would share his beautiful, virile body only with her. At last she had a man who truly loved her, who would support her through the worst life might hand them, a man she could trust and depend on.

"God has been too good to me," she said then, breaking into tears of blissful fatigue.

Ramon kissed at her hair, keeping her close. "He has given you what you deserve," he answered, "what we both deserve. This is the way it should always have been."

They drifted off to sleep, while the rest of Denver was just waking up.

For two days they did not leave their hotel room, which had a private bath. They bathed together, washing each other, touching, exploring, sharing bodies and souls. They refused to see anyone but the waiters who brought their food and the maids who brought clean linens. Ramon had left strict orders at his company that no one was to contact him with any problems short of a life or death emergency. The children were being looked after, and outside their window the citizens of Denver went about their daily routines.

Ramon and Irene's routine temporarily became one of making love, bathing, eating, talking, making love again. They explored not only each other's bodies, but their hearts, their needs, their thoughts and beliefs. Irene wondered if it was possible to love another person any more than she loved Ramon Vallejo. He was not just her magnificent lover. He was also her best friend, and always had been.

It was midmorning of the third day since the wedding when Ramon answered a knock at the door to see Kirk waiting outside. The man seemed a little embarrassed as he removed his hat. "I'm sorry to bother the two of you," he told Ramon, "but Bea is worse. I thought Irene ought to get over to the house."

Irene hurried to the door, wearing a ruffled, silken robe. Kirk was struck by her radiant look. She had never before appeared more beautiful or happy, and he knew her marriage to Ramon was the best thing that had happened to her in a long time. "What happened, Father?" she asked, as Ramon opened the door wider.

Kirk ignored the tumbled bed. "Bea collapsed. She's asking to see you, Irene."

The joy left her face. "We'll be right there!"

She hurried away to dress, and Kirk moved his eyes to Ramon. "You're good for her, Ramon. I can see it. I'm glad she has you."

"I love her very much." Ramon touched his arm. "You go back to the house. We will be along shortly." He closed the door, feeling suddenly very sorry for David Kirkland, realizing what a miserable personal life the man had led in spite of his riches. He had lost a son he had never even gotten to know, and two of his living children had all but deserted him. He had been married for thirty-one years to a cold, demanding woman who Ramon was sure had never given the man any real pleasure in bed. Now that woman could be dying. It seemed strange to think someone like Bea Kirkland could have the same frailties as other human beings, that she was just as susceptible to old age and death as anyone else. Still, she was only forty-seven.

"It's her heart," the family doctor explained to Kirk and Irene. "It's just giving out, and there isn't anything I can do about it. She could last a couple of weeks or only a couple of days." He looked at Irene. "She keeps asking for you."

"How could this happen?" Irene asked. "She's always been so strong."

"Not the last few months. I've seen this coming. She's been taking tonics and other medicines, but nothing has helped." He looked at Kirk. "If you want my opinion, I'd say the woman has simply worked herself to death. Bea has always been an over-achiever, always fretting about the company holdings, the children and all." He glanced at Irene. "I hate to say it, but bearing up to the remarks and gossip that surrounded your divorce and the discovery of your Indian blood also took a toll on her."

"That isn't Irene's fault," Kirk spoke up quickly, as Ramon moved a supportive arm around Irene. "It was keeping it a secret from her that took its toll on both of us. Bea has always just been too concerned about making impressions on other people and with being at the top of society. Those things never mattered to me, so when the news broke it didn't affect me nearly as deeply as it affected Bea."

The doctor sighed. "I never meant that it was anyone's fault. I'm just saying that Bea's basic nature and the very things you just mentioned can be harmful to a person's health. She has always worried too much and has worked much too hard. It's all catching up with her now."

Irene turned to Ramon. "Go and get John, will you? He was supposed to leave today. Tell him he'd better stay a while longer. And find Red. Have him tell Elly. I want her here, whether she likes it or not, even if you and Red have to drag her here. Tell her if she says anything to hurt Mother—" she looked at Kirk, "she'll never see a dime of Kirkland money."

Kirk nodded, and Irene looked back at Ramon. "She's going to be nice to Mother, even if I have to bribe her to do it."

Ramon grinned sadly, walking up and kissing her cheek. "I won't be long, *mi querida*," he said, squeezing her arm. "Do not worry about anything but taking care of your mother. I will watch after the children."

Her eyes teared. "How can you be so good about this after the way she treated you?"

"She is your mother, perhaps not by blood, but she has loved you the same, and I know that in spite of some of the things she has done, you love her, too. Now go to her."

He quickly left, and Irene went into her mother's bedroom, a huge, high-ceilinged room decorated elegantly, with the most expensive carpeting and wallpaper, a French chandelier, gas lights and heat throughout the castlelike home. She thought how the outrageously ostentatious structure fit Bea Kirkland, but now Bea would never get to enjoy it.

She approached the huge, four-poster canopy bed; and for the first time in her life her mother looked small and frail. She almost gasped at the sight. This was not the Bea Kirkland she had always known. The woman's face was so pale, and dark circles surrounded her eyes. Her big-boned body was the same but had a slightly shriveled look to it. She realized Bea had looked thinner at her wedding, but to see how a person could change in just three days was shocking.

The woman opened her eyes as Irene came closer then. Bea managed a weak smile, opening her hand. Irene took it and sat down carefully on the edge of the bed. "What are you doing lying around like a lazy woman?" Irene tried to tease. "I thought you hated lazy people."

Bea took a deep, weary breath. "I guess . . . I should have been lazier myself over the years." She studied her daughter. "You look wonderful, Irene. You're happy, aren't you?"

Irene smiled through tears. "I'm very happy, Mother. I've loved Ramon most of my life."

Bea tried to squeeze her hand, but it was a weak gesture. "I know, Irene. And I . . . don't want to die with you . . . hating me . . . for keeping you apart. Ramon never told you . . . that I sent him away all those years ago, when he suddenly left Denver . . . did he?"

Irene frowned. "No. Wasn't it his choice?"

Bea blinked back tears. "Elly saw you kissing. She told me . . . and I thought then he was just a Mexican boy . . . taking advantage of my beautiful daughter. I went to him . . . threatened to take away his grandfather's ranch if he tried to keep seeing you. I was counting on . . . the Mexican pride in family. I knew . . . he wouldn't do something to hurt his grandfather."

Irene shook her head. "But . . . you still took the land a few years later."

"I've done a lot of things others might consider wrong, Irene. Maybe they were." The woman spoke slowly, as though every word was an effort. "I wish I could make up for some of them, especially for . . . hurting you, Irene. I thought Chad . . . would be so good for you . . . was so much more right for you. I've always . . . tried to do what was best for my children . . . and because of it I've lost their love."

A tear slipped out of one eye and down into her ear. Irene leaned closer. "You haven't lost my love, Mother. I know what a sacrifice you made in the early years, marrying a man you hardly knew, taking in his child and loving her as your own. I know you thought some of the things you did were best for us."

Bea sniffed, studying Irene lovingly. "Of the three children, I used to think you were least suited to taking over K-E, Irene. Now I can see . . . you are the best suited. I gave John . . . all that education . . . and he squandered it on whiskey. Elly is a selfish, rude, ungrateful child who would quickly destroy everything I worked so hard to build. Kirk doesn't care anymore, Irene. He's changed . . . ever since finding Yellow Eagle and losing him to death. When I'm gone . . . he'll carry on, but not with the enthusiasm we both once had. I've . . . put it in my will, Irene. When I'm gone, Kirk will remain chairman of the board . . . but you will be president of K-E."

Irene frowned in surprise. "*Me*! Mother, I have four children now, and Ramon and I want to have more."

Bea smiled. "My darling Irene. You . . . are everything I always wished I could be. If anyone can run a company . . . and still be a good, attentive mother . . . it's you. You have Ramon. I can see he will be a much bigger support than Kirk was for me. I . . . had to do it alone, Irene, except for Kirk handling the gold mines. I'm not . . . blaming him. It was something I wanted, but he didn't. Kirk never understood . . . the business end of it. Ramon has a thriving business of his own. He understands. He's a strong, intelligent man. Together with Ramon . . . you will make K-E stronger than ever. Just hire good men, Irene. Don't neglect the children . . . the way I did. Make time for your family. You . . . can do it."

"But, Mother—"

"You can do it, Irene. Just tell me you love me . . . that you forgive me for all the hurt I caused you."

Irene swallowed back a painful lump in her throat. "You know that I do, Mother."

Bea smiled sadly, looking around the room. "This house . . . I wanted it so badly. But Kirk . . . he won't want something so big once I'm gone . . . and this house doesn't fit you and Ramon. I suppose . . . it will be sold."

"In years to come, Mother, people will know who originally built it. The Kirkland name will always be well known in Denver. You'll probably be mentioned in history books."

Bea sighed deeply again. "Do you think so? I wonder . . . what Cynthia would think of that."

Irene fought an urge to break down in tears. "She will be outrageously jealous, Mother," she assured the woman, amazed that she still wondered about the mysterious cousin named Cynthia. "The Ritter name will never be mentioned generations from now, but yours will."

Bea closed her eyes, letting go of Irene's hand and putting her hand to her chest. "I want . . . to see Kirk."

"I'll get him," Irene told her, almost choking on the words. She hurried out to get her father, going into another bedroom to cry.

Kirk entered the bedroom warily, surprised that the thought of Bea dying left him feeling as if he were a lost little boy. He moved to the bed, leaning over her. "Bea?"

She looked up at him, smiling. "Do you know . . . what always irritated me most about you?" she asked. Kirk shook his head, his eyes tearing. "The way you always stayed so damn handsome," she told him, "while I just got uglier and fatter and older."

Kirk sniffed, quickly wiping at his eyes. "I never noticed that much."

"Of course you did." She frowned. "I always wondered . . . if you would grieve for me . . . like you did that O'Day woman. Now I see tears in your eyes."

"A man doesn't spend thirty-one years with a woman and not feel something when he thinks he's going to lose her," Kirk answered. He took one of her knobby, work-worn hands into his own. "God knows we've had our differences, Bea. But we gave them hell, didn't we? Denver might have gone the way of so many other ghost towns if not for us. It's been a rocky road, but we stayed together through it all, and we were good friends and business partners."

Her eyes teared more. "We were husband and wife, Kirk. I'm . . . so sorry that I could never be the kind of woman . . . you needed. It was always so hard for me . . . to express my love. But I did love you, Kirk. I have always loved you. It was just . . . something inside . . . I could never show it for fear of losing you, I guess. I've always been afraid . . . of losing something."

"I know. I loved you, too, in my own crazy way. So many times you made me so damn mad. But right now . . ." He sniffed. "I don't want to go on without you, Bea."

"You'll be just fine. Maybe you'll even marry . . . a woman who will make you truly happy."

He shook his head. "No. I won't marry again." A tear slipped down his cheek.

"So handsome," Bea said then. "I was always . . . so proud to call you my husband. I loved the jealous look . . . in other women's eyes."

He smiled bashfully, rubbing at her hand. "Thank you, Bea . . . for marrying me in the first place . . . for taking in Irene. You think you have a lot to be sorry for . . . but so do I. I should have told you Red knew. I should have told you about Yellow Eagle right from the beginning."

"It doesn't matter . . . anymore. Just keep the company alive, Kirk. Don't let everything I worked so hard for . . . be lost. Irene will help you."

"Don't worry about the company, Bea. Just try to get well."

"I'm not going to get well," she answered. "I just . . . want you to do something for me. I just want you to lie beside me . . . hold me. It's been such a long time . . . since you held me."

He turned away, wiping his eyes. He got up and removed his jacket and shoes, then went around the bed and crawled in beside her, pulling her into his arms. She settled against him. "When was the last time we made love, Kirk? Oh . . . such a long time ago . . . I can't even remember. I'm so sorry about that. So . . . sorry."

"Do you want me to go in with you?" Ramon asked.

Irene stared at the door to her mother's study. Elly was there, waiting to talk to her. Irene's remark to Ramon that he and Red might have to drag the woman here had turned out to be not so much of an exaggeration as she had thought. "No," she told Ramon. "I'll talk to her alone."

Ramon drew her into his arms. "I am here if you need me. I am sorry about your mother, Irene."

Her eyes teared, and she kissed him softly. "I know. Thank God I have you. I'm the one who's sorry, Ramon. I didn't plan for the first week of our marriage to turn out like this."

He held her close for a moment. "We knew it could happen soon. In a while it will be over, and we can get back to just being together."

"But she expects me to take over K-E. I don't know if I can handle all that, Ramon. I don't even want to."

"Irene." He pulled away, grasping her arms. "You can hire good men. I will help you. We will not let K-E take over our lives the way it did your mother's and father's. Now quit fretting about it and go and see Elly."

She smiled sadly, kissing his cheek quickly before leaving him. She entered the study to see Elly pacing nervously. She turned to face Irene then, standing as tall and overpowering as her mother once had. It was the first time they had seen each other since Irene first left Denver and divorced Chad. Irene was almost shocked at the hatred that spilled from Elly's dark eyes, thinking how it should be she who hated Elly. "What gives you the right to force me to come here?" Elly sneered.

Irene could hardly believe the words. "The fact that our mother is *dying* gives me the right. She's your *birth* mother, the woman who raised you and gave you everything you ever wanted."

"The woman who kept me from having Chad for myself—you and she both," Elly bit back. "To think that all the time Mother knew you were part *Indian*, that you weren't even hers by birth, yet to treat you as though you were the most beautiful, wonderful thing that ever happened to this family . . . it makes me sick! Don't you know how much I *hate* her, *and* you? And now—now you've chased Chad out of Denver just to turn around and marry your Mexican *lover*! You must be very thrilled that again you have everything you want while robbing me of everything *I* ever wanted!"

"Is that why you have refused to see me since I came back to Denver?"

"Of course it is!" She stepped closer. "I *loved* Chad! I'm sure John has told you all of it by now."

Irene met her eyes squarely. "Yes, he told me the lurid details of how my own sister was a whore to my husband!" Elly's eyes widened with indignation. "There is no other way to put it, Elly. A woman who would sleep with her own sister's husband deserves no respect. Perhaps you loved Chad, or thought you did; but I can guarantee Chad never loved you, because he was incapable of loving *anyone*! If he truly loved you he would not have left Denver, and you know it. As far as any unhappiness you have ever had, Elly, none of it was ever my fault. You brought it upon yourself!"

She thought for a moment Elly might hit her as she clenched her fists. She held her chin haughtily then. "I'm happy enough. Red built me a home nearly as grand as this one, and he buys me jewels and furs and anything else I want! We've been to Europe and San Francisco and New York, and we have entertained some of the most important people in the country."

Irene turned away, moving behind a desk. "I'm glad you think those things can make you happy, Elly. You carried on for years with my husband, as well as sleeping with half the men of Denver; you married poor Red for spite, a man you don't love at all; you have no children of your own and you've abandoned the only people who really love you."

Elly folded her arms. "No children? Maybe you should know I was pregnant once, dear sister—by Chad!" She watched Irene's eyes widen in shock. "Yes. When I went off to school I discovered I was pregnant."

"To school! You were only seventeen!"

Elly smiled. "That's right. And I had already been sleeping with Chad for three years, before you even *married* him! He was my first man. *I* had him *first*, Irene. What do you think of that?"

Irene struggled to keep her composure. Fourteen! To realize the extent of Chad's lurid infidelities, the extent of his lies and lust . . . how could she have been so blind, so trusting? "I think the most notorious prostitute in Denver might be considered an angel compared to you," she answered. She turned away, hardly able to look at her sister. "What happened to the baby?"

"I had an abortion. The man who did it botched it up and I had to have an operation that left me unable to have children. *That's* the reason I've never had any, dear sister. *That's* the sacrifice I made for Chad."

Irene shook her head. "I hardly think it was a sacrifice on your part. It only left you free to carry on with him without the worry of pregnancy." She finally faced her again. "Why didn't any of us know about it?"

"Because I didn't *want* you to know. The school, of course, was quite happy to keep it quiet." She set a parasol aside. "As far as Mother dying, you might guess I am not overly upset by it. At least now I can get back into K-E and run it *my* way. John certainly isn't capable, and you're too concerned about being the good mommy and wife. I'm the only one qualified."

Irene was suddenly happy over her mother's decision to put K-E in her hands. She had not wanted it, until now. "It so happens I *have* been put in charge," she told Elly calmly. "Mother already told me it's in her will. I am to be president of K-E."

She could almost hear thunder as Elly's face began to turn nearly purple with rage. "*You*! You aren't even her real daughter!"

"The few things she turned over to you, you lost. You don't know how to make money, Elly. You only know how to spend it."

"I won't stand for it! I'm a *Kirkland*!"

"That never seemed to matter to you before."

"I deserve a share of that company! I deserve to be in control of some of it!"

Irene smiled bitterly. "Are you afraid poor Red is going to run out of money? You told Mother once that you didn't need K-E, that you would wait for your inheritance. Father is still a healthy man, Elly. He could live another twenty years, and that's how long you will have to wait for some of the money, unless he cuts you out of his will. If you refuse to go see Mother and be civil and kind to her, he just might do it."

Elly nearly trembled with rage. "I won't do it! I *want* her to die knowing I hate her!"

Irene held her eyes, hardly able to believe her ears. "Maybe you do. But I'm not going to let that happen. You're going to go to Mother and tell her you're sorry for hurting her and that you love her. You'll do it, even if I have to bribe you. I'll give you a share of K-E, Elly. I'll sign over a couple of the mines, some of the businesses, one of the banks—put it all in your name, free and clear, if you'll go see Mother. We're big enough to. get along without some of our branches. That way you'll never have to answer to me for anything, and you'll never have to darken my doorway again, nor I yours."

"You'd actually sign part of the company over to me just to go tell Mother I love her?"

"I would. I'm sure Father would agree. Do *you* agree?"

Elly frowned in astonishment. "Don't you know Mother is the one who kept you and Ramon apart?"

"I know. And I know you're the one who told her you saw us kissing. Life is too short to carry hatred in our hearts forever, Elly. I will not let Mother die with a broken heart. She might not have handled things quite right, Elly, but she thought she was doing the best thing for us. I was old enough at the time to remember how she scrubbed clothes from dawn to dusk for over a year back in California, waiting for Father to find his gold. We owe everything we have to Mother, like it or not. And if you want any part of what she has left to us, you'll go to her right now and you'll make her *believe* that you love her. That shouldn't be hard for you. Like Chad, you've always been good at acting."

Elly stiffened. "All right," she said, holding her chin high again. "I'll go see her. But I want two of the warehouses and three of the supply stores. I want to sit down and see how the gold and silver mines are doing and I want the right to pick which ones I get to keep."

"Fine. It's the coal mines that are beginning to emerge as more important anyway."

"There will never be anything more important than gold and silver! I also want one of the banks—the Colorado State Bank, I think. And I want twenty-five percent of our stocks in the gas company and the railway companies. I also want the Kirkland Hotel and the theater—and the smelting plant. I need to see that at least *part* of K-E doesn't fall into the hands of that stupid Indian nephew of yours. The way things are going, nothing but Indians and Mexicans will run K-E someday, and I want no part of them!"

"Fine. We'll have to sign everything over later. Right now every minute counts. Mother is not expected to last through another night."

Elly drew in her breath, picking up her parasol. "Show me to her room then."

Irene just stared at her a moment, wondering how the girl managed to live with herself. "I am really sorry for you, Elly. I never hated you, you know. I wanted so much for us to be close, but you would never let it happen. I truly am sorry you always felt so left out and unloved. I felt that way myself sometimes, but I guess you thought it was just you."

Elly sniffed. "You've always led the life of a fairy princess. *You* don't know what unhappiness *is*! Now, if I must go and see Mother, let's get it over with." She turned and walked out in a huff, skirts rustling. Irene just stared after her a moment in disbelief. Ramon came into the study then.

"Are you all right, Irene?"

She closed her eyes. "I'm not sure." She turned away, and in the next moment Ramon had her in his arms. "My God, Ramon, she was sleeping with Chad before I even married him. She was only fourteen."

The room hung silent for a moment as Ramon just held her. He sighed deeply, kissing her hair. "It is done now, Irene. It cannot be changed, and you will not change the way she is, nor are you responsible for it. All that matters now is us, just us and the children."

She met his eyes, his dark, loving, true eyes. "Yes. That's all that matters." He met her lips, again erasing the ugly past, again renewing her strength and her trust in the future, a future that would see Irene Kirkland Jacobs Vallejo as the new president of Kirkland Enterprises.

The funeral for Beatrice Kirkland was one of the biggest Denver had ever seen. Not only was it attended by the governor of Colorado and the mayor of Denver, as well as the top representatives of Denver's most important businesses and industries; but it was also attended by the owners of many smaller businesses who were connected to or dependent on Kirkland Enterprises. Mining representatives, as well as miners themselves, many of them friends of Kirk's, railroad executives, reporters and many people from the general public also went.

People overflowed the church and formed a huge parade through the Denver Bea Kirkland had helped build, a Denver that was plagued with the problems of city growing too fast. It bore the many signs of proud progress, four- and five-story brick buildings, hotels, theaters, restaurants, churches, shops, industries, schools, trolley cars, and now men were working on bringing in telephones.

But there were many drawbacks to the city's burgeoning population, which had grown in only ten years from five thousand to nearly thirty-six thousand. The streets were still not bricked, and dust rolled over the sad procession that made its way to the city graveyard. Black smoke and coal dust from smelters on the north side of town darkened the air, the streets were still much too littered, and when the wind was just right, the smell of raw sewage that was dumped into the Platte River stung the nostrils. A city-wide sewer system was sorely needed, a project Bea had been working on before she died. Irene was determined now to finish it.

Men walked ahead of the funeral procession shoveling up horse dung from the street, and in the distance one could hear the whistles and clatter of trains moving in and out of Union Station. Various gangs of homeless children stared at the "rich lady's" funeral from alleys, as did many of Denver's poverty-stricken adults. Irene caught sight of some of them as the carriage in which she rode with Kirk, Ramon, and the children made its way behind the hearse. She vowed that now that Bea was gone, she would donate more money to shelters to help the growing numbers of jobless people who had come to Denver to find their dream, only to discover it was a mirage. Some, especially Denver's Italians, were left jobless by the hundreds after being hired by the railroad, then let go once the railroad projects were finished. Irene wanted to do more to make hospitals and schools available to the poor as well as the rich, and to continue to help erase prejudice against foreigners and their exploitation by big business. K-E had been one of the worst, and she intended to change that.

There was so much to do, but she reminded herself she had Ramon. He and Kirk would help her hire more men to run the daily business, but she had promised her mother she would protect K-E, and she was determined to do just that.

She stared at the hearse in front of her, vowing she would never let K-E take control of her life, that she would never become a Bea Kirkland. She loved her mother, in spite of the things she had done, but she did not want to be like her. "I'm sorry, Mother," she whispered.

Red and Elly rode in their own carriage behind them, and John rode in yet another. The procession of carriages and people on foot stretched for several blocks along Larimer Street, past new K-E offices, past many K-E businesses, including the first bank Bea had ever founded, one that had survived both the fire and the flood.

They reached the graveyard, where Elly and John stood on one side of the black hole that would hold their mother, Elly wearing a black veil that was not necessary, for there were no tears in her eyes. John just stared at the coffin, shivering for a drink, tears coming to his eyes only out of a longing to cry out to his mother and ask her why she had never tried to understand what he really wanted out of life, why she never understood that in the early years he had done what she wanted just to please her and win her approval. But he had never pleased her. He had only disappointed her. What his mother had begun destroying in the beginning, he had finished destroying with liquor, on which he had been totally dependent to soothe the inner wounds since before leaving for college. Liquor was his life now, all he cared about, liquor and the women of Old Colorado City, who made him feel important.

He glanced over at Irene, loving her, admiring her strength. Irene had become the backbone of the family, and he was more than happy to see K-E fall into her and Ramon's hands. He was glad she was finally happy, married to the man she had always loved.

Irene turned to Kirk, placing her arm around his waist. He put his arm around her shoulders, and she felt him shudder with silent tears. The minister spoke his eulogy, people expressed their sympathy and headed for the Kirkland mansion for food and visiting. Elly hurried after them, anxious to get away from the depressing grave, eager to put on a show of the grieving daughter.

John stared at the coffin a moment longer, then broke into tears and walked away.

Kirk and Irene remained beside the grave. "I figured she'd be around long after me," Kirk said brokenly then. "She was always so strong, like an unbending steel post. I never realized how much I really needed her, Irene." He rubbed at her shoulder. "Don't ever let things come between you and Ramon, especially the company."

"I won't, Father."

He sniffed, reaching out to touch the coffin. "Thirty-one years," he sobbed. "We . . . sure had our fights . . . but in a lot of ways we had a hell of a good time. I never dreamed . . . when I brought a little baby Indian girl to a young woman I hardly knew back in Kansas . . . that it would all turn out like this. I never thought we'd build a city . . . with practically our own two hands. She wanted so much . . . and I wanted so little." He shook his head. "I just . . . can't believe she's gone. I can't imagine walking into K-E without her being there. I'm going to see her . . . everyplace I go, hear those skirts rustling . . . hear her complaining. Would you believe a man could miss a complaining woman?"

She smiled through tears "Yes. I can believe it."

He placed a rose on top of the coffin, one he had carried from the church and which was beginning to wilt. "Good-bye, Bea."

Irene noticed a bouquet of flowers at the grave she didn't remember from the church, although there had been so many it would have been easy to miss one. Out of curiosity she leaned down to read the card: "In deepest sympathy from Uncle Jake and Aunt Marlene Ritter, Cousins Charley and Cynthia, Kansas City."

"My God," Irene whispered.

CHAPTER
FORTY

January 1888

Irene stood holding two-month-old Miguel as she peered out at the raging blizzard. She hoped that seventeen-year-old David, who was up at Colorado State University at Fort Collins, was safe and warm, and she was glad for the marvelous invention of the telephone. She would try calling him later this afternoon, when he was finished with classes.

She walked over and turned up an oil lamp, thinking how nice it was going to be when they finally had electricity here at the ranch. Denver and other foothill communities had long ago changed from gas lights to electric lights, and now electricity was being used for many other purposes, replacing steam power.

Ramon had brought her here to the ranch to give her a long rest after giving birth to Miguel, the sixth child Irene had delivered since marrying Ramon eleven years ago. Two of the six had died, one at birth, the other, a little boy, of measles at two years old. Their little graves were not far from the ranch house, and Irene tried not to dwell on their deaths, but rather to be happy for those who had lived. Combined with her own children and Ramon's son, as well as little Sam and one other adopted child, Irene and Ramon had nine living children. Irene had no doubt there would be even more before her child-bearing years were over.

Eight of those children were with them now at the ranch, while

David was up at Colorado State. The winter winds kept them inside, and she turned to watch them playing in the great room, thinking how fast time passed, how rapidly things had changed in the twenty-nine years since she and her family had first come to settle in the little log community along Cherry Creek in '59.

Denver was a huge city of a hundred thousand people now, not drifters and miners, but stable, stationary citizens. K-E remained a huge enterprise, but other industries and businesses had moved in, and new antitrust laws were making it difficult to hold a monopoly. A good share of K-E had been broken down into smaller companies, some of the businesses sold, and several of the gold mines now sat idle, most of the precious ore already taken from their bowels. In some respects Irene was glad for the changes. She had discovered many questionable acquisitions and borderline-legal moves on the part of K-E, and she wanted no part of them. She had made the company reputable and had even made amends with a few businessmen who had been scalded by K-E.

So many things had changed. The huge Kirkland "castle" had been sold to one of the many new businessmen who'd come to Denver, which now attracted the very wealthy from many parts of the country. Kirk lived in a suite at the Denver Inn, still working at K-E, but not with the enthusiasm he once held.

"Now be fair," Irene spoke up then to thirteen-year-old Sharron, who sat playing checkers with twelve-year-old Sam. Alex, also twelve, sat near the fireplace carving a piece of wood. He had inherited his father's talent, and already talked about joining Vallejo Construction as soon as his schooling was finished. David wanted to be a teacher.

What the rest of the children did with their lives was still undecided, most of them too young to really know. Eduardo was ten, Elena seven, Anna three, the two daughters named after Ramon's dead wives. The new son in her arms had been named after Ramon's grandfather.

And then there was eleven-year-old Ben, whom Ramon and Irene had adopted off the streets of Denver in 1882, when he was only five. He was a little Italian boy who didn't even know his last name. Joblessness, prejudice, and segregation had grown rampant in Denver, and Irene and Ramon were doing what they could to help. Chinese riots in 1880 had led to bloodshed and hangings, and now most of the Chinese had fled Denver. But there were still too many homeless children running the streets.

In his quest to help curb the problem, Ramon had built an orphanage, his own labor and nearly all material donated free of charge, to provide a home for the children who ran wild through Denver's alleys, a home where children of all races could find shelter. Slowly but surely the wealthy white community began to understand. Something had to be done or Denver would suffer the shame of it, as well as suffer from the rising crime rate.

The last eleven years had been hectic, what with all the changes in the company, building the orphanage, Ramon's busy schedule. Denver was now the warehousing center of the West, and K-E still held a warehousing monopoly. Denver had a sewer system now, and efforts were being made to try to clean up the Platte River. A new college had been built in Colorado Springs, which was now also a fast-growing city giving Denver a run for its money, but Irene was confident Denver would remain the Queen City of the West. The city now had parks, a museum, and a baseball team. There were annual fairs, rodeos, and horse races; Elitch's Gardens offered roller coaster and carousel rides, and even a zoo for children, as well as concerts, operas, and plays for the older people.

Along with rapid growth and progress, Denver had had its share of scandal. Bill Byers had been shot at in the street by an angry "other woman" with whom he had been having an affair. The scandal had cost Byers a Republican nomination for Governor of Colorado.

And there was the shocking scandal of H. A. W. Tabor, the silver baron who had come to Denver to build the grand Windsor Hotel, which not only had the elevator and the ballroom floor hung on cables that Ramon had told Irene had been proposed years ago, but even had a swimming pool and steam baths. Before coming to Denver, Tabor had built a firehouse, an opera house, a street railway and a telephone company in Leadville. Now a Denver citizen, besides the Windsor Hotel, Tabor also had a magnificent mansion in Kirkland Hills and had hired Ramon to build an opera house in Denver. The theater sported carved Japanese cherry-wood, huge French mirrors, a chrystal chandelier in the entryway, embroidered silk draperies, one wall of stained glass, and a huge picture of himself that he had put up to replace a picture of Shakespeare.

Tabor had left the wife who had supported him through their years of poverty and then modest wealth to marry a young blond divorcée named Elizabeth McCourt Doe, called Baby Doe by most.

The Baby Doe and the Byers scandals were not the only sources of gossip for Denver citizens. Elly Kirkland McKinley had also provided news when she was caught by her husband, Red McKinley, in bed with the president of a railroad supply company. The divorce, two years ago now, had been so scandalous that Irene had retreated to the ranch with the children to get away from probing reporters. Elly had committed a grave error in demanding years ago that parts of K-E be put directly into her name, an even graver error in testing Red's patience to the point of divorce. Property laws were in Red's favor, especially since it was Elly who had committed adultery. Elly had lost nearly all her holdings, which had been awarded to Red. She had taken what little money she had remaining and had left Denver, announcing to Irene before she left that she was going to try to find Chad.

Irene wondered what her mother would think of Red McKinley now owning a good share of what once belonged to K-E. How strange that the people she had tried hardest to destroy, Ramon and Red, were now rich, powerful men who, after Kirk's death, would between them own all of K-E. She kissed little Miguel, remembering again Kirk's explanation of the Indian belief in the circle of life. It was so true. Things always seemed to come around and catch up with themselves.

"When can we go outside and play, Mother?" Eduardo asked. "I'm tired of playing with my counting beads."

Irene looked out the window again, a sickening dread moving into her soul at the horrible wind and blinding snow outside. The cattle! They had lost so many the previous year in the record forty-below temperatures. Now this. This was no ordinary storm. It had descended upon the plains in a matter of minutes, the day beginning with a calm, warm morning. In the last hour the temperature had dropped nearly one degree per minute.

"There will be no playing outside today," she told the boy. "I don't want to see any of you outside. Is that understood? It's much too dangerous. This is a very bad storm, children. You'll just have to keep yourselves occupied in the house until this is over."

Ramon came into the great room then, smiling as he weaved his way among the seven children who sat scattered across the floor. "If David were here and that little one in your arms were on the floor, I could not get to you without stepping on a body," he joked.

Irene smiled as he came closer, putting his arms around Irene and Miguel and kissing Irene softly. Irene wondered how she would have survived the past eleven years of changes without Ramon, who had remained steadfast and true, her friend, her magnificent lover, a dependable father and a capable business-man. "Did you finish your blueprints?" she asked him.

He turned with her to look out at the storm. "*Sí*, I am done. But how am I going to get back to Denver to present them to the man who asked for them? I have a feeling the little vacation we decided to take here at the ranch will turn into something much longer than we planned."

"I'm a little worried about David."

"He will be fine. He is inside those brick buildings at the university with many others around him. We are the ones who are isolated. If this keeps up, we'll be pinned down here for days."

"We have plenty of wood and plenty of food." She kissed the baby again. "It might even be fun for us and the children, a chance to really be together. It's just that I'm worried about the cattle, Ramon. Most of them are out there on the range with no protection. This could be a disaster for the ranch."

At times like this she couldn't help thinking about Hank, wondering what he would do. Her eyes teared. "This ranch is the only part of K-E I've ever really cared about."

Ramon rubbed at her shoulder. "Irene, when this is over and the snow is gone, the land will still be here."

"But so much has changed. So much has interfered with the cattle industry already. The government has forced us to break up and sell off some of the land, farmers are putting up that awful barbed wire—"

"Irene, I said the land, all the land that still belongs to you, will still be here. If the cattle business is becoming too complicated, then do something else with the land. Your mother once farmed potatoes on part of this land. Why not do something like that with it again?"

She watched the snow rapidly piling up under the window. "It's strange that you should say that. I've been thinking about that very thing, but I didn't know what you would think of it."

"Growing potatoes?"

"No. Sugar beets."

Ramon grinned. "Sugar beets?"

"Sugar beets have become big business in Colorado. K-E even owns a mill for processing them. Why not grow them ourselves, in addition to buying them from other farmers. We could build *another* mill, gradually make sugar beets one of K-E's biggest assets instead of beef. We could still raise Palominos, and some beef." She shivered. "At least if we lost a crop, we wouldn't be losing precious life. When you lose a cattle crop, you're talking about a lot of poor, dead animals."

He smiled sadly, stroking her hair. "You are like your mother sometimes, thinking about ways to improve K-E. But your mother would not have thought that losing cattle was sad. She would think only of the monetary loss."

"We have already lost so many, but we're still thriving. I don't need to own it all the way Mother did."

He rubbed at her neck. "I know. By the way, isn't it time for Miguel's morning nap?"

She sighed. "Yes. I've already fed him."

"Then come away from the window and stop fretting. You cannot stop the storm, so you might as well try to think about something else."

She agreed, turning to go to their bedroom, where they kept little Miguel's bassinet. She heard dear, dependable Rose talking to the children then, offering to read to them, trying to find a way to keep them occupied. The bedroom door closed as she lay Miguel down for his nap. Ramon came over to put his arms around her from behind. Because of the weather Irene had not even gotten dressed yet, and still wore her satin robe. Ramon slipped a hand inside it to caress one milky-full breast gently, feeling a trace of wetness at her nipple.

"Ramon, I have to get dressed. The children are all up."

"Rose is watching after them. We will be snowed in for days. There will be plenty of time to spend with the children."

She smiled. "We can't do something this hour of the morning."

"Is there a law stating when a man can make love to his beautiful wife?"

She closed her eyes as he pushed her hair aside and began kissing her neck. He pulled the robe away and kissed at her shoulders. After eleven years she still could not resist his touch. He had remained romantic and persuasive, still a virile, handsome man at forty-seven. She was proud that at forty-two she was still beautiful, at least in Ramon's eyes. After bearing a total of nine children, including the three who had died, her waist was a little thicker, and her breasts and hips bore stretch marks, but none of that seemed to matter to Ramon. With each child she always worried she would lose her ability to please him sexually, but every time they had intercourse after another child, Ramon seemed to fill her to ecstasy. She supposed that what youth and firmness she had lost through childbirth, they both made up for in simple love and desire that seemed to help them overcome any physical changes. Now, after a long recovery from giving birth to Miguel, she wondered if that would again remain true.

He pulled her robe open. "The bed is not made yet," he told her softly. "I came to bed last night late and tired, and you were already asleep, so I did not disturb you." She breathed deeply as a strong hand moved over her belly. "We have not made love in nearly four months, Irene. Do you think you are finally healed and recovered enough from Miguel's birth?"

She turned, moving her arms around him. "I always think each time that we'll be able to abstain so there won't be any more children for a while." She leaned back, looking up at him and smiling. "But what God wants us to have, He will give us, Ramon. I waited too many years for you. I don't intend to waste one moment of these years we've had finally to be together."

He met her lips. "It is the same for me," he told her between kisses. "But I worry, after what happened with Anna. If something happened to you in giving birth, I would blame myself."

"No, Ramon." She touched his hair. "It would be just as much my fault, because I want and need to be one with you as much as you need it. If I can't make love with my Ramon, I might as well not even be breathing."

He picked her up and laid her on the bed, then stood up and removed his clothes. Already that most manly part of him was swollen in magnificent desire. He climbed into bed beside her, smothering her with kisses as his fingers began to work their magic, urging forth the silken juices that helped him slide his fingers inside of her to prepare her for what was to come.

This was always an anxious moment for her, the first time after having another child. He sensed her fear of pain, her bigger fear of not pleasing him, and he searched her mouth suggestively as he gently probed her lovenest, awakening the wonderful urges he was always able to bring forth so magically. He moved on top of her then, carefully entering her, knowing by her gasp that he had brought her some pain, but that he also could still fill her to her satisfaction. She did not realize that he had his own fears of not pleasing her after so many children, but always both their fears were alleviated with that first intercourse that told them nothing had been lost.

They moved in sweet rhythm, their love as strong and beautiful as ever, their desire as intense as that first night of their marriage. Understandably, with their busy schedules, their many children, and the years they had been together, they did not do this as often as they had that first year of marriage; but when they did make love, it was just as thrilling, just as exotic and fulfilling as ever.

He surged deep inside her, and the groan of the wicked winter wind outside died away for both of them. They were warm and cozy, their bodies soon heated to a steamy sweat, as they both discovered this most important part of their marriage was as good and sweet as ever. Little Miguel had not changed a thing.

The blizzard of '88 became known as the "schoolchildren's storm," since it hit during the middle of a schoolday and trapped many prairie children in their remote one-room school buildings. Many died trying to get home; some teachers became heroines for finding ways to protect the children from the horrible cold, even if it meant burning school desks for heat.

It was the worst winter storm the United States had ever seen. Many lives were lost, both human and animal. The B&K lost ninety percent of their cattle, and the following spring the air was filled with the stench of thawing carcasses. The storm had virtually put an end to the era of ranching magnates and the overabundance of beef. Some big ranchers did not even know how many cattle they owned. Several of the most powerful ranchers went bankrupt.

Irene refused to fold. Her mother would not have given up, and neither would she. She turned to sugar beets, and within two years the B&K was a thriving sugar beet farm, and whenever she visited Hank's grave, she could not help wondering what he would think of what she had done. She was almost glad now that he had not lived to see the kind of life he had loved most slowly fall away to new government regulations, farmers, and the terrible blizzard. A good deal of Colorado's eastern plains remained cattle country, but the industry would never know the tremendous power and success it had enjoyed in the sixties and seventies and early eighties.

In 1890 Denver was a thriving metropolis, with buildings now rising to seven and eight stories, electricity lighting the entire city, telephones connecting them to Wall Street. Churches became more numerous, finally meeting the strong competition of the saloons, and prostitution had been outlawed. The population rose to one hundred thirty-five thousand, and street cars were run by electric cables instead of horses.

The Dawes Act of 1887 had brought more devastation to the Indians. The government had ruled that reservations should be broken up into parcels of land to be awarded each Indian family outright, to be farmed. The idea was to civilize the American Indian and bring him gradually into white society. As Kirk once predicted in an angry fit when the law was passed, it was a dismal failure. No one in Washington understood the Indian's nature, that it was not in the Indian's blood to be a cultivator. He was a hunter. His social form of living was communal, not individual. No Indian wanted to become a homesteader. The average Plains Indian gave no thought to tomorrow, did not know how to plan ahead and still did not know how to farm.

Landgrabbers and speculators took advantage of the act, easily convincing many Indians to sell them their parcel of land for whiskey, food, and beads. In a single year the total acreage of Indian lands was reduced by 12 percent. Some Indians were allowed to lease their land, which real estate developers would rent for eight to ten cents an acre, then turn around and lease to white farmers for one to two dollars an acre, making huge profits while the Indians who had leased the land originally were left shiftless and homeless. More and more turned to whiskey to drown their sorrows, and in 1890 the Sioux came upon one last hope—the Ghost Dance religion—by which they believed that one day soon their ancestors would all rise, as would the buffalo, and they would be strong again and would chase the white man out of their land.

This belief, and the wild dancing that accompanied the new religion, led to new fears of an Indian uprising and to misunderstandings that culminated at Wounded Knee, South Dakota, in December of that year, when soldiers massacred over two hundred Sioux, mostly women and children. It was considered the last great Indian "uprising," the last Indian "battle."

Fifteen-year-old Samuel was already planning to go to college to become a teacher, like twenty-year-old David, who now taught black children in Denver. Samuel intended to go and teach on what was left of the reservations, to help his people learn how to take care of themselves so that they would not be financially raped by land grabbers and developers.

"They need their own schools instead of being sent away from their families," he often lamented. "They need teachers of their own race, so they feel they can trust them. They need someone who understands white society like I do, but who also understands how they think and feel."

Samuel was just one small, bright hope for his people, and Kirk could not be prouder of his grandson, glad that indirectly, through Samuel, he would one day be back with the Sioux and Cheyenne, that he would be doing something to help them. He thought what a wonderful job Ramon and Irene had done with all their children, how he could go to his grave knowing K-E and what was left of his family would be in good hands.

In 1892 Irene bore her last child by Ramon. Complications left it impossible for her to bear any more children, something that grieved her but relieved Ramon, who worried that giving birth in her forties was much too dangerous. They could enjoy their love now without the constant fear of losing another child, or losing Irene. The little boy she delivered, who they named Ernesto was healthy; and once Irene got over the depression that followed the child's birth, Ramon convinced her that her condition was God's way of telling them enough was enough. Counting their own children as well as those they had brought to the marriage, the adopted boy Ben and Yellow Eagle's son, Sam, their children now numbered ten.

Irene was recovered and healthy again when yet another tragedy struck in 1893, and K-E, Denver and Colorado, indeed, the whole country, was put to the test by a stock market crash and a severe depression. The collapse of a major British banking house caused thousands of British investors to sell their American securities, which put a drain on America's gold reserve, as well as hitting Denver hard, since the area banked heavily on British investments. The stock market collapsed, and to make matters worse for Colorado, the government voted to go to the gold standard, undercutting Colorado's now-primary staple—silver. Besides the U.S. Treasury's halt to buying silver, India, a great consumer of the metal, stopped making silver coins.

Silver mines closed overnight. As in '73, many businessmen committed suicide. Silver barons, like H. A. W. Tabor, crashed into ruin, losing everything, and unemployed miners flooded into Denver. Kirk, Irene, and Ramon were forced to meet with K-E representatives to determine just which businesses could stay afloat and which could not. Ramon's contracting business came to a temporary standstill, and only sound investments and substantial savings would help them get through yet more hard times.

Several of K-E's important holdings in Colorado Springs were lost, due mostly to John's careless handling and poor bookkeeping. When the panic of '93 hit, they discovered some of the southern holdings were much deeper in debt than anyone had realized. Irene blamed herself, for not keeping a closer eye on John. She had thought he was doing better. After all, he was forty-five years old. He had been running things at Colorado

Springs, albeit with help, for over twenty-three years now. But not long after the crash of the stock market, they received a telegram from K-E Colorado Springs, telling of the losses, as well as informing them that John had stopped coming to work all together. It was decided that in spite of how busy the family was with the financial crisis, someone had better go and talk to John. Irene insisted it should be she, since she was usually the only one John would listen to.

"I have a terrible feeling about this," she told Ramon when she boarded the train at Union Station.

He squeezed her hands. "Just remember that we have all tried to help John over the years, especially you. His problems come from the inside, Irene, not anything we have done. It's the drinking." He kissed her tenderly. "I love you. Everything is going to be all right."

Her eyes teared. "Everything is such a mess, Ramon. What if we lose it all?"

"Irene, we are not going to lose it all. Remember what your father told you . . . and even your mother before she died. Do not let K-E take over your life. Whether the company thrives or crumbles, it does not matter. We still have each other, the children, our love. That is all we ever need. Always remember that."

His words stuck in her mind as the Denver and Rio Grande rumbled its way south, past fields of sugar beets, one part of K-E that had remained stable. She looked across the plains, trying to remember how many years ago she had ridden out there with Hank, rounding up cattle . . . twenty-three years! Had Hank really been dead that long? She still could not think of that time in her life without remembering the horror of life with Chad, and she pushed it all away. Ramon was right. They had each other. That was all that mattered.

The train came into the station at Colorado Springs, and Irene rented a buggy to John's apartment in the Kirkland Hotel. He was not there. The desk clerk caught sight of her as she came from his room and called out to her. She thought he looked rather pale and shaken as she came closer. "You're looking for your brother, Mrs. Vallejo?" the man asked.

"Yes. Do you know where he is?"

The man sighed, his eyes looking misty. "I'm sorry, ma'am. Some men from K-E came looking for him yesterday, too. He'd been gone for four or five days. One of them came back in here just this morning to tell me they found John. He's at the hospital.

I'm afraid . . . they don't expect him to live. I expect by now they've wired K-E up in Denver. You must have just missed the news on your way down."

Irene felt her heart tighten. John. In spite of all his faults and weakness, he had remained a loving brother. "What happened?" she asked.

"Well, ma'am, it seems he went on quite a binge in Old Colorado City. You, uh, you know how he drinks. The men I talked to think it was the depression that set him off . . . losing so much of K-E. He blamed himself. I guess he got to drinking and couldn't quit. Reports from Old Colorado City are that he was gambling, running with the . . . well, the loose women . . . and getting into fights. He was found in an alley . . . stabbed. It's not likely they'll ever find out who did it. They took what was left of his money, even took his clothes."

Irene closed her eyes, horrible grief welling up inside her. John! What a hideous way for his life to end! So unhappy. He had always been so unhappy. "Thank you," she said quietly, walking on shaking legs back outside and ordering the driver to take her to the hospital. How she got through the next few hours, she was not sure. She only wished she had Ramon with her.

At the hospital she discovered the rumored diagnosis was true. John was not expected to live much longer. She went into his room, wanting to cry out at his sick, grayish-yellow coloring. The doctor told her someone had stabbed him with a good-size knife, cutting deep into his bowels and kidneys. There was no hope.

Drawing on that strange, deep strength that always seemed to come forward to help her through a crisis, she approached the bed, leaning over her brother and touching his brow. "John?"

He opened bloodshot eyes and managed a half grin. "Hey, sis." It was all he managed to get out.

"I'm right here, John. I love you." She gently took hold of his hand, and he managed to squeeze hers, letting her know he was aware of her presence. For several minutes nothing was said. He was dying, and they both knew it. He only needed to know she was there. Memories stabbed at Irene's heart, memories of her and John and Ramon talking and laughing at the old mansion when she first met Ramon; of John talking with her after she married Chad, telling her he would never tell anyone she still loved Ramon; of the day he had come into her room and held her after Hank had been killed. John had always understood, always looked out for her.

"Mother . . . she'd sure . . . rail me for . . . this," he

suddenly spoke up in a raspy voice. "But . . . she wouldn't . . .
realize this is . . . because of her."

"John, Mother loved you. She couldn't have stopped you in
your later years if you wanted to do something else with your life.
It's the whiskey that did this to you, not Mother."

"She's . . . the reason I drank . . . then I couldn't stop. Sorry
I disappointed you . . . Irene. . . . Glad . . . at least . . . you
are happy . . . now." He grimaced then, clasping her hand so
tightly that it hurt. "My God . . . the pain," he groaned then, a tear
slipping out of his eye. The words tore at Irene's heart.

"I'm right here, John."

He breathed in deep groans for a moment before answering.
"You're . . . always here for me. You're the best one, Irene. I'm
glad K-E . . . is in your hands . . . Ramon's. . . . Hope
Mother . . . knows Red . . . got his share, too. Elly . . . she
got what she deserved . . . nothing. I wish it all could have been
different. I should have . . . defied Mother. I . . . should have
been . . . a carpenter." He started crying. "That's . . . all
I . . . wanted to do."

"John, you still can. If you can just pull through this, Ramon
will help you any way he can. You know that. We'll all help you
stop drinking and you can do whatever you want with your life."

He grimaced again, squeezing her hand as though desperate.
"My God . . . I see her," he groaned. He suddenly smiled, and
his eyes opened. An amazing, peaceful look came upon his face.
"Mama," he whispered.

The breath wheezed out of him then, and Irene sensed there was
suddenly no life in his hand. She leaned forward and closed his
eyes. "Good-bye, John, my good, sweet brother," she said softly.
She lay her head on his shoulder and wept.

Kirk was inconsolable. His only other living son was dead now,
and he felt partially responsible, blaming himself for never being
able to get close to John. It was a bleak time for Irene, with the
depression taking its toll on the business and John's death taxing
her emotional stamina. Through it all there was Ramon. Always
there was Ramon.

John was buried beside his mother, in the same graveyard
where the first baby Irene lost was buried, where Ramon's first
two wives and his little son were buried, where Mary O'Day was
buried, after dying in the Denver fire back in '63 . . . and where
Susan Stanner rested in peace. The newspaper had been polite

about how John died, not mentioning he had been on a drunken binge, but most people suspected.

It was two hours before Irene and Ramon could convince Kirk to leave the grave. Kirk was seventy-two years old now, still a strong, imposing man for his age, but suddenly seeming to age considerably after the economic collapse and John's death.

"Bea and I . . . we had it all once, didn't we," he groaned. "Look at what it got us. I have two dead sons, and a wayward daughter I'll probably never see again." He turned to Irene, tears staining his face. "But then there's you. When I think of you, Irene, I know everything is going to be all right."

He sniffed and wiped at his eyes.

"You'd better come home and rest, Kirk," Ramon told the man. "You come to our house. You shouldn't go back to that hotel suite alone."

Kirk shook his head. "No. I'm not going back to either place. I've made up my mind." He looked at Irene again, seeing the fear in her eyes. "I'm going to be all right, Irene. I'm going back to the mountains, deep into the Rockies, beyond the mining towns, beyond civilization."

"Father—"

He put a finger to her lips. "It's something I need to do, Irene. You should understand that better than anyone. I'm going back to my mountains, and I'm going to live the way I used to live, before all this." He waved his arm in the direction of downtown Denver. "I want to remember what it was like before men like me allowed this to happen . . . what it was like when it was just the Indians, and trappers like myself. I'm going to the mountains, and nobody is going to stop me."

"Father, you aren't the young man who once roamed around out there. You know how cold it gets up there, how thin the oxygen is, how dangerous that country can be."

"I damn well *do* know, and I remember how to take care of myself." His eyes teared anew. "Irene, I don't want to die down here in a city. It's true I helped build it, but only because I wanted to stay here, wanted to please your mother. It's done now, and K-E is in good hands. I've done all I can do for this town. It's somebody else's turn now, and I'm tired. All I ever wanted was to be in those mountains, and I've been afraid I'd never get the chance to go back. Now I'm going to do it. Please understand. If I *do* die up there, I'll die a hell of a lot happier than if I die here."

"Let him go, Irene," Ramon told her. "You know that he is right."

Irene broke into tears, embracing her father. "Take me with you," she sobbed. "You never took me back to the mountains like you promised, Father."

His arms came around her, and he smiled sadly as he patted her shoulder. "No, I never did, did I? But I think you will find your own way in those mountains one day. You'll go, Irene, and when you do, you'll know that I am with you." He noticed an eagle fly overhead then, and he pulled away, pointed to it. "Look up there, Irene."

All the children who were lined up beside Ramon, some of them crying, looked up at the bird their grandfather had pointed out.

"It's an eagle—a good sign. The sign of the eagle means everything is going to be all right. It's good luck, especially to an Indian, and most all of you children have Indian blood."

Irene met his eyes. "Once you go, you won't be back, will you," she said quietly, more a statement than a question. "I'll never see you again."

Kirk touched her face. "Maybe not, but I'll always be with you, Irene. Every time the mountains cast their shadow across Denver, I'll be watching over things. You can't bury a man's spirit, Irene, only his body. His spirit lives on, in the things he loved, and in his children and grandchildren."

He pulled her close, and the eagle let out an almost piercing call, as though to beckon those to whom the land truly belonged. Sam looked up at the magnificent bird, thinking about his grandfather's words. Yes, perhaps spirits did live on. Perhaps the spirit of his father, Yellow Eagle, lived in that beautiful bird that floated above him. He was seventeen now. Soon he would get his college degree and he would go and teach his people. It was surely true, then, about the circle of life. He would go back to his own, and his grandfather would go back to the mountains from which he had come.

CHAPTER
FORTY-ONE

All the children were present for Ernesto's first birthday August 30, 1893. Irene hired a photographer to take a family portrait. She sat near the fireplace of Ramon's beautiful Spanish-style home, which they both had shared in Denver for sixteen years now, sixteen of the happiest years of Irene's life, in spite of the problems with K-E, with Elly, in spite of John's death, and her mother's. She knew now she could bear anything life handed to her, because she had Ramon . . . and the children.

She held little Ernesto on her lap, and Ramon, now turned fifty, stood behind her, still handsome and virile, the touch of gray at his temples only making him look more distinguished. Irene, forty-seven, had a fuller, but still lovely, well-rounded figure. Her hair was showing only slight touches of silver-gray, and there were a few tiny lines about her eyes. But what age tried to take away from her, elegance, kindness, and sophistication made up for. She was a woman who needed to love and be loved, and Ramon and the family they had raised together fulfilled all the needs that had been denied her in her early years.

The children took their various places, according to size and age: David, twenty-two; Sharron, eighteen; Alejandro, nearly eighteen; Samuel, seventeen, his hair still shoulder-length; Eduardo, fifteen; Elena, twelve; Anna, eight; Miguel, five; one-year-old Ernesto on Irene's lap; and the adopted son, Ben, now sixteen, sitting to Irene's left.

Irene was proud of her ten children, her heart longing for the three she had lost. David was teaching now, and Alejandro was working with his father at Vallejo Construction. Samuel was preparing for college and would leave them to teach on a reservation when his schooling was finished. Sharron was a rare beauty, a well-schooled, elegant, exotically beautiful young woman who lately had developed an attraction to Alejandro that was more than sisterly. The two of them had completely different sets of parents, so Ramon and Irene had no objection to the sudden new love Ramon's son and Irene's daughter had found. They both well knew how deep and abiding young love could be, and they were not about to make the mistake with their children that had kept them apart when they were young.

Irene refused to compel any of the children to become active with K-E. She had long ago determined that if none of them wanted anything to do with the company, then it would simply be sold off at her death. Her own mother's driving determination to devote everything to K-E, and her insistence that her children do the same, had destroyed John and Elly, and had nearly destroyed Irene. David showed some interest, as did Ben and Eduardo, and both worked part-time for the company; but Irene made sure it was solely of their own free will. She wondered sometimes, always smiling at the thought, what her mother would think if she knew that someday K-E might belong to a man fathered by Hank Loring, one fathered by Ramon Vallejo, and another having absolutely no blood relation to either Ramon or Irene, a man who had once been a poor, orphaned street urchin who could only dream of such riches.

The photographer snapped the photograph, the flash powder exploding and making some of the children scream and laugh. Ernesto started crying, and Irene held him close and patted his bottom. Someone knocked at the door, and Rose answered it, ushering Red McKinley into the huge dining room, where all the children had taken their places around the table to eat birthday cake.

"Red!" Ramon hurried over to shake the man's hand. "What brings you here? Come in and have some cake. We are celebrating Ernesto's first birthday."

Red moved his eyes to Irene. "Your wife sent for me," he told Ramon.

Irene set Ernesto in a high chair and moved to embrace Red, whose hair and mustache now showed more gray than red. He was seventy years old now, but still amazingly solid and agile for his age. Irene guessed it was due to the rugged, active life he once led, the same kind of life that had kept her father stronger than his age should allow.

"I didn't think you'd be able to make it so quickly," Irene told him, stepping back. "It's so good to see you, Red. You don't come visit nearly enough."

"Well, I stay pretty busy with all the different businesses, you know. No retirement for me. Men like me have to keep going or die." He looked from Irene to Ramon and back to Irene. "So, what is it you wanted?" he asked.

Irene looked at Ramon, a worried look in her eyes. "I'm afraid even Ramon doesn't know about this," she answered. "I was going to tell him tonight."

"Tell me what?" Ramon asked. He knew that one thing Irene had learned from her mother was a fierce independence. He saw a look in her eyes that told him she had decided to do something of which he might not approve. "What are you cooking up now, Mrs. Vallejo?"

Her eyes suddenly teared. She turned to Rose, telling her to give the children their cake. "And give some to the photographer, too. We'll have ours in a few minutes." She turned to Ramon and Red. "Come with me into the study," she told them.

Ramon frowned and Red just shrugged, both men following her into the study she and Ramon shared. Three walls were made up of bookshelves from floor to ceiling, and in one corner sat a desk inundated with drawings and blueprints, while in the other corner was Irene's desk, neat and tidy. She moved behind her desk and sat down, asking Ramon and Red to take chairs also. Ramon eyed her closely, going to his own desk and taking a cigarette from a wooden box. "I think I had better stand," he said. He brought the box over to Red and offered the man a smoke.

"I'm sorry, Ramon," Irene spoke up as both men lit their cigarettes. "With the party planned and all, and you getting home late today, I just haven't had the chance to tell you." She took a deep breath. "I talked to the family doctor today. Something about Father suddenly deciding to go into the mountains six months ago kept bothering me, especially when he talked about not wanting to die here in Denver. After all, I know his heart was broken over John, but he was still a strong, seemingly healthy man who could live another ten years or more. I badgered Dr. Aimes until he finally admitted Father didn't have that much time left at all. In fact—" She hesitated, the painful ache returning to her throat, "in fact, he could already be dead, or dying."

Both men looked at her in surprise. "Kirk," Red asked. "Lord knows I never saw much of him these last several years, considering the hard feelings between us, but what I did see of him, he seemed as robust as ever."

Ramon came around to stand beside Irene, putting a hand on her shoulder. "What is wrong, Irene?"

She swallowed back the tears that wanted to come. "Dr. Aimes said Father has a disease called cancer, that it was slowly eating at him and there was nothing that could be done about it. Father knew. That's why he went to the mountains."

Red shook his head. "I can hardly believe it. Kirk—after all the brushes with death he had back in our old days of hunting and trapping and fighting Indians." He looked at his own wrinkled hands. "Of course, I guess none of us is immune from getting old and dying."

Irene reached up and touched Ramon's hand. Oh, how she prayed they would both live to be very, very old. She could not imagine life now without him. "No, none of us will escape it," she answered. "I asked you here, Red, because there is something I want you to do for me. I know you and Father were not the best of friends these last few years, but you were once; and I think that deep inside you both still are. You're just too stubborn to admit it."

Red grinned slyly. "I think you always knew both of us pretty good, Irene."

"I always felt bad about how the friendship ended." She sighed deeply before continuing. "I want to find my father, Red. You're the only one I can think of who might have some idea where he would have gone. You traveled with him once, lived with him, hunted and trapped and fought Indians by his side. You know the country he loved best. I know it's a lot to ask, and maybe you aren't up to it physically—"

"Hell, I'm just as able as I was forty years ago," he protested, sitting up a little straighter. "You know I'd do anything for you, Irene, but Kirk went off alone on purpose. He *wants* to die up there. What good will it do for me to find him?"

"If we find him, and he's still alive, he won't die alone. I can't bear the thought of not giving him a last good-bye, Red. And I can't bear the thought of him just dying up there alone to be eaten by wolves. I want at least to be able to bury his body. I wouldn't ask him to come back home. I know he wants to die in the mountains. I just can't stand the thought of never knowing what happened to him, where he is. He should be properly buried."

"Well, I can give it a try—"

"Wait a minute," Ramon interrupted, kneeling beside Irene. "What's this about 'we'? You aren't actually planning to go *with* Red into the mountains, are you?"

She looked at her husband warily. "Please, Ramon, I have to do this."

"Irene, it's nearly September! You know that from here on the weather up there is totally unpredictable! You could be caught in a blizzard!"

"I know." Her eyes began to tear more. "Ramon, I *have* to go! All my life I've wanted to go back into the mountains. It's like . . . like Father is keeping his promise to take me. Even if I find him dead, it will be as if we were together again. I need to do this, Ramon. With the proper horses and gear, Red and I will be fine. He knows all about how to survive up there."

Their eyes held for a quiet moment. Ramon took a drag on his cigarette, shaking his head. "Not Red and you."

"Ramon, please understand—"

He put his fingers to her lips. "I do understand. But I refuse to let you and Red go alone. And I will not let you suffer what you might *find* alone, either. I am coming with you."

She stared at him in surprise, and a tear slipped down her cheek. "You mean you aren't going to try to stop me?"

He smiled sadly. "*Could* I stop you if I wanted to?"

She smiled in return. "Probably not."

He leaned up and kissed her cheek. "We will all go, and we will take along some pack mules and a couple of extra men. We have ten children who will be back here in Denver waiting for their mother to come home to them. I do not intend to let anything happen to her. Besides"—his eyes softened—"I could not live without you myself. If I did not go along, I would go crazy sitting here waiting and wondering and worrying." He looked over at Red. "Do you think you can find him?"

Red sighed. "All I can do is try. It's been a long time since I've been up there, you know. With all the gold towns and all, things have changed some. There is one place he always liked best. He told me once that if a man had to die, he couldn't think of a better place for it to happen, up at Bear Lake, by Hallett Peak. I have to warn you, though, you're talking some of the highest mountain range in Colorado, in the whole country, for that matter."

"It doesn't matter," Irene replied. "Besides, I've always

wanted to get into the really high country myself before I'm too old to manage it."

Red grinned. "We might all of us already be too old." They all laughed, but a feeling of sadness hung in the air. "When do you want to leave?" Red asked.

Irene rose. "Well, Sharron is playing the piano in a concert at the opera house in three days," she answered. "I'd like to leave the day after."

Red nodded. "I'll start getting together the proper gear and mounts."

"Don't spare anything," Ramon told him. "I want the best. I don't want anything to go wrong."

Red got up from his chair. "I know what to do." He sighed deeply, crushing out his cigarette. "I'm sorry about Kirk, Irene. I wish we had patched things up before he left. Maybe I'll still get the chance." He shook his head. "It's amazing what all has happened since that day he left Bent's Fort carrying you in his arms. How old are you now?"

"Forty-seven."

Red closed his eyes. "My God. Was it really that long ago? It's strange how we never know where life will take us, isn't it?"

Irene clung to Ramon's hand. "Do you ever hear from Elly, Red?"

He looked at them, his smile turning bitter. "No. Bill Byers told me he got a letter from her asking him to start send the *News* to some hotel in San Francisco, so I guess that's where she is."

Irene sighed. "She always said she'd go back to California. I wonder if she ever found Chad."

Red put his hat on. "They can have each other." He breathed deeply and headed for the door. "I'm going to get started on this. Takes some planning, you know. I'll pass on the birthday cake." He nodded. "I'll see myself out."

"Thank you, Red," Irene told him, tears in her eyes.

He gave her a wink. "You always were a favorite of mine." He walked out and Irene turned to Ramon. He pulled her into his arms. "Thank you for understanding," she told him.

He kissed her hair. "I think it is crazy, but I understand why you have to do it. I just hope what you find isn't more than you can handle. That's why I'm going with you."

She looked up at him, touching his face. "But you're so busy."

"I have good men who know what to do. I couldn't stand waiting here for you, worrying about you. Besides, I haven't done any hunting in a long time. I used to go up into the mountains west of Denver and hunt elk and bear, before I had such a large family to care for, remember? I'll take my gun along and we'll hunt our own food and live like your father used to live. In fact, perhaps it would be a good idea to take the three older boys along. It would be especially good for Sam. He likes to hunt. He would be able to see what it is like living the way his people used to live. And I haven't taken David and Alex hunting in years."

She smiled. "I love you so much, Ramon."

They embraced, and her worry for her father was quickly interrupted when Anna came running into the study, shouting that little Ernesto had just smeared chocolate frosting onto his face and into his hair. Outside Red drove his buggy toward the livery to see about renting the best horses and mules for mountain travel. His heart ached at the thought of Kirk dying, and he was disgusted with himself for letting the rift between them remain so wide.

"Damn you, Kirk, men like you don't die," he muttered, a tear slipping down his cheek.

They took the Denver-Pacific north to Loveland, then mounted their horses and gathered their pack mules, heading west into some of the most magnificent country Irene and Ramon had yet seen. Ramon had hired two men who were experienced at traveling in the mountains, and their three oldest sons, David, Alex and Sam, had eagerly agreed to come along.

They made their way through Thompson Canyon, hardly able to hear each other talk because of the roar of the Big Thompson River that was made louder by the high, majestic, rocky walls of the canyon. Rocks seemed to literally dangle precariously above them where the red-rock walls bulged at the tops as though ready to fold over them and bury them any moment. Green fir trees seemed to sprout right out of the rocks, making one wonder how on earth the trees' roots managed to find any soil.

The three sons gaped and pointed, excited at what they were seeing, craning their necks to see to the tops of the canyon walls, where huge pine trees appeared tiny. Occasionally everyone had to scatter when a rock came crashing down. Irene would feel near panic for the boys, but they all would just laugh, thinking it was exciting and adventurous. It brought the three of them, none of whom were related by blood, even closer. David was Irene and Hank's son, Alex was Ramon and Anna's son, and Sam was Yellow Eagle's son. Yet the way they got along, one would think they had all been blood brothers.

In spite of the danger, Irene was glad now they had come. The trip was good for them, especially Sam, who was seeing some of the country the Cheyenne had loved most, although he would go even deeper into the mountains than even any Cheyenne had ever gone. They were actually moving into Ute and Shoshone country, although as with the Cheyenne, there were no Indians left here.

They followed the twisting canyon, camping one night there, then went into the sleepy little town of Estes Park, the last sign of civilization before moving into the higher mountains just beyond it. The state of Colorado was presently contemplating designating the area into which they would travel a national park, and Irene hoped it would happen, for the country into which they rode then was some of the most magnificent any man could behold.

They traveled for days, following Red in one long pack train, picking their way among rocks, following hard, narrow pathways left by Indians and fur trappers, weaving through thick groves of deep green pine and aspen, breaking out onto mountain ledges and gasping at how high up they were.

Whenever they broke into the open they would just sit and stare at the glorious view. Autumn had turned the aspen leaves to a brilliant gold, and when the wind blew the leaves fluttered from their gold side to their white side, giving the impression they were glittering. It was almost as if they were telling people that gold was what had built Colorado.

"And so it has," Irene thought. Just before leaving, they had learned of a new gold strike near Pikes Peak, and yet another wild, new gold town called Cripple Creek was already exploding with new prospectors. Irene had thought the days of the big gold strikes were over, but it was happening all over again. K-E owned a lot of land and mines near the area of the strike, and Irene did not doubt that new veins of gold would be found. It was rumored this was one of the biggest finds yet in the whole state, and the discovery was turning Colorado's financial woes, as well as K-E's, into celebration.

Irene wondered if Kirk knew about the new find. In the old days, he would have immediately left to do his own prospecting and stake his own claims for K-E. But she knew deep down that he didn't care about those things anymore. David Kirkland had done his share, found his gold, built a city, kept and raised his little Indian daughter. She breathed deeply of the rich scent of pine. This was Kirk's first love, the only thing that really meant anything to him.

They all wore heavy fur coats now. The days were cold and the nights colder. Three days into the mountains a wicked snowstorm hit, bringing a howling wind and stinging sleet and snow. They quickly erected tents and huddled inside them, wondering if they would be buried there until spring. But after two days the storm abated. The sun returned, and although the snow did not melt, the days became clear and bright again, and they continued their journey, although the snow and ice now made everything more dangerous. Yet it also made the scenery even more beautiful. Puffs of snow clung to the pine trees and capped rocks. The thick blanket of snow on the ground muffled the hooves of the horses so that a rich silence hung in the air. They passed glittering waterfalls, and the sights and sounds were so beautiful that it sometimes made Irene shiver.

David, Alex, and Sam were not the least bit alarmed or threatened by the weather and the danger. Whenever they made camp the three of them immediately began pelting each other with snowballs and wrestling into drifts. Whenever Sam would get one of his brothers down, he would stand up and raise his arms, letting out a yelp of victory, reminding Irene sometimes of Yellow Eagle and the day he had attacked her.

Although Sam had a streak of white blood in him, one would never know it. He was all Indian, his black hair falling nearly to his waist, his skin so dark. The bit of white blood he carried only slightly softened the hard Indian lines, making him a most handsome young man, one whom Irene suspected the young Indian women on the reservations would find most attractive. Sam had already decided that when he married, it would be a Sioux or Cheyenne woman. He would surely have his pick once he was old enough.

Alex already talked about marrying Sharron. To Irene and Ramon, they both seemed such children, and now Irene understood how her own mother might have looked at her and Ramon the same way. She could understand in some respects why Bea had been concerned, but she also remembered how she had felt then. She was not going to stop young love. If Alex felt the same way when he turned eighteen, which would only be two more months, they were going to allow the marriage. Alex was already doing well at Vallejo Construction. It was obvious he was talented enough to take it over completely when Ramon was gone.

The thought made her look back at Ramon, who gave her a grin. "Keep your eyes ahead, woman. This is a dangerous path."

"This horse doesn't need me to guide it. I think she knows the way better than the best mountain man. I just wanted to make sure you were still there," she answered.

"I will always be here, right behind you the rest of your life."

She smiled, turning to look ahead again, taking comfort in the words.

They bent their heads against wicked winds, fought snow and sleet, then rallied in bright sunshine, moving through Limber Pine, past lichen-covered rocks, trying to steer horses away from the sharp needles of Juniper shrubs, constantly climbing until it seemed they should be able to touch the heavens.

Irene began to feel a strange warmth in spite of the cold, an inner warmth. She felt as though Kirk was with her now. This was his country. He had not brought her here this time, but he had beckoned her. She could hear his voice in the wind that groaned and howled through canyons and crevices, feel his soul in the howl of the wolves at night. His heart lay in this vast wilderness, this magnificent land that still belonged only to God. Man would never totally invade and conquer this rugged terrain.

They passed areas of stripped-out fir trees, where avalanches the previous spring had ripped down the mountainside, tearing away everything in sight. This was a land of ancient order, a land whose history drifted far back beyond man's short time on earth, a land that would not change for generations to come. It was vast, overwhelming, magnificent beyond man's small imagination. Range after range of mountains seemed to stretch out into eternity.

Ramon taught Alex and Sam to shoot, and all three boys and their father practiced whenever they got the chance. Once Sam shot a buck, and he let out a wild war whoop that echoed against canyon walls, bringing to mind the days when Indians roamed and hunted these rugged mountains.

Red and Ramon showed the boys how to skin and clean the deer, and they ate roasted venison for the next three days, packing the rest of the meat in leather bags Red had brought in case they got stranded and had to hunt for their food and store meat. They stuffed the bags with ice and snow to preserve the meat, and Sam kept the deerskin.

"I'll show you how your people cleaned and dried animal skins soon as we get back," Red promised the boy.

In the still, cold nights, Red told stories around the campfire, stories of his days of hunting with Kirk, stories of Indian fighting and rendezvous. Irene had heard them before, but she didn't mind listening again, enjoying the enraptured looks on her sons' faces.

After five full days since leaving Estes Park, they finally reached Bear Lake, a pristine, deep blue body of water that was partially iced over. Rich green pine and colorful rocks decorated the lake's edges, and all around it more snow-capped peaks rose as though to protect the area from outsiders. They made camp, and Red began a search, insisting on being allowed to go alone.

For two more days the boys practiced shooting; Ramon and Irene took walks, Ramon keeping a constant eye out for bears. Irene felt even closer to Ramon here in the high country, away from all the distractions of Denver and everyday business. "This is even more peaceful than at the ranch," she told him. "Here we're truly alone. It's as though the rest of the world doesn't even exist, isn't it? It's as if we've made it to heaven. I like to think heaven would be something like this—all beauty, unspoiled by man and sin."

Ramon moved to put his arms around her from behind. "It is beautiful," he answered. "I am glad we came, in spite of the reason. This has been good for you, good for the boys. We will come again, maybe not into quite such dangerous territory, but we will come, and we will bring the rest of the children."

They stood together, wrapped in thick, fur coats and in each other's arms. There was no sound but the moaning wind in the pines. It was a strange, sweet, special moment, one of those moments one knows will never come again. Irene leaned against Ramon's chest. "As soon as we get back, I want to find out what's being done about making this a national park, Ramon. We have to make sure it happens."

He grinned. "Another one of your pet projects?"

"I want to do it . . . for Father. He'd be glad to know the prettiest part of Colorado will remain untouched, will stay the way it was when he hunted and trapped here." She turned to face him. "He's dead, Ramon. I feel it." She leaned her head against his chest. "But it's all right. It's what he wanted. He's happy now."

Two hours later Red came back to camp, his face pale, his eyes watery. He held Kirk's old rifle in one hand. "I found him," he announced. "He was . . . sitting against a tree, his gun beside him." He handed the gun to Irene. "You'd best stay here with the boys till Ramon and the other men and I get him buried. He'd want you to remember him the way he was when he left, Irene, not the way he looks now. One thing I can tell you, the way he was sitting there, he died happy, Irene. He sat down under a nice big pine, where he had a grand view of the lake and the mountains beyond it, and he just let it happen."

Irene nodded, handing back the rifle. "This old flintlock was his favorite—out-dated, but he liked it because it reminded him of the old days. Bury it with him, Red." She looked at Ramon. "I hate to give you such a burden, but I wish you and Red would bury him alone—then come get me—just me. I don't want anyone ever to know exactly where Kirk is buried. The fewer who know it now, the better. If the children don't see the grave, they can't say for sure where it is and won't feel pressured by others to tell."

She looked at the boys and the two extra men. "I don't even want you to mention Bear Lake to anyone, is that understood? Your grandfather—" she looked at the two men, "David Kirkland, died in the Rockies and is buried up here somewhere. That's all anyone needs to know. I won't have people coming up here looking for his body, claiming they own David Kirkland's old rifle or his jacket or buckskins. I know how vile and sacrilegious some people can be. Kirk came here to be alone, to die alone. Now I want to be sure he's left alone in death. You are never to mention exactly where he was found. Is that understood?"

They all nodded, Sam wiping at sudden tears, struggling not to cry in front of the others. He turned away and walked off by himself. Ramon and Red took shovels from their gear, and Ramon came over to kiss Irene's cheek before mounting up to follow Red deep into the pines and out of sight. By the time they returned it was too late to go back. They camped again for the night, then returned to the grave the next morning with Irene, who knelt beside the pile of rocks that covered the grave so that wild animals could not dig it up.

"I can make a marker," Ramon offered.

"No," Irene answered, touching the rocks, her throat aching. "It would just make it easier for someone to find it. This way, even if it is found, no one can be sure who is buried here."

An eagle floated above, its shadow moving over the grave. Irene looked up at the magnificent bird. *I came back, Father*, she thought. *You always said you'd bring me back to the mountains, and now you have*. She stood up, picking up a handful of dirt and small rocks and sprinkling them over the grave. "Another one of life's circles is complete," she said aloud. "Father is truly home now, back where he started from. Sam will go back to his people, and you have gotten back the land your grandfather loved, Ramon." She looked at him. "And I have you." She reached out and took his hand. "Father once said the eagle is a good sign. I believe him. I'm all right, Ramon. I'm glad we came here, glad we found him. I think he wanted me to come."

Ramon pulled her close. "*Fue muy triste lo que le sucedió, pero también bueno,*" he told her gently, telling her what had happened was sad, but good. It was what Kirk wanted. "*Yo te amo, querida. Vámonos a casa.*"

She looked into his eyes. "We *are* home, Ramon. Wherever we are, as long as we're together, we're home."

He smiled sadly. "*Sí, mi vida.* Your father needed these mountains, but all we need is each other."

A quick wind suddenly moaned through the pines, kicking up snow, and the eagle flew quietly away, heading for a distant peak.

The earth is all that lasts.
The earth is everywhere in me
Even when I'm gone.

NANCY WOOD
*"War Cry on a Prayer
Feather"*

CHAPTER
FORTY-TWO

 Irene looked out from a top-floor window of the new K-E offices, which had been built just two years ago. From her seventh-floor perch she had a grand view of Denver, including the gold-domed capitol building. She looked out at a street many blocks long, lined with other buildings as high as K-E's, electric poles strung along the way. Denver was a thriving city now, competing in size with such places as San Francisco and Chicago. Many of the streets were paved, and several city parks had been developed. It seemed incredible that her family had been part of the reason for the city's phenomenal growth over the past thirty years. No other town could quite compare to Denver when it came to rapid progress and a stubborn refusal to die.

How many times had this city been on the brink of disaster, ready to fold as had so many other gold towns? There had been the terrible fire in '63, the flood in '64, the shock of discovering the Union Pacific would not come to Denver, the panic of '73, the recent depression, gold mines that played out, the crash of the silver market. But a combination of luck and stubborn citizens who refused to buckle had won again. The gold rush at Cripple Creek was having its repercussions on Denver, and again they had bounced back from doom.

She wished Kirk could have lived to know about the latest

discovery, one of the biggest ever. K-E would thrive once again, and a couple of the older gold mines had been reopened. But there would be no celebrating today. Today was the reading of the will. Elly had been located and had returned, looking a little ragged. She had very little left, and Irene knew the only reason she had come was that she hoped to find new riches through her inheritance.

Irene's heart ached at the news Elly had brought with her. She had found Chad in San Francisco. He had died the previous year from a venereal disease, a horrible death, a near-insane man at the end. It was a sad yet strangely fitting end for a man who had led the sorry life he had. Much as Irene wanted to hate him, she could not. She felt sorry for how he had died, sorry for his brutal, painful childhood. If only he had shared his problems with her, let her try to help him get over them. There was a time when she might have understood, might have been able to love him.

Ramon came into the office then, followed by Robert Slade, the company attorney who had handled Kirk's will. Elly came inside the room, standing stiffly toward the back. To his surprise, Red had been asked to attend the reading. He came inside, glancing at Elly with a look of bitter sorrow. She raised her chin and looked away from him. All of Irene and Ramon's children were ushered inside, as well as some of the servants and the old black carriage driver, Jim Washington, who had worked for the Kirklands and for Irene and Chad for so many years before finally retiring.

Irene walked over to pick up little Ernesto, then sat down with him on her lap, ordering the rest of the children to gather around her and be very quiet. Everyone else but Elly took chairs, and Slade, himself an old man now, opened the will and began reading.

A hefty sum of money was willed to old Jim, as well as each of the servants, even more to Liz Thomas, who had been Bea's personal maid for years. A considerable amount of money was designated to the Cheyenne River Indian Reservation, as well as Rose Bud and Pine Ridge reservations, to be put into a special fund and used for improvements such as schools, better farm equipment, a museum to preserve Indian artifacts, clothing, weapons, and the like. "My daughter, Irene, will be executor of this trust until such time as my grandson, Samuel 'Jumping Bear' Kirkland, is of the age and ability to take it over. I will leave Irene in charge of deciding when Sam is capable of same."

Sam's eyes teared, and Elly scowled, fury and frustration building in her eyes. Irene took Sam's hand and squeezed it. Elly nearly gasped when Slade read that Kirk willed fifteen thousand dollars back to Red McKinley, "money I never would have demanded be repaid," the will read. "If you needed more, Red, I would give it," Slade read from the will. "But you already own a good deal of what was once K-E. This money is simply a token of the friendship we once shared, in hopes it will erase hard feelings from the past. Perhaps one day you and I will walk together again in the mountains, in a place where hard feelings and hatred do not exist."

Red took out a handkerchief. "If that's it for my part, I'd like to be excused," he told Slade, his voice sounding ready to break.

"That's all," Slade answered.

Red quickly left, putting the handkerchief to his eyes as he went out. Slade continued the reading, leaving fifty thousand dollars to Elly. Elly stiffened, her eyes widening in indignation. "You once owned much more, Elly, but you squandered it all and were careless in such a way that you lost most of it," Slade read. "The rest fell into your ex-husband's hands, and rightly so. You brought nothing but pain, sorrow, and disgrace to this family, and part of the reason for your mother's death was because of the worry you caused her. If you spend wisely, fifty thousand dollars should see you to old age."

"Old age!" Elly nearly screamed the words. "How *dare* he do this to me! Irene and I are the only remaining children. I should get half of *everything*!"

"This was Kirk's wish, Elly," Slade told her. "I was with him when he made out this will, and he was perfectly sane at the time. I can attest to that if you plan to fight this. It was before John died, so you can't say he made it out under grief or duress. In fact, there is a clause here for John, to whom he willed a hundred thousand dollars and nothing more—with the same reasoning—that John had his chance to work with K-E and prove himself but did not."

"Then why would he give John *twice* as much as me?" Elly fumed.

"He doesn't say," Slade answered. "But I imagine it's because John did not do anything to deliberately hurt a member of the family. I think it's fairly common knowledge what you did to Irene."

Elly sniffed, glaring back at him. Anna and Miguel glanced at their aunt, then scooted closer to their mother, afraid of the tall, overbearing, dark-eyed woman in the black taffeta dress. "Finish the will," she sneered at Slade.

The man sighed, glancing at Irene. "Go ahead, Robert," she told him.

Slade cleared his throat. "The rest of my estate, all K-E holdings, all personal property and any cash holdings I give to my daughter, Irene, and her husband Ramon Vallejo, discounting a trust fund of twenty thousand dollars each to be set up for Irene and Ramon's children, David, Sharron, Alejandro, Samuel, Eduardo, Elena, Anna, Miguel, Ben, and Ernesto; with the understanding that everything else bequeathed to Ramon and Irene will one day be divided equally among said children upon the deaths of their parents. By this will—"

"It isn't fair," Elly spoke up, stomping forward. "My *mother* built most of this, and Irene wasn't even her daughter! She's half Indian! And those children—they don't even all have Kirkland blood! One of them was just a street orphan! One is Ramon's, not Irene's! And Sam—Sam is an *Indian*! It isn't right that the bulk of the entire estate should go to Irene and Ramon and children who aren't even directly related—"

"That's enough, Elly," Irene said, rising and handing Ernesto to Ramon. "I'll not have you insult my children in front of them! They are *all* my children, *legally*; more importantly they're ours in our hearts. They're good, loving young men and women who deserve anything Father wanted them to have! You have caused me enough sorrow over the years! I will not let you cause them sorrow, too! The will is legal. You can fight it in court, if you so choose, but I guarantee that *I* would win, because I would be fighting for what belongs to my children! If you want to use up a good deal of your inheritance paying a lawyer in a losing battle, that is your choice!"

Elly stiffened. "You always win, don't you," she said, her voice a low hiss.

Irene shook her head. "No, Elly. You continue to defeat yourself by your own behavior. I used to blame myself for your hatred and bitterness, but I stopped doing that. It's something that is deep inside of you, and I feel terribly sorry for you, but there is nothing I can do about it, except to tell you that if you ever want to make amends, we're here. You can't make me hate you. I won't let your venom spill out onto me or my children. I will not let you teach them to hate. We're your family, and if you ever want to be a part of it again, you will be welcome, but only if you come with love and an open willingness to be a real sister and a loving aunt. The children would accept you, welcome you and love you, because they have been *taught* to love and forgive and be understanding of others. For the moment I will not allow you to stain their hearts and thoughts with your hatred. Your part of the will has been read. You might as well leave."

"I don't have to—"

"Get out." Irene spoke the words calmly but sternly.

Elly blinked, realizing this woman was far different from the Irene she had known in her younger years. She could not hurt this Irene, and there were no avenues left by which she could defeat her. She felt a sudden, ridiculous urge to cry. "I hate you," she said, surprised at how weakly the words came out of her mouth, with a quiver in her voice.

"No, you don't, Elly," Irene answered sadly. "You hate yourself. It's yourself you can't live with. You try to direct that hate to others, because it's too painful for you to face the truth of the kind of life you've led, the people you've hurt. Please just go. Remember what I told you. We're here if you ever really want to come home."

Elly swallowed. For one brief second Irene saw her sister soften, saw a spark of surprise in her eyes at Irene's offer. She quickly erased the look, putting her nose in the air then. "I have no home," she said aloud. She looked at Slade. "I'll be back tomorrow for my money. Have a check ready." She stomped out of the office, skirts rustling. Irene watched her, smiling sadly. "She'll be back." She looked at Ramon. "She just needs to make it look like it's her idea and not mine. She'll think of some excuse to save her pride. She's like Mother that way, so stubborn, refusing to admit she might be wrong."

He rose, handing Ernesto to Sharron. "Are you all right?"

She held his eyes. "I'm fine." She looked at Slade. "Is that all of it?"

He nodded. "Oh, there's a little legal mumbo jumbo left, but that's it as far as who gets what."

The servants and old Jim stood there feeling awkward at the confrontation between Irene and Elly. They began thanking Irene, expressing their sorrow over Kirk's death, their joy at their newfound riches, nervously leaving the office.

"This is a sad time, Miss Irene," Jim told her, taking her hand. "But this is also a wonderful thing for my family. My wife, she's been ailing, and my grandson, he wants some of that fancy schooling. Now he can have it. Your father was a fine man, Miss Irene, and you were the best child. I've been proud to know you, and I'm happy for your fine family."

"Thank you, Jim." To his surprise she leaned up and kissed his cheek. "Come and visit anytime. You're always welcome."

"Thank you, ma'am." His eyes teared, as he remembered the night, not long after Irene delivered Sharron, when Chad Jacobs had ordered him to take him to Milicent Delaney's house. Oh, what a sorry marriage that was. But now she had Ramon.

Jim left, and only Irene and the family remained in the office with Robert Slade. Irene walked to a window, looking out at Denver again, her eyes moving to the mountains beyond. Kirk lay buried up there, back where he belonged. She loved him for bequeathing so much money to the Indians. Again a circle had been completed. An old mountain man who had once lived among the Cheyenne would be with them again in spirit, would be helping the people he had once loved.

"I'd like a monument erected to my parents," she said, still staring out the window, "maybe a big granite rock placed along one of the roads heading west of Denver, somewhere closer to the foothills. It could be engraved, telling about Bea and David Kirkland, how they were among the original founders of this city. I want something special said about Father, a kind of dedication, perhaps something along the lines of David Kirkland watching over Denver whenever the mountains cast their shadow over the city." She looked at Ramon. "He told me that once, that whenever the mountains cast their shadow over Denver, he would be watching over us."

"That would be very nice," Ramon spoke up. "You decide what you want it to say, and I'll see that it gets done."

She studied her handsome Ramon, struck with love at the sight of him standing there surrounded by all the children. There was a time when she thought happiness was only for others, not for herself. Now her heart overflowed with love and joy. She thought how the circle of life goes on forever, how death changed nothing. For every death there was new life. All the children before her were the proof of that. She looked at Sharron and Alejandro, who stood beside each other.

"There has been enough sadness over your grandfather's death," she said aloud. "Now is a time to celebrate again . . . with a wedding."

Their eyes lit up. "Do you mean it, Mother? We can get married?" Sharron asked.

Irene looked at Ramon, who grinned the handsome grin she had loved for so many years. Both of them were remembering young love . . . a stolen kiss . . . the pain of being denied their passion.

"Yes," she answered. "I mean it, if it's all right with your father."

Ramon held her eyes, stepping closer. "*Sí, mi querida*. It is all right with me." He folded her into his arms, and for a moment the memory of that young love was rich and sweet and vivid. She was sixteen again, in a forbidden embrace.

EPILOGUE

1989

 Carl Ritter watched the changing signs of Highway 76 carefully as he drove his red, late-model station wagon toward Denver. He was tired, especially after the long, monotonous drive through Iowa and then Nebraska.

"We're flying next time," he complained to his wife.

"Oh, Carl, it's much nicer this way, being able to stop wherever we want. If we want to get a real feel of the West, it's better to drive. This will be great for the children."

Carl ran a hand through his thinning hair. "Kids don't appreciate these trips as much as you think." He looked into the rearview mirror, spotting fifteen-year-old Tom sprawled among luggage and duffel bags at the rear of the station wagon, holding a small portable tape player and wearing earphones. One foot was wiggling rhythmically.

"They'll remember—especially once they see the monument," Betty Ritter told her husband. "Be sure you get on 87 South. It might also be I-25. They seem to be one and the same on the map here. After we head south, look for Highway 6 West. That's the one the monument is supposed to be on. Six runs right back into Interstate 70, and that will take us farther into the mountains."

Carl frowned, more confused than ever. The Ritters were from a small town in Kansas, and Carl hated driving in city traffic. He tried to keep his attention on cars that zipped onto the highway on both his right and left sides, more irritated with his wife when she let out a little gasp that startled him.

"Oh, look! There they are! You can see the mountains now." Betty turned to twelve-year-old Rebecca and seven-year-old Irene, who sat in the back seat playing a game of magnetic checkers. "Look, girls. See the mountains? Give your brother a nudge."

"Betty, don't bother them yet," Carl grumbled. "There's so damn much smog you can't see them all that good yet. That's the trouble, everybody wants to come here. They build their cities and end up destroying all the beauty they came out here for. I've heard there was a time you could see those mountains a hell of a lot sooner. They ought to do something about this."

"I'm sure they're working on it, Carl. There! There's I-25 South."

Carl took the exit, and the red station wagon moved into the southern flow of traffic, Carl Ritter nervously watching the signs while his wife and two daughters gaped out the right-side windows at gray and purple snow-capped peaks that sprawled unendingly beyond the city. Young Tom raised his head long enough to glance at them. "They don't look very big from here," he mumbled.

"They'll be real big when we get up close," Irene told him.

"Yeah? What do you know, squirt?" Tom lay back again to listen to his music.

The Ritter car joined thousands more that weaved their way along I-25, exhaust fumes adding to the light gray smog that hung over the city, giving a ghostly cast to tall buildings in the distance. Minutes later the highway wound its way amid the skyscrapers, and the Ritter family gawked and pointed, as they got a closer view of downtown Denver.

"Look! That one's all glass," Rebecca said. "And it's not even square. It's round."

"So much of the city looks so new, Carl," Betty said softly. She spotted some older buildings, noting the stark contrast between the old red-brick four- and five-story buildings, and the towering new buildings that rose behind them in an almost threatening pose. Betty pictured them as tall, powerful warriors, ready to crush the old ones in the name of progress.

Now that they were in the heart of town, it seemed there was no smog at all. Betty realized one had to be farther away to really notice it. Here it was sunny, and glass towers sparkled. In the distance Betty caught sight of the golden dome of the capital building.

"This is a pretty city, Carl. It feels kind of funny to see some of those older buildings with the high rises behind them. I'll bet some of those older ones were here when Bea Kirkland was alive."

"Could be. I wonder what she'd think of Denver today."

"I wonder what *all* the pioneers would think. Oh, I'd love to bring some of them into today and show them what they built."

Carl thought about a news broadcast he had heard earlier, about how smog from Los Angeles was destroying redwoods and cacti hundreds of miles away, and acid rain was killing all life in pristine mountain lakes. "I'm not so sure they'd be happy to see our idea of progress," he answered.

"Look, Mom," Rebecca spoke up. "That building is shaped like a cash register at the top."

Irene laughed and Betty grinned. "It is. Must be a bank. Just think, girls, all this is the result of a handful of people finding gold in a little creek. I think it's called Cherry Creek, and it still runs through the heart of downtown Denver. That's what brought David Kirkland out here."

"It wasn't just the gold," Carl interrupted. "He came here because he loved the Rockies. That's why they built the monument—not just because he was one of Denver's founders. His children knew how much he loved the mountains, and they wanted him always to be remembered that way. He's even buried up in the mountains somewhere. No one knows where his grave is. Only his daughter Irene and her husband knew, and they never told anyone."

"The Indian daughter," Rebecca asked.

"Yes," Carl replied, searching for the sign that would lead him to Highway 6.

Tom had finally taken off his earphones. "How are we related, Dad?" he asked. "I keep getting it mixed up."

"Well, it's pretty distant, but we're related, nonetheless. My great-great-great grandfather was Jake Ritter. He owned a supply store in Kansas. When his brother and his brother's wife died from cholera, they left one daughter, Beatrice—she was my great-great-great grandfather's niece. She married a mountain man, David Kirkland, and they ended up striking it rich in gold in the California gold rush. Then David Kirkland came back to this area because he loved it so much. They helped build Denver and the Kirkland name became pretty well known. They were wealthy, powerful people, but the name died out through marriages and deaths and such. Only one daughter survived, and she supposedly married a Mexican man. There's some big construction company in Denver that's supposed to be a part of the old Kirkland empire, quite a few other businesses, too, I guess. My family says that at one time the Kirkland daughter and her Mexican husband owned half of Denver. It's probably just an exaggeration."

"Am I really named after the Indian daughter?" Irene asked.

"Yes, you are," her mother answered. "She's the daughter your father is talking about."

The station wagon weaved along the highway, other cars snaking their way in and out of exits as people moved along in daily routines. They passed Mile-High Stadium, gawking at the white horse that reared a pose to signify the home of Bronco-mania. Carl found Highway 6 and took the exit.

Carl turned left onto a two-lane road dotted on both sides with small industrial buildings, a few houses here and there. Tom took off his earphones and leaned over the backseat, helping everyone else look, none of them sure just what they were supposed to find. The road began to climb. After another mile they found another sign with another arrow, and they turned onto a dirt road that took them into an area surprisingly remote for being so close to a big city. Red rock formations stood out vividly against dark green pines and shrubs. Finally they spotted an opening where a huge piece of granite sat with something carved on it. Nearby was a copper plate on a pedestal.

Carl stopped the car and everyone scrambled out. The spot was pleasantly quiet, in spite of its location. Carl stretched and looked to the east. "Look at that," he told his wife. She turned to see Denver sprawled out below. "Some view, isn't it," Carl commented.

"Yes." Betty followed after the children, who ran over to the granite monument dedicated to a man who would never seem real to them. Rebecca began reading the copper marker aloud.

". . . one of the founding fathers of Denver," she was saying. "David and Beatrice Kirkland came to Cherry Creek in eighteen fifty-nine . . ." Her voice dropped as she continued reading to herself.

Carl and Betty walked to the monument, studying the polished surface that held the dedication.

"In honor of David Kirkland," Carl read, as the children suddenly quieted. "Each day when the mountains cast their shadow over this spot, the citizens of Denver will know that David Kirkland is watching over them. He loved Denver, but his first love was the Rocky Mountains. Now those mountains have claimed their own, and David Kirkland will walk among them forever.

"In loving memory . . . Irene."

*E*ven the seasons form a great circle in their changing, and always come back again to where they were. The life of a man is a circle from childhood to childhood and so it is in everything where power moves. Our tipis were round like the nests of birds and these were always set in a circle, the nation's hoop, a nest of many nests where the Great Spirit meant for us to hatch our children.

—Hahaka Sapa (Black Elk),
Oglala Teton Dakota Sioux
From "Touch the Earth"

From the author:

I hope you have enjoyed my story. If you would like to know about other books I have written, feel free to write me at 6013 North Coloma Road, Coloma, MI 49038–9309. Include a stamped, self-addressed envelope, and I will send you a newsletter with personal information as well as a list of published novels and what you can look for in the future. Thank you!